MW00442896

THE FURYCK SAGA

WINTER'S FURY

THE BURNING SEA

NIGHT OF THE SHADOW MOON

HALLOW WOOD

THE RAVEN'S WARNING

VALE OF THE GODS

KINGS OF FATE
A Prequel Novella

THE LORDS OF ALEKKA

EYE OF THE WOLF

MARK OF THE HUNTER

BLOOD OF THE RAVEN

HEART OF THE KING

Sign up to my newsletter, so you don't miss out
on new release information!

http://www.aerayne.com/sign-up

HALLOW WOOD

THE FURYCK SAGA: BOOK 4

A.E. RAYNE

Cover design & artwork by A.E. Rayne.

ISBN: 9781729440360

For more information about A.E. Rayne
and her upcoming books visit:

www.aerayne.com

/aerayne

For Beau

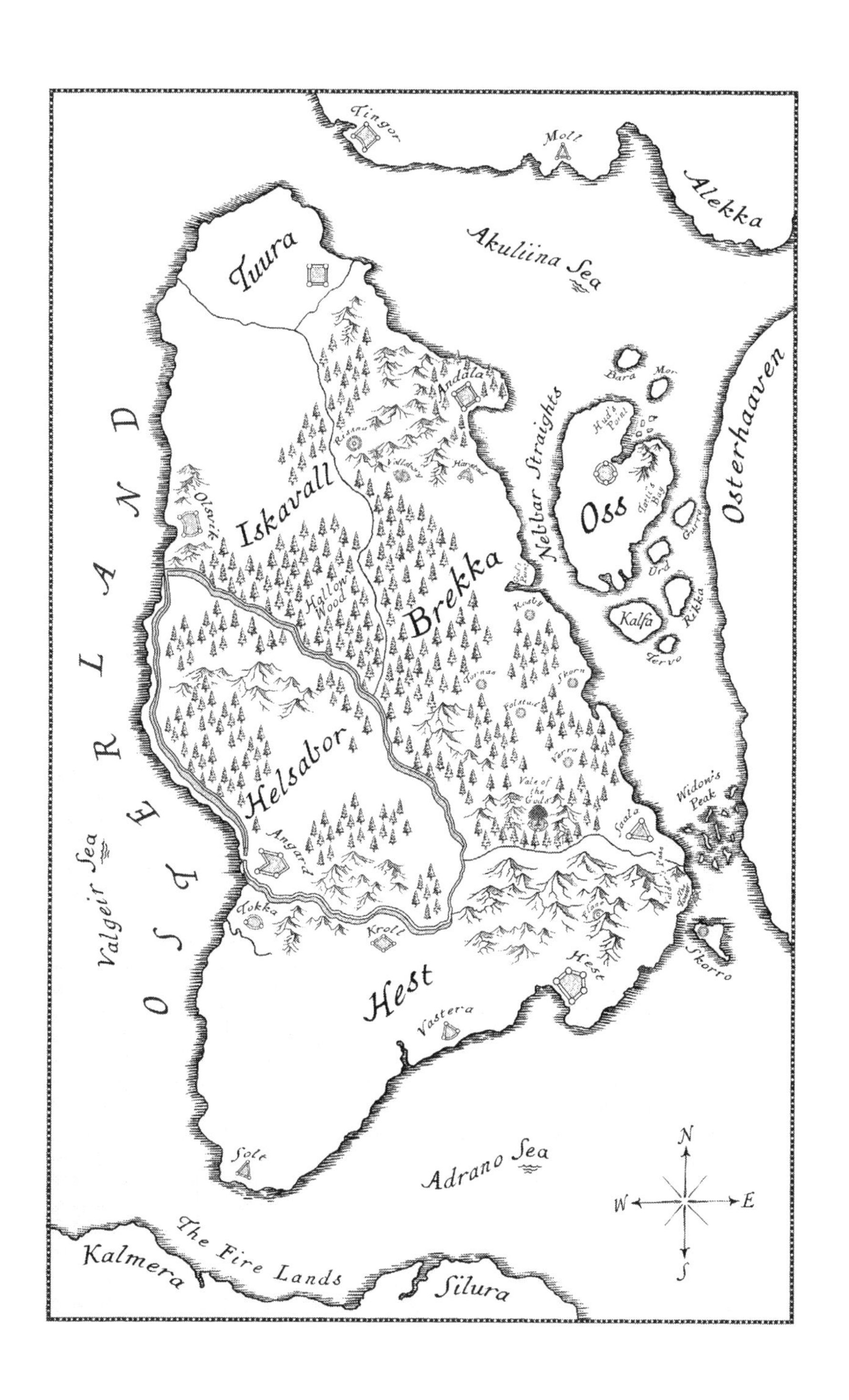

Tingor
Moll
Alekka
Akuliina Sea
Tuura
Andala
Harstad
Bara
Mor
Hud's Point
Osterhaaven
Neltbar Straights
Oss
Iskavall
Olsvik
Hallow Wood
Brekka
Kosby
Skorn
Verra
Vale of the Gods
Kalfa
Urd
Rikka
Tervo
O S T E R L A N D
Valgeir Sea
Helsabor
Widow's Peak
Saala
Angard
Tokka
Kroll
Hest
Skorro
Hest
Vastera
Solt
Adrano Sea
N
W
E
S
Kalmera
The Fire Lands
Silura

CHARACTERS

On Their Way to Andala

Queen Jael Furyck, Queen of Oss
Aleksander Lehr
Axl Furyck, King of Brekka
Gisila Furyck
Gant Olborn
Edela Saeveld
Eydis Skalleson
Brynna 'Biddy' Halvor
Entorp Bray
Amma Furyck
Fyn Gallas
Marcus Volsen
Derwa Fylan
Alaric Fraed
Kormac Byrn
Branwyn Byrn
Aedan Byrn
Kayla Byrn
Aron Byrn
Beorn Rignor
Oleg Grenal

CHARACTERS

In the Kingdom of Hest

Jaeger Dragos, King of Hest

Draguta Teros

Morana Gallas

Meena Gallas

Yorik Elstad

Else Edelborg

On the Island of Oss

Eadmund Skalleson, King of Oss

Thorgils Svanter

Bram Svanter

Isaura Skalleson

Ayla Adea

Bruno Adea

Evaine Gallas

Morac Gallas

Runa Gallas

Torstan Berg

Sevrin Jorri

Tanja Tulo

Arlo Horst

CHARACTERS

Attacking the Island of Oss
Ivaar Skalleson
Borg Arnesson
Toki Arnesson
Rolan Arnesson
Erl Arnesson
Rork Arnesson

Escaping the Kingdom of Hest
Bayla Dragos
Haegen Dragos
Irenna Dragos
Karsten Dragos
Nicolene Dragos
Berard Dragos
Hanna Boelens
Ulf Rutgar

In Saala
Rexon Boas, Lord of Saala

In the Kingdom of Iskavall
Raymon Vandaal, King of Iskavall
Getta Vandaal, Queen of Iskavall
Ravenna Vandaal

PROLOGUE

Her fingernail was long. Sharp. It dug into the baby's chest, and he whimpered.

She smiled.

It was dark in the chamber. Only a single lamp burned, its flame flickering frantically as the wind fought its way in around the window frame; under the door.

The storm was loud.

The woman didn't notice as she trailed her finger over the baby's chest, tracing the same shape three times before moving up to his forehead. She didn't want to leave a mark, so she lifted her nail, using the pad of her finger as she continued drawing the symbol.

Chanting.

Low, murmuring, threatening sounds.

The baby squirmed but did not cry. His lips quivered, though, so she bent down, whispering in his ear. 'You will never know happiness. You will never know joy. You will never fulfil your destiny. Not while there is breath in my lungs.'

'Morana!'

She straightened her spine, swallowing in annoyance as she turned to the doorway. 'Eirik.' Morana fixed the king with a cold smile, shuffling towards him, her black robe sweeping the scattered reeds behind her.

'What are you doing in here? Where's Eskild?' Eirik's frown was deep, his skin prickling as he scanned the dim chamber. *His* chamber. His and his wife's, and now, their newborn son's.

'*Eskild*?' Morana forced that name through yellow teeth. 'I do not know.' She stared at Eirik, challenging him with dark eyes. 'Her servant let me in. I wished to meet your new son.'

'Well, I shall have to get rid of the girl,' Eirik growled. 'She obviously doesn't know how things stand in *my* hall. You will leave this chamber, and I will never see you with my son again. Do you understand me?'

Morana dropped her head, her wild black-and-white hair hiding a smirk. 'Of course. As you wish.' And she edged past him, slipping through the door.

Eirik turned to watch her go, shivering.

PART ONE

A Secret

CHAPTER ONE

'I want those barricades in place now! *Now*!' Eadmund bellowed from the ramparts, turning back to squint at the stone spires guarding the entrance to Oss' harbour. His heart quickened, his body tensing in anticipation. 'Morac!' He turned to the old man who emerged, panting, from the tower below. 'Go to the hall! Get the fires burning high! Have them prepare for wounded men!'

Morac swallowed, his beady eyes unusually big and blinking. 'Are they here?' Turning to the headland, he could see the distant signal fires glowing against the dull morning sky.

Eadmund wasn't listening. 'Sevrin! Go to the square! Find Ketil and Una. I want their fires burning too. Heat the water! Wet the hides!' He turned to Arlo, his head archer, who already had his men lining the ramparts, bows in hand, quivers slung over their shoulders, flaming braziers nearby. 'Is there anything you need?'

Arlo shook his head. 'We're ready, my lord.'

Eadmund turned his attention back to the harbour, staring at the towering stones that threatened anyone who dared to attack them.

Thorgils was lighting the signal fires on his way back to the fort.

And Ivaar was coming.

***

Ivaar spat over the side of *Shadow Blade*. His second ship, *Iron Wolf*, followed closely in its wake. He wanted to vomit, but his men were already looking at him sideways, and he didn't want to give them another reason to lose confidence in his leadership.

He was no lord anymore.

He was trapped in the service of the man preparing to take the crown meant for him. The man who would steal all the gold and glory he had promised his own men.

Borg Arnesson.

The man who had, in the end, proved even more ambitious and ruthless than he was. The man who was about to beat him at his own game.

And there was nothing Ivaar could do about it.

He wiped a cold hand across his blonde beard, which had grown wild since his days as the Lord of Kalfa, and leaned towards his helmsman. 'Seppa, don't get too far ahead of that idiot. We need him ready when we are.' It was the last thing he wanted to say. The humiliation of his fall had been compounded by having to follow the youngest and thickest of the black-haired brothers from Tingor: the dim-witted Toki Arnesson.

Ivaar peered up at the familiar dark cliffs rising along their port side. His father had turned the wild cluster of islands into a kingdom, envisioning a legacy of Skalleson rule for centuries to come.

He would never have expected such a sudden end.

Ivaar tried to shake away the image of Eirik's body, slumped in that chair in Saala; wine dying his white beard a deep, deathly red.

But he couldn't.

***

'We're not going to make it!' Torstan screeched as he rode beside Thorgils, who was bent over Leada, red curls bouncing in the freshening breeze.

Thorgils worried that his friend was right.

There were eight of them charging up the island, racing against the line of ships they could see weaving around the stone spires. If they didn't arrive back at the fort in time, there would be no hope of getting inside before Ivaar and his men were on the beach.

Thorgils glanced at Torstan. 'Then let's go faster!' he grinned, though his throat had gone dry with thoughts of what Ivaar would do if he took the fort. And digging his heels into Leada's flanks, he urged her on. 'Come on, girl! Faster!'

***

Isaura was trying not to panic as she gripped Leya's little hand, pulling her up off the hall floor. Her youngest daughter had tripped over, and though there was only the slightest of grazes on her knee, she was wailing as though she had lost her entire leg. 'Ssshhh, now,' Isaura soothed distractedly, her eyes focused on Ayla, who was helping Bruno to a table by the fire. 'It's just a scratch.' Bending down, she smiled quickly. 'Why don't you go and see if you can find where that white cat has gone? Perhaps she's already had her kittens? Go on, go and see.' And standing up, she motioned for Selene to come and take her little sister, who had quickly ceased her crying, easily distracted by the thought of kittens.

Isaura hurried to Ayla, who looked unusually pale. 'Is it Ivaar?' she asked, shivering, though it was a warmer than usual summer morning on Oss. 'Is he finally here?'

'Yes,' Ayla nodded, pouring a cup of water for Bruno, noting the fiery spark in her husband's eyes at the sound of that name. 'He's here.'

'But where is Thorgils? Will he make it back in time?' Isaura panicked, glancing at the hall doors, which had remained closed since Morac's arrival. 'It's a long ride from Hud's Point.'

Ayla started to smile reassuringly at her friend, but she could feel her body shudder in protest. 'I'm sure he will. Thorgils would do anything to be here to protect you. Now come, let's go and help Runa get everything ready.' She took Isaura's hand, pulling her towards the kitchen. Soon, many men would be injured, she knew, and they needed to be ready to help them.

Evaine bumped into Ayla as she raced towards her father. 'Watch where you're going, dreamer!' she snapped, shaking her head, irritated by Ayla, and by her father, who seemed more interested in talking to Runa than anyone else.

Morac was giving his wife a long list of instructions about preparing the hall, and Runa was having trouble remembering them all. 'Morac!' she interrupted. 'I have to make a start. I will come back to you once I've prepared the tables. For now, though, you must let me begin!'

'Yes, yes, of course.' Morac felt anxious. Everything they had worked so hard to achieve was about to be destroyed. And where was Morana? Why hadn't his sister come into his dreams, offering her advice? Telling him what to do?

'Father!' Evaine hissed as she strode past Runa, grabbing Morac's arm. 'Where is Eadmund? I need to see him. Those men won't let me out of the hall!' She pointed to the doors, which were now blocked by two armed men.

'We're keeping everyone where I can see them. I can't have children running around distracting the men out there while they're working with boiling liquid. It's unsafe. And once Ivaar and his allies reach the walls, they will fire into the fort for sure. It's too dangerous.'

'But I must see Eadmund!' Evaine was frantic. 'He left before I woke. I must see him. If something happens... I haven't even said goodbye!' she sobbed.

Morac wasn't about to be moved by a few tears, but he did need to placate his daughter before she consumed what little time he had to prepare, so gripping Evaine's other arm, he bent to her ear. 'Nothing will happen to Eadmund. Morana will be watching, keeping him safe for you. We need Eadmund, don't we? All of us. He will not be hurt. Not now that *she* is here.'

Evaine was confused. 'Who? What do you mean?'

Morac glanced around, but the hall was filled with a heady din of activity, and no one was looking their way. 'Last night, they were planning to raise the woman. Draguta. She will stop anything from happening to you and Eadmund. She will protect us all.' Morac frowned, not sure if that was the truth, but he spoke with such calm authority that he could see Evaine's face relax as she stared up at him.

'You're sure?'

'Of course,' Morac said with some effort. 'Morana will know that we're in danger here. You've nothing to fear.'

***

Morana bent over the bowl.

She had been vomiting all morning. Her head felt as though it was being banged with an iron rod. The constant pounding made her wince as waves of nausea rolled over her aching body. She could barely lift an eyelash without cringing.

Though she'd never felt happier.

'You're sure you wouldn't like some water?' Yorik wondered from his position by the door. 'Or wine?' It was a humid day, and the stink of the chamber, and of Morana, most of all, was turning his stomach. He was desperate to leave, wanting to inhale some fresh air, but he felt obliged to make sure that she was alright.

After what she had achieved?

He'd never felt happier.

'No,' Morana croaked, sitting back against the bed and wiping her mouth. She glared at him. 'You shouldn't be here! You must be with Draguta. We cannot afford to have her and Jaeger plot against us. Remove us from the next stage. *We* must be the ones she trusts to guide her now. You and I.'

Yorik nodded, certain she was right.

He couldn't stop thinking about her.

Draguta.

She was exquisite. Unexpectedly delicate. Ageless. Intoxicating. The most powerful being he had ever met, yet surprisingly human. Yorik was overcome with an urgency to be by her side, assisting her. Caring for her. Helping her familiarise herself with life again –

'Are you listening to me?' Morana barked, disturbed by the dreamy look on Yorik's grizzled face. He appeared utterly dazed, although, after the ritual, she was hardly surprised. The complex mix of herbs and seeds had created such a powerful trance that she still felt half trapped in the Dolma.

Morana smiled. The Dolma. Such dark bliss, death, and emptiness.

Raemus' prison.

But not for long.

'Yes, yes, I shall go to her,' Yorik said eagerly, opening the door and taking a welcome breath. 'Shall I send your niece? Perhaps she could attend to you while you are... incapacitated?'

Morana grinned. 'Well, if you can convince Jaeger to let her go, then yes, I'm sure she'd be happy to come and clean out my sick bowl.' She watched the door close, then gripping her belly, she groaned in misery, reaching for the bowl.

***

Meena stared at the stain on the flagstones, trying not to inhale the stench of death in the chamber or the odour wafting up from her armpits.

Jaeger was stumbling about, hurrying to dress. She could sense his desperation to leave to be with her.

That woman.

And she was indeed a woman.

Meena had thought that Draguta would resemble some sort of decaying monster, like the ones in her nightmares, but she was beautiful.

Beautiful and evil.

Meena could feel it.

She swallowed, gingerly touching her swollen face. It hurt to blink, and she was trying hard not to, but she was so terrified when she thought of what would happen next that her eyes wouldn't stop twitching.

'You will wait here,' Jaeger muttered, almost to himself as he tugged on his boots. 'I shall send someone up with food. Someone to clean up the mess.' He glanced briefly at the enormous bloody stain covering his chamber floor, ruing the loss of his servant, Egil, who had been with him for longer than he could remember. But, he was easily replaceable, Jaeger knew. He stared at Meena, who was almost completely still as she sat at the table. It was unusual to see her not tapping her head. 'We will talk when I return. About what will happen next.' He smiled, then yawned. His throbbing head was a confused mess, and he was struggling to see straight.

Meena didn't even nod.

Standing, Jaeger walked towards her, and touching her bruised face, he felt momentarily troubled by what he had done. 'Everything will be better now that Berard has gone. Now that they've all gone.' Jaeger kissed the top of her tangled mop of red hair and strode towards the door, suddenly ravenous. 'You'll see, Meena. Everything will be better now.'

Meena watched him go, wishing she'd left with Berard and

his family.

Listening as Jaeger turned the key in the lock, she dropped her eyes back to the flagstones, to the stain Egil had made as he died.

Knowing that she'd killed him.

She had killed him and stayed behind for a reason, and turning towards the book that lay open on the table before her, Meena knew very well what that reason was.

***

'How many ships?' Bram stood on the ramparts beside his old helmsman, Snorri, who had a better pair of eyes than him. It was drizzling, and his beard was dripping down his tight-fitting mail shirt. He looked up accusingly at the darkening sky. No one needed rain now.

Not when they had invaders to burn.

Eadmund eyed Snorri, who appeared to be holding his breath, squinting into the distance.

'Ten. Maybe twelve,' Snorri said, at last. 'Maybe more hiding behind the spires. They're going in and out. It's hard to keep track.'

Bram's eyes widened. That was a lot of ships.

'Go and find Ayla. I need to speak to her,' Eadmund said to Bram. He turned to Sevrin, who was squeezing his way along the ramparts, past the archers, heading for his king. The ramparts around Oss' fort had always been too narrow for anyone's liking, but there was nothing Eadmund could do about that now. 'Are the fletchers at work?'

Sevrin nodded. 'They are.' He looked across the harbour, watching as the dark shadows of enemy ships bobbed around the spires. The wind was picking up, and their visibility was reducing rapidly.

'And you've men watching the rear of the fort?'

'All around,' Sevrin said. 'Any sign of Thorgils and Torstan?'

Eadmund shook his head, eyes wandering back to the narrow neck of land that rose alongside the harbour, stretching out far past its entrance.

Those ships would be here soon.

He hoped his friends would hurry.

***

The currents around the jagged, black stones were wicked. Like his mother.

Twisted and dark. Hidden and mysterious.

Borg Arnesson laughed at the looks on the faces of the men around him: grey with fear as they glanced up at the tall shards of rock that threatened their chances for glory. His mother had seen him breaking into that fort, though, so Borg felt no such terror. He felt confident that his destiny would not have him ending up as Ilvari's supper. Turning around, he was pleased to see his brother's ship, still following closely. Borg hoped he'd made the right choice sending Toki with Ivaar Skalleson. That conniving bastard wasn't a man to be trusted, but he was heavily outnumbered now, and Borg knew that Ivaar had no choice but to follow the man who would soon be his new king.

Smiling as his confidence rose, Borg caught a glimpse of flames up on the cliffs, knowing that they were expected. 'We land fast!' he cried, scanning the grim faces of his dark-haired crew who bent over the oars, hoping they'd make it to land. 'Beach quickly! Shield walls! Archers at the rear! We'll take them off the ramparts, then work the gates and wait for Toki and the Bastard to break in from the other side!'

His men barely grunted in acknowledgement. Borg didn't notice as he turned his gaze up to the stone fort that sat atop the hill in the distance.

Soon, this would all be his, and his enemies would loosen their bowels as his fleet swarmed the harbour. 'Victory!' he shouted joyously, thinking of how quickly he could get his bride into his new bed; his queen, he corrected himself. Queen Falla of Oss. 'Victory will be ours!'

***

'Faster!' Thorgils screamed into the rain; the heavy rain that had turned the ground soft and slowed their progress. He could see the fort now, but he could also see the first ships entering the harbour. Leada was tiring beneath him, and Thorgils didn't blame her as she snorted and blew furiously, her legs struggling up the long incline towards the fort. She had the heaviest weight to lug up the island, and he was asking her to do it at the fastest speed possible.

But he had to get everyone back in time.

Thorgils kicked her again, hearing Leada grunt in protest, feeling the thunderous pounding of her hooves, the shuddering of her muscles as they stretched to their limits, propelling them both forward.

'Faster!' Torstan yelled beside him, panicking, his face numbed by the wind, his vision blurred from the driving rain.

Turning around, Torstan saw the fear in their men's eyes.

Terrified, just like he was.

They weren't going to make it.

***

'Do you see anything? Any sign of Jael coming?' Eadmund

wondered, peering into Ayla's eyes in the dim light of the windowless tower room. He had not wanted her up on the ramparts, where everyone could hear their conversation.

Ayla shook her head. 'No, I've not seen anything.'

Eadmund sighed, unable to hide his disappointment. 'Well, go back to the hall, then. But if you see anything, have someone bring you back. Even if I'm sleeping, have me woken, Ayla. I need to know.'

'Of course,' she said quietly, jumping at a sudden bellowing from above.

Eadmund was quickly distracted, eager to get back to the ramparts. 'Erdon, see Ayla back to the hall,' he said, motioning to the man who was struggling in through the door with a large cauldron. 'I'll take that.'

Erdon nodded, and lowering the cauldron onto the dirt floor, he motioned for Ayla to follow him.

'Grab a shield, man!' Eadmund barked. 'I need you to keep her safe!' And, picking up the heavy cauldron, he turned towards the stairs.

***

Shadow Blade sailed past the tiny cove.

It was far in the distance, almost entirely hidden behind a pair of jagged black rocks which rose out of the frothing sea to shield it from view. Not many knew it was there. Not even his helmsman, it seemed, as Seppa's attention was fixed straight ahead.

Ivaar knew Oss' coastline well. He knew the safest place to climb the cliffs, the fastest route up to the fort, the best place to beach their ships.

But he wasn't leading Toki near any of them.

And he didn't know why.

***

'Open the gates!' Eadmund cried, watching the horses crest the hill. His eyes darted back to the beach where the first ships were being rushed onto the black stones, watching as swathes of dark-haired, heavily tattooed men jumped into the water, shields up, swords and axes at the ready. 'Arlo! Pin them down on the beach! Sevrin, take command! I need ten shield men! Three archers! Bram, get your bow! With me!' And Eadmund ran to the stairs, his men grabbing their weapons as they scrambled after him.

By the time they made their way out of the guard tower, the gates were already being dragged open. Eadmund pointed to one of the guards. 'Get more men. You're going to need to close them in a hurry! I want you ready with the beam as soon as we're through!' And he turned, shield up, running away from the fort towards the straining horses, his small group of men charging after him.

'Shield wall!' Eadmund bellowed as a wave of arrows whistled from the ramparts towards the men swarming across the beach, who stopped, quickly forming their own walls. Crouching behind his shield, Eadmund could hear the sound of hooves rhythmically striking the ground, the vibrations intensifying as the horses and their riders approached.

Thorgils saw the shield walls on the beach, certain that his heart had stopped. He swallowed, watching as more men flooded the stones, battering their weapons on shields as they raced to join the walls. Arms started pointing in their direction. 'Watch for arrows!' he screamed, urging Leada on. He needed to get her behind Eadmund's wall and into the fort.

'Archers!'

Thorgils could hear the call from the beach. 'Go!' he yelled, kicking Leada one more time, and despite the length of their journey and the challenge of the long hill, she dug in deeper, straining, spurred on by those open gates.

Eadmund, Bram, and their archers ducked as arrows shot towards them from the beach. The shields held as the arrows struck, thumping into wood. Eadmund could hear the horses getting closer. 'Archers! Fire at will!'

Another volley of arrows flew towards the riders.

Torstan grimaced, head low, waiting for the impact, but it was Thorgils who went down ahead of him.

'Aarrghh!' Thorgils cried, feeling Leada jerk in shock. And quickly slipping his feet out of the stirrups, he threw himself clear of her falling body. Cracking his elbow on a rock as he hit the ground, he rolled away from Leada, who was roaring in pain, already trying to get back to her feet.

Torstan yanked his reins, skirting the tumbling white horse and her red-haired rider, trying to avoid falling with them.

'Leada!' Eadmund pulled out of the shield wall, running towards his injured horse, relieved to see Thorgils back on his feet. 'Archers!' he called. '*Fire*!' Eadmund waved Torstan and the rest of the riders onwards, towards the open gates.

An arrow had punctured Leada's neck, and she appeared to have stunned herself in the fall. She was shaking her head, blowing angrily, trying to keep to her feet, but she looked ready to fall down again.

'Come on!' Thorgils urged, tugging her bridle as Eadmund grabbed her reins. 'Come on, girl!'

Bram was there now. 'We have to hurry!' He rushed around to Leada's rump, slapping her on it. 'Go! Go!'

Eadmund and Thorgils ran alongside the limping horse as the arrows flew in endless waves from the ramparts; Arlo working hard to give their enemies no chance to emerge from their shields until Eadmund and his men were safely inside the fort.

'Shields! Back up! Let's get inside!' Eadmund yelled as he hurried Leada towards the gates. 'Ready the beam!'

***

Borg crouched behind his shield wall, assessing his options, watching the gates close, twitching as another clattering of arrows stabbed into the shields protecting his head. He was happy to let the Osslanders use up their arrows. If that old fool, Frits Hallstein, had been right, they wouldn't have many to spare.

And when the arrows were gone?

Borg smiled, knowing that soon there would be nothing stopping them from getting into Eadmund Skalleson's fort.

CHAPTER TWO

Jael jerked around, knocking heads with Aleksander, who had fallen asleep on her shoulder. It was the middle of the day, or somewhere near, but they had been awake for much of the night and were only now catching up on some sleep.

'What? What is it?' Aleksander asked throatily, blinking himself awake.

'I had a dream,' Jael panted, rubbing her eyes, checking on Fyn, who lay to her right. He was still asleep. Sunshine streamed through arrow holes in the walls of *Sea Bear's* wooden house. They had finally sailed away from Tuura during what felt like the longest night she could remember, and now they were well on their way to Andala. The wind was strong, and Jael hoped to arrive by the following morning.

They had to get catapults fitted to two ships, gather all the sea-fire that Aleksander and Edela had hidden away, and sail for Oss to help Eadmund defend the island.

'What did you see?' Aleksander wondered, glancing at Axl, who was talking to Amma on the other side of the narrow house. Gisila was sleeping beside them, Biddy and Edela next to her. Eydis was curled up with the puppies, her head on Edela's knee.

'Ivaar,' Jael said, turning to him with a weary smile. 'I saw Ivaar.'

***

'The book?' Jaeger's fingers drummed against his legs. 'You want me to give you the book?' He had been so distracted by the breathtaking beauty of the woman that he'd not listened to anything she'd said.

Until now.

Draguta Teros perched upon the dragon throne of Hest, eyeing him coldly. A tall, slender woman of middle age, she possessed an almost fragile beauty. Her ivory skin glowed beneath a crown of flowing black hair, accentuating a pair of almond-shaped eyes, icy blue and penetrating. Her body was rigid; the determination in her gaze iron-strong.

Jaeger couldn't take his eyes off her.

But the book?

Draguta studied him, feeling the smooth skull armrests beneath her palms, thinking of her son, Valder Dragos, who had been the first man to sit upon the dragon throne of Hest. Though she was elated to be free from the Dolma, her return felt bittersweet without him by her side.

The man who stood before her wasn't Valder, but he was big, angry, and determined to be the king. Though... she could sense weakness.

Fear.

She could smell it on him.

'It is *my* book,' Draguta breathed, lips barely moving. 'Mine. And it belongs in my chamber now. With me.'

Jaeger swallowed, glancing at Yorik Elstad, who stood to one side of Draguta, cowed, avoiding his eyes, almost servant-like in his demeanour. It appeared that Draguta wasn't used to being told no. 'The book revealed itself to me,' Jaeger tried, suddenly desperate for wine. He saw a vision of his father on the throne, mocking him, and shaking his head, rolling back his thick shoulders, Jaeger remembered how he had run his sword through his father's chest the night before.

That cheered him.

Draguta laughed as she stood, smoothing down her dress of light-blue silk, pulling on the ill-fitting sleeves. Bayla Dragos' dress, she thought dismissively. It was loose, a little too short, a little... tasteless. 'Of course it was revealed to you,' she purred, gliding towards him. 'Once I knew your part in the prophecy, I made sure of that. And because of you, I am finally home. But you, my dear Jaeger, you look quite unwell. After what you gave for me last night? All that blood? You really should be in bed, recovering your strength. I will have great need of you soon, so you must get stronger for me.' Reaching up, she stroked his unshaven cheek, feeling the sharp ridge of his prominent cheekbone. 'There is much we will achieve together, you and I. This kingdom? This will be the *only* kingdom in Osterland soon. We shall both see to that.'

Jaeger shivered. Her touch was like ice, her eyes so demanding that he couldn't look away; so intense that he felt himself drawn to her, unable to do or say anything at all.

He felt powerless.

Yorik was still there, hovering behind them both, and Draguta turned to him. 'See Jaeger to his chamber, then bring me the book. I shall wait here for you.' She dismissed the two men with an impatient wave of an elegant hand and turned to the row of slaves standing mutely against the wall, their shaven heads bowed, waiting to be called upon. 'Wine!' Draguta exclaimed. 'I think I should like to try some wine!'

Yorik hurried towards the entranceway, turning to wait for his new king.

Jaeger forced his feet to move and reluctantly followed him, fleeting memories of Berard's anguished face flashing past his eyes. He blinked them away and kept walking, his thoughts returning to the book.

He would not give it up. He would not part with it.

The Book of Darkness was meant for him.

***

'How far away are we now?' Bayla demanded, rounding on the old helmsman.

Ulf Rutgar rolled his eyes, already tired of the nagging drone of the queen who would not let him be. He had not expected to be ferrying the Dragos family to Saala, but he realised that there was a chance of more gold at the end of the journey now. And, if that was the case, then it was worth enduring Bayla Dragos' endless stream of sharp-edged questions. 'We should arrive late tomorrow night if the wind stays this angry, my lady.'

Bayla sighed. That sounded like forever. It was a wreck of a ship, in need of repair. And the crew looked like swarthy, murderous beggars. But, she had to admit, not as murderous as her youngest son. Tears welled in her eyes, and she turned away from Ulf, into the wind, quickly wiping them away. She didn't want to think of Haaron, and of what Jaeger had surely done to his father. She didn't want to imagine what would become of them now.

They just needed to get to Saala. To get Berard some help for his injured arm.

Bayla shuddered. It wasn't an arm anymore.

'Are you listening?' Karsten wondered, nudging Hanna, who was watching Bayla try to pull herself together.

Hanna shook her head. 'Sorry, what did you say?'

'What will you do once we reach Saala?' Karsten repeated. 'What should *we* do?'

'We convince Rexon Boas to give us men!' Haegen insisted from his other side. 'We go through the pass. We take back the castle!'

Karsten snorted, adjusting his eye patch. 'You think a few hundred Saalans can help us do that? If Jaeger didn't kill Father, those guards would have, and then they would've killed all of us. You saw the way they were. The Following has control of the city now. We can't go back until we have a real army behind us.'

Haegen shook his head, tired and confused by everything that had happened. He didn't want to imagine his father's final moments, facing down Jaeger and his giant sword. There was no way that Haaron could have survived a fight with his largest, most violent son. No way that Jaeger would have shown him any mercy.

Not after what he'd done to Berard.

'We need to head to Andala once we get Berard some help,' Hanna said. 'We all do. You won't be safe in Saala for long.'

Karsten glanced at Nicolene, who was trying to stop their two sons crawling over Berard as he lay shivering against the gunwale, wrapped in cloaks and furs. '*Andala*? You think we'll be safe there? You think we'll be safe anywhere? After what you've said about this prophecy?' He lowered his voice. 'Sounds to me as though no one will be safe while The Following has that book.'

'We don't know what has happened in Tuura,' Hanna said. 'But we can go to Andala and find out. They might know. We need to find Jael. She is the one the prophecy says will stop the Darkness from coming.'

Karsten snorted again. 'Jael Furyck? Ha! You think *she* can stop Jaeger? Or this woman? Or The Following?'

Hanna winced as Berard roared in pain again. 'I think we need to get as far away from The Following as we can. The best thing we can do is find Jael and my father. They will know what to do next.'

***

Isaura threw her arms around Thorgils' neck in relief, stretching up on her tiptoes as he bent down to her. 'You're alright,' she breathed. 'You're alright!' Squeezing him tightly, she could feel his chest rising and falling against hers. It felt wet. Standing back, she looked him over and saw blood. '*Are* you alright?'

'It's Leada's,' Thorgils frowned. 'She took an arrow in the neck. I'm going to check on her, then head up to the ramparts. Although, maybe I'll just grab something to drink first.' Glancing around, he saw Torstan and their sodden men gathered around a table, filling their cups, and he headed towards them.

'Ivaar's here, then?' Isaura asked, hurrying alongside Thorgils, ignoring Mads, who was bellowing for her.

'On the beach,' Thorgils nodded, taking the cup Torstan offered him. He drank quickly, wiping a hand through his wet beard. 'But we've got them pinned down. They won't be going anywhere for a while.'

Isaura stood on her tiptoes again, pushing away Thorgils' straggly wet curls, searching for his ear. 'What about Jael? Any sign of her?' she whispered.

Thorgils shook his head, sensing Isaura's disappointment. 'Not yet. But don't worry, there's no more stubborn creature in Osterland than Jael Furyck. If she said she's coming, nothing is going to stop her from getting here.'

***

Jael stood by Tig, running her hand down his smooth dark back as he swayed anxiously with the ship. He was secured to a pole that ran from the house to *Sea Bear's* prow, and he whinnied constantly, utterly miserable, struggling with his balance, disturbed by the whistling wind.

He hated sailing almost as much as Edela.

The weather was gloomy, and the air was brisk, and although the Akuliina was a notoriously difficult stretch of sea, it was nothing compared to sailing across the evil Nebbar

Straights.

Jael shivered, knowing that she needed to be on Oss. Now. But there was nothing she could do to get them to Andala any faster.

She couldn't stop thinking about Eadmund. He would be working hard to keep the invaders at bay, but there were so many of them. Jael could feel it. She could almost see them surging across that familiar stone beach like a black mass, desperate to break down the gates.

Wanting to kill Eadmund.

She'd seen him in her dreams: Borg Arnesson, the Alekkan lord with a face so ruined by scars that he could barely see. Those mangled eyes burned brightly with ambition, though.

He wanted Eadmund's throne.

But first, he wanted Eadmund's life.

Jael rested her head against Tig's, trying to convince him to stay still. Hoping to calm them both down. But she couldn't. Not until she was standing with *Toothpick* in her hand and Borg Arnesson on the ground, the tip of her blade at his hairy throat, would she feel any better.

***

Their shield wall was more of a shield house, and the Alekkans hid inside it, creeping along the black stones, wishing they'd come to an island with a sandy beach. It would have been kinder on their feet, and their knees.

But Borg was still smiling.

He turned to Rolan, punching his shoulder. 'They won't have arrows for long! And we have enough shields to make a real house here. Build a fire! Cook a meal!'

Rolan tried to look as relaxed as his older brother, but he was growing uncomfortable. The fort looked strong. He peered between their shields, cringing as the arrows showered over them whenever they edged forward.

A strong fort with thickly packed ramparts.

'They won't have arrows for long, Brother!' Borg repeated, laughing at Rolan's frowning face. 'Forward!' he ordered, noticing that the arrows had stopped again. 'We *want* them to attack us! We're safe in here, but let them think they can hurt us! Let them fire all the arrows they like! Again!' he cried. 'Forward!'

***

Jaeger held the book in his big hands, pushing his boots down onto the flagstones. Yorik stood before him, reaching for it, but Jaeger could not bring himself to let go.

It was his book.

His.

'She must have the book to bring Raemus back,' Yorik tried, desperate to hurry back to the hall.

Jaeger glared at him, irritated by his eagerness to please Draguta. 'And what will she do, when Raemus comes back?' he wondered, gripping that cool black cover more tightly than ever. It was as though the book was pleading with him, not wanting to be reunited with Draguta. 'What use will you have for her or me then? Any of you?'

Yorik dropped his eyes to the book. He had answers, of course, but Jaeger wouldn't want to hear them.

Jaeger could almost read his thoughts, though. 'And if I don't give it to her? Surely the only page she needs is not even in here?' he tried. 'She ripped it out, didn't she?'

'I... she...' Yorik stumbled, not wanting to debate anything, not while Draguta was waiting for him. 'She was the mistress of this book for a long time, my lord. And when Raemus returns, it will be up to him to decide what becomes of it. Not you, or even her. Raemus will decide everything soon.'

Jaeger narrowed his eyes. 'Raemus?' he sneered. 'You're so confident that he'll deliver you to this place of darkness you want so much. But what if you could be happier in the light? With unlimited wealth? A lord in this land? *My* lord? Hest has plenty of towns and villages. You could choose one. Rule as you wished. As a rich, powerful man.'

'That is not our goal, my lord.'

'No,' Jaeger sighed in resignation, releasing his hold on the book so that Yorik could finally snatch it away. 'No, it's not, is it?'

'We will claim the ultimate power when Raemus returns. We will destroy your enemies. All of your family. All of Osterland,' Yorik breathed. 'It will be everything you imagine. The Darkness will surround us all. Set us free! You will be as powerful as you always dreamed!' His eyes were glazed with ecstasy as he stared up at Jaeger's scowling face.

And as Jaeger looked down at Yorik, watching as he edged towards the door, the Book of Darkness in his hands, he realised that he had made a terrible mistake.

***

'How is he?' Karsten wondered as Irenna swayed before them, rubbing her eyes.

'The bleeding has slowed down,' she sighed, glancing at Haegen, who was jiggling their two-year-old daughter, Halla, in his arms. She was proving to be an even noisier sailor than Karsten's son Kai. 'We're going to need more cloth, though. I've already ripped off the bottom of my dress. You're all going to have to tear some strips off your tunics. I have to change the bandages often.'

They nodded, both quiet, still shocked by what Jaeger had

done.

There had always been an unspoken hostility between the Dragos brothers, even as children. It was as though they knew that they were jostling for the prize of one day being the King of Hest. Although, just below the surface, it wasn't jostling at all, but full-throated ambition; a desperation to claim the dragon throne by any means necessary.

And now, here it was.

The unspoken thing had finally been revealed, and the consequences were far worse than any of them had imagined.

Now they had no father, no kingdom, and Berard had lost an arm, and if they couldn't get help for him soon, perhaps he would lose his life too.

***

'Hold your fire!' Eadmund barked, fed up with the crouching shield houses as they edged forward, then crept back. 'They just want to waste our arrows! Let them crawl along the stones all they like. Save the arrows for when they're coming up the hill!'

Sevrin nodded his agreement, shielding his eyes from a burst of late afternoon sunshine. 'There's nothing to report from the rear. No sign of anything happening anywhere but here.'

Eadmund took a long drink from his waterskin before handing it to Sevrin. 'But where's Ivaar? In one of those houses?' He shook his head. 'I didn't see him. None of those ships looks Kalfan. And why isn't he at the front, leading his men? Taunting me?' He frowned, unable to shake the nagging worry that Ivaar was up to something. Though that wasn't unexpected, he supposed. Ivaar was always up to something. 'Keep everyone alert. They'll try and outflank us somehow.'

'If they're stupid enough to climb the cliffs, there probably won't be many of them left by the time they're outside the walls,' Sevrin snorted derisively. 'Good luck to them!'

But Eadmund didn't stop frowning. 'No one's more determined to take this fort than Ivaar. He'll do anything, use any way he can to get in here. Where Ivaar's concerned, we'd be fools to rule anything out, so go! Make sure the men have everything they need. Keep regular watches through the night. Everywhere! Make sure the braziers are burning. We can't afford to miss a thing!'

***

'What do you think?' Toki Arnesson called over the gunwale, his youthful face bursting with energy despite the treacherous journey down the Nebbar Straights.

Ivaar sighed as he clung to *Shadow Blade's* prow, his eyes up on the sheer, dark cliffs of the island he knew so well, his shoulders like lumps of stone. 'That's not a climb to make in the rain or the dark!' he called back, trying to raise his voice over the intensifying howl of the wind.

Toki frowned, instantly disappointed, but he could hardly argue with Ivaar's logic. Those cliffs looked slick, and the sun was already heading down behind the island. Soon it would be dark. 'We beach in the cove, then. Head up at first light!'

Ivaar nodded, turning away to give Seppa his instructions, not inviting any further discussion. Toki was an idiot, and Ivaar was surprised that he was even listening to him, but, he supposed, it was impossible not to notice the threat those cliffs posed. He swayed back down the ship, calling to his helmsman. 'Follow the Alekkans in! We'll sleep on the beach tonight. Tomorrow, we climb!'

And though they could hear their lord, not one of his men even lifted their eyes.

***

Despite the cold and the wind and a sudden downpour, Borg was happy with how the day had gone. The Osslanders had loosed enough arrows for their stores to be getting low, and by the time the sun rose, he felt confident that he'd be sitting in his new hall, warming his toes by a blazing fire.

Especially when Toki and the Bastard arrived at that secret door.

'Stay sharp!' he growled to his men as they edged back to their ships, shields up, protecting themselves, though there was little possibility of another attack now. They were edging out of range, and the sky was darkening rapidly.

The bodies of his and his cousins' dead men lay along the beach, peppered with holes, their wounds leaking onto the stones. But no arrows. Borg had sent his men out to collect those.

They were going to need every arrow they could get to take those men off the ramparts.

***

'Do you think they'll try tonight?' Thorgils wondered, turning to Bram as they watched the enemy creep back to their ships. 'Makes sense to try and surprise us.'

Bram grunted. 'They can try, but once we stick them with a few fire arrows, there'll be plenty of light to see by!'

Thorgils grinned, rubbing his numb elbow. He was worried about Leada. She had collapsed in her stall, and he'd left Askel tending to her wound, which didn't look good. He wished Entorp or Biddy were there to help Askel prepare some sort of healing salve.

'We'll take shifts through the night,' Eadmund said,

squeezing along the ramparts. 'We need sharp-eyed men on every section of the wall. They'll try something for sure.'

'Or maybe they'll just wait for us to run out of arrows?' Thorgils suggested. 'They won't have long to wait!'

Eadmund frowned. Thorgils was right, but there was little he could do about it now. They didn't have enough arrows. They would just have to use what they had to hand and hope to hold them out as long as they could to give Jael a chance to arrive with more men.

Watching as the shield houses edged back towards the ships, Eadmund tried to focus, but his mind was weary, and his doubts kept floating into it. He closed his eyes, shutting them out, listening instead to his father's gravelly voice urging him on.

He had to protect the island.

He had to save his people.

'Ivaar came planning to break in,' Bram said quietly, 'so, likely, he'll know how to go about doing it. We should make sure the gates have enough behind them to hold. Enough to trip them up if they break in.'

'Do it,' Eadmund said. 'We can't let them get through. And Thorgils, go and check on everyone in the hall. Tell Evaine that I'll be there soon. I'm going to walk the ramparts a while longer.'

Thorgils and Bram nodded, watching as Eadmund strode away from them.

Bram put his hand on Thorgils' arm. 'If Ivaar gets in,' he whispered, 'I'll try and get you out.'

Thorgils blinked. 'What do you mean?'

'You, Isaura, and the children. There'll be a way, I'm sure. In all the ruckus, maybe you'll be able to slip away before Ivaar realises what's happening. So, if it comes to that, be ready. You can make it to Tatti's Bay. You can take a ship. Escape.'

Thorgils watched his uncle's face disappear into shadow.

He swallowed, not wanting to think about what would happen if Ivaar got in.

CHAPTER THREE

'You think they're in the fort yet?'

Toki wouldn't leave Ivaar alone.

Ivaar had planned to camp with his own men, keeping to themselves, but Toki quickly came to sit beside him, sharing his measly fire. 'In the fort?' Ivaar shook his head. 'It's a well-built fort, so I doubt it. And if my dreamer saw us coming, then they've had time to prepare. Time to make arrows. So no, not yet.'

'Good.'

Toki looked like a small-eyed, long-limbed ferret. One who had been dropped on his head at birth. His mad eyes were almost crossed, and Ivaar looked away from them, warming his hands in front of the fire. The wind was a bitter gale, and the flames blew away from him.

Not even they wanted his company.

'Good?' Ivaar grunted.

'If we're the first ones into the fort, we'll be the ones sung about!'

'Around our pyres, you mean,' Ivaar snorted. 'If we get in before your brothers, we'll have to fight like we're twice as many men.'

'We'll get to the gates, open them up. Borg and Rolan will come in! All the men we need will be right there, waiting outside,' Toki insisted, draining his cup.

'Sure, those who don't have arrows through their necks.'

Toki shrugged, not wanting his excitement dampened by Ivaar's sour mood. 'Well, unlike you, Bastard, I trust my family. They're *real* warriors, not like your drunken brother. I'd be surprised if he can mount much of a defense without his bitch wife!' And with that, Toki scrambled to his feet, searching for more ale, deciding that Ivaar was better left to his own miserable company.

Ivaar sighed, doubting that any amount of ale would help him become as lost as he wanted to feel. He thought of Ayla, remembering the feel of her body in his arms. Such a beautiful, useful woman, but always so sad.

Did she see him coming?

Turning around, he realised how alone he was. His men were clustered together, murmuring amongst themselves as they handed out pork biscuits and salt fish, not one of them seeking his company.

Staring at the flames, Ivaar shivered, barely noticing as the rain grew heavier.

***

'Are you alright?' Jael wondered as Edela yawned from her fur-covered box. She suppressed a yawn herself, eager to get some more sleep. Once they arrived in Andala, there would be little time to race through everything they needed to do before they left for Oss.

'No,' Edela murmured, wriggling her arms away from the wooden sides of the very narrow bed she had been stuffed into. 'No, I'm not. Not until my boots are on a pier will I be alright!'

It had been a fast journey from Tuura, aided by a brisk wind, but that had left her sea-hating grandmother in a constant state of terror. 'It won't be long now, Jael promised. 'If you can get some sleep, you'll wake up in Andala.'

'How is young Fyn?' Edela asked, ignoring her granddaughter's advice. 'How are *you*?' Her second question was more pointed, and Jael turned away before she could pry further.

'I'll go and see how Fyn is,' Jael muttered. 'You go to sleep.'

Edela frowned after her, but there was little she could do, trapped in her prison of a bed. She sighed, closing her eyes, cringing at the constant groaning and creaking sounds of the ship, trying to focus her mind on her old cottage and how nice it would feel to be back home again.

Jael smiled at Entorp, who was sitting on one side of Fyn. Eydis sat on the other, trying to keep herself awake. 'Eydis, you should get some sleep too,' she insisted, crouching down to peer at the patient. 'Fyn isn't going anywhere.'

Eydis didn't move.

'Well, why not just lie down beside him at least?' Jael tried, glancing at Entorp, who had his hand on Fyn's forehead.

'He feels cool,' Entorp said quietly. 'And his body is working hard to heal itself, so listen to Jael, Eydis. Get some sleep. Fyn would want you to take care of yourself. There's nothing you can do now.'

Eydis couldn't argue with that, as much as she wanted to.

'And besides, it would be good to have a dream, don't you think?' Jael suggested craftily. 'We need all the help we can get to see what's coming next.'

Realising that Jael was right, Eydis nodded. 'I'll try.'

'Good,' Jael said, yawning again. She looked around at Aleksander, who was staring at her with slow-blinking eyes, almost asleep too. He looked terrible, she thought. Scratched and bruised. Torn to pieces by ravens and wolves.

Much like the rest of them.

Standing up, Jael walked back to where he sat, tripping over her mother's foot and stumbling down onto his lap.

Aleksander laughed as he caught her in his arms. 'Looks

like you're the one who needs sleep,' he smiled, staring into her eyes. One was still barely open, swollen and bruised. He touched her face. 'What happened? Was that in the temple fight?'

Jael brushed away his hand and sat down next to him, leaning her head against the wall. 'No, that was me losing my edge.'

'Oh, you had an edge, did you? I didn't know.'

Jael frowned at him. 'You obviously feel better than you look.'

'Ha! No, I can promise you that I don't. But I am ready to go home.'

'But not for long.'

'No, not for long.' Aleksander closed his eyes, almost comfortable as he lay his own head back against the breezy wall. 'Go to sleep. Find some more dreams yourself, dreamer,' he smiled, imagining how much she was scowling at him.

***

Thorgils held Isaura close as he walked her into the bedchamber, towards Jael and Eadmund's enormous bed.

She was shaking.

'Ivaar won't hurt you,' he whispered over the top of her head. 'You're the mother of his children. He won't hurt you. I'll tell him that it was all my fault. That *I* took you. Forced you to come here. Don't worry.'

Isaura kept shaking. She knew that she needed to stay safe for her children, but she wanted to keep Thorgils safe too. She couldn't lose him. They had been apart for so long. After all those years without him, they were finally together again. She couldn't lose him. Not now.

'Bram thinks there's a chance we could escape,' Thorgils murmured, easing her down onto the bed, ignoring her protests.

'Come on, just lie down for a while. Just for a while.'

'Escape?' Isaura was fighting to stay upright. 'How? They will see us.'

Thorgils shrugged. 'They might, but perhaps not. And if there's a chance, we have to take it and get to Tatti's Bay. The ships are still there, waiting.'

Isaura stared up at him, gripping his hand. 'If there's a chance, then we go. All of us.'

***

'Not thinking of escaping, are you?' Eadmund wondered as he crept up behind Jael, placing his hands on her shoulders.

She jumped, sliding away from him.

No matter how many years since that night in Tuura, she didn't like to be surprised. She didn't enjoy being touched most of the time.

Even by Eadmund.

'Escaping? Maybe,' Jael said, leaning on the rampart wall. The sun was sinking, and the sea was rolling noisily in the distance. It sounded like an angry monster was out there, guarding the harbour.

Eadmund wanted to touch her. It was hard to stop himself, but she was avoiding his eyes, already uncomfortable with his closeness. 'I hope not,' he whispered, leaning over the wall next to her. 'Thorgils would miss you.'

Jael tried not to smile. 'He would. And you?' She turned to him, and the last rays of sun revealed flecks of gold in her eyes.

'Me? I would get the whole bed to myself. No more cold feet. Not such a loss.'

'Well, I'd take the bed with me. Eirik made it for me, you know.'

'For *us*,' Eadmund whispered, reaching for her hand.

And frowning, Jael gave it to him. 'And the puppies.'

'I'm not sure he knew that at the time,' Eadmund grinned, bending down for a kiss. 'Don't run away,' he murmured, his lips touching hers. 'Don't leave. I like it when you're here. Everything's better when you're here, Jael.' He brought his hands up to her face, holding his breath as she stayed perfectly still, staring at him with those intense green eyes.

'Well, since you ask so nicely,' she sighed, kissing him, 'I'd better stay here, then. With you.' Jael blinked, and suddenly there was no Eadmund, and she was alone, staring out at that familiar harbour, listening as the waves crashed against the stone spires and the sun slowly slid from view.

She turned away, into the darkness, wanting a different dream.

***

'I can't stay long,' Eadmund said wearily, sitting down on the bed, wondering if he should bother taking off his boots. He'd only wake Evaine if he tried to get them on again in a few hours.

'But you need to sleep!' she insisted, sitting next to him, her arm around his waist, pulling him closer. 'Your men can keep watch, can't they?'

'How's Sigmund?' Eadmund asked, wanting to distract her.

'Sleeping, as you should be. All night, with me!' She wasn't about to be distracted.

Eadmund laughed. 'You're very persistent.'

'Of course. I want you to be safe.' Evaine slipped off her shoes, hopping onto the bed. 'I want this all to be over with. For you to defeat Ivaar, so we can get married, and *I* can be the Queen of Oss.'

Eadmund froze.

It made perfect sense for Evaine to suggest such a thing. For her to want to be his wife. They loved each other. They were meant to be together. She was all he could think about when he wasn't thinking about Ivaar and the invasion.

It made perfect sense, but Eadmund felt unsettled.

Turning to Evaine, he swallowed, watching as she wriggled under the furs, plumping the pillows, looking so very beautiful. And he remembered that this wasn't his bed. And he remembered his own house, with his puppies, and his wife with cold feet.

'Eadmund!' Evaine scolded. 'Are you going to fall asleep sitting there?'

Eadmund shook his head, trying to smile, but his eyes remained sad. He turned back to his boots, deciding to take them off after all.

Evaine was a heavy sleeper.

She murmured behind him, talking about wedding dresses and thrones, but he heard none of it. His shoulders felt oddly heavy, and he could almost see his father staring at him from the chair by the fire, pulling on his long white beard, sharpening those bushy brows with such disappointment.

'Know your enemy, my son.'

It was one of Eirik's favourite sayings. 'Know your enemy.'

Eadmund shivered, hurrying to join Evaine under the furs.

***

'Well, what did you expect?' Morana sighed, irritated that Jaeger had barged into her chamber. 'That book was hers before it was yours. And as we no longer need you, I hardly think anyone cares whether you have the book or not!' She was still tired, and her tongue was loose.

Jaeger strode across the chamber, jamming his hand around Morana's throat, lifting her off the ground. 'No longer need *me*?

Are you so sure about that?' he snarled. 'Perhaps the greater truth is that no one needs you? Not now. You've brought her back, and now it's up to her. What use are *you* to anyone?'

Morana coughed and spluttered as he squeezed, her mother's vengeful cackles ringing in her ears. She glared at him, her dark eyes popping open like black stones before closing.

Moving her lips. Murmuring.

Jaeger dropped his hand, stumbling backwards. 'What did you do?' he spat, shaking his hand. It was burning. He looked around for water. His hand felt as though it was on fire. 'What did you *do*?'

Morana staggered, gripping her throat. 'Me?' she rasped. 'I am not my mother! You may try to kill me, but I will not go quietly. I did not escape your chamber with a *key*, Jaeger Dragos! That book has been very helpful to me. There's a lot more I can do now. And if you want me to help you remain relevant to anything that is about to happen, I suggest you show me some respect!'

Jaeger tried to ignore the burning sensation in his hand as he glared at the stooping, shaking mess of hair and flying spittle before him. 'I need the book back,' he said quietly. Desperately. 'Can you help me do that?'

Morana hid her sneer. She felt much the same.

The Book of Darkness was intoxicating, and as much as they both wished to claim it for themselves, the only one who could bring Raemus back was Draguta. She had ripped the ritual page out of the book. Only she knew where it was. 'No, I cannot. But you can make yourself useful to her, and she will let you be around the book, I'm sure. That is what we both must become now. Useful.'

It wasn't what Jaeger wanted to hear. There was no power in scraping about on his hands and knees, begging to be of service, hoping that Draguta would bring Raemus back. Raemus, who would then destroy everything he wanted.

But without the book, what choice did he have?

'Leave me now,' Morana grunted, pointing him to the door. 'I must sleep. As must you. We both gave a lot last night, and we need to gather all the strength we have for what lies ahead.'

Jaeger couldn't disagree. He was feeling increasingly light-headed, and his ears hadn't stopped ringing since he'd woken up. So, trying to put the book out of his mind, he turned for the door. 'Come to my chamber in the morning, then. We can discuss how to approach her. Together.'

Morana nodded impatiently, already shuffling towards her bed, her need to dream like a thirst she had to quench quickly.

***

Borg crept around the sloping deck of the beached ship, looking for Rolan. He'd caught a few hours of sleep and was ready to make something happen. He knew that Toki wouldn't attack the fort at night, but what if there was no need for Toki and the Bastard? What if all the songs could be sung about just the two eldest Arnesson brothers?

Recognising Rolan's thunderous snores, he kicked his brother's leg. 'Wake up, you slobbering idiot!'

Rolan jerked awake, reaching for his sword. 'What? What?' he panted, trying to focus on the shape looming over him. The weather was foul, and it was still a shadow moon, so there was nothing to see but shifting shades of darkness. 'What are you doing?' he croaked, recognising Borg's voice.

'I've been thinking that we don't need to wait for Toki. We can attack tonight.'

Rolan sat up, clearing his throat. 'They have too many arrows.'

'Maybe, but it's dark, harder to see your target. Especially with what I have planned,' Borg smiled.

***

Jaeger's body was heavy with exhaustion, but sleep would not come. And nothing he did with or to Meena made him relax. His mind was alert. Irritated.

Thoughts of the book raced around his aching head.

Thoughts of Draguta.

Of regret.

'What can you do, Meena?' he whispered hoarsely, rolling over to face her. She was so oddly still. No tapping. No twitching. But he knew that she was lying there just as wide awake as him.

Meena blinked. 'D-d-do?'

'To help me? To help us? What can you *do*?'

'I... I don't know.' She didn't want to say nothing, which was likely the truth, but she wasn't sure what he wanted from her.

Jaeger frowned, reaching out to touch her swollen face, feeling her flinch beneath his hand. 'I kept you for a reason. You are here to help me. I feel it.'

Meena squirmed, wanting to recoil from his touch, but she fought the urge and kept her face as still as possible. 'I will do anything I c-c-can,' she stuttered.

'Good,' Jaeger sighed, drawing her into his arms. 'There must be a way to get my book back. I can't be without it, Meena.' He ran his hand over her hair, bringing her face towards his. 'You can feel that, can't you? We are meant to be together, you, me, and the book.'

Meena tried to stop herself shaking as she nodded obediently. She tried to stop herself cringing as he kissed her, his stubble scratching roughly against her aching face.

But she couldn't.

***

Berard was on the verge of tears. He could barely think through the intense waves of pain, though part of him was still numb, not really believing that Jaeger had cut off his arm. He wondered how his brother had become so evil, so corrupted by that book? To have disfigured him? Killed their father?

Berard shook all over, wriggling, trying to get comfortable. The sky was so utterly dark that he felt unsettled, desperate for a light of any kind.

Hanna's kind voice was low and soothing. 'You need to lie still,' she urged. 'You can't knock your arm. You need to keep it still.'

Berard wasn't inclined to stay still at all, but he was too weak to argue. 'I can't believe Meena stayed behind,' he said. 'Why? I want to go back. I need to rescue her!'

In the darkness, Hanna couldn't see Berard's eyes, but the panic in his voice and the passion with which he spoke about Meena told her everything she needed to know. 'You can't. We have to get you help. We have to get your family to safety. We can't do anything. Not yet.'

Her calm words blunted Berard's urgency, and he sighed, finally lying still. 'He will hurt her, you see,' he whispered. 'And it's my fault. If I knew how to use a sword properly, if I was stronger, better, I could have defeated him. It would have been different. Father wouldn't be...' He closed his eyes in shame.

Hanna reached under the furs and found Berard's hand. It felt like ice, and she squeezed it gently. 'A father's job is to protect his family. A king's job is to protect his people,' she tried. 'I didn't know your father, but I imagine he'd make the same choice again if he had to. That he'd give his life to protect all of yours. To know that you were safely away from danger.'

Berard felt tears running down his cheeks. His father hadn't even liked him, he was sure, but when it had mattered, Haaron had stood up for them all.

Him included.

And Berard planned to do everything he could to show his father that he hadn't sacrificed his life in vain.

***

Morana walked through the square, almost itching with discomfort. This wasn't the dream she needed to have.

Oss.

She wanted to spit.

Eirik's wife, Eskild, had turned him against her; made him banish her all those years ago.

But now, Eirik was as dead as his bitch wife.

Morana smiled, then frowned, wondering what she was seeing.

A crowd of Osslanders had gathered in the muddy slop of the square, jeering and yelling. Ignoring them, and walking straight through them, she emerged into a little clearing, gasping in surprise. Morac was there, his face as grey as the bleak sky above. His ankles were chained together, his hands shackled behind his back.

Evaine was screeching behind him, almost drowned out by the jeers.

Eadmund turned, trying to encourage someone to take her away. Turning back around, he ordered Morac to lie down on a thick, stained stump of wood. He didn't look happy, but he glanced at Jael Furyck, who nodded at him, urging him on. So, inhaling sharply, Eadmund turned back to his prisoner, lifting his voice above the tumult. 'Morac Gallas! For the murder of my father, our king, I hereby sentence you to death!'

Evaine screamed, fighting against the men who were forcing her away as Eadmund raised his sword.

Morac, lying on the stump, head turned towards his sister, screamed. 'Help us, Morana! Help us!'

CHAPTER FOUR

'There!' Eadmund blinked, certain he'd seen a shape moving in the darkness.

Arlo was beside him, squinting. 'My lord?'

'Can't you hear that?' Eadmund frowned, listening. 'Go back to the harbour side. Light it up!' He drew an arrow from his quiver, and leaning against the rampart wall, he nocked it to his bowstring, dipping the pitch-soaked arrowhead into the brazier. 'On your way, get Mak to do the same. I'll go round to Erland.' Pulling back his bowstring, Eadmund pointed his flaming arrow up to the black sky and released it, watching the tiny burst of flame illuminate the eastern side of the fort.

No one was there.

Or were they?

Eadmund squinted some more, holding his breath, but nothing moved.

Sighing, he turned to leave, nodding at a young man as he stooped to collect his quiver of arrows. 'Eyes open, Darri, I'll be back soon.'

The arrow whipped past him like a speeding bird, and Eadmund dropped to the rampart walk, hearing the thud of Darri's body as it fell, the arrow protruding from his forehead.

Eadmund crawled with speed, leaving his dead man far behind. And when he reached the signal bell, he slipped out his knife, banging its wooden hilt against the hanging iron bar with force. The clattering din made his own ears ring. 'Eastern side!' he bellowed. 'Eastern side! Bring the pitch!'

***

Morana couldn't stop coughing as she struggled out of her low bed, her head swirling with the memory of the dream, her body still weak from the ritual. But she had no time for weakness. She needed to find whatever herbs she had to hand and get a fire going quickly.

It was time to dream walk.

***

'Western side!' came the frantic cry.

Eadmund wasn't surprised. 'Bram, help Erland! Sevrin, let's get that pitch up and over! Bram, do the same!'

'Southern side!'

'They're surrounding us!' Thorgils called, racing towards Eadmund.

'Go help Mak!' Eadmund called back. 'Drop the pitch on them! Burn them!' Bending down, he grabbed one side of the cauldron, ducking his head as a volley of arrows flew over the ramparts. 'Now!' The cauldron, full of stinking, sticky pitch, was heavy, but with Sevrin's help, he managed to tip its boiling contents over the men below.

Eadmund could hear screams of horror as the hot pitch scalded their attackers. Quickly choosing a fire arrow, he nocked it, frowning as the clouds in his head finally cleared. 'It's a diversion!' he roared. 'They're going for the gates!' And leaning over the rampart wall, Eadmund shot the arrow in the direction of the sizzling pitch. It exploded into the night sky like a brilliant-red bonfire, intensifying the screams. 'Stay here!' he ordered, rushing back to the signal bell, bashing it with his knife. 'The gates!' he bellowed, throat straining. 'To the gates!' And leaving Sevrin and his men to deal with those who survived the pitch fire, Eadmund ran.

***

'But where will we go?' Morac asked, blinking at his sister, who had hurried into his dream. 'We are trapped on Oss. We're under attack!'

'If you don't leave, Brother, you will die on that stinking island. Jael Furyck will see to it when she returns. She will tell Eadmund the truth about Eirik's death. I have seen it. You will lose your head.' Her warning was as stark as she could make it, and Morana hoped that Morac would heed her warning and not dither about. She could feel her grasp on the dream fading more quickly than she would have expected. She felt faint, everything clouding, before Morac's fretful face slipped away.

'But...'

'Morac!'

Morac frowned as his sister disappeared. He turned back to his dream, watching Evaine crawl around on the hall floor by his feet as he sat next to Eirik, drinking ale, reminiscing about their youth. It was his favourite memory of Oss, before it had all changed. Before Evaine had become the creature she was today.

Before...

'Morac!' Runa shook him again. 'They're attacking from everywhere! Can't you hear it? Please, you must come to the hall. We need to know what to do!'

Morac sat up quickly, rubbing his hands down his long

face. 'Get my swordbelt. Find my boots,' he croaked, suddenly wide awake. And dragging himself to the edge of the bed, he pressed his bare feet onto the floorboards.

He needed to think quickly.

***

Boom!

They had a battering ram.

The men wielding it were wrapped in wet hides. Shielded by their companions, they were making a determined assault on the fort, swinging the thick, wooden beam back and forth. Slamming it against the gates.

'Where's that pitch?' Eadmund roared, peering at the entrance to the stairs, furious that it was taking so long. He turned back, lighting another arrow. 'Get me that pitch! Archers! Kill those men! Fire at will!'

They shot arrow after arrow at the attackers - hitting some, Eadmund was sure, if the howls of pain were anything to go by - but the battering ram kept swinging.

Boom!

At last, the cauldron of steaming pitch made its way up the stairs. 'Torstan! Over here!' Eadmund cried. 'Quick!'

Torstan shuffled towards his king, panting with the effort of lugging the heavy load up the steep stairs.

Eadmund hurried towards him, and together they raised the cauldron over the rampart wall, dropping its hot black liquid onto the men and their giant weapon. He was out of arrows, but he turned to Arlo, who was already calling out the drill to his archers. He could hear screams from around the fort, but he couldn't leave his position, doubting that any incursion would cause them as many problems as a breach of the gates. The pitch burst into flames, and Eadmund thought of Jael and the sea-fire, hoping that she was bringing some with her.

Hoping that she was coming at all.

***

It was well before dawn when Jael stepped down onto the pier, though she was still reminded of the wintry morning she had left Andala all those months ago. Once, it had felt as though she would never return, but now, with her boots barely touching the wooden boards of the familiar old pier, she couldn't wait to leave. 'You're going to have to work by torchlight,' she said, running through the list of things they needed to organise.

'We need to beach the ships,' Beorn grumbled beside her.

'There's no time. We'd have to sail around to the cove. We don't have time, Beorn,' Jael insisted, clinging onto Tig's reins. He was almost pulling her off her feet, eager to head into the fort, which, she supposed, made a pleasant change.

The puppies were hesitant, though, tangling themselves around Beorn's legs as he continued to grumble beside her. 'I'll need someone to show me where everything is. Tools. Wood. Fixings.'

Aleksander was walking on Jael's other side. 'I'll take Tig to the stables if you like? Meet you in the hall? Hopefully, there's a fire going, and we can get something to eat. Work out who'll do what.' He turned back to Gant and Kormac, who balanced a limping Axl between them. Entorp and Biddy followed with Edela, who was eager to get away from *Sea Bear* as quickly as possible. 'I think we could all do with something to warm us up.'

'Alright,' Jael muttered, handing Tig's reins to Aleksander. She glanced up at the sky, eager to see some stars or a hint of the moon. The total darkness wasn't going to help Beorn and his men work quickly, but they had no choice. She had seen it in her dreams. Oss was under attack, and they had to gather what they needed and be on their way before it was too late.

***

Oss' hall was filled with panic as everyone charged around, getting in each other's way, checking on the cauldrons, which simmered continuously with water and oil. The fires in the square were busy heating the pitch. With so many different points of attack now, they had to use everything at their disposal.

Runa was working with Ayla, tending to the wounded men who lay on the beds that lined the hall walls. Isaura was helping Elona Nelberg, who, though utterly useless in Runa's estimation, was better than nothing.

Most of the injuries were not life-threatening, but two young men had died, and Runa felt her panic rise as she tried to help another who was writhing around on a bed as she attempted to sew up his cheek. Ayla was holding him down, but he was disoriented, wanting to get back to the ramparts and help. Runa murmured soothing words, trying to calm him, not noticing that Morac had grabbed Evaine and hurried her behind the green curtain.

'What do you mean *leave*?' Evaine hissed irritably. 'What are you talking about?'

Her hissing was too loud for Morac, who rushed a hand over her mouth. 'Ssshhh,' he implored, glancing at the curtain, but they were still alone in the dark corridor. The chambers were empty too. Even Bruno Adea was out in the hall, doing what he could to help. 'Morana has seen it. We are in danger, you and I. We must slip away before it's too late.'

Evaine ripped his hand away. 'You've gone mad! We're perfectly safe here with Eadmund,' she insisted, suddenly aware of her son's cries in the distance, wondering where

Tanja had disappeared to. 'I'm not going anywhere without Eadmund. Besides, how could we? The gates are barricaded, and those men are trying to get in. We can't get out! Not now!' she sneered.

'Perhaps, but Morana has seen it. They will get in.'

'And hurt Eadmund?'

'That's not what she's saying. You must gather some things. I will come for you when it's time.'

'But...'

'Evaine, you must be ready to leave. If you want to be Eadmund's wife, you will have to do what Morana tells you. And she is telling you to leave with me.' Morac turned away before she could protest further. He would not be going without her, no matter what she said.

***

'Pull back! Pull back!' Borg screamed, watching as a handful of his men danced around in fright, on fire and panicking, dropping the battering ram to the ground with a hefty thud.

The flames helped the men on the ramparts to see, and moments later, another hail of arrows showered over them.

'Get back to the beach!' Rolan Arnesson cried, charging after his brother, shield over his head, his flaming men running after him.

Borg skidded down the hill, slipping in the mud. Furious.

But not ready to admit defeat yet.

Not when he had Ivaar the Bastard up his sleeve.

***

'I'm sorry,' Fyn whispered.

'You've nothing to be sorry for,' Jael insisted. 'Now, lie back down, or you'll be in trouble with Biddy,' she smiled, trying to reassure him quickly, conscious of how much she had to do.

News of Axl's ascension to the throne had been greeted by both surprise and cheer in the fort. The Andalans had hurried out of their beds, servants rushing into the hall, bringing the fires around the tables and in the kitchen back to life. Ale had flowed quickly, and the smell of fresh bread and roasting meat was already wafting down the corridor and into Fyn's chamber, reminding Jael of how long it had been since she'd last eaten. But there was an urgency to talk, make plans, and prepare now. And Jael knew that she had to be back in the hall, taking charge of it all, for despite Axl being the King of Brekka now, he was going to need guidance, especially while he recovered from his injuries.

'You rest now,' Jael said, patting Fyn's hand. There was no time for anything else. Not yet. But he was warm and safe, tucked away in one of the smaller bedchambers behind the hall. 'I have to go. Biddy is coming, and no doubt she'll bring Eydis. They'll get anything you need. I have to get ready to go back to Oss now.'

Fyn's eyes widened, and he attempted to push himself up again.

'No! You can't come. You can't help. Except to stay there!' Jael said firmly, standing up. 'And you know that your mother would say the same. So, stay there!' And turning away, she gave Fyn no further opportunity to protest.

He slumped back onto his pillow, watching her walk out of the chamber, gasping at the sudden sharp pains in his belly.

Jael hurried down the corridor, pulling back the grey curtain, stepping into Andala's cavernous hall. She smiled, happy to see no sign of Lothar or Osbert for the first time in years. It was a wonderfully familiar place, all aglow with smoky, warm orange light. More than anything, the King's Hall made her miss her father. This was where he had ruled his people; listening to their concerns, dispensing justice, drinking with his men, telling stories.

Listening, with a frown, to those told about him.

Jael blinked, leaving her memories behind as she made her way to the map table where everyone was waiting for her. 'We have to leave as soon as the catapults are finished. We can't delay. But while we're gone, you'll need to work on protecting the fort, Axl,' she said, seeking out her brother, who didn't look well. His eyes were almost blank, his face unusually pale, though whether from his injuries or nerves, Jael couldn't tell. She moved her attention to Gant, who stood behind him. 'You'll have to try and shore up our defenses.'

Opposite her, Marcus nodded. He had been thinking about that on the journey from Tuura. About how they could use symbols to protect them in the same way that he had protected the secret room.

As had Edela, who sat next to Axl, certain that she was still swaying from side to side. 'That woman will come for us,' she warned. 'The one The Following raised. And likely with more than the ravens or wolves Morana Gallas was playing with. We need to lock her out.'

'Yes, now that she is reunited with the Book of Darkness, she will want to destroy you,' Marcus said, staring at Jael. 'The prophecy says that you stand in her way. She will need to come for you.'

'But what of Raemus?' Jael wondered impatiently. 'Won't she be focusing on bringing him back?'

'Perhaps,' Marcus frowned. 'We cannot guess as to her true intentions, but I imagine she'll discover that you sent someone to steal the book. She'll want to kill you quickly to prevent you trying again.' He shuddered, thinking about his daughter, Hanna. Wondering whether she was safe.

Jael focused on Gant again. 'You'll need to gather everyone together to help Entorp and Kormac. Aedan and Aron too.

They know the symbol we carved into the towers in Tuura. We need that symbol here. The one that keeps the dreamers out. It should be carved into the walls of the fort, wouldn't you say, Grandmother?'

'Yes, I would,' Edela agreed, smiling at Alaric and Derwa as they entered the hall. Theirs was the last ship to arrive from Tuura, and they both looked ready to fall down as they staggered towards the nearest table, still half at sea. 'We must do what we can to keep The Following out of our thoughts and our plans. We must shut them out of the fort entirely!'

***

'Safe for now,' Thorgils sighed, feeling his shoulders loosen ever so slightly.

'For now,' Bram agreed, watching their enemy retreat to their beached ships. The fires burning in front of the gates gave off enough light for them to see what they were up to. The incursions around the walls had all been extinguished now, and the fort was almost quiet for the first time in hours.

'Ivaar knows this fort. He knows the gates. He knows how many men we have,' Eadmund said quietly. 'And he knows we don't have enough arrows.'

Bram looked confused.

'Skorro,' Thorgils grunted. 'We've only just had a big battle against the Hestians. Ivaar was with us, and he's many things but not an idiot. He knows that he just needs to empty our arrow stores. And, if things continue like this, before long, he will.'

'You sound as though you're ready to crawl to him on your hands and knees!' Bram snorted. 'That's not our way! You don't think we can defeat a self-serving turd like Ivaar Skalleson? Like those murderous Arnessons? Ha! What would Eirik say if he were standing here? He never let anyone take this fort from him in all the years he sat in that stinking old hall. And I'm not about to let him down by handing the keys to the gates to any of them!'

Thorgils grinned, lifted by his uncle's throaty growl, certain that Eirik would be smiling down on them from Vidar's Hall.

***

'Ivaar! What are you doing here?' Eirik grabbed his son's cloak before he could scamper away. 'Why aren't you in bed?'

'I couldn't sleep,' Ivaar mumbled, ducking his head as he turned back to his father. 'I thought something was wrong.'

'Wrong?' Eirik smiled, ruffling his son's blonde hair. 'No, nothing's wrong. We are just doing secret things in the dead of night. It's the best time to do secret things, don't you think? When only the moon is watching you?'

Ivaar, only six-years-old, nodded slowly.

Eirik bent down. 'Don't you want to know *what* secret things?' he whispered conspiratorially.

Ivaar nodded some more.

Eirik took his little hand, walking him back through the stables, into an alley where he could see Morac and three other men gathered around a hole in the wall.

A hole?

'You see, our secret is this very secret door. One day you'll be king here, my son, and you might have to make use of this door. If you need to escape. If the enemy is breaking down the gates. You'll be able to leave through here and head towards the cliffs. There's a path we've been working on. It leads down to a tiny cove where a ship is hidden.' Eirik straightened up and smiled. 'That's a very clever secret, wouldn't you say?' He rested his hands on his son's tiny shoulders. 'But we mustn't tell anyone. No one. You never know who might become your enemy, Ivaar. And we can never let anyone take Oss from us, can we? This is our home. The islands will always belong to the Skallesons. We will never let anyone take them from us. Not while there's breath in our lungs and a sword in our hands. I would happily die to protect these islands, and one day, my son, so will you.'

***

Aleksander leaned over the map table, only half concentrating. His eyes kept wandering to the tall elderman as he hovered awkwardly by the fire, not knowing where to put himself.

'You're not listening,' Jael huffed, elbowing him.

'I'm listening,' Aleksander insisted, clearing his throat, eyes on the faded map of Osterland that Ranuf Furyck had had painted on a long wooden table when they were children. Aleksander and Jael would crawl up onto it when no one was around, pretending they were at war, moving the little figurines of ships and men around, trying to defeat each other before Gant or Ranuf caught them and sent them scurrying from the hall. 'Tell me again.'

'You'll take your ships through the stone spires, here. If the catapults are finished quickly enough, we can leave later this afternoon. That should have you entering Oss' harbour tomorrow morning, which means you won't have to navigate those spires in the dark.'

Aleksander was pleased to hear it.

'I'll cross the straights over here, aiming for a cove on this side,' Jael said, pointing to Oss' western coast. 'Beorn knows where to go. Once we get up the cliffs, we'll be marching to the fort. Probably through the night. That should see us arrive around the same time as you. No doubt we'll hear your commotion on our approach.'

'Well, I'd better make some noise then, hadn't I?' Aleksander grinned, trying not to yawn. Dawn was coming, and his eyes felt as heavy as his body and ready for bed. 'If we're not too late.'

'We won't be too late. Now, what about the sea-fire?' Jael wondered impatiently, shutting all thoughts of being too late out of her head.

'I hid ten jars under Edela's floor. That's all we can take. We don't have the time to make any more.'

Jael nibbled her bottom lip. It tasted like salt. 'Well, we need to start making more now. And constructing catapults too. Once we return from Oss, we'll have to make plans for how to get the Book of Darkness and destroy this woman.'

Aleksander nodded, thinking about the Widow. He needed to talk to Jael about her. 'There's a lot we have to discuss.'

'Agreed, but not now. Now, we have to go!'

***

'You smell terrible,' Evaine fussed sleepily as Eadmund hunted around the chamber for his cloak.

He'd left without it, but it was cold up on the ramparts, and he was planning on staying up there for hours yet. Placing one hand on top of Evaine's head, he smoothed down her hair. 'Ssshhh,' he soothed. 'Go back to sleep.'

But Evaine couldn't sleep. She was thinking about Morac's insistence that they leave the island. 'Are you alright?' she wondered. 'Has something happened?'

Eadmund sighed, realising that he was never going to be able to slip away until Evaine was asleep. 'I'm fine. And nothing has happened that I wouldn't have expected. They're trying to break in, we're trying to stop them. They won't succeed.'

'Ivaar, you mean?'

'Ivaar, yes.'

'He will try to kill you if he gets in. Perhaps we should leave? Now?'

'They won't get in, Evaine, so you don't need to worry, but you do need to sleep,' Eadmund urged. 'In the morning, things will get harder. Sleep will help.'

Evaine wanted to protest, but she could feel Eadmund's urgency to leave, so reaching down, she pushed her small hand inside his large, cold one.

Morana had warned Morac that they would die if they stayed.

But if they left, what would happen to Eadmund?

***

Edela was thrilled to be back in her cottage, lying in her own comfortable bed, but she couldn't sleep. Her body rolled nauseously, and her mind was alert, flitting about from one idea to the next like a hungry bird. She had wanted to stay in the hall and help, but she had fallen asleep so many times that, in the end, Biddy had bustled her and Eydis away to the cottage, ignoring their sleepy protests.

Edela smiled as she listened to Biddy's cacophonous snoring from the low bed that Aleksander had moved into the cottage when he was staying with her. It was hardly sleep-inducing, but then she thought of nearly losing Biddy in Tuura's burning fort; reminded of how close they had all come to being killed by Gerod and The Following.

It was such a relief to be safe in Andala. Now they had a chance to find answers. To find a way to stop this woman. A way to destroy the Book of Darkness before it was too late.

Edela was convinced that she was too anxious to sleep, but eventually, tiredness overwhelmed her, and she slipped away into her dreams.

And there she found the woman waiting for her.

CHAPTER FIVE

The sun wasn't up, but Ivaar was wide awake, too uptight to sleep. He wasn't where he should be. He wasn't in the secret cove where his father had hidden that ship all those years ago; where a small group of Osslanders had spent years carving out an easier path up to the fort for their king. Ivaar had brought Toki and his men much further around Oss' western coastline.

But why?

All he had to do was show Toki the secret door. Help the Arnessons take the fort. Defeat Eadmund. Kill Eadmund.

It was all he'd ever wanted.

Rolling over, Ivaar stared at the fire. It was nothing but charred logs and cold embers now. He shivered in the absence of flames, thinking of his old fort and his comfortable bed on Kalfa. He even thought about his miserable wife, who had never been much company. But she had been company, at least.

Ivaar sat up, wanting to clear his head. To see things differently.

But instead, he saw his dream, and he remembered his father, and he felt the loss of that six-year-old boy who had idolised Eirik Skalleson as though he were Vidar, King of the Gods.

***

'Draguta! Where are you going? You can't leave us!' her sisters wailed in unison.

'Ssshhh,' the young woman whispered, turning away from the door. 'I am going for help. I will come back for you. They are coming! I must go!'

'Sister, please!' Diona sobbed, her hands chained behind her back. 'Please! They are going to kill us! Please don't go!'

'Do not worry, I will return,' Draguta smiled, her long dark hair swishing behind her as she spun and disappeared through the door after the man who had come to rescue her.

***

Borg Arnesson farted, cracking his neck, stiff from the bitter cold and the sloping, wooden deck he'd stretched out on for a few hours sleep. His head was clearer now, and he was ready for the next day of the siege to begin. 'They don't have an unlimited supply of pitch or arrows. We've made them waste most of them by now, I'd wager. So we try again.'

Rolan looked less confident than his older brother. He'd been splattered with the stinking pitch, and his face and arms still burned. He wasn't keen on getting close to the fire arrows again. Frowning, he turned to his cousin Erl, who was wider and shorter than any man he'd ever met, and, comfortingly, in possession of a much cooler head than Borg. 'Do you think we could work the ladders now?'

Borg lifted his eyebrows in surprise but held his tongue.

'I think little Toki should be at the back door today. And we need to make sure we get ourselves inside, or else those Osslanders will be laughing as they piss all over him and that

Skalleson bastard,' Erl rumbled, running his whetstone down the meaty blade of his axe. 'Ladders make sense, for now. We'll draw them to the gates and pick them off, one by one. Soon they'll run out of men up there. And arrows, I'd say.'

His twin brother, Rork, who wasn't the talker in the family, nodded mutely.

Borg wanted to argue, but he couldn't. Still, he glared pointedly at Rolan as he spoke. 'We need to eat. Drink. Then we'll bring out the ladders. The archers will stay on the beach, behind a shield wall. As Erl says, we can keep them busy. Pick them off until there's no one left to throw anything at us.' And with that, he turned away to piss over the side of the ship, hoping that Toki and Ivaar would find their way to the secret door soon. He wanted to sit on his throne and sup wine from a goblet like the king he was about to become.

***

'Draguta?' Marcus had repeated the name three times now. 'You're sure it's this woman you saw in your dream? The one they raised from the dead?'

'Yes, when she was young. Perhaps no more than twenty-years-old. Her sisters are the ones I've been dreaming about since last winter. They were beheaded by the elders, but she escaped,' Edela said, pausing to swallow another mouthful of honey-drenched porridge. 'I felt her eagerness to leave. And she had no intention of coming back for them.'

Marcus had not touched his own bowl of porridge which sat steaming before him. He looked much gaunter than when Edela had first met him. Dark shadows rimmed his amber eyes, and his serious face appeared to have sunk, revealing sharp, high cheekbones. He was worried about many things, she knew, but most of all, his daughter, Hanna.

'And she had the Book of Darkness?' Marcus wondered.

'It was given to her by a man,' Edela said. They were sitting at the high table, and though there were many others seated nearby, she realised that there was no point in keeping secrets anymore. They were all in this together now, and everyone needed to know what she did. Well, almost all of it, she thought, glancing at her granddaughter. 'I don't know who the man was or where he got it from, but for a time, the sisters used the book together. To destroy Tuura and beyond. They were eventually captured and sentenced to death by the elders, but Draguta escaped just before her sisters were beheaded. And as they didn't find or destroy the book, we can only assume that she hid it somewhere.'

'And now she's been brought back from the dead, so she'll have the book again,' Axl said, frowning as he gripped Amma's hand under the table. He could feel her leg shuddering against his.

'Yes, and this Draguta will know how to employ its dark power much more effectively than Morana Gallas ever could,' Marcus breathed. 'It was her book.'

'Then we must find a way to take it from her,' Axl insisted, determined to sound like a king, though he didn't feel like one. Not yet. Not in his father's hall, with his sharp-eyed sister always one step ahead of him.

'We've tried,' Jael said. 'And we'll try again. But we're going to need more men. We have to put together an army capable of overthrowing Hest, or we'll have no chance of getting to the book.' She stood, grabbing a couple of flatbreads, eager to check on Beorn's progress with the catapults.

'You are,' Edela almost whispered.

'What?'

'I said, you are, Jael. *You* are the one who must raise an army. *You* are the one who must defeat her. That is what the prophecy says.'

That had everyone's attention.

'You and Eadmund,' Marcus added. 'You must do it together, so you will need to retrieve your husband first.'

***

Toki jiggled about, shaking in the cold. 'It's going to be hard to climb when we can't even feel our hands!' he laughed.

Ivaar knew that the idiot was right.

He swallowed his last piece of salt fish, running a hand over his mouth, brushing hair away from his lips. He was used to the feel of freshly shaven skin, so the hair sticking up his nose and hanging in his mouth was a gnawing irritation. But still, not as much of a gnawing irritation as Toki Arnesson. 'At least it's not raining,' he muttered, glancing up at the jagged cliff face.

Toki grinned, wrapping his swordbelt around his leather tunic. 'True! I'd say that means the gods are with us!' And with that, he headed off to organise his men.

'My lord?'

Ivaar turned, surprised to see Enok, one of his more experienced men, standing before him. 'What is it?'

Enok stared at the wild-eyed, tattooed Alekkans clustered around Toki, arguing over who would end up sleeping in Oss' hall and who would find themselves dreaming in Ran's arms after they tumbled off the cliff, into the sea. 'The men, my lord. They are... unhappy.'

Ivaar's temper flared, and he spat on the ground. '*They're* unhappy?' he snarled. '*They're* unhappy?' He kept his voice low, but his eyes were bright with anger. 'I'm glad to hear it, Enok, because so am I!'

***

Eadmund was back on the ramparts with a swollen-eyed Thorgils, who'd been unable to sleep. His worry about losing Isaura was a tight pain in his chest, and the threat of Ivaar hung over him like a low-lying snow cloud.

He was struggling to see straight.

'Ladders,' Thorgils mumbled.

'Well, they'd be piss-poor invaders if they hadn't packed ladders!' Bram laughed, nudging his nephew.

Thorgils didn't laugh as he watched their attackers organise themselves on the beach, just out of range. He felt anxious about their rapidly depleting arrow stores; about how vulnerable the gates had felt against that colossal battering ram. 'Four ladders,' he grunted.

'We can handle their ladders,' Eadmund assured him. 'Stop thinking about the arrows. We have more than arrows to keep them at bay.' He glanced at Sevrin, who had just joined them. 'Make sure the cauldrons stay on the boil in the square, and the hall. And more. We need to heat everything we can throw on them. Get every house fire going too. Everyone needs to be boiling something. I want you to start bringing the cauldrons up to each side of the ramparts. Keep them coming. And send Morac to me when you see him.'

Sevrin nodded, disappearing back down the stairs.

Eadmund turned his attention to the harbour entrance, hoping for a ship.

A fleet.

A queen.

Thorgils followed his gaze. 'Do you think she's coming?'

Eadmund swallowed. 'Yes.' Only half of him believed it now, but that half was holding firmly onto his dream, remembering Jael's eyes as she promised to come; trying his very best to ignore the taunting voice warning him that she would be too late

***

'It's not perfect,' Beorn growled wearily as he looked over *Sea Bear's* almost-finished catapult with his queen. 'But it will do what we need. And luckily, we still had boxes for the jars, so once we finish up, we'll be ready to go. We just need some archers.'

'Don't worry, we've plenty of those,' Aleksander grinned.

Beorn harrumphed. He didn't feel confident about this plan at all. And it was strange to see another man - a Brekkan - walking all over his ship, preparing to take her out without him.

'You can trust Aleksander with *Sea Bear*. He knows what to do. And I need you with me,' Jael insisted, glancing up at the sky. It was gloomy, dark clouds chasing each other on a gusting wind. That would help them get across the straights in a hurry. 'Come and find me as soon as you're finished, Beorn. I want to depart quickly. We need to take advantage of this wind.'

***

The trek up the cliff was taking a long time.

It had started raining heavily when they set off, and even Toki had approached their climb with caution. The ledges leading up the cliff were a mix of natural shelves of rock and man-made paths. Some had been created by crumbling rockslides, and they could ease their way along in single file, but then they would come to a heap of stones and mud, and it would take some time to dig out their path again.

This side of the island was notoriously wet, and after a morning of enormous effort and little progress, everyone was soaked to the bone and exhausted.

While his men hurled rocks over the edge of the cliff, trying to clear the path, Toki shook out his straggly hair, stomping back to Ivaar. 'You're sure this was the only way up to the fort?'

'The *only* way?' Ivaar frowned, choosing his words carefully. 'No. It's one way, but not the only way.' He kept his feet firmly planted on the narrow ledge, and stretching out his neck, he peered down. They were far enough up now that he could barely see the cove they had spent the night in. Above them, the cliff was jutting out so far that he could only guess they were halfway there.

'But are there *easier* ways? This path is getting worse! With all the rain – ' Toki stopped and lifted his head, listening.

Ivaar's eyes quickly followed; he'd heard the rumbling too. 'Back against the cliff!' he cried as the rocks came tumbling down.

The Kalfans and Alekkans flattened their backs against the cliff's sharp edges, but not all of them were in time. One Alekkan was hit by a boulder, and it knocked him off the ledge with a loud crack, sending him flying out of anyone's reach.

'Gert!' Toki screamed as the rocks rained down, taking his friend with them, his voice disappearing under the roar of falling rubble.

When the avalanche finished, and their throats were clogged with dust, and their faces were covered in mud and filth, and their path was now more blocked than before, Toki turned to Ivaar. 'We have to keep going! Borg will be waiting for us.' He looked anxious now.

Ivaar was pleased to see it. Not so pleased by the ever-increasing threat of death, though. He hadn't thought that the old path would have deteriorated so much over the years. He was starting to doubt what he was even doing. What point was there in delaying Toki and his attack on the fort?

Ivaar shook his head, realising that he had long since run out of options.

The point was to live, he reminded himself, not to get swept to his death like that unlucky Alekkan. 'I'm sure he will,' Ivaar sighed, looking around. 'But we can't go back, and until the men clear the path, we can't go forward, so no point worrying. If I were you, I'd stay still and keep your ears open. Who knows when the next rockfall is coming!'

Toki swallowed, peeling himself off the cliff, daring to look up into the pouring rain; imagining his brother's scarred face as he waited for them, purple with rage.

***

Morac was acting strangely, but Runa wasn't sure that she should care anymore.

She found an empty bench and sat down with a groan, eager to take the weight off her aching feet, hoping to enjoy a bowl of porridge in peace.

'You've been working hard,' Morac noted, sliding onto the bench beside her. 'You had a long night.'

'We all did,' she mumbled, not wanting to encourage his company.

'You're a caring woman, Runa, helping people as you do.'

Runa turned to her husband. 'Are you unwell?'

Morac snorted, trying to mask his discomfort. 'Is that who we have become? That I'm ill if I show some affection? Some interest in you?'

Runa frowned. 'It's just a strange time for it. With all that's going on.'

'Well, perhaps it's what's going on that's making me feel a certain sense of unease,' Morac tried, glancing down at his leaking boots. The rain was pelting down again, and he was wet through. 'We are so vulnerable. They have a lot of men out there.'

'What are you saying?' Runa panicked, forgetting all about her porridge. 'Do you think they'll get in?'

Morac sighed. 'I...' He shook his head. 'I'm just saying that being under threat like this, it makes you realise what you have. What you are reluctant to lose. But, I suppose, we must all say goodbye, eventually. Not many of us are given any warning about our end.'

'Morac! What is going on? What do you know?' Runa put down her spoon, grabbing his forearms, wanting to understand where he was trying to lead her.

'Morac!' Thorgils called from the doors. 'Eadmund wants you up on the ramparts!'

Morac turned to his wife. 'Stay safe, Runa. And finish your porridge. You need to take care of yourself now.'

Runa had lost her appetite, though, watching as Morac weaved his way through the injured and their carers, hurrying towards the doors.

***

'Aarrghh!' Rolan bellowed as he was knocked into the tip of one of the wooden spears the Osslanders had hammered into the ditch around the walls. His men were in a rush to get up the ladders, elbowing their way in between the deadly spears. 'Watch where you're fucking going! We need to get up the ladders in one piece!'

The spear-tipped logs of wood were not making it easy to manoeuvre the ladders into place. Not with the barrage of arrows firing at them as they tried.

And then there was the constant stream of liquid.

'Aarrghh!' the man in front of Rolan howled as boiling fat splashed his face. He scrubbed his hands over his melting cheeks, stumbling away, letting go of the ladder he was holding.

'No!' Rolan pushed his way through his men, but not in time as the ladder tipped slightly to one side – only slightly –

but just enough for the change in balance to unsettle everything. Within moments, it was tumbling over, six Alekkans crashing to the ground with it; two impaled loudly on the wooden spears.

And then the boiling pitch was thrown from the ramparts.

Followed almost instantly by a flaming arrow.

'Back!' Rolan cried, turning to run, shield over his head as the pitch burst into flames behind him.

***

'Save your arrows,' Eadmund muttered to Arlo, who motioned for his archers to lower their bows. 'Let them run. They'll come again.' He felt tense despite their success at keeping the invaders at bay. Something was troubling him.

Something he hadn't thought of.

And it was likely something to do with Ivaar.

The fact that he hadn't seen or heard from his brother yet continued to bother Eadmund. They'd been scanning the island to the east, south, and west of the fort, but no one could see anyone else coming.

So, was Ivaar with the men attacking the gates?

They were mostly dark-haired, broad-chested Alekkans. And no matter how many times Eadmund squinted at the harbour, fighting to see through the driving rain, he couldn't see Ivaar's ships either.

'Torstan!' he called as his friend brought up a cauldron of boiling water. 'Take over from me! I need to go and check around back.' Eadmund couldn't stay still. He couldn't take his eyes off what he was certain was staring him straight in the face.

The threat he couldn't see.

But it was there. He could feel it creeping silently towards him like fog on a dark night.

***

Jael turned to Axl, who was leaning on Gant, first in line to say goodbye. 'Keep everyone busy making weapons. Sea-fire. Arrows too. Get that symbol carved around the walls. And talk to Amma about sending a note to Getta. I doubt she'll be inclined to help us. Not after we killed her father and brother. But still, it would be better for her and her husband if they agreed to become our allies willingly.'

Gant nodded. 'Don't worry. Keep your mind on Oss. We'll still be here when you return.'

Jael turned to her mother. 'Make sure you take care of Eydis, or perhaps have Biddy look after her instead?' she suggested, remembering her own childhood, where her mother's interest in her would often wane. Biddy, she knew, could always be relied upon. 'And Edela. Don't let her do too much. She should rest as much as possible.'

Gant grinned. 'I believe your husband is waiting for you to rescue him, Jael. Which you can't do if you don't stop talking to us!'

Jael scowled, turning to Marcus, who she hadn't managed to speak to yet. 'We'll talk when I return, about Hanna. Don't worry, I'm sure she's alright. She's brave and smart. She'll find her way here.'

Aleksander stilled beside her, but Jael didn't notice.

Marcus looked worried. 'We have no idea what might have become of her. If she failed to get the book, was that because she was hurt? Or worse?' He swallowed, barely able to meet Jael's eyes.

'Talk to Edela. Give her something of Hanna's. I imagine she's too weak to dream walk, but she can still dream. She might find her for you.'

Marcus shook his head. 'Hanna has the symbol stones. No dreamer will find her now.'

Aleksander shuffled his feet, trying to keep his mouth shut. He was desperate to know what had happened to Hanna, but not ready for anyone to find out why.

'There'll be some way to see what's happening,' Jael said quickly. 'And when I return, we'll find it, but for now, Gant's right, we must go.' She inclined her head towards Gant, who handed Axl off to Kormac and walked her towards the ship she would be taking to Oss.

'Good luck,' Gant said quietly. 'Hopefully, we'll see you all back here soon.'

'Look after Axl,' Jael said, raising a hand to her brother. 'It's not the best moment to put him on the throne. He's desperate to prove himself, but he's no king yet. '

'He will be, though,' Gant assured her, pushing her towards the ship. 'Soon. Now, go!'

CHAPTER SIX

No one had seen much of Draguta since that first day, and Yorik was becoming anxious. From the whispers of gossip he'd caught, he discovered that she had commandeered Bayla Dragos' old bedchamber and organised herself a staff of servants. Those servants were roaming the markets, bringing back candles and flowers, silks and linens, furs and ornaments. Every tailor had been ordered to the castle, quickly ushered up to the first floor, and sent away with a list of demands.

Draguta, it seemed, had her mind set on becoming a queen.

It did not sit well with Yorik. 'Perhaps she is tired?' he wondered, walking higher into the winding gardens with Morana.

'Well, I certainly am!' Morana panted. 'Why did I let you bring me this way again? I need something to drink! It's far too warm to be outside like this, even with the sun going down.'

Yorik couldn't help but agree. His tunic was clinging to his back, and he had no idea why he was still wearing his heavy woollen cloak. Vanity, he supposed. Wanting Draguta to see him as the leader of The Following, though his shabby cloak hardly revealed that. And it appeared that she wasn't interested in anything to do with The Following anyway.

'This was her home,' Morana sighed, and spying a stone bench, she scurried towards it. 'She is familiarising herself with it. With the book too. She is remembering who she was. Deciding who she wants to become,' she rasped, flopping onto the bench. 'It is wise not to rush that. A woman like her? As powerful as she must be? That woman will break you into pieces if you cross her.'

Yorik sighed, taking a seat beside Morana. 'I imagined more than this,' he said dolefully. 'After all this time? I thought she would be different somehow. Not so much of a... lady.'

Morana laughed, her temper easing. 'You would prefer an ugly old crone? I hardly think it matters how she looks, Yorik. Stop being so impatient! She must find her feet, as must we. Everything has changed now that Draguta is here. And everything will change again, for the better. And best of all, she has taken the book from the Bear!' Morana smirked, remembering the misery on his handsome face. 'You should have seen how desperate he was to get it back.' Her words rang hollow, though, as she had some sympathy for Jaeger.

For she wanted the book back too.

***

Jael stood in *Silver Tooth's* bow, hanging onto the curling dragon prow, guessing that the sun was sinking. It was hard to tell. It had been a grim, cold afternoon, and night was coming, chilling the air even further. She wondered what Ranuf would have thought of her leaving Brekka behind to save Oss. She could almost see the displeasure carved into his stern face as he glowered at her. But he would have told her to go anyway, Jael knew. Ranuf Furyck had understood the importance of protecting those you loved. Of keeping your kingdom safe.

And Oss *was* her kingdom now.

And one day again, Eadmund would be hers.

If she could just get to him in time.

'Over there!' Beorn called from the stern.

Jael turned, blinking the rain out of her eyes. There was barely any indentation in the sheer cliff face, but when she squinted, Jael could see a tiny cove hiding beneath the mist-covered rocks in the distance.

She shivered in anticipation.

It wouldn't take long to get there at all.

***

Toki threw himself onto the flat ground in relief. He'd started to worry that they wouldn't live long enough to make it to the top of the cliff. They had spent hours digging out the path, sheltering against the cliff face as mud and rocks slid past them, before climbing again, higher and higher, in the never-ending rain.

He'd had never been so happy to see grass; wet, boggy grass; flat and wide, with no falling boulders in sight. He scrambled to his feet, hurrying away from the edge of the clifftop. After watching as two more of his men lost their footing and their lives, Toki was certain that he'd not be volunteering for such a mission again.

Ivaar crested the rise, leading his drenched, terrified men onto the welcome grass, frowning as Toki and the Alekkans congratulated each other on still being alive. 'We should camp here for the night!' he called.

'What? What do you mean?' Toki cried in surprise as he loped towards Ivaar. 'We have to get to the fort! We took too long to get up that fucking cliff! Borg will be waiting. We have to get to the fort!'

'We do,' Ivaar agreed calmly. 'But soon the sun will be gone, and there'll be scant sign of the moon again. I'm sure you don't want to accidentally walk near the cliff edge. In the dark, it's hard to tell where you're going up here. And the terrain gets tougher ahead. Slippery, sharp. More rocks.'

Toki stared up at the darkening sky. Torn. Worried that he'd kept Borg waiting for far too long already. 'We have time before night falls,' he tried, glancing around at his men for support, but none of them looked keen for a hike in the freezing, wet darkness; not after the day they'd endured.

'We do, and if we're smart, we'll spend that time collecting what we need to make a fire and have a meal. Unless you want to sit about in the cold with an empty belly?'

They had left their supplies, their ale, and most of their food down in the cove. There would be nothing to eat tonight that they didn't find themselves.

And being young, and permanently hungry, Toki thought that sounded like a very miserable prospect indeed.

***

The rain had a bite to it, and Eadmund was sure that he should be shivering, but he felt as though his face was on fire. Sweat mixed with raindrops as it dripped down his temples. 'Here they come again! Down!' he shouted, ducking a volley of arrows. The archers on the beach had them within range now, and they didn't need to come any further if their goal was to pick his men off the ramparts.

But if they wanted to break down his gates?

Well, they were going to have to get closer than this. And even though the sun was sinking and the rain was pouring down, Eadmund and his men would be waiting for them.

***

Jaeger felt better being near the book again, but he was uncomfortable being near Draguta. Her physical presence was both intoxicating and intimidating, and he perched on the edge of his chair, barely touching the wine she had poured, wondering what she was going to say next.

They were eating supper in his mother's chamber, and that unsettled Jaeger further. He thought fleetingly of his family, especially his mother, who would hate him for what he had done to Haaron and Berard. And she would've been horrified to see how Draguta had transformed her bedchamber. Everything had been tossed out, bar the bed, and Draguta's servants had worked quickly to redecorate the room.

Which shone.

Every surface was covered with dripping candles and glowing lamps. The candles in the sconces were burning brightly too. Even the fire was blazing.

It was a warm evening, and Jaeger had to keep wiping sweat out of his eyes.

'You do not like wine?' Draguta murmured, raising a golden goblet to him. 'It is good wine, I think. Although, after so many years of being a corpse, I would imagine that even water would taste good!' Her smile was broad and gleaming, her blue eyes sparkling in the candlelight. Even though it was barely dusk, Draguta had insisted on the candles being lit, not wanting one moment of darkness to come between day and night.

Not after so long spent in that cave.

Draguta licked her red lips, drinking from the goblet, enjoying the velvety smoothness of the liquid as it warmed her throat and settled in her chest. It was taking some time to become accustomed to the castle again, to feel as though she was alive, though she often wondered if, in fact, she was still dead.

It was hard to tell.

But she could sleep, eat, drink, feel.

Almost as alive as the hulking man who sat frowning before

her. If only she could taste the wine she was so eager to drink or the food that looked and smelled so appetising.

'You wish to be king here?' Draguta mused. 'Worried that my return has ruined your plans?'

Jaeger's tongue tangled around the words he was reluctant to speak out loud.

Draguta laughed. 'You and I are *family*, Jaeger. I will not stand in the way of your ambitions. The throne of Hest? The throne of Osterland? The death of the Furycks? The end of Tuura and Brekka?' She smiled, her eyes glistening at the mere thought of such destruction. 'We want the same, you and I. And we can achieve it together. There is no need for you to fear me. No need for you to crave the book any longer. I am its mistress again, and all three of us can get everything we want. Together.'

Jaeger tried to smile. It *was* everything he wanted, yet he wasn't prepared to simply let her have the book. If he was to be king, it felt only right that he should have it. *He* was its rightful master. The book felt as though it belonged to him. That it understood him. But one look at Draguta's determined face told Jaeger that it was a futile argument.

She would not be moved.

He frowned, thinking of Morana and Yorik; of The Following and their one true goal. 'What about Raemus? When will you raise him?'

Draguta's smile froze on her face, then promptly twisted into a scowl. 'Raemus?' she sneered. 'Father of the Tuuran Gods? That Raemus?'

Jaeger nodded.

'What need do we have of him?' Draguta laughed.

***

They had beached the two Brekkan ships in Eirik's secret cove, and though the sun had long since gone down, Jael and her men were quickly preparing to climb the cliff. There was no choice. Spending the night in the cove would delay them for too long.

They had to get to the fort before it was too late.

'Keep your eyes open!' Jael called to her men. 'It's a fair path from what I can see, but the rain will likely send rocks tumbling down, so eyes open and stay away from the edge!' She swallowed, glancing up at the shadowy cliff face, wondering what was lurking above them.

It was a long way up, but the ledge that had been painstakingly chipped out of the dark rock was wide enough for at least two across, and there was some comfort to be found in that. Although, without any moon to speak of, they wouldn't be able to see much. 'Keep one hand on the cliff!' Jael bellowed as she stepped up onto the path, feeling a strange twinge in her belly. Ignoring it, she started walking. 'Single file!'

***

'Another day down,' Thorgils sighed wearily, clapping Eadmund on the back as they surveyed Oss' storm-whipped harbour. 'You want to get some rest? I can take the first watch.'

Eadmund nodded. 'I think I should. They'll try something tonight. Probably the battering ram again.'

'I imagine so.'

Bending towards the brazier, Eadmund held out his numb hands. The wind was only getting wilder, and the flames blew in every direction. 'We're low on pitch. Low on fat too.' They had been tipping hot liquid over the ladder men all day, surprised by how persistent they were.

'There's still water.'

'Mmmm, we should boil it all. We can survive on ale and wine. Milk. Anything, until Jael gets here. But if they get in...'

Thorgils shook his head. He didn't want to even see the shape of the fear they both knew was lurking in the darkness. 'They can try. But we have enough men to take them, even if they do. Swords, spears, axes. We have more than pitch and water in here!'

Eadmund smiled, cheered by Thorgils' attempt to distract him. 'I'll be back as soon as anything happens. I just need to close my eyes for an hour or two.' He couldn't see straight, but he was worried about Evaine. He wanted to check on his son too.

If they couldn't hold them out. If Jael didn't make it back in time...

He needed to think about what would come next.

***

'I've had enough of this shit!' Borg spat, hunched under his cloak, wishing he had a fire and Falla's warm, soft body to wrap his arms around. He couldn't stop shivering. 'They're in *our* hall! Sitting around *our* fires! Drinking *our* fucking w-w-wine!' His teeth jammered together as he glared at Rolan.

It was too dark for Rolan to see Borg's angry scowl, but he could feel his brother's spittle as it sprayed his face.

'We need to get inside that fort!' Borg growled, spitting some more. 'No more cowering like dogs! This is not how we've risen! This is not who we are! This is not who we want to be!'

There were a few weary murmurs of agreement. Most were too cold and defeated to say much. The fort was solid, and so was the Osslanders' plan to defend it. Borg was growing sick of the stench of burning bodies and pitch.

They all stunk.

The smoke was in their hair. The drifting remnants of death gusted towards them in the howling wind, reminding them that, so far, they'd failed to do little more than send countless men to Vidar's Hall.

'We can sit here and cry into our ale, or we can get up and make ready!' Borg snarled, shaking off his cloak and clenching his tattooed fists. 'We need a plan! A better plan! We *will* be in that fort by morning! Do you hear me, you slack-balled bunch of shits! By morning!'

***

It had been another long day, and it was a freezing, cold night, but Bayla's tense shoulders finally dropped in relief as the man jumped onto the pier and hurried to tie the ship's rope around the thick post.

Saala.

Their neighbours, who they had been desperate to defeat for as long as she could remember. But she had never been happier to think that they hadn't. That Saala remained in Brekkan hands. That there was hope of finding help here.

And answers.

They needed both of those.

Bayla turned to Karsten, who stood by her side, fiddling with his eye patch, adjusting his sword. 'Stay behind me, Mother,' he muttered, watching as a group of torch-wielding Saalans started down the pier. He looked back at Berard, who had remained barely conscious for much of their journey, then up at Haegen, who walked past him, jumping down onto the pier.

Karsten quickly followed.

'My lords?' Rexon was puzzled, squinting into the darkness as he stopped before the Dragos princes, who waited, side by side. He noticed the queen being helped down onto the pier by a familiar face. 'Ulf?' Rexon swallowed, on edge. He had ten men behind him, but even in the faint glow of their torches, it appeared that the Dragos' had only brought one ship.

This was no invasion that he could see.

Unless it was a trap?

Haegen cleared his throat. 'My father has been murdered,' he began. 'Hest is no longer...' His voice broke, and he found himself unable to speak the truth of their situation.

'Hest has been overthrown by The Following,' Karsten said. 'By Jaeger too.'

Rexon stilled in surprise.

'We need your help,' Haegen said, recovering himself. 'My brother, Berard, he is badly injured. Jaeger took off his arm.' He turned back to the ship, watching as Berard was carefully lifted over the side. 'He needs a healer. Quickly.'

'Of course,' Rexon nodded, turning to his men. 'Torman! Go and find Alvida and Pria. Send them to the hall. Wake my wife too. We'll need to find beds for the queen and her family.' He bowed to Bayla, who nodded back stiffly.

'And some wine, I think,' Karsten added. 'I think we're all going to need some wine.'

***

Eadmund kissed his sleeping son's tiny head. He smelled good in a way that he couldn't explain. Like a puppy. Like a field of flowers after the rain. A smell that was so innocent. So new.

Smiling sadly, he stepped away from Sigmund's woven basket, walking back into his chamber, hoping he could keep him safe.

Knowing he had to.

'You're leaving already?' Evaine panicked, watching from the bed as Eadmund tied his swordbelt around his waist and reached for his cloak, throwing it quickly over his shoulders, wishing he'd thought to dry it by the fire.

He nodded, bending towards her, taking her soft face in his rough, smoky hands. 'Yes, time to give Thorgils a break. I didn't mean to take this long.'

'Then maybe you can stay longer? At least until the sun comes up?' Evaine pleaded, pushing herself up, sneaking her arms around his waist. They reached so much further than they used to, Eadmund being half the size he'd been a year ago. 'Don't go yet. Not yet. Come back to bed.'

Eadmund kissed Evaine slowly, feeling the intense pull of her chip away at his resolve. 'I have to go. And you have to stay here. Keep Sigmund safe for me. I'll be back soon, I promise.' And easing her out of his arms, he turned towards the door.

Evaine watched him go, feeling her discomfort intensify. She didn't want to leave Eadmund, but if she didn't, she worried what would become of her if Jael Furyck ever returned.

***

Jael bent over, hands on her thighs, sucking in a long, cold breath.

It had been an arduous climb, but the path had been surprisingly solid underfoot, and they hadn't encountered many problems, nor, thankfully, lost any men, which was surprising considering that it had been so dark.

Dawn was stirring, the sky lightening above the horizon, and they had to get moving. 'Eat! Drink something quickly, then we walk!' she called, standing up, rubbing her frozen hands together. She thought of Aleksander, hoping that the wind was with him. That he would arrive at the fort in time.

That they both would.

'Do you smell that?' Beorn wondered, peering around in the darkness.

Jael sniffed the air, shaking her head. 'No.'

'Sure I can smell smoke,' Beorn mumbled, digging into his leather satchel for a wedge of cheese.

'Smoke?' Jael smiled, sniffing again. 'That's good.'

***

Boom!

The Alekkans swung their enormous wooden ram into the gates over and over again.

Boom!

The noise shook the fort, undoing the Osslanders' confidence with each loud, echoing sound. For every Alekkan that fell off the ladders, scalded, on fire, and screaming, two more were ready to take their place.

The day had begun, and it was grey and cold, full of wind and rain, and the men on the ramparts glared up at the sky, weary and irritable.

'Find me more arrows,' Eadmund grumbled to Bram, wanting to keep his voice low. 'There must be more. Can you pull them out of the men who fell inside the fort?'

'Already have, and there aren't. Any more arrows, that is,' Bram sighed. 'We're just going to have to keep trying to scald them to death.'

'Or burn them?' Thorgils suggested as the ram hit the gates again. He cringed, sick of the deafening sound. 'We can tip the braziers onto them. We can bring torches. Anything with a flame.'

'Do it,' Eadmund urged. 'Bram, you go too. Gather whatever you can find. Thorgils, you need to get the men together in front of the gates. Get them ready. Build up the barricades. Prepare for a breach.'

Thorgils nodded, working his jaw, and clapping Bram on

the shoulder, he followed his uncle to the stairs.

Boom!

Their enemies were working under cover. Eadmund could see that in the flames that burned on the ground in front of the gates. A giant, hide-covered shield wall was in place now, protecting the rammers from every side, from whatever they tried to throw at them.

'Spears!' Eadmund shouted at Torstan, who was edging his way towards him. 'Bring me some spears!'

CHAPTER SEVEN

As soon as a house had been found for the Dragos', and Berard was tucked into a bed, fussed over by the two old healers, Karsten and Haegen took Hanna to the hall to speak to Rexon. They both insisted that she be the one to explain about the book and The Following, which had surprised her, and she was nervous, to begin with. The Lord of Saala had listened intently and patiently, though, and Hanna became more confident, strengthening her voice as she sat at the table, clasping her hands around a welcome cup of ale.

Saala's hall was full of industrious noise and appetising smells, and Hanna's stomach growled in anticipation of the hot breakfast that was on its way.

'Do you think this Following will come here?' Rexon wondered quietly.

'They will, yes,' Hanna said. 'They want to control everyone, every part of Osterland. Their goal is the total destruction of us all. Of everything that lives.'

Being a man with a newborn son, a wife he loved dearly, and a village of people he was tasked with protecting, that news chilled Rexon to the bone.

'Perhaps your people will be safer in Andala?' Hanna suggested, sensing his concern. 'From memory, it has an enormous fort.'

'And that's where you'll head next?' Rexon asked, pushing

a bowl of hazelnuts towards Hanna.

'We have to,' Karsten said, reaching over to grab a handful of nuts. 'If we're going to take back Hest, we'll need an army behind us.'

Haegen blinked in surprise. 'You think Axl Furyck will make an alliance with us to take back *our* kingdom? After how we treated him? After everything that's happened between Brekka and Hest?'

Karsten turned to glare at his brother. 'You don't think Axl Furyck wants to kill Jaeger? That he's not dreaming about ripping out his throat?' He shook his head, exhausted and impatient. 'It's probably *all* he's thinking about. Night and day! Imagining what Jaeger did to his woman. Seeing her lying in his bed, his big hands all over her!' Karsten ignored the surprised rise of Haegen's eyebrows as he turned his head to the fire, staring at the flames. 'I can promise you, Brother, Axl Furyck will stop at nothing to help us kill Jaeger.'

***

Boom!

Morac's skin prickled as he watched Thorgils bark at the men gathered behind the barricades. They had hammered stakes of every shape and size into the ground, pushing them against the shuddering wooden gates. He thought of Eirik, remembering how hard they had worked to strengthen those old gates over the years. Eirik had always worried that they weren't strong enough.

And now they would find out.

Morac shook his head, turning away, reminded of the secret door. They had worked hard on that too, keeping it hidden from everyone, lest its presence be revealed. Knowledge of that entrance would undermine their safety, Eirik had insisted. It was an option only to be used in the direst of situations.

He had not even trusted Eadmund with the secret.

Morac felt a flush of guilt. Eirik had made him promise that when it was time, and if he couldn't, Morac would be the one to reveal it to Eadmund. He would help him escape.

Boom!

Morac hurried back to the hall. His things were packed, and now he just had to wake Evaine and prepare her to leave.

***

Toki shook Ivaar awake. 'We need to move! It's morning! We need to move now!'

He sounded worried, Ivaar thought, rubbing his eyes, surprised that he'd managed to sleep at all. Struggling to his feet, he shivered, his wet tunic clinging to him under a heavy mail shirt. 'Alright, alright, we can leave. Calm down.' He held up a hand, trying to placate Toki, who was a jerking, shaking mess before him.

Toki wasn't placated. 'Now!' he growled. 'We need to leave now! My brothers will kill us if we're not in the fort soon. We should have been at that door by now. We need to go!'

Ivaar turned to his rising men. 'Get yourselves together! Gather your things! We march to the fort now!' He took a deep breath, realising that as much as he had wanted to delay Toki's attack on the fort, he had no choice but to lead him there now.

He had no choice but to help the Arnessons take his throne.

***

Jael's feet were ready for a warm fire. They had left the boggy ground behind hours ago, and they'd been clambering up, down, and around increasingly rocky terrain as they headed for the rear of the fort.

No one had spoken in hours, and because of the silence, Jael felt as though she was completely alone. They were all too tired to talk, and their progress felt slow as their energy waned, but it was better to be well on their way to the fort than only just waking up down in the cove.

Still, Jael knew where they were, and she knew that they still had a long way to go. 'Keep going!' she called hoarsely, turning around to bellow at her men, eager to make up time.

***

'Again!' Borg roared, a wide grin stretching his scarred face. 'Listen to that cracking! Again!'

Rolan was next to him, exhausted but relieved. They had been hammering at the gates all night long, and he could hear the cracking too. It was the first sign that they were making progress. And he could tell that the Osslanders were getting nervous. The arrows had stopped, and it had been some time since any liquids had been poured from the ramparts. Rolan smiled, knowing that they were likely preparing to be breached. 'Be ready to charge when the gates break!' he cried. 'They'll be waiting for us! We'll need a shield wall as soon as we're in! Be ready, men!'

***

Eadmund could hear the cracking of the gates as he hurried to the stairs, sword drawn, his heart pounding against his old mail shirt.

Morning was here, and so was the enemy.

***

'Do you have your things ready?' Morac whispered urgently, gripping Evaine's arm. 'It's time. We must go. Now!'

Evaine pulled away from him. He was hurting her.

Frustrated by her reluctance, Morac bent forward, trying to get her to see reason. 'Morana has seen what will come if we don't leave, Evaine. We must trust her. You will see Eadmund again, but for now, neither one of us is safe here. We need to get away from Oss. Quickly!'

Evaine sighed reluctantly, trying to move away from him. 'Alright! I'll get Tanja to wake Sigmund.'

'What? *No!*' Morac hissed, shaking his head. 'We cannot bring the baby. We must slip away. A crying baby and a whimpering girl will not help us do that!'

'But,' Evaine protested, frowning at her father, 'I need to take him. Eadmund will come for us if I take him!'

'Eadmund will come for you because you are soul bound,' Morac reminded her, glancing up and down the corridor. They were hidden behind the green curtain. Everyone had left their beds early, congregating in the hall, and they were alone. 'He will have no choice. Now, hurry!' He could hear the booming of the battering ram. The urgent voices. The panic.

The shattering of wood.

***

Eadmund heard the roar of victory as one of the gates broke, the battering ram bursting in through a well-earned hole. The broken gate jerked forward, but the wooden beam securing both gates held it in place. 'Archers!' he cried, standing behind a row of shields. 'Nock!'

The ram crashed into the gate again. They could hear the raised voices of the men on the other side who could sense that victory was near. They were not about to stop until they were standing inside the fort, and there was little any Osslander could do now but wait.

Eadmund glanced up at the ramparts, watching his archers positioned above the gates. 'Draw!'

Boom!

Thorgils tightened his grip on his shield.

Waiting.

The battering ram smashed through the hole in the gate again.

'Aim!'

Eadmund didn't blink. The gates were about to cave in; he could feel it. But there was no way those Alekkans were getting past his men. No way he was letting them claim Oss.

The surging mass of bellowing warriors pushed and pushed on the broken gate, finally shunting it open, squeezing in through the narrowest of gaps, only to be met with rows of pointed stakes and blazing fires, and behind them, a densely-packed shield wall that extended across the muddy square.

'Ramparts! Fire at will!' Eadmund roared, the men behind him lifting up shields to cover their heads. Eadmund had reserved some arrows to make a last stand at the gates. He had archers behind him, but he would let Arlo and his men on the ramparts pick off the invaders first.

The leading men went down in an explosion of arrows. Those still standing retreated quickly, flattening themselves back against the gates, trying to stay out of range. The archers above them hung out over the rampart wall, trying to find targets, but the angle made it hard.

'Archers!' Borg barked from a crouched position near the hanging gate, his shield over his head, watching as the men on the ramparts took aim again. 'Archers!' he yelled. 'Bring those fuckers down!'

Borg's archers quickly formed outside the gates, firing up at the ramparts. Arlo and his men heard the whip and whistle as the bows released, but some weren't quick enough to get down. Two Osslanders were killed instantly, tipping over the rampart wall, straight down onto the blazing fires.

Eadmund felt his body jerk, wanting to rush forward and save them, but neither man was screaming. There was nothing he could do.

He didn't move.

But Arlo did. 'Turn!' he cried to his men, realising that they had to defend themselves now. 'Nock!'

Eadmund watched as Arlo's men turned away from the square, and the tattooed men crouching by the gates suddenly rose; some bare-chested, most in mail; none wore helmets.

All of them were yelling.

But where was Ivaar?

'*My* archers!' Eadmund roared. 'Nock!' He peered between the shields, watching the Alekkans fight their way through the barricades, crying out when some of the archers on the ramparts briefly turned their attention back to them. But more and more were surging through the gap in the gates now. The sun was turning the sky a dull, yellowish-grey, and Eadmund could see his enemy clearly for the first time.

And his brother wasn't leading those men.

He hoped that Torstan was keeping a close eye on what was happening at the rear of the fort.

'Push! Push through!' Borg screamed from behind his shield, urging his hesitant men on through the barricades. 'Get that other gate open! We need every man in here! Now! Shield wall!' And he slapped his shield over Rolan's, the men behind them covering their heads with another row of shields, waiting for the next wave of arrows. 'Archers! Aim for their wall!'

***

'Where's Morac?' Bram called, scanning the hall. 'He's supposed to be organising you all in here! What's happening?'

No one seemed to know what they were doing, except panicking. Runa, Ayla, and Isaura were tending to the wounded, trying to keep the children under control and out from under their feet.

'They've breached the gates,' Bram said, grabbing Runa's arm. There was no time for Morac now. 'We need to barricade the doors. Quickly! Leave those men. Isaura, come here! Help me move the tables. We have to barricade the doors!'

Isaura swallowed, glancing at Ayla, hoping to see some sign that the dreamer could see how things would go.

Ayla felt terrified. She couldn't see a thing, except Ivaar.

Ivaar was getting closer.

***

'Hurry! Hurry!' Toki implored. His legs were long and young, and he ran ahead of them all like a spring foal, but no one had the urgency he did.

Not even his own men.

But Toki could see the rise of the fort in the distance now, and he wasn't going to be held back by Ivaar any longer.

Ivaar turned with a heavy sigh, ready to implore his men to pick up their feet.

He froze, coming to a halt.

'No!' Toki was furious as he spun around. 'What are you

doing? *No!*' Then he followed Ivaar's gaze towards a row of men in the distance.

Men, who were moving towards them with speed.

***

Both gates were twisted open now as the remaining Alekkans squeezed between them, flooding into the space behind Borg's ever-growing shield wall.

There were too many of them; the barricades wouldn't stop them now.

Eadmund swallowed, pushing his boots into the mud.

There were no Kalfans that he could see. No Kalfan colours, banners, or shields. They didn't look like anything other than Alekkans. But it hardly mattered who they were. There were a lot of them, and, unlike his men, they appeared to have a never-ending supply of arrows.

'What do you think?' Thorgils wondered from beside Eadmund, sucking in a breath as an arrow whipped over the top of his shield. He ducked down further, glad to be wearing his battered old helmet.

'I think they don't get through us,' Eadmund growled. 'We hold here. We don't let them anywhere near the hall. We don't give them our fort!'

'Hold the wall, men!' Thorgils bellowed, spinning around to glare at his crouching warriors. 'Let them come. If they want a glorious battle death, we'll make their dreams come true! We'll kill them all! For Oss! For Eirik! We'll kill them all!' And then another shower of arrows, and Thorgils was bracing himself against his shield, dropping his head, hoping that none would find their way through.

***

Evaine sobbed, tears streaming down her face as Morac dragged her through the fort, avoiding the square. He could feel himself panicking, worried that they'd be seen, but no one was near the stables where Eirik had been smart enough to hide the secret door. No one was worrying about horses now.

Morac hurried Evaine to the back of the stables, ignoring her noise, looking for the carved roof beam that indicated where the door was hiding. And, finding the tiny pair of ravens that Eirik had roughly chiselled into the beam, he dropped Evaine's arm and his full leather satchel, and ran to grab the axe he'd brought into the stables earlier in the day.

Swallowing, Morac indicated for Evaine to move back as he swung the axe, slamming it into the old wattle and daub wall. The wall panel under the ravens was just for show, he knew. The wattle had been loosely threaded to create enough of a structure for the daub to stick to, but one that would quickly crumble when any pressure was applied.

And Morac was applying some pressure with his axe.

Soon, there was enough of a hole for them to crawl through. 'Come on!' He threw away the axe, slung his satchel over his shoulder and grabbed Evaine's hand. 'We need to hurry!'

Evaine reluctantly ducked through the hole after her father, into the narrow space between the fort's rear wall and the rear of the stables. She waited as Morac dug into his satchel, listening to the building noise coming from the square. Worrying about Eadmund.

Finally, Morac pulled out an old key and turned to the wall, digging beneath the thick vines of a determined creeping bush that had covered the door, spreading across the wall, until he found a keyhole.

***

'Bitch! We're going to kill you, bitch!' Toki Arnesson spat into the wind, which promptly blew the gob straight back into his face. He shook his head, not bothered in the slightest, pointing his sword at the men in the distance who had stopped running now.

At the woman who stood waiting in front of them.

It wasn't hard to guess who she was, or why she was there, but there was no way she was going to stop him from getting to that fort. He glanced at Ivaar, who hadn't moved since they'd seen the row of warriors fanning out across their path. 'Get your men together, Bastard!' Toki shrieked. 'We attack now!'

He looked like a pecking chicken, Ivaar thought: all bulging eyes, swivelling head, tiptoeing about on his long legs. A confused idiot, screeching like the inexperienced child he was.

Ivaar turned around, motioning to his men.

Jael watched them, her body still, her heart pounding after the run.

'You were right, then,' Beorn muttered from her left.

'So far, at least,' Jael murmured, tightening her grip on *Toothpick*. 'We'll see.' She ran her eyes over her own men: her Osslanders and her brother's Brekkans; two shiploads of warriors ready to get inside that fort and have a well-deserved drink of ale around a hot fire.

Only half as many men as were waiting across the stretch of stepped rock with Ivaar.

Ivaar thought of the frozen waterfall.

Remembering how he'd tried to kiss Jael; so confident that she'd felt the same at that moment. Remembering her scorn and triumph when she'd turned against him, stealing the throne, plotting with his brother.

Yet, she had stopped Eadmund from killing him when his father died. She had defended him then, believed him when most hadn't.

He heard Eirik's voice in his ear. He could almost feel his father's big, rough hand gripping his, leading him to that secret door. *Their* secret, Eirik had promised in that gravelly voice, his eyes twinkling in the moonlight.

It would be *their* secret.

Ivaar sheathed his sword and drew out his knife.

CHAPTER EIGHT

'Hold!' Eadmund roared, trying to stop his foot sliding backwards, but the man on the other side of his shield was almost as wide as its round, iron-edged rim, and he was shunting hard. 'Hold!' he cried through teeth that were grinding, feeling the burn in his forearm as it pushed back against the crushing weight.

'Watch your flanks!' Thorgils warned, scanning the sides of their wall, worried about Torstan guarding the south of the fort. 'Keep both eyes open! This is our home! They will not take it from us! Not this bunch of inbred fucks!' He swerved to the side as a blade sliced through a narrow gap between the shields.

Borg laughed. He could understand him. He could understand all of them as they panicked before the power of his fearless Alekkan warriors. 'Forward!' And his men pushed harder against their own shields, banging them into their enemy's. 'Spears!' Borg yelled. 'Stab the bastards!'

Eadmund tried to clear the vision of his father's anxious face. 'Forward!' he ordered, feeling the weight of the Alekkans weaken his own wall. 'Push forward!' He thought fleetingly of Jael, wondering where she was, knowing that it was too late for her to help them now.

***

Ivaar flicked his hand, releasing the knife.

Toki Arnesson screamed, gripping the back of his head, too shocked to speak as he spun around, his mouth twisting in agony before he staggered and crumpled to the ground.

Dead.

Ivaar drew his sword. 'Kill them!' he ordered, watching as Jael and her men advanced at a run. 'Kill them!' And his Kalfans turned on Toki's confused men, who quickly backed into each other, caught between one enemy, and a rapidly approaching second one.

Ivaar leaned back, slicing an Alekkan across the thigh, avoiding his mail tunic. The man howled, jerking forward, and Ivaar hacked his blade into his neck, watching as he dropped to the ground, his pained cry quickly lost amongst the loud clanging of blades. Ivaar spun, holding off the sword of a hulking giant who was spitting furiously all over his helmet.

He couldn't remember his name.

'You treacherous bastard!' the giant growled, two hands around the hilt of his long sword. 'You'll pay for this!'

Ivaar jumped back, avoiding the sharp threat of the blade as it cleaved the air before him. He stumbled on a rock, twisting his ankle, grimacing in pain, both eyes still on the giant with the big sword.

The giant who was smiling now that his prey was limping.

And then he wasn't smiling at all as he felt the sharp bite of a blade across his ankles, which quickly unbalanced him, and he staggered forward, feeling the kick in his back before he fell.

'Ivaar,' Jael growled, stabbing the Alekkan through the neck before he could roll over. 'We need to get to the fort. Now!' And spinning away, she brought *Toothpick* down across the arm of the next charging man.

'Kill them!' Ivaar cried, urging his men on. 'Kill them quickly!' And he wheeled away from one bellowing Alekkan, raising his sword, holding off two more who were screaming for him, axes swinging.

Jael turned back, dropping to the ground, sweeping her leg around, knocking one of Ivaar's attackers over as Ivaar chopped his sword into the throat of the other. Jael was back on her feet, spearing *Toothpick* through the fallen man's groin. 'Perhaps we should do this together?' she panted, noticing how many more Alekkans were surging towards the two of them. 'Might make it quicker?'

Ivaar nodded and backed into Jael, both of them lunging forward.

The rain had gone, the wind was dropping, and the morning was no longer new.

Jael could feel it.

They had to hurry.

***

'Axes!' Borg yelled, turning to Rolan. 'Get back outside! Bring more axes! I want their shields down! Archers! Fire another round!'

'Whoever that shit is, I don't like him,' Thorgils muttered, sick of crouching and hiding behind their wall. He wanted to stand and fight. But he kept a firm grip on his impulses, imagining Jael's stern face, knowing that they needed to bleed the Alekkans of their arrows before they showed themselves. The Osslanders had none left now. They would be shot to pieces if they abandoned their shield walls too soon.

'Ha!' Eadmund laughed, his body shuddering against his shield. Their wall was still holding, though he wondered if he'd ever feel his arm again. Then he heard the furious ringing of the signal bell from the rear of the fort; Torstan's panicked voice rising in the distance. Eadmund wasn't smiling then. 'Up! Up! Now!'

Thorgils was quickly standing beside him, his shield over

his head as the arrows flew. 'Keep covered!' he roared. 'Keep your heads, you filthy Osslanders! You're going to need them!'

'Spears!' Eadmund cried, stepping aside to let his spearmen through. 'Charge them!'

'Archers!' Borg yelled again, only to be met with a mumbled report that they were out of arrows. He didn't care, though. He could hear the clanging of the signal bell too. 'Up! Kill them! Toki's here! Kill them!'

***

Aleksander held his breath as *Sea Bear* sailed too close to one of the stone spires. The gaps between the towering stones guarding the entrance to Oss' harbour were unsettlingly narrow, and he waited to hear the hull scraping across the dangerous rocks lurking beneath the churning water too.

Looking up, trying to take his mind off the next spire, Aleksander noticed the plumes of smoke in the distance, drifting up from the fort. As much as he wanted his helmsman to take his time and approach the next stone with care, he knew that they couldn't delay.

They had to get into the harbour quickly.

***

'Stay away from the doors!' Bram warned, listening to the howling clamour of clashing swords and shields; the blood-curdling cries of men dying out in the square. He had ten men with him. It wouldn't be enough if it came to a fight, but that wasn't why he was here.

Bram knew this hall. There was a door leading off the

kitchen, and he had a man stationed there in case Ivaar and the Alekkans had any plans to lock them in and burn them down. He knew of men who had done such evil things, and one of them had been the Arnesson's weasel father. He didn't put it past them to betray Ivaar, who was surely not cruel enough to burn his wife and children alive.

'Bram!' Ayla rushed up to him, brown eyes wide and blinking. 'Quick! Help me! You need to come with me. Now!'

***

Borg exploded out of the shield wall like a wild boar: all sharp teeth, foaming spittle and wild eyes, ploughing forward, thirsty for blood. Sword swinging, he charged for the biggest man he could find.

A red-headed tree of a man.

Borg chopped his blade towards one of the man's colossal thighs.

Thorgils frowned, stepping back, just out of reach. *This* was the fiercesome leader who had been giving him a headache all morning? 'You?' he roared. 'Ha! You think *you* can take me down, little man?' And Thorgils lashed out with his shield, which, he was sure, was bigger than the frothing Alekkan leader.

Slipping to the right, dodging the shield, Borg slammed his boot into the side of Thorgils' knee. Thorgils grunted, staggering, and Borg was quickly slicing his blade towards his waist.

'Shut your big mouth!' Eadmund yelled, throwing himself between Thorgils and Borg, blunting the Alekkan's strike with his own shield.

Borg growled in frustration, his eyes darting to the right, watching as Thorgils shook off the discomfort in his leg and rejoined the fight. 'Grrrrr! Island bastards!' he spat, throwing his shield away and drawing his second sword, glaring at Eadmund. 'I promised to leave you for your brother, but unless he hurries, there'll be nothing left of you except scraps! Something to feed the dogs tonight!'

Thorgils gripped his shield tightly, keeping it low enough to protect himself from the small man's twirling swords. He drew back his own sword, ready to strike, catching a flash of black out of the corner of his eye. 'Eadmund!'

Eadmund spun, ducking a swinging axe, throwing his shield up to bat the man away. But the Alekkan shook off the blow and kept coming, and so did another, and another, and Eadmund couldn't look around to see what was happening with Thorgils anymore.

***

Bram was torn.

Torstan was bellowing from the ramparts above them.

But Ayla was insistent.

'Please, Bram, trust me,' she pleaded, gripping his hand. 'Open it! Open the door!'

***

Aleksander sighed in relief, turning to watch the remainder of his fleet clear the spires. He could see the fort now. Smoke billowed up from its stone walls, and before the fort, a long stretch of ships leaned over, beached along the black stones.

'Dig in!' he called to his men, who'd been pulling slowly on the oars as they navigated the swirling currents around the craggy spires. Now that they were free, they had to pick up speed. 'We need to hurry! Catapult crew to me!'

***

They were fighting like angry bears. Tearing at them. Vicious. Loud. Led by the angriest bear of all, who was still intent on killing Thorgils. Axes were flying, and the Osslanders were slowly being pushed away from the gates.

Towards the hall.

Eadmund glanced at Sevrin, who was fighting off two men, ducking and weaving with his sword. He could see blood running down Sevrin's face, and slamming his shield into the forehead of the nearest Alekkan, Eadmund pushed his stumbling body out of the way, trying to get through to his friend. 'No! Sevrin!' he screamed as a spear slid straight through Sevrin's mail, pushing into his chest. His father's face flashed before his eyes as Eadmund ran, aiming his sword at Sevrin's attacker's neck.

The man jumped back, avoiding most of the impact, but Eadmund was on him quickly, ramming his sword into his thigh, swinging his shield into the man's throat, listening to his choked grunt as he jerked backwards. 'Sevrin!'

But Sevrin had fallen, his eyes fixed open, and Eadmund couldn't reach him through the melee of bodies and swords and roaring Alekkans.

'Eadmund!'

Eadmund spun, hearing the warning in Thorgils' voice. The big-mouthed, black-haired leader had slipped away from his friend, who suddenly had three more Alekkans to deal with, and he was charging towards Eadmund instead. 'Sevrin!' Eadmund cried, swinging his sword up to parry the fast blows of the double-sworded Alekkan leader.

'You have something I want, Drunkard!' Borg panted,

grinning maniacally.

'What? A better-looking face?' Eadmund spat, ducking, kicking out at Borg, but Borg was light on his feet and quick, and despite Eadmund's recent training, he still wasn't as sharp as he used to be, and he could feel the strain of trying to draw air into his lungs as he fought to catch him.

Borg kept up the pressure, swinging his swords back and forth across Eadmund's chest until Eadmund snapped. All thoughts of Ivaar and Evaine and Jael and his father were gone. All he could think about was ending this annoying shit who had been terrorising him and his people for days. He jabbed his sword straight through Borg's swirling blades. His arm was longer, his reach was greater, and the tip of his sword almost touched Borg's chest.

But not quite.

Borg smiled.

But Eadmund wasn't done. 'Grrrrr!' he snarled, and dropping to the ground, he skidded through the mud, ramming his boots into Borg's ankles, knocking him over with a sickening crack of bone.

Rolling and jumping to his feet, Eadmund leaned over Borg, who was stunned, shaking himself awake, his mouth wrenched open in pain. Eadmund lifted his sword, preparing to drive his blade down and end the sneering little shit, then everything went black.

***

'Load the sea-fire. Wait for my call,' Aleksander said calmly, working his way around his catapult crew, signalling for the next ship to do the same.

He had brought five ships, but only two had catapults.

Five jars of sea-fire each.

He turned to his archers. 'Nock and hold. We need to get closer.'

***

'We have your king! Throw down your weapons!' Borg shouted, spitting a great gob of blood onto the ground. 'We will kill him!' He shook his head, wondering if Eadmund Skalleson had broken his ankle. He could barely stand.

Rolan had his arm around Eadmund's shoulder, his knife at his throat, and there didn't appear to be much that Eadmund could do about that. He was awake, though he couldn't see properly, but he could feel something wet dripping down his neck. He couldn't hear anything except a loud buzzing in his ears.

It felt as though he'd been hit by a hammer.

Thorgils glanced at Eadmund; at Sevrin, who lay dead at his feet; at Otto, who stood frozen beside him, his sword dripping with Alekkan blood.

'What? You can't understand me, Osslanders?' Borg spat, scanning the hesitant men as their eyes darted around the bloody carnage, deciding what to do; most of them looking at Thorgils. 'Or, perhaps it's that you don't care much for *this* king?' he laughed, turning to punch Eadmund in the stomach.

Thorgils clenched his fist as Eadmund sagged forward, groaning.

'Throw down your weapons!' Borg demanded again, his eyes wild with impatience.

Eadmund tried to get Thorgils' attention. He tried to shake his head, not wanting him to surrender, but he could see three Thorgils', and none of them appeared to be looking his way.

'Ahhh, you've come! Finally!' Borg smiled, his attention diverted by a commotion at the other end of the square as Ivaar and his men appeared. 'I suppose I'll leave this one for you,' he said, pointing to Eadmund, who was barely able to stand on his own now. 'You may have your revenge, and then I will have my throne.' Borg frowned, noticing that there were no Alekkans with Ivaar. 'Where's Toki?'

Thorgils looked around in horror.

'Toki?' Ivaar murmured, glancing at his brother. 'He's coming.'

Borg looked relieved.

'Oh, did I say he's coming?' Ivaar frowned. 'I meant that he's *not* coming,' he said as Jael emerged from behind him. 'I brought someone else instead.'

Thorgils blinked in confusion, tightening his grip on his sword.

'Who the fuck are you?' Borg spat, feeling his belly clench as Jael strode towards him, Ivaar on one side, Torstan and Bram on the other; her men filling the square behind them.

Jael stopped and stared at Borg Arnesson, her hands by her sides.

'This is the Queen of Oss, you mad cunt,' Bram smiled widely. 'I'd show her some respect if I were you!'

Borg licked his lips, tasting blood as he limped forward, his hand sweaty on his sword grip. 'You *betrayed* me?' he snarled at Ivaar. 'For *her*?'

Ivaar didn't speak. He didn't know how he felt.

But Jael did. 'You have my husband,' she said coolly, watching Eadmund struggle to keep his eyes open, his head drooping onto his chest, not even noticing that she was there. 'I'd release him if I were you.'

Borg snorted. '*Release* him?' He shook his head, straightening his narrow shoulders, ignoring the pain in his ankles. 'I'd rather kill him!' And turning, he aimed his sword at Eadmund's belly.

Jael quickly lifted her arms, flinging the two small knives she'd been holding, hidden in her palms. The first one hit Borg in the neck. The second struck his brother Rolan between the eyes.

They both screamed.

No one moved as Rolan fell to the ground, releasing his hold on Eadmund, who tumbled over with him.

Borg spun towards Jael, grabbing his neck. 'Get them!' he gurgled wetly, before faltering. He tried to move his legs, but they wouldn't work, and he stumbled down onto his knees. Seething with rage and spitting blood, he reached for the knife, yanking it out of his neck, but Jael was already running towards him, *Toothpick* in her hand. 'Kill... them!' Borg gurgled, struggling back to his feet, swinging his sword at Jael, listening as the clash of blades resumed all around him.

Jael could see the fear in Borg's eyes as death approached, but he would not go down easily; the scarred mess of his face told her that. She swayed to the left, avoiding the slow arc of his sword, then lashed out, slamming her boot into his knee.

Borg screamed, feeling the crack on his kneecap, but he refused to fall. Not for that bitch. He staggered, limping, swinging again, but the blood pouring out of his neck weakened him further.

There was no power in his arms. No strength in his legs.

Jael could see that.

The fire in his eyes was quickly blowing out.

She spun around, roaring as she released *Toothpick*, taking off his head with one enormous, hacking blow.

Borg's surprise stayed on his face as his head flew in one direction, and his body collapsed to the ground in the other.

Jael held up her sword. 'Your lord is dead!' she cried. 'His brothers are dead! Put down your weapons and live!'

The Alekkans heard her, but Borg's cousin Erl urged them to continue their fight. 'We'll take this fort for Borg!' he yelled, charging her. 'For Rolan! For Toki!'

Jael watched the wide man barrelling towards her, two thick dark braids flapping around a grizzled red face. He was still confident that they had the men to finish what Borg had started, and one look at his twin brother, Rork, told him that he agreed.

Then the first ship exploded.

Erl stopped in his tracks, mouth gaping open, head swinging towards the broken gates, watching the fireball rise up into the iron-grey sky.

'Surrender to us now!' Jael urged. 'The Brekkan fleet is in the harbour! They will burn your ships!'

And then another explosion.

The Alekkans were looking at Erl for direction, but he had not moved. Slack-jawed and wide-eyed, he hesitated, his axe blade hovering near his ear.

'I won't kill you!' Jael insisted loudly. 'I need your men. Surrender now and take an oath to me!'

'To *you*?' Erl spat. 'To Oss?' He laughed, conscious of the sound of his ships exploding in the harbour. How hard they had all worked to command such an impressive fleet. And soon, it would all be ash.

'I'm building an army to take Hest,' Jael said quickly. 'There'll be gold waiting for you there! Plenty of reward for your loyalty to me.' She sought out Thorgils, who was kneeling beside Eadmund. 'Tell Aleksander to stop burning the ships now! They've surrendered!'

Erl was certain that he hadn't surrendered, but he didn't move to attack Jael, and his brother and their men didn't move either. Everyone stood like statues before each other, apart from Thorgils, who raced through the tangled piles of bodies, towards the twisted gates.

'Isn't that why you joined your cousins in the first place?' Jael asked, watching in fascination as Erl's eyes revealed his thoughts to her. 'Gold? Fame? Why not live and claim a great hoard with me? There's no gold waiting for you in Vidar's Hall, Erl Arnesson.'

'How much gold?' he wondered.

And Jael smiled.

CHAPTER NINE

Berard frowned. 'But why would she have wanted to stay?' It was a question he couldn't stop asking.

Karsten rested his head in his hands as he sat on the edge of his brother's bed. He'd slept for a few hours, but he still felt tired, worn down by grief and worry. Unable to stop thinking about his father. 'I don't know,' he admitted, looking up. 'Perhaps she loves Jaeger?'

Berard shook his head, more awake now that his pain was under control. The healers had cauterised what was left of his arm, which was now no more than a small stump hanging off his right shoulder. The pain had been excruciating, but they had dosed him with enough mandrake to keep him from feeling the worst of it. 'She doesn't,' he insisted. 'She wanted to leave with me. She killed Egil. She took the book!'

'*Meena* killed Egil?' Karsten was surprised.

'She wanted to leave!'

'Well, perhaps she stayed for the book? Perhaps she thinks she can still get it away from Jaeger somehow?'

Berard panicked, worried that he had exposed Meena to even more danger. He didn't imagine that Jaeger would take her attempted escape very well. 'We need to go back!' he insisted, trying to push himself upright.

'Back to Hest? Now?' Karsten snorted. 'Us? You with one arm, me with one eye, and Haegen with one ball?'

'I *can* hear you,' Haegen grumbled from a nearby bed.

They were all grateful for the privacy the small house by the hall provided, but no one was enjoying the close proximity to five small children who had barely slept, demanding to be fed or held. Refusing to stay still.

Bayla had insisted that Irenna and Nicolene take the children outside for some fresh air, leaving Berard to recover in peace. It was much quieter without them, but the silence gave her more time to think of all the things she didn't want to think about.

Everything that mattered to her had gone.

Well, almost everything, she supposed, glancing at her three remaining sons. But she had lost enough to know that life would never be the same again. 'We cannot go back to Hest without help, Berard,' Bayla sighed, walking over to check on him. His colour appeared to have improved, though without his arm, he was no use to them now. 'Your brother has turned into something...' She shook her head, trying to get Haaron's last words out of it, but they echoed constantly, as did the dull ache in her chest. 'We must go to Andala now,' Bayla said, clearing her throat. 'As soon as you're better. We must head for safety. It is decided.'

'What? Andala? But Meena! We can't leave Meena in Hest!' Berard panicked, staring at Karsten. Surely, Karsten would never want to abandon Hest? Leave their kingdom in Jaeger's hands?

'Mother's right,' Karsten said. 'We've decided to go to Andala, to ask for the Furycks' help.' He felt sick, hardly believing his own ears. He didn't want to imagine how it would feel to actually say those words to Axl Furyck himself. Though, perhaps he'd get Haegen to do the begging and scraping, him being the rightful King of Hest now. 'The only way you're going to see Meena again is if we go to Hest with an army, and we don't have one anymore.'

***

'You're back, then?' Thorgils noted wryly, glancing at Jael as she dug through the bodies, trying to find anyone still alive; listening to the women and children rushing about desperately, calling for their men, their fathers and brothers. 'Just in time.'

'Well, not quite. Not in time to save Eadmund from that hole in his head. Not in time to save poor Sevrin.' Jael felt sad, watching as the bodies were carried away, piled up, ready for the pyres they would have to build quickly before the rain returned; disappointed that she had not arrived earlier.

Thorgils felt sad, too, recognising many of the men lying dead around his feet. He lifted his eyes, avoiding the haunting looks on their ruined faces. 'But Ivaar?'

Jael glanced around. Ivaar and his Kalfans had gathered on one side of the square. Erl and Rork Arnesson and the Alekkans had moved to the other. Neither group of men appeared to know what to do. And then there was Eadmund, who had been carried into the hall, unconscious. Jael was eager to get inside and see how he was. 'Ivaar changed his mind.'

'So it would seem.'

Jael could sense his worry. 'He won't take Isaura.'

Thorgils snorted. 'You don't know Ivaar very well if you think that.'

'We have more to worry about than Ivaar,' Jael muttered. 'But Ivaar won't take Isaura. He's my man now. His loyalty belongs to me. I'm his queen. And I won't let him hurt Isaura or you.' And she looked towards Aleksander as he came through the collapsed gates. 'Let's start putting the fort back together!' she called loudly. 'We need the gates repaired quickly. Torstan, you work on the pyres! Thorgils, you take charge of the gates. And you...' she frowned at the large, bushy-bearded man who stood almost shoulder to shoulder with Thorgils. 'You, I don't know. But I'm grateful to you for opening that door. It would have taken a while to get through it without your help.'

Bram grinned at Jael. 'You can thank Ayla for that. She's a very useful woman to have around.' He glanced behind himself, but Ayla was bending over a wounded man, quickly tearing off a piece of her dress to tie around a gash in his thigh.

'This is my Uncle Bram,' Thorgils announced, clapping Bram on the back. 'He's visiting.'

'Am I?' Bram asked, shrugging. 'I suppose I am. Although I must admit, it's been nice to be back on Oss. Might stay a little longer, if you'll have me?' He glanced at Jael.

Jael nodded distractedly, her eyes drifting towards Runa, who was tending to another injured man, knowing that she needed to speak to her about Fyn. 'Of course. Perhaps you can help Ayla now? Start getting the injured into the hall. I'll meet you there. I need to go and check on Eadmund.' And without waiting for a reply, Jael hurried towards the hall steps, holding her breath, hoping her husband was alright.

***

As pleased as Axl was to be back in Andala, he had quickly become frustrated with his injured leg. He couldn't walk without help, so he was overly reliant on Gant and a stick to get around the fort. It wasn't how he'd imagined his triumphant return to Brekka.

Not in the slightest.

Yet, here he was, sitting in his father's hall, a king at last.

'What do you think I should say?' Amma wondered from his right. She had been poised over the piece of vellum for a while, not knowing how to begin the note to her older sister, Getta. Amma had always believed that they were close, yet the illusion she'd had of her family was destroyed now, and she realised that Getta had always been just like Osbert. Just like their father. A self-serving bully, determined to rise to power, and not caring who she had to step over to get there.

It was unlikely that she would choose to help them.

Axl frowned, turning to her. '*Say*? Well, perhaps we need to arrange a meeting, on the border? You could say that we should meet to discuss the safety of our kingdoms. Something about a great threat and the need to unite our armies to defend Osterland. That both our kingdoms are in grave danger.'

'That sounds good,' Amma murmured. 'But what do I say about Osbert and my father? About their deaths?'

'Oh.'

Axl, who was sitting in Lothar's chair, which would have been Osbert's had they not all agreed to have Gant murder him, could see her point. 'There's not much you can say. Would she really believe you were sorry? You can hardly pretend that we didn't have anything to do with their deaths.'

'No.'

'Perhaps it's better coming from me?' Axl suggested, reaching for the quill. 'I can write the note. We need to get it off today, I think. Although, I doubt any response we receive will be positive. We all remember Getta.'

Amma handed over the quill with a grateful smile. 'She was especially close to Father, of course, but Raymon may not be inclined to follow his wife's advice.'

Sent away from Brekka by his father for being an embarrassment to the Furyck name, Lothar had made himself valuable to the rulers of Iskavall instead. The Vandaals were one of the oldest families in that kingdom, and once Hugo Vandaal had been crowned king, Getta had made a point of becoming very attentive to his only son, so that by the time he was ready to ascend to the throne himself, she was waiting dutifully beside him as his wife.

Raymon Vandaal had always seemed like a pleasant boy, Amma thought, though perhaps a little timid. And Amma knew her sister well enough to guess what that would mean for him. 'But, then again,' she murmured, 'it would make sense for them to agree to meet with you and Jael. I can't imagine they'd want to start a war when Brekka and Iskavall have been allies for so many years.'

Axl nodded, hoping she was right. They needed to keep the allies they had if they were to attack Hest and get that book away from The Following. And more importantly, where he was concerned, kill Jaeger Dragos.

Feeling another sharp sting in his leg, Axl shivered, remembering the wolves and the ravens and the threat of what was to come.

***

'You should be careful about trusting them,' Ivaar murmured, inclining his head to where Erl Arnesson and his brother, Rork, huddled with their men, watched over by Bram and a handful of tired-looking Osslanders.

'Oh, that's coming from you, is it?' Jael said tartly, turning to him as they looked on from the hall steps.

Ivaar narrowed his eyes, annoyed that he would still feel anything for her after all that she had done to crush his ambitions. But she had saved him from becoming the Arnesson's lapdog, and he was grudgingly grateful for that. 'How did you know that I'd be there? How did you know what we were planning?'

'I had a dream. I saw you. I sensed your reluctance. You didn't want to give them the island. I saw you with your father when he showed you the door. I felt how much that meant. How much *he* meant to you.'

Ivaar's eyebrows were up. 'You're really a dreamer, then? I thought that was just a game.'

'I am,' Jael sighed. 'Makes it much harder for you to betray me now, wouldn't you say?'

'It does.'

'Not many will welcome you here, Ivaar. Eadmund certainly won't. Nor will your wife, or your dreamer,' Jael suggested. 'But you'll have my protection. And you and your men will come with me to Andala. The Alekkans too. And who knows, perhaps you'll redeem yourself in the eyes of the Islanders? Perhaps you'll make amends to all those you've hurt?'

'Andala?' Ivaar was confused. 'Why are we going to Andala?'

***

Jaeger kept thinking about his brothers, wondering what they would do next. After his talk with Draguta, he realised that there was little he could do but wait upon her. She had his book, and she seemed intent on taking her time, deciding how to use it and on whom. But in the meantime, he had to ensure that Hest was ready to protect itself against Haegen and Karsten, for surely they would not hide away like beaten dogs for long?

They would come for him, seeking revenge.

And he needed to be ready to kill them when they did.

Jaeger glanced at Meena, who stood silently beside him. 'Can you ride?' he wondered. The stable hands were grooming his father's horse, checking his teeth, untangling his long chestnut mane. Haaron had treated his horse better than any of his sons, and Jaeger was looking forward to taking him out for a ride.

He could almost see his father's scowling face, red with rage.

Meena visibly shuddered. 'I... I have not...' She swallowed, starting again. 'I rode a pony once.'

Jaeger burst out laughing, reaching for the reins. 'Well, best you stay behind, then, until I can find you a pony. I don't want to kill you yet, Meena. Not while I may still find some use for you!' And pushing his weight down onto his ankle, which he'd slipped into a stirrup, he threw himself up into the saddle, patting the silken coat of his father's beloved horse, Bakona.

His horse now. 'Ha! Ha!' he roared, kicking him sharply.

Meena watched Jaeger disappear up the road, the horse's hooves lifting up clouds of red dust all around her. She wanted to run after him, out of the city, far away from Morana and Draguta, but she couldn't.

Not while that book was still in Hest.

And sighing, thinking of Berard, she turned around, trudging back to the castle.

***

Oss' hall was echoing with the noise of too many people squeezed into a space that wouldn't accommodate them all; ringing with shrieks of pain. The doors had been wedged open, but the smell of blood and bowels, wet boots and smoke was overpowering.

Jael tried not to inhale as she glanced around. 'How many of their ships survived?' she asked, turning back to Aleksander, who was taking a moment to warm his hands over the flames.

'We only used two jars in the end, so... ten, I think?'

Jael nodded. That was a good number of ships to add to the ones Eadmund had sent around to Tatti's Bay, as well as the Brekkan and Kalfan ships still down in the coves. It looked as though there were enough Alekkans standing, ready to sail them to Andala, but whether she could trust them was another matter. Putting together an army of her enemies didn't sound like the wisest plan she'd ever dreamed up.

'Do you think you can trust them?' Aleksander asked, watching her eyes narrow on Erl Arnesson, who appeared to be enjoying his cup of ale on the other side of the hall.

'Probably not,' Jael admitted, holding her own hands out to the fire. 'But we either kill them all or let them go back to Alekka. Neither of those options sounds good to me. There are hundreds of the bastards! And we need the biggest army possible to attack Hest. Besides, for now, they're outnumbered. And they don't have the gold they came here for. I'm sure they'd rather not return home empty-handed, or they'll have a lot of disappointed wives to answer to!'

'You're sure the Dragos' will hand over their gold so easily?' Aleksander wondered, taking a seat on the nearest bench.

Jael smiled, remembering Haegen Dragos' miserable face the last time she'd forced him to part with his father's gold. 'Who knows? If my dreams are to be believed, everything has changed in Hest now.' Frowning, she joined Aleksander on the bench. 'We have to secure Oss and leave as soon as we can. As soon as Eadmund is back on his feet. The longer we leave The Following with that book, the more trouble they're going to cause.'

Aleksander noticed how worried she looked.

Jael grabbed a cup of ale from one of the servants and handed it to him. 'Here, you look like you could do with a drink. I'm going to go and see if Eadmund's woken up yet. By the look of the hole in his head, he's lucky it's still sitting on his shoulders. But then again, he has got a very thick skull!' She tried to sound light-hearted, but her eyes darted around the packed hall, worried about Eadmund, thinking about everything they needed to do before they left.

Wondering what had happened to Evaine.

***

Morac had tried to shut out his daughter's endless whining. He was used to it, of course. She had been making a fuss since she'd learned how to talk, interested only in that which affected her, oblivious to that which did not.

And always, always, completely obsessed with Eadmund.

It was as Morana had planned, but sometimes it was just too much to bear. 'Evaine!' he snapped. 'Will you be quiet!'

They had walked with speed after escaping through the secret door; changing course quickly at the sight of the warriors battling across their path in the distance; forced to abandon their plans and head to Tatti's Bay instead. Morac felt panicked, expecting to be caught at every turn, terrified they'd be hunted down. But perhaps Ivaar and his allies had captured the fort? Perhaps there was no one to come after them anymore?

It was what Evaine feared most of all.

She had not wasted a moment worrying about her son. She'd thought only about Eadmund and whether he still lived. Her anxious breaths rushed from her lips as she stumbled along behind Morac. They were soul bound. Surely she would know if Eadmund was injured or dead?

Surely she would feel it?

'We're nearly there,' Morac panted, relieved to see the edge of the ridge that would lead them down to Tatti's Bay. 'Just a little further, and you'll be able to rest, I promise. Just a little longer, and we'll be on our way.' He hurried her along, glancing over his shoulder so often that he felt a twinge in his neck, hoping upon hope that they wouldn't be caught.

Morana had seen death coming for them both.

They had to escape Oss quickly.

***

'Morana Gallas,' Draguta smiled. 'Yorik has told me all about you. About how you were the one who used my book. How you brought me back.' She couldn't take her eyes off the strange, hunching woman.

Morana, peering at Draguta through her wild black-and-white hair, could tell that it wasn't a genuine smile. There was no amusement in those icy blue eyes. 'Yes, I did.'

They were sitting outside on Draguta's balcony, watching the sun set over the harbour. It was a beautiful, warm evening. A gentle breeze took away the humidity, cooling Morana's flushed face, but she was irritable and tired. Still weak. And becoming more unsettled by the moment.

It was apparent that Draguta wasn't just taking her time to adjust to life again. She was, in fact, not who they imagined she would be at all.

'You are still loyal to Raemus,' Draguta stated, offering Morana a goblet of wine before picking up her own.

Morana took the goblet but did not drink from it. 'I am, of course.'

'And why is that? What did he promise you? What did he promise anyone? I have often wondered why you all chose him as your master,' Draguta mused. 'You and your kind... always so ready to burn yourselves at Raemus' stake. For what? Immortality? Death? Darkness?' she scoffed. 'Yet what do any of you truly know of it?' Leaning forward, she picked up a fig from a silver tray, imagining how it would taste. She had eaten two now and was becoming frustrated by the lack of flavour. There was simply no pleasure in eating if there was nothing to taste. It was just a chore to endure. 'I have lived all of it. Immortality. Death. Darkness.'

Morana leaned forward, brushing hair out of her eyes, her body tingling in anticipation.

Draguta laughed. 'Shall I tell you what is better than any of it? Power,' she breathed. 'And with my book and your help, I shall become more powerful than Raemus. You should think about that, Morana. You should think about who you want to give your loyalty to. About which master you truly wish to serve.' Biting into the fig, Draguta closed her eyes, her body sagging in frustration.

***

'Eadmund?'

The gash in the back of his head was deep, and he had remained unconscious as they cleared the bodies from the square to make room for the pyres; as the fletchers returned to work, and Jael checked over their stores with Thorgils; as Ivaar kept out of everyone's way, avoiding his wife and Ayla; and as the Alekkans gathered around Erl and Rork Arnesson, happy, for the most part, to still be able to sup from cups of cool ale, unlike their men whose bodies were being roasted out in the square.

But now, as night was beginning to fall, he finally opened his eyes.

Jael smiled at him.

'Evaine?' Eadmund murmured.

Jael frowned.

'Where's Evaine?' he asked desperately. 'And the baby?'

It was a good question. The baby was asleep in the next chamber, but nobody had seen Evaine, which, Jael supposed, was no surprise. She assumed that the annoying girl had made herself invisible until Eadmund was back on his feet and able to protect her. 'I don't know,' she admitted, not wanting to talk about Evaine.

Eadmund panicked, sitting up. He tried to move to the edge of the bed. 'I need to find her!'

'Eadmund!' Jael got off her stool, pushing him back down. 'You have a hole in your head. Lie down!'

He grimaced as the pain finally kicked in, his ears clanging so loudly that he had to close his eyes. Covering his face with his hands, he sunk into the pillow. 'She may be hurt,' he mumbled.

'Why would she be *hurt*?' Jael sighed, irritated now. 'The Alekkans didn't get out of the square. They didn't breach the hall.'

'Sevrin!' Eadmund exclaimed, opening his eyes. 'What about Sevrin?'

Jael shook her head. 'He died. He was dead when I arrived.'

Eadmund swallowed, feeling the pain of that. Sevrin had been at his father's side since before he was born. He had spent his whole life looking at that rugged face, listening to Sevrin's throaty voice telling him off. Guiding him. Helping him. He closed his eyes, trying to think straight. 'And the fort?' he asked, clearing his throat. 'What happened?'

'It's ours. The Alekkans are ours. Ivaar and the Kalfans are ours. Their ships are ours too.'

'Ivaar?' Eadmund looked confused. 'I never saw Ivaar. When did he get here?'

Jael smiled. 'It's a long story, but Ivaar is with us now. Under my protection. He betrayed the Arnessons to save Oss. Or, at least, to save himself.'

Eadmund was sure that the clanging in his head had affected his hearing. 'What? *Ivaar*?'

'He sought the Arnessons' help to take the throne from us, but they had other plans. They wanted it for themselves. Seems like that was something not even Ivaar could stomach, so he helped me. He helped us.'

Eadmund frowned. 'But...'

Jael reached out a hand as he tried to sit up again. 'You need to stop worrying about Ivaar and Evaine and just lie back and rest. We have a lot to talk about. A lot of decisions to make. There's so much you don't know. So much I have to tell you before we leave.'

'Leave? Leave for where?'

CHAPTER TEN

Meena had lain in the crook of Jaeger's arm for hours. His breathing had finally evened out to a steady rhythm, and she was desperate to move to the other side of the bed. Her face ached, and she felt cold, wanting to reach down and pick up the furs, but she was afraid of waking him.

She closed her eyes, remembering how Berard had offered her a way out, wondering why she'd refused to take it.

She had been blinded by something impossible to describe.

Not love.

Perhaps her own stupidity? Perhaps her grandmother had cursed her, determined to stop her from ever being happy? Never allowing her to find the path that would lead to a different life.

Away from Hest.

Meena frowned, convinced that choosing Jaeger was nothing to do with Varna at all.

Finally, she slid to the very edge of the bed, holding her breath. Jaeger didn't stir, so she reached down to the floor and grabbed a discarded fur, quickly wrapping it around her chilled body, curling into a ball. Despite feeling more terrified than ever, Meena had not tapped her head since that night. Not since Haegen Dragos had carried Berard down to the ship, and she had chosen to stay with Jaeger.

For all her fear, she felt a stirring of strength deep down

inside herself.

When it had counted, she had killed Egil and taken the book.

And she could do it again.

If only she could find a way out of Hest.

***

Isaura was convinced that she hadn't taken a breath since Ivaar had walked into the hall.

The children had rushed towards him, surprised and excited to see their father again. And Ivaar had almost looked pleased to see them too, she thought, but he didn't acknowledge her. He kept to the opposite side of the hall, standing with his men, trying to appear as if invisible.

Thorgils insisted that she had nothing to fear from Ivaar - that he had chosen to help defeat the Alekkans in the end - but that did little to unwind the knots in her shoulders or steady the galloping of her heart.

Ayla stopped beside Isaura with a sigh. 'We need more water,' she said, wiping her bloody hands on her apron, keeping her eyes on Bruno. She had warned him away from Ivaar, but he hadn't stopped staring at the man who was responsible for imprisoning him. The man who had taken his wife.

Isaura blinked. 'I'll organise it.'

'He won't hurt us,' Ayla said wearily, noticing Isaura's tension. 'Not now.'

'But how can you be sure?'

'I feel it. Ivaar made a choice. He changed his path.'

Isaura wasn't convinced. 'For now.'

Ayla smiled. 'Yes, of course, for now. And he is not to be trusted, but perhaps if he had not made that choice, we wouldn't be standing here tonight? So I'm glad he did. No matter what has gone before, I'm glad that we're here to talk about what to do with Ivaar, and not lying out on those pyres with those poor dead men.'

They were standing near the green curtain, with a good view of the doors so they could both see the look on Thorgils' face as he walked in with Bram, past Ivaar and his four happy children. Isaura could see the disappointment and anger in his eyes; perhaps even jealousy.

Yet, they were all safe, and surely, that was what mattered most?

'How's Eadmund?' Thorgils asked as he reached Isaura, pulling on his beard, trying not to turn around and glare at Ivaar.

'He's awake,' Jael yawned, emerging from behind the curtain. 'You should go and see him. He's asking about Evaine.'

'Oh.' Thorgils looked awkward.

'Has anyone seen her?' Jael asked with some reluctance.

They all shook their heads, thinking that there were far more important things to worry about than where Evaine was.

'Well, I can't say I'm disappointed,' Jael said. 'Hopefully, she'll stay wherever she's hiding until we leave.'

'You're leaving again?' Isaura was surprised, glancing at Thorgils. 'But you only just arrived.'

'We'll all be leaving, I'm afraid,' Jael warned her. 'Once Eadmund is on his feet, and we can secure the fort.' She turned to Thorgils. 'We'll need to find someone to command the garrison too. Without Sevrin...'

Thorgils nodded sadly, looking at Bram. 'I'll have a think.'

'Good, well I'd better go and talk to our new friends,' Jael grinned wearily, and she strode off towards Erl and Rork Arnesson, who were both eyeing her expectantly.

***

Morana sat slumped over at Yorik's table.

He had prepared a fish stew, which smelled enticing, but they sat before full bowls, neither of them possessing much of an appetite.

'It is as I feared,' Yorik murmured, breaking the lengthy silence. 'Draguta does not want to bring Raemus back.'

'No, she doesn't,' Morana sniffed. 'Which is a problem, as she is the only one who knows how to. Or, at least, she is the only one who knows where that missing page is.'

'Everyone wants to know what will happen now. I've been receiving messages all day. The Followers are desperate for me to hold a meeting. They want to hear from Draguta herself, but what do I tell them? That she has no interest in them? In any of us?' Yorik pushed away his bowl and stood, too disturbed to sit still any longer.

'Draguta appears to have her own plans,' Morana said slowly, staring at the grey lump of stew in her bowl, watching it slowly congeal. She didn't lift her eyes, not wanting to reveal to Yorik how bad things truly were. 'The Following still has a part to play, I'm sure. Call the meeting for tomorrow night. Draguta has asked me to come to her chamber again in the morning. Hopefully, I'll find out more then.'

Yorik frowned, unsettled, his mind flitting about like a desperate moth. 'And our daughter?' he wondered distractedly. 'What of her?'

'She is coming. Morac will follow my orders. They will be here soon, don't worry.'

But Yorik did look worried, though not about Evaine.

If Draguta wasn't willing to bring back Raemus, what were they going to do?

***

Jael was only half listening. She kept wanting to go behind the curtain and check on Eadmund, though he was likely sleeping again, and hopefully, would be until morning.

'You'll not break into Hest easily,' Erl Arnesson grunted, gnawing on a pork bone, not liking the sound of Jael's plan.

Aleksander smiled. 'No, we have some experience of that, being Brekkan.'

'It will be easier if we have the Dragos' help,' Jael suggested.

'And what makes you think you will?' Ivaar wondered, trying to avoid Erl's angry eyes. Trying to avoid Thorgils and Bram and Torstan too. They all wanted to kill him, he knew.

'I've had a few dreams. Jaeger Dragos has taken over. He has the Book of Darkness, and the book has him. Haaron is no more. I imagine Jaeger's brothers will be desperate to reclaim Hest and avenge their father.'

'You're a dreamer?' Erl asked in surprise, his cavernous frown finally clearing.

Jael shrugged, convinced that she would always feel uncomfortable admitting such a thing, but realising that she could hardly run from the truth any longer, she sighed. 'I am.' She stared up at the smoky rafters, listening to a sudden downpour hammering the roof. That wouldn't help the pyres, she thought distractedly. 'We need to get to Andala and start building an army. The biggest army Osterland's ever seen. One that can get us into Hest so I can take the book.'

Ivaar looked puzzled. 'And what can this book really do?'

'Well, I know what it could do when it was in the hands of Morana and The Following,' Jael began. 'But what this Draguta woman could do with it?' She shrugged. 'I'd hate to think.' And she told them about the raven attack, and the temple guards in Tuura, and Aleksander told them about the wolves, and when they had both finished, no one spoke.

'They will not give up a book like that easily,' Bram noted, the shock of it still on his face. 'And they're likely not going to be stopped by swords and axes.'

'No, they're not,' Jael agreed, finding a lot to like about Bram Svanter already. 'But we have other weapons at our disposal. And we'll use them. For now, though, we have to focus on what lies in front of us. We need to secure the fort, then we can prepare to leave. Erl, Rork, what about your men? You're sure they're ready to follow us to gold and glory?' Jael stared at the square-jawed men whose thick braids framed two almost identical, deeply serious faces that had yet to break into even a hint of a smile.

'*Our* men?' Erl growled, narrowing his gaze until his black eyebrows touched like a pair of ferrets. 'Well, I suppose they're all ours now, aren't they? Without our cousins, who you murdered...'

Thorgils glared at him.

'But, they would have done the same to you, I'm sure,' Erl continued, glaring back. 'And we Arnessons are not known to turn down a hunt for gold and glory. Especially one that leads to the richest kingdom of all.'

'Good. And think of what it will mean for you. You can return to Alekka a wealthy man, with more ships and men than you left with. And a chance to take the throne from Ake Bluefinn. If, of course, you had a mind to do such a thing?'

Erl's eyes narrowed, wondering if she could see inside his head. He had never worn his ambition like a bright cloak as his cousins had. But now that Borg and Rolan were gone, he had his chance. His brother would follow him. His men would follow him. And, he decided, with a gruff nod in the queen's direction, he would follow Jael Furyck.

***

Draguta sat at her round table, encircled by the flickering glow of dripping candles, and slowly opened the book.

She assumed that it was very late, but she had no real awareness of time yet, and although she was slowly adjusting to life, she doubted that she'd ever truly feel like herself again.

The Dolma had changed her.

It was a deep void. A dark hole with no edges. No hope of escape.

And she had been imprisoned there, inside that endless cave for centuries. Shivering, she glanced towards the fire, motioning for her servant to add another log. She found it hard to get warm, even in Hest's balmy weather.

Turning her attention back to the book, Draguta ran her alabaster hand over the familiar, crisp vellum pages. She smiled, feeling a sense of peace flood her body.

With the book, everything felt possible.

The Following thought it belonged to Raemus, that his return would realise their dreams. But they were wrong. Salvation did not exist in the Darkness of Raemus' time but in the pure, dark magic of the book.

The book had been given to her, and she was its mistress.

And she had spent all that time in the Dolma planning her return. Imagining everything she would do to claim her revenge, piece by bloody piece.

Knowing exactly where she would begin.

Draguta turned the pages, warmed by the memories of the spells and rituals, as familiar as old friends; reminiscing about the destruction she had wrought with her sisters, and then, with her son, Valder, when they had ruled Hest together, eliminating their enemies, one by one until...

Draguta blinked, not wanting to remember the betrayal.

Then, as a smile curled her red lips, she found the page she was looking for, finally ready to begin.

***

'Jael?'

Runa felt hesitant. Jael looked ready to fall asleep as she approached the curtain. Runa felt much the same, but she had not wanted to return to her house until she was confident the man she was caring for would live. At least through the night.

Jael was slow to turn around. She'd found reasons to avoid Runa all day, though she wasn't really sure why. 'Runa,' she sighed. 'Come, sit down.'

Runa immediately threw her hands over her mouth.

'Fyn's alive,' Jael said quickly. 'He's injured, but he's alive. When I left him in Andala, he was recovering. Entorp was with him, and Biddy.' She helped Runa down onto the bench, pouring her a cup of water. 'We were in a battle in the Temple of Tuura, against men who wouldn't die.'

Runa frowned, confused, impatient to hear what had happened to Fyn.

'Fyn fought bravely, but he was stabbed in the stomach. It was a bad wound, but he was never going to die. He's far too stubborn for that.'

Runa felt sick, wishing she was in Andala. Wanting to see for herself.

'Don't worry,' Jael tried, though Runa only looked more frantic. 'I'm sure he'll be up and about by the time I get back there.'

'Perhaps I should come with you?' Runa suggested eagerly. 'I could help take care of him.'

'Of course,' Jael said. 'You should. Fyn would want that. I'm sure Biddy and Edela would be glad to see you again. Eydis too.'

'Edela?' Runa's eyes popped open. 'She's alive? That's wonderful news, Jael! You must all be so relieved?'

'Yes, it was well worth the visit to Tuura in the end,' Jael said, still in shock that they had managed to escape the fort. 'We found out a lot of things we didn't know before. Speaking of which, where's Morac? I don't remember seeing him today, but perhaps that's no surprise. I'm sure he hasn't been looking forward to my return. With good reason,' she frowned, remembering her conversation with Marcus about Eirik's death.

Runa swallowed. 'That's what I came to tell you, Jael. I think Morac has left the fort and taken Evaine with him.'

***

Tatti's Bay was abandoned, much to Morac's relief. The men recalled to the fort had left in a hurry, leaving behind food, ale, and furs. Everything they would need for their journey to Hest was waiting for them in the row of enormous ship sheds that Eirik had spent years building to protect his fleet from Oss' bitter Freeze.

Including most of his warships.

But Morac couldn't helm a thirty-man warship with only Evaine's help, so he chose a small boat mainly used for fishing, hoping it was hardy enough to get them through the Widow's Peak and past Skorro in one piece.

'And what will happen when we get to Hest?' Evaine grumbled. 'Why do you think we'll be safe there?'

Morac muttered irritably to himself as he hurried towards the boat with a basket of overripe fruit, stale flatbreads, some salt fish and half a round of cheese. Evaine had been nagging him with questions since they'd arrived in the bay. 'Because Morana will be there, of course. She will keep us safe.'

'But what about Eadmund? What about my son?' Evaine slumped onto a large rock in a miserable, sodden heap. It had started raining, but she didn't even care to seek shelter. Her heart was an aching pain in her chest, and she was oblivious to everything else.

She needed Eadmund. Nothing would feel right until she was with him again.

'Eadmund will care for him,' Morac puffed, his breath swirling before him as the air cooled down. He lifted the basket over the side of the boat, turning back to her. 'And then he will come for you. Don't worry, but do be patient, Evaine. Morana knows what she's doing. She knows how to bring Eadmund to you when it's time. And, more importantly, she knows how to keep us both safe.'

Evaine pulled her white fur cloak tightly around her neck. She couldn't stop shivering. She was supposed to be the Queen of Oss, sitting next to Eadmund on their matching thrones, not running away like a thief, wondering if she would ever return.

CHAPTER ELEVEN

Jaeger had slept well for the first time since the ritual, and he smiled as he dressed, eager to head down to the hall for breakfast. He felt strong. His ears weren't ringing. He could breathe easily. Even his ankle had stopped aching. If it wasn't for the loss of the book, he would have almost felt happy. 'Come!' he called to Meena, pulling his tunic over his head. 'Come and eat in the hall with me. You can meet Draguta.'

Meena recoiled in horror. She had spent a day in Morana's chamber after the ritual, caring for her aunt, listening to her taunts about what Draguta would do to her, and she had no intention of meeting the terrifying woman at all.

Jaeger laughed, grabbing her hand. 'You needn't be afraid of her. She will know that Berard forced you to take the book. That *he* killed Egil.' The thought of what his brother had done - of how he'd betrayed him - burrowed its way under Jaeger's skin like a hungry tick. He felt an intense burst of rage when he thought of Berard, the one brother he'd believed had cared for him.

But he had been proven wrong.

Meena looked even more worried. 'I, I...' She fought the sudden urge to tap her head. 'I need to clean the ch-chamber.'

Jaeger pulled her towards him. 'There's no need. I found a new servant. She will come this morning. Now, stop arguing and let's go. I'm starving!'

Meena felt ready to vomit as she stumbled after him. Visions of Egil's dying body flopping to the floor came rushing back, and she knew that if Draguta was any sort of dreamer, she would certainly discover the truth.

***

Jael smiled as Eadmund opened his eyes. 'Are you hungry?' she wondered, pulling the curtain away from the window, letting in faint rays of sunlight. 'I brought you some bread and honey. It's still warm.'

Eadmund frowned at her, shaking his head. He felt odd. His dreams of Evaine had been so vivid that he was surprised to find that she wasn't there. But Jael was, wearing a blood-stained, faded blue tunic, her dark hair tied back in those familiar braids, her face battered and bruised.

His wife.

Jael tried not to feel disappointed by his sleepy scowl. 'Or some milk?' She placed the tray of food on the table by the bed and leaned over. 'Here, let me help you up.' Eadmund brushed her away, but she ignored him, pulling him slightly upright before handing him the cup of buttermilk.

'Where's Evaine?' Eadmund asked, ignoring the cup. 'Did she come while I was asleep?' He noticed the hurt in Jael's eyes which she quickly masked, and he felt guilty, not wanting to hurt her. She had done so much for him and Oss, but he needed to see Evaine.

He loved Evaine.

'She's gone,' Jael muttered. 'She left the fort with Morac. They disappeared during the battle.'

'What?' Eadmund lurched forward, cringing at the sharp stab of pain in the back of his head. 'How? Why?' he demanded, gritting his teeth as he shuffled towards the edge of the bed, ears buzzing, black patches flashing in front of his eyes.

'I don't know why. Perhaps Morana warned them of what I would tell you? Of what you would do?'

Eadmund swayed, worried that he was about to pass out. Jael shoved his head down between his legs. 'What would you tell me?' he mumbled, taking a quick breath. 'What?'

'When I was in Tuura, I spoke to the elderman. He told me that Morac had killed your father. That Evaine stabbed Edela because she was trying to stop her from telling anyone. She meant to kill her, just as Morac had killed Eirik.'

Eadmund sat up slowly, still light-headed. '*What*?' He shook his head, wondering if he'd misheard her over the intense noise in his ears. 'What? Morac? Why?'

'I imagine it was a plan between him and Morana, but yes, Morac did it. It wasn't Ivaar who poisoned that wine, it was Morac. And now he's disappeared, taking his things with him. And Evaine.'

Eadmund was in shock. 'My son?' he asked suddenly. 'Where's Sigmund?'

'He's still here,' Jael assured him. 'With Tanja.'

Eadmund wanted to sigh with relief, but he couldn't. Evaine had gone, and Morac had killed his father. He felt ready to snap. 'I have to get up!' he insisted. 'Can you see my trousers? I have to find them! They can't have gotten far.'

Jael shook her head. 'I sent men to look for them last night. They would have tried to escape the island. If they're still here, we'll find them. Morac knew of the secret door, so he knew of the cove where your father hid the ship. And if he didn't go there, he may have gone to Tatti's Bay.'

'Secret door?'

Jael smiled. 'Why don't you lie back and drink your milk, and I'll tell you all about it.'

***

Berard shuddered, unable to shake the memory of Jaeger's blade lopping off his arm. He could hear the noise so clearly. He could still feel the shock of his body as it collapsed to the floor without his arm; his father's voice, so calmly controlled as he stepped in to try and stop Jaeger.

Haaron had never thought much of him, Berard knew, but he felt the loss of his father deeply. They had been a family once - broken parts, perhaps; everyone grumbling and arguing amongst themselves - but a family. And they'd had a kingdom with a king and a queen and a certainty that had kept them all believing that they were safe. Safe and powerful. Berard had had three giant-sized brothers and a father so fiercesome that he'd never given his own role in the family much thought. Not when he knew that they were there. That one of them would protect him when it was time. That they would keep Hest safe.

But now?

Berard reached a hand towards his stump, squirming in discomfort. His arm felt as though it was still there, but he could see very plainly, even in the dim glow from the lamps, that it was gone, just as his father was gone, and neither of them were coming back.

And Jaeger had taken both of them.

And Jaeger had Meena.

Berard rolled over, suddenly exhausted. Somehow, despite the grizzling children, and Nicolene and Karsten's sniping, and the noisy stream of people coming in and out of the house, he needed to find some sleep.

He had to get stronger if he was going to kill his brother.

***

Draguta studied the odd, trembling creature who sat at the high table, eating her breakfast next to Jaeger. The Gallas' looked like a family of hairy trolls, she smiled to herself, bemused by Jaeger's interest in the girl. She was at best ugly and at worst grotesque. Perhaps the book had warped his mind? It was powerful enough to do so, she knew, from experience. Though it was so long ago now that Draguta could not remember the girl she had once been.

She drank from her long-stemmed silver goblet and leaned forward, narrowing her eyes at Meena. 'You tried to steal my book,' she announced. 'Yet, once you were caught, you did not escape. Why? You could have, but you didn't. Why?'

Jaeger froze, turning to Meena, feeling her leg shaking against his, just as interested in her answer.

Meena's eyes rounded like full moons. She felt so uncomfortable sitting at the high table as though she were a lady, near this... creature. For all appearances, Draguta looked like the most beautiful woman she had ever seen, but Meena was worried that she wasn't even a person at all. Her skin looked so oddly pale, like a frozen lake you could almost see through. 'I, I... Berard, he...' Meena knew that it was never wise to try and fool a dreamer. 'He asked me to help him steal the book. I didn't know what to do.'

'But you did not need to help him,' Draguta mused, slowly running her finger around the rim of the goblet. 'Did you?'

'He, I...' Meena spluttered, her cheeks hot, her arm-pits moist. 'I could not refuse. He is a Dragos. A prince. I, I could not refuse him.'

Jaeger turned to Draguta, whose smile was as fixed as her eyes were cold, hoping she'd be satisfied with that answer.

'I suppose you could not. It is a good story, at least. And you seem so... pathetic.' She grinned widely, and both Jaeger and Meena could see how white her teeth were. 'It is hard to imagine you putting up much of a fight against anything. Yet, you refused their offer to leave, so you do not do everything the

Dragos princes ask of you, do you, girl?'

Morana almost spat as she crept into the hall, horrified by the sight of her niece sitting at the high table next to Jaeger.

What was she playing at?

What did anyone want with *her*?

'You are here!' Draguta smiled at Morana as she stood. 'Good. We have much to organise today, you and I. We must prepare to cast a spell, so I shall require your help to find everything I need.' Ignoring Morana's irritated scowl, Draguta turned to Meena. 'And you, strange girl, you will come along too. I think I would like to get to know more about you. And besides, one can never have too many dreamers to assist them. Isn't that right, Morana?'

Morana shook her hair, scrunching her lips into something between a grimace and a smile, before frowning, suddenly realising what Draguta had just said. '*Dreamer*?'

Draguta laughed. 'You didn't know that your niece was a dreamer?'

Jaeger's mouth hung open as he turned to Meena. 'You're a *dreamer*?'

Meena was too stunned to speak.

'You may stay and finish your meal, Jaeger. We ladies shall be on our way.' And cracking her fingers together, Draguta bent towards Meena, demanding her blinking eyes focus on her. 'Come along, girl. We have much to do.'

Meena gulped, scrambling to her feet, hurrying after Draguta as she strode across the hall, trying not to step on the swishing train of her long white dress.

Jaeger stared after them, his shock turning to happiness.

Meena Gallas was a dreamer!

***

Eadmund stood next to Thorgils and Bram, just outside the broken gates, watching Jael issuing orders down on the beach as she inspected the ships with Aleksander. They had been down there since breakfast, monitoring the supplies being brought on board, talking with Erl and Rork Arnesson about their ships and their men. Behind them, Islanders, Brekkans, and Alekkans were hard at work repairing the gates.

The island was consumed with a flurry of activity.

Eadmund and Thorgils barely noticed, though. Their attention was constantly being pulled back to Ivaar. Thorgils was convinced that if Bruno Adea could walk properly, he would be standing there with them, all three of them deciding how to exact their revenge.

It wasn't how anyone had expected things to turn out.

'Why does your wife have so much faith in that slippery turd?' Thorgils grumbled.

Eadmund could barely hear him over his rising panic about Evaine, but he wondered the same thing. 'She was right about him not killing Eirik, if the elderman is to be believed,' he admitted reluctantly. 'But as for everything else, I don't know. I don't think Jael really trusts him, but from what she said, it seems as though every hand is needed for now.'

Bram frowned. 'For now, sounds right to me. When all the battles are done, it will be time for Ivaar Skalleson's reckoning.'

'Mmmm, I've a feeling there'll be a long line waiting to take a turn at him, including those Arnesson twins. They don't look happy that Ivaar betrayed their cousins,' Thorgils noted, crossing his arms over his broad chest. 'Though it worked out well for us in the end.'

'It did,' Bram agreed. 'Still, Ivaar has a lot coming his way. For what he did to Ayla and her husband. For Isaura.'

'For Melaena,' Eadmund added.

Thorgils lifted his eyebrows. 'Well, you know what Jael says about that...' he tried.

Eadmund turned to him. 'What? You think Morac killed

her too?'

Thorgils shook his head, ready to laugh, before stopping himself. 'No, but with Morana, anything's possible, I suppose. She hated Eirik. She hated your mother. It may be that she hated you enough too. Ivaar certainly didn't hate Melaena, did he? It's hard to imagine anyone killing someone they love. Even Ivaar.'

Bram shivered. His memories of Morana Gallas, though decades old, were still fresh enough to unsettle him. She had been a terrifying creature even as a young woman. He hated to think what had become of her now.

Eadmund didn't want to agree with Thorgils. He didn't want to think of Morana being Evaine's mother at all. His head was aching, and as much as he wanted to ignore it and get moving, he couldn't think clearly. 'Have the riders returned?' he muttered.

'Not yet,' Bram said.

Eadmund rubbed his eyes, turning to Thorgils. 'And how's Leada?'

'She's up,' Thorgils smiled. 'Not happy, but up. It's a good sign. Askel says her wound will heal. The arrow seems to have missed the important bits.'

Eadmund almost looked happy. 'Good. That's good.' He turned back to the beach, frowning at his wife. He wanted to feel pleased to see her. He was relieved that she had come and saved the fort, and him, but all he could think about was Evaine.

Jael looked up at Eadmund, sensing his frown.

'Where do you think Evaine has gone?' Aleksander wondered, following her gaze.

'Well, I don't think you need to be a dreamer to work that out.'

'No. At least she left her baby behind.'

'Mmmm,' Jael agreed, chewing on a piece of salt fish. 'Though, I hardly think she thought twice about that. I doubt he'll even notice she's gone.'

'She won't let Eadmund go, no matter how far away from

him she gets. The pull of her will be intense,' Aleksander warned, turning to watch the Alekkans who were checking through the charred shells of their ships, seeing if there was anything worth saving.

'Until we break the spell,' Jael said. 'I don't believe you can cast a spell that can't be broken. And between Edela and Eydis and me, one of us must be able to dream about that book and find an answer.'

Aleksander nodded as Jael handed him a sliver of salt fish. 'I hope you're right. Although, perhaps there's someone else who could help us as well? Someone who might know more than anyone.'

Jael stared curiously at Aleksander. 'Who?'

***

Hest's winding gardens were colourful and surprisingly lush for this time of year. The city had been battered by intense storms for weeks, experiencing more rain than they would have expected to fall in an entire year, and the gardens had flourished.

Draguta couldn't stop bending down to touch each plant as she glided along the narrow gravel paths that meandered through rows of flowers and bushes, beaming as though she was being reunited with old friends.

Morana tried not to stare or let her thoughts about the book or Raemus run to the front of her mind. She had the sense that Draguta could tell what she was thinking, and Morana was determined to prove herself a useful ally. When she thought of Yorik, biting his fingernails in his little cottage, and Evaine and Morac, who were on their way, it made sense for her to make herself as valuable as possible.

'Your daughter is a rare beauty,' Draguta smiled, straightening up and placing a cutting into Morana's basket.

'Such pretty hair. A real lady. Not like your unfortunate niece here.'

Morana bit her tongue.

Draguta turned to stare at Meena, who stooped over beside Morana, trying her very best not to look away. Draguta laughed, amused by the hideous gurning on the girl's battered face. 'What happened to you?' she wondered, staring at Meena's bruised eyes, and her swollen nose. 'You look as though you've been in a battle. You're not a warrior like Jael Furyck, are you?'

Meena shook her head, trying to hide her face, still struggling to come to terms with Draguta's announcement that she was a dreamer. Despite the thick canopy of leaves and branches that had woven together above the winding gardens, the sun had forced its way in, and she felt exposed in the harsh morning light.

Morana glanced at Meena, not bothered by her bruises but suddenly very interested in the idea that she was a dreamer. How was that possible? Varna had never mentioned it. Nor had Meena. Morana shook her head, straightening her back with a creak, wistful for the miserable gloom she had enjoyed on Rikka. She sighed, remembering the cottage where she had lived so peacefully all by herself.

How complicated people made everything.

Though people, it seemed, were her only route to bringing Raemus back.

Draguta frowned sharply at Morana, watching as she tried to conceal her thoughts. 'If you find me some mugwort, then we can leave here and move onto the next place. And I'm going to need some blood,' she said icily, not taking her eyes off the black-and-white haired dreamer; trying to decide whether Morana Gallas was going to be more trouble than she was worth.

***

'Who?' Jael asked, rounding on Aleksander, pulling him out of the path of two Osslanders struggling over the stones with their sea chests.

Aleksander suddenly felt uncomfortable, wondering if it was the right time to have this talk. 'The Widow.'

Jael frowned. 'Why do you think she could help us?'

'She's been coming to me. In my dreams.'

'*Your* dreams?' Jael was surprised. 'You're sure it was her?'

Aleksander nodded, flapping his hand at a cloud of midges. 'She helped me. Warned me about the ravens and the wolves. Told me that you were in danger. That we needed to go to Tuura.'

'*That's* why you came?' Jael shook her head, realising that, in the hurry to get to Andala, and then Oss, she'd never had a conversation about why Aleksander had turned up in Tuura. Not a real one where he didn't just mumble into his ale, ignoring her questions.

Aleksander nodded. 'She's trying to help. She spoke about the prophecy. As though she knew it. I... I believed her.'

'And you think she might know of a way to save Eadmund?'

'I think she knows more than we do. And from the way she tried to warn me, I think she sees a lot too. So, yes, if anyone is going to be able to help Eadmund, I think it's the Widow.'

Jael turned back to the fort, watching Eadmund. His head moved constantly, scanning the beach, the headland, the rugged land to the right of where he stood with Thorgils and Bram, thinking about Evaine.

Jael could feel it.

Every part of him was being pulled to wherever Evaine was.

And she had to do something to cut those threads before it was too late.

***

Jaeger ran his eyes over the practice matches in the training ring, too distracted to join in. He kept thinking about Meena, wondering when Draguta would release her. He was desperate to talk to her.

The idea that Meena was a dreamer...

It was all he could think about.

Everything was starting to fall into place, and he could finally see a path ahead - a way back to the book, with Meena by his side.

Draguta may have it for now, and perhaps she would be useful - especially if she could defeat the Furycks - but eventually, he would have no need for her.

Draguta was just a dreamer who could use the book.

And soon, he wouldn't need her at all.

***

Edela patted Eydis' hand. It was cold, which was surprising as the weather in Andala was much warmer than anything they'd experienced in Tuura. 'Why don't we leave Fyn to sleep now,' she urged softly. 'The more sleep he can get, the quicker he'll heal.'

Eydis nodded and turned to Biddy, who she knew was standing behind her. She was desperately worried about Fyn, and nothing anyone said would reassure her. Not until he did so himself.

'Come on, Eydis,' Biddy smiled, grabbing her hand. 'We need to find you something hot to drink to warm up these little hands. They're like ice!'

Eydis didn't smile as she was led out of Fyn's chamber and back into the hall. She had tried to imagine what it looked like, and although Entorp had described it to her in great detail, she had not formed an image of it in her mind yet. Voices echoed loudly, up into the smoky rafters, and it wasn't warm. It felt too spacious. So different from the familiar closeness of her father's hall on Oss. She thought of Jael and Eadmund, hoping they were both safe. Eager to see them again.

And then she felt fluffy tails curling around her legs.

'Ido! Vella!' Biddy grumbled. 'Move out of the way, you hairy creatures!'

Edela yawned as she walked alongside them. 'I see Amma sitting by the fire. Would you like to join her?' Edela was ready to sit down herself. Her energy was still low, and she wondered if she would ever feel like herself again.

Likely not, she supposed. Not at her age.

'Hello, Eydis,' Amma said. 'Here, come and sit by me. Axl has grown bored with my company, so he's sent me away, over here.' She laughed, but Eydis could hear the tension in her voice. She sounded worried. Eydis supposed that they were all worried but trying to be brave, especially around her. She wasn't a child, though, and she wished that they wouldn't continue to treat her like one.

'You sit here, Eydis,' Biddy said, helping her down onto Amma's bench. 'I'll go and make us all some cups of tea.'

Edela nodded eagerly.

Biddy smiled and hurried away. She was enjoying being home, freed from the oppressive terror of Tuura and The Following, and so happy to think that Andala had no more Lothar or Osbert in it, tipping their lives upside down.

'I've been thinking about Aleksander,' Edela announced as she squeezed onto the end of the bench next to Eydis. 'I'm not sure why. How about you, Eydis? He is your cousin, after all,' she smiled. 'Perhaps you have some thoughts about him?'

Amma stared at Eydis, but she shook her head. 'Do you think it's because of the Widow?' Amma wondered. 'Because of his dreams?'

Edela peered at Amma, the wrinkles on her forehead folding up like a fan. 'Aleksander is having dreams?' she wondered, feeling the thud of her heart quicken. 'About the Widow?'

'Didn't he tell you? The Widow is the one who told him to go to Tuura. She helped us escape the wolves.'

'Oh.' That was a surprise. 'Well, it seems that you have much to tell me, Amma Furyck,' Edela said, getting herself comfortable. 'Now, why don't you start at the beginning...'

CHAPTER TWELVE

Ivaar wiped a hand down his beard, catching the eye of a man he'd not seen in some time. Another man who wanted to kill him.

But perhaps this one more than any other.

Turning away from the dark-eyed stare of Bruno Adea, Ivaar tried to pick up the conversation. A group of them were standing around the map table as Bram described Helsabor's coastline. Being that he was the most widely travelled of them all, they were listening eagerly, except for Eadmund. His attention was focused on Ivaar, uncomfortable with his brother's presence at the table.

In his hall.

The hall that Ivaar had just tried to claim for himself.

Jael nudged Eadmund, sensing how distracted he was. 'I had thought of asking you to look after Oss, Bram,' she said. 'But you may be the very man we need in Andala. You seem to know your way around the coast.'

Bram smiled. 'It's like the shape of a woman's body to me. All those nooks and crannies have taken me years to discover and appreciate!'

Thorgils clapped his uncle on the shoulder. 'You'll have Jael blushing if you're not careful!' he laughed.

Even the stern-faced Erl Arnesson looked amused.

Bram grinned, eyeing Jael. 'I doubt that, Nephew. Now

listen, you can't climb most of Hest's coastline. It's like this.' He held up a straight palm. 'You can only get in by going through Helsabor, unless you're going to try the pass or think you can attack their harbour. But Helsabor... well, last time I was there, Wulf Halvardar had a fleet that would make your eyes water. Don't know why. The old coward's never fought anyone! He's a strange bastard. Collects things. Hoards treasure, as you'd expect, but also weapons. It's as though he's planning on being attacked by the gods one day. They talked about Haaron sitting on a pile of gold, but I'd wager old Wulf would've gone toe to toe with him for who was the richest man in the South.'

Erl's beady eyes glistened. 'So we take Helsabor as well?' he asked eagerly.

Jael smiled. 'We want to take Hest, but we need more men to do it. If Helsabor or Iskavall want to help us, we'll have plenty of allies, but if not...' She shrugged. 'My father always had a good relationship with Iskavall. There's a reasonable chance they'd want to continue their alliance with us, but equally, Raymon Vandaal might have other plans. We just need to concentrate on what we have to do. And *we* have to build an army any way we can.'

Eadmund frowned, taking a sip of ale, wishing his pounding headache would go away. 'Go and ready your men,' he said, inclining his head towards Erl and Ivaar. 'We'll leave tomorrow. And Thorgils, have a think about who can stay and watch the fort. I agree with Jael, Bram should come with us.' He grabbed Jael's hand, ignoring his brother, resisting the urge to simply thump him and throw him to the ground. 'We need to talk.' And drawing Jael away from the table, Eadmund led her towards the hall doors. He wanted to feel some cold air on his face. It felt strange to be around his wife again. He could talk to her about so many things, except the one thing he suddenly wanted to talk about all the time. So, trying to avoid all thoughts of Evaine, Eadmund turned to Jael, lowering his voice. 'Perhaps I should stay behind? We almost lost the island. Leaving it now seems risky.'

Jael shivered. It was dark, and the air was ice-tipped, chilling her quickly. She could hear her stomach rumbling, though she was sure that she'd only just eaten. Digging into her pouch, she wondered if she had any salt fish left. 'You have to come with me. It's part of the prophecy. *You* are part of the prophecy.' And happily, she pulled out another hard sliver of dried fish. 'You have to help me kill the woman.'

'Who told you that?'

'The elderman. He said that we have to do it together. Attack Hest. Get the book. Kill this Draguta. End any hope of the Darkness returning.'

'Me?' Eadmund was stunned. 'I... didn't know.'

Jael sighed, gripping his arm. 'No, you didn't. Everyone has kept it from you, waiting until you were ready. And now, you're not ready at all. You think you love Evaine. You want to run away and find her. But it's all part of their plan to stop us from destroying them.' She gripped his arm even tighter as Eadmund squirmed. 'It doesn't matter what you say. I know what we have to do. And when it's over, and Draguta is hanging off the end of my sword, go back and find Evaine. Be with her and your son if that's what you still want.' They were hard words to say, and Jael wasn't sure if she felt mad or sad as she said them, but she needed Eadmund to accept his role. She couldn't control what he felt, but she needed to convince him to trust her.

Eadmund relented, staring at her face, but it was just a shadowy mass, and he couldn't see her eyes. He was grateful for that, though; Jael's eyes had a way of confusing him. 'Evaine has likely gone to be with Morana.'

'I imagine so.'

'But what about Oss? What about the islands?'

'We need to send word to the lords. They must meet us in Andala too. Now that the Arnessons are ash, and we have the twins and Ivaar on our side, I don't see many contenders to steal Oss away, do you? You've never had any problems with the Alekkans before now.'

'No,' Eadmund admitted. 'Ake Bluefinn had an alliance with Eirik. He hasn't threatened us in years.'

'Well, then?'

Eadmund nodded slowly, his head clearing in the brisk night air. 'Alright, I'll come.'

***

'I'm ready to leave!' Berard insisted again as he sat up, swinging his legs over the side of the bed. 'The sooner we leave Saala, the sooner we can get back to Hest!' He grimaced, feeling the pain in his stump.

'We, Little Brother?' Karsten snorted. '*We*?'

'You don't think I'm any use now? Now that I've only one arm?' Berard challenged, looking from Karsten to Haegen, and then to his mother, who sat in a chair by the fire, watching milk heat in a small cauldron, hoping it would soothe the restless children. 'You never thought I was any use to begin with, so what does it matter what you think now?'

Berard wasn't wrong, though Bayla felt uncomfortable acknowledging the truth.

She looked away.

'You've lost your sword arm,' Haegen reminded his angry brother. 'That will make things harder.'

'I imagine so,' Berard said frankly. 'But a man does not need a sword to be useful. There are things I can do. Ways I can help.' He glanced at Hanna, who didn't know where to look as she hovered behind the Dragos', wanting to give them some privacy, which was hard when they were all squeezed into the same small house. 'We need to leave for Andala quickly, wouldn't you say?'

Hanna nodded. 'Yes. We must find out what is happening. What we can do to make ourselves safe. And useful.'

Haegen frowned. Berard didn't look well, but he was agitated and not likely to stay in his bed unless they strapped him into it. 'Do you think you're well enough for another sea journey? Perhaps we should stay one more day?'

'No!' Berard insisted. 'I'm not dying, and my stump will heal. I have the tincture the healers left. That will help with the pain. We shouldn't stay. We're not safe here!' He glanced around the house, feeling weak but determined. 'I shall need a new tunic. Perhaps you could find me something, Mother? Something that's not covered in blood.'

Bayla blinked at her son, surprised to be called upon. She had not wanted to be near his stump at all. Blood and sickness of any kind made her want to retch, but she could hardly say no. 'I will find one of the healers. They can help you,' she muttered, turning away before he asked her to do anything else.

'Good!' Berard said, standing up. 'And, Hanna, make sure that your helmsman is ready to depart in the morning. Straight after breakfast.'

Karsten and Haegen eyed each other as Hanna nodded and disappeared through the door after Bayla, just as eager to leave herself.

'You're sure?' Haegen wondered as his daughter Lucina ran over to say goodnight to him, throwing her arms around his legs, her little sister, Halla, toddling after her, sucking on her fingers. He smiled down at them, then turned back to his brother.

'I want to rescue Meena. She's Jaeger's prisoner because I failed her!' Berard cried. 'And I will not fail her again!'

***

'What happened?' Jael looked worried as she held out the torch, checking Leada's neck, peering down her legs, running a hand over her back.

'That would be the Arnessons,' Thorgils muttered, his hands twitching at the thought of what they had done to the gentle white horse; Eadmund's horse, he knew, but Leada had always been particularly good to him. And she had worked so hard to get him up the island in time to save his life. He held out a carrot, which she sniffed but didn't eat.

Thorgils frowned.

'She looks like she'd rather go to sleep to me,' Jael said softly, noticing Thorgils' worried face as she walked past him with the flaming torch, returning it to its sconce. 'Her wound is clean. Askel has been doing a good job with it. Don't worry.'

Thorgils took the carrot away. 'So, you've decided on Arlo, then? To take charge of the fort?'

Jael nodded. 'He's got the wisest head in the place now. Makes sense to leave him behind. Although, Otto did suggest himself,' she smiled. 'I don't think he's keen on coming to Andala.' She turned towards the stable door, suppressing a yawn, certain that it was far too early to be tired. 'Hopefully, the gates will be back on in a few days, and Arlo can get those fletchers working overtime. I've sent men down to the coves to bring back our ships. Ivaar's too. They should be here by midday tomorrow. The rest will head to Tatti's Bay and sail from there.'

Thorgils shuffled his feet in the hay, not knowing how to approach what he really wanted to talk about. Then he thought of Isaura and just jumped in. 'And Ivaar? What are you going to do about Ivaar?'

'*Do* about him?' Jael looked confused. 'He's coming with us. Him and the Kalfans. You know that.'

'I mean, for what he's done. For what he tried to do. To Ayla, Bruno... Isaura. He tried to take the fort. He would have killed Eadmund. Maybe his son. Me.'

Jael could sense Thorgils' urgent need for answers. For certainty. It was understandable. He had Isaura and their future to think about now. 'Ivaar will be judged when we return,' she said. 'So it depends on what happens while we're gone.'

'Meaning?'

'Meaning that everything Ivaar has done to hurt people will be weighed against everything he does to help us now.'

Thorgils didn't say anything, but his lips disappeared beneath his beard.

'I know what you want me to say, but I can't,' Jael insisted. 'He backed out of his alliance with the Arnessons. He didn't kill Eirik. He didn't kill Melaena. He's hurt Ayla, mistreated her husband. I know all of this, Thorgils. But I also know that he will help us now, and we need all the men we can get. In the end, it's up to Ivaar how much he chooses to even up his ledger.'

'And Isaura?'

'Isaura can't be forced to be with Ivaar,' Jael said. 'And from memory, Ivaar doesn't want to be with her either. So I don't see any problems there. Eadmund and I will grant them a divorce. We can do that, I imagine, being king and queen?' She smiled, listening to Thorgils huff and puff. 'Ivaar is not the enemy we need to fight now,' she reminded him. 'Leave me to worry about him. When this is all done, we'll talk about Ivaar.'

Thorgils sighed, realising that there was no budging a woman as stubborn as Jael, and it was hard to argue with her logic, as much as he was desperate to. 'Are you alright?' he asked. 'You look... different.'

Jael froze. 'Different?' she asked lightly, reaching for the door. 'Oh, you mean the black eye? You don't think it suits me?' She disappeared quickly ahead of him, leaving Thorgils to reach for the torch and slip out after her.

'It's an improvement, for sure,' he grinned. 'I would hate to see what the man who did that to you looks like!'

Jael laughed, thinking of Baccus, the temple guard who'd refused to die for a time, but who, eventually, had.

Minus his eyes.

'Yes, you would.'

***

Morana was irritable. She had followed Draguta around the city all day as though she were a little dog. Holding every item she gathered, showing Draguta where everything was, nodding and scraping like a servant.

Surely, that was what Meena was for?

'You think that it's *beneath* you to assist me, Morana?' Draguta wondered from her right. They had moved the small round table next to the fireplace, and now the three women sat around it, blinking in the dazzling glow of the candles and lamps that Draguta had ordered placed around her chamber. 'I can assure you that many would leap at the chance of assisting me.' She stared at Meena, who gulped and looked away, trying to ignore the drop of sweat she could feel hanging from the tip of her nose.

Morana swallowed, cursing herself for being so loose with her thoughts. She was also dripping from the heat of the fire, which was almost too much to bear on such a warm evening. 'I do not, no,' she insisted moodily. 'But the book... I used it myself for a time. I am not used to assisting another.'

'Well then, you should feel even more honoured that I have chosen you to be of use to me,' Draguta decided, lifting her goblet and motioning for them to do the same. 'You see, there is great power to be found in the number three. But of course, you know that, Morana. Three pairs of eyes see much better than one. That is what my sisters and I discovered,' she said, without a hint of sadness or regret. Diona and Dalca had been useful for a time, but eventually, her ambition had outgrown theirs. And the book had made it very clear who its true mistress was.

And it was never going to be anyone but her.

'That is part of this ritual. Seeing. And I'm not ashamed to admit that I would like all the help I can get. The person I'm trying to find is very good at hiding, you see. Better than anyone I know.' She smiled, and her teeth glowed brightly in the candlelight. 'Now, drink up, my miserable assistants, for it is time to begin!'

***

Jael had walked Thorgils to her house, where she had left him with Isaura and the children. As much as she was desperate to sleep in her own comfortable bed, it didn't feel right to take that away from them. Nor would it feel right without Eadmund lying next to her. But he was no doubt in Eirik's old bed, wishing that Evaine was in his arms.

Aleksander had followed Jael as she wound her way through the fort, up to the ramparts, and now he crept up behind her as she stood staring out at the dark harbour, resisting the urge to wrap his arm around her shoulder. He would never have considered it, even when they were together.

Jael had never welcomed anyone touching her.

'You have secrets,' she said, turning to him, listening to the familiar sound of waves crashing against the stone spires in the distance. 'From me.'

Aleksander blinked. 'Can you read my mind?'

Jael laughed.

'It's a serious question!' he insisted. 'Can dreamers read people's minds?'

'I don't know. I'm finding it hard to even think of myself as a dreamer. It's still too strange,' she admitted. 'I've always been able to tell what people are feeling. Usually, from knowing someone well. But I suppose it was always more than that. I can hear the things they don't say. I don't think that's mind-reading, though. Just being observant.'

'Maybe a little more than observant.'

'Maybe, but now I'm observing that you're avoiding my

question.'

'You didn't ask me a question that I recall.'

'Hmmm, must be a very big secret if you're avoiding it this much,' Jael decided. 'I have one too. I'll tell you mine if you tell me yours.'

She sounded playful, and it made Aleksander smile, but he didn't offer anything.

'I'll go first then, shall I?' Jael said, shivering. 'Although, perhaps we should leave it till we're in Andala. Let's get back to the hall and a fire.'

'No!' Aleksander grabbed her arm. 'What secret do you have?'

Jael looked into his eyes. 'I had a dream about your mother.'

***

Draguta had refreshed her memory by studying the book that morning, but she hadn't needed to. It felt like only days since she had drawn such a circle.

Morana looked on with interest as Draguta dipped her finger into the small bowl of blood and herbs they had prepared that day. Lifting up her bloody finger, Draguta carefully drew symbols around the edge of the table. Morana could hear her chanting, though Draguta's voice was low and deep, as though she was concealing the actual words from them, not wanting to reveal her secrets.

Meena didn't want to watch, but nor did she wish to incur Draguta's wrath by looking away.

Once the seeing circle was complete, Draguta sat back and smiled dreamily, gripping Morana's and Meena's hands. 'Now, let us see who we can find!'

***

Ayla sensed that Bruno wasn't breathing as he lay beside her. She wasn't sure that he had moved since she'd blown out the lamp.

And Ayla knew what that meant. 'You can't keep thinking about Ivaar.'

'He should have been on one of those pyres,' Bruno growled, wishing that he even remembered how to swing a sword. His arms had wasted away because of Ivaar, and now he was too weak to kill him.

But he would. No matter what the queen had decided.

He would.

'For what he did to us, he will pay,' Ayla whispered. 'In the end, we all pay, don't we? Sometimes, in ways we never see. I often think that Ivaar has been paying his whole life. His father abandoned him. His mother killed herself. The woman he loved was murdered –'

'You're making *excuses* for him?' Bruno didn't want to get angry with his wife, but he was desperate for her to feel as bitter and vengeful as he did. He knew that Ayla was more inclined to find the good in people, but surely she could not see the good in this?

Not after what Ivaar had done to her.

Ayla sighed, knowing that she could talk herself in circles, but that, ultimately, nothing she said would dampen Bruno's fire. He was determined to make Ivaar pay, and she could only hope that he would be prepared when he did confront him.

Laying her head on Bruno's chest, Ayla closed her eyes, hoping that Jael knew what she was doing.

***

Aleksander blinked away tears, listening to Jael's rumbling stomach. He tried not to smile, but it was a non-stop interruption. 'Do you really think my mother acted that way because she was spellbound?' he asked breathlessly. Hopefully. 'That she didn't know what she was doing when she sent that note?'

'I have no doubt,' Jael said firmly. 'I watched her in my dream. I saw inside her, and she wasn't herself. Fianna was gone. She did what they made her do. She would never have hurt you, or me. Or your father. Never.'

Aleksander dragged Jael into his arms, squeezing her tightly before she could protest. She squirmed against him, as she usually did, but he held on anyway. 'Thank you,' he whispered in her ear. 'Thank you.'

Jael pulled herself away from Aleksander, desperate not to have him press against her belly. She didn't want anyone to notice her changing shape. She didn't even want to see it herself, but Thorgils wasn't wrong; she felt different, and Jael could only assume that she looked different too, and if Thorgils had noticed, then Aleksander certainly would. Or feel it. And that wasn't a conversation she wanted to have.

No one could know.

Jael's stomach rumbled again, and Aleksander laughed. 'Has anyone ever been as hungry as you?' he wondered with a happy grin, feeling lighter than he had in months. 'Let's go to the kitchen. I'm sure you can find something to eat before you keep the hall awake tonight!'

Jael smiled as she turned to follow him, but her smile quickly fell away as she readjusted her cloak, covering her stomach. As soon as they arrived in Andala, she would have to talk to Edela and decide what to do about the baby.

***

It was a rushing wind that blew past her face.

Draguta had not thought that she would ease into it so quickly, but it was who she had been for so long.

It was who she was meant to be.

The three women sat around the table, holding hands, eyes closed. Draguta had worried that she wasn't strong enough to perform the spell alone, which is why she'd wanted the two ugly trolls to stay, but now?

Now, she could fly into the darkness.

It was as though no time had passed at all.

But then she frowned, realising that the clouds would not part. They were dark and stormy. There was no light coming through. There was nothing to see but thick clouds blocking her path. She took a deep breath, intensifying her focus, but nothing would break those clouds.

Opening her eyes, Draguta wrenched her hands away from Morana and Meena, who opened their own eyes, neither of them daring to look her way. They could feel her disappointment raging, hoping they wouldn't be blamed.

Standing, Draguta smoothed down her white dress. Her body was rigid. The fragrant smoke from the fire tickled her throat, but she didn't react. She could feel her anger building, flowing over her like a heated waterfall. 'Leave.'

She said it so darkly that Morana hurried to her feet, almost running to the door, leaving Meena to stumble after her.

Draguta looked down at her elegant hands. Taegus had always liked her hands. She was born to be a queen, he would say.

The queen.

Picking up the copper bowl, still half-full of bloody potion, Draguta hurled it against the stone wall. The dark-red liquid ran down the stones, the bowl dropping to the floor with a clatter.

Where was she?

Hiding?

'I will find you!' Draguta screamed. 'You think that you can hide from me? From *me*?!' Her face twisted with such fury that she felt a sharp pain between her eyes. 'After what you did to me? I will find you!'

CHAPTER THIRTEEN

Meena had lain awake for hours. Or she had not slept at all. She didn't know which. Her thoughts tumbled like storm clouds, her fears and memories swirling around her as she desperately tried to avoid having to face them.

Jaeger rolled over, woken by all her twitching. He squinted at her pale, anxious face and smiled. 'You're a dreamer,' he croaked. He couldn't stop saying it. And reaching out, he touched Meena's bruised eye. '*My* dreamer.'

Meena held his stare, though he was hurting her eye, and she didn't want to be so close to him. She swallowed, not knowing what he wanted her to say. She didn't know how to be a dreamer, but she could see how desperate he was for her to be one.

'Don't worry,' Jaeger reassured her, 'there's plenty of time. You'll learn. Go and get some of Varna's books.' He edged closer. 'You can read them, so read, and learn from her. Learn how to be a dreamer, and then...' He narrowed his eyes and lowered his voice. 'And then, we'll take the book from Draguta. You and me. Together.'

Meena's eyes bulged, and her lips parted, and her body shook, and Jaeger ignored all of it as he pulled her into his arms and kissed her.

***

It was still early, and Jael would have slept for longer, but the baby's crying had woken the entire hall, and when he wouldn't settle, she had come into Eadmund's chamber to see what was wrong.

Eadmund held his squirming son against his chest, frowning as he paced the room. Sigmund's crying was relentless. Not even Tanja had been able to soothe him. 'He's missing his mother,' Eadmund decided.

Jael was sure that Tanja was rolling her eyes, though the dawn light from the window was too dim for her to see much more than shadows across the room where the young girl hovered nervously by the door. 'Perhaps he's hungry?' Jael suggested awkwardly. She had no idea why the baby was crying, and she was reluctant to offer any advice, but without Evaine, he was her responsibility too.

Eadmund walked towards Jael, jiggling his son. He had barely slept. The pain in the back of his head was a constant reminder of Evaine's sudden departure. If he hadn't been knocked out, he would have looked for her. Sent men earlier. He might have been able to stop them from leaving. But the riders had finally returned to report that one of the ships in Tatti's Bay, along with a basket of supplies, was missing. It was what they had all suspected, and Eadmund wasn't surprised. He just hoped that Morac would get Evaine safely to Hest. If that was where they were heading.

Eadmund peered at Jael, resigned to her being there instead of Evaine. 'Will you try?' he asked, desperate for a respite from the noise.

Jael froze.

'It's easy enough,' he insisted, sensing her discomfort. 'Hold him against your chest, head over your shoulder. Put your hand under him, and the other on his back. Like this.'

Jael didn't look any keener, but neither did she move as Eadmund placed Sigmund into her arms. Grimacing, she tried to adjust her hands so as not to drop the squawking baby.

He was so light. His little head lolled about, and Jael rushed a hand up to secure him over her shoulder, worried that he was about to flop onto the floor like a fish. Sigmund didn't stop crying, though, so she jiggled him as Eadmund had, walking quickly around the chamber, feeling as uncomfortable as she did the first time she held him.

Thorgils burst out laughing as he stopped in the doorway. 'Well, that's a sight I never thought I'd see!' he hooted, laughing even more at the unfamiliar expression on Jael's face as she turned to glare at him. He was so used to that look of moody confidence in her eyes, but she appeared terrified.

Sigmund stopped crying instantly.

'You have a way with babies, it seems. You should hold him,' Jael declared, reaching out with Sigmund, watching as Thorgils' mockery quickly turned to awkwardness as he struggled to take hold of the baby himself.

'Hand on his back!' Eadmund grumbled, not happy having his son passed around like a mead bucket. But Sigmund was so fascinated with Thorgils and his bushy red beard that he'd not started crying again, and they were all grateful for that.

Jael watched as Thorgils adjusted his grip on the fair-haired baby. It was hard not to see him as Evaine's son. But he was Eadmund's too. 'We should bring him,' she said suddenly, turning to her frowning husband. 'We shouldn't leave him here.'

Eadmund sucked in a breath as another pain shot through his head. 'Do you think he's in danger?'

Jael shrugged, suddenly unsettled as she glanced at Thorgils. 'I don't know, but I think it's best if we're all together. You should bring Isaura and the children too, and Ayla and her husband. Who knows how powerful this woman is. We need to stick together. Keep everyone we care about close.'

Thorgils was quickly at ease with the baby, and thinking so hard about Isaura that he didn't notice that Sigmund hadn't uttered a peep, and was starting to fall asleep on his shoulder. 'I think Jael's right. They'll be safer in Andala with us.'

Eadmund looked at his son as he struggled to keep his little eyes open. He nodded, wanting to do everything he could to keep his son safe for Evaine's return.

***

Jaeger could almost feel the book calling to him as he sat opposite Draguta, trying very hard not to reach out and caress its dark cover. It felt as though another man had stolen his wife, and he was powerless to take her back again.

He scowled irritably. That had happened too.

'Tell me about our fleet,' Draguta smiled, pouring Jaeger a cup of water. She had sent a servant to find more wine, but in the meantime, water was all she had to offer.

Jaeger was surprised by the question. He lifted his eyes from the book, noticing how intently she awaited his answer. Watching his eyes. Never blinking. 'The Furycks destroyed everything we had. My father had us rebuilding. I...' He tried to remember the things Haaron had said about their fleet. 'We need more shipbuilders. Progress has been slow.'

Draguta lifted a dark eyebrow. 'Well, what are you going to do about that, then?' she wondered, drumming her sharp nails on the table. 'We will require many ships, Jaeger. More than you have ever imagined. Hest must rise and conquer all of Osterland. And for that, we will need ships.'

'I'll send for more builders today.'

'Yes, you will,' Draguta said. 'And the ones we have now? They must work twice as fast if they wish to live. Remind them of that. I want them building day and night. Our harbour must be full, and quickly!'

Jaeger nodded, preparing to leave. 'I will go to the sheds now.'

'But we are not finished,' Draguta smiled coolly, pulling the book closer, watching jealousy flare in Jaeger's amber eyes. 'We must talk about how we are going to rule here. Together. For you wish to be king, and yet, now that I have returned, you feel an uncertainty. A terror. Wondering what will become of you. Wondering what I will do with you. *To* you.'

Draguta was so mesmerising to look at that it was often easy to become distracted by her beauty and ignore her words, but Jaeger blinked himself awake and nodded.

She laughed. 'You may be the king here, but you will be *my* king. You will take my orders, do my bidding, and kneel before me, for I will be the true queen.'

Jaeger looked confused as Draguta's smile widened.

'I will be the Queen of the Gods!'

***

'It's not that cold!' Edela grumbled as Biddy tried to tuck a fur neck-warmer around her shoulders.

'Perhaps, for most people, but most people haven't almost died twice recently!' Biddy grumbled back as Edela slipped through the door, the puppies charging past her, eager to escape the tiny cottage.

Edela ignored Biddy, enjoying the pleasant sunshine that greeted her as she wandered down the path. It was warm and bright and such a welcome change from the storm-chased, bitterly cold Tuuran weather. Frowning, she saw visions of the fire that had decimated the fort, destroying Tuura's ancient temple. It was a sad end for what had been her home for many years.

Biddy hurried after her. 'Why are you in such a rush this morning? And not telling me anything either!'

'You haven't asked me anything!' Edela grinned. 'And besides, it's best if I talk to the elderman first. I want to keep my thoughts in order in case they fall out of my ears as they're wont to do now that I'm so old and doddery!'

Biddy slipped her arm through Edela's as they came to a muddy puddle. 'Here, come this way,' she urged, pulling her towards a wooden path. 'I didn't know that you and Marcus had become friendly.'

Edela snorted. 'We have not, as you well know, but he's a man with greater knowledge than any of us, and I've had a dream I need his help with. We should find Eydis on our way. I need all the dreamers I can find!'

***

It had been a brief respite, Bayla thought, as she waited impatiently for her sons to finish speaking with Rexon. But only a respite. The stark reality of their situation was becoming more apparent with each day.

There was no home to return to. No castle or kingdom.

And, for Bayla, no husband.

They had to crawl to Andala, begging the Brekkans for help.

The *Brekkans*?

She shook her head, turning to Nicolene, who was trying to stop her eldest son from running away before he could be lifted onto the ship after his cousins.

Nicolene glared at Karsten, who appeared oblivious to the trouble Eron was causing as he screamed and ducked behind a barrel.

Karsten took the note from Rexon, slipping it into his pouch. 'Best you prepare to defend yourselves. My brother will be at your gates before long, wanting to conquer you too.'

Rexon nodded, worried by the thought of Jaeger Dragos coming anywhere near Saala. 'Well, he won't have an easy time if he tries it.'

'You must look out for more than just armies, though,' Hanna suggested shyly. 'The threat Jaeger poses with that woman and The Following is not something you'll expect. We don't know what they can do with the power of the book.'

'Well, I imagine it won't be pleasant,' Haegen frowned, turning to Irenna, who had secured their three children on board and was looking impatiently at him. They had to leave, he knew, yet, much like everyone else, he was reluctant to head to Andala.

Nothing felt certain anymore. Their brother was now their enemy. Their enemies were now, hopefully, their allies. It was confusing, and he felt on edge, worried about how he was going to keep his wife and children safe; worried about his kingdom too, for, without his father, Hest *was* his kingdom now. Yet Jaeger was there, sitting on the dragon throne, this mysterious woman by his side. And everything he'd heard from Hanna made him fear what that would mean for them all.

'I wish you a safe journey,' Rexon said as Karsten left to help Berard onto the ship. 'With this wind, you'll be in Andala within two days, I'd say.'

Haegen nodded, only half of him pleased by that statement. 'Thank you,' he said, clasping Rexon's forearm. 'For your hospitality.' He wasn't as thick-headed as Karsten, but still, it was hard to say. It all felt so unfamiliar. He couldn't stop thinking about his father. 'We are grateful. All of us.'

Rexon smiled, following Haegen to Ulf's ship. 'Well, perhaps it won't be long till we see each other again. Hopefully, you'll bring the Brekkan army with you, and we can get rid of that book once and for all.'

Berard, standing by the prow, dropped his head, trying not to imagine how different everything would've been if he had defeated Jaeger and taken the Book of Darkness.

***

Jael looked back at the fort, seeing the lines of smoke snaking up from the pyres that had been lit that morning. Some were still smoking from yesterday afternoon. It was hard to think about how many had lost their lives trying to defend the fort. How many more would die, never to return to Oss?

It wasn't an especially cold day, but Jael shivered, wrapping her cloak more tightly around her chest as she turned away, walking past Runa, who jiggled a fur-wrapped Sigmund in her arms as she talked with Isaura and Ayla, deciding who would sleep where. Most of them were going to be joining Jael and Beorn on *Sea Bear*, owing to the protection provided by the wooden house, and Isaura and Ayla's desire never to set foot on *Ice Breaker* again.

Not after their journey from Kalfa.

'Feels strange to be leaving,' Thorgils said quietly as he fell in beside Jael, turning his own eyes up to the old stone fort on the hill.

The only home he'd ever known.

Jael followed his gaze, thinking of Eirik, hearing his grumbles, imagining his displeasure at their mass departure. Eirik had trusted her to look after the islands, and though it was a risk to sail away, leaving nothing but a small garrison behind, if she didn't try to defeat Draguta and destroy the book, there would be no islands to come back to.

'Better to be doing something about what's coming, than waiting for it to come,' Bram grinned, tugging on his swordbelt as he prepared to board *Red Ned*. 'We can't be safe here if the world around us is on fire.'

'Exactly,' Jael agreed. 'We can't. And while that book

remains in Hest, no one's safe.'

Thorgils nodded, his eyes on Isaura, watching as she ran a hand over her golden hair, which was coming undone, pulled apart by Mads, who had been attached to her hip for most of the day. 'I hope your brother will have room for all of us.'

Jael smiled, wondering how Axl was coping back in Andala. 'I'm sure we'll all squeeze in somewhere.' She froze, feeling a sudden wave of nausea rising.

'What is it?' Thorgils asked, concerned by the strange look on her face.

'Nothing,' Jael said quickly, clearing her throat. 'I'm just going to check on Eadmund, and make sure those Arnessons aren't planning to slip away to Alekka, then we should head off.' Her stomach lurched further. She wasn't looking forward to crossing the Nebbar Straights.

Hurrying across the foreshore, Jael sucked in some deep breaths of cool air.

'Ready?' Eadmund called as she approached.

'I think so. You?'

'We're ready,' Eadmund said, uncomfortable with the idea of leaving. Or, at least, uncomfortable with the idea of going to Andala. His mind was on Hest and Evaine. His need for her was so great that it felt as though he was being pulled apart. It was the strangest sensation.

'Eadmund?' Jael frowned, sensing his unease.

Eadmund ignored her. 'Did you check on the Arnessons? And Ivaar?'

'No, but I will, then let's go. You lead us out.'

Eadmund nodded. 'I hope you know what you're doing with Ivaar and those Alekkans. They might just sail away from us. Come back and claim Oss. '

'Well, they have a chance for gold and fame, and a future that isn't a pyre. It's their choice. If they betray us, they'll soon regret it. With Brekka as our ally, we have a big enough fleet to destroy anyone who tries to take Oss from us.' Jael wasn't as confident as she was trying to sound. Everything told her that she needed men, but she didn't trust Ivaar or Erl. Or even Eadmund.

She could see that Evaine's disappearance was torturing him, and Jael didn't know how long she could keep him focused on what they needed to do. His heart and soul were bound to that desperate girl.

And she didn't know how to set him free.

Eadmund stared at her as though she was a stranger, and Jael felt the knot in her stomach tighten like a clenched fist.

It didn't matter, she told herself.

Not yet.

***

Jaeger stood at the edge of the harbour wall with Yorik.

In his desperation to get another audience with Draguta, Yorik had sought out the new King of Hest, who had been surprisingly eager for his company. They were both suffering from the paralysing confusion of how to approach their new roles, with Draguta as their mistress.

It wasn't how either man had expected to feel.

'She doesn't want anything to do with Raemus,' Jaeger said, watching the men scramble around the barely-built piers with rising irritation. The builders and their workers didn't appear to be going slowly. They looked industrious, and he rarely saw them taking breaks, so why were they making such little progress? He barely remembered his father's own frustrations, but now the kingdom was under his rule - his and Draguta's, according to her - and he was responsible for preparing a fleet worthy of a true Dragos king. And he wanted to do it quickly.

Yorik swallowed, not pleased, but not surprised either. 'She *told* you this?'

Jaeger nodded. 'You need to approach her yourself, Yorik. I have no interest in being your messenger.' His body tensed just thinking about Draguta's hands all over his book. But then, remembering that soon Meena would be able to help him, he relaxed, turning back to the castle, wondering where she was.

Yorik looked worried. 'But what does she want?'

Jaeger walked away from him, shaking his head. 'More than you can imagine.'

***

'Have you been hiding from me, Morana?' Draguta cooed, pleased to have finally found the grumbling dreamer crouched over in one of Hest's hidden gardens, looking like a black-and-white bush. 'Thinking I wouldn't find you? But I can see you with my eyes both open and closed, Morana Gallas. I can hear your thoughts, even when you're not with me. There is no secret you can keep from me. No place that you can hide.'

Morana swallowed, shaking the hair away from her scowling face as she straightened up, daring to look into Draguta's emotionless eyes. There was no other way, she realised, but to speak her thoughts. Anything else would just trap her in a lie, leaving her exposed and vulnerable. Better to be bold. 'I don't know what you want from me,' she admitted. 'We brought you back from the Dolma. *I* did. We thought you wanted to bring Raemus back. That you sought a return to the Darkness as we do. The Following... we have worked together for centuries to return Raemus to his rightful place. We assumed that you shared our goal.'

They were standing in one of the herb gardens her mother had expertly cultivated over her long lifetime. An ancient olive tree dangled its thick leaves over their heads, granting them a shady respite from the sun, but Morana could still feel sweat pooling in the crevice between her sagging breasts.

Draguta laughed. 'You did, didn't you? Which is good for me, otherwise I'd still be in the Dolma!' She shuddered, unable to keep the horror of that place off her face. 'But the Darkness is a pointless wish!' she scoffed. 'Why would anyone welcome a dark, empty hole? Where you will never die, but exist in an endless world of nothing. Where there is no light or warmth. No life! And you seek *that*?' she sneered, smoothing her shining black hair over her white dress. 'You were all sold a lie, you and your pathetic Followers. As if the Darkness was better than anything this world could offer! Raemus sold you a lie, and you all foolishly built that lie into an illusion so grand that you can no longer see the truth!'

Morana frowned, pushing back her tense shoulders, eager to defend their vision of the Darkness. Ready to proclaim her loyalty to Raemus.

'Raemus never cared for his followers!' Draguta raged, her eyes bright now. 'He sought your help to defeat the humans, yes, but he had no intention of giving you anything in return. He used you in his war against Daala! Against the gods!'

'How could you know?'

'*Me*?' Draguta wasn't sure whether she wanted to laugh or cry. 'I know more about Raemus than most. If you want to throw yourself on his ash pile... if you want to join him in his prison, go ahead! But know that I can offer you more than he ever could.'

Morana frowned. Raemus had always been her guiding force. Reuniting him with the Darkness he so desperately sought had been her sole motivation since she was a child; a destiny drummed into her by her mother and the leaders of The Following. They had sent her and Morac to Oss as children, foreseeing that one day Eirik Skalleson's son would stand in the way of Raemus' return. It had been their job to stop him. If Morana hadn't fallen in love with Eirik, she would have killed him years ago, before it had all come to this.

She closed her eyes, not wanting to revisit the shame of her weakness.

Draguta had turned away, seeking the sunlight. 'I want you to see, Morana. I want you to see how much I can offer you. You and the girl will assist me tonight. We will go to the Crown of Stones. I will cast a spell. Something to make you change your minds. Come to my chamber when you are done here and bring the girl with you,' Draguta smiled as she walked down the path.

Morana didn't move, but she did frown.

She would never turn away from Raemus, and nothing Draguta showed her would convince her otherwise.

***

Oleg had finally arrived in Andala with the Brekkan army and the Tuurans, who had decided that they wanted to be as far away from the burning mess of their fort and the curse of the ancient temple as possible.

The sudden influx of people had kept Gant busy, and he'd spent most of the day running around the fort with Gisila, popping into the hall to talk with Axl, working to assign everyone accommodation. Those who could fit within the fort were given whatever cottages were available, but most were moved into a hastily constructed tent village outside the walls. It wasn't ideal, but they believed there would be time to bring the Tuurans into the safety of the fort if an attack came.

Marcus was happy to have been given his own cottage, which was big enough for his needs and warm too; furnished simply and more than he had expected, but, as grateful as he was, he could barely raise a smile.

Edela had finished speaking, and she stared at him, waiting for an answer. He seemed so far away that she wondered if he was even listening.

'Yes,' Marcus sighed, at last, bringing his attention back to the room; back to the warm cup of nettle tea almost hidden in his giant hands. 'There is another copy of the Book of Aurea.'

Edela whooped happily, squeezing Eydis' arm.

'*Two* copies?' Eydis' serious face broke into a smile.

Marcus hurried to curtail their enthusiasm. 'I was given one copy by your grandmother, Eydis, but Samara didn't tell me where the other one was. It was important to keep its location hidden. Protected. The fewer people who knew, the better.'

'But there *is* one,' Edela said. 'And that's the main thing. All hope is not lost. You and I just need to keep trying to dream on it, Eydis. And if we can find it, we may be able to free Eadmund.'

Marcus glanced over at the cauldron, busy heating a rich-smelling mutton stew. Axl had provided him with a servant, and she was bustling around the cottage, getting things in order. He felt awkward with her there, but he certainly wouldn't have enjoyed his own cooking. 'I hope so. While Eadmund is bound to Evaine Gallas, he is a danger to everything we are trying to achieve. If we cannot free him soon, I fear that we will never stop Draguta.'

'I agree,' Edela murmured, picking up her cup and taking a quick sip of the warm tea. 'The threat she poses is like a dark cloud, and when I close my eyes, I see it creeping towards us. She is vengeful. Seeking justice. She wants to destroy her enemies.'

'What enemies?' Biddy wondered.

'The ones who killed her family all those years ago.'

'The Tuurans? But Tuura is already destroyed,' Biddy reminded her.

'The Tuurans killed her sisters, yes,' Edela began. 'But Draguta's quest for revenge started well before her sisters were beheaded. She blames Brekka for the deaths of her parents, particularly the Furycks. The very first King Lothar killed her father. He was another greedy king. Greedy for more land. He broke all peace accords, robbing the Tuurans of their holdings. Killing their people. Forcing both sides into endless wars.

Draguta's father led the Tuuran army into battle to face him, and he was killed.'

Marcus was surprised. 'You dreamed this?'

Edela nodded. 'Yes. I've been sleeping well since I returned to my own bed. I've seen much of Draguta as a girl. When her father's death was announced, her mother killed herself, so she lost both parents within days of each other. She blames the Furycks for everything.'

'And now she will come here,' Eydis said quietly. 'Won't she?'

'Oh, yes. She will come. And soon.'

PART TWO

Andala

CHAPTER FOURTEEN

'I'm sorry,' Hanna said haltingly. 'For what happened to your arm. I shouldn't have asked you to try and take the book. Your brother... I should have realised how dangerous he was. What the book had done to him.' She was sitting beside Berard, their backs against the gunwale. It was the only way to escape the worst of the wind, but it was still bitterly cold as they sailed up the Brekkan coast.

'You weren't to know,' Berard murmured. Kai was curled up next to him, wrapped in a thick fur, his head resting on Berard's knee. Berard didn't want to wake him. The little boy had cried himself to sleep, and they were all desperate to keep him quiet for as long as possible. 'You weren't to know what the book had done to him.'

Hanna sighed. 'All that my father told me was passed down to him from the eldermen who came before. From the dreamers too. I'm not sure that anyone really knows the depths of the book's evil, though. I imagine it's even more dangerous than we realise.'

Berard closed his eyes, trying not to give in to the demanding pain in his stump; trying not to see the vicious sneer on his brother's face as he chopped off his arm; the hate in his eyes.

Not the brother he remembered at all.

'Then the only thing we can do is destroy it. It's all that matters now,' Berard insisted. 'Destroy the book, and worry about Jaeger when it's done.'

Hanna nodded, encouraged by Berard's determination, but wondering if he realised that there was little chance of Jaeger ever letting them near the book. He had killed his father and tried to kill his brother to keep it, so Hanna was certain that there was nothing he wouldn't do to stop anyone taking it from him.

***

'My queen,' Yorik murmured, bowing his head before Draguta, who did indeed sit upon the dragon throne looking like a regal queen.

But it wasn't her throne; not the one she wanted to claim.

No throne could represent the immense power she would soon wield.

'Yorik Elstad,' Draguta smiled, lifting a hand towards him. 'Come. Come closer.' Yorik looked uncertain as he stepped forward, and Draguta's smile grew, enjoying his discomfort. 'I am casting a spell tonight, at the Crown of Stones. It will be a true spectacle,' she said mysteriously. 'I want The Following there. I want you to see for yourselves what I can do. You may think that the Darkness is your one true goal, but I intend to change your minds.'

Yorik tried very hard not to frown, which was hard because her words disturbed him. 'We shall be there, my lady,' he said quickly. 'Of course.'

'Good!' Draguta stood gracefully and glided towards him, her white dress billowing behind her. 'I have high hopes for you, Yorik. Especially you. I believe that you can be a very valuable assistant to me.' Reaching out, she trailed an elegant finger down the side of his bristly face. 'You are a man of great wisdom, though so misguided. But I will show you the right path to follow. Tonight.'

Yorik shivered. The intensity of Draguta's eyes had the hairs on his arms standing on end. It was as though she was peering into his soul, and he blinked, afraid of what she would find. His belief in their one true goal was unwavering. It had been carved into his soul since birth. Raising Raemus was all he had been taught. All he had ever desired.

To abandon that now?

But when Yorik stared into Draguta's penetrating eyes, he was unable to look away. 'Tonight,' he breathed, feeling his head nod in agreement.

***

Despite the surprisingly even-tempered mood of the Nebbar Straights, neither Isaura nor Ayla were able to relax. Memories of their last journey were never far from their minds, and every wail of the wind had them both jumping with nerves.

They were sheltering in *Sea Bear's* wooden house with Bruno and the children; with Runa and Tanja, Isaura's two servants, and Sigmund too. This time Isaura's children were more settled, comforted by the fact that their father was nearby on his own ship, coming with them. When they were taken out on deck and lifted up, they could see him standing in *Shadow Blade's* stern; sometimes even waving to them.

Isaura felt confused. She didn't want Ivaar near the children, yet they were so much happier now. And she didn't want to make them miserable just because she hated Ivaar and wished that they'd left him behind on Oss, sizzling on a pyre.

Jael poked her head in the end of the house. 'Everyone alright?'

Isaura and Runa nodded, smiling at her as Ayla staggered out of the house, eager to stretch her legs. 'It's a much quieter journey than our last time at sea,' she sighed, following Jael to the stern.

'Yes, I heard about that,' Jael said. 'Sounds as though they were lucky to have you on board.'

Ayla looked surprised, her eyes suddenly evasive. 'Me?'

'According to Bram, you're a powerful dreamer,' Jael said, stumbling as she reached out for the small dragon prow. 'Stopping a storm like that.'

Ayla's eyes darted around, but none of the crew was within hearing distance. 'It wasn't me who stopped the storm.'

'But you asked someone to? Who?' Jael was curious. They were going to need all the help they could get to defeat The Following; dreamers as much as warriors. 'The gods?'

Ayla's eyes widened, and she took a deep breath, trying to release her tension. Jael Furyck was no enemy; she could feel that. 'Yes,' she admitted. 'I was taught how to speak to the gods, though it doesn't always work. They are... cautious. They don't trust humans.'

'Why?'

'Many humans sided with Raemus against them. They followed his teaching, practiced his magic, became The Following. Eventually, they wanted to destroy the gods as much as Raemus did. They distanced themselves from the humans after Daala killed him. They retreated. Hid away.' Ayla rubbed her hands together, wishing she'd thought to put on her gloves. 'Though now they're worried that Raemus will return. They are trying to warn us.'

Jael frowned. 'And if he does?'

'With the help of The Following, he would destroy them all. Once he was finished with us, of course.'

'Well, hopefully not if we get to Draguta in time. If we stop her, then he can't return, can he?' Jael turned at the sound of Sigmund's crying; a noise that was quickly becoming familiar. 'Without Draguta, no one can bring Raemus back, isn't that right?'

Ayla shrugged. 'I don't know. But if we destroy the book, then perhaps he has no way of returning?'

'If we destroy the book,' Jael muttered. 'If we get into Hest. If we defeat the rest of The Following...'

'It won't be easy. They'll do anything to keep the book.'

'And I will do anything to take it,' Jael said firmly, turning back to the house to check on Sigmund.

***

'I don't think you're strong enough,' Gisila warned as Axl let go of the table and pushed his foot onto the hard mud floor. 'You may do more damage to that leg if you try too soon!'

'Oh, stop fussing,' Edela chortled. 'I don't know where you and your sister get it from, but you're the fussiest women I know! Axl is ready. Can't you see?'

Gisila turned around to glare at Edela, but her ire was quickly extinguished by the happiness on her mother's face. She almost looked like herself again.

Branwyn laughed. 'Well, I'd say that it comes with being a certain age, but it must have passed you by entirely, Mother.'

Edela nodded cheerily. 'And I'm glad for it. I have better things to do with my time than fuss over all of you. Like making sea-fire! But for that, I'm going to need my assistant.' She glanced at the hall doors, but there was still no sign of Kormac.

'He won't be long. He went with Entorp to check on progress with the symbols,' Branwyn said, sensing her mother's impatience. 'But you can have Aedan and Aron. I think they'd like to give their hands a break from all that carving. It's not easy, carving into stone.'

'No, I'm sure it's not,' Edela muttered distractedly. 'Well done!' she smiled as Axl reached his chair. 'Seems that leg of yours is ready for more than just sitting and ordering us about all day. I'd say you just need someone to make you a proper crutch and you'll be able to get about by yourself.'

Axl sighed with relief. He had started to wonder if it would ever be possible to walk again, and despite the discomfort, he felt ready for more.

'But perhaps you still need to do plenty of sitting while it heals properly?' Gant suggested as he walked around the tables, up to Axl's throne. 'There's a lot to prepare. And soon, Jael and Aleksander will return. We need to have those catapults ready. More sea-fire. More arrows. Spears and shields too.'

Axl nodded. 'Has there been any word from Iskavall?'

Gant shook his head. 'Not unless Gerber taught his horse to fly! Be patient. He'll return with a message soon enough. Maybe three or four more days? Everything's underway. Now we just have to wait.'

Axl looked impatient at the thought of being patient. He peered around the hall. 'Where's Amma?'

'She's with Eydis, visiting Fyn,' Edela said. 'I left them with Biddy, in his chamber.'

'How is he?' Axl asked.

'Not as impatient as you!' Edela laughed. 'But improving. Slowly. It will take him a long time to recover his strength, so I don't imagine he'll be going with Jael and Aleksander when they leave.'

'Do you think they'll have to leave?' Gisila panicked. 'All of them?'

'To get the book? Oh, yes, they will. We cannot sit in this fort and hope that Draguta and The Following will simply get bored and go away. If we ever want to feel safe again, we're all going to have to fight. Every single one of us is going to have to fight to make Osterland safe again.'

***

Yorik felt troubled, looking for Morana's advice, but she was barely listening as she walked beside him, head down, eager to escape the castle. She could feel Evaine getting closer, and that gave her a sense of relief, but it was the only thing she had to feel relieved about. The situation with Draguta was a rising irritation.

'But what does she hope to achieve?' Yorik wondered as they walked past the rows of tiny cottages carved into Hest's bleached cliffs. 'Without Raemus? Without the Darkness?'

'You think there's nothing without either of those things?' Morana snorted, listening at last. 'Have you ever looked around this place? At that castle?' she said, pointing behind them. 'Most people crave wealth and power. Most people desire beauty and love. There are not many who dream of dark things, not as we do. But they don't know what is truly possible. What that book can do.'

'But Draguta does,' Yorik murmured. 'And she doesn't want Raemus or the Darkness.'

'She has returned from the Dolma, where everything was dark for so long. Her soul craves light and warmth. In time, perhaps she will come to see things as we do. She may start to want what we want when she realises how pointless this life is. How pointless these people are,' she sneered, flapping her arms at a ragged-looking family passing them on the road.

'And if she doesn't?' Yorik asked, turning to Morana, grabbing her arm. 'What are we prepared to do to stop her?'

Morana hesitated, knowing very well that to speak so would only cause problems. 'She will not be stopped, Yorik,' Morana insisted carefully. 'And those who try will fail. Know that.'

Yorik stared at her, more troubled than ever.

'Tonight, Draguta will show us what she can do. Perhaps we'll both change our minds then?' And shaking off his arm, Morana crept onwards. She wondered if she believed that herself, but she was wise enough to know that if she wanted to stay alive, there was no other thought she could consider.

Not while Draguta was poking around her head.

***

Karsten glanced at his wife, unsure whether he wanted to hold her in his arms or tip her over the gunwale. Nicolene glared at him, and he frowned. She had yet to apologise to him or beg his forgiveness. He wondered if she ever would? Whether she even cared that she had betrayed him with his brother?

He couldn't stop thinking about it.

The thought of them together tortured him, but this far away from Jaeger, there was nothing he could do.

'I'd say we're in for it soon,' Haegen noted, watching the dark storm clouds gathering in the distance.

Karsten yawned, scratching his beard. He thought of his father, who had ruled for so long. For what? His kingdom and his life taken; his family sent away, running to their enemies like frightened children.

It wasn't the future Haaron Dragos had worked so hard for.

'Might help us get to Andala quickly,' he grunted, trying to smile as Eron toddled towards him, his stubby legs struggling as the ship rolled. Karsten lunged forward, grabbing the little boy as he stumbled. 'Not that I want to be in Andala!'

Haegen laughed. 'No, but the sooner we get there, the sooner we have the chance to reclaim Hest. And right now, after what we've been through, I don't care whose help it is. As long as it gets us home. As long as we can destroy Jaeger and take back our throne.'

'*Our* throne?'

Haegen glanced at Eron, giggling in his father's arms, and he lowered his voice. 'Alright, *my* throne. I'll be the king when we kill Jaeger, and you know it. You want to cross me and take it for yourself, go ahead. But wait until we get rid of our little brother. Wait until we kill The Following and destroy this book, and we're standing in front of each other in our own kingdom with swords in our hands. If you want the throne that badly, Karsten, be patient. Put *their* needs before your own ambition,' Haegen muttered, inclining his head towards their children, their wives, and their mother. 'Think about someone other than yourself for a change.' And feeling himself losing his temper, he walked towards Irenna, who was checking on Berard's stump again.

Karsten watched his brother go before looking down at his son, who was staring up at him with big blue eyes full of confusion. He had wanted the throne since he could remember, believing that he would walk over any member of his family to take it for himself when the time was right.

But now?

When he thought of what Jaeger had done to their father and Berard, Karsten felt sick, doubting his own appetite for taking a throne that didn't belong to him in the first place. Unless it was to take it from Jaeger, of course.

He smiled, meeting Nicolene's eyes before she quickly turned away.

***

'Tonight?' Jaeger was excited, eager to be reunited with the book. 'At the Crown of Stones?'

'I doubt she'll want you there,' Morana grunted, scratching her head. Draguta had revealed nothing about the spell she planned to cast. She wanted her help, and Meena's, but she was keeping everything so closely guarded that Morana had no idea what she was helping Draguta prepare for.

'Well, she has no choice. *I* am the king here. If I wish to join in, she can't stop me,' Jaeger growled. 'I don't see why she would.'

Morana ignored him, turning to Meena while Jaeger continued to mutter to himself. 'Get your things, little mouse. I have Draguta's list, and it is long. We don't have much time to gather everything for tonight.'

'Meena?' Jaeger was instantly irritated, glancing around at Meena, who stood with her back to them, looking down at the harbour, wishing she couldn't hear what they were saying. 'Why do you need Meena?'

'Draguta has requested our help,' Morana said mutely, desperate not to acknowledge her true feelings. Not even to herself. 'So we must help her.' She glared at Meena, urging her to look around.

And eventually, feeling her skin crawl, Meena did.

'You will come for me tonight, Morana,' Jaeger demanded as he walked them to the door. 'Do you hear me? I *will* be there. You can tell Draguta that.'

Meena blinked nervously at Jaeger before Morana shoved her into the corridor. She didn't want to go to the Crown of Stones again.

Not one part of her wanted to see what Draguta could do.

***

Eadmund closed his eyes and saw Evaine. Her hand was out, reaching for him. Her eyes were drawing him to her. Needing him. She was smiling, so excited to see him, and then her face twisted in pain, and she was crying, tears rolling down her cheeks as she slipped away, calling his name.

'Eadmund?' Villas asked as he swayed down the deck towards his king, disturbed by the anguished look on his face. 'Is something wrong?'

Eadmund opened his eyes, shaking his head, almost surprised to realise that he wasn't alone. It had been nice, just for a moment, to disappear. To escape the pain in his head and the ache of Evaine's absence in his heart. 'No. Nothing. Just that hole in my head. Hopefully, I'll find a soft pillow in Andala.' He tried to sound different than he felt. He was furious and bereft at the same time. Though at who and why he didn't know.

'Likely you will, being a king,' Villas winked as he swayed back to his tiller. 'Won't be long now!' He'd closed his eyes for an hour and was still half asleep but eager to get back to his rightful place. He never felt like himself without that wooden stick in his hands.

Eadmund didn't even notice him go. He was busy thinking of how quickly he could get to Hest and find Evaine.

***

It was like a thread, and she could feel it pulling from her heart to Eadmund's.

Tugging so urgently that she couldn't breathe.

Evaine stared up at the sky, watching the clouds chase each other above her, trying to count how many there were; trying to do anything to take her mind off the throbbing need to be with Eadmund again. It was as though she was hungry but could never eat. But her body needed Eadmund, just as it needed food.

She sighed, losing count of the clouds again, wondering how long it would be before Eadmund came for her. And he *would* come, she knew. If that bitch didn't try to stop him, he would come for her soon.

CHAPTER FIFTEEN

They were getting closer; Aleksander could feel it.

The sun was going down, and he was hopeful that they'd arrive in Andala's harbour before the rain started. He'd seen the clouds, and they promised a wet night. Laying his head back against the stern, Aleksander closed his eyes, trying to think. Something had been nagging at him all day, but he didn't know what. Except, of course, the loss of the woman he loved, the threat to his home and his people, the worry over what was to come, and the weight of responsibility he felt to try and stop it.

And Hanna.

He couldn't stop his mind from returning to Hanna.

'Aleksander!'

He thought he was awake, but he'd fallen asleep, and the voice sounded muffled. Aleksander spun around, confused, not knowing in which direction it was coming from. Or where he was. He turned and turned as though he was in the clouds, seeing nothing but dense, foggy shapes that finally cleared and revealed a tiny wooden cottage hidden amongst tall trees.

The Widow's cottage.

He remembered it, though not fondly.

'Aleksander!'

The voice was more insistent now. It was suddenly clear, and Aleksander heard its urgency. He felt his legs carry him forward, even though he wanted to remain where he was.

Danger lurked in that house, he was sure.

Or was he?

He remembered his dreams of the Widow. She had helped him, he reminded himself as he was pushed closer and closer to the door.

And then it flew open, and she stood there.

'Aleksander,' she sighed impatiently. 'Come! Come inside. We don't have much time.'

***

Morana was growing irate. They had gathered the items on Draguta's list, but when they returned to her chamber, the door was locked. There was no sign of Draguta, and no one Morana asked knew where she'd gone. 'She can't have just disappeared!' she grumbled, glaring at Meena as they headed back down the corridor, carrying their weighty baskets.

'Perhaps she went to the Crown of Stones?' Meena suggested boldly. 'To prepare it for tonight?'

It was one idea, but Morana didn't want to trek all the way out to the stones only to find the place empty and then be sent back again later to prepare it themselves. She shook her head. 'We'll take one more look around the castle, then try the winding gardens. I'm not going up to the stones if I don't have to.' Morana frowned, catching a glimpse of a familiar face up ahead. 'That's one of her servants, isn't it? Whatever her name is.'

Meena had terrible eyesight, so she simply shrugged and followed her aunt.

It *was* Draguta's servant Brill, and she led them around the castle towards the heated baths where Draguta lay, submerged, enjoying the hot water of the ancient pool, her head resting back on the stone walkway.

'My assistants,' Draguta smiled, opening her eyes. 'Do you have everything I need?'

'We do,' Morana muttered, trying to contain her irritation.

'Wonderful! Now, go and start the preparations, and I shall join you when I'm done. Brill can unlock the chamber,' she sighed, lifting her head as her sour-faced servant slipped a pillow under it. 'Ahhh, perfect. This water is so gloriously warm. Filled with salt, you know. Perfect for purifying oneself, wouldn't you agree, Morana?'

Meena's eyes were wide, watching the steam rise from the pool. She had never dared to venture into the Dragos' private bathing area before, not even when she could be sure that it was empty. Her mouth hung open, her eyes transfixed by the inviting water.

Morana elbowed her in the ribs. 'Close your mouth, girl, and let's get going!' she hissed. 'I don't have time to stand about waiting for you.'

Draguta smiled as she listened to them scurry away, feeling her body unwind, and her mind with it; all thoughts of the seeing circle floating away.

That was for another day.

She needed to turn her attention to tonight.

***

Aleksander swallowed, blinking in surprise.

When he'd last seen the Widow, she'd been hooded, shielding her face from him, leaving him to assume that she was hiding some sort of decaying, ghoulish face. But she looked like an ordinary middle-aged woman; much as he imagined his mother would look if she were still alive.

'The symbol won't work,' the Widow said urgently. Her dark hair was short, shot with strands of silver. It sat at her shoulders, which were slightly rounded. She stooped forward; not an old woman, but a defeated-looking one. 'The symbol won't work on Draguta.'

'What do you mean? Why not?'

'You must bring Jael to me,' she went on, ignoring him. 'When you return to Andala, bring her to me, Aleksander. It is time she knows everything. And there is something I must give her. I have the other copy of the Book of Aurea. She needs it. But for now, come closer, and I will show you another symbol. You must use it, all of you, before it's too late. Before Draguta sees things she shouldn't.'

Aleksander stepped towards the table where she waited. He bent down to stare at the symbol carved into the wooden surface - deep and old, as though it had been burned into the table itself. And when he looked up again, he could see the symbol all around them: in the walls, etched into the door frame, carved on the floor too.

'Wake now, Aleksander, and carve this symbol for Jael. Find something. Make it for her now. It is very important. She is not safe. Draguta will see what she is trying to hide. You must make this for Jael, now!'

Aleksander opened his mouth, determined to ask more questions, but she drifted away from him, her arm still outstretched, her voice fading into the clouds that swarmed around them both. 'Now, Aleksander! Wake up! Before it's too late!' she cried.

***

Jael woke up, thinking about Eydis. Hoping she was alright.

She wasn't sure if everything she saw when she was asleep was some sort of message, or whether it was just a dream. But she had seen Eydis as a little girl. She was on Oss, with her mother and Eirik. They had been holding Eydis' little hands, smiling down at her as she toddled along between them.

Jael felt sad, realising how much Eydis had lost.

And now, Eadmund had left her too.

'You must have been tired,' Runa murmured, rocking Sigmund in her arms. 'I didn't think anyone would fall asleep through this one's noise.'

Jael blinked at Runa, surprised herself. She didn't usually fall asleep during the day. Yawning, she stood, hitting her head on the roof of the house. The noise frightened Sigmund, who promptly burst into tears again. 'Sorry,' Jael mumbled as she skirted the sleepy children and servants, and headed out of the house, leaving Runa to try and coax Sigmund back to sleep.

'He likes to make a lot of noise,' Beorn noted, rolling his eyes at the ear-splitting sound. 'Must take after his mother.'

Jael smiled, noticing how dark it was getting. She strained her eyes and was pleased to see the faint shapes of Brekka in the distance. 'Nearly there.'

Beorn looked just as pleased. It had been a smooth journey, and he had almost enjoyed himself for the first time in Jael's company. He frowned, noticing *Silver Tooth* pointing straight for them. 'Over there!' he called to Jael, nodding towards the fast approaching ship.

Jael walked to the row of shields lining the gunwale and leaned over them, watching Aleksander flap his arms at her. 'Slow us down, Beorn!' she cried, turning to him. 'Slow us down now!'

***

Eydis couldn't stop yawning.

Fyn smiled at her. It hadn't been long since Branwyn had

brought him supper, yet Eydis appeared ready for bed. 'Are you alright?' he wondered gently.

Eydis sat up straighter on her stool, nodding, feeling embarrassed. She was nearly fourteen-years-old; everything embarrassed her. She reached down, feeling paws on her knees.

Ido.

She tried to pick him up, but he was far too heavy, so he jumped onto Fyn's bed instead.

'No!' Fyn yelped as the little black dog hopped on top of him.

Biddy bustled in, holding two cups of steaming passionflower tea in her hands. 'What's going on in here? Ido! Get down! What are you doing, you naughty boy!'

There wasn't much she could do with no hands free, but her sharp tone was enough for Ido, who leaped off the bed, scampering out of the chamber in a black blur.

'I'll have to keep that door shut,' Biddy grumbled, placing the cups on the table by Fyn's bed before taking a good look at him. He was still very pale. His eyes had sunk into his face, and his cheekbones were jutting out. There was a deep sadness about him that she could only guess was the disappointment at being left behind. Worry too, not knowing what was happening on Oss with Jael, and his mother. 'How are you, then?' Biddy asked cheerfully, glancing at Eydis before bending forward to try and prop Fyn up. 'Entorp will be here soon to check on your wound and slather on more of his balm, no doubt, so don't go to sleep yet!'

Both Eydis and Fyn wrinkled their noses.

'Well, I'm sure it will wake you up, Eydis. You look half asleep,' Biddy said, handing Fyn the cup of tea. He was tucked in a small chamber just off the hall. It was relatively peaceful, and close to the kitchen too, which meant that Biddy could rush about, checking on Edela and Axl and Entorp without having to be too far away from him.

Eydis looked uncomfortable, dropping her head to her chest.

'What is it?'

'Well, I, it's... your snoring,' Eydis mumbled. 'Yours and Edela's. It's hard to sleep in the cottage.'

Fyn burst out laughing, spluttering hot tea all over his chest, grimacing at the excruciating stab of pain in his stomach.

'Here, let me take that,' Biddy said quickly, grabbing the cup and looking around for some form of cloth. 'And I don't know what you mean about snoring, Eydis. I've been sleeping like the dead since we returned!' Lifting up her apron, she dabbed Fyn's chest. 'Perhaps we should swap places tonight? I can sleep on the floor. We need you dreaming, Eydis. You must see if you can find that book.'

Eydis nodded eagerly, feeling the same way. She was worried about Eadmund. Whenever she saw his face, he looked like a stranger, and she could feel how desperately lost he was. But if she could dream and find that book again - see the symbols, perhaps even read the words - then maybe she could save him. She yawned again, feeling Biddy grab her hand.

'Right, you're coming with me, young miss! I'm going to

put you in the hall with Amma. You can curl up on a bed near her while I finish up what I'm doing, and then we'll head back to the cottage.'

Fyn smiled at Eydis as Biddy tugged her towards the door. 'I'll see you tomorrow, Eydis!' he called out as she disappeared. His head sank back into the pillow, and his smile vanished. He couldn't stop thinking about Jael, wondering what she was doing. She certainly didn't need his help, but he'd wanted to be there, by her side. It meant something that she valued him. That she thought he was good enough to stand beside her. It meant more than almost anything.

But now, trapped in bed like an invalid... he felt worthless again.

***

'What is it?' Jael shouted, waiting for the ships to be pulled together. Ropes had been thrown from *Silver Tooth* to *Sea Bear*, and now her crew was busy pulling them in.

Aleksander didn't say anything until they were almost face-to-face; until he could reach out and touch her hand. And he did, placing a small piece of wood into her cold palm. 'The symbol on the stones won't work on Draguta. *This* is the symbol that will keep her out. You need to make yourself safe!'

Jael's eyes rounded in surprise. 'How do you know?' she called, but Aleksander was already turning away, bellowing at his helmsman. 'We have to get to Andala quickly! They're not safe. They're carving the wrong symbol into the walls!'

Jael turned to her men, standing by the gunwales in confusion. 'Release the ropes! We have to fly!' She looked up at the darkening clouds knitting together above her head, remembering the ravens.

***

Eadmund watched Jael flapping her arms at Beorn, wondering what she had been talking to Aleksander about. The wind was picking up, and they were getting closer to Andala's harbour, he knew. It hadn't been a long journey, but he was thankful that it was nearly over.

He was consumed with worry for Evaine, and unable to think clearly, not knowing whether she was safe.

Jael was watching him now, and as much as Eadmund could feel his body clenching uncomfortably, he didn't turn away. His head pounded, and he thought back to the attack on Oss, reminded that Jael had arrived just in time, saving him from having more than a small hole in his head. If Borg Arnesson had had his way, he wouldn't have a head at all.

Eadmund frowned, turning away, finally uncomfortable.

***

Edela felt strange.

Sometimes her dreams were like open doors, and she could walk through them and find the answers to the questions she had posed. Other times, they were locked, and she didn't even know what the question was in the first place. But it was there. Unspoken. Nagging at her, scolding her, trying to get her to see what was right in front of her face.

A problem.

There was definitely a problem.

'We made good progress with the symbols today,' Kormac smiled, passing his mother-in-law a bowl of wild plums. 'Hopefully, we'll get close to finishing the walls tomorrow.'

Edela had eaten two bowls of mutton stew for supper, and

she shook her head distractedly.

Gant, sitting to Kormac's right, nodded. 'The sea-fire is coming along too. We'll get another batch going tomorrow. We should be in good shape when Jael and Aleksander return.'

Edela didn't look pleased.

'What is it, Grandmother? Is there something else we should be doing?' Axl wondered, reaching for his ale.

'Doing?' Edela frowned. 'I imagine there's always more we can be doing, but no, I'm just having dreamer problems. Nothing you can do about that.' She grimaced, her stomach scar aching as it often did in the evenings. 'I can't think of anything else for us to do but wait for Jael and make our plans. And hope to hear from your sister soon, Amma.'

Amma looked up, smiling awkwardly. She was convinced that Getta would refuse to help them, and she doubted that there was any chance her husband would have much say in the matter. The Getta she remembered had wound Lothar around her little finger, time and time again.

'Yes, and we need to think of what to do if we don't hear from them,' Axl suggested, sensing Amma's unease. 'Or if they don't want to help. We need more men to attack Hest. It won't be enough to just have the Islanders join us, will it?'

'No,' Gant agreed. 'So, there's your first big decision as king, then. Are you prepared to conquer your neighbours to save Osterland?'

Axl swallowed, thinking of his father. Ranuf Furyck had always appeared in complete control of his kingdom, and Axl realised that he must have been making decisions constantly. It was just what a king did. What a king had to do to keep his kingdom safe and prosperous. He sighed, wondering if he would ever feel as though he was in charge of anything.

Eydis gasped loudly, lurching up from one of the beds along the far wall, her hands out in front of her. 'Biddy?' she called. 'Edela?'

Edela turned her head as Amma got up from the table and

hurried to the bed, gripping Eydis' hand.

'What is it, Eydis?' Edela asked as Amma led Eydis towards her. 'Here, you take a seat and tell me what you've seen.'

The only sound in the hall was a popping fire. Even the servants had frozen, wanting to know what the little dreamer had seen.

'I, it's the symbol,' Eydis whispered, conscious of everyone's attention. 'The symbol is wrong.'

Edela's face finally cleared. The locked doors she had been staring at were suddenly wide open. 'Yes, it is, isn't it. But tell me, Eydis, did you see a new symbol? One we can use?'

***

The sky was dark, sprinkled with stars as the fleet of ships nudged Andala's piers, one after the other.

Gant stood waiting by the first mooring post, his frown digging deep into his forehead as Jael jumped down onto the pier and strode towards him.

'The symbol is wrong!' she cried. 'You have to get everyone into the hall! We need to use a different symbol!'

Gant held up his hands, trying to stop her. 'We know.'

Aleksander, who had joined them, looked at Gant in surprise.

'Eydis,' Jael said, turning as Eadmund, Thorgils, and Bram walked down the pier towards them.

Gant nodded.

'What's wrong?' Eadmund asked.

'We have to get to the hall. Thorgils, have Askel take Leada to the stables. Bram, make sure the Arnessons and Ivaar come to the hall. We have a lot to discuss and not much time.'

Bram and Thorgils glanced at each other, wondering where the hall and the stables might be.

'Oleg!' Jael called, recognising his familiar face. 'Get the women and children to the hall!'

'You've brought a lot of ships,' Gant noted, seeing how quickly the piers had filled up. 'Perhaps we should send them around to the cove?'

'I'll leave that up to you. I need to speak to Axl.'

***

'You are so very good at this,' Draguta purred, running her eyes over Morana and Meena's preparations. She dipped a finger into the potion, touching the bloody liquid to her lips, inhaling its pungent scent before sucking slowly on her finger. 'So very useful.'

Morana blinked, relieved to hear it.

They had ground Draguta's ingredients into a paste, mixing it with fresh blood to form a thick liquid while she carried on her purification ritual. But now, dressed in a new white dress, her hair brushed, oiled, and scented, and glowing like polished ebony, Draguta was finally ready to do her part.

For she was the one who would cast the spell.

She was the one who would show The Following what she was truly capable of.

CHAPTER SIXTEEN

'The Widow came to you too?' Jael didn't know how she felt about that, but there was little time to dwell on it now.

'We can trust her,' Eydis insisted, squeezing Jael's hand. 'She helped us get out of Tuura. She helped me read the book.'

'And you've got everyone making this new symbol?' Jael asked Axl.

He nodded from his throne. 'We set them to work as soon as Eydis drew it. But it's taken days to get the other symbol around the fort, so now we're back at the beginning.'

'Well, I've brought you a lot of new helpers,' Jael grinned. 'We need quills, vellum. We need everyone to have a copy of the symbol. Everyone needs to be carving it. What about in here?' Glancing around the hall, Jael almost expected to see her father emerge from its smoky corners, his great fur cloak draped over his broad shoulders, barking orders at someone. It was strange to be back. She blinked, trying to focus. 'Let's carve the symbol in here too, just to be safe. If we can't protect the whole fort in time, at least we could lock her out of the hall.'

'Good idea,' Aleksander said, smiling at Biddy, who'd just handed him a cup of something hot to drink. 'In my dream, the Widow had the symbol all over her cottage.'

No one knew what to make of that. The Widow's name had inspired fear for centuries, and Aleksander suddenly felt awkward, exposing his dreams, revealing his connection to her in such a large gathering of people.

Many of whom were strangers.

Erl Arnesson broke the silence. 'Why are we to believe a symbol will protect us?' he sneered. 'Why should we trust what this woman says? Legend has it that she's a murderous bitch!' He puffed up his broad chest, trying to impose himself on the group of mostly strangers gathered before the throne. He felt intimidated by their tall stature, determined to stake a claim for his Alekkans.

Ivaar had no inclination to speak at all. He had chosen to follow Jael and helped her defeat Borg and his brothers. She had seen inside his dreams.

He saw no reason not to believe her.

'The Widow has proven herself to be an ally,' Aleksander said firmly. 'For the prophecy to be realised, for Draguta to be defeated, Jael must be kept safe. The Widow is trying to protect her. And all of us too.'

Jael took a deep breath, trying to remain focused. 'We have little time for discussing what we think of the Widow. Not now. She's trying to warn us. We're in danger from Draguta and the book. And whatever we think of the Widow, we'd be fools to ignore her warning.' She peered at Edela, who sat next to Amma, her hands wrapped around a cup, her brow furrowed. 'We need to prepare now before it's too late.'

'I agree with Jael,' Edela said. 'Something is coming. We must prepare to be attacked. Soon.'

Axl was overcome by a sudden fog, intimidated by his sister and the warriors who were busy glaring at her. 'I agree,' he muttered, trying to deepen his voice, hoping to sound more like a king. 'Jael, I... I think you and I need to talk.'

Jael turned to her brother in surprise, but seeing the barely-masked panic in Axl's eyes, she nodded.

***

Runa didn't want to cry, but Fyn looked so pale. So weak. She gently touched the scratches on his face, blinking away her tears. 'What is this from? What happened to you?'

Fyn grinned happily, so pleased to see her. 'Ravens.'

'Ravens?'

'You don't want to know, Mother.'

'It's what they say is coming now,' Thorgils mumbled from behind Runa. 'Ravens, wolves. Something magical.'

Fyn wriggled, trying to sit up.

'Best you stay there, my long-legged friend,' Thorgils growled. 'This hall will be the safest place to be soon. And you're right where your mother can keep an eye on you.' He turned to Bram, who stood beside him. 'Come on, Uncle, we need to see what we can do to help. It's going to be a long night.' And winking at Fyn, he patted Runa on the shoulder. 'I'll be back in the morning to see how you're both faring. Nothing much you can do now but try to get some sleep.'

Bram smiled at Runa, nodded at Fyn, and turned to follow his giant nephew through the door.

Fyn glanced at his mother, who suddenly looked as though she was about to faint. 'Are you alright?' he wondered weakly. 'Mother?'

'Yes, I am. Now, are you sure that I can't find you something to eat? You do look very thin.'

***

Jael helped Axl to a chair, then hurried back to close his chamber door. She felt impatient, wanting to check on Fyn, needing to talk to Eadmund, eager to speak to Edela and Eydis. But Axl was the King of Brekka now, and she couldn't dismiss him as just her annoying little brother anymore.

'You look better,' Jael said, taking the seat opposite him, warming her hands over the fire that burned between them. It wasn't an especially cold evening, but the sea wind had numbed every part of her, and she was grateful for the warmth of the flames. 'How's your leg?'

'Healing,' Axl said. 'But I didn't want to talk about me. I wanted to talk about you.'

Jael frowned. '*Me*?'

'You need to lead us,' Axl said plainly. He looked down at his leg. 'I... can't. Not like this. Not yet. If Father were alive, he would choose you, we both know that. I don't know why he ever thought to make me his heir in the first place.'

Jael leaned towards him. 'Not even Father knew how to be a king at first. You just need some time. I'll help you. We can work together. And when this is over, when we get that book and defeat Draguta, you'll have the time to find your way. Don't worry, it will come.'

'I want Jaeger Dragos,' Axl said suddenly, his eyes sharpening. 'Can you do that? Can you kill him?'

'I hope so,' his sister smiled. 'I think I have to.'

'Good. If there is anything I can do to help you, I will, but for now, Jael, you must lead us.'

***

Jaeger smiled as he squeezed Meena's hand. It was a balmy night, and her fingers were slippery. She shook uncontrollably as she walked slowly next to him, almost fighting against him as he led her away from the castle. They were following the black-robed figure of Morana, who had no intention of waiting for either of them.

Jaeger felt a sense of anticipation stirring, eager to discover what Draguta had planned. Neither Morana nor Meena could tell him, but his hopes were high. He had seen what Morana could do with the book, but she didn't know it like Draguta, and his body tingled at the thought of what destruction she would unleash. 'Hurry,' he implored, tugging Meena forward. 'We're the last ones!'

Meena didn't want to hurry, but Jaeger was hurting her. He was so strong.

She had no choice. No choice at all.

Draguta had said that she was a dreamer, and it was all Meena could think about. She wondered if Draguta was merely teasing her, as Varna had, as Morana did, for how *could* she be a dreamer? She couldn't see anything, even when she closed her eyes and tried. All she found was darkness.

Morana spun around, glaring at her. 'Hurry up, little mouse! I'm sure you don't want to keep Draguta waiting!'

***

Jael could almost hear her father's voice bellowing orders as she watched the helmsmen steering their precious ships out of the harbour, around to the neighbouring cove. The night sky was dark, now threatening rain, but Jael's mind was alert, eager to start their preparations, ignoring her body's need to head for the nearest bed.

Andala had been under attack countless times when Ranuf Furyck was the King of Brekka, and he had scrambled his well-drilled warriors quickly. Many of them were still here. They knew how to prepare. None more so than Gant, who was shepherding everyone around with ease, his familiar frown carved deep into his forehead.

Andala would never feel the same without her father, but

having Gant there made everything easier. And soon, it would for Axl too.

Jael scanned the piers, searching for the familiar shape of Eadmund.

She found Ivaar instead.

'Perhaps I should have gone with Toki after all,' Ivaar said wryly, watching his two ships leave the harbour. 'It would have been the safer choice.'

'You never struck me as someone who wanted safe.'

Ivaar laughed, trying to avoid her eyes. He didn't even want to admit to himself how much power she had over him. Yet, here he was, ready to do whatever she asked. Jael Furyck's oathman now.

Not a lord, nor a king. Barely a man.

'No, that's true,' he admitted. 'But I do prefer to be alive, and it seems that this Draguta woman is intent on killing us all.'

'She is.'

'And you think you can keep her out? With a few symbols?' Ivaar wondered, his shoulders tightening as Eadmund strode towards them.

'We've done it before,' Jael said. 'When The Following used the book against us in Tuura. They're more powerful than you know. We can only hope this new symbol will work and keep them all out.'

Ivaar edged away, but Jael reached out, grabbing his arm, keeping him there as Eadmund stopped before them. 'We must be united in trying to survive,' she urged, looking from one brother to the other. 'You both have children. If you can't think of any reason not to try and kill each other, think of them. If we're fighting ourselves instead of Draguta and The Following, we're just putting everything we care about at risk.' Jael shivered suddenly, feeling an unexpected urge to touch her belly, but she sucked it in instead and pushed back her shoulders. 'Let's line the catapults around the walls. Make sure each one has some sea-fire jars beside it. Check if any are ready yet, otherwise, we'll need to bring the leftover jars back from *Sea Bear*, which we should do anyway. Every catapult will need someone commanding the crew and the archers. I'll leave you two to sort that out between yourselves.'

And realising that she hadn't spoken to Marcus yet, Jael turned back to the fort, striding away from them both.

Ivaar and Eadmund looked after her, neither one knowing what to say.

'Well, this is awkward,' Thorgils muttered as he walked up behind them, deciding that there was little he could do to avoid Ivaar, and there was no point even trying until things returned to normal.

'Ahhh, the man who stole my wife and children. My dreamer too,' Ivaar snarled, unable to stop himself. 'You look well, Thorgils. And happy. I'm not surprised.'

'According to our queen, Isaura won't be your wife for long,' Thorgils growled, pushing his chest towards Ivaar. 'And your dreamer was never yours, to begin with, and as for your children...' He loosened his shoulders and stepped back, realising that there was more to consider than just his feelings now. 'They are yours, and always will be. I have no desire to claim them.'

Ivaar was surprised by the change in Thorgils' tone. He sighed. It was very late, and he felt too tired to argue. 'Good. I have no wish to lose my children, but you are more than welcome to my wife.' Fighting the urge to walk away, Ivaar glared at his brother. 'We should go and move the catapults. Work out whose men should be positioned where.' His lips barely moved, and his eyes were cold, but his boots remained on the wooden boards of the pier, deciding that it was time to stop running away.

***

Draguta stood before the sparking bonfire, watching as the long row of Followers slipped through the stones, one by one. Their familiar black robes made her frown.

She remembered these people.

They had been allies once. Well, in their minds, at least.

The book had been hers, but The Following had wanted her to use it for their own ends, always wanting to find their way to Raemus. It had not ended well back then. And now?

Draguta smiled, listening to their scrambled thoughts.

They were so desperate for their master. So suspicious of her.

And confused. Wanting her to want Raemus and the Darkness as they did. Unsettled that she did not. They were suspicious but also curious. Eager to see what she could do. Excited by the prospect of using the book again.

And they did not like Morana Gallas. Or her niece. Or even Jaeger Dragos.

An untrusting bunch of self-serving men and women then, Draguta thought, lowering the hood of her cloak. It was white, to match her dress, trimmed with white fur.

Pleased to finally see Morana and Meena, she motioned them forward. 'You will serve the potion,' she said, enjoying the grimace on Morana's face. There was enough light from the sliver of moon for her to see that. 'And then make the symbol as I showed you.'

Morana nodded obediently, clearing her mind.

Meena dropped her eyes to the ground, feeling a surge of nausea. The fragrant smoke from the fire blew towards her.

She tried not to inhale it.

Morana elbowed her. 'You carry the bowl,' she hissed, and picking up the copper cup, she led her niece towards the Followers who had quietly taken their places around the enormous blood circle that Draguta had cast.

Meena gripped the bowl, avoiding Jaeger's eyes as she passed.

'Shall I join the circle?' Jaeger asked.

'Why?' Draguta snorted, wondering why he was there at all. 'Do you think that *you* can help us? With what power? Are you a dreamer, Jaeger dear?'

'I have seen what they have seen,' Jaeger insisted. 'When Morana cast her spells, I saw everything. I experienced it as the Followers did.'

Draguta laughed. 'Well, you may drum for me, I suppose. That would be helpful. You can do that, can't you?'

Jaeger looked offended, but he dropped his eyes and said nothing. There was, he had discovered, little he could say to move Draguta in any direction that she didn't wish to go.

'Good!' Draguta smiled as Jaeger walked over to the drum that lay near the fire. 'Stay in the middle of the circle!' she called after him, running her eyes over the hooded figures. They sought her attention and shunned it at the same time. Not Yorik Elstad, though. His eyes were fixed on her, inviting her company.

Draguta walked over to him, taking his rough hands in her smooth ones. 'You will see everything in a different light soon, and then you will no longer think of Raemus.' And dropping his hands, Draguta took a deep breath, turning back to the book, which sat on the ancient sacrifice stone, waiting expectantly for her to begin.

***

Marcus had remained in the hall, hoping to find a moment to speak with Jael, but she had been in and out, checking on everyone and everything, and eventually, his eyes felt so heavy that he wondered if he should just head for his cottage and try to see her in the morning.

But then, there she was.

'I think Hanna is safe,' Jael said quickly, motioning for him to sit opposite her. She leaned forward, grabbing a handful of nuts from the bowl that sat between them.

'You had a dream?'

'I did,' Jael mumbled. 'The Dragos family has left Hest on a ship. I think Hanna is with them, but she has a stone, so I can't see her. It's more of a feeling.'

Marcus wanted to let out a huge sigh of relief, but he knew that he wouldn't be able to until Hanna was standing before him. 'And where are they headed?'

Jael frowned. 'I don't know. If Hanna's on the ship with them, I imagine she'll take everyone to Tuura, but I hope not. She strikes me as clever, and it would not be clever to go to Tuura until she knows it's safe.'

Marcus nodded. 'She is. Clever.'

'Then, all you can do is wait. Give it a few days. She may send word, or they may come here. I wish I could tell you more.'

He looked worried, Jael thought. Panicked.

They all did.

It was hard not knowing what was coming next. Yet, with four dreamers in the fort now, she could only hope that one of them would discover another clue, and quickly, before Draguta found a way to hurt them all.

***

The rasping hiss confused Yorik. He couldn't tell if it was coming from Draguta. She was chanting. He could see her lips moving, but he didn't think it was her making that noise.

It sounded like a snake. An adder. He had seen one as a boy, on a trip to Silura with his father. He had never seen one in Hest, though the merchants from the Fire Lands brought every kind of luxury and oddity to tempt their wealthy Hestian customers, many of whom had an appetite for the exotic.

But here? At the Crown of Stones?

A snake?

The smoke was more potent than anything Yorik had experienced before, and the drumming was disorienting. The dull, rhythmic beat felt as though it was pounding straight through his body.

He wondered if it was the sound of his heart.

But that rasping?

And then he felt it.

Morana, standing next to him, gasped. She had felt it too: the slithering, wet creature weaving its way around their legs. She shook her head, confused, desperate to look down, but Draguta would be furious, she knew, if one of them broke the flow of her chanting with a sudden movement.

Was she chanting? It sounded like someone else.

A man's voice, almost hissing.

Not human at all.

Morana squeezed Yorik's hand, feeling as though her feet were no longer on the ground; as though she wasn't inside her body anymore.

Then the hissing stopped, and she could hear Draguta's voice.

'You seek power!' Draguta cried. 'The power to be free! To live in the Darkness with your master! To exist as limitless, lifeless beings, freed from the oppressive yoke of humanity! You seek the blissful mercy of that dark void. Desperate to be reunited with the Father of the Gods! But why do you think that *he* is the one to gift you this salvation?' Draguta's arms were wide, her eyes glazed, searching the circle, but the Followers were thick in the mire of hypnotic smoke, and no one even blinked an acknowledgement of her words.

Jaeger's head was hazy as he watched from the middle of the circle. He glanced at Meena, whose eyes were big and terrified as she swayed next to Morana. He blinked. Perhaps Meena always looked that terrified, he thought dreamily, trying to keep his hand tapping the drum in time to Draguta's voice.

'You wish to be reunited with Raemus?' Draguta called. 'Well, let me change your minds!' And she started chanting again, leaving the fire now, and walking around the circle, touching the blood symbol that Morana had drawn on each Follower's forehead. Placing her hand over the symbol, she closed her eyes, murmuring, before moving on to the next Follower, and then the next.

Draguta stopped before Morana and Meena. They were as lost as the rest of them, their eyes attempting to focus on the white-robed woman before them.

Cocking her head to one side, Draguta smiled, and turning back to the fire, she held up her hand, motioning for Jaeger to stop drumming.

Into the silence that crept around them like mist, Draguta laughed and clapped her hands together.

And one by one, the Followers dropped to the ground.

***

Jael's eyes felt heavy as she looked at Eydis, who lay under a pile of furs on one of the beds along the side of the hall. But there was too much to do. There would be time for sleep when they had made themselves safe.

Jael took the piece of wood Aleksander had carved for her out of her pouch, running a finger over the symbol, wishing she knew why the Widow was helping them.

Wondering who she was.

'You're a hard woman to pin down,' Aleksander grinned. 'I've been looking for you everywhere.'

'Why?'

He glanced at the piece of wood. 'To talk about that.'

Jael was intrigued, glancing around the hall, still full of

people and noise, even at this late hour. She was amazed that Eydis was sleeping at all. 'Let's sit over there.' And slipping the wood back into her pouch, Jael headed for an empty table in the darkest corner of the hall.

'You're sure you have the time?' Aleksander wondered with a smile. 'Being in charge of everything as you are?'

'I'm sure,' Jael said impatiently. 'Now, tell me about your dream.'

'The Widow wants you to come to her. She has things to tell you. She has the other copy of the book you need.'

'The book?' Jael's eyes widened, then narrowed suspiciously. 'The Book of Aurea? *She* has the other copy?'

Aleksander nodded.

'Sounds like a trap.'

'She's our friend,' he tried. 'I don't think it's a trap.'

'We're using this symbol now because she came to you in a dream, but what if it's all wrong? What if she's playing games? Luring us closer? Acting like a friend when she's really the enemy?'

Aleksander had thought the same thing, many times. 'I don't know,' he admitted. 'But she helped me. Saved my life. And when I was little, my mother used to tell me about her. About how she was the person I should turn to if I ever needed help. Whenever I doubt the Widow's intentions, I always come back to that.'

Jael stared at him. 'Well, that's if Fianna wasn't bound when she told you that.'

Aleksander swallowed, not wanting to think about what The Following had done to his mother. She had killed herself because of them, he was sure. He still couldn't get the image of her horrific death out of his head.

'Aleksander?'

He swallowed. 'Think about it. We can talk again tomorrow. It's a risk, I know, but if the Widow can help us defeat Draguta and destroy The Following, then it's worth it, don't you think?'

***

The Followers didn't get up, and Meena wasn't sure they ever would. She held her breath, looking from Jaeger to Draguta and then Morana, who was the only other person still standing in the collapsed circle of black-robed bodies.

Jaeger, still holding the drum, was speechless, his mouth hanging open.

Morana thought she'd pissed herself.

She blinked slowly, wondering for a moment if it was an illusion, part of the spell, but looking down at Yorik's face, she could see very clearly that he was dead. The symbol was twisting like a snake on his forehead, covering his face with spreading red lines. Consuming him in a burning, heated rush.

Draguta didn't stop laughing as the symbol worked its magic, destroying each body, one by one, until they were standing in the middle of a large circle of hot red ash.

The smell was unbearable, and Jaeger spluttered, unable to stop himself retching.

Morana didn't move as Draguta turned back to her. She thought she could hear that hissing again, but she didn't dare turn her eyes away from her mistress.

For that was who Draguta was now.

'You have changed your mind, Morana!' Draguta exclaimed. 'I am pleased!' She rubbed her hands together. 'And hungry. Aren't you? Let us head back to the castle and see what we can find to eat! I must make my plans for the Furycks, then you shall gather what I need. Tomorrow, we will return and carry on with our work. One by one, we will destroy everyone who stands in our way.'

Morana's legs wouldn't move, but Draguta didn't notice as she glided back to the book. Eventually, glancing down at the smoking pile of ash that had been Yorik, the only thought that entered Morana's head was how glad she was that it wasn't her.

CHAPTER SEVENTEEN

Edela frowned as she held onto Alaric. He was supposed to be walking her to the hall, but she wondered who was actually helping who. He seemed unsteady on his feet. What had happened in Tuura, and what felt as though it was about to happen in Andala, had left him shaken, and Edela could feel fear coursing through his frail body. She patted his arm. 'You're safer here than you ever were in Tuura,' she reassured him. 'With all of us. With Jael. She will keep us safe.'

Alaric turned to Edela in surprise. 'Well, I... yes, I suppose you're right,' he conceded. 'It all feels so strange, though, what is happening. Although, I suppose it is nothing that hasn't happened before. But it was so long ago now. I think we all started to believe they were just stories. Not things that actually happened.'

Alaric was mumbling, his sagging chin on his chest, and Edela wondered if she'd heard him correctly. 'What do you mean? What stories?'

Alaric's eyes narrowed as he turned to her. 'The dark magic. The powerful dreamers. The gods and their creatures. I used to write about them all. Read about them too.' He felt wistful, remembering the familiar sound of his quill scratching across vellum as he sat in the scribe's chamber in the temple, working by candlelight, day and night. 'The dreamers saw a lot, but I was never sure if their dreams came true, or if they had just been imagining the things I read about... the prophecies I wrote down. Perhaps they were simply telling stories to amuse the elders?'

'Well, I'd say we're about to find out,' Edela whispered, stopping just before the hall steps, seeing Aedan and Aron hard at work carving symbols around the thick frame of the doors.

'I hope not,' Alaric shivered. 'What I read? That is the stuff of nightmares!'

***

Jaeger had no appetite, and glancing at Morana and Meena, he could see that their own bowls were untouched. He had expected to come away from the Crown of Stones feeling exhilarated, but he had lain awake for much of the night, his head reeling from the smoke, too disturbed to even speak to Meena.

He thought of the book and how different he'd felt when it had been his.

How vulnerable he was without it.

They all were.

'But you are all so quiet,' Draguta murmured, peeling an orange. She could smell the sweet juice and was desperate to taste it, but even with all the power she had, she knew that she could not. She popped a segment into her mouth anyway, savouring the pleasant sensation as her teeth pierced the fruit's thin membrane. Draguta held out the orange to Morana. 'Have some.'

Morana frowned, not wanting any, but she took it and tore off a segment, shoving it into her mouth with barely any awareness of what she was doing. She kept seeing Yorik's face as it crumbled to ash. She had never seen anything like it.

To think that all the Followers were dead...

It didn't feel real.

Morana had barely tolerated their incessant, whining

demands on Yorik, but she took no pleasure in their deaths. They had followed Raemus and sought his return as eagerly as she had, but for some reason, Draguta had chosen to save her and Meena while she burned the rest of them.

Morana wondered why.

'And you, girl,' Draguta smiled at Meena. 'What are you thinking about?' But looking at Meena's morose face, so plain and in need of a good scrub, she turned away in disgust, wondering why she had let her live. Help, Draguta reminded herself, reaching for her goblet. She needed assistants to help her prepare for spells and rituals. To do those menial things that were beneath her. The two hairy trolls had proven useful, so she would let them live for now.

Enjoying the silence, Draguta sipped her wine, feeling a warm glow in her chest as it trickled down her throat, still basking in her victory over The Following.

How easily she had led them to their deaths.

Those black-robed fools were long overdue their end. And now they were where they belonged: in the eternal darkness of the Dolma.

Not the Darkness.

But it would be dark.

Draguta laughed. 'Well, I'm not sure what company you're going to be, but at least you'll be busy, preparing what I need for my next spell. And Jaeger, while these two miserable creatures assist me, I expect to see you out on the square, down at the piers. I want to know that our warriors are preparing. That our ships are filling the harbour. To conquer all of Osterland, we are going to require a great many things, but none more important than an army of one hundred thousand men!'

Jaeger blinked, turning to Morana, who stared back at him in surprise.

It sounded impossible, but neither of them dared tell Draguta that.

***

Breakfast was a rushed affair, but it gave everyone a chance to discuss who needed to do what as they grabbed a flatbread and smothered it in honey or soft cheese, or, where Thorgils was concerned, both.

'Maybe you need to take a plate with you?' Biddy suggested, watching how many flatbreads Thorgils was trying to carry through the door; securing some under his bearded chin.

He couldn't even mumble back because his mouth was full, but he winked at her, motioning to the table with his head, indicating that he would certainly be returning for more.

Biddy laughed as she helped Eydis inside, trying to decide where to put her.

'I'm not a puppy,' Eydis muttered, sensing that Biddy was trying to decide where to put her. 'Or an invalid.'

'No, of course you're not,' Biddy said, moving her out of the way of Erl Arnesson as he barrelled past with his equally wide brother, arms flailing about. 'But you don't know Andala yet, do you? And if you're not careful, you'll be knocked over by one of these men who don't appear to notice anyone who isn't as tall as a tree! Now, come on, I see Ayla and her husband. I'm sure you'd like to sit down and talk to her?'

Eydis forgot all about being irritable and nodded eagerly, barely remembering the time when she had been frightened and suspicious of Ayla.

'Hello, Eydis,' Ayla smiled. 'Here, sit on the bench beside me. You'll make better company than Bruno, who won't stop moaning about staying in the hall. He wants to get out there and move catapults about!'

Bruno frowned at his wife. 'I don't think I said that, but yes, I'm a bit tired of being treated like an invalid. I'm sure there's something I could do to help.'

'Well, why don't you sit somewhere and carve a symbol?'

Biddy suggested, pouring Eydis a cup of buttermilk and placing it next to her hand. 'I can get Entorp to gather what you need.'

Bruno smiled gratefully at Biddy. 'I can't promise that I'd be any good at it, but it's worth a try. As long as my healer won't get cross with me?'

Ayla kissed his hairy cheek. 'I'm sure she won't.'

Eydis was pleased to hear how happy Ayla sounded. Not at all like the sad dreamer she remembered from her time on Oss.

'How about a bowl of hot porridge, Eydis?' Biddy asked, glancing over at Edela, who was eating her breakfast with Alaric and Derwa. She ran her eyes quickly around the rest of the hall, reminding herself that she needed to see how Fyn was and then check on Axl's leg. And she couldn't remember if she'd even given the puppies something to eat before she'd left the cottage.

Eydis nodded, starting to recognise some of the sounds of the hall now. She could hear Amma in the distance, and Gisila, both of them talking to Axl, but no Jael or Eadmund.

Eadmund had barely spoken to her since they'd arrived.

'Do you know Samara?' Ayla asked suddenly, surprised by her question. The image of her aunt's face had suddenly popped into her mind.

'Samara?' Eydis stilled. 'My grandmother was called Samara. Samara Lund.'

'Was she?' Ayla felt a burst of happiness. She couldn't stop smiling.

'I never knew her,' Eydis murmured. 'Why?'

'Samara Lund was my mother's sister,' Ayla said. 'I didn't know about her until recently. After my mother died, I thought all of my family was gone, but now, it seems, I have you.' She put her arm around Eydis' shoulder, bringing her closer. 'I always thought you were special to me, Eydis, and now I know why.'

Eydis heard the warmth in Ayla's voice, felt the comfort of her arm, and then the tears rolling down her cheeks.

***

'And?' Aleksander whispered as he snuck up behind Jael, who was heading out of the fort towards the harbour to check on what Gant was up to.

'*And*?' Jael turned around, shielding her eyes from the sun. It was a warm morning, and she felt the urge to remove her cloak, but she didn't, not wanting to reveal what she was hiding beneath its loose-fitting fabric. At least she had thought to leave her thick bear-fur cloak behind on Oss and bring her old, much thinner, woollen one. But still, her cheeks were burning, and it made her irritable. 'And what?'

'Have you thought about what I said? About going to the Widow?' Aleksander asked, nodding at Kormac as he wandered past with Aron.

Jael shook her head. 'No, not yet. I don't know what I think about it. About her. It's hard to see how we can just leave. Axl needs both of us.'

'True. But it feels important. *She* feels important to what's about to happen. She wants to help you, and if the book she mentioned is the one you're after...'

Jael spotted Gant walking into one of the sheds by the piers, but she stopped and turned back to Aleksander. 'I'll think about it. And maybe even dream about it, if I ever get a moment to sleep again!' And grinning wearily at him, she disappeared after Gant.

***

'Jael,' Draguta sneered. 'Jael, Jael, Jael. What sort of a name is Jael?' She turned to Morana, expecting an answer.

Morana scratched her nose, not knowing what to say. 'I...

it's a stupid name,' she muttered dutifully.

'But even people with stupid names can cause problems,' Draguta warned, running her hand down the stalk of a flowering yarrow plant. Slicing through it with her knife, she handed the cutting to Meena, who carefully placed it into her basket. 'So we must stop her, and quickly.'

'She killed everyone in the temple,' Morana warned. 'All the Followers in Tuura. The dreamers and elders too.'

'Well, she has my thanks for that!' Draguta laughed. 'One less thing for us to worry about. The fools in that temple conspired for far too long, hoping to break Raemus out of his prison. Ha! And now they are there, shuddering in the darkness with him!' Draguta's eyes popped open as she rushed through the garden towards a long-seen plant. 'Oh, my dear friend, how I have missed your sweet scent!' Sighing, she bent down with her bone-handled knife and dug into the warm earth, feeling around the roots with her blade, easing them loose. 'There,' she said contentedly, lifting the plant towards Meena, who reached for it, but Draguta flapped her hand out of the way and laid the cutting into the basket herself. 'You do not have the hands for such delicate work, girl. Those hands look perfectly suited to my pestle, though. I shall have you grinding day and night. And you can kill a horse too. We are going to need a lot of blood!'

Meena gulped, terrified by the thought of what Draguta was planning next.

She had not believed it possible for things to get worse, but now she was trapped with someone more evil than Varna and Morana combined, and one wrong word, or look... one move in the wrong direction, and she would be as dead as Yorik and his Followers. Every raised hair on her arms told her that.

Nodding at Draguta, Meena dropped her eyes, trying her very best not to think of Berard.

***

'What do you think he's done to her?' Berard wondered quietly. His stump was throbbing, and he was trying to take his mind off the pain. The Saalan healers had given Irenna a tincture for when it became too much, but he'd already taken more than half of it, and Irenna was worried that they wouldn't have enough to get him through to Andala.

Staring across the white-capped waves, Karsten frowned. 'I don't know,' he admitted. He remembered the sight of Meena's battered face, and what Jaeger had done to his first wife. He didn't want to give Berard false hope, especially as Hanna believed that the book would slowly consume Jaeger's soul – if there was anything left of it now. 'He seems to want her company. Without you there, it will be easier for her. He has no reason to be jealous anymore.'

Berard was comforted by that thought, though not by the idea that he wasn't there to protect Meena. 'She is strong, you know.'

Karsten rolled a toothpick around his mouth.

'The way she killed Egil? Deciding to stay? She is strong.' Berard stumbled, groaning as he drew his stump towards his chest. He didn't like to touch it, to feel that there was nothing but a small lump of flesh hanging off his shoulder, but the pain was intense at times. He gritted his teeth.

'Come on, Brother,' Karsten said. 'I'll take you to Irenna. I'm sure she can spare another few drops of that tincture. I remember what it was like when I lost my eye. You just have to take the edge off, then you can think clearly again.' Karsten had spent all his time after his injury thinking about how he would gut the woman who had taken his eye.

Jael Furyck.

And now he was sailing towards her, asking for her help.

He clamped his teeth down on the toothpick, snapping it

in half.

***

'Have you seen Eydis this morning?' Jael wondered, stifling a yawn as she hurried to catch up with Eadmund, who was heading for the harbour gates.

Eadmund barely heard her. His mind was busy with thoughts of Evaine. 'No, not yet. Why?'

Jael was surprised by the disinterest in his voice. 'She was looking for you. And last night too. Have you spoken to her at all?'

Eadmund wasn't slowing down. 'I'll speak to her later.'

'Eadmund, wait!' Jael called, running after him.

He stopped, turning around, jiggling his leg, wanting to leave.

'Are you alright?' It wasn't what she wanted to say.

'Alright? As alright as everyone else, I suppose. There's a lot to do today. I've got things on my mind.'

Jael doubted there was anything on his mind other than Evaine and how quickly they could be reunited. It was getting worse. She could feel it. She could see it in his eyes, which were glaring at her as though she was his brother, not his wife.

'We need to build more catapults,' she said, trying to focus. 'If we're going to take a fleet down to Hest, we want to be able to attack them with sea-fire. We need to start getting more catapults onto the ships.'

Eadmund nodded. 'I'll talk to Beorn. See what he thinks is possible.' And spinning around, he disappeared before Jael could say another word.

***

Draguta opened her eyes and sat back, exhaling slowly. She was annoyed, but her anger did not burn as heatedly as it had before. Despite casting the seeing circle a handful of times now, she had seen nothing but clouds.

Unhelpful clouds.

She had tried using many different symbols, turning every page in the book, searching for help, but nothing would part those clouds.

It was so hot in Draguta's chamber that Morana was dripping with sweat as she waited by the fireplace, her long dress clinging to her like a wet rag. Her wild hair was defeated, hanging limply around her face. She could barely breathe, desperate to open the doors to the balcony, for surely fresh, cool air waited out there.

It wasn't just from the fire either. Draguta's servants had filled the room with beeswax candles, so as well as being too bright, it was unbearably sweet smelling.

She wanted to vomit.

But she kept her mouth closed, determined not to draw any attention to herself as she waited to be called upon. She felt imprisoned by an unfamiliar sense of fear. Being around Draguta felt as though she was walking across a soft ice lake, listening to the cracks, never knowing if the next step would be her last.

'She thinks she can stop me,' Draguta sighed. 'That she can simply hide away as though I have not even returned. But I will make her reveal herself. Tonight.' She turned to Morana, who nodded mutely. 'Now go and see where your niece has disappeared to. I want that blood! This spell will take us all day to prepare, but it will be worth it, Morana. You'll see!'

Eager to escape the glowing sauna and the threat of Draguta's wrath, Morana scurried to the door, gripping the handle with her hot hand.

'And Morana, you will do well to remember that I will reward your loyalty and your obedience. And, just like your friend, Yorik, I will also not hesitate to punish your deceit. It is best not to let your thoughts wander too far from where they need to be.'

Swallowing, Morana pulled open the door and hurried away.

***

After talking with Beorn about how many catapults they needed to build for the ships, and walking him around to the cove to look over their fleet, Eadmund finally headed back into the fort, realising that he hadn't eaten breakfast. He wandered towards the hall, trying to keep his focus on catapults and symbols and arrows.

It was impossible, though.

No matter how hard he tried, he couldn't stop seeing Evaine's terrified face. She was always crying out for him, urging him to come to her.

Needing him.

Eadmund clenched his jaw as he reached for the hall door, pulling it open, unable to think about anything except Evaine. It wasn't until he caught sight of his little sister, sitting all by herself, that he blinked, allowing himself to feel something that wasn't frustration or anger.

She looked so sad and alone, and he remembered their father and how brave Eydis had been after his sudden death; how scared she must feel in this new, big, loud place. And he started walking towards her, looking around to see if he could find an apple. Eydis loved apples more than anyone he knew. And, finding a bowl, he picked the reddest one and turned back to see that Amma had grabbed Eydis' hand and hurried her to the back of the hall, no doubt taking her to visit Fyn.

Eadmund sighed, biting into the apple, his mind quickly returning to thoughts of Hest and Evaine.

***

Meena stood over the horse, too upset to move.

She hadn't been able to kill the poor creature herself. She had dithered in the paddock all morning, not even daring to approach one of the horses until Morana arrived and led both her and the feeblest looking horse to Skoll's Tree. There, she had tied it to a low branch, puncturing its neck with her knife. And the slumped body of the old grey horse had been leaking its lifeblood ever since.

Turning away, Meena thought she might vomit.

'You think *this* is bad?' Morana hissed as she handed Meena the full bowl of blood and quickly replaced it with another. The horse was on its side now, its slow death approaching like a painful whisper. 'This is nothing. Nothing compared to what she will do to us! You want to end up like Yorik? Like the Followers?' Morana shook with discomfort, not taking any pleasure in draining the blood from the dying animal.

Not taking any pleasure in anything.

Her limbs jerked with fear as she tried to keep her mind on Draguta and the task she had set them. She was desperate for a breeze, but the air was still, trapping her in its humid grip.

She thought of Evaine and Morac, knowing that soon they would have company out on the ice.

CHAPTER EIGHTEEN

Jael watched her brother limping ahead of her next to Aedan and Aron. He seemed happy in their company; much more relaxed around people his own age, who didn't require him to make decisions every few minutes.

'You look like a woman who needs something to do!' Thorgils boomed, making her jump.

Jael turned around, eyeing him moodily. 'What are you doing sneaking up on people?'

'Sneaking?' Thorgils grinned. 'You couldn't hear these enormous boots of mine?'

'It's been too long since I gave you a good beating,' Jael decided, ignoring the muddy old boot he was determined to lift up and show her. 'If only you weren't so busy...'

Thorgils dropped his boot and lifted an eyebrow, tempted by a wooden sword and Jael Furyck in the training ring, but he sighed. 'You're right, I've got to get back to catapult making. Although, looking at that sky, I think it's about to piss down!'

Jael had noticed how dark it was too. It was only mid-afternoon, but the sky had suddenly turned an ominous dark grey, and she could sense a storm approaching. 'Best you hurry before you're building catapults in the rain, then!' And turning to the right, she left him to head in the other direction.

'A lucky escape for you, my queen!' Thorgils bellowed after her. 'I'm feeling particularly vicious today!'

Jael smiled, but she didn't look around. She felt strange, as though everything around her had blurred. As though time had slowed down so much that she could see what usually went unseen. And what she saw was a thick mist creeping towards her, curling around Andala.

Creeping closer.

Jael blinked, and her focus sharpened, but she didn't stop shivering.

***

The waves were as high as walls now.

Bayla clutched Kai to her chest, sliding into Irenna and Hanna, trying not to panic as she listened to the shrieking wind, peering at the worried faces of the crew. She heard Berard crying out as the ship rose up, slamming down onto the angry sea with a thump. Karsten and Haegen were on either side of him, trying to keep him still, but the waves were tipping over the deck now, and they were finding it hard to keep a firm grip on their brother as they sought to control their own bodies.

Bayla had no idea how far they were from Andala, but any hesitation she'd had about going there had been swept away by the growing storm. She closed her eyes and pushed Kai's little head closer to her chest, covering his exposed ear with her numb hand. The furious noise of the wind was a constant reminder of the threat they faced, and he didn't need to hear it.

Haegen glanced at Irenna, who had her arms around their two daughters; at Hanna, who had his son, Valder, on her knee; at Nicolene, who had a wailing Eron in her arms. Their faces, hiding beneath their hoods, were pale and wet; terrified eyes jumping around in the dark afternoon.

The ship was creaking, and Ulf, the helmsman, was wiping the rain out of his eyes, and Berard was whimpering next to him, desperate for more of the tincture. But there was none, and Haegen wasn't sure that it would even matter soon.

Hanna could feel Valder shuddering against her. She had wrapped her cloak around the boy, trying to keep him warm, but she didn't think that it was the cold making him shake. The ship groaned, tipping to the side, and she knocked into Irenna.

Peering up at the clouds, Hanna tried to see if it was a real storm.

Or something else.

She wasn't sure if she wanted to know the answer.

***

Jael rubbed her cold hands together, eager to get to the hall, but wanting to check on Tig and Leada first. Turning for the stables, she banged into Marcus.

'Oh!' he exclaimed, looking embarrassed, holding up his hands. 'I'm sorry.'

'Are you lost?'

'No, just taking a break, trying to feel my fingers again. And my back.' He smiled awkwardly, not knowing what to say to her. 'I think I'd better go and carve another symbol before that storm hits.'

'Mmmm, I'd be quick if I were you. Looks like it's almost here,' Jael said, turning away into the dark afternoon, shivering. It was suddenly so cold. Her breath puffed out from numb lips, and she picked up her pace, pulling her hood down over her face.

It felt even colder in the stables, and Jael didn't stop as she hurried to Tig, already thinking about warming herself by a blazing fire in the hall. She paused, surprised to see Eadmund standing outside Tig's stall.

'How's Leada?' she asked.

'Happy not to be on that ship, I think,' he said, noticing his breath smoking. 'Though it felt warmer at sea. Where did summer go?'

'It's the gods,' Jael said, surprising herself.

Eadmund frowned. 'When did you become a dreamer?'

'When I was born,' Jael admitted, holding her hand out for Leada to nuzzle. 'I just tried very hard to ignore it. Edela knew, but I wouldn't listen to her, or it. I didn't want to be a woman in a robe, telling fortunes. Having visions. I'm no healer. I don't even like people. It wasn't the life I wanted.'

The stable doors rattled loudly, and Tig whinnied, nudging Jael with his cold black muzzle, reminding her that she had come to see him too. She stroked his cheek, digging into her pouch with her other hand, looking for a treat.

'Well, I think everyone around here is going to be grateful for whatever you can see about this Draguta woman, and what she plans to do to you,' Eadmund mumbled, looking away.

Jael gave Tig half a stale flatbread. 'To both of us, Eadmund. We must defeat her together.' She edged closer, searching his eyes. 'You're still in there. And if you can just hold on, we'll find a way to set you free.' She touched his arm.

Eadmund froze. He saw Evaine's face, and part of him wanted to shake Jael's hand away, but he didn't. 'You think I can be free?' he asked harshly. 'I've never been free, Jael.'

Jael blinked, trying to hold on to what she'd just seen, but it disappeared too quickly, and she was left confused.

Eadmund moved away from her, at last. 'I have to find Gant. There's still a lot to do.' And turning his head, he hurried out of the stables.

***

Meena swallowed as the balcony doors shook, then flinched as

Morana hit her on the back of the head.

'You expect me to do this by myself?' she growled, sick of Draguta's chamber, and even more sick of Meena's irritating company. She had twitched and sniffed all afternoon, still moping over the dead horse, barely lifting a finger to help her prepare Draguta's potions.

What was wrong with the idiot girl?

'I was just listening to the storm,' Meena mumbled. 'How are we going to do the spell in this weather?'

Morana shook her head dismissively. 'It's never stopped us before. And I can't imagine that anything will stop Draguta. She seems to have a way of getting what she wants.' Morana saw Yorik's face and felt strange. Almost sad. Rubbing the sweat out of her eyes, she shook her hair and straightened up. 'Now, start grinding those bones. I need to check on the cauldron.'

Meena nodded obediently and grabbed the stone pestle, pushing it down into the bowl to break up the little bones Morana had scattered into it, grinding them slowly into dust. Morana had collected the bones herself, and Meena could still see little bits of flesh on some. She looked away, not wanting to imagine what poor creature they had come from.

'Why does Draguta think you're a dreamer?' Morana asked, stirring the cauldron, inhaling the rancid odour of the potion. It made a wonderful respite from the stink of beeswax. 'When have you ever had a dream?' She peered at her niece, trying to see anything inside that thick head of hers, but she couldn't.

Meena shrugged. 'I haven't.'

'And if you did?' Morana scowled. 'I doubt you'd even know what to do with it!' She cackled as she joined Meena at the table, ripping up a handful of wormwood leaves and adding them to the bowl. 'Keep going, little mouse. Don't stop now. Before you know it, Draguta will return, and we don't want to incur her wrath, do we? Not when we've seen what that wrath can do!'

Meena shuddered, the smell of the Followers' ash still in

her nostrils.

***

They huddled around the hall's roaring fires, disturbed by the sudden drop in temperature; by the violent storm shaking the old walls, and the booms of thunder crashing overhead too.

'Bet you wish you'd brought your fluffy cloak,' Thorgils grinned, offering Jael a cup of ale.

She shook her head, then tried to nod it at the same time. 'Right now, I'd rather have something hot to drink,' she admitted, shivering. 'But yes, I do miss my other cloak. Maybe you could lend me yours?'

'Not likely. Isaura's already made plans to join me under mine!' And with a wink, Thorgils slipped away to find Isaura, which was easy – he just had to follow the sound of Mads' bellowing voice.

'I'd offer you mine, but it looks no better than yours,' Aleksander smiled.

'Well, it used to keep me warm enough when I lived here,' Jael said. 'But this feels as cold as Oss.'

'I agree,' Biddy muttered, handing them cups of honeyed milk. 'Here, these will warm you up. I was making one for Eydis, and I thought you two might like something hot to drink.'

'You're perfect, Biddy,' Aleksander said, kissing Biddy on the top of her curly head.

She brushed him away. 'Least I can do for the two people who rushed into a burning fort to save my life.'

'Well, it's the least *I* could do for the person who rushed into a burning fort to save my dogs,' Jael smiled, raising her cup, jumping as another clap of thunder exploded above the hall.

Biddy looked nervous. 'Sounds like the gods are angry.'

'Mmmm,' Jael murmured, thinking the same thing. 'Though, hopefully not at us.'

***

Draguta stood in the middle of Hest's empty cobblestoned square, her arms raised to the dark storm clouds swirling above her head. She was wet through, her white cloak and dress clinging to her tall, slender body, her dark hair trailing down her back like snakes. But she was smiling as the rain washed over her face. 'You think you can stop me?' she laughed, shivering in the darkness. 'But you are powerless against me! Powerless against my book!' She glanced at Jaeger, who wasn't smiling as he stood before her, drenched and cold.

Jaeger had no idea who Draguta was talking to, but he wanted to get inside and have someone light a fire. It felt like winter.

He shook his head.

Winter in Hest never felt this cold.

'Come, we must go to the catacombs!' Draguta said happily, ignoring his grumbles as she strode past him, eager to see if she still remembered the way. 'There is one more item I need!'

***

When the storm first appeared on the horizon, Ulf had quickly aimed his ship for the Brekkan coastline. And though the clouds, the wind, the rain, and now, the night sky had conspired to keep him from retaining a clear picture of where they were, he had trusted his gut and kept going, knowing that their only chance for survival was to get to shore quickly.

His ship was his livelihood - his and his men's - and he wasn't about to see it wrecked by the beast of a storm coming their way. Squinting, Ulf followed the line of his man's arm. Rain lashed his face, the howling wind trying to push him backwards, but he was sure that he'd seen a glimpse of land. And, gripping his tiller even tighter, he pulled it back, watching as the ship slowly turned.

Hanna cringed as another bolt of lightning lit up the black sky. She had heard of someone struck by lightning, and it didn't sound like the sort of death she would welcome. The ship rocked, and she rocked with it, trying to soothe the little boy who was sobbing against her now, just as desperate as she was for the deafening noise to stop.

It was so cold that Hanna couldn't feel her face, though she was certain her nose was running down it.

Closing her eyes, she tried to take her mind off the storm. She thought of Aleksander, remembering when she had said goodbye to him as he darted out of her bed all those months ago. His eyes were so full of pain, and yet, part of her felt as though he'd almost wanted to stay.

At least that was what she told herself.

Wherever he was, she hoped that he was safe.

***

Entorp sipped his ale and sighed, happy to be out of the storm; relieved that its noisy arrival had meant a break from carving the symbol for a while. His hands were blistered, and his back was aching from crouching in all sorts of strange positions over the past few days, though he knew that he would have to get back to work as soon as dawn broke. They had not yet carved enough of the new symbol around the walls. But they had made a useful beginning, and he was hopeful of finishing it tomorrow.

He didn't have a good feeling, though, when he looked around the hall. Edela kept glancing up at the rafters, when her eyes weren't fixed on the doors. Eydis looked worried as she stood yawning beside her, waiting for Biddy, and the other dreamer, Ayla, appeared just as tense. He hadn't seen Jael for some time, but he imagined that she'd look much the same.

Entorp took a deep breath, realising that there was little any of them could do now but wait. He glanced to his left, conscious of someone staring at him.

'You going to keep that jug all to yourself?' Erl Arnesson growled.

Entorp shook his head, pushing the ale jug towards him.

And grabbing it with a grunt, Erl refilled his cup. They had good ale in the King's Hall, he decided. It wouldn't be the worst place to die if the ale kept coming. He turned back to Thorgils and Bram, busy debating the best way into Helsabor, while Ivaar sat opposite them, trying to avoid the unwavering stare of Bruno Adea, who, Erl thought, looked ready to kill him.

Having some experience of the devious ways of Ivaar Skalleson now, Erl was sure he had good reason.

'We don't know what else they can do,' Bram insisted. 'This woman? The Following? They can control people. Make them do things.'

'So they say, and I believe them. I mean, look at Eadmund,' Thorgils sighed.

Ivaar frowned, suddenly more interested in the conversation.

Thorgils edged further away from him, scanning the hall for Isaura. She had disappeared some time ago to help Jael's mother and aunt, who were busy making sure that everyone had a bed for the night. She hadn't returned.

Perhaps she didn't like the company he was keeping?

'What's wrong with Eadmund?' Ivaar wondered.

Bram glanced at Thorgils, ever so slightly arching an eyebrow in warning.

Thorgils turned to Ivaar, his eyes as angry as the storm

rattling the hall. 'He's got a brother who keeps plotting to kill him and take his throne. A brother who won't accept the fact that his father didn't choose him.'

Ivaar smiled, ignoring the insult, but feeling the sting of it nonetheless. His instinct was to fight back; to lurch off his bench and wrap his hands around Thorgils' thick throat, but he bit his teeth together and said nothing, looking instead at Erl. 'Where's your brother, then?'

'Don't look at me for company, Bastard!' Earl spat. 'Your treachery killed my cousins, and you'll pay a heavy price for that one day. Not even the gods will forgive a worthless piece of shit like you!'

Thorgils blinked, trying not to laugh, but when he glimpsed Ivaar's face, it was suddenly easy, because he saw Mads.

Entorp frowned, deciding that it was better to go and get some sleep rather than sit and listen to the battle of insults. Instinct told him that it would only get worse.

He stood, nodding to the men, and took his leave.

***

It had been a long time since Draguta had seen the catacombs. They were not as she remembered them. The skulls lining the crumbling walls of the tunnels were new. New but grotesque, Draguta decided as she glided after Jaeger. It was as though the entire place had been crudely made by ham-fisted slaves.

Jaeger would have to do something about it.

They reached the antechamber, where Yorik had brought Jaeger only days before, and he swallowed, reminded of The Following's violent end. He wasn't sorry that they were dead, but he was acutely aware of how quickly he could become the next heap of ash that Draguta stood laughing over.

Draguta cleared her throat, pointing to the archway. Jaeger

walked ahead of her, his flaming torch lighting the way. 'I'll take that,' Draguta snapped, reaching for the torch, not wanting to be without the light. 'What we need is under there.' And she motioned towards her coffin. It was still open, its thick stone lid lying beside it on the ground. She shuddered, not remembering the experience of being entombed in there, but not welcoming the reminder of her lengthy fate imprisoned in the Dolma.

Jaeger peered into the empty stone coffin. There was nothing inside it except the lingering stench of death and decay.

Draguta rolled her eyes. '*Underneath* it,' she said slowly. 'There is a crypt. You will have to move it out of the way.'

It was a long coffin with thick sides, but Jaeger was a powerful man, and he shunted his shoulder against it, sweating with the effort as Draguta stood behind him, impatiently tapping her foot.

Scuffing his boots in the dusty gravel, Jaeger grunted and hissed through gritted teeth, finally scraping the coffin across the floor. Stepping back, he panted, trying to catch his breath, his arms shaking as the dust clouded around him.

Draguta smiled, delighted to see the little trap door she remembered so well; untroubled by the thick clouds of dust swirling around them both. 'Open it,' she ordered, nodding towards the door.

Jaeger couldn't stop coughing as the dust caught in his throat, his eyes quickly watering, but one look at Draguta told him that she wasn't in the mood to be kept waiting. He flipped open the wooden door and took the torch from her hand, leading the way down the narrow stone steps.

The crypt was dark and airless, and it smelled even worse than Draguta's coffin.

Like fish and rats. Old and rotten.

Draguta took the torch back from Jaeger, eager to find what she was looking for. There were different shaped boxes stacked all over the dirt floor: square, long, wooden; many made of stone. All of them were laced in thick cobwebs, hidden beneath layers of centuries-old dust. Draguta eventually found the one she was looking for, and, motioning for Jaeger to come, she pointed to it. 'Open the lid,' she sighed in anticipation, staring at the intricately carved stone box, her heart quickening. 'It is time to begin.'

***

'I want to come with you,' Fyn insisted, trying to move.

The flame from the lamp beside his bed danced around precariously. Wind was coming in from somewhere, threatening its very survival, which was to be expected, Jael thought, listening to the wild roar from outside. 'I wish you could,' she said quietly, seeing how tired he looked. 'But you need to be sharp in battle. You don't want to make mistakes. You don't want your opponent to sniff out your wounds or your weaknesses, do you? And who knows what we might be facing. A whole army of men who won't die again?' Fyn looked even more disturbed, and Jael shook her head, wishing that thought hadn't popped out of her mouth. 'You'll have an important job to do,' she said quickly, trying to distract him. 'Staying with Axl. He'll need your help.'

'Will Axl be staying?' Fyn looked cheered by that thought.

Jael nodded. 'His leg will take some time to heal properly. It's hard to go into battle if you can't walk. At some point, you have to get off your horse! Besides, someone needs to look after the fort.'

Fyn yawned, lying back more comfortably now.

'Sleep,' Jael said, yawning herself. She had no idea how late it was, but her eyes were ready to close. 'I'll go and find Runa. She's going to sleep in here with you tonight. You can keep an eye on her.' And winking, Jael squeezed his arm and stood.

'Jael,' Fyn whispered. 'Thank you.'

Jael looked surprised.

'You saved my life,' he murmured, closing his eyes. 'Again. Thank you.'

Jael stared at him for a moment, feeling guilty that she'd put him in that position in the first place. Again. She turned away as Runa came in. 'I think he's almost asleep,' she whispered in passing.

Runa nodded. 'Sleep well, Jael.'

'You too,' Jael mumbled, overcome by the sudden need to go outside.

***

The storm was buffeting them with ever-increasing ferocity, and Meena glanced at Morana, wondering what hope their fire had. The flames blew in and out, disappearing every few heartbeats, and they were both conscious of Draguta's displeasure every time she turned around to glower at it.

Jaeger stood well out of Draguta's way, tapping distractedly on the drum, trying to stop his attention from wandering to the book. But he could see it, and he could hear the call of it. Yet it would not be his hands stroking its perfect pages tonight. It wasn't him who was careless enough to bring it out in a storm.

Draguta looked up from the book, glaring at him.

Jaeger swallowed, turning his eyes to the drum.

Morana hovered in front of the bowls of horse blood, trying not to remember what had happened the previous night. It wasn't just horse blood, she knew. They had ground up all manner of herbs and seeds into it; crushed bones and bark, adding berries and mushrooms. But all she could think about was what had happened the last time Draguta had brought them up to the stones. And how few of them were left to make the long walk back to the castle.

Draguta tried to ignore them.

She closed her eyes, picked up the long black fang she had retrieved from the crypt, and dipped it into the first bowl of blood. 'Girl! Come here! Bring the bowl!' she called into the wind. 'Follow me!'

Meena turned away from the warmth of the fire, hurrying to pick up the bowl, trailing behind Draguta, who was casting a circle with the bloody fang drippings. Every few steps, she would turn back to the bowl, dipping the fang into it before continuing with the circle, murmuring continuously as though she was already slipping into a trance.

Morana glanced over at the book, trying to remember seeing anything in its pages that mentioned a fang.

She couldn't.

Meeting Jaeger's eyes, she looked away, not wanting to share in what he was feeling. They both missed the book, she knew. Yet it would do neither of them any good to pine for it.

It was no longer theirs.

Having completed the circle, Draguta returned to Morana, her white cloak splattered with the blood that still dribbled from the enormous fang. 'Come! It is time.' She reached for a cup and dunked it into the second, smaller bowl. 'Drink!'

Morana's mouth gaped open, her chest tightening as she reluctantly held out her hand and took the cup, pouring the thick liquid down her throat, wondering what was about to happen.

***

Jael felt drawn to the storm as she walked away from the hall, out of the fort, towards the harbour. The dark sky was an explosion of noise above her.

All around her.

She shivered, her fingers quickly numbing as her braids whipped against her face. It was so cold that she couldn't stop her teeth chattering, so she wasn't surprised to look up and see flurries of snow floating down towards her. And in the distance, a sudden burst of lightning.

And then that voice.

Like a rusty bucket, rough and worn, and so instantly familiar.

She turned around, not expecting him to be there.

But he was.

'Get out!' Ranuf cried, reaching out a hand. 'Now, Jael! You must get everyone out!'

CHAPTER NINETEEN

Edela, Eydis, and Biddy had hurried back to the cottage, eager to escape the frigid night air. It was so cold that they slipped into their beds as soon as they were inside, desperate to feel warm again.

'Do you need another fur, Edela?' Biddy wondered, shivering beneath her own; trying to warm up her feet by rubbing them together. 'You can have mine. I have more meat on my bones for sure.'

Edela chortled. 'You think I'd have you chattering away over there all night? How would I ever get to sleep?' She froze.

Biddy couldn't see Edela in the darkness, but she heard her voice catch. 'What is it?'

'We must get dressed!' Edela cried, shuffling out of bed. 'I will come and help you, Eydis. Put on your boots, Biddy. Find our cloaks. Tie those puppies together. Hurry!'

***

The blood ran down her forehead, and Meena wanted to run before Draguta could put her hand on the symbol, but Draguta didn't come near her. She was too busy swaying around the circle, swooping her arms in rhythmic, wave-like motions.

Chanting. Her head back.

It was as though she was calling.

Calling?

Calling who?

***

'We have to leave!' Jael yelled, bursting into the hall, wondering how to get the children, and the injured Axl and Fyn out of the fort in a hurry. She had to find Edela, Eydis, and Biddy. Tig, Leada. Sigmund too. 'We have to leave!'

Thorgils was off his bench in a flash, knocking over his ale, his eyes quickly finding Isaura, who had come back from the bedchambers. 'What is it?' he asked, readjusting his scabbard.

'Get everyone out of here! Gant! We need to open the main gates. You take Axl and Amma! Eadmund!' Where was Eadmund? 'Entorp! Help Runa get Fyn to the door. I'll bring the horses around. You have to head up the hills! To the caves! We need to wake everyone in the tents. Get them moving! Now!'

Aleksander was there, tying up his swordbelt; Eadmund behind him, Sigmund in his arms. Jael remembered her father. She had to stay calm. 'We have to leave! Everyone has to leave the fort! Aleksander, get into the square, ring the signal bell! Get the horses out. Everyone! I have to find Edela and Biddy.'

'Eydis!' Eadmund panicked, handing Sigmund to Tanja and quickly tying his cloak into some sort of sling that she could use.

Jael hurried to help him, and together they managed to make something secure enough to hold the baby. She looked at Tanja and Eadmund. 'Get to the stables. Get Leada and Tig. Go through the main gates. Head for the hills. There are caves there. Axl will show you. I'll get Eydis!' Jael spun around. 'Amma! Where's Eydis?'

***

The land was a teasing mistress, coming closer with open arms and then drifting away, and they had all become frustrated by the endless game. The wind was too powerful, and the ship would not push forward in the direction they needed to go, no matter how tightly Ulf gripped the tiller.

The storm was loud, pounding them with unrelenting waves and heart-stopping noise. They couldn't hear each other.

They couldn't hear themselves think.

Haegen crawled down the deck, checking on his family, leaving Karsten to hold onto Berard. His son was now curled into the chest of one of the crew, who had much bigger arms and a thicker cloak than Hanna. Hanna had happily taken Halla instead, who, being two-years-old, was much easier to contain, although she made a lot more noise. Haegen smiled sympathetically at Hanna, knowing that sound well. 'There, there,' he soothed, running a wet hand over his daughter's hood, though his voice was lost before she could hear it, he was sure. Haegen was focusing on trying to calm his daughter, so he didn't notice what was happening behind him, but Hanna did. She frowned in confusion, not sure what she was seeing.

Halla stopped crying, her eyes popping open.

Haegen spun around, his own eyes just as wide. A thick white mist was creeping towards them, threatening to cover the ship. 'What's going on?' he wondered, standing and striding towards Ulf, whose bulbous nose was red with cold, his beard covered in ice.

Ice?

'The sea's freezing!' Ulf called, the whites of his eyes bright against the dark sky. 'Look!'

And turning towards the bow, Haegen could see that Ulf was right. All around the ship, the storm-whipped sea was hardening into thick ice.

***

Morana could feel something slithering around her again. She sensed warm breath on her legs. She didn't dare move. Her head was swimming with waves.

It was as though she was in the sea, riding the ocean like a whale.

A giant black whale. Sleek and supple. Diving and reaching and curling under the waves. Long and black and...

Not a whale.

***

The fort erupted in panic, though the roar of the storm was louder than any noise they could make.

'What's coming?' Eadmund demanded, grabbing Jael's arm as he waited by Tanja, who was sitting astride a horse, Sigmund tucked into the sling draped over her shoulder. Leada was next to him, not well enough to be ridden yet.

'I don't know!' Jael cried, turning away, searching for Askel, who was dragging Tig behind him. 'You ride Tig!' she said to her stable hand. 'Pull Leada behind you. Follow everyone up into the hills! You'll be safe up there!' She swallowed, hoping she meant it.

'Jael!' Edela and Biddy hurried forward with Eydis, dragging the nervous puppies behind them.

Jael's mind was jumping around, trying to remember where her chest was.

She needed armour. Weapons.

She wouldn't be leaving.

'Hurry!' Jael called to Biddy. 'Go! Now!'

Biddy grabbed Edela's arm, trying to pull her away towards

the gates, but Edela wasn't ready to leave yet. She had just seen the strongest image of *Toothpick* in her mind. 'Your sword, Jael! You must use your sword!'

Jael blinked, only half listening as she watched Branwyn and Gisila coming towards her with Aedan, Aron, and Kayla, who was clutching her baby daughter to her chest. 'Follow everyone out! Get horses if you can! You have to leave now!'

Kormac was there too, holding onto Alaric, who was panicking, and Derwa, who looked half asleep. 'Shall I stay?'

Jael shook her head. 'No, I need you to make sure that everyone's safely away. Help Entorp with Fyn.'

'Jael!' Axl was on his horse, looking down at her.

'Get everyone into the caves, Axl! You lead them out of here and stay there! Wait until we come for you!'

Entorp and Thorgils carried Fyn out between them. He was trying to stand, but he had no hope.

'Kormac, help Fyn onto the horse!' Jael urged.

Runa was there with Ayla, both of them ushering confused children ahead of them. Isaura was hurrying behind with her servants. Ayla moved out of the way of a rearing horse, grabbing Jael's hand. 'It's the gods,' she warned, watching the puffs of cold white air stream from her mouth; listening to the boom of the storm overhead. 'They're here.' She turned away as Bram came down the hall steps, helping Bruno. They needed to find him a horse quickly. He wouldn't be able to walk far.

Aleksander ran back to Jael, who was still staring after Ayla. Thorgils was there, and Gant too.

'What do we do?' Aleksander asked.

All eyes were on Jael, but she didn't know what to tell them.

What was coming?

***

Karsten couldn't stop shaking. His breath rushed in and out his mouth in frigid waves. The ice had hardened so rapidly that the ship was trapped.

They were trapped.

Bayla was beside herself. 'How is this p-possible? What is h-happening?' She pulled Kai closer to her chest, trying desperately to warm them both up. Her teeth were banging together, and she couldn't stop them.

Hanna was sitting next to Berard, too worried to speak. The storm was so loud in her ears that it was hard to think, but whatever thoughts entered her head were dark ones.

Then she heard it.

It wasn't thunder or lightning. It was coming from below.

A loud, cracking noise.

'What is *that*?' Haegen cried, hurrying to the stern.

Irenna's mouth fell open in horror. 'Haegen! *Noooo*!'

Haegen turned, listening to his wife's scream.

It was the last thing he heard.

***

Morana's mouth hung open.

It was the most astounding thing she had ever seen.

And for the first time in days, she smiled.

***

'Haegen! Haegen!' Irenna sobbed hysterically as Karsten pulled her away, forcing her down to the bow where everyone was sheltering. 'No! Haegen! Karsten, go after him! Please! Help him! Haegen! No! *Please*!'

But Karsten wasn't going anywhere.

He thought he was going to piss himself.

'What was th-th-that?' Berard yelled, gripping Hanna's arm. 'Where's Haegen? Where is he?'

Hanna shook uncontrollably, listening to the cracks beneath their broken ship; feeling the tremors moving further and further away; jumping at the shards of lightning striking the ice nearby.

They all ducked their heads, protecting the children, trying to keep Irenna from running to the empty stern.

Back to where the ship had been ripped open, and Haegen had disappeared.

Karsten had seen it.

He wasn't going over there.

***

The fort was almost empty now, bar the warriors who were remaining behind with Jael.

Kormac, Entorp, and Gant were shepherding the women and children, and the old and injured after Axl, who sat atop his horse, leading the way across the fields and up into the hills.

It would take some time.

Most of the warriors had stayed behind to make sure they would have it.

They'd quickly gathered everything they could find, shrugged on armour and helmets, dragged out bows and arrows, and set fires going in the braziers around the square.

Eadmund, Aleksander, Thorgils, and Bram checked that each catapult had sea-fire jars nearby. And then they followed Jael through the harbour gates, towards the piers, though not even Jael knew why she was heading in that direction.

The snow flurries had gone, replaced by cold, hard rain, which was freezing all around them as it fell. Freezing them.

Freezing the harbour.

Thorgils swallowed, gripping his sword as the icy rain streamed down his face. Bram shuddered beside him, uncomfortable in his mail tunic. Thorgils didn't even notice that Ivaar had joined them, walking on his other side, pushing his helmet onto his head.

Jael stopped before the entrance to the piers, listening. She looked up at the storm clouds swirling angrily above her head, trying to see anything, hear anything, but the wind was too loud.

And then, suddenly, it wasn't.

There was complete silence.

And they could all hear it.

The ice was cracking.

***

'Hurry! Move faster!' Axl implored as the shuffling Andalans and Tuurans made their way up the hills towards two large caves, which he knew were big enough for his Andalans. He didn't know whether they could fit the Tuurans who had been camping in the tent village as well. The clouds rushed across the moon, and the stormy sky was dark, and the grass was wet and icy beneath their feet, and the violent wind pushed them back and made the horses nervous. Axl nudged his horse onwards, grateful for the sudden absence of noise, but wishing that he was down in the fort, defending it with his sister.

Amma rode beside him, Eydis sitting in front of her.

'It's coming,' Eydis whispered, shivering against Amma. 'Can you feel it?'

Amma couldn't feel anything except cold terror. Every part of her was frozen solid. She glanced back at the fort – just a big shadow in the distance now – worried about what was going to happen. Relieved that Axl wasn't down there, trying to defend it.

Hoping they would make it to the caves in time.

***

Eadmund stood beside Jael, shivering as the cracking intensified.

It sounded like a forest being crushed by giants.

'Get back to the fort!' Jael roared, turning and running for the open gates. 'Catapult crews ready! Archers ready! Secure the gates!'

And then the storm exploded above them again.

***

Seawater.

Ice cold, freezing seawater was flooding the ship.

The ship that was quickly sinking.

'Abandon ship!' Ulf ordered, flapping his arms, trying to get them all up on their feet. 'Abandon ship!'

Hanna blinked, ready to follow him, but Nicolene grabbed her arm, shaking in terror. 'But what about that thing? What about...' Sobs rose up into her throat, and she couldn't speak.

'We're leaving the ship!' Karsten cried, wrapping an arm around his wife's waist. He had Kai on his hip. Nicolene held Eron. Both boys were silent, too cold and scared to cry now. 'It's sinking!'

'Onto the *ice*?' Bayla was in shock, unable to move. 'What about Haegen?' The tears that leaked from her eyes, froze on her face.

'Get out of the ship! Now!' Karsten roared, urging everyone

forward, past Ulf, who was determined to be the last man off.

'Hurry!' Ulf shouted. 'We need to find land!' He'd seen land again just before it happened. They all had. It couldn't be too far away.

The crew helped Bayla, Nicolene, and Irenna hoist the children over the side of the tipping ship as it quickened its descent into the sea.

Ulf pushed Berard towards his brother. 'Hurry!'

Hanna and Karsten helped Berard up and over the side, jumping out after him as the ship groaned and creaked beneath them. Ulf scrambled up the deck as the bow rose, throwing himself over the gunwale just before the ship slid away into the watery abyss.

***

The creature burst out of the ice. A gigantic black serpent, shrieking as it lurched forward, crashing over the piers, crawling towards Jael as she raced for the gates.

'Secure the gates!' Jael screamed, running into the fort. Glancing over her shoulder, she watched as the serpent lifted its long neck, its mouth open, hissing at them; enormous glistening fangs bared, ready to attack.

That thing wasn't going to be stopped by any gates.

Jael held her breath as six men hurried to drop the wooden beam in place, locking the gates, though she doubted they would hold for long. 'Load the sea-fire!' she yelled, running for one of the guard towers, hoping that Axl was still hurrying everyone up into the hills. 'Archers! Head for the ramparts! Use the fire arrows!' And ducking her head, she ran inside the tower, up the stairs, and out onto the ramparts overlooking the harbour.

The creature looked like something from her childhood nightmares, but it wasn't Ilvari, Ran's three-headed sea monster that was surging towards them. This beast had just the one colossal head, swivelling from the top of a body longer and thicker than the oldest tree in Andala's forest; black as the sky above it, with cat-like golden eyes flickering hungrily from either side of its scaly face as it sought its prey.

It crawled over the piers on four solid legs, snapping them like toothpicks, its ridged tail sweeping away everything in its wake.

Sensing movement on the ramparts, it shot forward, rearing up, its huge nostrils twitching, inhaling the frosty air. Opening its mouth again, Jael could see lethal black fangs hanging down, its tongue rolling out as it screeched.

'Fire the catapults!' Jael roared, running around the ramparts, away from the harbour, listening to the whistle as the catapult arms snapped back, sending the jars flying over the walls. 'Archers! Nock! Draw! Aim for the creature!'

Some jars crashed against the serpent. Some fell to the ground.

'Fire!' Jael screamed as lightning burst through the rumbling clouds, shooting into the serpent who roared angrily, shaking its head, turning to glare up at the storm.

Knowing what those gods were trying to do.

***

Draguta stood in the circle, gripping Meena's and Morana's hands, though she wasn't really there at all.

She could see Andala's walls.

She could feel the burn of fire and the sting of lightning; smell the reek of fear from the humans, who were cowering behind their pathetic defenses.

She was Sabba, one of Raemus' beloved monsters who had been destroyed by Daala. One of her fangs had been retrieved by the ever-loyal Followers, planning for Raemus' return; dreaming of a time when he would rule alongside his evil creatures again.

Draguta was grateful for the gift.

Now she was hers.

And together, they would destroy Andala and end the Furycks.

Ravens? Wolves? What small ambition Morana had, Draguta smiled to herself.

Sabba would swallow Andala whole.

***

The sea-fire and lightning had slowed the serpent down. Confusing it.

Momentarily.

Ivaar, Eadmund, and Bram were running the catapults, barking at their crews, but down in the fort, behind the towering walls, they were blind when the serpent was crawling around, relying on those up on the ramparts to be their eyes.

The serpent snapped its head around, shaking away the pain, hissing white streams of ice-cold breath onto the flames, extinguishing them in a flash. Irritated now, its glowing eyes returned to the walls of the fort as it slithered forward, swaying from side to side.

'Again!' Jael roared. 'Catapults! Fire again!'

***

'What do you see, Eydis?' Edela asked desperately as their horses nudged into each other. They were far up the hill now, and the caves were within reach, but it was a struggle. The horses, especially, were slipping in the darkness, trying to find sure footing on the craggy slopes, disturbed by the strength and noise of the storm. 'Do you see the book?'

Eydis turned her head towards Edela's voice, feeling Amma shaking against her back. 'No, I can't see anything.'

'What about you?' Biddy wondered as she walked carefully alongside Edela's horse, holding onto its reins, unable to feel her hands.

'Nothing,' Edela said anxiously, glancing at Marcus, who was gripping Alaric's arm; he had already slipped over twice. 'You?'

Marcus shook his head. 'I don't know what's happening. But something to do with the book, I'm sure.'

'Yes, I feel that a great power is here. This weather?' Edela shuddered. 'How is it possible if not for magic?'

'It's the gods,' Ayla said from behind Edela, where she walked by Bruno's horse. 'They have come to help Jael.'

CHAPTER TWENTY

Jael ran towards Aleksander, who had emerged from the guard tower and was bellowing down into the fort, trying to get the catapults to move. 'It's going to come through the gates! Pull back! Pull back!'

Eadmund leaned on his catapult, pushing it backwards, signalling for his men to join him.

Ivaar was doing the same. 'Back! Back!'

The gates would not hold.

'I have to kill it with my sword!' Jael yelled at Aleksander as thunder crashed above their heads.

They both jumped.

'What?'

'Edela said that I have to kill it with my sword!'

The roar of the serpent blew a trail of cold air over them, and they turned towards it.

'Get down into the fort! Point the catapults at the gates! Load them with sea-fire!' Jael cried. 'Wait for my call!'

The serpent roared again, and Jael glanced over the rampart wall towards the harbour, surprised to see that it had stopped, rocking from side to side, waiting just outside the gates.

***

Draguta spat in fury, looking up and down the wall.

Symbols.

Her magic could not pass those symbols. Sabba could not pass those symbols.

She smiled and crawled around the side of the fort, clambering over the ship sheds and buildings, smashing everything with her enormous clawed feet and fiercesome tail, looking for a way in.

***

'Follow me! Quickly!' Ulf shouted as he ran and slipped across the ice.

It felt hard underfoot, and normally that would have given him confidence, but he had seen the serpent break through that ice, smashing his ship, taking Haegen Dragos. He didn't know what was lurking beneath their feet. It was dark, and the storm was too loud for him to hear any warning of what might be coming next. But he knew that whatever happened, they had to get off the ice.

'Mother!' Karsten cried as Bayla slipped, falling to her knees. He rushed forward, adjusting Kai in his arms, reaching out a hand to pull her up. Ulf was there too, lifting the queen back to her feet. 'Hurry!' Karsten implored, his face numb from the cold, his son frozen in his arms, the terror of his brother's death too shocking to acknowledge.

He could barely breathe, but they had to find land.

They had to get off the ice.

***

Jael ran around the ramparts, following the serpent's path, trying to keep out of its line of sight.

It was crawling around the walls, slapping its spiky tail in irritation. She needed it to stay still. In one place. The sea-fire would be wasted if they shot at a moving target.

Eadmund joined Jael on the ramparts, his eyes popping open at the sight of the colossal serpent. Jael put a finger to her lips. 'It can't get in. The symbol is working,' she whispered, though she didn't look confident.

Eadmund nodded, as worried as his wife.

They both knew that the symbol had not been added everywhere yet. There were parts of the eastern wall that were missing it entirely.

'I have to kill it with my sword. If I can get it where I want it.'

'How?'

Lightning shot into the harbour, and the serpent shrieked, snapping its tail. They could hear another building shatter as the storm rumbled with renewed fervour overhead.

Jael grinned. 'We're going to take out its foundations!'

Eadmund blinked in surprise, remembering how worried he'd been about her fighting Tarak. Yes, she'd taken out his foundations, but Tarak had nearly killed her. And Tarak Soren had been as big as one of the serpent's fangs.

'Come on!' Jael called, running to the west side of the fort. 'Hurry!'

***

Entorp had a firm hold on the puppies' ropes as he stood by the mouth of the bigger of the two caves, trying to soothe Ido and Vella, who couldn't decide if they wanted to go inside the foul-smelling dark hole.

Entorp knew that he didn't. He'd never liked caves, having been lost in one as a child, so he was happy to watch from the entrance, despite the bitter cold.

He could hear the great roar in the distance. As could everyone else who passed him by, shaking and shivering, wishing they'd stopped to find furs and cloaks, their boots thick with ice, their hands and faces chapped, their beards frozen.

They could all hear the roar.

'It's just thunder,' Entorp smiled encouragingly as Amma hurried past, leading her horse with one hand, gripping Eydis' hand with the other. 'Just a bad storm.'

Eydis turned towards his voice, hearing his lie, knowing that what was attacking the fort was no storm.

***

Jael knew that she had to draw the serpent away from the one place it could get into the fort. 'You want *me*?' she shouted, trying to make herself heard. The thunder quickly died away, and Jael shouted again. 'I'm here! Over here!' Her heart was banging in her chest with such force that it felt as though it would burst through her mail shirt. Not one part of her wanted to call that creature closer.

She unsheathed *Toothpick*, hoping that it wasn't some form of dragon.

A fire-breathing dragon.

The serpent didn't hear her. It kept sliding away, towards the eastern wall. Jael swallowed, shaking her head, watching her frozen breath stream out before her.

Down in the fort, Aleksander had everyone pulling the catapults into position in front of the harbour gates, loading more sea-fire jars. They were blind, though, and could only hope that Jael would lure the serpent back. It was hard to know where it was, though the screeching, hissing noise certainly helped.

Aleksander picked up his bow and held his breath, frowning as Jael tried to get its attention. 'Jael!' he cried, though his voice was lost under another shudder of thunder. 'Jael!'

She turned, staring down at him.

'The piece of wood I gave you! Throw it down to me!'

Jael looked confused, then realisation dawned. She sheathed *Toothpick* and dug into her pouch, pulling out the rough piece of wood that Aleksander had carved the symbol onto. Stepping to the edge of the ramparts, she threw it towards him.

Sabba's nostrils were in the air, quickly smelling her.

'I'm here!' Jael shouted, flapping her arms. 'You want me? Draguta? Morana? You want me? I'm here! Come and kill me!'

***

At last.

Draguta could smell her. See her. She could feel Sabba's heavy body swing around, surging back towards the tiny, helpless figure of Jael Furyck as she peered over the rampart wall, glimmering in her helmet and mail.

Draguta could feel the serpent's enormous jaw unlock, her fangs prising themselves apart.

Salivating.

Gobs of thick saliva dripping from her spear-like teeth.

She paused, confused, then smiled.

Jael Furyck had a secret.

***

The ice was melting. Cracking. It was no longer safe to stand on, and Karsten was doing everything he could to move his family and Hanna towards the shore as quickly as possible.

They could see it now: the dark shapes of hills in the distance, the promise of a beach. Solid land beckoned. Karsten could feel it getting closer, but the ice was softening rapidly, and no one was moving fast enough. 'Hurry!' he yelled, catching Ulf's blinking eyes. 'Mother, give me Eron! You'll go faster without him. Pick up your cloak. Watch your footing!'

And as Karsten reached for his eldest son, he heard the cracking. He only had the one arm free to grab Eron – Kai was in the other – and he had no way of snatching his mother as well. But in a heartbeat, she was gone, dropping through a hole, straight down into the icy sea. 'Mother!'

'Mother!' Berard cried helplessly, too far away to reach her.

But Ulf was there, sliding down onto the ice, reaching into the hole for Bayla, who had thought quickly enough to push her arm up as she sank. Wrapping his fingers around her wrist, Ulf plucked her sodden, frozen body out of the water in one big rush.

Bayla was spluttering, shaking, and very much alive, but not for long if they didn't get her in front of a fire. None of them would be safe if they didn't get off the ice.

'Move! Go! Go! Go!' Karsten urged, hurrying forward. 'We need to get to shore. Hurry!'

***

Aleksander's eyes were on the ramparts, waiting for Jael's signal. 'Hold!' he called to Ivaar, Thorgils, and Bram; to the Arnesson brothers and Torstan; to Eadmund, who had come back to join them, and the men who were waiting by the gates, ready to lift the beam. He held up his hand, preparing to drop it when Jael did, his eyes never leaving her. 'Hold!'

The storm was holding too.

The only noises anyone could hear were Jael's taunting screams and the serpent's shrieking hiss.

'You will not defeat us!' Jael yelled, trying to lure the serpent closer, but it had stopped, not quite where she wanted it to be. She needed to irritate it into moving just a little more to the right. 'That's what the prophecy says, doesn't it, Draguta? That *I* will be victorious over you! You think this little worm can hurt me? Ha!' she laughed. 'But you don't know *me*!'

Sabba edged closer, her nostrils flaring angrily, her black head rising up to meet Jael.

And Jael threw down her arm, running for the stairs.

'Now!' Aleksander shouted. 'Fire! Archers, light your arrows!'

The sea-fire jars soared over the wall, crashing onto the jagged ridges of the serpent's flicking tail, smashing into its spitting mouth, breaking as they hit the ground.

'Archers! Fire at will!' Aleksander cried before turning back to his men. 'Load the catapults! Again! Again!'

Jael ran out of the guard tower as the serpent reared up, screeching furiously, snapping its head around. Lightning pierced through the clouds, helping to spark the sea-fire alight; flaming arrows following quickly.

Fire exploded across the serpent's back.

Jael knew that she didn't have long, but if the catapults and the arrows and the lightning kept up, the serpent would have little time to notice her. She ran for the gates, where Aleksander was already waiting. Eadmund was quickly beside her, sword drawn. Thorgils, Aedan, Aron, Beorn, and the Arnessons hurried to join them.

'Keep it busy!' Jael yelled to Ivaar, who was running all the catapults now with Oleg and Bram. 'Open the gates!' she called to the men who waited, ready to lift the wooden beam.

'Hold!' Ivaar bellowed at the catapult crews. 'Hold!'

And above their heads, the storm exploded, lightning striking Sabba over and over as thunder rumbled menacingly in the distance.

The serpent appeared so distracted by trying to put out the fire along its back that it didn't notice their approach at first. But it felt the tear of flesh as Jael and her men rushed around, slicing through each of its four solid legs.

Sabba roared, head back, jaw open, spittle flying everywhere.

They scattered as another bolt of lightning lit up the sea-fire along the serpent's back.

'Move!' Jael cried, not wanting her men to be crushed as it spun, swinging its flaming tail towards them. 'Back to the wall!'

And when they were flattened back against the stone wall of the fort, watching the serpent screech and twist itself into angry knots, Jael called out. 'Ivaar! Arrows!'

More arrows shot over the ramparts, stabbing into Sabba's face, one piercing her eye. She swung her head in pain, trying to put out the flames, but the lightning struck again, keeping her alight.

Blood was leaking from the serpent's legs now, and Jael hoped that it wouldn't simply freeze in the cold, but she realised that it wasn't as cold anymore. She wasn't shivering, but perhaps that was merely the heat from the flames that rose up from the ground all around them? The sea-fire was burning everywhere. 'Again!' Jael yelled, running for the serpent's back legs, conscious of its sharp claws digging into the melting ice, trying to keep its balance.

Dropping her head to the ground, Sabba swept it quickly to the left, trying to hit her attackers as they approached again. But they were too fast. Eadmund, Aleksander, and Thorgils ran, sliding to the left, swords out, slashing the serpent's leg. Jael, Erl, and the rest ran to the right.

'Again!' Jael cried. 'Again!'

***

Gant stood at the entrance of the smaller cave, watching the storm rage over the fort. Kormac waited anxiously next to him, worried about his sons, wondering what was happening, listening to the strange, screeching noises.

Surely it wasn't the storm?

Biddy and Edela joined them, unable to stay still inside the cave.

Biddy swallowed nervously. 'What is *that*?' It sounded as though something was in pain.

'That,' Edela said quietly, gripping hold of Biddy's shaking arm. 'That is *Toothpick*.'

***

Jael could see that only *Toothpick* was making any headway. The other swords didn't appear to have any bite as they jabbed and sliced the serpent's legs. It was only when *Toothpick's* blade cut its skin that the serpent would roar in pain.

She knew they didn't have long before the giant beast tired of their game, but there was only one *Toothpick*. So everyone took turns trying to protect Jael as she ran around the serpent's legs, chopping into its scaly skin with her sharp blade.

Sabba, furious and in pain, dropped her head to the ground, lashing out to the right, knocking Thorgils flying into the fort wall.

'Thorgils!' Jael yelled as Sabba flicked her head again, screeching in frustration, swinging to the left. Aedan ran to avoid getting hit, but he smashed straight into Erl Arnesson, who wasn't as fast as him, and they both tumbled to the ground.

Jael watched as the serpent opened its jaw, aiming for the

fallen men. 'Draguta!' she screamed. 'I'm here! Come and get me!'

Sabba swung back quickly.

Jael wrapped both hands around *Toothpick's* hilt and ran towards the serpent, dropping to the slippery ground, sliding underneath its head, just before it smashed down onto the ground.

Lifting *Toothpick* as she slid, Jael stabbed the tip of her blade through the underside of the serpent's long throat, tearing it open. Pulling *Toothpick* out, she rolled away, slipping under its legs, feeling its enormous body shudder in shock, tilting to the right. 'Back!' she cried, wiping the foul-smelling blood and muck out of her eyes. 'Into the fort! Ivaar! *Now*!' And running for the open gates, Jael could feel the rush of air as the serpent spun around, blood and bits falling out of its throat, splattering over the white ground.

Sabba was weak from the leaking wounds in her legs, and now, the gaping hole in her throat. The sea-fire jars crashed against her hard body, cracking open, and then the lightning and arrows followed, and she tried to turn her head, but it felt so heavy now. She tried to open her mouth, desperate to extinguish the exploding fire as the flames fanned towards her face in a sudden gust of wind. But when she wrenched open her massive jaw and tried to blow, she couldn't.

No air would come from her ruined throat.

And she wobbled, spent, her legs failing. Turning, she slipped, her claws stuck in the ice, twisting awkwardly. Her body tangled like a slithering black knot, falling to the ground in a heap of skin and fangs and exploding flames.

***

'No!' Draguta roared, on her knees. 'Get up! Fight! You must kill her! We have her! She is there. Right there! Get up, you stupid creature!'

She was squeezing Meena's hand so tightly that Meena jerked out of the trance, wincing, trying to rip her fingers away before her bones shattered. But Draguta only clamped down more tightly, still lost in the trance, swaying, trying to help Sabba hold on to her fading lifeblood.

***

'Wait!' Jael called as her men moved to shut the gates. 'Aleksander! My symbol!' Jael spun, grabbing the little piece of wood from him, slipping it into her pouch. And squeezing through the smallest hint of a gap between the gates, she ran back across the melting ice towards the dying serpent whose black tongue had flopped out of its mouth. One big golden eye was fixed open, dilated, leaking blood from the arrow speared through it.

But Jael had to be sure.

The flames were burning up the serpent's back, charring its hard shell, burrowing into the arrow holes, scorching its soft flesh.

Jael ran up the serpent's wide spiky nose, not feeling any reaction. And standing between its eyes, feeling the intense heat from the flames all around her, she lifted *Toothpick* into the air and brought him down with a crack, spearing the sharp blade straight through its head.

CHAPTER TWENTY ONE

Draguta held out her hands, long and pale and covered in blood.

Shaking with fury.

She turned her head up to the sky. 'This is just the beginning!' she seethed. 'You think that you can stop me? That *she* can? Your little puppet?' Spinning around, she watched as Morana and Meena tried to blink themselves out of the trance; wet through, shivering, suddenly aware of the intense cold.

Jaeger held the drum, frustrated that he hadn't seen anything.

Not invited into the circle, he had been left drumming again like a servant. His head was muddled with the herbs from the fire, but he had not seen a thing.

'I will find you!' Draguta yelled as she spun away, stalking towards the book, and scooping it into her arms, she hurried away from them all, desperate to get back to her candles, her lamps, her bright warm fire.

'What did she do?' Jaeger asked throatily as Morana approached. 'What did she do?'

'She raised a creature,' Morana murmured, still in shock. 'Raemus' serpent. Sabba.'

'The book showed her how to do *that*?' Jaeger was incredulous, watching Draguta's white dress disappear into the darkness.

Morana nodded. 'She knows the secrets of the book.

Everything Raemus hid in there. It all belongs to her.'

'And so do we. For now,' Jaeger muttered, his mind quickly turning to thoughts of capturing the book with Meena; thoughts of defeating Draguta and ruling Osterland too.

'But not if Jael Furyck gets her way!' Morana spat, dropping her hood over her face before turning into the rain.

Meena let Jaeger grab her hand without protest as they followed Morana, eager for a fire, a fur; anything but this incessant icy rain. How did she ever stand a chance of getting the book away from someone as powerful as Draguta? Meena sighed, thinking of Berard. Wishing that she'd sailed away with him.

What had she been thinking?

***

'Aarrghh!' Another man fell through the ice.

Two of the crew ran back to help him, dragging the shaking man out of the water before the cold took him.

Karsten didn't turn around as he urged Nicolene on. For once, she was quiet, too terrified to complain. She gripped Lucina's hand, pulling the little girl along, both of them stumbling and shaking. Utterly silent.

Everywhere they looked, the ice was melting, cracking, sinking into the sea.

'There!' Ulf cried, squeezing Bayla's frozen hand as he hurried her towards the shore. The storm clouds had lifted. The night sky was suddenly littered with stars, and they could see.

They were nearly there.

And then Irenna went through the ice, holding little Halla in her arms.

'Irenna!' Berard screamed, dropping Valder's hand and running towards where he'd last seen his sister-in-law.

'Irenna!' Karsten lowered his sons to the ice and ran to join Berard, whose one arm was already down the hole Irenna had just made.

'I can't! I can't!' Berard grunted, trying to keep hold of Irenna's wrist, feeling his fingers numbing, his grip loosening as he slid towards the hole.

More men were quickly there, helping to keep Berard on the ice.

Karsten shoved his arm into the water, wrapping his fingers around Irenna's wrist, yanking her up with Berard's help.

She was still clutching a terrified toddler to her chest.

Ulf was there, bundling Irenna into one of his men's cloaks; Bayla already had his cloak draped around her shoulders. Hanna hurried forward, helping Halla out of Irenna's arms. And pulling her to her chest, she hoped to warm her with the little body heat she had.

She was still breathing.

They both were.

'We have to go!' Ulf warned, turning back to his men. 'We need to get to shore! Now!'

***

Jael was too stunned to speak as she stared at the serpent. Its burning body sprawled lifelessly over the flattened ship sheds and the broken piers. Its legs, splayed at odd angles, were ripped open, still leaking blood.

'You're sure it's dead?' Thorgils wondered, rubbing the back of his head.

The serpent's eyes had glazed over, covered by a milky film. Its black tongue appeared to be hardening.

There hadn't been a twitch since it went down.

Eadmund and Aleksander walked around its snaking body,

poking and prodding, avoiding the sea-fire flames that burned with intensity, sending great plumes of smoke into the night sky, but there was no sign of life.

Bram shivered, clapping his arms across his chest. 'We might need a drink after that!'

Jael felt a sharp twinge in her belly, fighting the urge to touch it.

Eadmund watched her. 'Are you hurt?'

Shaking her head, Jael cleared her face. 'No.'

She wasn't the only one shaking her head.

Erl Arnesson came to stand beside her. 'I might have changed my mind about wanting to be in your army,' he grumbled, tugging on his long black beard. 'If that's the sort of enemy we're going to be facing.'

'But it couldn't get past the symbols,' Eadmund reminded him. 'So there are ways to make ourselves safe. And what do you think you're going to do in Alekka if we don't fight here? You think they won't go there next?'

Jael looked down at *Toothpick*, still dripping with the serpent's dark blood. 'Draguta wants to destroy us, all of us, so we're going to have to do everything we can to stop her. We need men, weapons, and dreamers. And when we defeat her and The Following, the gods will know our names. Do you want them to laugh about you, Erl Arnesson, as the man who ran away? Or as the one who slayed the mighty beasts they sent to kill us?' She watched his black eyes considering things, almost completely hidden as he screwed up his leathery face.

'Well, as you say, better to be sung about as a hero than a feckless coward,' Erl growled, shrugging his broad shoulders as he turned back to the gates. 'Bring out the ale!' he cried, eager to settle his jittering nerves.

'I'll go to the caves,' Aleksander said, finally sheathing his sword.

'Are there any horses left?' Jael asked.

Aleksander shook his head and grinned, which was

preferable to vomiting, though his stomach was swirling about like a ship in a storm. 'But I don't mind the walk. I could do with some thinking time after that.'

Jael nodded, her shoulders loosening as she considered everyone in the caves.

Wondering how she would keep them safe now.

Wondering how quickly the next attack would come.

***

Karsten lowered his sons onto the icy shore, pointing at them to stay, making Eron hold Berard's frozen hand as well as his little brother's. He ran back for Nicolene and Hanna, who were leading the rest of the children. Ulf had Bayla and Irenna. Irenna had been slow – reluctant to move after falling through the ice – so he'd picked her up, carrying her the rest of the way.

They had made it, and as they stood on solid ground, they could hear the ice breaking up in the distance.

It was still cold, but the wind had finally dropped.

The Dragos' sheltered in front of a tussocked bank, shivering beside each other while Ulf and his men scoured the area for driftwood and grass; anything that would help them get a fire going.

Hanna wrapped her arms around Halla, trying to keep her warm. Karsten had his mother, and Berard, though he only had the one arm, wrapped it around Irenna.

Irenna was too numb to speak. She kept seeing the moment Haegen had been pulled out of the ship, those long black fangs ripping him away from her. She hadn't cared when she'd fallen through the ice. If she hadn't been holding onto Halla, she wouldn't have even reached for Berard's hand.

Without Haegen, she didn't want to live.

Hanna frowned, feeling Halla shivering against her chest,

wondering if she was crying. She felt sick. Terrified. She didn't know where they were or what they were going to do now. 'Ssshhh,' she murmured gently. 'Ssshhh.'

'It's warming up,' Ulf noted, trying to rouse a smile from Bayla as he knelt on the ground, making a circle with stones as his men returned with what they had gathered to make a fire, but she wouldn't even move her head as she stared at the slushy ground before her.

'But how was it even possible?' Karsten asked blankly, struggling to think just as much as he was trying not to. 'To freeze like that? Is your book that powerful?'

Hanna glanced at him, desperate for Ulf to get the fire started. 'I don't know.'

'We have to get to Andala quickly,' Berard insisted. 'Someone will be able to help us, to tell us what's happening.'

'But where is Andala from here?' Nicolene panicked. 'Where are we?'

Ulf frowned. 'We'll see soon enough. Let's just warm ourselves up, and when the sun rises, it will help make sense of things, I'm sure.' He wasn't sure at all. It was summer, and yet his ship had sunk in a frozen sea. Two of his men had been lost, falling through the broken ice before he could save them. And Haegen Dragos had been eaten by a monster from the deep.

Ulf Rutgar wasn't sure about anything anymore.

***

It took some time for everyone to make it back from the caves, but they were all eager to return to the fort and see what had sent them from their beds in the middle of a cold, stormy night.

And when they saw the serpent, they were not disappointed.

Axl's mouth hung open as he stared at the enormous head that had come to rest just outside the harbour gates. 'And *you* killed this?' he breathed, turning to his sister in the slowly building light of dawn. She looked tired, he thought, and he didn't blame her.

'We all did,' Jael sighed.

'With your sword?' Gant's eyes were wide. 'Your little sword killed that?'

'Well, he's not that little,' Jael said indignantly. 'My sword, the gods, the sea-fire, and everyone else. Somehow, we got it down.'

Gant shook his head, blowing out a long smoky breath. 'How did you know it was coming?'

Jael glanced around, but only Axl and Gant were paying any attention to her. 'Ranuf.'

Axl was surprised.

Gant was not.

He had known Ranuf Furyck better than anyone. If he could have, Ranuf would have found a way to help save Andala.

'You *saw* him?' Axl breathed, leaning heavily on his crutch, trying to keep himself steady on the slippery ground.

Jael stared at her brother, wondering what she had seen. A dream? A vision? She didn't know what to call it, but her father had been standing there, warning her. She had seen him for just that one moment, and now she felt the enormity of his loss all over again. 'Yes,' she said haltingly. 'And we don't have time to stand around here admiring this victory. That thing could have broken through the fort if it had found the section of wall with no symbols. We need to get back to work quickly. This is only the beginning.'

***

Jaeger pulled Meena close, and, for once, she didn't want to recoil from him. His big arms were almost comforting. She couldn't stop shaking as she listened to the racing beat of his heart that kept pace with her own. He hadn't said a word since they'd returned to his chamber and crawled under the furs.

It was no longer that cold, but Meena thought of how nice it would feel to sit before a warm fire. The chamber was so dark. Jaeger hadn't even wanted to light a lamp. He just wanted to lie in bed and try to think.

But it was hard to think clearly after inhaling all that smoke.

'What did it look like?' he asked, remembering the size of the fang they had taken from the crypt.

Meena shivered. 'It was big. Like a giant snake. Like a dragon without wings. With a long tongue and fangs. Big fangs.' She swallowed, remembering how Varna had enjoyed torturing her with nightmares about Raemus' creatures before she went to sleep. Her grandmother's detailed descriptions and the terrifying dreams that ensued were so blood-curdlingly real that Meena would often wake up crying.

Varna could never take the amusement out of her voice as she barked at her to be quiet.

'And she brought it to life with a spell from the book?'

Meena nodded.

Jaeger could feel his breathing slow, remembering when the Book of Darkness had sat on his table; imagining how it would feel to hold it in his hands again. 'You could do it, couldn't you?'

Meena froze.

'You could read the book. You could cast the spells. Look at Morana. She's just a dreamer, yet with the book, she possessed those ravens. Those wolves. She went into the Dolma and brought Draguta back, so why couldn't you?'

Meena was ready to argue with every bit of strength she had, but then she realised that it was what she wanted as well.

It was why she'd stayed behind.

'I could try.'

***

The sun was barely up, but Andala's fort was already humming with activity. There was a renewed urgency to prepare themselves. To protect the walls. To make more sea-fire. To grow their stores of arrows at a faster rate. And seeing how well the symbol had worked, the focus on carving it everywhere had intensified.

No one was complaining about blisters and aching hands now.

Aleksander and Gant were busy overseeing the men who had been given the task of getting the serpent out of the harbour. They were working to carve off its head, deciding that there was little else to be done with it except pull it back into the sea, which was now, thankfully, free of ice.

But first, they would remove its head.

Just in case.

Jael had left them to it, checking on Fyn and Eydis before disappearing to speak to Edela.

She trekked up the familiar, well-worn path to her grandmother's little cottage, remembering that night all those months ago when she had stormed up there, full of barely-controlled fury, desperate for answers.

Not satisfied with any she'd been given.

The wind chimes announced her arrival, and Edela was opening the door before her granddaughter had even reached out to knock on it. 'Your stool is waiting for you,' she smiled, her eyes twinkling in the bright morning light.

This wasn't a talk Jael had ever wanted to have, but sighing, she ducked her head and slipped inside.

***

Draguta ate her breakfast without a smile.

No one dared speak to her.

They could all feel the heat of her rage.

Jaeger glanced at Morana, who scowled at him, turning towards her plate, wishing that she was in her chamber, still asleep, but Draguta had sent a slave to fetch her.

To fetch all of them.

'We have challenges,' Draguta said, at last, sipping her wine. She had no wish for porridge, bread, cheese or cold meats. She was ravenous and had ordered a wild boar on the spit as soon as she'd returned from the stones, and now, as the four of them sat at the high table with the morning still new, the slaves were serving plates of sizzling roast boar and honey-glazed vegetables. 'We are few against many. But despite the small victory they achieved last night, they will not win the war against us. For, although poor Sabba could not defeat them, she was not sacrificed in vain.' Draguta smiled for the first time since they'd sat down. 'We gained much more than Jael Furyck realises.'

Morana lifted her head and frowned. She had no idea what Draguta was talking about, and she wasn't even sure that she cared. Blinking, she quickly cleared her mind, sensing Draguta still beside her.

'Let them think they can keep themselves safe. Let them think they can keep us out,' Draguta mused, stabbing her knife into a succulent slice of roast boar. She lifted it to her lips, thinking about Jael Furyck.

Imagining that she was stabbing the knife into her stomach.

***

Berard left the fire, walking towards Karsten, who stood on the edge of the sandy beach, staring at the waves rolling gently towards him. There was no ice now. He could feel his hand again, and his body was almost warm, but he hadn't stopped shaking yet. 'What do you think it was?' Berard wondered, trying to ignore the demanding pain in his stump. 'That creature? Why did it take Haegen? Why didn't it take us?'

Karsten sighed. He had been wondering the same thing himself.

Why Haegen?

Was it something to do with Jaeger? Was he trying to kill off anyone who stood in his way? The throne was Jaeger's now. What did he care about his family anymore?

'Ulf says that we're not far from Andala,' Berard went on. 'He thinks we can make it in a day's walk.'

Karsten frowned, looking back to a bereft Irenna, who didn't appear inclined to go anywhere in a hurry. Her three children huddled next to her, terrified, tired, and hungry.

She didn't appear to notice them.

Bayla sat beside them with Hanna, trying to keep the children warm.

Berard was desperate for Karsten to come back to them; he didn't know what to do. 'Haegen would want us to get to Andala quickly,' he tried.

'*Haegen*?' Karsten spat, spinning around. 'Haegen doesn't exist anymore! There is no Haegen, just like there is no Father! They're gone! And you have one arm, so you're completely useless to me! And we have no ship! And we're nowhere!' He could feel anger and grief consuming each other as tears burned his eyes. 'We're nowhere!'

Berard reached out, braving Karsten's fury as he gripped his brother's shuddering arm. 'But you're still here. And you can lead us, and we can take the throne back from Jaeger. We can take revenge for Haegen and Father if you lead us, Karsten. And then you can be king.'

Karsten threw off Berard's hand and stormed down the beach, not wanting anyone to see him cry.

***

They were alone.

Jael sat on her stool, which wobbled. She looked at her wedding band and wondered where Eadmund was.

'She saw you,' Edela began.

'What?'

'When you removed your symbol, Draguta saw you,' Edela said quietly, picking up her cup of cold chamomile tea. 'She knows about the baby.'

Jael sighed. 'That's why I'm here. We need a plan. I think I have a plan.'

Edela leaned forward, her eyes sharpening with interest. 'You do? Tell me.'

'No one can know about the baby.'

'*No one*?' Edela frowned. 'What about Biddy? She will need to help me when the time comes. I'm not as much use as I once was.'

'Alright, Biddy, but no one else.'

'I think you're right, but is it possible? You must have seen a woman about to give birth. It's hard to hide being so heavy with child. I don't think any amount of cloaks will do that.'

'There's no choice, Grandmother. No child of mine will be safe. Until Draguta and The Following are defeated, the baby has to remain a secret. We can't trust anyone. It's safer that way. Besides, pregnant women are all different shapes, aren't they? Hopefully, I won't look too obvious.' She cringed, not wanting to imagine how she was going to look soon.

'Well, stand up then, and let's have a look at you. Let's see how far along you are.'

Jael hesitated. She had tried to ignore her body entirely, as though it wasn't even hers. For a long time, she hadn't wanted it to be real. She had ignored the aches and pains, and the swell of her breasts and her belly. And the sickness and the hunger and the odd tiredness and heavy limbs, but she couldn't hide from it any longer. Not if she wanted to keep the baby safe.

Standing, she unpinned her cloak.

'You're going to need a new tunic,' Edela noted, seeing the strain of the faded blue fabric as it stretched across Jael's breasts. 'Take it off,' she smiled at her awkward granddaughter. 'Let me see you properly.'

Frowning, Jael tried to tug her tunic over her head, which wasn't as easy as it used to be. Edela was right; she could barely fit it anymore. 'Is the door locked?' she asked quickly.

Edela nodded, running her eyes over Jael's rounded belly. She stepped forward, placing her hands on it.

Jael flinched.

'Sorry,' Edela murmured, closing her eyes, keeping her frozen hands on either side of Jael's belly button. 'You are further along than I thought. This child will come in the winter. She will be a winter baby like you.'

'She?'

'Yes, she,' Edela said gently, conscious of the need to keep her voice low, just in case. 'Cover yourself up now, and we will think of what to do. You cannot go into battle with Draguta and her beasts when you're about to give birth. And perhaps now she will know that.'

'And if she does?'

'Well, I imagine she'll do everything she can to draw you out. Wanting to hurt you now. Sensing that you are vulnerable. There will come a time when you won't be able to fight at all, Jael, no matter how good you are or how powerful your sword is. It would be too dangerous for you and the baby.'

Jael sighed. It was her greatest fear: not being able to protect herself or the people she loved. 'We'll have to take the fight to her, then. Now. Defeat her before the baby comes,' Jael said, yanking her tunic back over her head and reaching for her swordbelt.

Edela didn't like the sound of that. The notion that Jael

would be fighting to defeat Draguta and destroy the book whilst trying to keep her unborn child safe filled her with terror. 'Or you wait. Build your army. Prepare. Plan your attack.'

'I don't think Draguta is going to let that happen, is she? I imagine she's already making plans to attack us again. There's no reason for her to wait.'

'No, I suppose you're right, and now that she's seen the baby, she may be even more inclined to defeat you quickly.'

Jael tightened her swordbelt, suddenly aware of the strong odour of serpent in her hair and on her clothes. She frowned, wondering what creature Draguta would send for them next.

CHAPTER TWENTY TWO

Morana, Jaeger, and Meena stood on one of the newly built piers.

All that there was of the newly built pier.

It would take some time to complete, but there was enough for the small ship to bump against.

Morac jumped down onto the wooden boards, sighing in relief as he picked up the rope and looped it around the solitary mooring post. He was amazed to think that he'd navigated his way from Oss, through the Widow's Peak, and around Skorro, with only Evaine's help. He had been pleased to discover that he still retained enough memory from his years raiding with Eirik to find his way. They'd spent more time at sea than on land when they were young, savouring the freedom of the waves after a childhood spent in chains.

Evaine had been a constant, whining nightmare on their journey, and Morac was looking forward to spending time with someone who wasn't her. Even his scowling sister promised to be more enjoyable company than Evaine. 'Morana!' He embraced the stooping black-and-white-haired figure before him, unable to keep the smile off his weary face. She didn't look happy, though, as she stepped back and frowned. 'My lord,' Morac nodded towards Jaeger, before turning back to help Evaine out of the ship.

Jaeger almost gasped.

Evaine Gallas, with her flowing blonde hair, and her perfectly round face set off by two big blue eyes and a delicate snub nose, was the most beautiful woman he'd ever seen.

Meena, standing beside him, felt a fresh breeze lift the hem of her dress, and she wondered if that was a sign of hope. If Jaeger could fall in love, perhaps he would no longer force her into his bed? Though now that he wanted her help to take the book from Draguta, perhaps that would cause problems? As frightening as it sounded, she needed to remain useful to him.

It was the only way she could imagine getting close to the book.

'You took your time,' Morana grumbled, barely acknowledging Evaine as she turned and headed back to the castle, her black cloak swishing angrily behind her.

Evaine blinked in surprise, then realising that Morana wasn't stopping, she hiked up her dress, hurrying after her. 'But what about Eadmund?' she cried frantically. 'Why did you make us leave him on Oss? I thought we were supposed to be together!'

Morana stopped, irritated and impatient, snapping her head around. 'Did you *want* to die? Either of you?' She glared at Morac, who didn't wish to be lumped in with Evaine. 'Because that was what was coming. After Eadmund took Morac's head, his wife would have tried to take yours!' she hissed. 'Would you have rather stayed and let that happen? Let Jael Furyck become the mother of your son?'

Evaine's eyes flared. 'She's already doing that. You made me leave him behind!'

'Yes, but you have a chance of getting him back, don't you?' Morana sighed. 'Now, let us hurry. Draguta wants to meet you, and she is not a woman to keep waiting.' Morana frowned as Jaeger and Meena joined them. Her dark eyes sought out her niece's, and Meena was surprised to glimpse the fear in them.

It mirrored her own.

***

Thorgils rolled his shoulder, still shaking his head in shock, struggling to believe that he'd been battered and bruised by a giant serpent from the sea.

Isaura hovered nearby with a worried look on her face, Mads trying to pull her outside. He wanted to play by the serpent. Far from being terrified of it, as his three sisters were, he was desperate to watch as the Andalans, Islanders, and Alekkans gathered around it, waiting for the burning sea-fire to die down on its back and tail, preparing to drag it into the harbour water. 'What if there are more lurking in the sea?' Isaura panicked, keeping her voice low. 'What if more creatures are coming for us?'

'Well, we've worked out a plan to stop them now,' Thorgils grinned, winking at Mads, who ignored him. 'Should be easier next time.' He shovelled another slice of bread and soft cheese into his mouth. He was tired and ready for his bed, but just as happy to sit in the hall and eat and drink for a moment before he headed out to start fixing the broken harbour.

Isaura turned to Ayla, who sat beside Thorgils, braiding Leya's hair. 'Do you think there are any more?'

'I imagine so,' Ayla said quietly. 'The stories my grandmother used to tell me were filled with monsters. I never thought I'd actually see one of them, though.'

Bruno frowned, finishing his cup of small ale. 'And you think this woman can control them? Through the book?'

'It seems that she can. When Raemus wrote the Book of Darkness, he wanted The Following to help him kill the humans. And it seems that he came up with many different ways to do just that.'

'Mmmm, I'd hate to imagine what's coming next,' Thorgils mumbled through a mouthful of bread. Catching a glimpse of Ivaar walking into the hall, he frowned. 'But we have Jael, and she has her sword. And we have the symbols too. So this Draguta can try what she likes, but we're not just going to sit here and suck our thumbs, are we?' he smiled at Mads, who was busy sucking his thumb.

Mads scowled and hid his face.

***

'How weary you both look after your long journey!' Draguta cried as she shepherded Evaine and Morac towards the high table, snapping her long fingers at a cowering slave. 'Bring us some wine! Something for our guests to eat too!'

Morana had given Morac no warning about what had happened to The Following. She hadn't known what to do, except bring him to Draguta and let everything unfold as it must. They were all Draguta's now, to do with as she wished, and Morana couldn't see through the weeds in her head to find a way out for any of them.

Evaine was transfixed by the beautiful woman. As was Morac. They took the hastily delivered goblets of wine, barely able to keep from staring at her as they sat down.

Morac glanced at his sister, sensing her tension. Morana would not even look his way. He was quickly becoming unsettled. 'And where is Yorik?' he wondered, taking a sip of wine, surprised by its potency.

He coughed.

Morana stiffened.

Jaeger's eyes widened.

Meena had taken a seat at the very end of the table, wondering why she was there at all.

'Yorik?' Draguta snorted dismissively as she took her place between Evaine and Morana. 'We had no need for Yorik and his kind, did we, Morana?'

Morana shook her head mutely, keeping her thoughts at bay.

Draguta smiled, raising her goblet. 'Now that we are all together, we can talk about Jael Furyck and how we will kill her. There are just so many spells we could try.' She drank her wine and sighed. 'So many ways that we could end her. The prophecy holds her up to be some sort of god. Yet what is she really but an angry woman with a sword? Just a woman. A woman who will soon be dead!'

Morac tried to catch his sister's eye, but she had her head down, hiding beneath her hair. He could feel his chest tightening uncomfortably as he listened to Draguta's cackling laughter and the deathly silence of his sister, which spoke loudest of all.

'Jaeger shall find you somewhere to stay. We have more chambers in this castle than we'll ever need, so you may take your pick, Evaine dear,' Draguta cooed. 'And, of course, there will be servants and slaves to tend to your every need. Everything you could wish for is right here.'

Evaine swallowed. The wine had burned her throat, but it had warmed her insides, and after days on that stinking ship, listening to Morac's lectures and worrying about Eadmund, she suddenly felt brighter. 'Thank you, my lady.'

'How very polite you are,' Draguta smiled. 'And how truly lovely.' She reached out to touch Evaine's hair, which was tangled and wild after her sea journey. 'I shall send someone to bathe you and brush your hair. You must look your most enticing for when Eadmund arrives.'

Evaine's face glowed with happiness.

Jaeger looked on with a frown.

***

After Jael had left her cottage, Edela had tired quickly. The night had been exhausting and long, and she had forced herself to stay awake, hoping to be of some use, and now she couldn't stay awake any longer. So she retreated to her bed, sleepy but anxious.

Jael was in more danger than ever. Yet, if she didn't go after the book and Draguta, they would all die. But if she did...

Edela sighed. Her bed was cold, and her feet were frozen, but she wriggled under the furs and closed her eyes, hoping that her dreams would find their way to her.

But when they finally did, she wished they hadn't.

***

It had taken until the sun was high in the sky for the sea-fire to finally die down. And when it had, they tied ropes around the headless body of the charred serpent, preparing to drag it into the deep water of the harbour, hoping that it would drop like the dead weight it was, down to the bottom, never to return again.

Axl frowned at Gant, not convinced that it was the right approach. 'Perhaps we should make a pyre and burn it instead?'

'Ha! If that sea-fire didn't turn it to ash, nothing's going to,' Gant laughed, looking over the dire state of the piers, which the serpent had shattered into kindling; relieved that they'd sent the ships around to the cove. He turned around, happy to see the high stone walls still standing.

'Luckily, it didn't breathe fire,' Axl said, reading Gant's mind.

'Indeed, but maybe the next one will?'

Axl turned away, leaning on his crutch, eager to get back to the hall to take the weight off his leg for a while. 'Next one?' He didn't like the sound of that. 'How quickly do you think they'll try again?'

'Hopefully, not before we're ready. The symbol kept the serpent out, so maybe we need to put some up around the caves too? It makes sense to protect ourselves as much as possible.'

Axl nodded as they walked towards the gates, stopping before Aleksander, who was carving a symbol into the wall. 'We can't go to Hest by sea. We'd be too exposed out there.'

'Axl has a point,' Aleksander said, placing his tools on the ground and removing his cloak. The weather had righted itself, and he was sweating as he worked. 'If it was the gods who froze the sea to try and keep the serpent trapped, it didn't work, so if we're out on a ship, we'll stand no chance of defending ourselves against something like that. The sea-fire might help, but the fleet would be in pieces before it took effect.'

'Mmmm, after last night, I don't think the sea's for us,' Gant agreed. 'We're just going to have to find a way to keep ourselves safe overland to Hest.'

'Jael's looking for you!' Oleg called as he approached. 'She's gathering everyone in the hall.'

Aleksander picked up his cloak and grabbed his waterskin, eager to hear what plan she was cooking up.

***

Morac walked away from his meeting with Draguta in a state of shock.

He was still shaking his head as Morana closed the door to her chamber and turned the key. Feeling the tension in her body start to ease, she dragged a stool towards the charred remains of the fire, trying to think.

'She killed Yorik? And what of the others?' Morac took a stool opposite his sister, leaving Evaine to pace irritably around them, her eyes appraising the stark stone chamber with disdain.

'They're all gone,' Morana muttered. 'All of them.'

'She *killed* them? How?' Morac was incredulous. '*Why*?'

'You don't want to know, trust me,' his sister shuddered. 'She had no need for them, I suppose. She doesn't want what they did. What we did.'

Morac frowned. 'Are you saying that *we* no longer want Raemus' return? Either of us?'

Morana raised her head, glaring at her brother. She had kept a lid on her frustration for days and was ready to burst. 'What we want no longer matters! Draguta is our ruler now. We do as *she* bids. Have you not realised that yet?' she shouted, not caring who heard. Draguta would surely be listening, no matter how far away she was, ready to pounce on any hint of disloyalty.

Morac glanced at his daughter, wondering if he'd made a mistake bringing her here. But then he remembered Morana's warning, and he realised that he'd had no choice. 'And what will we do now?'

'Yes,' Evaine said, sitting down on Morana's bed, eager to steer the conversation towards the only topic she cared about. 'What will we do about Eadmund? When will you bring him here?'

***

Eadmund couldn't concentrate.

He stood at the map table, trying to listen as Jael walked around it, pointing at various places, making suggestions for how they could approach Hest overland. Aleksander kept shaking his head, irritating her, Eadmund could see, but he felt no jealousy watching how comfortable they were with each other anymore.

All he could think about was Evaine, and how quickly he could see her again.

'The only place to take shelter around there would be in Hallow Wood,' Gant suggested, pointing to the middle of Osterland, near God's Point, where a great swathe of dense woodland covered much of their approach to Hest. 'And no one wants to go in there.'

Axl glanced at Aleksander, thinking about the wolves.

'No, the wood won't be safe. But nor will the sea, the fields, the wetlands, the mountains. Nowhere will be safe if Draguta and The Following can see us,' Aleksander muttered.

'Well, not The Following,' Edela interrupted, pushing her way through to the table.

'What do you mean?' Jael asked. 'Why not them?'

'She's killed them,' Edela said loudly enough to be heard over the frantic bustle of the hall. 'Draguta has killed them all!'

'*All* of them?' Marcus was there, beside Entorp, their faces matching pictures of shock and confusion.

'Well, she saved Morana Gallas and a strange-looking girl,' Edela frowned. 'But everyone else... yes, she turned them to ash with a symbol. With a spell. I saw it. It was truly awful. They all burned alive.'

No one spoke.

'But what about Raemus?' Jael asked. 'Isn't that what they all wanted? For her to bring Raemus and the Darkness back? Doesn't she need their help?'

'It appears not,' Edela said. 'She has her own plans, and from what I saw, they no longer include The Following.'

***

Draguta turned away from the seeing circle and opened the book.

The woman she was looking for was doing her very best to stay hidden.

Draguta was surprised by her stubbornness. Her cowardice.

Well, she wasn't really surprised by that.

But she didn't have the Book of Darkness. She didn't have anyone or anything listening to her thoughts.

Showing her the way forward.

Helping her.

Draguta ran her eyes over the page and smiled. 'You can try and protect them with your pathetic symbols, but there are ways around them. You'll see.'

***

Aleksander swallowed, watching Jael watch Eadmund as he stood by the hall doors, talking to Bram and Thorgils. She looked sad, not imagining that anyone would notice.

But Aleksander did.

'We might gather the greatest army in Osterland, but Draguta could destroy us all before we're anywhere near her,' Jael sighed irritably, turning to him. 'We can carry the symbol with us. Put it on our shields, our catapults, even our swords, but would it be enough? Would she find a way around it?'

'The serpent couldn't see you when you had the symbol on you.'

'It's still a big risk. We could lose everyone if Draguta finds a way to see past it.'

Aleksander reached for the jug and filled his cup with ale, reminded of the dream he'd had when they were crossing the Nebbar Straights. He glanced at Jael, who had a very familiar look on her face. 'What?'

Jael frowned, reaching for a slice of cheese, glancing around, pleased to see that they were alone. 'Do you remember where the Widow lives?'

Aleksander nodded. 'Her cottage is deep in Hallow Wood.

I went in through the western side, near Iskavall. I think I can remember my way there.'

'It's hard to think about leaving now,' Jael admitted, her eyes back on Eadmund as he banged into Ivaar. The tension between them was starting to boil over. 'Draguta will likely send something else to attack Andala while we're gone. Maybe you could go? On your own?'

'I don't think she's going to give me that book. Not without you.'

'You're sure?'

Aleksander nodded. 'I think it's about more than a book. She must have answers to everything. Everything you need to know about how to defeat Draguta. She wants to talk to you.'

But Jael had stopped listening. Her eyes were on Eadmund, who had just followed Ivaar outside.

***

Ivaar walked away from the hall, still thinking about the serpent; about what an unexpected turn everything had taken. It wasn't how he'd imagined things going when he'd made his alliance with Borg Arnesson. By now, he should have been sitting on Oss' throne, inhaling the stink of his brother's pyre.

Savouring his sweet success.

Ivaar frowned as he walked down the wooden path that wound its way through the rows of almost-identical thatched cottages, past the men and women who were working hard to carve symbols into their doors, out into the open again, and past the workshops where the armourers and blacksmiths were hard at work, forging more tools and weapons.

He walked to the western corner of the fort, where it suddenly became quieter, and there were no more wooden paths to keep his boots dry. And that was where Ivaar finally turned around. 'Brother,' he smiled, but his eyes were hard, and his body was tense as he waited for Eadmund to reach him.

'Brother?' Eadmund snorted, stopping an arm's length from Ivaar. 'You were coming to kill me! To take everything from me! Again! And you think that we're still *brothers*?'

'I think that we're on the same side now,' Ivaar said carefully. 'So say what you need to, and then let us focus on what we're all here to do. It won't help anyone if you're distracted by your need to punish me.'

Eadmund laughed. 'You think I want to punish you? For what *you've* done? Just punish you?'

'And what exactly have I done, Eadmund? I didn't kill Father, you know that now. I didn't kill Melaena, so what have I done to you?' Ivaar challenged. 'Seems to me that you're the King of Oss. You have a wife, a home, riches and an army. *I'm* the one with nothing! No home. No wife. No crown!'

'And whose fault is that?'

'I would think it's yours, Eadmund!' Ivaar roared. '*You* made Father banish me! *You* convinced him that I'd murdered the woman I loved! I lost her and everything else! You lost her, but no one sent you away! What did you think I should do? Forgive you? I didn't kill Melaena! I wanted her to be my wife!' He was surprised by the tears that came as the pain of her death burst in his heart again. 'I wanted to take her away from you, to run away with her. I didn't kill her! She loved me. She wanted to be mine!'

Eadmund didn't even blink. 'So I should pity you? Feel sorry for you? You who wanted to kill me! Eydis! Father!'

'I wanted *revenge*. I was never going to kill Eydis. I wanted *you*!'

Eadmund shook his head. 'I don't believe you, Ivaar. You may have fooled Jael, but I know you. I remember our childhood, the things you did, the games you played. It's who you've always been. Jael doesn't know you. She doesn't know who you are. And Jael won't be around much longer to protect you.'

Ivaar blinked. 'What? What does that mean?'

CHAPTER TWENTY THREE

Karsten had barely spoken since they'd left the beach behind and begun the long trek towards Andala.

The ice and snow had turned to muddy slush, and eventually, as the air warmed, it started to melt away, and even Bayla stopped shivering. But despite feeling warmer, everyone remained frozen in shock.

Berard and Hanna trailed at the back of the group as the sun slid in and out from behind a gentle gathering of clouds. Berard was feeling weak, and he didn't want to slow anyone down. Karsten hadn't noticed. No one had except Hanna, who hung back to keep him company and urge him on. He was morose, blaming himself for Haegen's death; for all that had befallen his family since he'd tried to steal the book and failed.

'If only I'd told someone about it before,' Berard mumbled, his eyes down as he navigated the rocky terrain. As far as the eye could see, there were wide steps of rock now, mostly flat, but very slippery, and with only one arm, Berard was struggling to keep his balance. 'I should have turned Jaeger away from the book before it took hold of him. I wasn't seeing things clearly. He was so desperate to get Father to notice him. To treat him better. Both of us were, I suppose. I didn't think that the book had any real power,' he sighed. 'I thought it was just a myth. Jaeger was so happy. I didn't want to upset him.'

Hanna remained on his left side, ready to grab him if he

slipped. 'You weren't to know, Berard. And I don't think you'd have been able to stop Jaeger if you had. Your brother... he seems like an intimidating man. It would have been hard to force him to do anything he didn't want to do.'

'But what has he become? Do you think he sent that creature to kill Haegen?'

Hanna shrugged. 'I don't know. We don't know that it was the book at all. But hopefully, someone will have answers and a bed and a fire in Andala. We just need to focus on getting there.'

'And if they don't?'

'Then we go to Tuura. We find my father and Jael Furyck. They'll be able to help us. Don't worry, Berard.'

***

Jael and Aleksander joined Edela and Marcus at a table in the corner of the hall, eager to discuss their plan to find the Widow.

'I don't know much about her,' Marcus admitted. 'Nothing that isn't known publicly, at least. She came to Tuura, trained as a dreamer, but she was found to be a member of The Following. I believe she was banished by the elders. No one heard from her again until things started happening. Murders. Strange occurrences. All sorts of sickness. Crop failures. People thinking they were cursed. Spellbound. Her name started being mentioned, and, I suppose, after that, it never stopped.'

Edela looked puzzled. 'I didn't know she was in The Following.'

'Yes, she was, so it could be a trap,' Marcus warned, glancing at Aleksander. 'Perhaps she is their true leader? Pretending to be an ally? Waiting for the right time to spring her trap on you?'

Aleksander squirmed under Marcus' intense stare. He didn't know what to believe. 'My mother trusted her,' he said quietly. 'As my grandmother did before her.'

'But that turned out badly for both of them, didn't it?' Edela said, patting his arm. 'And we don't know how much of that was down to the Widow, do we?'

Marcus nodded. 'She has helped you, I know, but to what end? What does she want? Who does she serve?'

Edela frowned, looking at Jael. 'Well, none of this is making things clearer, is it?'

Jael's mind wandered to Eadmund and Ivaar; neither of them had returned. She felt her leg twitching, eager to leave. 'I think we have no choice but to go. If there's even a small chance that she has the other copy of the book, we have to go. We have to try and protect everyone. And we need to save Eadmund.'

Aleksander felt relieved that a decision had been made. 'It should take us eight or nine days to get there and back, I'd say, so we need to leave as soon as possible.'

Jael nodded, worried about taking her sword away from the fort for that long.

'Well then, it seems that the Widow gets her wish. She gets you, Jael,' Edela said, clasping her hands in her lap. 'But before you go, we're going to have to put our dreamer heads together and think of all the ways we can make both you and the fort as safe as possible.'

***

Ivaar was unsettled by the dead look in Eadmund's eyes.

'Jael won't be my wife for much longer,' Eadmund insisted coldly. 'I plan to make Evaine my queen. Soon, Jael won't have any say in what happens to you. When we return to Oss, she won't be coming with us. She won't be able to protect you then.'

'Does Jael know that?' Ivaar couldn't keep the surprise out of his voice.

'What Jael knows or doesn't know is between us. She is Oss'

queen for now, but Brekka is her true home. She belongs here, and Evaine belongs with me.'

Ivaar remembered what Thorgils had said about something being wrong with Eadmund. And there was something very wrong with Eadmund. He knew his brother. He had seen him with Jael; Eadmund was in love with her. 'Well, as you say, you've the right to choose your own wife, being a king, but until then, Brother, I shall enjoy my freedom.' And he turned away, wondering if Jael knew about her husband's plans.

He doubted it.

Eadmund watched Ivaar leave, surprised by his own words, which had burst forth in such a passion that he'd almost had no control over his tongue. But it was true, he realised, turning away from the horror he could imagine in his father's eyes. Eirik had chosen Jael to be the Queen of Oss, but she didn't belong there.

And he didn't want her as his wife anymore.

***

Evaine was overwhelmed by the sheer size and luxury of the grand chamber Jaeger had chosen for her. 'It's enormous!' she breathed, lifting her eyes up to the stone ceiling which curved high above her head. 'Are they all like this?'

Jaeger was unsmiling, forcing himself not to notice anything about the chamber at all. He felt unsettled being in it, not wanting to think of Haegen. Not wanting to imagine the hatred his brothers would feel for him now. 'No, not all of them. This was my brother's. I should think that it will do?'

'Oh, yes!' Evaine rushed to the bed, which was twice as wide as her own. Opposite it, two doors led to a balcony overlooking the harbour, a cool breeze rustling the pale-yellow curtains framing either side. 'It's perfect. Thank you!' Her thoughts skipped to Eadmund and how soon he'd be able to share it with her. She wondered if the adjacent chamber would be suitable for their son. He could sleep in there with Tanja.

That would make Eadmund happy.

'A servant will come soon and help you with everything you need. I must be going.' Jaeger hesitated as he watched her, struck by how exquisite Evaine was, though she hardly noticed he was there as she hurried through the doors, out onto the balcony, marvelling at the view of the square and the harbour beyond. Exquisite, he thought to himself, reminded of his own wife, who was equally desirable. His body pulsed with anger, knowing that she was still in the arms of Axl Furyck.

Jaeger had allowed himself to become so distracted by the loss of the book and the arrival of Draguta that he had lost his focus. But it was there, immediately: that strong appetite for revenge. He wanted to defeat the Furycks - all of them - and nothing would give him more pleasure than ripping Amma away from Axl Furyck's dead body.

He would have to speak to Draguta.

Surely, she'd be able to help with that...

***

Draguta felt weary, realising for the first time how much the serpent spell had drained her. She had been sitting at her round table for hours, staring at the seeing circle, flicking through the book, thinking, planning, but now she felt overwhelmed by tiredness. Walking to her bed, she yawned, reminding herself that everything she wanted was close. Closer than she could see right now. It was waiting for her on the other side of a door.

A door she needed to find a key for.

Wrapping herself in the thick white bed furs, she lay down, closing her eyes, hoping that the answers she sought would come to her in a dream.

***

Jael spotted Arnna, the tailor, shuffling into her cottage. She desperately needed to see her about a new tunic, but she would have to tell Arnna why she needed it, and then Arnna would want to measure her. And although Jael trusted the old woman, she didn't want anyone else knowing her secret.

Her boots remained stuck in the mud as she weighed her options. She could borrow one of Eadmund's tunics, or even Aleksander's. But everyone she asked would want to know why.

There was always Biddy, Jael supposed. Biddy had been mending her clothes since she was a little girl. Maybe it wouldn't be too much of a stretch for her to make a tunic? Turning away, Jael headed towards where she had last seen Biddy, bumping into Ivaar.

'Sorry,' Ivaar mumbled as Jael threw out her hands, not wanting him to hit her stomach.

He avoided her eyes, and Jael frowned. 'What happened with Eadmund?' she wondered sharply. 'I saw him follow you.'

Ivaar opened his mouth but closed it quickly. He was no fool. Jael had not saved him for any other reason than her need to keep Oss and Eadmund safe. She may have said that she needed his men, but ultimately, they were expendable. As was he.

He was powerless.

But Jael was not. Not yet, anyway.

'Eadmund...' he began, drawing her away from the busy square where people rushed industriously around them, conscious that the afternoon shadows were lengthening. 'Eadmund threatened me. Told me about his plans to get rid of you.'

Jael was so surprised that she didn't have the time to clear her face of any emotion. 'Get rid of me? He *said* that to you?' She didn't doubt Ivaar. For some odd reason, and despite his reputation, Ivaar had a way of telling her the truth. Jael glanced around, not wanting anyone to hear. 'Let's walk to the cove. I want to check on the ships before it gets dark. You can tell me everything he said.'

***

'Meena!' Jaeger strode through the castle doors, catching a flash of her dress as she hurried up the stairs. 'Wait!'

Meena gulped, wishing that he hadn't spotted her. She had enjoyed the blissful silence of being ignored by everyone for a few hours; the freedom to roam the castle unobserved and in peace.

'Where have you been?' Jaeger grumbled, grabbing her arm. 'I've looked everywhere.' He glanced around, but there were only a few slaves nearby, on their knees, scrubbing the hall floor. 'Morana left for the markets with her brother. There's no one in her chamber, so get up there and find some of Varna's books!'

Meena blinked rapidly, terrified by the thought. 'But, but... she will know I was there,' she tried, squirming away from him.

'And?' Jaeger let go of her arm, pushing her up the stairs. 'If she has any problems, she can come and speak with me. Now go!'

Meena panicked, not wanting to go to Morana's chamber, but then she remembered that Draguta had said she was a dreamer, and dreamers were powerful people. So if she could actually learn how to *be* a dreamer...

Taking a deep breath, Meena scrambled up the stairs.

***

Evaine's eyes glistened in the afternoon sun as she entered Hest's vibrant marketplace. The bright colours, the exotic fragrances, the variety of fabrics and the number of jewels on offer had her head swinging in constant motion. The sheer explosion of noise and activity was so different than anything she had experienced before.

She wanted everything she saw.

Morana scowled as she followed her excited daughter, annoyed by the noise and the heat; irritated by the crush of bodies and the impatient elbows of merchants and customers alike. But Evaine appeared oblivious as she rushed ahead, admiring every necklace, every cord of shimmering silk. It gave Morana a chance to speak to Morac freely. She only hoped that Draguta wouldn't be able to hear them in the middle of the humming throng.

'But what can we do?' Morac sighed morosely.

Morana didn't know. She wanted to scream. Her shoulders were tight with tension, and her mind was blank. 'We are powerless. The book has many spells. *I* know many spells, but Draguta...' Morana shook her head. 'She would be able to stop anything I tried. She can read minds. She would discover whatever we were planning.'

Morac swallowed, wiping his brow. He had left Hest as a small boy. His memories of the place were abstract images of buildings and people, but he certainly had no memory of it being this unbearably warm. He unpinned his cloak as he walked. 'Then what can we do?'

Morana glanced around, watching as Evaine took the small cake offered by a crafty merchant who was eager to sell her a tourmaline necklace. 'There's nothing we can do to stop her, but perhaps... someone else can?'

***

It was a long walk around to the cove, but Jael didn't mind. It was nice to escape the noise and the people, and she was eager to find out if the serpent had done any damage to their fleet on its way to the harbour.

'Eadmund plans to make Evaine his queen,' Ivaar announced when they were far enough away from the fort. 'To divorce you, I suppose. He said that you belonged in Brekka.'

Jael was quickly irritated. 'Did he?' It was hard to see straight. Straight was where Eadmund was powerless and unable to help himself. But to think that he was planning to divorce her still hurt, and she couldn't contain the spark of anger that sharpened her eyebrows. 'Well, there are things about Eadmund you don't know.'

'So I hear.'

'You do? From who?'

'Thorgils said something, but nothing that made sense.'

'Morana Gallas has done something to him. Helped Evaine do something,' Jael said quietly, wondering what she was thinking, trusting Ivaar, though she doubted it could make anything worse. 'She put a binding spell on Eadmund. He thinks he's in love with Evaine. They are soul bound.'

Ivaar stopped, frowning in confusion. 'What does that mean?'

'It means that Eadmund believes he's supposed to be with Evaine. As though they're destined to be together. He feels nothing for me anymore.' She stared at Ivaar, ignoring her own words. 'But he forgets himself if he thinks that I'll be pushed off the throne without a fight. I was made the Queen of Oss by Eirik. Eadmund's only the king because of me.'

'Yes, I remember how it went,' Ivaar said drily, turning back to the path. 'You were so happy about that.'

'You wanted to kill everyone, Ivaar,' Jael reminded him.

'Are you someone else now? Not that man? You thought that you'd kill your whole family and take the island. Were you that desperate? Or evil? The things you planned...' She shook her head, walking ahead of him, doubting her own instincts that had kept Eadmund from killing him.

'But I didn't!' Ivaar called, hurrying to catch up with her. 'When I had the chance, I chose not to. So think what you like, but I chose to walk away from the Arnessons and follow you.'

'Ha!' Jael laughed, looking over her shoulder. 'Do you really think you had a choice, Ivaar Skalleson?' She turned back around, disappearing over the small hill. 'Come on! It'll be dark soon!'

Ivaar growled, dropping his head as he followed her.

***

'What did you find?' Jaeger asked softly, placing his hands on Meena's rounded shoulders.

Meena bit her tongue, wanting to wriggle away from him, but she pushed her boots onto the flagstones and stayed as still as possible, trying to meet his eyes. 'I... I took two books. Hopefully, Morana won't notice.'

'Good, then you must start reading them. Now. And when you're done, go back and swap them for two more,' Jaeger urged. 'I want you reading all day long, Meena. Every night too. You are going to teach yourself how to be a dreamer. *My* dreamer. And then we'll be free, you and I.' His eyes were feverish as he stared into hers. '*I* will be free to rule Osterland. All of it! With you beside me.'

Meena tried to hold his gaze, but it burned too intensely, and she turned her eyes to the floor. 'I will try,' she mumbled. 'I will try.'

***

Morac's attention had been commandeered by Evaine, who had her heart set on the tourmaline necklace. She had rushed back to interrupt his conversation with Morana, and Morac knew that he would not be free of her until she was admiring the necklace as it hung around her neck.

And so, soon, Evaine was happily pushing her way ahead of them again, the necklace sparkling in the late afternoon sunshine, leaving Morac and Morana to resume their conversation.

'Who?' Morac wondered, glaring at a well-dressed woman who had elbowed him in the ribs. 'Who could help us?'

'Raemus,' Morana whispered. 'The Followers are gone. Only you and I have any chance of returning him to his rightful place now.'

Morac was confused. 'Without the book? Or Draguta?'

'*I* have been to the Dolma, Brother,' Morana reminded him with a hiss. 'And I can do it again if we can find that missing page.'

Morac glanced around. 'The one Draguta ripped out of the book? But that was centuries ago, wasn't it? How would it have survived?' He frowned. 'Wouldn't she have burned it?'

Morana smiled as the clouds in her head finally parted. 'I don't need to hold it in my hands to read it, Brother. Not if I can find it in my dreams!'

***

They made camp for the night on the eastern edge of a copse, hoping the small cluster of trees would shelter them from the worst of the wind. Half of Ulf's crew had worked to build a large fire while the rest hunted and foraged amongst the trees, returning with a few furry carcasses and some handfuls of nuts and berries.

After a long day of walking, they were all starving.

Ulf had kept them near the coast for much of the day, only deviating inland when the beaches and coves had turned into sheer cliffs. When morning came, they would skirt the edge of the copse, and hopefully, arrive in Andala within the day.

Bayla peered at the craggy helmsman as he threaded a squirrel onto a stick, resting it on top of the hastily assembled spit. Its tiny skinless body didn't look appetising, and despite the endless gurgling of her empty belly, Bayla doubted that she could stomach it. She nibbled on nuts instead, comforted by Ulf's assurances that they were on the right path to Andala.

Bayla offered Karsten some nuts, but he shook his head, looking away. He was trying to calm Kai, who he'd carried for most of the day, and who wasn't so enamoured with the dark, spidery trees that rose up behind them. When Kai had fallen asleep in his father's arms, they had been by the sea where everything was open and light, and now they were in darkness, and he was terrified, reminded of the storm and the creature and the horrifying death of his uncle.

Nicolene made no move to help her husband. She was trying to keep their other son asleep, with one eye on Irenna, who had been just as silent as Karsten. Irenna's three children clung to her, hoping to get her attention, but she stared straight ahead, ignoring their pleading voices and constant crying.

'Valder,' Hanna smiled at Irenna's only son. 'Why don't you come and sit by me, and we can guess what's making those noises. Have you heard an owl before? Or a cricket? What about a hedgehog or a fox? All sorts of creatures make homes in the trees, you know. And some of them sleep all day, just so they can wake up and explore all night.'

Valder stopped crying and stared at Hanna, intrigued. He stepped away from his silent mother, towards Hanna's outstretched hand.

'Sit down here, there you go, and we can close our eyes and try to guess what's making each sound.'

'But will they hurt us?' the little boy wondered, his eyes darting around fearfully.

'No, they are likely too scared to even try,' Hanna said softly. 'They are wary of us, just like that squirrel should have been. Because we want to hurt them, don't we? We want to eat them, and make clothes from them. Furs for our beds too.' Her eyes met Berard's. 'So they have to do what they can to make themselves safe. They have to escape. They have to disappear so they won't be found by all the people and creatures trying to hurt them. They have to protect their families, and keep them safe from harm.'

Karsten looked up, listening, feeling his son finally go limp in his arms. He glanced at Irenna and her devastated children; at his mother, who looked terrified, nibbling on her nuts, jumping at every sound.

At his one-armed brother who was being braver than any of them.

And Karsten realised that he was the man destined to become the King of Hest now. His family was his to care for, and he had to do everything he could to keep them all safe.

CHAPTER TWENTY FOUR

The King's Hall was a bubbling cauldron of Andalans, Alekkans, Tuurans, and Islanders celebrating their victory over the serpent. Finally freed from the shock of it all, they were sharing their stories - heavily embellished and more heartily told after a few cups of ale and mead - but their smiles didn't quite reach their eyes, as they all knew that this was only the beginning, and all of them feared what would come next.

'Have you heard from Raymon Vandaal?' Jael asked Gant as she tried to chew her way through a stringy piece of chicken, though she was too distracted to have much of an appetite.

'I think we have to give them a few more days,' Gant suggested. 'Though I don't have a good feeling about it.'

'No, nor do I, but hopefully, Raymon's mother can talk some sense into him. She always seemed nice enough, unlike her stupid husband.'

Gant raised his eyebrows and reached for his cup.

Jael noticed but didn't say anything. She was trying to remember what she needed to check on before she left with Aleksander in the morning. She saw Eadmund watching her and frowned, remembering her talk with Ivaar.

'How long will you be gone?' Gant wondered.

'Hopefully, only about nine days,' Jael mumbled, finally giving up on the chicken. 'We'll be as quick as we can. If we can stay away from the wolves, that is.' She caught Aleksander's eye and winked at him.

'And ravens,' he added. 'Serpents too. I wouldn't mind a rabbit, though. Maybe a fish. Something small and edible.'

'Unless Draguta sends thousands of them to attack us,' Jael grinned. 'We'll have to make sure we pack everything we can think of, just in case.'

'Not sure there's anything that could help us,' Aleksander admitted, remembering the ravens. 'Just you and that sword, maybe.'

Gant frowned. They would miss Jael and her sword, but he could only hope that what they would gain by losing her and Aleksander for a few days would help them in the end.

Eydis was quiet as she sat beside Jael, not interested in her supper at all.

'Are you alright?' Jael wondered, bending to whisper in her ear.

Eydis jumped, then shrugged.

'No one is listening,' Jael assured her. Amma was on Eydis' other side, busy talking to Axl. Gant and Aleksander had started discussing the fort.

No one was looking their way.

'Not Eadmund?' Eydis murmured.

'No,' Jael said, glancing at her husband, who sat wedged between the square frames of Erl and Rork Arnesson, frowning at whatever they were arguing about. 'Not Eadmund.'

'I'm worried about him,' Eydis said sadly. 'When I see him in my dreams, he's drifting away. And when I hear him, he sounds like a different person.'

'That's why Aleksander and I have to leave to see the Widow. She has the other copy of the book. Hopefully, it will save him.'

'But what will happen while you're away? To Eadmund? Or to the fort?' Eydis dropped her head, lowering her voice even further. 'I don't know how to keep him safe.'

'Eadmund?'

Eydis nodded.

Jael stared at Eadmund, who was now looking her way. His frown deepened before he dropped his eyes to his plate. 'I'll talk to Thorgils. He's very experienced at looking after Eadmund, isn't he?' she smiled, trying to lift her voice. 'And Torstan. Bram too. They'll watch him. And Aleksander and I will return as quickly as we can.'

Eydis bit her lip, not comforted in the slightest.

***

Getta Furyck may have been the Queen of Iskavall, but she wasn't content to sit by her husband's side and simper agreeably as the queens before her had done. Her husband, Raymon, was younger than her - only seventeen-years-old - and he needed her guidance. No, not her guidance, Getta realised. It was more than that. He needed her approval. It helped him to feel calm and in control. To know that he had pleased her; that she was content with his decision making.

He was young but trying so desperately to prove himself worthy of her love, worthy of his father's crown too. Though Getta knew that Raymon wasn't worthy of anything yet, but one day, perhaps, with her guidance, he would be.

If his mother didn't get in the way.

'You must hear them out,' Ravenna Vandaal insisted, dabbing her mouth with a napkin. 'Jael and Axl are your cousins, Getta. Amma is your sister. You can't dismiss their words so lightly. And nor can you, Raymon. Not as the king. You must consider the safety of our people, and the friendship of our neighbours will always have great bearing on that.'

Getta snorted, leaning back as her servant removed her plate. 'You think we should consider the words of *murderers*?' she sneered, turning to Raymon, demanding his loyalty with the strength of her hard brown eyes. 'Those who killed my father? My brother?' She shook her head, reaching for her husband's hand. 'It will do us no good to listen to murderers, Ravenna. They will come here next,' she insisted. 'They will try to take your throne, my love, and I will never allow that to happen!'

Ravenna sighed. She disliked her daughter-in-law almost as much as she'd disliked Getta's father, Lothar. No, possibly more, she realised. Getta had set her sights on becoming the Queen of Iskavall as soon as Raymon became heir to the throne. And poor, sweet Raymon had never stood a chance.

Getta was a plain girl; soft, round, and small. There was no warmth about her, no gentleness or agreeability. No kind heart or inviting smile.

Yet Raymon was besotted.

'Getta is right, Mother,' Raymon said firmly. 'Jael and Axl Furyck have murdered two kings. We can't speak to them as though we're still allies. They have committed crimes against their own kingdom. They have killed my queen's family!'

Ravenna felt sad, watching her son's gentle hazel eyes darting about beneath a serious pair of dark eyebrows as he looked from his mother to his wife. He had always been so eager to please, even as a small boy. She knew that he didn't want to disappoint either of them, but if there had to be a choice, Ravenna was well aware that her opinion stood no chance. 'They have, yes, but we must hear them out at least. Ranuf was a loyal friend to the many Kings of Iskavall, including your father. Our kingdoms have supported each other in times of war for as long as I can remember. I do understand why you are upset, Getta, but if there is danger coming for the whole of Osterland, we cannot ignore it, whether we feel offended or not. The lives of our people may depend upon it.'

Raymon glanced at Getta, who puckered her lips irritably, then at his mother, who stared at him with desperation in her kind brown eyes.

He swallowed. Caught.

***

The lords and ladies of Hest were on edge.

They had been invited to the castle for a grand feast, yet it felt wrong to be celebrating, when Haaron Dragos had been murdered by his own son; when Berard had been disfigured, maybe killed; and when The Following had emerged from the shadows and run the rest of the Dragos' out of the city.

And now, a strange woman had appeared, acting as though she was their mistress, ruler of even the new king himself.

No one knew how to behave or where to look, but they drank Haaron's wine and nibbled the exquisite food the slaves ferried around the hall, keeping their questions to themselves and their eyes fixed upon each other.

Draguta didn't notice. She was far too busy enjoying herself.

Happy with the brightness of the candles and the delicate melodies of the musicians, who meandered through the guests, blowing on their flutes and pipes, Draguta glided around, admiring the fine elegance of the company.

She wasn't the only one.

Draguta watched as Jaeger escorted Evaine around the little clusters of Hestians and Silurans, noticing the envy of the ladies who were old or ugly or too plain to be noticed, and the desire of those who could not take their eyes off Evaine, so breathtaking was her beauty.

Draguta observed it all with amusement, enchanted by how utterly vapid and self-involved Evaine was. So exquisite to look at, and yet, so empty. So vain and calculating. So desperate to be adored.

And so obsessed with Eadmund Skalleson.

Smiling broadly, Draguta floated towards her, ignoring Morac and Morana, who hovered awkwardly on the edge of the little group, wondering when they would be allowed to leave. 'What a beautiful necklace,' she cooed, admiring Evaine's new piece of jewelry. 'How well it suits you.'

Evaine's flawless face shone. 'Thank you,' she smiled. 'There were so many wonderful things in the markets. I think I shall go every day!'

Draguta nodded, but she was watching Jaeger, noting how his eyes continued to find Evaine, despite being deep in conversation with an old Siluran merchant. She frowned, sensing the desire coursing through his body. It would not help things for him to get in the way, and the sooner he realised that, the better. Evaine was meant for a very particular purpose, and he wasn't going to ruin that. 'Come to my chamber tomorrow after breakfast,' Draguta murmured. 'And we will talk about how quickly you can become the Queen of Oss.'

Just thinking about Eadmund made Evaine shiver in anticipation. It was a feeling that welled up from deep inside her, leaving her almost giddy.

She quickly nodded her head.

'Good,' Draguta said, running her eyes over Morac, who smelled like fear. 'I've no need to kill you, have I?' she wondered sweetly. 'You're not plotting against me with your sister?' Draguta laughed, watching Morana's face crumple in annoyance.

Morac shook his head, spilling his wine. 'No. No, you don't, and we're not. I... it was a surprise. Things were not as I expected when we left Oss. It has been a shock... what happened.'

'Ohhh,' Draguta soothed, 'you poor thing, having to run away before Eadmund Skalleson murdered you. And he would have, I saw that. Then his wife would have killed poor Evaine and Morana too. She wants us all dead, you know, so we must put our heads together and come up with a way to stop her before she is outside this castle, trying to run her sword through us all!'

***

Thorgils left the noise of the hall behind, eager to ensure that Isaura and the children were comfortable in their new cottage. And safe. As safe as he could make them. Memories of the serpent attack were burned into his mind, and he couldn't stop thinking about what that woman would try next.

He was so lost in his thoughts as he hurried along the path, that he didn't hear Jael approach.

'Lucky I wasn't a murderous fairy,' she grinned, tapping him on the arm. 'You would have been skewered on my sword by now.'

Thorgils spun around with a frown. 'You're telling me that fairies are real? I should be looking out for fairies as well as giant snakes? What about elves? Trolls? Dragons? Anything else you want to tell me about, Jael?'

It was dark now, but there was enough moonlight for Jael to see that he had a twinkle in his eye. 'You know as much as I do. More than either of us ever wanted to know, I'm sure.'

'Well, at least we're surrounded by that symbol now. Though how a little symbol is powerful enough to keep a giant monster like that away...' Thorgils shivered, pulling his cloak around his chest, though it wasn't a cold evening. 'It just doesn't seem possible to me.'

'Well, for some things it might be enough. I don't know if flying things would be stopped.'

Thorgils blinked. 'Flying things?'

Jael nodded. 'Yes, you'll have to keep an eye out for those too. Watch the clouds. They might not always be clouds, and if so, you won't have long to react.'

Thorgils stopped, grabbing her arm. 'Are you being serious?'

'I am, unfortunately. If Morana could send thousands of ravens to attack us, who knows what Draguta could do. But you'll have three dreamers here. Hopefully, one of them will see what's coming and give you some warning.'

'Yes, but the dreamer with the sword is leaving, and that's

the dreamer I'd much rather have here,' he sighed, dropping her arm.

'It's nice to feel wanted.'

'Well, you could leave your sword behind,' Thorgils suggested. 'It's not you I'm going to miss as much as *Toothpick*.'

Jael laughed and punched his arm, enjoying his company again. Thorgils had been so busy with Isaura, and she had been so preoccupied with Eadmund and the fort that it felt as though they'd barely spoken since they'd arrived in Andala. 'Ivaar said that Eadmund plans to divorce me,' she said suddenly, not smiling anymore. 'Apparently, he's going to make Evaine the Queen of Oss.'

Thorgils looked horrified. 'Ivaar said that? And you're trusting Ivaar now, are you?' He shook his head. 'I'll never understand what you see in that slimy shit.'

Jael ignored him. 'Eadmund threatened Ivaar, said I wouldn't be able to protect him for long. That Evaine would be the queen soon, and I'd be staying in Brekka, where I belong.'

'Oh.' Thorgils wasn't thinking about Ivaar anymore.

'You're going to have to watch him closely,' Jael warned. 'His need to be with Evaine has been growing stronger since they've been apart. Eydis is worried about him. He may try to leave.'

'*Leave*?'

Jael shrugged. 'I don't know, but it makes sense to watch him. He's being controlled by Evaine and Morana. When we were in Tuura, the dreamers were controlling the temple guards. One of them tried to kill me in a training match. He had his hands around my throat, and when I looked into his eyes, they were blank, like Eadmund's. A dreamer had bound him, making him do that.'

The valley between Thorgils' eyebrows only deepened. 'I'll keep an eye on him. We all will, don't worry. Just get back as soon as you can. I don't like the idea that we're sitting here just waiting for something to happen. I'd rather get out there and kill this Draguta bitch. Take that evil book away from her for good!'

Jael smiled. 'Me too. And we will. Soon.'

***

Heavy with child, Getta had tired after supper, waddling back to her chamber, so Ravenna took a rare opportunity to spend some time alone with her son. He was her only child. She had fallen pregnant once, late in her marriage, and Raymon had always been precious because of it.

Ravenna was a tall, elegant woman, with long flaxen hair and a sadness about her that had only deepened over the years. Her marriage to Hugo Vandaal had been loveless, and she'd felt nothing but relief when he was murdered.

She only hoped that her son would not make the mistakes of his foolish father.

Ravenna slipped her arm through Raymon's as they walked towards the harbour, enjoying the mild evening. Iskavall's capital, Ollsvik, was small compared to Andala. Its three-sided wooden fort was wedged into a flat valley between a pair of majestic high-peaked mountains. Much of Iskavall was mountainous and uninhabitable, offering little opportunity for farming, and most who made their homes in the kingdom chose to do so on the narrow strips of arable land hugging the coastline. They fished and farmed and traded with Alekka to the North, and the Fire Lands to the South.

Yet, for a seemingly small, simple kingdom, Iskavall's rulers had left behind a legacy of turbulence and corruption, ensuring that no one who sat upon their ancient throne had the confidence that they would reign for long.

And Ravenna was desperate for her son not to fall victim to the same traps of greed and impetuousness that had felled his father. 'I understand why Getta is so upset,' she began, having eased herself into the conversation with general chatter about the new ship Raymon had commissioned, and the summer weather, which was warmer than usual. 'But as king, you can't make decisions just because your wife dislikes your neighbours.'

Raymon tensed, turning to his mother. 'Why not? Shouldn't it matter that her cousins killed her father and brother?' Raymon shook his long dark hair out of his eyes, glaring sternly at his mother. 'Getta is smart enough to see the truth behind their motives. She is no fool.'

Ravenna sighed. Her son was lovesick, and he would hear nothing but Getta's words, she knew. Still, she had to try. 'The Kings of Iskavall have never covered themselves in glory. This kingdom was begun by an adulterer who ran away from his own king after stealing his wife. It's as though the gods cursed every king who followed in punishment for his crime. None lasted long. They made poor choices, chose the wrong allies. They made many mistakes, your father included, and if you don't think this through, my son, your reign will end up as brief and ruinous as theirs.'

Raymon wanted to glare some more, but the quiet of the evening and the absence of Getta allowed him to think for himself for a moment. His mother wasn't wrong. His father had made mistakes, and, like many of Iskavall's kings before him, Hugo Vandaal had been murdered because of them. And choosing to dismiss the stark warning Axl Furyck had sent him could possibly be a very big mistake indeed.

Ravenna reached up, holding Raymon's handsome face in her hands. He was still growing, and the width of his broad shoulders told her that he would one day be as big as his father. 'It's a heavy weight a king carries. Making decisions that affect the lives, and possibly cause the deaths of thousands of people. But you are the king now, so you must ask yourself what sort of king you wish to be.'

***

Ivaar leaned back against the wall, enjoying a long drink of mead.

He was feeling more confident in his position after his talk with Jael. They were not friends, but he was beginning to think that they might almost be allies, and he saw no reason why that wouldn't continue. For the time being, at least.

Although, with Jael gone...

He frowned as Bruno Adea approached his table.

Ivaar had been expecting this.

Bruno appeared to have finally broken free of Ayla's shackles, and he now stood before him, glowering like a man thirsting for his long-dreamed-of revenge.

Ivaar knew how he felt. 'Think this through,' he began calmly. 'A time will come when we can face each other with swords in our hands, if that's your wish, but for now, you can barely hold a spoon, and I would kill you in seconds. I don't imagine your wife would want that.'

Bruno wanted to drag Ivaar from his bench and throw him out of the hall. He was ready to pick up a sword and fight him now; in his mind, at least. 'You think so?' he growled. 'You've never seen me with a sword, Skalleson.'

'No, and likely I won't for long. You'll be dead before you can even find the strength to raise it. Why not sit down, and ask someone to feed you some broth. You look ready to fall over.'

Bruno lunged forward, slamming his fist onto the table.

Bram was on his feet, by Bruno's side in a flash. 'You'd do well to come with me,' he muttered. 'Unless you want to get on the queen's bad side. I imagine she wouldn't take well to you picking a fight with Ivaar. He's under her protection, remember?'

Ivaar didn't think he needed protecting from a skeleton like Bruno Adea, but he was happy to have the irritation removed as Bram shunted a furious Bruno away.

Lifting his cup, Ivaar signalled to the mead girl, eager to stop feeling anything at all. She smiled and headed his way, but before she could get there, someone else reached him.

Ayla.

Ivaar squirmed on his bench, avoiding her eyes.

'I think it's time we talked,' she said softly. 'Alone.'

***

Jaeger's new servant, Else, was a soft-spoken, red-cheeked old woman. And one of the only people in the castle who had ever spoken to Meena as if she was a person, and not just some strange oddity to be ignored or ridiculed.

'Shall I bring you some supper, my lady?' Else wondered as she stopped by the table. 'I have filled the wine jug and left another one beside it. There is nothing else I can see to do for now.'

Meena wasn't even sure that Else was speaking to her, though they were alone in the chamber. 'I...' She shrugged uncomfortably. 'I'm not a lady.'

'Are you not, then?' Else asked kindly. 'Well, seems to me that living in the king's chamber might make you a lady.'

Meena frowned, biting a fingernail. 'I would...'

Else leaned forward. 'Yes?'

'I would like something to eat,' Meena mumbled.

Else smiled and straightened up, smoothing down her apron. Her children had all died before they were grown, so her natural instinct was to mother every lost creature she came across, and no one looked more lost than Meena Gallas. Over the years, she had watched as Varna dragged her granddaughter about, treating her as no better than a dog. But now, there wasn't even Varna. There was no one to bother about Meena at all. 'I shall find something in the kitchen and be back shortly,' she said, bobbing her head, happy to be of use.

Meena watched Else walk to the door. She didn't feel comfortable sitting in Jaeger's chamber, looking through her grandmother's books. She was convinced that Morana or Draguta would discover what she was doing; worried that she was wasting her own time, and Jaeger's. The first book had been hard to understand. Varna's light, spidery scrawls had made Meena's eyes blur, and her rambling thoughts had wandered far from anything that made sense. Meena felt panic flutter in her chest, convinced that Jaeger would open the door at any moment and demand to know what she had learned.

Closing that book and grabbing the next, Meena sighed and opened it, blinking at the title on the very first page.

Dreaming.

***

Ivaar was surprised that Ayla wanted to talk to him, and he was convinced that he wouldn't like anything she said, but he followed her out of the hall and down a path, away from the few stragglers who were still out in the dark, finishing their preparations for the night to come.

'You must not fight Bruno,' Ayla said quietly, once they were alone. 'You have done enough to him. To both of us.'

Ivaar felt the tension in his body ease as he listened to her familiar voice.

He had missed her.

But he didn't know what to say.

'There is no need for you to hurt him or kill him. Not anymore. Not anymore, Ivaar. You can have everything you want without needing to hurt anyone.'

Ivaar stopped, turning to her. The moon shone its luminous

beams towards her beautiful face, and he had to work hard to keep his hands by his sides. 'How? Why do you say that?'

'Jael has given you a chance. And if you prove yourself to her, then she will give you another. And another. And the more you do to earn her trust and prove that she was right in saving you, the more you will be forgiven. By most, eventually. It will take some time, but yes, you have a chance for a new life, Ivaar. People will forgive you. I see that.'

Ivaar couldn't hide his surprise. 'But not you?'

Ayla lowered her eyes. 'I can feel your pain. I've always been able to feel it, and I sympathise with you, but I didn't deserve what you did to me. Or my husband. You took time from us,' she said, looking up. 'You loved Melaena, so I know you understand the feeling of having someone you love taken from you. We are not given much time, Ivaar, and you stole mine. Mine and Bruno's, and I can never forgive you for that. For how you hurt him. He will never be the same again.'

Ivaar felt a rush of anger, but it was quickly dampened by sadness. He realised that it mattered if Ayla forgave him, and knowing that she never would was a sharp pain in his chest. He dropped his eyes, not wanting her to see his disappointment. 'I can't change what has been, but I have no wish to die, as it stands. Tell your husband to stay away from me, Ayla. And you too. I will not go after him, but I will defend myself if he comes, so tell him to stay away.'

Ivaar turned away, not wanting any further reminder of what he had done to her.

***

Jael couldn't stop shivering as she pulled the bed furs up to her nose. She'd found a spare chamber in the hall, next to Fyn's. Sleeping arrangements were all over the place, and would be for some time, but Jael was just grateful to be alone. Tanja had finally gotten Sigmund to sleep in the next room, and Jael allowed her eyes to close, enjoying the warm lump that was Vella, wedged against the backs of her knees.

They would be leaving in the morning, and Jael couldn't shake the worry that they were walking so eagerly towards the Widow.

Walking away from keeping everyone in the fort safe.

But she had a strong feeling that getting the Book of Aurea was important. She just hoped that the Widow actually had it.

That it wasn't a trap.

Jael yawned, feeling her body relax, trying to picture how Eadmund had looked before Morac returned to Oss, and everything changed. Sometimes it felt as though they'd never been married at all, and it was hard to remember who he had been or how they'd been together. But then she remembered the fur cloak he'd bought her and how it had stayed by the door of their house for so long, waiting for that moment when she finally stopped running away from him.

And she had, in the end, but now Eadmund was so desperate to leave her.

Jael reached down, feeling her wedding band, cold against her finger, trying to remind herself that Eadmund wasn't there anymore.

She closed her eyes, hoping the Widow would help her find a way to bring him back.

PART THREE

Hallow Wood

CHAPTER TWENTY FIVE

Draguta stretched languidly, staring at the ceiling. Since her return, she had awoken each morning with no memory of her dreams. At first, she wondered if it was her body strengthening itself. She certainly was beginning to feel stronger, her mind felt sharper too, but there had been no sign of her dreams returning.

Until now.

Smiling, Draguta eased herself out of bed, wrapping a fur around her shoulders as she walked towards the bright sunshine streaming into the chamber from her balcony. A clear, light-blue sky greeted her, and Draguta was pleasantly surprised to see that Jaeger was already out on the square, organising his men.

That was a promising start to the day.

Jael Furyck would not be easy to defeat, Draguta knew. The gods were doing their best to protect her. And, despite their pathetic weaknesses, they were powerful in their own way. Powerful enough to irritate her. To thwart any plans she might make.

Or were they?

Smiling, she turned back into her chamber, ready to dress and head down to the hall for breakfast.

***

Jael had skipped breakfast, eager to be gone, but Biddy handed her a large packet of food for the journey, staring at her intently. Jael could only assume that Edela had told her about the baby, as they both appeared to be fussing over her now.

'Are you sure that's enough food?' Edela wondered, glancing at Biddy.

'We're not going to spend all day eating!' Jael insisted, frowning at her grandmother. 'Besides, Aleksander and I are perfectly capable of finding our own food. This will be fine.'

'Perhaps I should go back to the kitchen and see what else I can find?' Biddy muttered, suddenly worried that Edela was right.

Jael rolled her eyes, glancing at her mother and Branwyn, wondering who else wanted to join in the mothering, but neither of them said a word. She looked down at Eydis, who stood quietly beside her. 'Edela and Biddy will take good care of you while I'm gone, Eydis. Biddy, make sure you find Eydis some cloth to stick in her ears, so she doesn't have to listen to your snoring!'

Biddy narrowed her eyes. 'I think Tig is getting impatient over there, so best you get going before he decides to leave without you.'

Jael smiled. 'I'll miss you too, Biddy. Take care of the puppies for me.'

'I will,' Biddy said, looking worried. The idea that Jael and Aleksander were going to see the Widow unsettled her. It didn't sound like the right thing to do at all.

'Keep Eydis and Ayla close, Grandmother,' Jael urged. 'If anything happens, you'll all need to come together to try and find a way to stop it. Just like in Tuura, Eydis. You'll have to find the book if you can.'

'I'll try.'

Jael could hear the anxiety in her voice. 'And don't forget to help Runa take care of Fyn for me. I want to see him out of bed when I return.'

Eydis nodded, eager for that to happen too.

Jael glanced around. Many people were waiting to say something to her, but if she spoke to each one of them, they wouldn't leave until midday.

'Be careful, Jael,' Gisila implored, sensing her daughter's impatience.

'I will, Mother,' Jael said, heading for Axl. He was leaning on his crutch, wobbling beside Gant, which was handy as Jael wanted to speak to him too.

'Axl,' Jael said, indicating for them to follow her to Tig. 'You must stay alert.' Her eyes darted to Gant, knowing that her message was mostly for him. 'An attack could come at any time. Hopefully, Draguta won't know that we've gone, but she may be planning to try again anyway. Keep an eye on Edela. Eydis and Ayla too. They're your best defense against her. And try to get that serpent into the water as quickly as possible. We need to rebuild the piers, and the sheds too. That's going to take some time.'

Axl nodded, wishing she wasn't leaving.

Jael turned to Gant. 'Keep the forges going day and night. We're going to need more weapons, especially arrows. Put the symbol on every shield too. Get the men training. Keep them all busy.'

Gant nodded, wishing she wasn't leaving.

'We'll be back as soon as we can,' Jael promised, watching Tig, now getting noisy in his impatience. She still felt uncertain about going, but part of her was eager to escape the confines of the fort and leave all the people and their problems behind.

To feel free from the responsibility of it all, just for a moment.

Aleksander, waiting by his quietly patient horse, Sky, looked just as eager. 'We should go,' he said, hoisting himself into the saddle. 'I think we're looking at rain soon. It would be good to get over the hill before it comes.'

Jael nodded, wanting to say goodbye to Eadmund, but there was no sign of him. That worried her, but then she spotted

Thorgils striding towards her, Eadmund and Bram trailing behind him.

'You can't slip away without saying goodbye to me, my queen!' Thorgils boomed. 'I'm still your loyal oathman. You can't just abandon me without a farewell hug!'

Jael squirmed. 'I don't think that's how it works,' she tried, letting Thorgils come towards her, his big arms extended. Despite her reluctance to be touched, there was something about Thorgils' arms that made her feel oddly comforted. But just as he started to wrap them around her, Jael backed away, thinking about her belly. 'We have to get going,' she muttered. 'If you're looking for hugs, I'm sure Eadmund will give you one!' And hurrying to Tig, she didn't look around again.

In the end, Jael had not had time to organise a new tunic, and she could feel hers straining across her breasts every time she moved her arms. It wasn't the most pressing problem she had, so she put it out of her mind and stuck her boot into Tig's stirrup, hoisting herself into the saddle, listening to him snorting and nickering impatiently, ready to head for the gates.

It had been a long time.

Thorgils frowned at Jael, but now that she was safely away from him, she could smile. 'Behave yourselves!' she ordered. 'And keep your eyes open. I want to see this fort standing when we return!' And easing Tig's head around, she followed Aleksander through the main gates, turning for one last look at Eadmund.

He stared after her, oddly disappointed that she hadn't said goodbye to him, but images of Evaine distracted him quickly. Turning around, he headed for the hall, wondering how Sigmund was.

Thorgils watched him leave, inclining his head towards Bram. 'I promised Jael that we'd keep a close eye on Eadmund. I'm going to ask Torstan too. Just in case he decides to escape,' he murmured. 'You get first watch!'

Bram turned to his nephew in surprise, but not quickly

enough as Thorgils was already striding down the path that led to Isaura's new cottage. Ready to grumble, Bram caught sight of Runa standing by the hall doors and suddenly changed his mind.

***

'That's Bog's Hill,' Ulf smiled at Bayla, happy to see that mountainous rise appear in the distance. It had been a long couple of days, and he was thirsty; desperate for a bench and a jug of ale and a fire to dry out his boots and warm his aching toes. 'And Bog's Hill means Andala!'

Ulf had been very attentive to the queen since he had pulled her out of the icy sea. And though Bayla thought that he looked and sounded like an old beggar, she was grateful for his care. Without Haegen and Haaron, she was feeling more vulnerable by the moment. Karsten was far too occupied with Berard and Irenna and the children to notice her at all. She nodded at Ulf, but her heart sank as she followed his gaze. Her feet were blistered and sore, and she didn't know how they were going to carry her to the bottom of the hill, let alone all the way up it.

'It's easy enough,' Ulf assured her, seeing the hesitation in her eyes. 'A gentle slope, I'd say.'

'You're sure you know where we are?' Bayla wondered anxiously. 'You not being a man of the land.'

'Well, it's true, I've spent most of my life on the sea, but I'm from Andala. I know this place. This is home.' And putting his arm around Bayla's slumped shoulders, he ushered her forward.

Karsten was grateful for Ulf's help with his mother. He had enough to worry about without needing to respond to her endless stream of complaints and questions. Irenna would barely move her feet, Nicolene had begun her familiar moaning, and the children were no better. Not one of them would walk without constant coaxing.

At least there was Hanna.

Karsten turned around, watching how she kept close to Berard, making sure that he had support. His one-armed brother was weaker than he would admit, and Hanna had helped him throughout their day and a bit of walking. Karsten turned back around, wishing he'd married a woman as capable and agreeable as she was. He felt like a different man than the one who'd been so desperate to get Nicolene into his bed.

There was a lot he'd do differently, given a chance.

And now that he was the rightful King of Hest, he would hopefully have the chance to make some changes.

Once he killed Jaeger.

'Keep going!' he demanded, lifting his voice over the rising moans and groans. 'Over that hill, we'll find a fire and something to eat! Keep going!'

***

Jael felt her head clear as she rode up the hill. She loved this lush, rolling place, and despite her attachment to the wild, barren landscape of Oss, she had missed her home more than she'd realised. Tig had too. He was pushing harder as he climbed, impatient to crest the hill, knowing that what waited over the other side was one of their favourite rides across the wide meadows that would eventually lead them into Hallow Wood.

'We'll know soon enough if she can see us!' Jael called to Aleksander, who rode beside her. It was as though no time had passed, and despite any awkwardness that had arisen since her marriage, it felt good to be together again.

Aleksander nodded, finding it impossible to keep the smile off his face. 'Hopefully, she won't cast any spells till it gets dark!'

Well, let's make sure we're out of sight well before nightfall, then!' Jael dipped her head, spurring Tig up the hill, smiling just as widely as Aleksander.

***

'How lovely you look this morning, Evaine,' Draguta purred, popping her eggs with a knife, watching their bright orange yolks flood her plate. 'Perhaps we should visit the tailors today? I imagine the King of Oss would prefer his new queen to look a little more... elegant. Though, of course,' she said quickly, 'you are hardly to blame. You did have to leave that little island in such a hurry. I don't imagine there was time to pack anything more suitable?' She glanced at Morana, who was bent over her own eggs, showing no interest in their conversation.

Draguta appeared the very picture of elegance herself. Hest's tailors had been hard at work creating a wardrobe of identical white silk dresses. They were the only ones Draguta wanted to wear.

And she preferred to wear a new one each day.

'No,' Evaine said. 'Oss' tailor had little skill to speak of, and such a poor selection of fabrics. I did the best I could, but I'm sure I look barely respectable.'

Draguta's expression told Evaine that she agreed. 'Good! Then we shall go, you and I, after breakfast, and we will talk on the way. There is much to discuss about you and Eadmund.'

Evaine beamed with happiness.

Jaeger frowned, bored with the constant talk of Eadmund Skalleson and the endless prattle about dresses. His dreams had tortured him with visions of Evaine, naked, writhing on his bed, and it was frustrating to have her so close, yet so utterly uninterested in him. He wasn't used to being ignored. 'But won't you have some argument from his wife?' he wondered sharply, reaching out with his cup as a slave brought around the jug of buttermilk. 'I don't imagine a woman like Jael Furyck will let her husband go without a fight. She seemed quite happy with him when they were here, and he couldn't take his eyes off her.'

Evaine scowled, irritated that Jaeger was sticking his nose into a conversation that had nothing to do with him. He was a powerful, handsome man, and the King of Hest, she knew, but Eadmund was nothing to do with him, and nor was she.

She refused to even look his way.

'His wife will be dead soon,' Draguta pointed out cheerfully. 'That is what we are all trying to achieve, is it not? All of us. Together. Our little group.' She glanced around. 'And where is the missing member of our group, Jaeger? Where is the strange girl?'

Jaeger swallowed, not wanting to draw attention to Meena's absence. 'She wasn't hungry. I left her in my chamber.'

Morana lifted her eyes, noting the change in Jaeger's tone, and when she peered at him, she could tell that he was hiding something. His leg was jerking beside hers, and his eyes were darting about. She looked away, deciding it was better to let him think that no one could tell something was amiss.

But something was most certainly amiss.

***

Reaching the bottom of Bog's Hill, Jael turned to Aleksander, sensing Tig's impatience to fly. 'Race to the stream?'

Aleksander grinned. She'd read his mind, and he pulled on Sky's reins, bringing her into line with Tig, nodding at Jael. 'To the stream.'

Jael felt Tig vibrating against her legs. He was ready, and so was she. So, ignoring the discomfort of her tight tunic and her tight mail, she touched her boots against Tig's flanks and bent low.

Tig burst forward, but Jael pulled up on the reins almost immediately, bringing him to a skittering halt. Aleksander stopped Sky beside him, both of them watching the large group of people who had suddenly appeared in the distance.

'Come on!' Jael cried, recognising who it was. 'Come on!'

Ulf stopped as the riders approached. They were moving fast, and he shifted his right hand towards his old sword. That weapon had not been tested in a while, though he knew how to use it well.

His men stopped behind him, mirroring his movement.

The riders did not slow down.

Berard stepped forward, squinting. He recognised that hair. 'Jael!' he called, throwing up his arm as he ran forward. 'Jael!'

Hanna blinked in surprise, hoping Berard was right. She hurried past Karsten, running after his brother, worried that he was going to fall. And, just as she thought it, he did. Tripping over a rock, Berard lurched forward, unbalanced, landing on his side with a thud.

'Berard!' Bayla cried, urging Karsten after his brother.

Karsten frowned, adjusting his eye patch, not looking forward to this. Swallowing, he strode forward as Hanna helped Berard back to his feet.

'Are you alright?' Hanna asked, watching Berard's face redden with embarrassment as she pulled him up. Turning to look at the two riders who had skidded to a stop before them, her own face quickly reddened as well.

'Berard!' Jael slid off Tig, hurrying towards him. 'Are you hurt?'

Berard shook his head, damp curls bouncing around his face. 'No, I just haven't mastered my lack of an arm yet, I'm afraid.' He pushed his cloak away, revealing his missing limb, ashamed that he hadn't managed to steal the book.

Though he wanted her to see that he had, at least, tried.

Jael swallowed, staring in horror at his pinned sleeve. 'Oh, Berard. I'm so sorry.' Her attention shifted to the man whose eye she'd taken. 'Karsten,' she said tightly. The last time she had seen Karsten Dragos, she'd been running her sword through his side. Or was it his leg? She couldn't quite remember.

That night, escaping Hest, had been a blur of Dragos princes and sea-fire.

'Looks like we're in the right place if you're here,' Karsten growled, finding it hard to look anywhere near Jael's face.

'You came from Hest on foot?' Aleksander wondered as he dismounted, joining the small reunion. He hadn't noticed Hanna at first, but when he did, his mouth dropped open in surprise.

Jael watched the way that Aleksander was staring at Hanna, feeling an unexpected rush of jealousy. She quickly shoved it to one side, noting the strain on Karsten's face. 'What happened?' she asked, running her eyes over the crew who had joined them; at the Dragos' who were missing. 'What happened?' Jael asked again, seeing the grief all over Irenna Dragos' face. On Bayla's too. They looked exhausted. Broken. Ragged and weary.

Karsten cleared his throat. 'Jaeger killed our father. Tried to kill Berard. We... we headed for Saala with Hanna, then sailed for here once Berard had been treated.' Images of Haegen being ripped from the ship stopped him from continuing. He coughed, trying to clear his throat and start again, but no words would come.

'There was a storm,' Hanna said, sensing Karsten's distress. 'The sea froze, trapping our ship. Then a creature came up through the ice. It tore open the stern and... it took Haegen.'

Jael and Aleksander exchanged a look.

'What is it?' Berard wondered.

'The creature... it was likely a serpent,' Aleksander said. 'It came to Andala, tried to destroy the fort. Jael killed it.'

Jael shook her head dismissively. 'Well, I had some help.'

'You did, but it was your sword that stopped it in the end.'

Karsten glared at her. 'Why did it take Haegen?'

'I don't know,' Jael said. 'She sent it. Draguta. The woman who's with your brother now. The one they raised from the dead.'

Hanna gasped. 'You *know* they raised her?'

Jael nodded. 'We killed Gerod and the Followers in Tuura. The temple was burned to the ground. The fort too. Gerod told me before he died that they would raise Draguta that night.'

Berard dropped his eyes, thinking of Meena, knowing it wasn't only the book that he'd failed to rescue.

'And my father?' Hanna wondered desperately. 'Is he alright?'

'Yes, he's in Andala, and many Tuurans with him.'

Hanna sighed in relief.

'Where are you going?' Berard asked, conscious of his mother and Ulf, who had come to join them.

'Ulf?' Jael was surprised. 'Where have you come from?'

Ulf bowed his head. 'My lady.' He looked up, smiling. 'I was the one who took young Hanna to Hest. The one whose ship the creature attacked. Seems like I ended up with more than I bargained for when I agreed to take her coins.' He looked sympathetically at Bayla, not minding for a moment about his ship at all. She was an attractive woman, though she had been a queen, and he was an old helmsman without a ship. Likely she wouldn't look his way once they were at the fort.

'Seems that you did, and more besides. We're going to need everyone's help now. Aleksander and I will return in a few days. We're trying to find some answers to how we can keep the fort safe,' Jael said evasively. 'We have some ideas, but nothing we can talk about yet.'

'And your brother?' Bayla asked, running a hand over her unkempt hair, trying to strengthen her weary voice. 'Will he help us? Will he give us somewhere to stay until we can find our way back to Hest?'

'Of course,' Jael said. 'We're preparing to attack Hest as

soon as possible. We need to get that book and kill Draguta.'

Karsten's eye glowed brightly at the thought of a war, especially one against his murderous brother. 'You won't have enough men.'

'We're working on that,' Aleksander said. 'Hopefully, we'll have Iskavall's army too.'

Jael snorted. 'Yes, we're hopeful rather than certain, but if they don't want to be our friends, then we'll make them our enemies. We're going to Hest with as big of an army as possible, and I don't mind how we get it.'

'And what do you plan to do in Hest?' Karsten asked, narrowing his gaze. 'Take it for Brekka?'

Jael shook her head. 'Lothar wanted Hest. My father never did. My brother doesn't, and nor do I. Jaeger seems to have his own plans for Osterland, so we have to stop him and take the book. If we don't, we'll all die.'

Ulf swallowed, glancing at Bayla.

Karsten smiled, his teeth gleaming in a sudden burst of sunlight. 'Well then, you'd better be on your way. The sooner you return, the sooner we can discuss how we take back our kingdom.'

Jael nodded, turning to Aleksander, who appeared in a daze.

She nudged him. 'We will. Ulf will get you to the fort, and Axl will find somewhere for you all to stay.' She glanced at the children, who were rubbing tired, swollen eyes, and at Irenna Dragos, who looked as though she could fall down and not care to ever get up. 'You'll be safe in Andala, don't worry.' And grabbing Aleksander's arm, she pulled him away from Hanna, back to the horses, hoping she was right.

CHAPTER TWENTY SIX

Draguta insisted that Morana and Morac join her and Evaine as they walked to the markets after breakfast, though Morana wondered why she had wanted them there. Draguta ignored them entirely as she helped Evaine choose which fabrics to send to the tailors before turning her attention to jewelry. And then there were decisions to be made about footwear, and cloaks, brooches and...

Morana tapped her foot, trying to stay under the shaded canopies of the stalls. Hot and irritated. Biting her tongue.

'You are bored, Morana?' Draguta laughed, turning to peer at her ornery face. 'Perhaps we should find something for you? A hairbrush, perhaps?' And she winked at Evaine, who giggled.

Morana frowned, keeping her mind clear. 'I don't require such a thing,' she mumbled, and, pushing her hair away from her eyes, she peered up at Draguta, who stood before her like a tall ivory statue.

Morac sighed. Morana was proving to be terrible company, which wasn't new. He missed Runa, who had been such a pleasant companion. Now he was stuck with a growling ogre and two gossiping women, who only wanted to talk about jewels or Eadmund.

Neither of which interested him.

'You are not enjoying yourself, Morac?' Draguta smiled. 'Though I'm hardly surprised. I have never known a man to take pleasure in the company of a woman. Not when she was fully clothed, at least!'

Morac looked down at the cobblestones, ignoring Draguta's tittering.

Draguta had enjoyed herself as much as Evaine. She had never had a daughter, and the pleasure of discussing dresses and hairstyles reminded her of her youth, when she had spent every waking moment with her sisters. They had been inseparable, growing even closer after their parents died.

Her face changed, her eyes serious now, and she tapped her fingers against her thigh. 'You will leave us, Morac. We must go to my chamber and make our plans for Eadmund. I'm sure you will find something to do. Perhaps Jaeger can make use of you? I'm not sure what skills you have, but he could use an assistant. He has so much to do, organising those slovenly shipbuilders. The stonemasons as well. We must prepare for the invasion, yet he doesn't seem to know how to go about it.'

'Invasion?' Morac was surprised.

'Oh, yes,' Draguta smiled, turning her face up to the sun. 'I mean to conquer all of Osterland.' She looked down at Evaine. 'When Eadmund comes, he will help us. He will help us get everything we want.'

Evaine's hopes were lifted by the certainty she heard in Draguta's voice.

When Eadmund comes...

She shivered with excitement.

***

Jaeger had left the chamber early, and Meena couldn't fall back to sleep, so she made her way to the table, opening Varna's book. She hadn't had any dreams, though what little she had read was already exciting her.

The book was very old, and Meena guessed that Varna had written it as a young woman. The scrawls were thicker, the ink more boldly applied, and the words themselves made more sense. Their clarity enabled Meena to understand how she could bring dreams to her, and she wondered if she could find something in Berard's chamber to see if it would work.

She was desperate to dream about him, and see if he was still alive.

The knock on the door made Meena jump. She quickly closed the book and hurried to the bed, hiding it beneath the furs before scurrying to open the door.

Else stood before her, holding a full tray. 'I thought you might like some breakfast, my lady.'

Meena was unable to disguise her hunger as she eyed the tray. There were flatbreads, berries, a pot of honey, a plate of cheese, and slices of cold meat. She spied three big figs too.

'Shall I come in, then?' Else asked. 'I saw the king eating in the hall earlier, but I didn't see you, so I thought I may as well bring something along with me.' She smiled, bustling past Meena with the tray, placing it on the table.

Meena glanced up and down the corridor before closing the door, her stomach gurgling impatiently. She was so used to feeling hungry that she barely noticed it anymore, but she rushed to the table with a nervous smile. 'Thank you,' she mumbled, taking a seat as Else looked around the chamber, her attention quickly drawn to the unmade bed.

'Well, I shall make a start, then,' she said, leaving Meena to eat. 'Oh, and I brought this as well.' And pulling a brush from her apron pocket, Else walked back to the table. 'I thought this might work better than a comb. Hair like yours can be trouble, I know. My daughter had similar hair, but a good brushing would tame it. I can try if you like?'

Meena didn't know what to think, but she found herself nodding as Else lifted the brush to her head and began to gently pull it through her tangled red mane.

***

Gant chewed his bottom lip as he led the Dragos family towards Axl's throne. He couldn't stand Karsten Dragos, but he did like Ulf Rutgar, and he'd listened with some sympathy to the helmsman's hasty explanation of what had occurred as they walked towards the hall.

And now it would be up to Axl to decide what to do about it all.

Karsten had taunted Axl when he was the Dragos' prisoner in Hest - more than taunted - and Gant didn't imagine that Axl would welcome the one-eyed man to Andala.

Although, perhaps once he'd listened to his story...

Leaving the Dragos' in an awkward huddle just before the throne, Gant strode to Axl's side, whispering in his ear. Amma sat beside him, immediately uncomfortable, not wanting to revisit the nightmare of her brief time in Hest.

Gant straightened up, nodded at Axl, and walked back to the Dragos', motioning them forward.

'I am sorry for your losses,' Axl said, not standing. Aedan had taken his crutch away to work on making it more comfortable, and he didn't want to appear weak by needing to lean on Gant - not in front of Karsten Dragos. 'You are welcome here. I will have someone find you a cottage. You can stay as long as you need. We plan to attack Hest as soon as we have a large enough army in place. As soon as we're confident we can keep them safe, but as my sister probably told you, we have no claims on your kingdom. We want the book, the woman, and your brother. The rest is up to you.'

'Sounds fair. We are... grateful for your help.' Karsten's lips barely moved, and he wanted to spit, but he couldn't deny that he needed Axl Furyck's help. And he couldn't deny that he wanted the same things the new King of Brekka did. 'And we will do what we can to help you in return.'

Bayla nodded, trying to overcome her own irritation at the sight of Amma sitting next to Axl Furyck. She was Jaeger's wife. She should be in Hest with him. Shaking her head, she reminded herself that Jaeger had killed Haaron.

There was no place in their family for him anymore.

Bayla glanced at Karsten, realising that he was the only person who could return their family to its rightful place now.

Gisila walked in from the kitchen with Axl's crutch, her eyes popping open as she spied the bedraggled Dragos family clumped together before the throne. 'What is going on?'

'The Dragos' are our guests, Mother,' Axl said. 'Gant will find them a cottage, but they will require help familiarising themselves with the fort. Perhaps Branwyn can help you show them around?'

Gisila nodded blankly, eager to talk to Axl alone and find out what was going on.

'And my son, Berard,' Bayla said, not enjoying having to stand in front of the Furycks looking like a dishevelled servant. She felt filthy, certain that she stunk too. 'He has lost his arm. He needs a healer.'

Axl stared at Berard in surprise. The Dragos' were draped in big cloaks that he supposed belonged to Ulf's crew. He hadn't noticed that Berard was missing an arm. 'Of course. Gant, can you find Derwa and Edela?'

Gant nodded, turning to leave.

No one knew where to look, or what else to say.

The silence quickly became awkward.

'You must be hungry,' Axl said, at last. 'Why don't you find a table while we sort out somewhere for you to stay. I will have food brought over. And something to drink.'

Karsten nodded, ushering his wife and the children towards the nearest empty table, turning back for Irenna, who had stayed where she was, eyes on the reeds scattered over the hall floor.

'Thank you,' Berard exhaled gratefully. His feet were aching, and his stump was throbbing, but for the first time in days, he didn't feel afraid. 'Thank you.'

***

Eadmund, Thorgils, and Torstan were helping Beorn build catapults near the main gates. They were all grateful to be able to do something useful. Something with their hands. Something that made sense.

'You think they'll be safe out there?' Torstan wondered. 'Jael and Aleksander? With only a couple of swords and shields?'

'Well, I think *Toothpick* seems like more than just a sword,' Thorgils grunted, lifting the arm beam into place. 'After what happened with that serpent?' He shook his head. Many men were still down at the harbour, trying to drag the dead creature back into the water. It would take some time to shift its stinking corpse.

'True,' Torstan agreed, handing Beorn a nail. 'But there are plenty of things a sword can't protect you against.'

'I suppose so,' Thorgils mused. 'But if anyone can take care of herself, it's Jael, and Aleksander seems handy enough, for a Brekkan.' He winked at Eadmund, who didn't appear to be listening. 'Eadmund?'

Eadmund stared at Thorgils, but his eyes barely focused. His attention wasn't on his friend, nor his task. He was imagining Evaine. He could almost see her in Hest, begging him to hurry to her side. She was trapped with Morana and Morac, and Jaeger Dragos.

The thought of that was a tight fist in his chest.

Eadmund didn't want Jaeger Dragos anywhere near Evaine.

***

Jaeger was irritated that Draguta had suggested he needed an assistant. Morac Gallas was a dour man – as dull as Morana was angry – and the last person he would have chosen for such a role. They were an odd family, Jaeger thought, frowning as he realised that he had no family himself anymore. His mind wandered to the last time he'd seen them, running out of the castle, Berard's blood dripping from his blade. And then his father's.

Jaeger shook his head, trying to distract himself with thoughts of Evaine. He turned to Morac, who walked beside him, hands clasped behind his back, his thin lips pressed tightly together. 'Why is your daughter so desperate for Eadmund Skalleson, then? Why him? Surely someone like her deserves better?'

Morac was surprised by the question. He lifted his eyes to meet the king's. 'She has been promised to Eadmund since she was a girl. She grew up thinking about nothing else. For Evaine, having Eadmund is the only thing she truly cares about.' He felt uncomfortable talking so openly, but now he was in Hest, Morac realised there was little point in keeping secrets anymore.

'Why didn't Morana just kill him? Why lead Evaine on? Surely it's torture to make her love a man doomed to die?'

Morac frowned. 'Those of us who follow Raemus believe that Eadmund is important for stopping the prophecy. For protecting Raemus.'

It was Jaeger's turn to frown. He glared at Morac, who was almost as tall as him, but only half as wide. 'Raemus' return is irrelevant now. Draguta has no intention of bringing him back, so why bother with Eadmund anymore?'

Morac swallowed. Jaeger's gaze was intense, and he dropped his eyes, fiddling with his cloak. 'I couldn't say. The prophecy warns that Jael Furyck will kill Draguta, but it also warns that she will kill you.'

'*Me*?'

Morac looked up. 'Yes, it speaks of the Hestian prince

who would try to protect the Book of Darkness. Who would ultimately fail and be killed by Furia's daughter.'

'And Eadmund can stop this? *He* can stop her?' Jaeger scoffed, remembering the man he had seen in Hest. He'd looked barely capable of pulling on his own boots. Jaeger shook his head. 'I don't need anyone protecting Hest or me.' He thought of his brothers and how he had conquered them all to take the throne. 'This is *my* kingdom now, and I don't intend to allow Jael Furyck anywhere near it!'

***

Else answered the door, staring at the muttering woman who stooped before her.

'Who are you?' Morana spat, elbowing her way past the elderly servant.

Meena spluttered in surprise, quickly dropping her eyes to her lap.

Morana gaped at her niece. 'What happened to *you*?'

Meena blushed, reaching up to touch her hair which Else had spent a good deal of time taming as she devoured the tray of food. It felt considerably different. Softer. Flatter. She guessed by the look on Morana's face that it didn't look any better, though.

'Who are you?' Morana asked again, turning on the elderly servant, who closed the door and walked slowly towards her.

'I am the king's new servant,' Else said.

Morana quickly dismissed her as irrelevant, turning back to Meena. 'Draguta wants you in her chamber.' And without waiting for her niece, she headed back to the door. 'Now!'

Meena swallowed, glancing at Else, who smiled sympathetically at her.

'And you'll bring that book with you, little mouse,' Morana

grumbled, inclining her head towards the bed. 'It does not belong to you.'

Meena's eyes popped open, her heart lurching up into her throat as she scrambled to her feet, and, with a heavy heart, hurried towards the bed where she had hidden Varna's book.

***

Edela watched from a stool by the fire as Derwa looked Berard over.

Eventually, the hunch-backed old woman harrumphed loudly, stepping away from his stump. 'I see nothing for us to do,' she declared. 'You are healing well. The wound is clean, and most importantly, your spirit is strong.'

'Derwa is right,' Edela said. 'A wound will dig deep if your spirit is weak, but you have a very powerful resolve. I feel it. You want to kill your brother, don't you?'

Berard nodded. He had left his family in the hall, accompanying Edela to Derwa's tiny cottage. There had been such an influx of Tuurans, Islanders, Alekkans, and now, Hestians, that Axl and Gant had been struggling to find accommodation for them all, but Edela had ensured that they found Derwa a comfortable cottage just along from her own, where she could practice her healing skills, and they could be almost-neighbours for the first time in more than thirty years.

'Well, that is spurring you on,' Edela decided. 'Your wound is responding to your mind. And your mind, Berard, is strong.'

Berard was pleased to hear it. 'But my brother,' he began, knowing that Edela was a dreamer, Jael's grandmother, and hopefully, someone he could trust. 'Will I be able to kill him? With only one arm? And the one I have left has never been of much use to me.'

Edela smiled. He was a funny young man. He almost cowered

before them, awkward and shy, but with a kind heart, she could tell. He wasn't like his brothers at all. 'I do not generally give advice about killing people,' she chortled as Derwa dipped her finger into a jar of Entorp's salve, applying it to Berard's stump while he was distracted. 'But I do believe that your brother will die. He has to. We need to stop Draguta and destroy that book. And he stands in our way. So don't worry, Berard, whether it's your left arm, or my granddaughter's sword, one way or the other, that brother of yours will meet his end soon.'

***

The weather stayed fair, though the terrain was heavy going after the snow and ice, and the horses struggled. But the air was mild, and the freedom was welcome, and Jael and Aleksander rode in a comfortable silence for most of the afternoon.

Eventually, though, it was time to give the horses a drink and themselves a chance to stretch their legs and have a bite to eat. They sat down on a pair of moss-covered boulders, unwrapping Biddy's packet of food, choosing a cold chicken leg each.

'I can't believe what happened to Haegen Dragos,' Aleksander said. 'I wonder why the serpent did that?'

Jael shrugged, watching as Tig drank from the nearby stream. 'I don't know. Makes no sense.' She shuddered, remembering the putrid stench of the serpent's throat as it opened over her; convinced that the smell of it was still in her hair, despite a vigorous washing. 'But if it was Draguta who brought it to life, she's not wasting any time. Makes you wonder what she's planning next.' It was meant to sound light-hearted, but Jael frowned, already feeling guilty for leaving the fort. She glanced at Aleksander, who looked just as troubled.

'Gant is there. He'll help Axl. Edela too,' Aleksander said, trying to reassure them both as he reached for his waterskin. 'All we can do is focus on getting to the Widow's cottage quickly.'

'How far into the wood is it?'

'I don't remember exactly, but quite far,' Aleksander said. 'It feels like you're in another place, as though you're going in circles once you get inside. You lose all sense of time.'

They let that unpleasant thought hang in the air, noticing how dark it suddenly felt as the clouds gathered above their heads; hoping it wouldn't start raining this early in their journey.

In a couple of days, they would enter the vast, creeping woodland that spread from the western cliffs of Iskavall, almost all the way to Brekka's eastern coast, though neither were looking forward to it. Hallow Wood was a place that most avoided because the tales told about it were so unsettling. Some said that it had grown at a time when the Furycks were pushing north, trying to claim all of what was once Tuura for themselves. That it was placed there by Daala as a home for the gods, and a way to keep the Furycks out. Stories were told of the armies who marched through the wood and became disoriented, lost, never to be heard from again.

Over the years, the Brekkan kings had felled trees along its eastern edge, creating a path for their armies to march up and down the kingdom without ever having to enter Hallow Wood. But Aleksander knew that they were going to have to ride deep inside it if they were to find the Widow's cottage.

He stood, offering his waterskin to Jael, who shook her head. 'Well, then, we should go. If there's rain coming, I'd rather get somewhere we can shelter for the night. And we're nowhere near a cave yet.'

Jael nodded, eager to make progress, not wanting her mind to wander to what might be waiting for them inside the wood.

***

Since his arrival in Andala, Marcus had tried to make himself useful by helping Entorp decide where to apply the symbols around the fort. After the serpent, they had come together to ensure that they were protecting as much of the fort as possible; both of them convinced that it was only a matter of time before the next attack.

Andala's piers had been destroyed – many of the sheds and buildings around the harbour too – but the serpent had not touched the fort itself. The symbol had worked, and they needed to ensure that it was applied everywhere they could think of.

Marcus was so busy frowning, trying to anticipate what Draguta would do next that he didn't hear the footsteps behind him.

'Hello.'

He spun around, his heart quickening as he pulled his daughter into his arms, sighing in relief. 'You're here.' His voice broke, and he squeezed her tightly, feeling his body slump in relief. Standing back, he looked her over. 'Are you alright?'

'Yes,' Hanna smiled, tears running down her round cheeks as he pulled her to him again. Her father had never been a demonstrative man, and she was quite overcome by the unfamiliar feeling of being in his arms. 'Yes.'

Marcus released her, stepping away. 'Jael told me what you tried to do. That it didn't work.'

Hanna looked crestfallen. 'No, it didn't. It didn't work at all.'

'Well, you were brave to try. It was a dangerous thing to attempt.'

Hanna's blue eyes filled with more tears. 'It was, it turns out, but not for me. Berard Dragos lost his arm trying to take the book away from his brother. Jaeger cut it off and killed his father.'

Marcus frowned. 'The book has claimed him, that much is obvious. For a man to hurt his own family like that?' He inhaled sharply. 'We don't know much about the book, except the one thing that matters. Whoever claims it and whoever it claims will try to bring an end to everything we know. One way or the other.'

***

'Do you have something from Eadmund?' Draguta asked, reaching over the table towards Evaine. 'Give it to me. Everything you have.'

Evaine dug into her purse, pulling out the lock of Eadmund's sandy hair that she'd tied to a small leather strap. She gave it to Draguta, then dipped her hand into her purse again, taking out one of his arm-rings. She had taken both items from Eadmund while he was sleeping. They were precious to her, but she had no hesitation in handing them over. She would do anything to be reunited with him. The pain of their separation was excruciating.

'Good,' Draguta smiled, passing them to Morana. 'That is just what we need to begin. You and Eadmund are connected by an invisible thread, from his soul to yours. And when Morana pulls hard enough, she will bring him hurrying to your side. Nothing will stop him once she starts pulling on that thread. He will fight anyone who tries to stop him from getting to you.'

Morana wriggled impatiently on her chair, sweltering in the intense heat of the chamber.

'Let us begin,' Draguta murmured, nodding at Morana, who stood, dipping the candle into the burning lamp, watching as it caught. She placed it in the centre of the small circle of symbols she had drawn on the table and closed her eyes, breathing deeply, inhaling the fragrant smoke from the fire, chanting in a low, rhythmic voice.

Draguta focused on Morana, watching as her face contorted, a frown dragging her wild eyebrows together.

Eventually, Morana opened her eyes. 'There is no way through. It's as though he's hidden behind a door. A locked door. I can't get through to him.' Morana was puzzled. 'Symbols,' she realised. 'They are using symbols to shut me out as well.'

Draguta stood immediately and picked up Eadmund's lock of hair and arm-ring, flinging them at the wall. Turning to the three women, she hissed with fury. 'Leave! *Now*!'

Evaine, Morana, and Meena scrambled to their feet in a rush as Draguta stormed around the chamber, sweeping candles and ornaments from the tables, her temper exploding in a blinding rage. 'You think you're better at this game than me, do you? Well, we shall see about that!'

CHAPTER TWENTY SEVEN

Getta went into labour during breakfast, and Raymon had paced around the fort all day and all through the night, unable to eat, too distracted to think. Ravenna had kept her son company, trying to reassure him that the length of time it was taking for his child to arrive was perfectly normal. But Raymon had remained in a constant state of anxiety.

Women died giving birth. Ladies, servants, queens.

Women died giving birth, and as much as Raymon was desperate for sons, he did not wish to sacrifice his wife for the pleasure of filling his hall with heirs.

'She is tired,' Ravenna said gently, watching from the ramparts as the sun made its slow climb into the sky. 'But very strong. She is a Furyck. They have strong women in that family.'

Raymon frowned, not enjoying the reminder of their neighbour's strength.

'You are so stubborn,' Ravenna laughed. 'The Furycks are not our enemies. We have fought alongside one another. Our families have been close friends. If you refuse to help them now, you'll be making a grave mistake. One your wife and child may suffer for.'

Raymon yawned, suddenly aware that he had been awake all night. 'What do you mean?'

Ravenna doubted that she could pierce the veil Getta had hidden her son beneath, but she had to try. 'Getta wants revenge. She wants to hold her cousins accountable for what they have done. But how do you know who was to blame? Lothar was an embarrassment to his family. His own father banished him. He led your father to make foolish decisions. He was always buzzing in his ear, convincing Hugo that his ideas were the best for Iskavall. But Lothar was only ever interested in enriching himself. And when Ranuf died, he stole the throne and ruled Brekka like a greedy tyrant. Osbert was no better. So what makes you think that *they* were the victims in any of this?'

Raymon thought of Getta. She was everything to him, but he knew that his mother was right. Many in Iskavall suspected that Hugo Vandaal's trust in Lothar, as his right-hand man, had ultimately led to his murder. Yet, Getta was determined to see her cousins punished for her father's death, not rewarded with their help. He turned to his mother, readying another impassioned defense of his wife when he noticed that Getta's servant had joined them on the ramparts.

'My lord,' the old lady panted as she bustled towards them. 'You must come. Now!'

***

'But what if Eadmund drinks the wine?'

'He won't.'

'You've seen this?'

'Of course I've seen it!' Morana snapped. 'He'll not drink the wine. She will serve him. He will wait for her. She will die.'

Morac sucked in a breath, almost choking on the putrid stench emanating from his sister's cauldron. 'And if Eadmund finds out that it was me?'

Morana snorted derisively. 'Why would he even *think* to suspect you?' She leaned forward, handing Morac the tiny glass vial. 'When I've spent all these years turning him against his own brother? Ivaar is all he sees now when anything goes wrong. Ivaar is the one he blames for everything. He is blind to anyone else. Eadmund loves Melaena. He hates Ivaar. He will be overwhelmed with pain. He will blame his brother, as he's always done, and slip away from his father, into a self-pitying abyss. I have seen how it will go, Brother,' she smiled.

Morac took the vial, slipping it inside his pouch. He frowned. Eirik was his best friend. Eirik loved Eadmund.

If he were to make a mistake...

Morana scowled, irritated by his hesitation. 'We must end this marriage before it even begins! We must break Eadmund! It is what I have been tasked with. When Evaine is old enough, he will be hers. Until then, he will fall into a thousand broken-hearted pieces, waiting to be picked up and put back together again. He is ours, and soon, he'll be Evaine's. He will never be free of us!'

***

Jael jerked awake, panting.

Opening her eyes, she saw that it was well past dawn. She yawned, stretching her arms above her head, relieved it wasn't raining.

'I thought you'd never wake up!' Aleksander called from under a tree, where he was feeding apples to the horses. 'Who knew the ground could be so comfortable?'

Jael didn't say anything as she hurried to wrap her cloak around herself. They had slept in a small, damp cave, and it was cold.

'Jael?'

Jael was still half asleep as she made her way to the fire. Her body felt stiff after sitting in the saddle all day, unused to so much riding. 'I had a dream.'

Aleksander laughed. 'I'm beginning to see a pattern here.'

'Well, do you want to know about it or not?' Jael grumbled.

Aleksander patted Sky, leaving her to finish munching her apple, and came to join Jael by the fire, picking up a long stick to poke the burning logs, wanting to see a few more flames. 'What did you dream about, then?'

'Nothing to help us, but it's another piece of the puzzle,' Jael said, and she told him about her dream. About how Morana and Morac had plotted to poison Eadmund's first wife, twisting it so that any blame would fall on Ivaar.

Aleksander handed Jael a waterskin. 'And Eadmund blamed his brother for her death?'

Jael nodded, taking a long drink. 'It's why Ivaar was banished from Oss. It's why he wanted to take his revenge on Eadmund, and why Eadmund fell apart. Morac Gallas killed his wife.'

'No wonder he ran away from Oss. Morana probably told him that you were coming for him now that you're a dreamer,' he said, picking up a handful of some of the berries he'd collected. 'Here, having listened to your stomach rumbling all night, I thought I'd better get up and find you something more to eat.'

'I'm sure your snoring was louder than my stomach, but thank you.' Jael took the berries, thinking of Eadmund. She felt a burst of anger. Morana and Morac had conspired to take his wife *and* his father from him. And, if Eirik was right, Morana likely had something to do with his mother's death as well. Taking a deep breath, Jael tried to calm down. There was nothing she could do about it now. 'How long till we get to the wood, do you think?'

'Hopefully, tomorrow morning, and then maybe another two days to her cottage. It will get tougher the closer we get, from memory. It's a real tangle of trees in there.' He wasn't looking forward to it.

Jael wasn't really listening, though. She was remembering

the glee on Morana Gallas' face as she talked about Eadmund.

Of how he'd never be free.

***

Meena rolled over, coming face to face with Jaeger, who frowned in disappointment. She wasn't Evaine Gallas, and he'd been dreaming about Evaine Gallas all night long.

But Meena didn't mind his frown because she'd had a dream.

'Why do you look so happy?' Jaeger grunted, pulling her towards him. 'And what happened to your hair?' He kissed her roughly, pressing himself against her.

Meena squirmed, tasting the sour tang of wine on his breath as his bristles scratched her lips. 'Else brushed it.'

'Who?'

'Your servant,' Meena mumbled between kisses.

'Oh. Why?'

Meena didn't know why. She shrugged, feeling Jaeger's warm hand slip up the inside of her thigh.

He stopped suddenly. 'Did you have a dream?'

Meena tried to look into his eyes. His nose was almost touching hers, and she felt trapped. She swallowed. 'No, but I think I can try tonight. I read about it. About how to do it.'

'Good,' Jaeger murmured. 'That is good, Meena.' He kissed her again.

'But what should I dream about?' Meena wondered, hoping to distract him.

Jaeger was instantly distracted. 'That's a good question. Hmmm...' He rolled away from her, lying back on the pillow.

'Varna's book said that I needed something. A thing to help me dream. Something to hold onto or put under my pillow.'

'Oh, well, it can't be the book, then,' Jaeger smiled, his eyes narrowed into slits. 'Unless... what if you were to touch it? Would that work?'

Meena didn't think so. She vigorously shook her head, hoping to dissuade him from that idea.

'But we could try,' Jaeger said eagerly, desperate to touch the book himself. 'And we could take something from Draguta's chamber. I've heard that she only wears her dresses once.' He sat up, feeling energised. 'We'll sneak into her chamber to touch the book, then we'll find one of her old dresses, and tonight, you'll dream!'

Meena opened her mouth, wondering what she'd walked into. After her dream, she was beginning to think that she might be a real dreamer, but not one part of her wanted to dream about Draguta and the Book of Darkness.

Shivering, she closed her eyes as Jaeger crawled towards her again.

***

Evaine knocked impatiently on Morana's door.

She had gone down to the hall for breakfast, only to discover that no one else was awake. Or, if they were, they weren't eating their breakfast in the hall. She quickly ate a few hotcakes and hurried up to her mother's chamber to find out what was going on.

Morana yanked open the door, glaring at her, not appreciating the interruption, the company, or the angry sneer on Evaine's face. 'Yes?'

'What is happening?' Evaine demanded, pushing past Morana and striding into the dark chamber. 'No one was in the hall. No one!' She rounded on her mother. 'Where is Draguta? What is going to happen with Eadmund? You've made me leave him behind, and now he's trapped! Trapped with that bitch!

You've given him to her!'

Morana wanted to cover her ears or slap Evaine across the face to make her shut up, but she patiently bit her tongue and crept back to her cauldron instead. 'Have you finished?' she grumbled when Evaine finally took a breath. 'Do you require any answers to your questions, or would you just prefer to listen to the awful sound of your own voice?'

Evaine looked suitably insulted, and she could see that Morana had no intention of saying anything until she calmed down. It took some time, but eventually, Evaine dragged a stool towards the fire and sat down. It was a cold, miserable chamber, and it reminded Evaine of being on Oss, which reminded her of Eadmund, and her eyes brimmed with tears. 'Where is Draguta?' she asked dolefully. 'When will she find a way to bring Eadmund here?'

Morana lifted the cauldron, tipping the steaming water over the dandelion flowers and poppy seeds she had placed in the bottom of her cup. Slipping it back onto its hook, she sat down on her stool with a groan. 'I don't know the answer to either of those questions. I imagine she's dreaming. I had no dreams myself, so I have no answers for you. Why not try knocking on Draguta's door? That would teach you a lesson!'

Evaine was furious.

Morana didn't care.

They sat in silence, simmering, both of them too irritated to speak.

'But what can we do?' Evaine asked eventually, her voice a plaintive whisper. 'I don't want to lose Eadmund.'

Morana snorted. 'The spell has not been broken. It *cannot* be broken. A spell like that? I dare anyone to break it! No, the spell is not broken, so there will be a way through, and Draguta will find it. Best you think of something to do while you're waiting. Having seen what Draguta does to people who irritate her, I suggest you try not to become one of those people!'

Evaine sucked on her bottom lip and sighed.

***

Eydis could hear Thorgils laughing with Bram, and it made her smile. They were sitting opposite her. Isaura sat to her right, fussing over the children, and Eadmund was on her left.

He had barely said a word since they'd started breakfast.

Eydis didn't know what to say to make him speak to her. She remembered how it used to be when he called her Little Thing; when he sounded as though he was smiling, despite the pain in his broken heart. No matter how he felt, he'd always made an effort to talk to her. To be around her and look after her. But now, when Eydis saw him in her dreams, he looked like a stranger.

Her images of him were growing faint, and it worried her.

'Well, we lived through another night!' Thorgils grinned.

Isaura glared at him, inclining her head towards the children, two of whom were gaping at him in horror. The other two were far too busy protesting the food on offer to even hear him.

Thorgils looked suitably embarrassed, turning his attention to Eydis. 'How about you, Miss Eydis... did you have any helpful dreams?'

Eydis shook her head, not wanting to think about her dreams, which had been full of her unhappy brother. She could see the threads pulling him away from them all, but she couldn't see a way to cut them.

Isaura smiled as Ayla walked towards them with Runa. 'Perhaps Ayla did?' she wondered, sensing Eydis' distress and cursing Thorgils' big mouth again. 'I imagine you'd get rather tired if you were always working on finding dreams while you're asleep!'

Eydis tried to smile, but she felt a building sense of dread. They were waiting for something terrifying to happen, knowing that it would come, but not knowing when.

But it was coming. Of that, Eydis was certain.

***

Raymon could feel his heart throbbing with joy as he cradled his mewling son. He felt nervous holding such a tiny, helpless creature but overcome with relief that both his son and his wife were safe.

They would name him Lothar. Lothar Vandaal, heir to the throne of Iskavall. Raymon thought back to his conversation with his mother and knew what she would think of that. He wondered what he thought of it himself, but Getta had endured so much to bring the baby into the world that he didn't want to complain, though he had assumed they would name him Hugo, after his own father.

Getta looked exhausted. And pale. Raymon handed the baby to the wet nurse and hurried to her side. 'You had a hard time,' he said quietly, running a hand over her lank brown hair. 'You must rest now.'

The baby squawked hungrily, and Getta's attention was immediately diverted to him. 'Maya, bring him to me,' she urged. 'I shall feed him.'

Raymon was surprised, having thought that his wife would employ a wet nurse as most ladies did, but Getta seemed eager to tend to her son herself. 'Is there anything you need, my love?' he asked as she sat up, trying to move into a more comfortable position.

Getta ignored him as she took the baby, lying him across a pillow, his small furry head resting in her hand. 'You should go,' she muttered wearily. 'I need to concentrate now.' And grimacing, she tried to force the baby's mouth onto her nipple.

Raymon felt a strange jolt of jealousy. His wife was asking him to leave his own chamber, preferring the company of his son. He shook his head, realising that he was being childish. 'Of course,' he murmured, backing out of the room. Reaching for the door, he paused, watching Getta with their son.

It was everything he had dreamed of, and he would do anything to protect them.

Anything.

***

'Do you think she'll try something?' Aleksander wondered from Jael's right, his eyes scouring the grim sky as they navigated the horses across a boggy field, sodden after so much recent rain. Dark clouds were creeping towards them. It felt mild, but more rain was definitely coming. 'Draguta.'

'Ha!' Jael laughed. 'I thought you meant Evaine.' She tugged gently on the reins, nudging Tig to the left of a hole. 'She'll do something. After we killed that serpent, she'll be angry, ready to try something else. But what? I'm not sure we want to think about it. Not when we can't do anything to stop it.'

Aleksander frowned, knowing she was right. 'Well, at least Edela's back to herself again. I imagine she's got everyone under control, preparing for what might come.'

Jael smiled, thinking of her grandmother, still surprised to realise that they'd saved her. 'She seemed happy to be home. Away from the sea!' Thinking about the sea led her mind quickly back to Oss. Morana Gallas had a lot to answer for, destroying lives as though she was playing children's games. And for what? To keep Eadmund broken? To keep him away from her? So they couldn't unite to defeat Draguta and destroy the book?

Jael felt the wind pick up, blowing a welcome breeze across her face. It felt like a lifetime ago that she and Eadmund were together. And only by defeating Morana and Evaine and breaking their spell would they be again.

***

Edela took Eydis' hand, leading her down the hall steps towards the table that Ayla had chosen, closest to the brazier. Biddy would be pleased to see that they were both sitting by a fire, Edela chortled to herself, though she couldn't deny that she'd been feeling the cold since she'd woken, grateful for the flames herself.

The sun was out, and it made a nice change to be sitting outside rather than stuck in the smoky hall.

'Hello, Eydis,' Ayla smiled as Edela helped her onto the bench.

'Hello,' Eydis said, pleased to be outside herself. Fyn had fallen asleep, and Runa had insisted she go and get some fresh air until he woke up.

'I thought it would be good to have a meeting of the dreamers!' Edela announced. 'What do you think? Can we put our heads together and share our dreams? See what we can come up with to help everyone?'

Ayla nodded eagerly. 'I thought the same. We need to try and focus on finding answers, instead of just hoping they will come. I haven't had any dreams for a while that I would consider useful, but hopefully, that will change soon.'

'Yes, we need to see what we can find out about Draguta,' Edela agreed. 'I'm the only one to have dreamed of her so far, so I think I must keep my focus on her. Perhaps you could turn your attention to the Book of Aurea, or the Widow, Ayla? See what is happening there. And Eydis...' Edela mused, turning to the dark-haired girl. 'Maybe you could help us with Eadmund? He feels very lost to me. As though he is slipping further away.'

Eydis swallowed, feeling tears coming, but she didn't

want tears. She didn't want to be a crying child they needed to comfort. 'He is,' she said, clearing her throat. 'He is angry and sad and desperate to be with Evaine. It's as though he can feel her. He can sense how much she wants him to come.'

Ayla frowned, looking at Edela. 'Do you think he's safe here?'

'I think the symbols we're using will keep Draguta out. And Morana too,' Edela said, kneading her cold fingers together. 'But I don't imagine they'll keep them out forever. Seems to me that clever dreamers with the use of that book will find the answers they need. Eventually.' Edela felt Eydis tense beside her, and she squeezed her hand. 'But we'll do everything we can to protect Eadmund, won't we? Jael has Thorgils looking after him,' Edela said, trying to reassure her. 'You don't need to worry about Eadmund.'

But Eydis could hear a loud voice in her head, screaming at her.

Screaming with laughter.

CHAPTER TWENTY EIGHT

Andala was much smaller than Bayla had imagined. Smaller and far less grand. After Hest's magnificent castle and her luxurious, private bedchamber, complete with its own balcony, it came as a shock to see the primitive accommodation they had been assigned.

Apparently, it was one of Andala's finest homes.

Bayla lifted her nose in the air as she considered its dusty corners and exposed, smoke-stained old rafters. A long firepit ran down the centre of the very plain one-room house. Narrow beds hugged the walls; barely enough to sleep them all. There was a rudimentary kitchen at the far end of the house, with a small table and chairs, and a door leading to a storage room that smelled of damp hay and ale.

It looked like the sort of place her slaves would have slept.

Berard, recognising the scowl on his mother's face, hurried to intervene. 'It is perfect, thank you,' he smiled at Gisila Furyck, who stood hesitantly by the door with her sister.

Neither Gisila nor Branwyn knew what to say to Bayla, who was obviously having a hard time keeping her disdain from her face. It was the best accommodation Gisila could find, though, and its longtime owner had not been pleased to be relocated to a small cottage while the Dragos' were in Andala.

Karsten was neither bothered by his mother's lack of manners, nor the size of the house. He was far more interested in getting out into the fort and helping with the preparations for their attack on Hest, but he felt trapped by his family. Nicolene was useless, as was his mother. Irenna, who had always been reliable, had not spoken in days and had yet to even acknowledge what had happened to Haegen.

And Berard?

Berard had one arm, and though he was doing everything he could to help, he still looked pale, in pain, and incapable of managing the children on his own.

'Hello?' Hanna poked her head into the house, smiling shyly.

Gisila eyed the door as Hanna slipped inside. 'We should be going,' she said quickly, nudging her sister. 'If you need anything else, you'll find one of us in the hall, I'm sure.' She didn't even wait for Bayla to acknowledge her as she pushed Branwyn through the door.

'Thank you!' Berard called after the quickly disappearing women.

'Well, this looks nice,' Hanna said, glancing at the miserable faces who didn't appear to agree with her. Only one person had a smile on their face, and that was Karsten, who stood by the firepit, grinning at her.

'You're just the woman I need,' he announced, walking towards Hanna, grabbing her elbow and pushing her back out the door.

Berard looked after them in surprise.

Hanna turned to Karsten once they were outside. 'What's happened?'

Karsten lowered his voice. 'I need your help. With them.' He inclined his head back to the house. 'Berard can't do much with the children, though he wants to. Irenna won't move. Nicolene is...' He closed his eyes, feeling disloyal, then wondered why he was bothering with loyalty after what she'd done. 'Nicolene is useless. She's always been useless,' he admitted. 'And my mother... well, I don't know what there is to say about her. But you are not useless, Hanna. I need to be out in the fort, talking with those in charge. Making plans for our attack on Hest. Doing what I can to help. I can't be stuck in there all day long. I'll kill someone!'

Hanna nodded, smiling. 'Of course. I'll stay and help.'

'You don't mind?' Karsten was amazed by her eagerness, knowing that he'd hardly offered her an appealing proposition.

'No, I don't mind. It will give me something useful to do,' Hanna admitted. 'And besides, the children know me. I think they even like me. It will be better if I can help them, rather than a stranger. Especially Valder and the girls. Losing their father like that? I can't even imagine how terrified they must feel. I'm happy to stay. You can go.'

Karsten couldn't quite believe his luck, and adjusting his eyepatch, he smiled, eager to be gone. 'I will. I'll come back soon, though, just to make sure you're still standing. Not everyone can stomach so much time alone with my mother!' And winking, he turned around, almost skipping away, relieved to finally have a moment to himself.

Hanna turned back to the house, listening to the sudden high-pitched scream that could only be coming from Kai Dragos.

***

Having finally gotten rid of Evaine, Morana went straight to bed. After two cups of her tea, she was feeling sleepy. Dandelion flowers and poppy seeds had always helped to induce her dreams, and she was eager to spend as much time asleep as possible, searching for that missing ritual page.

Nothing she'd dreamed of so far had proven useful.

What she really needed was something from Draguta's chamber. But what? Morana stretched out her legs, feeling the pleasant coolness of the linen mattress beneath them, listening to the cracking of her twisted toes. She closed her eyes, enjoying the distant hum of the markets, the constant hammering of the harried shipbuilders, and the men at work on the piers. It all blurred together in the most pleasant way, luring her eyelids closed, helping her body, and then, eventually, her mind, unwind.

And then a sharp knock on the door.

Morana growled, her eyebrows meeting in annoyance.

'Morana?'

Sighing, Morana dragged herself out of bed and trudged towards the door, yanking it open, not even wanting to speak. Morac looked worried as he walked past her, ignoring her crumpled look of displeasure.

It was nothing he wasn't used to.

'I can't find Evaine,' he fretted. 'She wasn't in the hall for breakfast, though apparently, she had been there earlier. One of the servants said that she'd come up to see you.'

Morana continued to glare at her brother, who dragged a stool towards the last embers of the fire.

'I heard her crying through the wall last night. She is very upset about Eadmund.' He turned to his sister, at last, wondering why she hadn't spoken. 'Are you alright?'

Morana shook her matted hair, peering at him. 'Do I *look* alright? I was almost asleep, you old fool! I was trying to dream! Trying to help us,' she hissed, glancing at the door. 'And I can hardly do that if you are here, blathering at me!'

Morac stood, smoothing down his dark-grey tunic. 'Well, I shall go then. I didn't realise. I'm just worried. Without Eadmund here, I'm not sure how to keep Evaine... under control.' He was looking for help. Support. Anything.

'Best thing you can do is hide from her,' Morana grumbled, pushing him towards the door. 'Why not go to the baths? I doubt you'll find anyone there in that disgusting hot water. Certainly not Evaine. Enjoy the peace, as I shall do once you leave my chamber!' And opening the door, she shoved Morac through it.

'You mustn't worry about the girl. Eadmund will come soon, and in the meantime, just ensure that you stay out of her way!'

And turning back into her chamber, she slammed the door.

***

They found Else washing Jaeger's tunics in the stream.

It was a warm day, and she struggled to her feet, wiping the sweat from her wrinkled brow. 'Hmmm, her servants keep very much to themselves, but I imagine they...' She paused, not wanting to get the girls in trouble. They were all nice enough. All of them terrified of Draguta.

'What?' Jaeger was impatient, squinting in the bright glare of the sun. 'What is it?'

'I imagine that they might sell the dresses to the merchants. Or, perhaps, back to the tailors. I have seen her servants here, washing them out. Not all can be saved, but those that can will surely be sold.' Else felt disturbed, remembering the dress covered in blood.

Glancing at Meena, Jaeger frowned; that wasn't what he wanted to hear.

Else pointed towards a tall girl bending over at the other end of the stream. 'There you go. There's one of them now.'

Meena's eyes bulged, watching as the servant dipped the elegant white dress into the stream.

'Hey!' Jaeger yelled. 'You!' It was hardly going to keep their quest a secret, but he didn't want that dress dunked all the way into the water. He ran towards the girl, who stood up in a panic, realising that the king was screaming at her.

And promptly dropped the dress into the stream.

Jaeger snatched it before the whole garment could slither under the water. One corner was still dry, and he tore it off, much to the servant's surprise. 'I need a piece of cloth,' he panted. 'I have an injured ankle, you see. This will do nicely.' And dropping the dress back into the water, Jaeger turned to Meena with a triumphant grin.

Meena gulped, hoping that she'd be able to dream something with the piece of Draguta's dress. Afraid of how furious Jaeger would be if she couldn't.

***

Hanna and Berard decided to give Irenna and Bayla some peace by offering to take the children for a walk around the fort. Nicolene had not wanted to come, deciding that even Bayla would make better company than either of them.

'What do you think will happen now?' Berard wondered, his eyes darting around as they walked, taking great interest in their new surroundings. 'In Hest? With Jaeger?'

Hanna shrugged, smiling at Kai, who seemed just as interested in the fort as Berard, and thankfully, very quiet as he sat on her hip, gnawing a carrot. 'I imagine he's planning to attack us,' she said quietly, conscious that Eron was walking beside Berard, though he was really too little to understand what they were talking about. Irenna's three children were further away, sticking together, enjoying the freedom of being out of the house.

Berard frowned. 'And Meena is there with him.'

'I think she must be very strong to have chosen to stay,' Hanna said. 'Valder! Don't go there. Those men might not see you!' She cringed, watching as the little boy ran towards a group of men who were sharpening the tips of giant logs with lethal-looking axes. Valder stopped quickly, backing away. 'She'll be doing everything she can to help, don't you think?' Hanna was quickly distracted again, her eyes on Lucina, who had hold of Halla's hand and was leading her out of sight. 'Come back, girls!' she called, walking faster. 'Hurry, Berard! I don't want them to get lost!'

Despite Hanna's urgency not to lose the children, Berard barely lifted his feet as he traipsed after her. His mind was back in Hest with Meena, hoping she would stay safe until he could find a way to rescue her.

***

Jaeger shoved the torn piece of silk at Meena, turning her towards the stairs. 'Go. See if you can dream,' he muttered, his eyes on Evaine Gallas, who had wandered into the castle, looking morose. All thoughts of going up to Draguta's chamber to touch the book with Meena were suddenly gone.

Meena was surprised, not expecting to have to dream in the middle of the afternoon. 'But, I...'

'Go!' Jaeger hissed and pushed her again, walking towards Evaine.

Meena stared after him, then started up the stairs, hoping that his interest in Evaine meant that she could enjoy an afternoon alone.

'You look bored,' Jaeger smiled.

Evaine was relieved to finally find someone to talk to. 'I'm not sure what to do with myself,' she admitted meekly. 'There's no sign of Draguta today. Morana is busy, and I can't see my father anywhere.' She sighed heavily, pursing her lips.

Jaeger thought that she might have the most perfect lips he had ever seen.

'Do you ride?' he wondered. 'I have to go and check on the progress of my walls. If you'd like some company, you may have mine.'

Evaine frowned at him, sensing that his idea of company wasn't quite the same as hers, but she was so desperate to talk to someone that she nodded. 'I can ride. And yes, company would make a nice change.'

Jaeger took her hand, slipping it through his arm, feeling a charge ignite his body, unable to think of anyone's company he wanted more.

***

Axl sat beside Fyn, happy to see that he looked alert. His cheeks had already filled out since Runa had arrived and started feeding him.

He was bored and eager to get up and be of use.

'My mother said I can try a walk around the hall,' Fyn said, glancing at Runa, who stood in the doorway, watching him. 'Didn't you?'

Runa didn't look as keen as her son, but she nodded anyway. 'I'll go and see if I can find Thorgils. He did say that he'd come.'

'Well, I'd offer my help, but I think we'd both end up on the floor,' Axl grinned.

Fyn was pleased to see him. He felt shut off from everything that was happening, and because his small chamber was behind the curtain, just off the hall, he could hear how frantic and busy everyone was, including his mother. It was hard not to be part of it. There was obviously a lot to do.

Runa smiled, and leaving them to talk, she walked back into the hall. She hadn't seen Thorgils for hours. He'd been trying to stay out of Ivaar's way, while keeping a close eye on Eadmund and worrying about Isaura. He was flitting about the fort like a dragonfly.

Runa wandered through the hall, out the open doors and down the steps, enjoying the warm sunshine that greeted her. She wasn't sure that she'd ever felt such warmth on Oss.

Bram waved her over to his table, where he had one hand in

a bowl of apples. 'You look lost,' he grinned.

Runa brushed a loose strand of silvery hair out of her eyes, tucking it behind an ear. 'Not lost, just looking for Thorgils. He promised to help Fyn take a walk around the hall, though I'm not sure how far he could really get. Maybe more around his chamber?' She dropped her eyes, suddenly shy.

'Thorgils is moving too quickly for me to keep up with today,' Bram laughed. 'I'll help your boy.' And taking his hand out of the apples, he stood with a groan.

'Oh no, no, you don't need to do that! I'll go and find Thorgils.'

'Runa, you stay right there. I haven't done anything useful all day. Besides, I like being around young people. Reminds me of when I wasn't so old and creaky.'

Runa smiled awkwardly as they walked up the hall steps. 'I suppose you must miss your own children? And your wife?'

Bram froze, and Runa froze with him, wondering what she'd said.

The pain in Bram's heart, though not new, was still as sharp as a spear, and he swallowed, not wanting to expose himself, but when he looked into Runa's kind eyes, his shoulders loosened. 'They died, I'm afraid.' And he walked ahead, leaving her stuck to the hall steps in shock.

Edela watched Runa shake her head and hurry after Bram. She frowned, trying to remember to check on young Fyn. Jael cared a lot for the boy, and she wanted to ensure that he was healed and happy when she returned.

'Have you seen anything of Jael?' Eydis wondered from her right. She was taking pieces of apple as Edela cut them with her knife. 'Or Aleksander?'

Edela handed Ayla a slice of apple too. 'I haven't. Have you?'

'No, but I did see one thing,' Eydis said slowly. 'I saw a forest. It looked scary and dark. There were so many trees. And lots of owls.'

'Oh, that would be Hallow Wood,' Edela smiled. 'It's like a maze, from what I hear, though I've never been in there myself.'

Eydis' eyes were round as she took a piece of apple, munching noisily.

'Yes, people often disappear in Hallow Wood,' Ayla added. 'They go in search of the gods, seeking their wisdom, looking for their help. But the gods don't welcome humans anymore. Most people avoid it these days.'

'They do,' Edela agreed. 'Though I don't think Jael and Aleksander will be too worried about the gods.'

'No, and I don't believe the gods would see them as a threat. They must know that they're trying to help us,' Ayla suggested hopefully.

Edela nodded, biting into the remainder of the apple. 'As long as the symbol holds, it will protect them from anyone who tries to hurt them while they're in there.'

Eydis wanted to offer something more, but she couldn't see anything except darkness. And darkness in itself wasn't frightening to her. But what lurked in the darkness was growing loud.

Creeping in from the edges.

She could almost hear the shuffling of feet and feel the cold breath of evil blowing on her cheeks.

Something was out there, hiding in the darkness.

***

Bram had Fyn's arm around his neck as he lifted him off the bed, trying to convince him not to take his own weight too quickly.

Runa fussed around them both, worried that Fyn looked pale, urging him to breathe deeply.

'Why don't you step back to the door, Runa,' Bram suggested, puffing at the surprising weight of the lanky young man. Fyn was almost as tall as him, and his floppy auburn hair hung in his eyes as he stood, focusing on the floor.

Runa reluctantly stepped back, hovering in the doorway, ready to help. And when Fyn finally righted himself with a relieved smile and a loud groan, she burst into tears, determined not to unbalance her son by throwing her arms around him.

'What's going on here?' Thorgils asked, popping his head over the top of Runa's. And then he saw Fyn, leaning on Bram, and he blinked in surprise.

***

Jaeger glanced at Evaine. She appeared nervous as she perched on her saddle, as uncomfortable as the horse she sat upon. 'You're sure you've ridden before?' he wondered with a grin.

'The horses on Oss are smaller,' she insisted, clamping her teeth together as her irritable horse shook his head, wanting her to loosen her hold on him.

'You need to release the reins,' Jaeger said. 'Just a little. You're pulling, and soon he'll get cross with you, and that won't end well.'

Evaine blinked, letting the reins rest in her lap. 'Like this?'

Jaeger nodded, smiling as he brought his horse alongside hers. 'Much better.'

Evaine didn't relax at all. She had barely ridden before, but she'd been so desperate for company and a chance to escape the confines of the castle that she'd not wanted to reveal that to Jaeger. Glancing around, she finally noticed the breathtaking view. 'It's beautiful up here,' she smiled, scanning the rooftops of the castle and the buildings that bordered the square, before lurching back around, tightening her grip again as her horse threw up his head.

'It is,' Jaeger agreed, watching her. 'Very beautiful.'

Evaine was used to the way men admired her, but she had little time for it. There was only one man she had ever wanted, and she saw no point in leading anyone else down a dead-end path. 'You have a wife?' she asked. 'In Brekka?'

Jaeger didn't appreciate the reminder, his expression souring. 'I do.'

'And will you try to take her back?' Evaine asked, eager to know more.

Jaeger shrugged. 'I have yet to decide. Perhaps I will? Perhaps I'll kill her and find a new wife?'

Evaine didn't blink, though she did swallow. 'Well, I'm not sure which she'd prefer.'

Jaeger laughed. 'You don't think she'd prefer to be my wife?'

'From what I hear, she loves another, and it's hard to imagine a life apart from the one you love. So, if you take her away from Axl Furyck, perhaps she'd wish she was dead?'

Jaeger was cheered by that thought. 'I think I'd prefer a different type of queen,' he said, his eyes on Evaine's perfect lips. 'A woman so fine that everyone she passed was struck dumb by her beauty. A woman who wanted to rule beside me. Who cared for fine jewels and elegant clothing. Who desired power and heirs and wealth. I don't believe that describes my current wife.'

Evaine looked away from his intense gaze. 'Well, I wish you luck finding such a woman. I can't imagine it would be hard. You describe a life that anyone would dream of. But it would all feel empty if there was no love. That is what you must look for first.'

Jaeger laughed. 'You truly believe in love?'

'Why would you say such a thing?' Evaine pushed back her shoulders, feeling offended. 'I love Eadmund, and he loves me. Of course I believe in love!'

'Is it still love if it comes from magic?' Jaeger wondered. 'If you have to trap someone with a spell, is that still love?'

Evaine's eyes flared with anger. 'Eadmund loved me before there was any spell!' she spat, shaking with fury. 'There was no need for me to put a spell on him at all. But we had to make sure he stayed away from Jael Furyck. She was trying to take him away from me! The spell was necessary. For Eadmund.'

Jaeger could hear her desperation, and he decided to stop teasing her. 'Of course,' he said softly, pointing to the left. 'We'll leave the road now and head that way.'

Evaine was too furious to reply, feeling the thundering of her heart; not wanting to admit for even a moment that Jaeger was right.

***

Bram walked Thorgils back to the main gates where they hoped to finish off the catapult they'd been making with Eadmund and Torstan.

'Fyn seems in good shape,' Thorgils said as they headed down a wooden path. 'No doubt he'll be thinking he can pick up a sword soon. Not sure Runa will be happy about that.'

'Well, you can't hold a young man like that back,' Bram smiled. 'These are the best years of his life. When all you want is to feel a sword in your hand, go on adventures, defeat your enemies, build a reputation. By the time you're our age, it's too late for anything like that.'

'*Our* age?' Thorgils snorted. 'When were *we* the same age, Uncle?'

Bram laughed. 'Well, true. Seems only yesterday when I was your age, but I suppose I'm an old man now.'

The sinking sun glinted in Bram's sad eyes, and Thorgils guessed that he was thinking of his dead wife and children. 'You're not that old. And it's never too late for anything. You're about to go to war against the biggest enemy we've ever faced.

It's the sort of story that'll be sung about for all time!'

'Well, perhaps that's the perfect way to end it all? A glorious battle death!'

'You're feeling optimistic, then, about how things will go?'

Bram smiled. 'If I get through this battle, I'm not sure what I'd do. I've no one to go back to in Moll now. I could keep sailing around with Snorri, trading, trying to bring in enough coins to feed our men. But sometimes you have to wonder what it's all for? Just to survive until I'm too old to sail the sea? Shitting my britches... a burden to everyone?'

Thorgils wrapped an arm around his uncle's shoulder. 'That doesn't sound like you. I think you'd be surprised by how much you have to live for. Just you wait and see. You'll find something to change your mind.'

Bram lifted his snowy eyebrows at Thorgils, but his nephew kept his conspiratorial eyes fixed on the path ahead.

CHAPTER TWENTY NINE

It wasn't long after they'd started riding that morning that Jael and Aleksander came to Hallow Wood. Neither of them felt pleased to see the long, densely packed treeline that snaked across the flat expanse of land before them. It looked more like a dark forest than any wood, Jael thought.

Not inviting in the slightest.

It was oddly quiet, except for the nervous whinnying of both horses, which wasn't the most encouraging sign.

Jael motioned for Aleksander to go ahead. 'After you, then.'

Aleksander smiled, nudging Sky forward. 'Won't be so bad,' he said over his shoulder. 'Plenty to eat in there!'

They had finished Biddy's packet of food, and Jael's eyes lit up at the thought of a hot meal, but every part of her wanted to turn around and go back to Andala.

Running away now wouldn't help anyone, though.

So Jael tapped Tig's flanks, and, with his ears twitching, he reluctantly followed Sky and Aleksander into the wood.

***

Morana was irritable and stiff, having spent nearly a whole day and night in bed, trying to dream. She had walked down to the hall, just to stretch her legs, but Jaeger had insisted she join them for breakfast, and now she was trapped at the high table, listening as he prattled on, trying to impress Evaine.

'Shouldn't someone go and find out if Draguta's alright?' Evaine wondered, glancing at Morana, avoiding Jaeger's eyes.

Morana lifted her head, scowling. 'You could try, but I imagine that anyone who interrupts her dreaming will regret it.' She pushed away her bowl of porridge which was far too runny for her liking.

'Is that what she's doing?' Morac asked. 'Dreaming?'

Morana shrugged. 'I'm not Draguta, but that is how dreamers find answers to their problems. Though, of course, the dreams do not always come,' she sighed, realising that she too wanted Draguta to emerge from her bedchamber. Morana knew that she would have far more success with her dreams if she could find something of Draguta's to dream with.

Something she wouldn't miss.

Jaeger turned towards the entranceway, wondering where Meena was. He had left her asleep in bed, hoping to keep her dreaming, though he wasn't sure why he was bothering.

Perhaps Draguta had just been playing games?

According to Meena, she had never had a real dream in her life, so why did he think that anything they did could coax one out of her now?

***

Meena kept dreaming of Berard.

At first, she had felt a lift, seeing that he was safe in Andala with the Furycks. She saw him with Karsten Dragos. With the queen. With his sisters-in-law and their children.

He looked sad, she thought. Worried. But apart from losing an arm, he appeared well, and that gave Meena hope, though those were not the dreams Jaeger was looking for her to have. But despite keeping the torn piece of Draguta's dress under her pillow, Meena hadn't seen anything of her.

After Jaeger left, she'd crept out of bed and dug under the mattress, pulling out a comb she had taken from Berard's old chamber, wondering if that was stopping her from seeing anything else. Varna's book had mentioned how you had to hold what you wished to bring to you in your mind. You had to see it, feel it, imagine drawing it to you. And Meena didn't feel that way about Draguta. She was terrified of her and didn't want to dream about her at all, so it took Meena some time to convince herself to fall back to sleep, holding the piece of white silk in her hand.

But two minutes later, she was sitting bolt upright, gagging in shock.

***

Hallow Wood felt odd.

Jael couldn't think of any other way to describe it. It was a winding knot of ancient moss-and-lichen-covered trees whose branches twisted so intricately around each other that it felt as if the only sky above them was made of leaves. They could barely see any sign of the sun. Even the air felt different. It was cold, but almost airless, as though no breeze could penetrate that dense canopy of leaves either.

Neither Jael nor Aleksander spoke. All of their attention was focused on watching where they were going, not wanting either horse to twist an ankle as they navigated the sprawling tree roots and holes hidden beneath a thick carpet of soggy leaves and twigs.

Jael rode behind Aleksander, wondering if he knew where he was going. Though how could he? Their path didn't look like an obvious path at all, just a way to get between the trees, with no real indication that anyone had been this way before. It was narrow, and there was no way they could ride beside each other. Not here. In some places, the horses were almost too wide to squeeze through the trees.

'Do you know where you're going?' Jael called, unable to stand the silence any longer, but Aleksander only nodded, and the silence continued.

Looking down at Tig, Jael noticed that his ears were swivelling. She glanced around, wondering what he could hear.

There was no one there. No one that she could see.

But it did feel odd.

***

Meena hadn't appeared yet, so, curious to find out if she had seen anything in her dreams, Jaeger headed up to his chamber. His new servant was there, but she had no idea where Meena had gone.

Jaeger frowned. He didn't like Else, though it was nothing he could put his finger on. She was just too... pleasant. Always smiling, trying to be helpful, but not in the way that Egil had been helpful. Perhaps that was it, Jaeger decided, turning to the door, leaving Else to sweep the floor in peace. Perhaps it was just that he was so used to Egil's effortless subservience.

There was nothing subservient about Else. It was more as if she was trying to mother him. Care for him.

Jaeger didn't know what to make of her.

Pulling open the door, he bit his tongue in surprise, not expecting Draguta to be standing there.

'Just the person I need!' she smiled, curling a long finger towards him. 'I have a job for you.'

***

Thorgils had left Torstan to keep an eye on Eadmund, so he could share a cup of ale and a slice of cake with Isaura in the hall, and when he'd finished both of those, he headed to the bedchambers to say hello to Fyn.

'Ahhh, this is where you're hiding,' he smiled at Eydis. 'Isaura was looking for you. I think she was wondering if you'd like to spend some time with your nieces and nephew?' He put his hand down as Ido and Vella stretched themselves awake and came to sniff him. They could smell the cake, but Thorgils held out his empty hands, showing them that they were out of luck.

Vella licked them anyway, just to make sure.

Eydis didn't think that she should leave, and Fyn could sense her reluctance to go. She had been a near-constant companion since they'd left Tuura. Everyone else was too busy to keep visiting, so it had been nice to have her to talk to. He was growing tired of being in bed, though, and now that he'd been able to stand, he felt confident that he could start sitting in the hall soon. 'You go, Eydis,' Fyn said. 'I think I might close my eyes for a while.'

He made yawning sounds, and Thorgils grinned, seeing that he was just trying to encourage Eydis to go and have some fun.

'Why don't I take you to find the children?' Runa said as she came in, bringing Fyn a large piece of cake.

Fyn's eyes lit up, and they didn't look sleepy at all.

'I'll come back later, then,' Eydis said shyly, letting Runa help her up. The puppies started to follow her, but the smell of cake quickly changed their minds.

Fyn smiled as Thorgils pushed them away before stuffing half the cake into his mouth.

'You're going to need a bit more than cake to get your

strength back,' Thorgils suggested. 'Though it's a nice cake!'

Fyn's mouth was too full to reply.

Thorgils frowned at him. 'Do you ever wonder what happened to Morac and Evaine? Where they disappeared to?'

'Wherever they've gone, I hope they both stay there. I never want to see them again. After what they've done?' Fyn shook his head, his face disappearing beneath his hair, which had grown long – almost past his shoulders now. He irritably pushed it away. 'It's hard to think of your father being a murderer. But after what he did to Eirik, I hope Eadmund kills him.'

'Well, he always was a strange bastard,' Thorgils admitted. 'I'm not sure many liked him. But they liked you and Runa, so no one wanted to say much about it.'

'They can now,' Fyn said, reaching for his cup of small ale. 'They can say what they like. He's dead to me. He never meant anything in the first place, but now, he's dead to me!'

Thorgils watched the anger in Fyn's eyes, and he smiled.

***

Jaeger was distracted as he followed Draguta out of the castle, through the narrow back streets of the city, down into the catacombs. Whether it was imagining the sweet taste of Evaine's perfect lips or wondering what had happened to Meena, he barely gave much thought to what Draguta wanted from him, but as they walked through the archway into the stinking antechamber, his curiosity was finally awakened. 'Why are we here?'

Draguta turned to him with a smile. 'I'm planning to cast another spell, tomorrow night. And this time, I will draw her out. This time she will have no choice. She will need to stop me. She will *have* to reveal herself.'

Jaeger frowned. 'Who?'

Draguta turned to him, her pale face aglow in the flame from his torch. 'My sister.'

***

Thorgils left Fyn to sleep, realising that Torstan had probably lost Eadmund by now. Quietly closing the door to the chamber, he turned around, surprised to see Runa walking up and down the corridor, jiggling Sigmund in her arms.

'You're getting a lot of practice for when you become a grandmother,' Thorgils whispered, eager to keep the baby quiet. He wasn't sure he'd heard a noisier child.

Runa looked horrified. 'Oh, I don't want to imagine that!' she exclaimed. 'Fyn's just a boy!'

Thorgils laughed as he walked towards the thick grey curtain that separated the bedchambers from the hall. 'It's been a long time since you looked at your son properly, Runa!' He reached for the curtain, then stopped, turning back, running his eyes up and down the corridor. 'You should tell him,' he murmured. 'Morac will never return to Oss. He knows that he's dead if he does. You should tell Bram.'

Runa blinked. It was dark in the corridor, but not so dark that she couldn't see the implied meaning in Thorgils' eyes. She opened her mouth, not knowing what to say. Wondering what he could know.

How he could know anything.

Thorgils shrugged. 'Of course, I'm just guessing. But I'd wager it's a guess that would earn me a fair return if I were a betting man. I saw them together, Bram and Fyn...' He let that hang there between them, watching the shock on her face turn to guilt before she dropped her eyes. 'You could make them both happy, Runa. Who knows how long we have with the trouble brewing out there. But you have a chance to make them both happy before it's too late.'

Runa closed her mouth, then opened it again, but she still didn't know what to say. It was a secret she had sworn never to reveal. She had judged herself harshly over the years for a brief moment of weakness, though it was a moment she had thought of with wistful longing, wishing she could experience that warmth again.

That kindness and desire.

Turning her eyes to the floor, Runa hid her face as it burned with shame and embarrassment.

Thorgils squeezed her shoulder and slipped away as Tanja pulled back the curtain, smiling in relief at the sight of an almost sleeping baby. Runa was distracted as she handed Sigmund to her, but not for long. Twenty-year-old memories were hurrying back, and she realised that, perhaps, it was finally time to face them.

***

'You're not going to say anything, then?' Jael wondered, bored now. The wood was becoming an even darker, more obstructive maze, and their progress had slowed to a crawl. They had taken turns leading the way as there was only one obvious path, and they had no option but to follow it as it meandered through the trees. Jael turned around to Aleksander, deciding that it was time to make her own fun. 'About Hanna?'

Aleksander frowned at the playful look on Jael's face. He didn't want to give her the satisfaction of thinking that she could make him uncomfortable.

Jael grinned, turning back around, just in time to smack her head into a thick branch.

Aleksander burst out laughing as Jael groaned, holding her head. 'What was that you were asking?'

Jael ignored him, deciding that they should probably swap places again as she could see a fork in the path ahead.

Aleksander glanced behind himself, a shiver racing up his spine. The darker the wood became, the colder it got, but he'd trekked through deep snow. It wasn't that sort of cold. It felt as though they were being followed, but even though he'd turned around countless times, he'd seen no sign of anyone or anything.

Though his senses remained heightened.

He didn't want to come across wolves again.

Leaning forward, he patted Sky, who was walking with some trepidation, her red ears rotating constantly.

Taking a deep breath, Aleksander tried to stay focused on what lay ahead, but, like his nervous horse, his ears remained open to what might be coming from behind.

***

Draguta refused to answer any further questions, much to Jaeger's irritation. Instead, she pointed towards the crypt which lay hidden beneath her coffin, demanding that he uncover it again.

Jaeger grunted and shunted, slipping in the dusty gravel, wondering why they had covered it up last time. Surely, with The Following now ash, there was no one else who could possibly know about this place? He frowned. Unless Draguta was worried about Morana?

'Should I be, do you think?' Draguta wondered.

Jaeger coughed loudly. He wasn't sure that she'd even spoken. '*Be*?'

'Worried about Morana,' Draguta murmured from behind him, leaning against the elaborate tombstone of some ancient Hestian king.

Jaeger froze, unsettled that she was reading his thoughts. 'I wouldn't trust Morana if I were you. I certainly don't. But after what you did to The Following, I think she'd be foolish to cause you any problems. And whatever else she may be, Morana Gallas is no fool.' He clenched his jaw, leaning into the stone coffin again, growling as he shoved it away from the hidden door.

'No, she is no fool,' Draguta agreed. 'And she is useful to me. As are you. Though I am not blind, nor deaf. I see much more than either of you realise, Jaeger,' she purred, walking up to him. 'About how things will go.' She trailed one hand up his arm, towards his face. 'There is still a chance to change your mind before it's too late.' And smiling, she turned her attention to the little trap door. 'Now, let us get inside. There is so much to do today!'

***

The tight knots of trees suddenly eased, and Jael edged Tig forward to ride alongside Aleksander. The horses were almost trotting now as they rode down the wide, clear path.

Jael turned to him, trying not to frown. 'You can tell me about Hanna. We've always been friends. Always will be.'

'I don't recall you ever wanting to tell me anything about Eadmund.'

Jael blinked in surprise. 'Hanna's like Eadmund, is she? *That* important?'

'No, I'm not saying that, but you won't talk to me about him. Not really.'

Jael sighed. 'I made promises to you when I left Andala. I didn't think it was fair to hurt you.'

Aleksander looked hurt. And confused. 'Hanna is nothing.' He shook his head, annoyed with himself. 'I mean, it meant nothing, what happened. I was drinking too much. Lost control of myself. It was a mistake.'

Jael didn't look at him. She didn't know how she felt. Mostly strange, though she wondered how she had the right to feel anything. She had left him behind and married someone else. She wanted someone else. But still, Aleksander had always belonged to her. He had only ever been hers. 'Hanna seems nice,' she mumbled. 'Smart. Brave.'

'I can't say that we did much talking,' Aleksander admitted.

'Oh, well, now you've said too much,' Jael squirmed, holding up a hand. 'I don't want to think about that!'

Aleksander grinned. He'd thought about it often. Mostly feeling guilty, though it had been nice not to be alone for a moment or two. 'I don't know anything about her, except that she helped me escape Tuura.'

'And now you know that she went to Hest to try and steal the Book of Darkness, so there's obviously something to like about her.' The words didn't come easily, but Jael's jealousy didn't override her admiration for Hanna. Not many would have volunteered for such a mission.

'I think so,' Aleksander almost whispered, remembering Hanna's kind face.

'See, we can talk about things –' Jael froze, pulling on Tig's reins, her eyes darting around, checking the trees. 'What was that?'

Aleksander thought he'd heard something too, but the wind swept through the trees, quickly covering any oddity with a loud rustling of leaves.

Neither Jael nor Aleksander returned to their conversation. They both remained on edge as they continued forward.

***

Meena was beginning to enjoy the freedom that her new status as Jaeger's dreamer afforded her.

Was that what she was?

She frowned uncertainly, walking down to the piers, listening to the cheerful sounds from the markets. It was a cloudless day, and the harbour sparkled under a bright sun. Meena watched the birds swooping down to the water, searching for fish, calling to each other, and she felt sad, thinking of how close she had come to leaving with Berard. But if she had left Hest, perhaps she would never have found out that she was a dreamer?

'Wishing you were somewhere else?' Morana cackled, creeping up behind her niece. 'Far away, with the armless hunchback?'

Meena flinched, not wanting her evil aunt anywhere near her thoughts. 'I was just watching the birds.'

'Ha!' Morana snorted. 'More likely wondering how quickly you could find your way out of here. But there is no way out of Hest, not while you're Jaeger's little toy. And no matter how much he may desire my daughter, it doesn't appear that he's letting go of you in a hurry.'

Meena wondered if she had to stay and endure Morana's company, but any thoughts of boldness were quickly squashed as Morana wrapped her bony fingers around her wrist. 'Now, come along, little mouse. Draguta has left the castle, and I want you to go into her chamber and take something for me.'

Meena's eyes bulged, and she quickly shook her head. Her hair had bounced back into a knotted bush again, and it vibrated with panic like the rest of her.

Morana leaned closer and narrowed her dark eyes, squeezing her fingers tightly, watching Meena grimace. 'You're *refusing* me?'

Meena squeaked, opening her eyes even wider.

'Ahhh, just the two creatures I was hoping to find!' Draguta exclaimed as she walked towards them with Jaeger. 'I have been dreaming the most wonderful things. So if you've stopped trying to kill your niece, Morana, we can all go to my chamber, and I will tell you all about them!'

Morana dropped Meena's wrist and quickly cleared her mind.

Meena closed her gaping mouth and lifted up her head.

And they both hurried off after Draguta.

CHAPTER THIRTY

Ulf poked his head around the door. He could hear the wailing, but nobody could hear his knocking.

Two of the three women who turned to him looked frazzled.

One of them was almost lifeless.

He smiled and walked inside, pleased to see the relief on Bayla's face as she strode towards him.

'Just the man we need,' Bayla sighed. 'We are trying to make this horrid little shack more amenable to our needs, but Karsten has disappeared, and there is no point to Berard anymore, so perhaps you can help us, Ulf?' She didn't notice that his hair and beard had been combed or that his old brown tunic had been washed as she pointed him towards the far corner of the house. 'We wish to make an enclosure for the children, so that they may sleep together and stop crawling all over their mothers and me.'

Ulf nodded, though he wasn't really listening.

Bayla grabbed his arm, and smiling at Irenna and Nicolene, she led him back outside. 'It's Irenna, you see,' she said in a hushed voice, once she'd closed the door. 'She is not quite here. And there is nothing we can do about that except give her some time.' Her eyes filled with tears, which irritated her, and she sniffed loudly, carrying on. 'I think that sleep will help her, but she cannot sleep with the children waking her throughout the night. And when they do, she does nothing, which wakes the rest of us. So we need to move one of the beds, but it is attached to the wall. You will need to break it off, move it, then attach it to a bed on the other side, thereby making one large bed for all the children. Do you understand?'

Ulf put his hand on her shoulder, trying to still the frantic jerking of her body. Bayla was upset about her dead son. About her dead husband too. 'I can do that,' he said calmly. 'Sounds like a sensible idea, but I'll need some tools. Perhaps you can walk with me to find them?'

Bayla frowned. 'Why would I do that?'

'Because you need to listen to something that isn't squawking children,' Ulf grinned, picking up her hand and slipping it through his arm, ignoring her sudden stiffness. 'You need some air, and I shall require some help carrying the tools.' Of course, he didn't really, but Bayla didn't need to know that.

***

'Here we are, together again,' Draguta purred, sitting at her table with Morana and Meena, excitement bursting from her fingertips as they pressed on her beloved book.

After taking the time to rest and recover her dreams, she was feeling powerful again.

Darkly so.

'Now, we must prepare ourselves for what lies ahead. We are getting closer. Closer to drawing her out. And when she reveals herself, there will be nothing to stop us, will there?'

Morana frowned at Meena, wondering if she'd missed something.

Meena met Morana's eyes, just as confused.

Draguta dismissed them both. Whether they knew what was going on mattered little to her. But their help would be invaluable. There was a considerable amount of work involved in preparing the potions she needed. Not the sort of work she had to do anymore. Not when she had such capable assistants.

'We will prepare everything for tomorrow night,' Draguta said, handing a folded piece of vellum to Morana. '*You* will prepare everything. And while you are foraging about on your hands and knees, I shall prepare myself.'

Morana squinted at the vellum and sniffed. The list was long, stuffed full of obscurities, and she could tell that it would take all day to gather them. And the next. She wasn't even sure if they would be able to find all of them.

'Well, then, you'd better make a start!' Draguta decided as she stood, walking to the balcony, eager to soak up the last golden rays of the afternoon, leaving Morana and Meena to bite their tongues and hurry to their feet.

***

The dead serpent was close to the water now, and Axl felt relieved.

For a time, he'd wondered if it would ever budge. It was impossible to start thinking about rebuilding the harbour while the giant black corpse lay there, decomposing.

He turned, ready to head back into the fort and check on the fletchers. Jael had been very concerned with their arrow stores, and he didn't want her to be disappointed when she returned. Lifting his crutch over a rock, Axl stopped, surprised to see Berard and Karsten Dragos standing there, watching as the men dragged the headless serpent ever closer to its watery grave.

He nodded to them, but they barely noticed he was there. Their attention was consumed by the serpent, and Axl didn't know what to say, so he limped past them, towards the gates.

'He's in there,' Karsten said haltingly, staring at the serpent. It was too hard a thing to imagine. He swallowed, turning to

Berard. 'Do you *think* he's in there?'

Berard sighed. 'I don't know. Perhaps not.'

'But it was definitely this creature, wasn't it?'

Berard nodded, remembering Haegen's final moments.

Karsten unsheathed his sword and strode towards the serpent. Gripping the hilt with two hands, he stabbed the black corpse over and over again. Everyone working around the serpent stopped, many of them confused, not understanding what was going on.

Berard burst into tears, wishing he could change everything that had happened. Blaming himself for everything he'd failed to do.

Karsten exhausted himself, eventually, and panting, his shoulders heaving, he turned around, sheathing his bloody sword as he walked back to his only brother now, tears running down his face. Looking up, he wiped them away, adjusted his eye patch and stared at Berard. 'We kill Jaeger as soon as we can. Any way we can. For this. For Father. For your arm. Meena. Nicolene. We kill Jaeger.'

Berard wiped away his own tears and nodded.

***

Evaine had decided to stay far away from Jaeger Dragos, visiting Morac in his new accommodation: Yorik Elstad's old cottage. 'Why are you staying *here*?' she asked incredulously, glancing around the tiny one-room hovel. It was absent every comfort they had been used to in their luxurious house on Oss. Or, at least, what Evaine had believed to be luxurious before she'd seen Hest's magnificent castle. 'This is awful, and it stinks!' She peered around. 'What is that smell?'

Morac shrugged. He had been wondering that himself. 'Morana thought it would provide me with some privacy. I hardly belong in the castle. And this cottage was unoccupied. It used to belong to Yorik Elstad, apparently.'

Evaine didn't care.

'But this is not what you deserve, Father. You should be in the castle with us. The chambers there are more than five times as big as this ugly little hole.'

'It is kind of you to worry, my dear,' Morac smiled, pouring hot water into a cup of peppermint leaves that he'd picked from Yorik's tiny herb garden. 'But I am enjoying the peace of being far away from everyone. The castle was too big for me. Too demanding of my attention. I like it here.'

Evaine frowned. 'Well, at least come back for supper. I don't want to be alone with any of them.'

'I will. I may be enjoying my own company, but I certainly won't enjoy my own cooking! Before I do, though, I'll just take a quick nap. I've been feeling rather weary since our journey from Oss.'

Evaine looked away as he yawned, deciding that there were plenty of places inside the castle where she could hide from Jaeger, and surely any of them would be better than enduring the stench of this disgusting place. 'Fine. But don't be late for supper. Draguta will expect you.'

Morac nodded as he ushered her to the door. 'I'll be there after my nap, don't worry.' And he closed the door quickly, eager to get back to Yorik's books which he had stowed under the bed when Evaine had knocked on his door.

Morana had set him the task of looking through Yorik's old journals to see if they mentioned the missing ritual page they were so desperate to find. Her dreams had revealed nothing, and they were both growing impatient to uncover any clues to help them in their search.

And that was something neither of them planned to share with Evaine.

***

'Hurry up!' Morana grouched as Meena bent forward, gently easing her fingers around the precious roots of the tall angelica plant, wiggling it slowly out of the warm soil.

Meena felt a great responsibility in collecting the items on Draguta's list. She didn't want to be the one blamed if the spell failed, so she was determined to take her time.

Morana was far less concerned, though she knew very well how important it was for the plants to be harvested with great care. 'You would make a good snail!' she grouched, rolling her eyes. 'What the Bear sees in you, I'll never understand.' She stood under a tree, banging her long wooden staff on the ground, wanting to get on with things. 'We have to hurry!' she grumbled. 'And I need to find a cat.'

Meena swallowed. 'There's a dead cat down by the stream,' she said sadly. 'I saw it yesterday.'

Morana's eyes lit up. 'Well, if it's still there, that would save us some time, so get moving! Remember, Draguta is always watching... especially snails like you. It's easy to crush a snail, isn't it, Meena? Because they move so slowly!'

Meena swallowed, not wanting to incur Draguta's wrath. She had seen it with The Following. And in her dreams.

She had seen what Draguta could do.

***

Once the sun started sinking, the wood became even colder as Jael and Aleksander hurried to prepare a fire and secure the horses for the night. A thick, cloudlike mist was creeping through the trees towards them, and they were both growing more unsettled by the moment.

Though neither knew why.

But their unspoken fears sounded loud in the silence.

Aleksander had discovered another packet of food that Biddy must have hidden at the bottom of his saddlebag. He happily pulled out a wedge of smoked cheese, some hard flatbreads, and a few slices of cured pork. He found four squashed plums in the bottom of his saddlebag too.

It would be enough for supper.

The fire was warm, and Aleksander admired it as he leaned back against the broad trunk of an oak tree. 'Makes a change to have real flames,' he grinned.

'Makes a change for it not to be raining,' Jael added as she bit into an overripe plum, which squirted dark-red juice over her cloak. Her back was aching in an unfamiliar way, and she tried to get comfortable, but the tree she was leaning against was disagreeable, its old warped bark jabbing into her wherever she moved.

'Well, it's definitely going to rain now!' Aleksander decided. 'The gods are always listening.'

Jael frowned, glancing into the gloomy distance, but there was nothing to see. The mist felt as though it was drifting closer, almost encircling them in the small round clearing they had found to spend the night. Jael couldn't see beyond it. It was too thick. 'I think you're right. But whether they're friends or foes, I don't know anymore.'

Aleksander grabbed the cheese, reaching for his knife. 'I'll take first watch.'

'I can. I don't feel like sleeping.'

'Me neither.'

Jael laughed, trying to relax them both. 'What's happening to us? It's like we're ten-years-old again, and Edela is telling us a scary story before bed!'

'I never slept after her stories.'

'Neither did I.'

Jael spat out her plum pit, staring at Aleksander. 'We're

deep inside this wood, you and me. With two swords, two horses, and no idea where we are.'

'Well, some idea.'

'Do you think she's watching us?' Jael wondered.

'Who?'

'The Widow.'

Aleksander swallowed. 'I hope so.'

***

Eadmund glared at his brother.

Ivaar sat at the next table, laughing with his men, looking more relaxed than he'd seen him since their arrival in Andala.

It irritated him.

He thought of Melaena.

It irritated him.

Reaching for another salted herring, Eadmund met Bruno Adea's eyes.

'Your brother seems to like it here,' Bruno noted coldly, filling his cup with wine.

'Seems that he does,' Eadmund said. 'Which is hardly surprising. Nice to be alive and free, isn't it? Not like Borg Arnesson and his brothers.'

'Or stuck in a rotting hole,' Bruno grunted, his body vibrating with rage. He had never been an angry man, but it was impossible not to imagine Ivaar hurting his wife. Touching her. Keeping her in his bed; his prisoner, just as he had been.

Yet there was no justice that he could seek. None.

Ayla thought highly of the queen. Everyone did. And Bruno was a well-travelled man, so he knew all about Jael Furyck, as he had her father. But she was making a mistake to let Ivaar escape punishment for what he had done.

It was a mistake she would likely come to regret.

Eadmund turned to Bruno, noticing how bent he was; how he almost curled over the table. Surviving a year and a half in a prison hole had changed him. But he was still alive. And there would be plenty of opportunity for them both to ensure that Ivaar received the punishment he deserved.

When Jael was no longer the Queen of Oss.

Eadmund ran the rolled herring around his plate, soaking up the last of the gravy.

'You look like you could do with some more,' Biddy smiled, bending down in front of him, blocking his view of Ivaar. She was worried by the intense scowl on his face. He didn't look like the Eadmund she knew.

'No, I've had enough, thank you.' And he pushed himself away from the table, ducking his head and walking quickly out of the hall.

Biddy stared after him in surprise, turning around to meet Edela's concerned eyes.

Eadmund was definitely getting worse.

Edela frowned at Gisila, who'd been talking to her for some time. 'I'm not really listening, my dear,' she confessed, 'so why don't we swap places and you can talk to the queen instead?'

Neither Bayla nor Gisila looked keen for that to happen, but Edela was already creaking to her feet, eager to be closer to Hanna and Marcus, who looked as though they were having a far more interesting conversation with Berard.

Squeezing along the bench, Edela smiled at Hanna, thinking what a lovely girl she was, and so familiar, though she couldn't put her finger on why. 'Let's hope that this end of the table is more interesting,' Edela whispered to her. 'I can't sit through another discussion about weaning!'

Hanna laughed and grabbed an empty cup, filling it with wine. 'Here, have something to drink.'

Edela smiled, taking the cup. 'Thank you.' She raised it to Alaric, who sat next to Berard, ploughing through his second plate of herring and turnips. His mouth was so full that he could only nod in reply.

'And how is that stump of yours feeling, Berard?' Edela asked. 'Your cheeks certainly have more colour in them than when you arrived. That's a good sign.'

'Yes, I do feel better,' Berard admitted. 'It's a comfortable house. Being at sea and then walking over the ice...' He shuddered, still remembering the frozen sea and the horrified look on Haegen's face; still hearing Jaeger's emotionless voice; watching him hit Meena.

'Berard?' Hanna asked. 'Can I pour you something to drink?'

Berard blinked at the kind faces staring at him with concern. He nodded.

'Your brother will not escape justice,' Edela assured him, taking a quick sip of the tart fruit wine. She shivered as it tingled down her throat. 'For what he has done, and for what he will do, he will pay a heavy price. Do not despair. The prophecy says that my granddaughter will see to that. Isn't that right, Marcus?'

Marcus looked surprised to be called upon. He was unused to so much company. Though he had lived in a temple filled with people for years, he had barely spoken to any of them. But as much as the conversation made him uncomfortable, he was well aware that only by helping each other would they defeat that which sought to destroy them all.

'Yes, the prophecy says that he will not survive,' Marcus said, nodding at Berard.

Edela frowned, catching something in his eyes that troubled her.

A lie.

***

Evaine sighed with pleasure as she bit into the slice of roast boar. It was mouth-wateringly tender. More flavoursome than anything she had eaten at home on Oss. She reached for her goblet of wine. The deep-red liquid was potent, and her head felt fuzzy. She could feel herself swaying as though she was on a ship, rocking gently in a light breeze. It was a pleasant sensation, reminding her of being in Eadmund's arms.

Glancing at Draguta, she accidentally caught Jaeger's eyes.

Evaine scowled, looking away.

'Tell me about your day,' Draguta said, pushing away her plate and turning to Meena. She had quickly become bored with eating. Eating without tasting was a chore. There was no pleasure to take in the act of simply shovelling food into your mouth. 'How is your foraging going?'

Meena was so surprised to be addressed directly that she choked on a bean, which lodged firmly in her throat, and though she grabbed her goblet and swallowed her wine, it would not move. She coughed and gagged and panicked, trying to breathe.

'Help her,' Draguta said, flapping her hand at Jaeger, bored with the performance. She turned to Morana instead. 'If your throat is still working, *you* can tell me.'

Morana forced herself not to scowl, but she did sigh as she began to recount what they had done that day in a bored monotone.

Jaeger slapped Meena on the back, and the troublesome bean popped out onto her plate.

Listening to the conversation, Morac tried to do what Morana had taught him: clear his mind to only that which lay before him. And at that moment, it was the head of a wild boar, challenging him from a silver platter. He focused his mind on those lifeless eyes, waiting, as the slaves glided silently across the front of the table, topping up their goblets.

'Are you unwell, Morac? You do not seem yourself tonight,' Draguta mused, noticing his stiffness.

Morac bit his tongue as he reached for his goblet, almost knocking it over. He felt Morana tense on his other side. 'I am...

I am missing my wife,' he mumbled, swallowing his wine in panicked gulps. 'It wasn't easy to leave her like that.' Turning to Draguta, he tried to still his shaking legs. 'We were very close. Since childhood.'

Draguta stared into his grey eyes, pleased to see so much pain in them. It explained a lot. 'But she was never like you, was she? She never wanted what you did?'

Morac sighed. It was true, he realised. For all that he had loved Runa, she was never going to embrace Raemus and the Darkness as he had been taught to. 'No. No, she didn't. Still, it is not easy to let go.'

Draguta smiled. 'Oh, but you will. You will see how much more I have to offer you than poor, pathetic Runa.'

Morac blanched, surprised that she knew Runa's name.

Draguta leaned over him, her eyes on Morana. 'You are not hungry, Morana? Is there someone you are pining for? Yorik Elstad, perhaps? Do I have an entire family of teary-eyed romantics sitting at my table?' she sniggered, looking at Evaine, who tittered nervously, trying to edge her leg away from Jaeger's persistent thigh.

Morana tightened her jaw. 'No.'

Draguta laughed, amused by Morana's sullen face. 'Well, I'm relieved to hear it. I require clear minds and hearts for tomorrow night. A unified focus to create the greatest thing seen for centuries. Something I have not even witnessed myself. But, I believe it can be done. And it's exactly what we need to draw her out of her little hole.'

Morana frowned. 'Jael Furyck?'

'No, not Jael Furyck,' Draguta whispered with a grin.

CHAPTER THIRTY ONE

The Widow awoke with a start, padding quickly to her table. Searching for a sheet of vellum, she didn't notice how cold it was. Her skin rippled with goosebumps, though perhaps that was because of her dream?

Dipping her tired old quill into the pot of ink, she took a deep breath and began to write.

***

'Any dreams?' Aleksander croaked. His throat was so dry that he could barely speak.

Jael turned around from where she was packing her saddlebag, yawning. 'No. And no nightmares either. Probably because I didn't close my eyes all night!'

Aleksander smiled, eager to leave the clearing as quickly as Jael. He reached for his waterskin, taking a quick drink. Wiping his wet beard, he stood. 'It doesn't feel right in here.'

'No, it doesn't.'

'Once we get to the Widow's cottage and she gives you the book, we might feel better.'

'Do you think she's just going to give it to us?'

'I don't know. But I hope so. She wants to help. The book is supposed to help, isn't it?'

'Mmmm, well, let's not worry about eating now. We can ride till we find somewhere less strange. Somewhere with a cloudberry patch might be nice. Maybe a little stream where we can fish?' Jael grinned, not waiting for Aleksander's answer as she stuck her foot into Tig's stirrup, hoisting herself into the saddle. She knew him well enough to sense that he felt the same.

Aleksander nodded as he kicked dirt over the last embers of their fire, checking that they hadn't left anything behind. 'Hopefully, we'll be there tomorrow,' he said without any confidence. So far, nothing had looked familiar from his last journey.

Nothing at all.

***

Jaeger pulled on his trousers, scowling at Meena. 'You don't know? Your answer to everything is, I don't know?'

Meena squirmed uncomfortably as she tied up her boots. There were so many holes in the worn soles that she wondered why she was even bothering. 'I'm sorry,' she mumbled. 'I don't know what Draguta is planning. She won't say. All we have is a list. Well, Morana has it...' Her voice trailed away, and she thought of her conniving aunt, convinced that she was up to something.

'And you've had no dreams either?'

'I have... had dreams,' Meena said, realising that she had to reveal something or Jaeger would start to get angry with her. Perhaps even violent.

Jaeger reached for his own boots, turning to her with sharp eyes. '*About*?'

'I saw your brothers,' Meena whispered.

Jaeger froze. 'Which ones?' He wasn't sure whether he wanted to know if Berard had survived. He felt nothing, except, perhaps, curiosity.

'Berard and Karsten.'

Jaeger frowned. 'And Haegen?'

'He's dead.'

That was a shock. 'How?'

Meena didn't know. 'His wife was sad, and they were talking about her. She doesn't want to live without your brother. She won't eat or talk to anyone.'

Jaeger barely heard her. 'Why are you dreaming about them? What have they got to do with Draguta? It's *her* dress under your pillow, isn't it?' Irritated, he yanked Meena's pillow off the bed, finding the scrap of Draguta's white dress still there.

He shook it at her.

Meena nodded, trying to think quickly, but her mind was thick with fog. 'Draguta is powerful,' she croaked. 'Perhaps she has... protected her dreams?'

'From *you*?' Jaeger looked doubtful as he stood with a moody growl, ready for breakfast. 'I hardly think she has anything to fear from you, Meena. Not yet, at least.'

Meena watched as Jaeger strode towards the door, not wanting to follow him.

'Well, come on!' he barked. 'If we don't get down to the hall soon, it will be you who has something to fear from Draguta!'

Meena scrambled to her feet and hurried towards him, eager to leave all thoughts of her terrifying dreams behind.

***

Eadmund watched Axl's face as he read the note.

His intense frown reminded him of Jael, but not even the smallest part of him missed her now. The pain of being without

Evaine was boring a hole in his heart. The sensation was so intense that he could barely eat or sleep. He felt sick; imprisoned in the fort. It was an enormous fort – more than five times as big as his own – but it felt as though the walls were closing in on him, and he couldn't breathe.

Everyone was waiting for Jael and Aleksander to return, but he didn't want to wait, he needed to act. The quicker he acted, the sooner he'd be reunited with Evaine.

'Iskavall will help us!' Axl said, looking up from the scroll with a relieved smile. 'Raymon Vandaal pledges his army to help us invade Hest!'

Karsten glanced at Berard, both of them as pleased as their host.

'When will we leave?' Karsten called out.

Axl frowned. 'Not for some time. When Jael and Aleksander get back, we'll hopefully have some answers for how to keep us safe, but until then, we do what we can to help those forging weapons, strengthening the walls. We store food. Collect wood. Everything we can do to prepare for the next attack.'

Karsten wasn't pleased with that for an answer, but Axl had turned away, whispering to Gant and Oleg. 'Why are we waiting?' he grumbled to his brother. 'If Iskavall is offering its army, why are we waiting?'

'Best you keep your opinions to yourself,' Thorgils suggested from behind them. 'You not knowing what they know. Kings who go after glory for glory's sake, usually end up dead. Just ask Lothar Furyck. No one has much patience for self-serving kings around here.'

Isaura, standing next to Thorgils, squeezed his arm in warning as Karsten slowly turned around, lifting his one eye up to meet Thorgils' bearded face.

'And you know all about kings, do you?' Karsten sneered, looking him over.

'I had a good king on Oss. A man who cared about his people more than he cared about any song sung about him.

More than he cared about the gold in his chests or the rings on his arms. And I'm thinking that if you want to be a better king than your arse brother, you'd better start thinking like a king who cares whether his people live or die.'

'He's right,' Berard said, trying to calm Karsten down, though siding with the red-headed giant was hardly going to do that. 'The book is dangerous. Axl has seen what it can do, and so has Jael. They won't send us out of the fort until they know they can protect us. There's no point in trying until we can be sure that we can even *reach* Hest. You want to get to Jaeger, don't you?'

Karsten glared at his brother and snorted, turning away from him, disappearing into the crowd before he lost his temper.

'Your brother looks ready for a fight,' Thorgils noted wryly.

'He does,' Berard agreed. 'I think he's just impatient to avenge our father. And, maybe more. Jaeger, he...' Berard ran his eyes around the hall, lowering his voice. 'He had his way with Karsten's wife.'

Isaura swallowed in surprise. She had spent the past few days in Irenna Dragos' company, trying to help both her and her children. Irenna was morose and never spoke, but her children had enjoyed the distraction of playing with the girls and Mads. Nicolene was sharp and unpleasant, though, and Isaura had struggled to find anything to say to her.

'Oh.' Thorgils found a morsel of sympathy for Karsten then. It was hard to expect any man to sit on his hands while his murderous, adulterous brother was ruling the kingdom he'd stolen. 'Well, even so, you'll have to try and calm him down. We're not going anywhere in a hurry. Best he realises that now.'

Berard nodded mutely, not having any idea how he was going to do that.

***

'You did *what*?' Getta flew around the bedchamber like a bird, pecking at her husband. 'Why? Why, Raymon? After all we talked about? Agreed upon! And now you *betray* me and the memory of my poor father! Offering our army to the Brekkans?' Getta was beside herself, forgetting how long it had taken to get their newborn son to sleep.

Little Lothar Vandaal immediately burst into tears, and Getta rushed to him, even more furious with her husband. 'How could you humiliate me like this?' She lifted the baby out of his woven basket, holding his swaddled body against her shoulder, cooing in his ear. 'There, there,' she said softly, glaring at Raymon as she sat down on the bed, patting Lothar's back. 'It's your mother, isn't it? *She* made you do it.'

Raymon would have quite happily blamed it all on his mother just to have some peace from Getta, but he felt the need to assert himself. He was younger than his wife and far less aggressive, he knew. But *he* was the King of Iskavall. He could not allow himself to be rolled out of the way like a boulder whenever his wife had an opinion. No one would respect a king without a spine. 'No,' he muttered, 'it wasn't my mother. I said we'd help them. I want to do what I can to make us safe here, and if there's a threat to the very existence of Osterland, then we'll not make ourselves safe by cutting ourselves off from our neighbours, who up until this point, have proven to be very useful allies!' His voice rose then fell, watching his wife's scowl intensify.

'They murdered my father! My brother!' Getta hissed, trying to calm her son, though he could surely feel the urgent thumping of her heart and hear the sharp screech of her voice, and he wasn't settling down. 'You should go. I must get Lothar back to sleep!' And standing up, and hurrying back to the baby's basket, Getta ended their conversation.

Feeling his resolve strengthen further, Raymon headed for the door, determined to seek out the head of his army. He would start making preparations for going to war.

***

Edela poked her head around the door, pleased to see that Ayla was alone. 'I wondered if you'd like to come for a walk? Biddy is busy with Entorp, so I'm looking for some company. Just in case I keel over in an alley again!'

Ayla turned away from making the bed. Bram had taken Bruno down to the harbour, and she was busy airing out their bedchamber. It was narrow and dark and had previously been used by servants, which wasn't so bad, but Ayla had dreams of a cottage, with room to cook, and sheds to raise livestock. Maybe a family too. It had always been her dream, though when she tried to see their future, nothing would come.

Just darkness.

It worried her, but she tried to brighten her eyes. 'I would like that.'

'Good! The weather's fine for now, though I see storm clouds gathering again, so I thought I would get out before the rain.'

Ayla followed Edela out of the chamber, through the busy hall, enjoying the smell of fresh bread wafting from the kitchen whose fires were burning day and night, trying to keep the influx of warriors and workers well fed. 'I don't think the gods have been happy for some time. All this terrible weather? The storms are a sign.'

'Mmmm, if things go as we suspect, we are going to need all the help we can get,' Edela muttered as Ayla grabbed her arm to help her down the hall steps. 'Including the gods'. They may not be able to stop the Book of Darkness or undo any of Raemus' spells, but hopefully, they can help us in other ways.'

Ayla shivered despite the sunshine that greeted them. 'I hope so. It feels as though something is coming soon,' she murmured, glancing around. 'I worry that it is. I'm not dreaming much. I don't see anything but a deep, dark hole.'

'Oh, I would happily trade your deep, dark hole for my nightmares of Tuura. All I see are flames. Hot, towering flames, devouring us all. I wake up with the smell of smoke in my nostrils. The memories of that night won't leave me alone. Though,' she mused, 'I'm pleased that it's gone. That temple. It was my home for years, but it appears to have always been corrupt. The Following hid the truth from most of us for a long time.'

'But now they are gone.'

'Gone?' Edela shook her head as she watched Eydis and Amma approach. Leaning towards Ayla, she lowered her voice. 'While Morana Gallas and her brother live, they're not gone. While there is breath in their lungs, they will still fight for Raemus and the return of the Darkness.'

'Though if what you saw of Draguta is true, there might not be breath in their lungs for long. She doesn't appear overly fond of The Following.'

The frown between Edela's eyebrows deepened. She doubted that Morana Gallas was a woman foolish enough to get in Draguta's way.

***

Jaeger watched Evaine walk away from the castle with Draguta, heading towards the markets. He stood on the steps, wet after a long swim in the cool water of the cove. His body felt refreshed, but his mind was still jumping with irritation. Evaine was intent on ignoring him, and nothing he tried seemed to get through to her.

He wasn't used to being rejected by a woman, though he comforted himself with the fact that her soul was bound to Eadmund Skalleson's. It would be impossible for anyone to break through such a powerful spell, he was sure. But it didn't stop him fantasising about taking Evaine to his bed.

If they even made it there.

She was exquisite. He had to have her.

'Meena!' Jaeger called, pleased to see her shuffling towards him, struggling with a large bronze bowl.

Meena froze. She'd been so lost in her thoughts that she hadn't looked up in time to avoid him. Morana had sent her to find more blood. She'd had to kill four chickens, and the memory of it was still upsetting her. Varna had sent her on many such missions, of course, but Meena had never enjoyed it. 'I've been with Morana,' she mumbled. 'Preparing for tonight.'

Jaeger's eyes glistened at the thought of what Draguta had planned. What she had retrieved from the crypt had piqued his interest. 'Mmmm, I'm looking forward to that, but in the meantime, Draguta has gone to the markets, so why don't you and I go and visit her chamber? Perhaps if you touch the book, it will help you dream?'

Meena's mouth made a series of strange shapes as she tried to express her reluctance. She shook her hair, wobbling the bowl from side to side, slopping blood over the edges, splattering her boots.

'Meena,' Jaeger soothed, pushing her up the steps. 'She won't even know we were there. Her mind is on other things.'

Meena stumbled before him, trying to keep the blood in the bowl, suddenly desperate to tap her head again.

***

'Looking for an escape?' Thorgils joked as he came across Karsten Dragos, who stood by himself, staring at the main gates. 'Likely, you won't get far. Not with Draguta out there watching.'

Karsten scowled, turning around.

'You'll be staring at those gates a while yet, I'd bargain,' Thorgils went on. 'Unless you want to do something foolish and get yourself killed? Don't imagine your mother would be very pleased about that. Maybe even your wife too.'

Karsten snapped, visions of Jaeger bursting into view. He lunged at Thorgils. 'What do you know about my wife?' he spat, jutting out his bearded chin.

Thorgils stuck out a hand, keeping Karsten back. 'I know she fell for the charms of your brother, and that can't be easy to bear. But I also know that she's here with you now, and your brother won't be alive when you get your hands on him.'

Karsten stepped back, seeing that Thorgils wasn't poking fun at him. There was no smile on his face, just sympathy. Still, he felt embarrassed. Angry. Stir crazy. 'He'll only get stronger,' he insisted. 'He'll repair the harbour, build ships, drill the army, make more weapons. Jaeger won't be waiting for us to come. He'll attack as soon as he's ready.'

Thorgils shrugged, turning away from the gates, hoping to convince Karsten to walk with him. 'I expect so, but what do you think we're doing here? And besides, our army will outnumber his. What chance will he have against all of us?'

Karsten followed him. 'If what you say is true, they'll have this Draguta woman, and who knows what creatures she'll have in her army. If she can bring that serpent to life?' He swallowed, remembering his brother's surprised face as he was yanked from the ship.

'True, which is why we need to take time to prepare. We don't know what we'll be facing, so we can't walk towards it with our eyes closed. We need to give Jael time to get that book. To find a way to protect ourselves.'

'And why do you have so much faith in what Jael Furyck can do?' Karsten sneered, swerving out of the path of a horse pulling a cart of firewood towards the armourers.

Thorgils stopped, staring at him. 'Well, Jael just happens to be the one person I have the most faith in. I've seen what she can do, and from what I hear, so have you. And if that's not enough for you, so did the person who wrote the prophecy all those years ago.'

Karsten scratched his beard and closed his mouth.

'We make ourselves safe, then we attack. It's the only way to survive.'

Karsten blinked, remembering his father. When Jaeger had railed against Haaron, wanting to rush to Saala with their army, desperate to take back his wife, his father had insisted that they make themselves safe first. He had been determined to strengthen their defenses before launching an attack.

Karsten dropped his shoulders. 'Well, you'd better give me something to do that involves a lot of smashing, then. It sounds as though we're going to have a long wait.'

***

'The soul spell is one of the strongest you can cast,' Draguta said as she walked with Evaine under the shade of the coloured awnings hanging over the market stalls. 'And you did well to follow Morana's instructions. I feel how strong the bond between you and Eadmund is.'

Evaine smiled happily, pleased to be talking about her favourite subject.

'You're not a dreamer, of course, but there are things you can do, ways to reinforce that bond. Morana will bring Eadmund to you soon, but in the meantime, you should take his things to bed with you. His hair. His arm-ring. Hold them while you sleep. Draw him to you in your dreams. Anyone can do that. Focus your mind on him, for it's imperative that we take him away from that woman.' Draguta shuddered as the clouds swept overhead, darkening the sky. She squeezed Evaine's delicate hand. 'Eadmund is meant to love her. To be with her. Their destiny was planned by the gods themselves. They thought to defeat me with two humans!' Draguta laughed loudly. 'Two humans, and another book!'

Evaine frowned. She wanted no part of what Draguta was planning unless it involved bringing Eadmund to her.

'You and Morac will come to the stones tonight,' Draguta purred. 'You may think that you want no part of this, my dear, but you'll change your mind once you see what is possible. They think that they can hide from us with symbols,' she said, narrowing her icy-blue eyes. 'But not tonight. Now let us go back to my chamber and retrieve Eadmund's things. Then you may start focusing your mind on bringing him here.'

***

Thorgils and Torstan watched from below as Eadmund walked the ramparts with Gant. They had been spending more time together, overseeing the shoring up of the fort's defenses, ensuring that there would be enough sea-fire jars and catapults for their assault on Hest, while keeping the Islanders from killing the Alekkans, and the Andalans from killing them both.

'He's been up there all morning,' Torstan muttered.

'Well, Gant seems like he's got a good eye on him,' Thorgils groaned, stretching out his back. 'You can go. I'll take over now.'

'You really think he needs watching all the time?' Torstan wondered, coiling a length of rope around his arm.

'Since I can remember, Eadmund has always needed watching all the time!' Thorgils laughed. 'Nobody gets themselves into more trouble than Eadmund Skalleson, except perhaps his wife. They do deserve one another!' He bent down to Vella, who had her paws up on his leg, sniffing his hand. 'You think I have a treat for you, young miss?' And reaching into his pouch, he pulled out a scrap of salt fish. 'Here you go.

Go make your brother jealous!'

Vella ripped the treat out of Thorgils' hand, tearing off into the crowd of men and women who were busy shepherding their livestock into the fort and sorting through the freshly harvested crops. If Draguta sent another creature to attack them, it could wipe out their winter stores, so everything was being brought into the fort in anticipation.

Eadmund peered down at his friends, and they quickly turned their eyes away, paying a lot of attention to the catapult they had just finished.

'He's spellbound,' Thorgils said hoarsely, looking up after a while. 'A man who's spellbound isn't in control of himself. Who knows what they can do to him? Who knows what he'll do in return?'

'But don't the symbols stop any spells from getting through the fort?' Torstan wondered, pulling a piece of salt fish from his pocket. It was covered in wood shavings, but he brushed them off and quickly started gnawing on it.

Thorgils shrugged. 'No idea. Makes no difference to us. We keep one eye on him day and night. That's not Eadmund anymore, so we have no idea what he's capable of.'

Eadmund frowned as he turned back to Gant, uncomfortable with the way Torstan and Thorgils kept staring at him. Every time he turned around, there they were. One or the other. Sometimes Bram. All three of them, watching him.

They were definitely watching him.

But why?

'There's not much more we can do,' Gant decided. 'Except wait. For Jael and Aleksander. For this woman to make her next move.'

Eadmund looked up, sensing the sudden retreat of the sun. He could see dark clouds edging in from the corners of the sky. 'For another storm.'

Gant frowned himself, watching the urgency of the clouds. 'That's the last thing we need.' He looked down into the fort.

'I'll get everyone moving inside. It looks like it will hit soon.'

Eadmund nodded distractedly as Gant strode away, his mind drifting to Hest as it did whenever he was alone. He remembered his time there with Jael, but those memories were faded now, barely mist, evaporating so quickly that they might never have happened at all.

All he could see was Evaine standing before him, her hand out, calling to him.

Urging him to hurry to her.

CHAPTER THIRTY TWO

'Do you know where we are?' Jael asked. Every row of trees looked the same, and the sky felt like a dark cloak draped above the tree canopy, making it hard to see.

'I don't think I do,' Aleksander admitted. He'd started to realise that they must have taken a wrong turn at some stage.

But when?

He'd been hoping that he would eventually get his bearings, but it hadn't happened yet, and he could hardly keep pretending anymore.

Jael eased Tig to a stop, desperate to get down and stretch her lower back. The ache was unbearable. Her body was irritating her in ways she'd never experienced before. She was used to wounds and scars, but the twinges and pains in odd places were wearing, and her mood was fraying quickly.

She dismounted and bent over.

'What is it?' Aleksander frowned, watching as Jael hunched up her shoulders, letting her braids touch the thick carpet of soggy leaves beneath her boots.

'We need to be going in the right direction!' she grumbled, straightening up. 'Why keep on this path if it's the wrong one?'

'What path?' Aleksander wondered irritably as he joined her down on the ground. 'The trees are closing in on themselves, blocking out the sun. I can't see what time of day it is or where we are. Can you?'

Jael peered up at the dense canopy. Aleksander was right. They couldn't see the sun. It could have been dusk or mid-morning. The only thing it wasn't, perhaps, was night. Her irritation peaked. 'Feed me and leave me!' she announced. 'I'll see what I can do.'

'*Leave* you?'

'I need to try and focus my mind,' Jael said, opening her saddlebag, hoping to find something to eat. 'Apparently, dreamers can find answers when others can't. So... maybe I can? Who knows, but it's better than carrying on like this.' She found nothing to eat and looked expectantly at Aleksander.

He dug into his own saddlebag, pulling out the last of the cheese. 'Alright, but I won't go far. We don't want to lose each other.'

Jael nodded. 'Here, have a drink.' And she passed him her waterskin. 'You don't need to go far. Just as long as I can disappear into myself a bit.'

Aleksander took the waterskin, which was almost empty; they needed to find another stream soon. 'Anything to help.'

Jael bit into the smoky cheese, watching Tig turn around, sniffing the air. She smiled, sensing that he was hungry too. 'You stay with the horses. I'll just walk into those trees over there.'

Aleksander watched her go, quickly grabbing Tig's reins before he could follow her, listening to the screech of a hawk somewhere above them.

Worried that wolves were coming.

***

Jaeger was pleased that his father had kept a spare key to every chamber in the castle. It made sense as Bayla and Berard had a habit of losing theirs.

Especially Berard.

Jaeger blinked, surprised by the unexpected warmth of his memories. He shut the door on them quickly, though, not interested in feeling anything for his family. They were irrelevant now.

Looking at Meena, shaking nervously before him, he frowned. 'Perhaps it's best if I go in by myself? You wait here and knock on the door if you see Draguta coming,' he whispered, not noticing how relieved Meena was as he pushed open the door and disappeared inside Draguta's chamber.

Meena stared at the closed door, then spun around quickly, glancing up and down the torchlit corridor, listening for footsteps.

Hoping that Jaeger would hurry.

Jaeger *was* hurrying as he ran to the small round table by the fireplace where the book lay closed, calling to him. He sighed with pleasure as he reached out, placing his hands on its dark cover. The room was overly warm, yet that cover was as perfectly cold as ever. He smiled sadly, feeling the weight of its loss. The book was no longer his, and Jaeger could feel it now. He couldn't understand the words on its pages; they were written by a god, meant for a dreamer.

And he was neither of those things.

But he was the king now, and surely he had the right to claim power over his kingdom? Especially now that he had the help of his own dreamer.

Looking around, he tried to see something of Draguta's to take for Meena.

Jumping at a sudden knock on the door.

***

When Jael leaned her head back against the dark-green moss of the tree trunk and closed her eyes, she immediately saw Eadmund, which wasn't particularly helpful. He wasn't going to show them a way through the maze of trees, so Jael knew that she needed to try again. She had to focus her mind on the problem in front of them, though it was hard to look away from the vision of her husband.

It made her sad.

She felt as though she could almost reach out and touch him as he sat on a bed, his head in his hands.

Looking up, Eadmund stared at her.

He was in pain.

And there was nothing she could do.

Sighing, Jael opened her eyes, trying to break the unsettling vision, ready to start again. The noises in the wood were loud, and oddly unfamiliar. Jael had been in woodland many times, but in here, nothing sounded as it should.

She was just about to close her eyes again when she saw a shaft of light breaking through the trees in the distance. Jael blinked, certain that she'd seen a woman, but when she squinted, there was no one there. The path was suddenly more obvious, though, and the shaft of light revealed that the afternoon was old, so if they wanted to make more progress before night fell, they would have to hurry.

'Let's go!' Jael called as she clambered to her feet, shaking the leaves off her trousers. 'I've found a way!'

Aleksander popped around the side of the opposite tree, a look of relief on his face. 'Where?'

And she showed him, pointing to the sunlit path in the distance.

'Who knew you were so useful?' Aleksander smiled, turning to Sky, eager to get going.

Jael followed him, reaching for Tig's reins, still seeing the image of Eadmund sitting on his bed, staring at her as though she was a stranger.

She hoped that Thorgils was keeping a close eye on him.

***

'Someone will see us!'

'Someone? What someone?' Thorgils mumbled between kisses, pressing himself against Isaura, who was leaning against the wall of an unused shed, tucked down a dark alley. 'I don't see anyone.'

Isaura pushed him away, smoothing down her pale-yellow apron. 'Ivaar.'

'Ivaar?' Thorgils ran a hand over his beard. 'Why do you care what Ivaar thinks?'

She sighed. 'I don't, but I'm still his wife.'

'Well...'

'I am. Until Jael and Eadmund grant the divorce, I am!' She glanced around, feeling unsettled. As much as she wanted to be with Thorgils, it didn't feel right.

Not yet.

'But Jael promised to grant you a divorce. Ivaar knows it. He's happy for us to be together.'

Isaura stood on her tiptoes, pushing a finger into his frown, trying to smooth it away. 'But we're not divorced yet. When Jael gets back, maybe you can ask her again?' She kissed him on the nose.

Thorgils frowned some more.

Isaura laughed. 'We waited eight years! You can surely wait eight more days?'

Wrapping his arm around her waist, Thorgils drew her close. 'I would wait the rest of my life for you, so yes,' he grumbled, 'I can wait. But as soon as I see Jael, I'm going to be asking about that divorce. I don't want one part of you to belong to Ivaar Skalleson anymore. You're mine. You've always been mine. No one's ever going to take you away from me again.' And he pulled Isaura into his arms, holding her tightly, trying not to think about how much danger they were all in.

***

Morac had been wandering the castle, searching for Evaine and Morana. The pleasure of Yorik's cottage had quickly turned to boredom, and he had tired of trying to find anything helpful in Yorik's books. They were hard to read, rambling scrawls of little substance. He'd found nothing that would lead them to the missing ritual page at all.

Morana wouldn't be pleased, but hopefully, she would find something in her dreams - if Draguta ever left her alone long enough for her to sleep.

After walking up to Morana's chamber and discovering that it was locked, Morac had tried to find his way to Evaine's and couldn't, which made him feel like a silly old man. Every corridor and door looked the same, and every turn seemed to lead him further away from the stairs he was trying so desperately to find.

'Morac?'

He gulped, stiffening at the sound of that voice.

Draguta was a beautiful woman, but her voice was harsh and cold, and it slid down his spine, weakening his legs. Spinning around, Morac lifted his thin lips into a smile. 'Ahhh, there you are, Evaine. I was looking for you, but I seem to have...' he shrugged sheepishly, 'gotten myself lost.'

Draguta laughed loudly. 'Is the castle *that* big?'

Evaine glared at Morac, feeling embarrassed. 'Why did you want me?'

'Oh, for nothing in particular. I was just looking for some company. I haven't been able to find anyone this afternoon. The castle feels almost deserted.'

Draguta glanced down the end of the corridor as Jaeger and Meena suddenly appeared, walking towards them. She frowned. 'And yet, here we all are. How interesting.' Narrowing her eyes, she peered at Jaeger, almost smelling the book on him. And then Meena, whose flaming red hair shook in terror. The stench of their guilt was unmistakable. 'Perhaps you should take Morac with you, Jaeger? He needs a friend. And Evaine, we must get to my chamber and find Eadmund's things.' She dismissed Morac and Jaeger with the wave of a hand, drawing Evaine away, down the corridor.

Jaeger exhaled, inclining his head for Morac to follow him.

Meena stayed where she was, trying to catch her breath, hoping that no one would notice her.

'And you, girl!' Draguta turned and barked. 'You will go and find Morana. She will need your help to prepare everything for tonight!'

Meena nodded quickly, almost tripping over her feet as she shuffled away.

***

Though Jael and Aleksander had a new path to follow, the wood continued to be a muddle of branches that seemed to be reaching out to one another, wrapping and twisting themselves into a wooden embrace. It felt as though a storm was coming, and the rustling of leaves and the scratching of branches became so loud that they were unable to hear one another. But they kept going, determined to find a big enough clearing to spend the night. Hopefully, one near a stream. Both of them were thirsty, and they knew that the horses were ready for a long drink too.

Aleksander recognised nothing, though he wondered if that was how it was meant to be. It felt as though the Widow was leading them in circles of confusion, keeping her exact location a mystery, even to those who had been there before.

'This hasn't been the best journey we've ever taken together!' Jael grumbled from behind him.

Aleksander laughed. Despite the frustration of the wood, he was quite enjoying being with Jael again. He didn't want it to end, though he knew that she didn't feel the same way anymore. 'Ahhh, but think of how much longer we've still got to go!' he called, grinning as he listened to her snorting behind him.

***

'I'm not going anywhere,' Eadmund insisted, reaching for another sausage.

Torstan looked down at his plate, suddenly very intent on organising his cabbage with his knife.

Thorgils grabbed his ale, taking a big gulp. 'So you're just keeping your eyes on the hills, looking for the next attack, then?'

Eadmund frowned. 'I'm not going anywhere.'

'Fair enough,' Thorgils grunted.

'No need to keep watching me as though I'm about to escape. I know Jael asked you to.'

'Do you blame her?'

'I think after we go to Hest and defeat this woman... I think Jael and I can talk then,' Eadmund muttered. 'Jael knows how I feel. If she wants to ignore it, that's up to her. It's not my intention to hurt her. I've never wanted that. But I don't plan on remaining married to someone I don't love. Not when I can be with the woman I *do* love.'

Torstan spat out his ale.

Thorgils tried to keep perfectly still. He could feel Isaura's hand on his knee, and it helped. 'Well, being the King of Oss now, you have the power to do as you wish.'

Eadmund was too angry to say any more. Jael had spoonfed his friends a bunch of lies, and now they were against Evaine too. Pushing away his plate, he reached for his ale, trying to calm down.

Trying to believe anything he'd just said.

Thorgils kept a firm hold of his tongue. He just had to keep Eadmund in the fort, he reminded himself. Jael would find a way to break the spell.

Turning to Isaura, Thorgils caught sight of Runa. She was sitting nearby, eating with Bruno and Ayla. She smiled awkwardly at him before looking away. Thorgils frowned, seeking out Bram, who sat between Ivaar and Karsten Dragos. He raised his eyebrows in sympathy at his uncle, who winked back.

Thorgils kept watching as Bram turned to answer Ivaar's question, and he saw his uncle's mask slip for a moment, revealing the sadness in his eyes. Looking back to Runa, Thorgils wondered what he could say to convince her to speak to Bram.

Wondering if it was even his place to try.

***

Berard had brought Hanna to the house. He was worried about Irenna.

They were all worried about her, he supposed, but no one seemed to want to do anything about it. Karsten appeared concerned, though he assumed that Nicolene or Bayla would do something, but Nicolene was struggling with all five children, and Bayla was little help, somehow making everything about herself, and always causing more drama than she resolved. And there was little Berard could do about any of it. With only one arm, it was proving difficult to take charge of the children. They ran around like a pack of wild, whining dogs, and he was worried that they would bang into his stump, which, although healing well, was still painful.

He needed Irenna.

Hanna had come to the house with a tray of roast apples, which she left on the table where Nicolene was trying to convince Valder to eat his cabbage. He had shoved his plate away, though, and was sulking. Lucina was attempting to spoon soup into Halla's mouth, although most of it appeared to have ended up on her face, and Bayla had Kai on her knee. He was almost happily gnawing on a bone, his face still wet with tears from his last tantrum. Eron was under the table, refusing to come out.

Karsten was in the hall, though no one really missed him. He barely spoke, and when he did, it was usually to yell at the children to be quiet, or to yell at his wife to get the children to be quiet.

Hanna held onto Irenna's hand, trying to get her attention.

Irenna lay in her bed, staring at the rafters. Berard sat on the end of the bed, one ear on what was happening at the table, realising that he would have to intervene if Eron didn't come out from under it soon.

'The soup looks tasty,' Hanna smiled, trying to think of what to say.

Irenna didn't speak. She barely blinked.

Hanna glanced at Berard, who looked worried. She didn't blame him. Irenna was very thin and pale, even in the warm glow of the lamps. Her dark hair was greasy, stuck to her face, and her lips were dry and cracked. 'I know you don't think you're hungry, Irenna, but if you eat something, you'll feel better. And if you can feel a little better, you might try to get up. Perhaps see the children? They miss you.' Hanna turned back to the table, seeing Valder watching his mother with big, terrified eyes, not wanting to lose her too.

But Irenna didn't move.

The wind rattled the door, whipping it out of Karsten's

hand as he pushed it open. It banged loudly against the wall, and the five children jumped as a broom clattered to the floor.

But Irenna didn't move.

***

Andala's hall was packed with weary men and women who had spent days dragging the serpent's corpse into the harbour water, carving symbols around the fort, cooking and caring for the influx of visitors.

Preparing for war.

Erl Arnesson and his twin brother, Rork, were arguing with Ivaar, and although Thorgils didn't think that he should insert himself into the conversation, he could almost feel Jael elbowing him off his bench, not wanting things to erupt. It would hardly help their plans if the Alekkans and the Kalfans killed each other. Thorgils didn't envy Jael trying to sort through that mess when she returned, but in the meantime, Eadmund didn't appear to care, and Jael wasn't there, so, he decided, it was up to him to save Ivaar from a well-deserved death at the hands of the square-jawed Arnesson twins. 'Alright! Alright!' And holding up his hands, Thorgils pushed himself into the fray. 'If we kill each other now, there'll be less of us to kill the Hestians!' he growled, shoving Rork and his equally weighty brother away from Ivaar, who was sneering and spitting and changing Thorgils' mind about rescuing him.

'You'd protect *him* after he stole your woman?' Erl growled. 'This prick?'

Thorgils laughed before glaring at Ivaar, who couldn't focus on him at all. 'Well, she's my woman again, and her children are his also. They quite like their father for some reason, so yes, seems that I am. Protecting him, that is.' He turned back to Erl, who stood almost two heads shorter than him. 'You got a problem with that?'

Erl blinked, bleary-eyed himself, peering at his brother, who shrugged. 'Seems that I don't.'

'If anything happens to this prick,' Thorgils grumbled loudly, elbowing Ivaar in the chest, 'I'll know who to send Jael after when she gets back. He's under her protection. And if I remember rightly, she didn't have a problem killing your cousins, so I doubt she'd lose any sleep about having to kill either of you two drunkards!' And pushing Ivaar away, he left Rork and Erl to frown at each other.

'That was brave of you, Nephew,' Bram laughed as Thorgils forced his way through the crowd, shunting Ivaar far away from any Alekkan.

Thorgils grinned. 'Not as brave as having to face Jael if I'd let them kill her pet.'

Ivaar turned on Thorgils. 'I don't need your help,' he slurred. 'Or Jael's!' He swayed into Bram, who pushed him upright.

Thorgils rolled his eyes. 'Maybe. But by the stink of you, you need the latrines and then a bed.'

Ivaar mumbled to himself, stumbling away from them, searching for the mead girl.

'I almost feel sorry for him,' Bram said, watching Ivaar go. 'It's not easy to lose your family, though I'd have preferred losing mine to a better man, than to that evil sickness.' He looked away, not wanting to bring on the memories again. 'Speaking of latrines...' And Bram clapped Thorgils on the arm, heading to the doors.

Thorgils watched his uncle leave as Isaura came up behind him, slipping her arm through his. He turned, kissing her on the head, feeling the warmth of her as he pulled her close.

So grateful that he had this second chance to be with her again.

***

'You *have* done well!' Draguta purred happily, running her eyes over the baskets and bowls that Morana and Meena had brought to her chamber. Bending over, she inhaled the pungent bouquet of aromas with an appreciative sigh. 'You've been so very busy. It all looks perfect. Now, leave me, and prepare yourselves for tonight. No food. No sleep. Just purity of focus.' Draguta glanced at Meena's bright red face, screwed up in confusion, heated by the glow of a table full of dripping candles, and embarrassment over not knowing what she was meant to do. 'Morana will show you,' Draguta laughed. 'Now, hurry along!' And she rubbed her hands together, looking around the chamber.

Morana ran to the door, eager to be gone before Draguta could make any further requests. She almost tripped over Meena, who was trying to get out before her.

But Draguta didn't notice; she had already shut them out.

Walking to the fireplace, she started to lose herself in the mesmeric dance of the flames. It was a balmy evening, yet she welcomed the fire.

The Dolma had been cold and desperate and so utterly lonely.

Light was hope.

And fire was death to her enemies.

***

Jael held her hands to the flames, eager to taste the meal that Aleksander was preparing. Tired of nibbling on nuts and berries all day, he had left Jael to make their camp and disappeared through the trees with his bow. And now he was busy cooking a rabbit stew.

'When did you learn how to do that?' Jael wondered, inhaling the appetising smells emanating from the tiny cauldron.

Aleksander smiled. He'd been listening to the cauldron banging against his saddle for days, so he was happy to finally put it to some use. He had foraged for herbs and mushrooms to add to the rabbit, and felt encouraged with the aroma rising up from the bubbling stew. 'After you left Andala, I ended up living with Edela. Looking after her.' He sat back, enjoying the warmth of the flames. They were in a tight little clutch of trees, which, thankfully, acted as a break against the swirling wind. 'It was nice for us both to have some company.'

Jael looked up, meeting Aleksander's hooded eyes, remembering their life together. How easy it had been, just the two of them, so comfortable that they could read each other's minds. Knowing every look, every unspoken feeling.

Brought together by the shared pain of that night in Tuura.

Inseparable.

'I'm glad,' she said, at last, feeling rain. 'It was hard to leave. Hard to be on Oss in the beginning. I was ready to get back to Brekka as fast as I could.'

Aleksander was pleased to hear her finally talking about it. 'You were?'

'Of course. It's all I could think about. But then... things changed, I suppose. I started to feel differently about Oss, the people, and, in the end... Eadmund.'

Aleksander didn't look away. 'Well, Edela saw that that would happen.'

'She did, but I didn't believe it would. He was a mess when I met him. He's... still a mess,' she smiled. 'But he's my choice, and I want to free him from Morana and Evaine and all that they've done to him. And if I can do that, maybe we can defeat Draguta and stop her bringing Raemus back.'

They weren't the words Aleksander wanted to hear, but he felt happy that she was talking to him again. Like she used to. It almost didn't matter what she was saying. 'Well, there's no choice, is there? When we get this book from the Widow, we'll have a chance to free him. And more. Hopefully, she can tell us what to do to stop Draguta. If she knows.' He leaned forward, deciding that their gurgling stomachs could wait no longer. 'Ready?' he asked with a grin.

Jael reached for their trenchers, feeling better than she had all day. 'Ready.'

PART FOUR

Death to My Enemies

CHAPTER THIRTY THREE

'Are you sure you don't want to stick something in your ears?' Biddy wondered, pulling the fur up to Eydis' chin.

Eydis smiled. 'No, I didn't hear any snoring last night.'

'Oh, you are such a polite girl, Eydis Skalleson!' Edela snorted. 'I thought that serpent had come back to life and was huffing and puffing around the cottage!'

Biddy harrumphed, blowing out the lamp as she crawled into her bed. 'You must have been listening to yourself, Edela, because thanks to your huffing and puffing, I was awake for most of last night!' And pushing Vella off her pillow, she wriggled down under the furs.

'Well, no wonder you've been in such a foul mood all day, Biddy Halvor. You should really try to get some more sleep!'

Eydis listened to Edela and Biddy's chatter as she rolled over in her little bed on the floor. Ido was tucked up next to her feet, keeping them warm, and Biddy had rolled up a blanket and pushed it against the bottom of the door, trying to shut out the noisy draft. Another storm was on its way, and the wind was already howling around Edela's tiny cottage, trying its very best to sneak in through the holes in the walls.

Sighing deeply and feeling her body start to unwind, Eydis thought of Jael, hoping she had found her way to the Widow.

Hoping she would find her way back to them soon.

***

Jael pulled her cloak over her shoulder, trying to adjust her swordbelt so that everything wasn't digging into her as she lay on the ground. Neither of them were inclined to take off their belts in case they needed their weapons in the night. If the fire died down, they wouldn't be able to see a thing.

But it didn't make for comfortable sleeping.

'Do you think they're alright in Andala?' Jael wondered, watching Aleksander banking the fire. They were conscious of not inviting too many creatures to their campsite, but while Aleksander sat there, taking the first watch, it would give off a little heat.

'Well, I'm no dreamer, so I don't know. I don't know what this Draguta wants at all, but maybe she'll need to wait between spells? When Edela dreamwalked, she was exhausted afterwards. Maybe Draguta needs time to recover?'

'It's a nice thought,' Jael yawned. 'But if you're powerful enough to bring a serpent to life, maybe you're not like the other dreamers? Especially not the little old ones.' She felt worried, thinking about her grandmother in her cottage. Edela was tough in spirit, Jael knew, but her body had been through so much recently. It was asking a lot to have her try and protect all of Andala from Draguta with the help of a thirteen-year-old girl.

Jael closed her eyes, hoping that Ayla would be able to help her.

'Hopefully, we'll get back before anything happens,' Aleksander yawned. The wind was strengthening, rustling the leaves all around them, and he was sure he felt rain.

'Mmmm,' Jael sighed, feeling herself relax, despite the discomfort of the ground and the tension in her body. She was desperate to find a dream and see if she could help too.

***

Morac was reluctant to go with his sister. The stories Morana had told him about the horrific demise of the Followers filled him with dread. 'But why does she want me there?'

Morana grumbled impatiently. She could hear the storm screaming around her brother's tiny cottage, the rain hammering his solitary window pane. She wasn't looking forward to the long walk to the Crown of Stones. 'You'd have to ask Draguta,' she snapped. 'And you can do just that on our way up to the stones!'

Morac frowned and reached for his cloak, glancing at Evaine, who was watching the rattling door, just as reluctant to head out into the storm.

'We are hers. We do as she bids,' Morana reminded her brother, lifting her eyebrows, hoping to convey more than she was able to say around Evaine.

Morac nodded. 'Of course. Come along, Evaine. We don't want to keep Draguta waiting.'

Evaine stood with a loud sigh, readjusting her white cloak, pulling her fur hood over her face in anticipation of the rain. 'I hope this will be worth it,' she grumbled.

Morana took a deep breath and opened the door, cringing as the wind blew the rain into her face. 'Oh, the one thing I can promise you about Draguta is that this will be worth it.'

***

Karsten ran a hand over Kai's soft hair, trying to soothe him back to sleep. Nicolene had made no move to comfort the boy, and Karsten realised that he would have to find a servant to care for the children. The only woman in the cottage who even liked children was Irenna, and he didn't know how to convince her to come back to them. Everyone had tried - even Bayla - but they couldn't wait any longer. He would have to ask Axl Furyck about getting a servant in the morning.

'Ssshhh,' Karsten murmured, thinking of Haegen. Trying not to. He left Kai to sleep, sighing heavily, not wanting to get into bed next to Nicolene. His mind was jumping, and he felt ready for a training match or a fast ride across a flat plain; anything to take away this unbearable tension.

Grabbing his cloak off the back of a chair, he opened the door and headed out into the storm, hoping to clear his head.

***

The storm had battered Hest all evening, but it began to intensify when they left the castle for the long trek to the Crown of Stones. The wind swirled around them, buffeting them with an angry urgency that had Draguta smiling as she strode forward, carrying a long wooden box.

It wasn't cold, but Meena couldn't stop shivering as she dragged her feet at the back of their small group. Not even Jaeger slowed down to walk with her. He appeared much more interested in keeping up with Evaine, who didn't even look his way as she held onto her hood, pulling it over her face to keep out the rain.

Morac and Morana walked next to Draguta, carrying bowls of her bloody potion, keeping their mouths closed and their eyes down, hoping she wouldn't talk to them. Neither knew what she was planning, and Morana was eager to keep it that way. She wasn't looking to be blamed for anything that might go wrong.

She hoped that nothing would go wrong.

When they arrived at the stones, Draguta set Morac and

Jaeger to work building a large bonfire while she lowered her box to the ground and opened the lid, her body tingling in anticipation. 'You will help me cast the circle, Morana! Bring me the blood!'

Evaine stood watching as Morana scurried to Draguta's side, soaked through, wondering why she'd been dragged all the way to this miserable heap of stones in the middle of the night. She shivered, hurrying to the fire as its flames burst into life, her hands over her ears, trying to shut out the screeching call of the wind.

'They will try again!' Draguta smiled as she finished the circle and glanced up at the dark sky, wet hair whipping around her pale face. 'But they know that ultimately, they are powerless! There is little they can do to stop my magic! The book does not belong to them! Its power is not something they can control!'

Morana swallowed, watching as Draguta strode over to the Book of Darkness, its pages flapping open on the ancient sacrifice stone. She hoped that Draguta had been convinced by her usefulness.

That she had proven to be a valuable assistant.

'Morana!' Draguta barked. 'Hand the cups around! I shall make the symbol. The rest of you, come! Join the circle! Jaeger, you will drum for me again.' She ignored his frown as she stood over the book, holding down the pages as the wind fought against her. As the gods tried to stop her.

But they couldn't. They wouldn't.

Not this time.

Morana shuffled around the circle, glaring at Meena, demanding her help. Meena had hoped to stay by the fire, unnoticed by any of them. She could feel the cold fingers of fear creeping up her spine, and ducking her head, she hurried to Morana's side, lifting up a bowl, wrinkling her nose at the acrid stink of the potion.

Blood and bits and herbs and seeds. Bone and skin and bark and mushrooms.

Meena knew what had gone into it.

She didn't want to drink it.

'Hurry!' Draguta urged, watching them dither. 'Hurry!' And closing the book, confident that she had committed the spell to memory, she walked to Evaine, who stood next to Morac, both of them wet and anxious as they considered the potion with distaste. 'Drink up! Drink up!' Draguta cried. 'It is time to begin!'

***

Aleksander couldn't fall asleep. The wind was a wailing nightmare.

Was it the wind?

He kept listening for wolves, hoping that he'd be able to discern their howls from the rising squeal of the storm. The horses were disturbed too, whinnying nearby.

Jael lay next to him, one hand on *Toothpick*, frozen by the growing certainty that something was coming.

The storm was so loud. Jael wondered if it was the gods.

Warning them?

Or coming for them?

***

Karsten squinted, recognising the figure walking towards him, and as she got closer, he smiled. 'What are *you* doing out in this weather?' he called into the storm.

Hanna looked embarrassed. 'I had to go to the latrines. I... think I ate something that disagreed with me.' Her stomach cramped again, and she wondered if she should turn around and head straight back.

A bolt of lightning shot down from the sky, and she jumped.

'Where are you staying?' Karsten asked. 'I'll walk you back!' The storm was getting violent, and he'd quickly changed his mind about wanting some air. Thunder rumbled ominously, booming and rolling like giant waves overhead.

Hanna had never liked storms, and she was grateful for the company. 'I'm staying with my father! I'll show you!' And turning to the right, she stumbled, dizzy, wondering if she was about to faint. Her ears were suddenly ringing so loudly.

Karsten grabbed her as she fell. 'Hanna? What's wrong?' But Hanna's eyes were closed, and she had gone limp in his arms.

***

'I've made mistakes,' Ranuf sighed, staring across the harbour, watching the fishing crews head out to sea. 'More than you know.'

Sitting on a barrel next to him, Jael frowned. Her father never spoke this way. 'What does *that* mean?'

'If I told you, I don't think you'd speak to me again. Not for a good while, at least, knowing your temper.' He ran a hand over his beard. It was so much greyer than the mop of black hair on top of his head, which still only had a few streaks of silver in it.

Jael was surprised. 'That sounds bad.'

'Well, you have your impression of me, Jael. The truth might be more surprising. Not as noble, perhaps?' Ranuf mused. He was feeling morose. Guilty. Old. 'I should get going. Gant's probably stalking the fort, looking for me. We should have left for Iskavall by now.' He stood and held out a hand to his daughter, helping her off the barrel, though she hadn't needed his help for years now. 'Anything I haven't told you? Anything you want to ask?'

Jael shook her head. 'Nothing I can think of. How long will you be away?'

'Ten days or so. Hugo Vandaal's not a big talker, but he does like to drink, so it depends on how many pointless feasts we have to sit through. No doubt Lothar will try to impress me, showing off as he likes to do.' Ranuf rolled his eyes, despairing of his pointless brother, happy to think that he was far away from Brekka.

Jael laughed. 'I don't envy you. I can't imagine I'd have the patience to deal with someone as idiotic as Hugo Vandaal.'

Ranuf turned to her. 'Everyone needs allies, Jael. Whether you're a queen or not. As much as you'd like to, you can't command an army of beasts!'

He turned around, and she could see the smile in his eyes. 'So you say, but I'd happily do it. We'd be unstoppable!'

'I have no doubt. Now, come on, walk me back to the hall, so I can remind you about everything again. I don't want to come back and find my fort in pieces!'

'*Pieces*?' Jael snorted. 'This fort? Nothing's getting through these walls,' she smiled confidently. 'You'll find them waiting for you when you return, Father, don't worry. I would never let anything happen to Andala.'

***

Draguta's chanting felt like a furious wind spinning around them all, mingling with the overpowering smoke that had quickly untethered their senses.

Evaine lost all awareness of what was happening. She felt adrift in the storm, and as terrified as she was sure she should feel, listening as Draguta's deep voice swept over her, she felt exhilarated.

It was as though she was riding the storm. Up high in the clouds.

Above all of Osterland.

She was flying.

***

Karsten laid Hanna on the ground, trying to see what had happened. She wasn't moving; her eyes remained closed. The rain was teeming down now, so he scooped her into his arms and peered around, trying to see, not knowing where the elderman's cottage was.

Eventually, ducking his head against the icy rain, he headed for the hall.

***

Silence.

For a moment, there was silence.

And then they could hear it.

Aleksander peered up at the treetops, trying to see anything in the darkness.

The screeching was loud. A gust of wind blew down towards them.

And then a bright burst of fire.

Jael was quickly on her feet, Aleksander next to her.

Glancing around.

***

The Widow sat at her table, trying to think.

But there was no time to think.

They would die if she didn't help.

Yet, they would die if she did.

She closed her eyes, trying to clear her mind. Eventually, standing, she gripped the Book of Aurea in one hand and walked to the door.

Opening it with a weary sigh, she strode out into the storm.

***

Jael blinked as the noise disappeared into the distance. 'Was that...' she started, turning to Aleksander, *Toothpick* in her right hand, sweat running down her spine, her mouth opening and closing. 'Was that a... *dragon*?'

Aleksander was too stunned to speak. He nodded slowly. 'I think so.'

'Heading for Andala!' Jael closed her eyes and tried to focus. If there was a way to reach Eydis. Or Edela.

She had to warn them, but how?

***

'Help!' Karsten cried, pushing against the hall door. 'Someone, help!'

He was loud enough to be heard over the storm, which appeared to have retreated for a moment, and before long, the curtain was pulled back, and a sleepy-eyed Gant was there, wanting to see what the commotion was about.

Karsten carried Hanna to a table, and Gant quickly cleared it of cups and lamps. 'We need a healer!'

Gant turned to Axl, who was limping towards them on his crutch. 'I'll go for Edela.'

Axl nodded as he was joined by Amma, who had hurried to the table, wrapping a blanket around her nightdress.

'What happened?' Amma wondered, brushing Hanna's wet hair away from her face.

Karsten shrugged. 'I don't know. She collapsed in the square.'

'Someone should get her father,' Axl said, looking at Bram, who had pulled himself up from a bed and was rubbing his eyes.

Bram grabbed his cloak. 'I know where he's staying.' And shaking himself awake, he disappeared through the doors after Gant.

Karsten looked down at Hanna, gripping her hand. 'Hanna?' he murmured. 'Hanna?'

***

'Eydis!'

Eydis opened her eyes. Ido was licking her face.

'Eydis!'

The storm boomed above her head, and she shook all over, but nobody was awake. Nobody was moving in the cottage.

Perhaps she was just having a dream?

Vella was there now, too; both of them urgently licking her face.

'Eydis!'

The voice in her head was familiar, and she sat up quickly, hearing its panic.

'Hurry! You must hurry! Get up now!'

And then a loud banging on the door had the puppies barking, and Biddy scrambling out of bed, and Edela blinking as she sat up with a start.

***

Her name was Thrula.

Thrula. A beautiful name.

Draguta felt peaceful as she embraced the power of those expansive wings, each one bigger than the mightiest warship. They flapped slowly and powerfully up and down, propelling her forward.

The storm made no difference.

Draguta smiled.

The storm made no difference, and as she looked down, she could see a blanket of darkness covering Osterland, and then, occasionally, a burst of golden light showed her where she was.

Where *they* were.

She hoped the storm would continue because soon it would show her where her sister was hiding too. She would not be able to resist revealing herself.

She would have to leave her symbols behind to help those pathetic creatures.

***

'What is it?' Biddy asked as Gant burst in, dripping all over the floor.

'It's the elderman's daughter. Something's wrong with her. She's in the hall. You'll need to come, Edela.'

Edela frowned, searching for her boots, though the fire was only embers, and she could barely see. 'Go and get Derwa, Biddy. I will need her help. Has someone gone for Marcus?'

Gant nodded as Biddy started looking for her own boots, pushing Ido and Vella out of the way as they tried to get her attention. But it was Gant who noticed Eydis sitting on the floor as though she was in a trance. 'Eydis?' he asked gently, a crash of thunder rolling over his voice. 'Eydis!' he called, more urgently now.

Biddy hurried past him, throwing her cloak around her shoulders. 'I'll meet you in the hall. Can you bring Eydis, Gant? I don't want to leave her alone.' It was too dark, and Biddy was too distracted to notice anything as she slipped out of the cottage.

Edela turned around, a shiver creeping up her spine. 'What is it?' she asked as Gant reached for Eydis, who was suddenly whimpering in panic, scrambling to her feet. 'Eydis, what can you see?'

***

'There's no way through,' Jael realised quickly. 'I can't get through the symbols around the fort! I'm locked out!'

The creature had gone now, but the noise of the storm above their heads was suddenly loud again.

Aleksander sheathed his sword and dragged Jael into his arms, trying not to think about what was going to happen.

***

Eydis was so scared that she couldn't get the words out. Gant and Edela were both talking to her, urging her to speak. The voice was in her head too, but it was confusing.

And then suddenly it wasn't.

'Dragon,' Eydis breathed in terror, feeling Edela's cold hand squeezing her shoulder. 'Dragon!'

CHAPTER THIRTY FOUR

Marcus ran to the hall, Bram following in his wake. He pushed open the door, hurrying towards Hanna, who lay on a table, completely still, her eyes closed.

'She's breathing,' Gisila assured him. 'My mother will be here soon.'

'I found her walking back from the latrines,' Karsten said awkwardly. 'She had an upset stomach. Something she'd eaten.'

Marcus frowned, grabbing his daughter's limp hand. It felt like ice. 'Hanna?'

Gant burst into the hall, blinking with urgency. Spotting Axl on a bench, he ran for him, grabbing his arm, whispering in his ear.

Axl's face quickly matched the horror on Gant's. 'Dragon?' he said, almost to himself. He was the king; he had to act fast. 'Dragon,' he repeated quietly, and then, pushing down on his crutch and struggling to his feet, he lifted his voice. 'We have to take shelter now! A dragon is coming!'

***

Eydis knew that Edela was there, sitting next to her, holding her hand. She knew that Gant had left to warn everyone. She could feel the thick sheepskin beneath her knees, the cold rush of wind under the door. She could feel Vella licking her other hand.

And then she saw the Widow, standing in a beam of moonlight, buffeted by a strong wind.

And she was holding the book.

***

No one moved.

'We have to shelter!' Axl roared, trying to make himself heard over the crashing storm. 'Gant! Eadmund! Go out and raise the alarm! Get everyone to shelter in their homes! Under their beds! Hurry!'

They were all up, running around the hall. Out of the hall.

'Eydis!' Eadmund called to Thorgils. 'I have to find Eydis!'

Thorgils was already at the doors, hurrying to get Isaura and the children.

'Eydis is trying to stop it!' Gant yelled, running after him. 'She's with Edela, in her cottage. Edela will keep her safe. Come on!'

Karsten scooped Hanna into his arms. 'Take me to one of the chambers! I'll slip her under a bed.' Marcus, still in shock, followed him.

Runa threw her hands over her mouth, looking around the hall for a familiar face. 'Ivaar! Help me with Fyn! I need to get him under the bed!'

Ivaar, who knew where Thorgils had gone, didn't hesitate. He followed Runa through the curtain to the bedchambers.

'The sea-fire!' Axl cried. 'We have to secure the sea-fire!'

Erl and Rork Arnesson nodded quickly and ran out of the hall, motioning for their men to follow them.

***

Draguta could feel the heat of Thrula's angry breath as she bellowed waterfalls of fire down onto the fort.

Inside the fort.

Setting the thatched rooftops on fire.

Listening to the storm and the panic. Smelling the terror.

But there was nothing they could do.

The symbols couldn't stop her now.

***

Eadmund ran across the rain-drenched square, fighting against the wind that was almost tearing his cloak off him. Looking up, he could see the great shadow of the dragon as it passed overhead, listening as it roared louder than the thunder. 'Dragon!' he screamed, though at this time of night, most were already in their homes, he knew. 'Dragon!' And he ran for the nearest house as flames shot towards him. Smashing his shoulder against the closed door, it burst open and Eadmund fell inside with a heavy thump.

Fire erupted over the sodden ground.

The rain teemed down so heavily, then, that Eadmund couldn't hear anything as he scrambled to his feet, ushering the surprised family under their beds. 'Hurry!' he cried, slamming the door shut against the flames.

***

Bruno wanted to see what he could do to help, but Ayla pulled him under the bed with her.

'Stay,' she urged, feeling a sense of calm steady her nerves as she listened to the rain hammering the roof, louder than any waterfall. 'The gods are coming.'

***

Eydis opened her eyes, gripping Edela's hand. 'I can't see her!' she panicked. 'She disappeared! Everything went dark. I can't see the Widow, Edela! She's gone!'

Edela could hear the deep roar of the dragon as it flew above the fort. She could feel her throat tighten with fear, imagining what was about to happen. Taking a quick breath, she sought to calm her nerves, knowing that Eydis was the only hope they had. 'Try again, Eydis. She may still be there, waiting for you. Try again. Close your eyes, there you go. Now, deep breath and focus on the Widow.' Edela jumped as thunder crashed above the cottage. 'She wants to help, doesn't she? So you just need to find her again.' She swallowed, glancing at the door as the wind rose, rattling it so violently that Edela wondered if it would come off its hinges.

Eydis nodded, her eyes squeezed tightly together, trying desperately to hear that voice again.

***

The children were wailing in terror, and Thorgils didn't know what to do. He'd ordered them under the beds with Isaura and her two servants while he remained by the door, so he could see very well that the cottages on either side of them were on fire.

And so was the ground outside Isaura's door.

The rain was doing its best to douse the flames, but they were spreading, rising like a wall, and Thorgils could smell smoke.

He looked back into the dark cottage, trying to think over Mads' screams, and his own panic, which was just as loud.

Thorgils could hear the dragon too - a great growling beast, flying above them all - and he remembered Jael's warning that they would be helpless against flying things. Blinking rapidly, he made a decision. 'Let's go!' he shouted. 'Out now! We're going to the hall! Quickly!'

***

Erl Arnesson ran across the square, glancing up, trying to see the dragon through the rain. It was like a slow-moving, dark cloud, but every now and then, he glimpsed a burst of flames as it turned its enormous mouth towards the fort and roared.

'Find the sea-fire!' he yelled to his brother and their men. 'We have to get it off the catapults! Spread out! Take it into the sheds!'

And then an explosion, and Erl was flying back through the air, landing on a rock with a thud.

***

Eydis had been silent for some time, and Edela was starting to wonder if they needed to seek shelter. The dragon seemed so close now. Her tiny cottage was almost shaking as it flew overhead.

Edela was certainly shaking as she knelt on the floor next to Eydis.

Eydis suddenly burst into life. 'Cut my hand, Edela!' she cried over the driving rain and the shrieking wind. 'I need blood! I must draw a symbol! Hurry!' She could hear the terrifying noise of the dragon too, and her heart pounded in terror, but she held onto the picture of the symbol she could see in the book and the words above it.

Edela pierced Eydis' palm with her blade, making a quick cut, trying not to hurt her, though there was little time to be gentle, she knew. Throwing away the knife, she rolled Eydis' hand into a fist and pumped it, trying to make her blood flow. And when she had, she reached for Eydis' other hand and dipped a finger into the blood. 'Here,' she said, pushing the sheepskin away. 'Draw, Eydis!'

Eydis felt the rough floorboard beneath her finger. She gritted her teeth against the sharp pain in her other hand and focused on the page the Widow was showing her.

Taking a deep breath, Eydis started chanting.

She could hear the Widow urging her on over the rain as she drew the symbol, chanting with the full-throated anger of a real dreamer.

'Put your hand over the symbol now, Eydis,' the Widow said faintly. 'Good girl. You have been so brave. Edela must hurry outside to check where it falls. She must keep you safe. I have to go now. Goodbye, Eydis.'

And then darkness and rain, and Eydis was panting, reaching out for Edela. 'Quick! It will fall! You must go and see!'

Edela struggled to her feet, yelping at a pain in her hip, leaving Eydis on the floor as she hurried to the door, peering through the rain, searching for the dragon.

***

Erl opened his eyes, feeling a hand dragging him along the ground. It was his brother, Rork. He blinked, pain rushing to the back of his head.

'Quick!' Rork yelled over the torrent of rain as he tried to lift Erl's substantial bulk. Then he heard a loud screech of pain, and he turned his face up to the stormy sky, staring in confusion for a moment before his eyes popped open. 'It's coming down!' he cried, yanking harder as the dragon spiralled towards the fort in ever-quickening circles. 'The dragon's coming down!'

Bram was there now, pulling on Erl's other hand, and together they got him to his feet, and the three of them ran through the mud as the dragon's wings dropped by its sides and it spun out of control, limp and lifeless.

Spinning around. Faster and faster.

'Run!' Rork screamed, glancing up, his voice lost in a powerful gust of wind that almost knocked him backwards. 'Run!' One eye on the dragon, he charged forward, slipping in the watery mud. So much rain had fallen now that the fort was flooding quickly.

And as the dragon fell and Rork ran, he lost his footing, tipping forward.

The storm was so loud that neither Bram nor Erl noticed that he wasn't following them.

Rork struggled to his feet, slipping, crying out, watching the dragon, his mouth open as he realised that the wind was blowing it away from the hall, towards them. 'Stop! No!' And he turned and ran in the other direction as the dragon fell into the fort, dropping with an explosion of head, wings, body, and tail.

Crushing everything in its path.

***

Axl limped outside, scanning the fort in horror, Gant beside him; Aedan and Aron hurrying after them.

The dragon had missed the hall, but not by much.

It had landed across the northwestern corner of the fort, crushing the wall near the main gates with its belly; its long tail curling across the fields; its dark, barbed head and neck twisted onto the square just before the hall steps. Everything in between was lost underneath the mammoth beast. And before it fell, the dragon had set their sea-fire stores alight with its last fiery breath.

Now they were exploding, sending red balls of fire up into the storm.

Thorgils came running towards the hall, ushering Isaura and her servants ahead of him, each one of them carrying a child. His red hair was stuck to his face, rain streaming into his eyes. 'We need help! People are trapped under the dragon! The sea-fire is exploding! Everything's on fire!'

Axl froze, feeling his breathing slow, watching as people panicked before him. Running past him. Running for the dragon.

Was it even dead?

It was suddenly so cold. Axl could see his breath streaming before him in frosty clouds.

Gant turned to Amma, realising that Axl had gone into shock. 'Amma, get Axl back inside the hall! You need to prepare for injuries. Fire, water, bandages. We'll need more beds too. Axl, organise everyone inside!' Gant grabbed Thorgils' arm. 'Show me!'

Thorgils eased Selene down onto the steps, and with one quick look at Isaura, he hurried after Gant. Karsten, Kormac, and Ivaar ran out of the hall, following them.

***

No one in the circle spoke.

No one could hear anything but the pounding of the rain as it doused the bonfire.

But they could feel Draguta's white, hot fury.

At first.

But then she lifted her wet face up to the storm and smiled.

***

It was snowing.

Eadmund tried to blink the wet flakes out of his eyes, but they were falling so heavily that he couldn't see as he ran across the square towards the dragon. The wind and rain had quickly turned into a blizzard, and his teeth started chattering.

He could hear someone calling, and he spun around.

There was nothing to see but the shadowy, mountainous shape of the dead dragon. Its body was so big that Eadmund couldn't see over or around it. And then he heard an explosion and saw flames shooting up into the white sky.

Sea-fire.

The snow fell even harder, making it impossible to see anything at all, but he had to find out who was calling. 'Hello?' he cried, running towards the dragon, hands out, trying not to bang into something or someone. 'Hello?'

And then he heard a familiar voice.

'Eadmund?'

'Bram?' Eadmund dropped to the ground, crawling towards the faint voice, cringing as more jars of sea-fire exploded nearby. 'Bram?' Eadmund felt the dragon's scaly skin, still warm, and he dug down beneath its body, finding a hand, but not much else. 'Bram! I've got you! I'll get you out of here!' He turned around, trying to see anyone.

'Eadmund!' Thorgils was quickly kneeling beside him.

'It's Bram! We need some shovels!' Eadmund shouted. 'We have to dig him out!'

'I'll be back!' Thorgils yelled, hurrying to his feet and disappearing into the snow.

'My brother?' Rork cried, dropping to the ground beside Eadmund. 'He was with Bram! Can you see him?'

'No!' Eadmund shook his head, feeling around in the snow near Bram as Rork started shouting for his brother.

***

Edela smacked into a rickety wattle fence. It almost gave way, but she managed to keep to her feet. The snow was swirling so angrily around her that it was like walking into a white wall. She couldn't see a thing, but she felt impatient to get to the hall, sensing how urgently they needed her help.

Tightly gripping Eydis' frozen hand, she moved them away from the fence, trying to get back onto the path; not feeling anything but deep snow beneath her soaking boots; wishing for the first time that her cottage wasn't so far away from the hall.

Eydis was holding onto the puppies who were trying to pull her in the direction of the buried path.

Ducking her head against the bitter onslaught of wind and snow, Edela focused on moving her feet after the puppies, deciding that they were her only hope of finding the hall. 'This way, Eydis!' she called, one hand out in front of her face, jumping as another jar of sea-fire exploded in the distance.

***

'Mother! Help me!' Berard cried. One corner of their house had collapsed. The roof had caved in, right on top of Irenna's bed, and he was trying to lift up the heavy wooden rafters to get to Irenna. Bayla was beside him, but she wasn't strong enough to offer much help. 'Nicolene!' Berard panicked, trying to see his other sister-in-law through the snow that was gusting inside the broken house.

He could hear explosions outside.

He could see flames through the collapsed roof.

Nicolene had pulled the children towards the door, except for Halla, who'd been sleeping with Irenna. 'Berard, come and stay with the children!' she ordered, rushing forward, deciding that her two arms would be more useful than his one.

Berard hesitated, then realised that she was right.

'Poke your head outside! Find help!' Nicolene screamed as she dug her hands under one of the rafters that had crushed Irenna, hoping that between her and Bayla, they could shift it. Gritting her teeth, she tried lifting the rafter, but it was too heavy. She peered at Bayla, her eyes darting through the holes in the wall to the flames that were blowing ever closer. 'I can't move it!'

'Get out of the way!' Karsten roared as he ran inside, pushing his wife to one side, quickly heaving the biggest rafter off Irenna. He gasped, turning away. It had landed on her face. 'Don't look!' he demanded, sending Bayla and Nicolene to the door as he threw the broken rafter to one side. 'Get outside!'

'But Halla!' Bayla sobbed, not about to leave. 'Where's Halla?'

Karsten suddenly couldn't see a thing as the snowstorm whirled around them with greater intensity, but he could feel the heat of the encroaching flames. 'Get everyone out of here!' he ordered, turning to Berard. 'Now!' And he felt quickly around the broken bed, trying not to look at poor Irenna's face. 'Halla!' he cried. 'Halla!'

And then he felt a tiny frozen foot.

And grabbing hold of it, Karsten pulled.

***

Thorgils and Eadmund carried Bram into the hall.

'Bram!' Runa rushed to them in horror, pointing to the nearest table.

'The dragon fell on him,' Eadmund panted as he eased Bram down onto the table before wiping the snow from his eyes. 'He must have been in some sort of trough, so he missed the worst of it, but he hasn't woken up since we pulled him out. We have to go back. There might be more people trapped.' Eadmund glanced at Thorgils, whose dripping boots weren't moving.

He didn't want to leave.

Isaura was quickly beside him. The children were safely tucked away in the chambers under Tanja's care now, and she was already helping Ayla and Biddy tend to the wounded. 'You have to go,' she urged. 'We'll take good care of Bram. He would want you to help everyone you can.'

'The fort is on fire,' Eadmund said, grabbing his friend's arm. 'The snow is helping, but we have to see if we can save anyone else.'

Thorgils shook the melting snow from his hair and looked away from his uncle, whose leg was bent at a strange angle, comforted by the fact that he was, at least, breathing. He dropped his head, turning to follow Eadmund out of the hall, almost knocking over Edela and Eydis as they were pulled inside by the puppies.

'Eydis!' Eadmund threw his arms around his little sister. 'Are you alright?' He stepped back, looking her over as she nodded quickly, shaking the snow out of her hair. 'Stay here with Isaura. I'll be back as soon as I can!'

***

The flames were fighting the snow.

The dragon's tail had smashed the shed housing their sea-fire stores, and the broken jars were leaking, catching alight, exploding in continual heart-stopping blasts.

'We can't do anything!' Ivaar yelled as he signalled for his men to move away. The heat from the flames was too much. Squinting, he saw that Gant had arrived. 'Nothing will put that fire out! Only the snowstorm stands a chance now!'

Gant nodded as Eadmund, Thorgils, and Torstan joined them.

'We have to get everyone away from the fire! If the snow doesn't stop it, those houses will catch!' Eadmund cried, pointing to the buildings near the flaming shed. 'Let's open the harbour gates. Get everyone out!'

Gant turned, motioning for Ivaar and his men to follow him.

Eadmund rubbed his eyes, trying to see through the snow. 'We have to check around the dragon!' he called as Aedan and Aron arrived with Kormac, who'd been smart enough to bring a flaming torch, which was still burning, despite the determined onslaught of the blizzard. 'There may be people alive, trapped under it still!' His teeth chattered, and his body shook, but he was grateful for the snow, hoping it stood a chance of putting out the sea-fire.

Eadmund spun around as realisation dawned. 'The stables!' He grabbed Thorgils' arm. 'Quick!'

***

Berard and Nicolene held the doors open as Karsten rushed into the hall with Halla Dragos in his arms. Her face was splattered with blood, her head covered in snow.

She had woken up and was yelling loudly, which was a good sign.

'Here!' Branwyn called, motioning to the nearest table. 'I'll take a look.' She nodded for Kayla to help her as Amma hurried to gather the rest of the Dragos children. 'Take them into the chambers, Amma. They'll be safe there.' And gently placing her hand on Halla's little head, Branwyn tried to keep her still. 'There, there, now, let's see what's happened to you,' she said, trying to smile, though it hadn't escaped Branwyn's notice that one member of the Dragos family was missing.

'Berard, stay with them,' Karsten urged, pointing to his mother and wife, who were dripping from head to toe as the snow started to melt, warmed by the hall fires and the throng of people rushing around tending to the injured.

Ulf hurried into the hall, one of his men leaning against him, a great gash in his head. 'My lady!' he cried upon seeing Bayla. 'Are you hurt?' And he handed his man over to Entorp and turned to Bayla, who immediately fell into his arms, sobbing.

CHAPTER THIRTY FIVE

Rork Arnesson couldn't stop shaking his head as he kneeled beside his brother's cold, snow-covered body, which Ivaar had helped him drag out from under the dragon. He couldn't speak. He didn't want to move, and eventually, he dropped his head to his hands, letting the snow cover him too.

'Come on!' Ivaar urged, grabbing Rork's arm, trying to pull him back to his feet. 'You can't do anything for him now. Not while it's like this! But I can hear someone over there!' he cried, pointing into the blizzard. 'They're stuck. Help me!'

Rork didn't want to move.

The sea-fire was exploding in the distance.

People were screaming, and the storm was wailing, and the snow was falling, and he didn't want to move.

His cousins were dead, and his brother was gone.

And he didn't want to move.

But he struggled to his feet, too numb to think, lifting his head as Ivaar pulled him away into the snowstorm.

***

Bram opened his eyes, yelping as Entorp and Derwa forced the bones in his lower leg back into place, before quickly passing out again.

'Well, he's alive for the moment,' the old woman muttered, holding her hand out to Runa, who quickly placed a torn strip of cloth into it. 'No,' Derwa frowned, shaking her head. 'I need you over here. Entorp and I will hold the leg in place with these sticks, and you're going to wrap the cloth around them.' Derwa picked up two sticks that Entorp had found and tidied up for her, and placed them gently on either side of Bram's lower leg.

Runa nodded, swallowing, her hands shaking.

'And then we'll take a look at his chest,' Derwa promised, watching as Runa took a deep breath to steady herself. 'Don't worry.'

Nodding again, Runa started winding the cloth around the sticks, her eyes meeting Marcus'. He looked worried as he bent over Hanna, who'd been brought back into the hall and was lying on a table, being examined by Edela.

'We need to take Hanna somewhere else,' Edela said softly. 'If she caught this sickness in Saala, it will spread quickly. We'll need to find somewhere to quarantine her and anyone else who might have it. I think outside the fort would be best. Are there any sheds still standing?'

Marcus swallowed, trying to think.

'A couple,' Axl said, turning to the doors as Gant strode into the hall, shaking snow from his cloak, wiping it out of his eyes.

'It's too thick out there,' Gant panted. 'We can't see a thing, but the snow appears to be dampening down the sea-fire.' He glanced at the worried faces. 'What is it?'

'It looks as though Hanna has the illness from Saala,' Edela whispered.

Gant froze. He looked down at Hanna, who lay perfectly still on the table before them. Her face was pale, but sweat was beading across her brow. 'Oh.'

'We need to quarantine her now. Out of the fort.'

'There are a couple of sheds still standing near the harbour.

Let's take her there,' Gant said hoarsely, shaking his head. This was bad timing indeed. He looked up at Berard, who stood beside Hanna. 'Gather your family together. You'll need to go too. We'll keep you in one shed, the girl in the other. We'll have to get Ulf and his men, try to contain it.'

Berard nodded, leaving to find his mother and Nicolene, wondering where Karsten was.

'I'll go with her,' Marcus said quietly.

Entorp had joined them, catching the last of the conversation. 'I'll come with you. I'm sure there's something I can do to make Hanna more comfortable.'

***

Andala's main stables were still in one piece, but near enough to the burning sea-fire to be under threat. Eadmund had his Osslanders hard at work, shepherding the horses out, moving them to the smaller stable blocks on the eastern, dragon-less side of the fort. Those that could not fit were being taken out through the main gates, past the tent village, which had just been missed by the dragon's tail, into the paddocks.

As the snow blew even harder.

They could barely hear themselves think.

Eadmund grabbed Thorgils' arm. 'You find Leada! I'm going to run around the dragon again! See if I can hear anyone else!'

Thorgils nodded, his breath puffing around him in big white clouds. He was worried about Bram, but there was too much to do. He couldn't go back to the hall and check on him yet, so turning into the blizzard, he stuck his hands out in front of his face, trying to find his way towards the panicking horses.

***

Karsten, Ivaar, and Rork were struggling to see; struggling to get their frozen hands to work at all as they dug under the dragon. Someone was calling faintly, but they couldn't find them. The voice was muffled, and it was hard to hear exactly where it was coming from.

'Here!' Ivaar called finally, feeling a finger, and then, an entire hand. 'I've got someone!' And he could feel life in that hand as it gripped his.

Karsten fought his way towards him, blinking snow out of his eyes, unable to see, but feeling around, he followed the hand down to a body trapped beneath the dragon's belly. If that hand had life in it, then there was hope for the rest of the body. 'We need to dig them out! I'll go and find help! You stay here!' And he ran into the blizzard, disoriented, not knowing where to go until he smacked straight into Gant Olborn.

Gant grabbed his arms. 'You have to come with me!' he yelled over the howl of the snowstorm. 'Now!'

Karsten frowned. 'What's happened?'

'I'll explain soon! Come on!'

Karsten looked back to where he had last seen Ivaar, but there was only a wall of swirling snow now. 'I need to get help! Someone's trapped over there. Still alive! We can dig them out!'

Gant nodded, grabbing Kormac as he came running up to them. 'Get some men and shovels and meet us back here!' He turned to Karsten. 'We'll wait for Kormac,' he shivered. 'Then we have to get you to your family. We're moving you all out of the fort!'

Karsten shook his head, wondering if he'd heard Gant correctly.

***

Eydis sat beside Fyn, both of them feeling utterly useless as they listened to the howl of the snowstorm and the rising panic and distress in the hall. All they could do was ensure that the puppies stayed in Fyn's chamber, out of everyone's way. After what had happened in Tuura, Eydis knew that both Jael and Biddy would consider it a worthwhile job, but still, she wanted to be out in the hall, helping.

So did Fyn.

'What do you think happened to Jael?' Fyn asked, breaking the worried silence. 'Do you think the dragon found her and Aleksander before it came here?'

They were sitting on the floor, their backs against the wall, Ido and Vella curled up on their laps, still shaking. Eydis shrugged. 'I don't know. I hope not.'

'What is it?' Fyn could hear the hesitation in her voice.

'The Widow, when she helped me...' Eydis began. 'It felt strange. She looked sad. And then, at the end, she said goodbye.'

'Goodbye?'

'Yes. It was as though she was leaving, and not coming back.'

For all the terrifying tales Fyn had grown up hearing about the Widow, it was still disconcerting to think that she might not be able to help them anymore.

'What about Jael and Aleksander?' Eydis panicked. 'What if she hasn't given them the book? If something happens to her, what will we do? She's the only one protecting us!'

Fyn looked worried himself. 'But the gods came again, didn't they?' he said, trying to reassure them both. 'They must have brought the rain and snow, trying to put out the sea-fire?'

Eydis nodded, but her fears were not eased.

The Widow was in danger.

She could feel it.

***

Draguta was weak.

Her limbs felt like a burdensome weight; so heavy she could barely lift them.

Thrula had been an immense beast, and the strength needed to control such a creature had depleted her. She felt her body sagging against Jaeger as they traipsed slowly back to the castle.

No one spoke.

Morac stumbled along in the dark at the back of the little group with Evaine. What they had witnessed was so stunning that even Evaine held her tongue.

What he had seen...

He shook his head, trying to catch his breath. Was it real? Had it actually happened? Or had the smoke simply made him hallucinate? Gripping Evaine's elbow, Morac pushed her forward to catch up with everyone else, trying not to let his mind wander too far. Draguta was so powerful that he didn't want to think anything untoward.

Not in her presence, at least.

Morana and Meena shuffled behind Jaeger and Draguta, their eyes hidden beneath cold, wet hair, flapping in the wind. Neither noticed the storm at all. Both were still transfixed by fading memories of the dragon.

A dragon?

Meena shuddered. It was as though she was trapped in her worst nightmare, never imagining that she would see such a thing whilst awake.

She wondered if she truly had?

And if so, what had happened to Berard and his family?

***

'The fire is under a mountain of snow,' Gant sighed, jiggling by the fire, eager to feel his fingers again. 'We've gotten everyone out around the dragon. Everyone we could find in the blizzard. We'll try again when it stops. When morning comes. Hopefully, by then, all the fires will be out too.'

Axl nodded distractedly from his throne. His mind was flitting about as he tried to think of all the things he needed to organise. He was finding it hard to focus. He wanted to be up, running around with Gant, checking on everyone, but his leg had weakened quickly, even with his crutch, and eventually, he'd had to sit down and give it a break. 'And the sickness?'

'We've got the Dragos' in one of the harbour sheds. Ulf and some of his crew are in another. There are a few missing. We won't know till morning where everyone is, though. If they're still alive.'

'What about the horses?' Axl asked Eadmund, who had just come in with Thorgils.

'The main stable block caught fire,' Eadmund said, rubbing his hands together, looking around for something to drink. 'But we got the horses out. It's under a mound of snow now. The horses that couldn't fit in the other stables are out in the paddocks.'

'Well, best if we all stay in here now and keep warm, wait out the blizzard,' Axl mumbled, watching Amma as she walked around the hall, seeing what she could do to help.

Eadmund nodded, slipping off his wet cloak as Thorgils left to check on Bram.

Gant frowned, turning away from his king, staring at the doors, wondering what they were going to do now. The fort was broken, the northwestern wall was smashed to rubble, and an enormous dead dragon was lying in the middle of it all.

The symbols couldn't protect them anymore.

***

'Do you see anything?' Aleksander asked hopefully. The rain had stopped, but it was still freezing cold, which was a worry. Though perhaps it meant that the gods were doing something to help Andala?

Jael had disappeared around a tree some time ago, sitting by herself, trying to see something. And, eventually, she had, and she walked back to Aleksander, pushing herself into his arms.

Aleksander blinked over her head in surprise, holding her shaking body tightly. 'What can we do?' he breathed into her smoky hair.

'Nothing,' Jael said sadly, hearing the desperate cries of panic and pain, images of the broken fort flashing before her eyes. 'Nothing.'

***

With no Egil sleeping in his little bed, anticipating his master's every need, there was no fire. There wasn't even any wood in the chamber, so Jaeger simply shrugged off his wet tunic and trousers and ran for the bed, slipping under the furs. The linen-covered mattress was cold, but the fur against his chest felt warm.

'Meena!' Jaeger called throatily. He felt drunk from the smoke which had dried his throat, but he was too tired to look for anything to drink in the dark. His eyes were already closed, but he knew that Meena was still standing where he'd left her, dripping on the rug. He would have to organise that servant to move into his chamber. It was far too inconvenient not to have someone always on hand, tending to his needs. 'Meena!'

And then Meena was there, naked and wet and shaking beside him as he pulled her close, wanting to share her body heat. 'Tell me,' he whispered sleepily. 'Tell me what you saw.'

Meena didn't want to.

She felt as though she was still flying, up in the clouds, watching the fire, listening to the screams.

Falling.

She was confused. It hadn't felt as though she *was* the dragon, but she had seen it, felt the heat of its fiery breath and the weight of its wings. She had spun with it, listening to its painful death cry, watching as it dropped onto the fort, crushing the Andalan people and their homes.

Draguta had killed many, and it made Meena sad. If she had escaped with the book when she'd had the chance, Draguta wouldn't even be here.

But had she killed Berard?

Meena closed her eyes, wanting to fall asleep, hoping to see if Berard and his family were still alive.

'Tell me,' Jaeger whispered again.

Meena could feel his heart beating as she lay her head on his chest. It was slowing down, and she hoped that he would fall asleep so that she didn't have to relive it, but then she felt his hand crushing hers.

'*Now.*'

***

Morana's eyelids drooped as she leaned over the fire, but she didn't want to fall asleep. There was too much to think about.

Morac perched on a stool opposite her. After helping Evaine to her chamber, he'd felt too tired to walk all the way back to Yorik's cottage, so he'd decided to spend the night with Morana, though she seemed more intent on talking than taking to her bed.

'It's not all bad,' she sighed, hanging her wet hair near the flames. 'She is doing our work for us. Killing the Brekkans. It's not all bad.'

Morac frowned. 'It seems as though her plans are hers alone, though. She has no grand vision, just personal grievances,' he whispered hoarsely, glancing at the door.

'Who doesn't have personal grievances?' Morana sniffed. 'I'd happily gut Jael Furyck. If only Draguta could find her!'

'We're not safe while Jael Furyck lives,' Morac muttered distractedly, reminded of how easily she'd twisted Eirik around her little finger.

Eadmund too, for a time.

'We're not safe at all,' Morana reminded him. 'Draguta has no interest in us. She might see me as useful, Meena too, but if we displease her... if she no longer needs us? She'll kill us. And I don't know why she'd want you around, Brother. Not once I'm gone.'

Morac saw Runa's face, remembering his fumbled attempt at saying goodbye to her. It was only now that he wished he'd said more. It was only now that he realised how much his old life had mattered to him.

He wondered if he would ever see her again.

***

'He opened his eyes a while ago,' Isaura said, looking from Thorgils to Runa, who stood by Bram, watching him with great concern. He was covered in furs, tucked into one of the beds lining the hall.

'Did he say anything?' Thorgils asked wearily, squeezing his hands together, trying to feel them again. They hadn't warmed up since he'd plunged them into the snow, digging out those who could be saved from broken cottages and from under the dragon.

And some had been.

But not many.

Isaura shook her head. 'He grabbed Ayla's hand, didn't he?' she said, smiling at the dreamer, who had stopped by to check on Bram.

Ayla nodded. 'He did. His leg is broken, but it will heal. He must have landed on something, which damaged his chest, so he's struggling to breathe. But he was lucky. Something stopped that dragon from crushing him. It could have been a lot worse.' She couldn't offer anything more than that. Everyone agreed that the injury to Bram's chest was a worry, and no one was confidently predicting his recovery yet.

Gant and Eadmund came through the doors, sleepy-eyed and wet through.

Dawn had been struggling to break through the snowstorm, but it had finally eased enough to give them a chance to check how things stood in the fort.

And it was even worse than they'd imagined.

'We need to set up more places to bring the injured,' Eadmund said, yawning as they walked over to Thorgils.

'Not just the injured,' Gant added. 'We have to find places for those who've lost their homes. It's too cold to be outside for now. The Tuurans in the tents will freeze. The sea-fire's almost out, but we don't know how long this blizzard will last. We have to bring them into the fort, find them somewhere warm to stay.'

Eadmund frowned instinctively as Ivaar emerged from behind the grey curtain. 'We need to move the sea-fire jars that are still intact,' he said, glaring at his brother. 'Can you and your men do that? You'll need to take them to the eastern side of the fort, away from the last of the flames,' he suggested, glancing at Gant, who nodded in agreement.

'We can,' Ivaar said wearily. He'd been hoping for a drink and a moment to thaw himself by a fire, but if the sea-fire wasn't stored safely, there'd be more flames than anyone wanted soon.

Eadmund clapped Thorgils on the shoulder. 'Can you come

with us? We need all the help we can get.'

Thorgils nodded, grabbing his cloak, which he'd left drying by the fire.

'Maybe you should try and organise some food?' Gant suggested, glancing at Isaura and Runa. 'For those who have an appetite, at least. Something hot in their bellies might be welcome.'

'Of course,' Isaura said, looking around for Biddy, who had mentioned the same thing earlier.

Eadmund blinked, following Gant and Thorgils to the doors, trying to keep the constant visions of Evaine out of his mind.

There was too much to do to listen to that desperate voice in his head.

***

As soon as the blizzard eased, Aron walked Edela and Eydis back to the cottage. Edela had looked ready to fall down from exhaustion, and Branwyn had firmly insisted that her mother would be more use once she'd had some sleep.

For once, Edela hadn't argued with the fussing. She could barely keep her eyes open. It had been a tragic night for Andala, and she had worked hard to help as many people as she could. There were burns and cuts. Broken bones. Crushed limbs. Homes were shattered. Part of the fort was destroyed.

And then there was the Widow.

Edela tucked Eydis into Biddy's bed and immediately crawled into her own, grateful that her kind grandson had stayed behind to light a fire. The flames helped to warm the cottage, and as she rolled over, they revealed how worried Eydis was. And Edela, despite needing sleep, was determined to get to the bottom of it. 'What do you think the Widow was scared of, then?'

Eydis frowned, running her hand over Vella's fluffy back. 'I don't think she was scared. It wasn't that. I thought she was crying.'

Edela shivered, suddenly worried about Jael. She took a slow, deep breath and exhaled, clearing her mind. Throughout Jael's life, Edela had always been confident in her granddaughter's safety, convinced that if something was going to happen to her, she would be warned. She opened her eyes, relieved to feel that same sense of certainty was still there. But as for what was wrong with the Widow... 'And she said goodbye to you? It seems a little odd. Unless she said it before, as a farewell?'

'No, never.'

Edela listened to the pop of the fire, thinking about the dragon. It was almost too unbelievable to be real.

'She helped us. She wanted to save us,' Eydis murmured.

'If she hadn't, that dragon would have destroyed the entire fort, burned us all to ash. I don't think the gods could have stopped it, even with all that wind and snow.'

Eydis yawned, feeling her mind drift. 'Maybe she's saying that she can't help us anymore?'

'You might be right, Eydis. And if that's the case, I fear what it means for us all. But especially...' Edela rolled over, yawning herself, curling into a frozen ball. 'Especially for Jael and Aleksander.' She closed her eyes, trying to get the terrifying sound of the dragon out of her head.

***

Meena's dreams were filled with dragons.

Nightmares of fire and death.

Her ears echoed with screams.

'And soon it will be your turn. If you're not careful, girl, soon

Draguta will kill you. Can't you see? Not much of a dreamer are you if you can't see what's right in front of you. That woman. Always watching.'

The laughter was old and familiar, scratching at her like branches against a windowpane.

'She sees everything. Hears everything too. And soon she will come for you!'

Meena jerked awake, panting in the darkness.

CHAPTER THIRTY SIX

As dawn forced its way in through the wood's canopy, Jael and Aleksander hurried to leave their campsite.

'The only thing we can do now is get to the Widow's cottage as quickly as possible,' Jael muttered, running her hand down Tig's face as he nuzzled against her, looking for a treat. 'We can't help anyone in Andala until we have that book.'

Aleksander nodded, hoping the weather would warm up again soon. 'We might get there by nightfall,' he suggested, adjusting his scabbard.

Jael peered at him, hearing the uncertainty in his voice. 'You don't know where we are, do you?'

Aleksander sucked in a smoky breath. 'Well,' he sighed, 'not at the moment. We've been turned around so many times now. I... can't get my bearings.'

Jael frowned, thinking of the vision of the woman she'd seen showing her the path. 'She wants us to come, so she'll lead us to her, won't she?'

Aleksander shrugged and stuck his foot in a stirrup, throwing himself up into his wet saddle. 'I hope so.' And he did. More than anything, he wanted to hear that voice in his head again, telling them where to go.

***

Bayla held her two-year-old granddaughter's tiny hand, wondering how much more her family would have to suffer.

Berard sat on Halla's other side, trying to calm her while Entorp dabbed a sweet-smelling salve over the cuts on her face. Some of them were very deep. The rafters had splintered, and Entorp had spent a long time pulling out each shard of wood, carefully stitching up the worst of them.

But Halla would recover, unlike Irenna.

Berard didn't want to think about Irenna. He didn't want to remember her dead body lying on the broken bed, entombed in snow. He tried to think of other things, such as what was happening in the fort or wondering how Hanna was. She was being kept next door in a smaller shed, away from everyone else. Her father was with her, caring for her. He was glad to think that she wasn't alone, but Hanna had only gone to Saala because of his arm, and Berard felt the heavy weight of guilt pushing down on his shoulders.

If he'd taken that book, Irenna and Haegen would be alive.

Perhaps, even his father too?

And Hanna wouldn't be sick.

'Berard!' Karsten called from his stool by the fire where he'd sat slumped over for some time. 'Go and eat something.'

Berard shook his head. Halla was so scared that he didn't want to leave her. She kept crying for her mother. It broke his heart. 'I'm not hungry,' he insisted.

Karsten got up from his stool, stretching out his aching back. 'You can't do anything now, except get stronger,' he groaned. 'It's the only way you can help us.'

Berard sighed, realising that Karsten was right. He squeezed Halla's hand, smiling at her before walking over to Nicolene, who was spooning what looked like porridge into bowls for the children. The smell made Berard want to vomit, making him wonder if he had the sickness too.

Karsten inclined his head towards Valder and Lucina, who were sitting together on a bed, eyes down, staring at their socks. Neither had uttered a word since they'd been moved into the shed. 'Come on, you two, come to the table and have some porridge.'

They didn't even raise their heads.

Karsten didn't blame them. They'd lost their father and mother now. It was too much for anyone, but they had to eat. 'I think Nicolene has some honey to go with the porridge, don't you? Maybe some berries?'

Nicolene nodded mutely, sprinkling a few raspberries into each bowl, though she had no appetite herself. The smell of the sea-fire smoke was strong in the breezy shed, but it wasn't as stomach-churning as the smell coming from Hanna next door. She clamped her lips together, trying not to inhale.

Karsten walked over to his niece and nephew, grabbing their hands and easing them off the bed. He didn't want to speak at all, but they had to help each other survive what had happened.

And prepare for what might be coming next.

***

Draguta peeled open one eye.

Bright morning light shone in through the fluttering curtains, but she was so weary. Not ready to wake.

Closing her eye, Draguta sighed, happy to think that she had finally drawn her sister out of her little hole. In the end, as predicted, she had not been able to resist helping those pathetic humans, saving them from the dragon. Well, not all of them, Draguta smiled. But if her sister hadn't revealed herself when she had, there would have been nothing left of Andala.

Nothing but warm ash and charred bones.

The Furycks still lived, but the symbols were useless against her now, and more importantly, Draguta had seen where her sister was hiding.

***

The snow finally stopped falling, but it still felt colder than Oss in the depths of winter, which was just as well, Eadmund decided as he watched Ivaar and his men working to move the sea-fire jars. He didn't want any of those fires sparking back to life. He blew on his hands, trying to get some feeling back into them. He hadn't packed his gloves, not thinking he'd need them in summer.

'Any idea how we're going to get this flying worm out of here?' Thorgils muttered, jiggling on the spot beside him, hungry, freezing, and half asleep.

Eadmund shrugged, still in shock as he stared at the dragon whose dead body curled around the fort like a range of snow-capped mountains. 'We're going to need a lot of rope.'

Thorgils nodded. 'A lot of rope... a lot of hands. Horses too. It's three times as big as the serpent!'

'At least. But we can't start repairing the wall if we don't get the dragon out of it. We have to move it quickly,' Eadmund said, turning to Gant and Oleg, who had joined them, shivering beneath thick fur cloaks.

Gant frowned, unable to stop staring at the dragon, still wondering if he was dreaming. 'It's going to take a long time to repair the wall. And in the meantime, we're exposed. There's nothing to stop them attacking us now. No symbols. No Jael.'

No one spoke, but Oleg could hear the anxiety in Gant's voice. He'd never heard him sound so rattled.

'We have to prepare what we can,' Eadmund said, glancing

around. 'We need to gather our armies. Organise a defense. We can't just sit here and hope that Eydis can stop the next attack. We don't even know what's happened to Jael and Aleksander. Whether they're still alive? Maybe Draguta's already killed them?'

Thorgils' grainy eyes widened in surprise.

There was no feeling in Eadmund's voice at all.

'Jael and Aleksander are the two most determined people I know,' Gant said, not liking the dismissive tone of Eadmund's voice either. 'Nothing will stop them from getting back here. Not a dragon or a Draguta!' He tugged on his beard, thinking of Ranuf, and of the years they had spent training Jael and Aleksander together. Training them to withstand every sort of enemy they could think of.

Except, of course, magic books and dragons.

***

'Hurry.'

It was barely a whisper, and Aleksander had almost closed his eyes as he rode through the trees, his head nodding in time to Sky's rhythmic walk. He jerked around in surprise, thinking it was Jael, but she was ducking a branch, not even looking his way. Turning back around, he quickly dropped beneath a branch of his own. Progress had been slow since they'd left their camp, which didn't trouble Aleksander as much as the fact that he still had no idea where they were going.

'Left. Go left.'

Aleksander swallowed, glancing to his left. There didn't appear any way through the thicket. He frowned, then looked again, his eyes brightening. 'This way!' he called, tugging Sky's reins.

He could see a path now.

***

Axl felt overwhelmed.

The dragon.

The giant hole in the wall.

The sickness.

Many of his people were dead. Their homes were crushed, burned to ash. His harbour was wrecked. He was struggling to think; frustrated that there was little he could do to help. But he had his cousin Aron and his crutch, and he hobbled around the snow-blanketed fort as quickly as he could, leaning on Aron when it became too much.

Kormac and Aedan walked with them.

'It will take some time to get that dragon out of here,' Kormac frowned. 'And we'll have to clean up the wall before we can start any repairs.'

Axl grunted, coming to a stop as he stared at the monstrous dragon whose wings had broken when it hit the ground, twisted and bent like mammoth sails. 'I...' He shook his head. 'Gant can show you where to find enough rope. Although, maybe we'll need to take it out in pieces? It's so big.'

Kormac puffed out a smoky breath, not liking the sound of either of those options. He turned to his sons. 'And we thought the ravens were bad!'

Gant came around the head of the dragon with Eadmund, skirting the long black tongue which had flopped out of the side of its mouth.

'Speaking of Gant,' Axl smiled in relief. He always felt better having Gant nearby. Gant seemed to know where everything was. Who everyone was. What needed doing and when. But Axl knew that, as king, he had to start making more decisions on his own, showing some leadership. 'We were talking about moving the dragon.'

'Good, so were we,' Gant said, inclining his head towards

Eadmund. 'I'll organise some crews, and we'll collect every piece of rope we have. I've a feeling we'll need to go to the ships for more. I don't think that dragon is coming out easy!'

Axl grimaced, feeling the bite of his crutch into his armpit.

'Why not go and sit down?' Gant suggested, noticing his strained face. 'We can organise this. It's going to take us all day, I'd say.'

'And more,' Kormac said. 'We should probably cut off its head too. Just to be sure.'

Axl felt embarrassed, but the pain was suddenly overwhelming. He was struggling to keep his balance in the snow. 'Good idea,' he muttered into his chest. 'I'll see how everyone is in the hall.'

'I'll send someone to give you regular updates!' Gant called after him.

But Axl had already left, limping through the snow.

***

Edela frowned as she guided Eydis into Fyn's bedchamber.

Fyn was sitting impatiently on the edge of his bed. He had grown bored with staring at the four walls of his tiny room, desperate to do something to help. His stomach wound ached as he sat there, though, and he suddenly doubted his ability to stand on his own.

'I don't think that's a good idea,' Edela said quietly, helping Eydis to a stool. 'You trying to walk. Not without help, at least, and I'm not the sort of help you need. We'd have each other on the ground in no time!'

Fyn's shoulders sagged. 'No, but maybe Thorgils or Aron could help me?'

'Aron is out there trying to move that dragon, and Thorgils...' Edela's voice trailed away.

Fyn sat up straight. 'What's happened to Thorgils?'

'His uncle was injured by the dragon,' Edela said. 'He's not very well, I'm afraid.'

'Oh.'

'But he's luckier than some. If the wind hadn't come and pushed the dragon further north, it would have fallen on the hall and all the houses around it. It could have been a lot worse.'

'But what can we do now? With the dragon breaking the wall? How are we going to protect ourselves?'

'She can see us,' Eydis murmured distantly.

'The Widow?' Fyn asked.

Eydis shook her head. 'Draguta. She can see past the symbol now. She can see Jael.'

***

Aleksander stretched out his legs, taking a long drink. They had finally come across a stream, and they'd hurried to fill their empty waterskins. Despite the bitter cold, they were both thirsty, and so were the horses.

'This looks familiar,' Aleksander said, peering around. 'I remember crossing this stream.' He stared at the trees curling around each other, making a tunnel in the distance. 'And over there. I've been here before!'

Jael's shoulders loosened slightly. 'So we're getting closer?'

Aleksander nodded, walking back to Sky. 'Only one way to find out for sure. Come on!'

Jael tucked her bulging waterskin into her saddlebag, seeing images of the dead dragon lying across Andala's square; wanting instead to see Eadmund, Eydis, and Edela. She was worried about all of them. Now that the dragon had broken the fort, the symbol wouldn't work, and as bad as that sounded, she hoped that she'd be able to see more of what had happened.

And hopefully, of those who were safe.

Taking a deep breath, Jael reached for Tig's reins, trying not to let her thoughts wander too far.

***

The woman shut the book and looked up at the man.

Morana frowned. It was very dark in this cottage. No fire, just a single lamp flickering in the corner, but even from behind, she recognised the woman.

She would know that woman anywhere.

'He wrote it so his followers could bring him back. He saw that his death would come. He wanted to return. To finish what he had started,' the man said with urgent eyes. He was handsome and young.

But there was something strange about him.

'And what would he do, Taegus?' Draguta asked, reaching for his hand. 'If we brought Raemus back? What would it mean for *us*?'

Taegus stared into Draguta's eyes, finding himself as lost as ever. In her. In the void between his father's expectations and his desperation to please the woman he loved. 'It would mean the end. Raemus lived in the Darkness with my mother. He wants it to be that way again. All his spells, the book, his followers... it was all so he could reunite with her in the Darkness once more. Just the two of them. As it was in the beginning.'

Draguta inhaled sharply, not liking the sound of that. 'But why would anyone agree to help him do that? And why would he still want to be with Daala? She killed him!'

Taegus shook his head. 'Even gods love. And love is rarely logical. He never stopped loving my mother. Everything he did was because of his deep love for her. His desperation to be with only her.'

'This book is *ours* now,' Draguta smiled sweetly, having heard everything she needed to. 'Yours and mine. Your father left it for you to find. He wanted you to use it, to know its secrets, its power.' Her pretty eyes were wide and insistent, urging Taegus to bend to her will, to see the future as she did. A future where they were together, and very much in the light.

Morana edged closer, wanting to see the book, hoping that Draguta would open it again and show her the page she longed to find.

'He wanted me to bring him back,' Taegus said, pushing back softly.

'But you can't,' Draguta purred. 'Can you? For if you did, you would lose me. You would lose all that we would create and destroy together, my love. For I have seen it in my dreams, the great kingdom that we will claim, the son that we will have. If you bring your father back, it will all turn to ash. He will destroy it all.' She could feel the tension in Taegus as he tightened his grip on her hand. '*You* are the God of Magic now. You don't need your father to return. Not when you have me. Not when I can give you everything you desire.'

Morana watched Taegus as he leaned forward to kiss Draguta, pulling her towards him. She scowled irritably, wanting to wake up from her dream, knowing that there was no help to be found here.

***

'How is Hanna?' Berard wondered, hurrying towards Entorp as he entered the shed.

Karsten was quickly by his side.

'I... she is very unwell,' Entorp said solemnly. 'Very weak. There is little to be done but to keep her cool and hope to get some broth into her. She cannot keep anything down, but I'll carry on trying.'

'Oh.' Somehow, Berard had been expecting better news.

'Her father is with her,' Entorp said. 'He will keep a close eye on her now. I will see her again this afternoon.' He nodded at them both, wanting to check on Halla before heading back to Hanna's shed for some sleep. Entorp couldn't keep his eyes open, and he knew that unless he took a quick nap, he would soon be the one in bed needing to be cared for.

Karsten sighed heavily. 'Well, things just keep getting worse. Seems as though we're cursed. Which one of us will be next, do you think? Me?'

He sounded so bitter, Berard thought, but when he looked in Karsten's eye, he could see fear and pain. They were helpless to do anything. Trapped inside a freezing shed. Waiting, while everyone else was outside, preparing the fort for the next attack. Though, Berard wondered, if they could send serpents and dragons to destroy Andala, what was the point in preparing for anything?

They were all just targets, ready for Draguta and Jaeger to pick off, one by one.

***

Jaeger threw his boot at the wall.

It was wet, and he couldn't find another pair to wear. He had some memory of Egil taking his boots to be repaired, but then Egil had died, and now Jaeger had no idea what had happened to them. But he knew that he didn't want to wear wet boots. 'You will find my boots, Else!' Jaeger shouted at the old woman. 'They are likely at the cobblers. I need them back! Now!'

Else didn't flinch as she waited for him to finish bellowing. Eventually, he did, and she nodded her head. She wore a light-grey scarf wrapped around her light-grey hair, and it rustled when she moved. 'I will go and find them, my lord,' she smiled calmly. 'Do not worry.'

Jaeger frowned, disturbed by how unflappable she appeared; how irritatingly agreeable. 'Well, hurry up about it! I shall wait here. I have no intention of throwing that at the wall too. 'And bring some food back with you! And wood! We need a fire in here. It's fucking cold!'

Else kept nodding and Jaeger kept frowning, but he did stop speaking, which enabled Else to slip out of the chamber and get on with her tasks.

With Else gone, Jaeger rounded on Meena, who immediately dropped her eyes to the flagstones. 'And what dreams did you have?' he growled. His own dreams had been torturous pictures of Evaine with Eadmund Skalleson.

With Draguta.

The three of them taunting him.

Draguta had put Eadmund on the throne of Hest. Evaine was his queen and Jaeger? Jaeger was made to watch it all.

He was in the foulest of moods.

Meena didn't dare reveal her dreams.

Jaeger had his hands on her shoulders in two strides. 'You are a *dreamer*!' he snarled, pushing his face towards hers. 'So tell me about your dreams!'

Meena swallowed. 'I saw the d-d-dragon in my dreams. What it did to Andala.'

Jaeger scowled. 'Why do I care about that? Why are you dreaming about that?'

'It... it was...' Meena didn't know. 'It was in my head when I went to sleep. A... nightmare.'

'And?'

'Irenna was killed. Her daughter was hurt.'

Jaeger blinked, quickly shutting away any feelings he might have had about that. 'And Draguta? Did you see her?' Jaeger's hands were squeezing her shoulders now, almost pushing them together.

Meena didn't know what to say.

She still wasn't convinced that she was a dreamer. Varna had never suggested that what she was dreaming might have been actual visions of things that had happened or images of what was to come. And now, she was confused, not knowing how to sort the truth from her own fantasies.

Finally, Meena shook her head, watching the fire in Jaeger's eyes intensify, almost sensing his hand move towards her face. Cringing in anticipation, she tried to think of something to say. 'I saw Evaine,' she mumbled quickly, hoping to distract him.

Jaeger's angry expression immediately changed to one of interest. 'What did you see?'

'I saw Evaine, with you.'

Jaeger cocked his head to one side and smiled.

***

It was so dark.

Cold.

Draguta tried to twist away, searching for light.

Why was she here again?

She couldn't breathe. It felt as though hands were clasped around her throat, squeezing.

Squeezing.

Yanking herself away, Draguta dropped to the ground, feeling the sharp rocks cutting into her knees. She started crawling, pulling herself forward, one hand at a time, clinging to the rocks, feeling her chest tighten.

And then the hands again.

Squeezing around her neck.

CHAPTER THIRTY SEVEN

Andala's hall was heaving with people.

Scorched and distraught, they came for the warmth and shelter of the hall. Some had lost everything, thanks to the flaming breath of the dragon and the exploding sea-fire that had devastated their homes and wiped out their livestock. Heaving too with the men and women who were standing around tables and leaning over beds, trying to give comfort and ease pain. There was no room for eating or drinking, but those with frozen bodies and numb, raw hands, who had spent the better part of the day trying to dislodge the dragon, needed feeding. And with the injured almost under control, the servants started ferrying food to the exhausted men and women who sat outside.

On the hall steps.

On benches and around tables that had been brought out of the hall and carried from nearby houses.

Isaura sat shivering beside Thorgils, waiting for him to finish his cup of ale, determined to refill it before she returned to the hall. 'You look ready to fall asleep,' she smiled.

Thorgils took another long drink, sensing her urgency to leave, watching as Mads toddled over to Ivaar, who sat some distance away on the hall steps. 'It's a big dragon,' he groaned, shaking his head at the giant beast. 'Can't believe I'm saying that, let alone trying to pull it out of the fort. It's not budging, though. Not sure it ever will. And the horses and oxen are no use. They're terrified of it.'

Isaura shook her head too, frowning as Ivaar ignored Mads and kept talking to Rork Arnesson, who had his head in his hands as he sat on the steps, still in shock over his brother's death. 'Well, I hope you get it out soon, though I don't suppose it makes much difference, does it? Not now. You can hardly rebuild that wall in a hurry.' Isaura's head was aching, and her throat hurt. She hoped she wasn't getting the sickness, though it was likely just the smoke from the sea-fire which hung over the fort like a dense cloud. She coughed. 'You don't think the dragon will come back to life, do you?'

Thorgils placed his empty cup on the snowy ground, pulling her onto his knee, eager to warm her up. 'No, they're going to take off its head soon, so you've nothing to worry about there. But there's not much we can do about the dragon either way, from what I can see. It's heavy, being a dragon, and a dead one at that. If only we had Bram. I'm sure he'd get it out of here. He was once the strongest man on Oss. Do you remember? When Eirik had that contest to see who could lift the heaviest weight? And Bram won. Ha! Eirik did like to hold a contest, didn't he?' His smile faded, thinking about his dead king and his injured uncle.

'Give me your cup. I'll fill it up, then I'll check on Bram.'

Thorgils shook his head. 'I'll fill it, you go on. Though you might need to grab Mads,' he grinned, watching as the little boy threw himself onto the snow in front of his father.

Isaura eased herself off Thorgils' knee as the familiar screeching started. 'I think I'd rather have filled your cup!' And walking off towards her tantrum-throwing son, she turned around and winked at him.

Thorgils watched her go, thinking about his uncle. He hoped Bram would recover. It had been so nice having him around again.

He didn't want to lose him.

***

'You look lost.'

Evaine reluctantly turned around. She wasn't sure that Jaeger Dragos was the right person to be talking to. The way he stared at her made her skin crawl. She was used to being stared at, of course, but not many of her admirers were that big and strong. And, apart from Eadmund, none of them had been a king.

One who was used to getting what he wanted.

It was an unpleasant day, yet despite that, Evaine had been eager for some fresh air, so she'd left the castle in search of a breeze, hoping to blow away the waves of smoke that had twisted her mind and dried her throat.

But she didn't want to go riding.

And she had quickly grown bored with the markets.

'Lost? No, I'm just going for a walk,' Evaine muttered irritably, wanting to send Jaeger on his way. Turning back around, she decided to go and find her father, who she'd seen walking towards the markets with Morana.

Jaeger walked with her.

Evaine stopped. 'Don't you need to check on something? Order someone to build you a ship or a weapon? Fight someone?'

Jaeger laughed. 'You'll make a good queen one day with insight like that.'

Evaine frowned, irritated further.

'Why don't you want my company?' he wondered.

Fingering her new necklace, Evaine tried to think of what to say, watching as the tourmaline beads sparkled, even in the dim light of the afternoon. Eventually, she sighed and started walking again, deciding that some company was better than no company at all. 'You're always staring at me.'

Jaeger smiled. 'And that's a bad thing? Being desired? A woman as exquisite as you? You should expect to be admired, for I have never seen anyone as lovely as you. It's hard for me to stop myself... thinking things. You make it impossible, Evaine.' He walked her past the ship sheds, heading for the winding gardens. It smelled so pleasant in there at this time of year, and he thought it would be the perfect place to... take in some fresh air.

Evaine pushed back her narrow shoulders, peering at him. 'Well, it is very kind of you to say, but that doesn't mean that I wish to be admired by you. I am Eadmund's woman. I will be his queen soon. He will come to Hest, and we will be married. Once Draguta has gotten rid of his wife!'

Jaeger's smile froze on his face, but he didn't let the irritation dig in too deeply. He was watching the way her eyes kept approaching his, the way her body swayed against him as she walked.

The way she had agreed to walk with him in the first place.

Evaine was doing little to dissuade him with her actions, so he was inclined to ignore her words. 'I will not stand in your way,' he said softly. 'It is meant to be. I've heard Morana and Draguta talking about it. You and Eadmund will be together soon.' Standing to one side, he motioned for Evaine to walk ahead of him, through the stone archway, into the gardens.

'What *is* this place?' Evaine wondered, inhaling the heady mix of scented flowers and herbs that drifted towards her on a warm breeze. 'It smells divine! Why haven't you brought me here before?'

Jaeger hurried to catch up with her as she ran up the path, enchanted by the pretty scenery. 'Why indeed?' he murmured, narrowing his eyes.

***

'He's struggling to breathe,' Biddy said wearily as Runa joined her at Bram's bedside. 'I'll ask Derwa to check him again. She had a brief look this morning. I'll see what she has to say now.'

Runa nodded anxiously, sitting down on the stool Biddy had just vacated. 'Please. I know Thorgils would be very upset if anything happened to him.'

'Just Thorgils?' Biddy wondered as Runa took Bram's hand.

Runa closed her eyes, ready to run away from that moment she'd always felt so ashamed of. She opened her eyes, staring at Biddy's kind face. 'No, not just Thorgils.'

Biddy smiled sympathetically and disappeared to find Derwa.

Bram's breathing was a strained rasp. It reminded Runa of how Odda had sounded before her death, and that didn't reassure her at all.

'How is he?' Ayla asked as she stopped by to check on Bram, wiping her wet hands on her apron.

'He doesn't sound very good to me.'

Ayla frowned and leaned over, her ear on Bram's chest. Looking up, she tried not to let her worry linger on her face. 'Derwa will help him, I'm sure.'

Runa blinked, hoping Ayla had a dreamer's insight that everything would be alright, but she slipped away before she could ask.

'Mother?'

Runa turned in surprise to see Fyn limping towards her on Kormac's arm. 'What are you doing?'

'He needs some fresh air,' Kormac said calmly, sensing Runa's panic. 'He needs to get stronger. A little walk will be good for him. Just a little one,' he reassured her. 'I thought I'd show him the dragon.'

Fyn looked down at Bram, who he barely remembered. Bram Svanter had come and gone from Oss as Fyn was growing up, and Fyn had few memories of him. 'Is he going to be alright?' he asked, knowing how much Thorgils cared for his uncle.

Runa looked at the way Fyn was staring at Bram and

promptly burst into tears.

***

Else returned, wielding two large baskets. One was filled with three pairs of newly repaired leather boots, and the other with a jug of buttermilk, a stack of apple pancakes, a bowl of soft cheese and boiled eggs, and a small side of pork.

Her arms felt ready to break.

Meena rushed to help her. 'Jaeger has gone,' she mumbled apologetically, hefting one of the baskets onto the table.

Else left the other basket on the floor, smoothing down her apron as she walked to the table. 'Well, more for you, then!' she said, lifting the jug out of the basket. It was barely half full now, having slopped about as she struggled up the stairs from the kitchen. 'Why don't you take a seat, and I'll make you up a plate. You look like you could do with a good meal, my lady.'

Meena's eyes darted to the door, not knowing if Jaeger was coming back. 'I... you must call me Meena.'

Else smiled. 'If you promise to eat something, I'll certainly call you Meena.'

Meena nodded reluctantly, sitting down, watching as Else pulled out her knife and dug into the pork, sawing off a thick slice.

'I've some cockles in here too. The kitchen was humming this morning. They're all on their toes, trying to make that woman happy. Things have certainly changed around here, haven't they?' She tried to keep the sadness from her voice, though it was hard to feel anything but sadness over what had happened. 'With the family gone.'

Meena realised that she recognised Else. She had been one of Irenna Dragos' servants, helping to care for her children. Nodding, she took the heavy plate Else offered her, and unsheathed her own knife, her stomach gurgling loudly.

Else pushed back the sleeves of her simple grey dress as she walked to the bed. Glancing at the fireplace in passing, she realised that she would have to go back outside and find some wood. 'These furs could do with an airing,' she noted, pulling the heavy bundle of bed furs onto the floor. 'Pity you don't have a balcony so I could hang them out for the day. But perhaps I could take them outside and give them a good beating? Unless you think the king would mind?'

Meena shrugged, her mouth too full to speak.

Else smiled. 'I will then.' And she continued to drag everything off the bed. 'It all smells a bit smoky to me. And as for this mattress...' She frowned. 'I'm not sure what that Egil did, but it looks as though he spent more time in the kitchen eating than he did doing anything in here!' Else tugged on the mattress, determined to flip it over, knocking Berard's ivory comb onto the floor with a clatter.

Meena jumped off her chair and hurried to the bed, trying to swallow a mouthful of pancake. 'I, that's... it's mine,' she mumbled as Else let go of the mattress and picked up the comb.

Meena snatched it out of her hand and turned away, feeling her cheeks redden, not knowing what to do or say. She held the comb to her chest. 'It's not mine,' she confessed, turning back around, realising that more than anything, she needed a friend. She didn't know if Else could be one or if she would tell Jaeger what she'd found, but she was determined to try.

Else took her hand, leading Meena to the bed. 'Why don't you sit down and tell me all about it?'

Meena swallowed, nodding eagerly, tears already flowing down her red cheeks.

***

'Why are you crying?' Fyn asked. 'Mother?'

Runa shook her head, trying to stop her tears, but they kept coming. 'I...' She didn't know what to say.

She did.

She did know what to say, but she was afraid.

Closing her eyes, she took a panicked breath, realising that she couldn't run away anymore. 'Sit down,' she said, opening her eyes. 'Here, you take this stool.'

Entorp helped Fyn onto the stool, then ducked his head and turned away, leaving them to talk.

'Morac and I couldn't have children,' Runa said softly, trying to meet his eyes. 'We tried, but I never once fell pregnant. He blamed me. He wanted a child more than anything. He thought it was my fault.'

Fyn frowned, feeling odd.

'They went raiding a lot when they were younger. Eirik loved it. Morac was always beside him then. Sevrin. Bram too, for a time,' Runa said, sighing wistfully as the memories came hurrying back to her. It didn't feel that long ago. 'One summer, Bram was ill. Very ill. He stayed behind when the rest of the men left. The illness took his brother, Ned. Thorgils' father. I cared for Bram while he was ill. I used to help Saari Nelberg. Bram was so sad after Ned died, but so sick himself. As he recovered, we became... close.' Runa swallowed and finally looked at Fyn, hoping not to see disappointment in his eyes.

'And?' Fyn asked quietly. 'What are you saying, Mother?'

Runa glanced at Bram, with his big, bushy Svanter beard and his broad chest and his kind face. And his hair that had once been a deep auburn red and his eyes that were closed, but she knew that they were blue, and she turned to her son. 'I'm saying that Morac isn't your father. And I wish I'd told you sooner. He didn't treat you well, and you deserved so much better. He is not a good man, but Bram,' she cried, reaching for Fyn's hand. 'Bram Svanter is.'

Fyn felt tears well in his own eyes, his mouth dropping

open in surprise.

***

'Oh.'

Meena glanced nervously at Else as they sat on the bed, wondering what she would say after hearing everything. Everything that had happened since Jaeger had first shown Meena the Book of Darkness all those months ago.

Else exhaled slowly. 'Well, you're certainly in a quickening mire, aren't you?' She glanced at Meena's tear-stained face. 'I'm not sure what to advise. That Draguta woman sounds terrifying, and if she can truly read minds and cast spells powerful enough to bring creatures back to life with that book...'

'But I'm a dreamer now,' Meena said quietly. 'Even though I don't know how to do much of anything, I'm not useless. I can't be.'

Else smiled, squeezing her hand. 'You're not, of course not, but how can you find a way to stop her? Your grandmother was an experienced dreamer, but I doubt that even someone like Varna could have stopped her.'

'Someone did.'

'Did what?'

'Stop her. Someone killed Draguta before,' Meena said, blinking rapidly. 'Someone knew how to do it. She was immortal, but someone killed her.'

Else lowered her voice. 'Do you think you could find a way to dream about that? About a way to kill her?' She shuddered, uncomfortable with speaking about such terrifying things.

Meena shuddered too, wanting to shake her head, though she found herself nodding it ever so slightly instead.

***

The air smelled sweet, and the birdsong sounded so delightful that Evaine didn't notice how close Jaeger was until it was too late. Or, at least, that was what she told herself, exclaiming in surprise when he put his hand on her knee, leaning his face towards hers. 'No!' she insisted, hurrying up from the stone bench. 'That's not why I came.'

'Then why *did* you come?' Jaeger asked breathlessly, his body throbbing with desire as he stood, grabbing her arms.

'I love Eadmund.'

'So you've said.'

Evaine tried to move, but Jaeger gripped her harder, leaning down to kiss her, pushing himself against her.

'No!' Evaine squirmed, wriggling, trying to break the hold he had on her arms, but Jaeger fought equally hard to keep her right where she was, her desperation to escape only urging him on. She panicked, hearing the warning loud in her ears, knowing that she was in trouble.

He was so strong, and she couldn't move. He was hurting her.

'No!' Evaine cried, though her voice was lost under Jaeger's forceful kisses. And then he was dragging her up the path.

Off the path.

And away into the bushes.

'Help!' Evaine shouted, shaking with terror as she tripped, twisting her ankle. 'Help me!'

Jaeger pushed her down to the ground. 'No one's going to hear you in here, Evaine,' he grunted, undoing his swordbelt and tugging down his trousers as she screamed, trying to get up. 'And if they did, what would they do?' he laughed, shoving her back onto the ground, laying his hulking weight on top of her.

***

Eadmund had no appetite.

He wanted to get everyone back to the dragon. They hadn't made any progress. Before long, the sun would head down, and they'd lose the light. He worried about what would happen when night fell. With the dragon lying across the wall, there was nothing to protect them from whatever plans Draguta was making next.

'You're wasting away!' Thorgils bellowed as he approached his friend, brandishing a leg of mutton. 'Thought you might like this.' White breath smoke swirled around his bright-red beard and his bright-red nose. 'Although, if you're not hungry...' And Thorgils slowly aimed the leg of mutton at his open mouth.

'Alright, I'll eat it,' Eadmund grumbled, snatching it out of Thorgils' hand.

'I'm thinking that we should get Ketil making mutton sticks,' Thorgils grinned, trying to take his mind off Bram. 'It's a tasty meat.'

Eadmund took a bite and swallowed, nodding his head. 'Mmmm, it is good.' He was hungrier than he'd realised, and he continued eating while Thorgils chatted away next to him. Thoughts of Evaine had intensified as the day wore on. Her voice was a panicked cry in his head now, and it was almost impossible to focus on talking or thinking anymore. Losing his appetite quickly, Eadmund wiped his mouth and turned to Thorgils, eager to get away from his distracting friend. 'Time to get everyone moving again. We've got to get this thing out of here before dark.'

Thorgils laughed. 'And you think that's possible, do you?'

'No, it's not. I doubt we'll even get it moved by winter. Not if we can't get the animals to go anywhere near it.'

'Perhaps she'll send a giant next? We could ask it to pick up the dragon and move it out of the fort before it kills us all!'

Eadmund shook his head as he walked to the next table, looking for something to drink. 'With stories like that, it's a wonder Isaura lets you near her children!' He frowned, thinking of Sigmund, which led his mind straight back to Evaine.

Hoping she was safe in Hest.

***

They kept glancing up at the sky, or, at least, at the leafy canopy, trying to guess how far along the day was. Eventually, it became apparent that they weren't going to make it to the Widow's cottage before nightfall.

'We're not far now,' Aleksander insisted, turning around to Jael, who hadn't spoken in hours.

Neither of them had. They were worried, hungry, cold, and irritated that the wood seemed to be sucking them into a trap.

Aleksander was yet to admit his fears, even to himself. He'd heard the Widow's voice in his head, directing him, but it had stopped some time ago, and now he was blind again.

'No, we're not!' Jael grumbled. 'If the Widow's cottage was anywhere around here, it could only be as wide as a tree! And I don't think that's likely. I'm not a child, Aleksander! Stop pretending that you know where we're going when it's obvious that you don't!'

Aleksander turned back around, leaving Jael to stew in her foul mood.

He pulled on the reins and dismounted. 'I need to piss.'

Jael frowned at him as she eased Tig to a stop. Her mail shirt felt as though it was crushing her lungs. She was struggling to breathe, and it had made her increasingly irritable. Reaching under her cloak, she tried to pull it away from her expanding belly and her expanding breasts, quickly realising that she needed to piss too.

Jumping down from Tig, Jael adjusted *Toothpick's* scabbard and froze.

A woman stood in the distance, motioning to her.

The same woman she'd seen before.

Aleksander walked out from behind a tree, disturbed by the strange look on Jael's face. He turned to see what she was staring at, but there was nothing there. 'What is it?'

'We have to go!' Jael said quickly, forgetting all about her bursting bladder and her foul mood. 'Now! We have to go. That way!' And she pointed in the direction she had seen the woman, sticking her foot into Tig's stirrup and throwing herself back into the saddle. 'Come on!'

***

It took some effort for Draguta to finally force herself out of bed. She felt light-headed, and her ears were ringing. Blinking slowly, she tried to open her eyes, but when she did, she realised that no lamps were burning in her chamber. There was barely any light at all.

Panicking, and remembering her dream of the cave, she searched the chamber, calling for a servant. But they were gone, and she remembered sending them all away, demanding to be freed from their pestering noises; wanting to sleep and recover for as long as she needed in total silence.

Feeling dizzy, Draguta reached for a chair, trying to catch her breath as she sat down, panting. The spell had drained her more than she'd realised, which wasn't what she needed now. And she was suddenly so cold. Her white silk nightdress was perfect for Hest's balmy nights, but it felt like winter in Tuura, and she frowned, getting angrier by the moment.

Draguta took a deep breath to steady herself and closed her eyes. She quickly opened them in surprise, and pushing herself up from the chair, she strode to the door, yanking it open, watching Meena Gallas scurrying down the corridor. 'Girl!'

Meena froze, too afraid to turn around.

'Girl!' Draguta called again. 'Come here! *Now*!'

***

Evaine hadn't spoken.

She hadn't moved when Jaeger stood and pulled up his trousers, tying his swordbelt, readying to leave.

And realising that she had no plans to stand at all, Jaeger reached down for her hand, dragging her to her feet. He glared at Evaine as she shivered before him, grabbing her chin, lifting her face. 'You wanted that just as much as I did,' he insisted, defying the truth he could see in her eyes.

Evaine felt limp and weak. Her legs were shaking uncontrollably, and she was ready to fall to the ground, but she had enough anger and strength left to spit at him.

Jaeger drew back his hand, striking her across the face.

Evaine flew backwards, landing amongst a row of flowering calendula, her head hitting the dirt with a dull thud.

'I'm the King of Hest, and one day soon, I'll be the King of Osterland too, so I will take what I want, when I want it. Best you remember that, you little whore!' And leaving her lying in the garden, Jaeger disappeared through the bushes, heading back to the path.

CHAPTER THIRTY EIGHT

Axl sat on the hall steps with Amma and Gisila, watching those heaving on the ropes, grunting and cursing, screaming and bellowing, trying to dislodge the decomposing dragon.

'I think it moved!' Amma exclaimed, standing up.

'Did it?' Gisila struggled to her feet, trying to see. 'I think you're right,' she said with a weary smile. 'I think it did, Axl.'

Axl didn't smile. If the dragon had moved, it was likely by no more than a fingertip. There was no way they were getting it out of the fort before nightfall.

'They'll have more luck tomorrow,' Amma assured him, seeing how worried he looked. 'Once the snow has gone, it will be easier, won't it? It's getting warmer. I'm sure it will melt tomorrow.'

Axl didn't want to say anything in case he revealed his fears of what the night might bring. With the wall shattered, and without his sister and her sword, they had little to protect themselves if Draguta tried something now.

***

Draguta eyed Meena as she vibrated before her, crouched over, staring at her boots. No one had ever looked as pathetic as this blithering mess. 'What were you doing outside my door?' she demanded sharply.

Meena felt ready to burst into tears, remembering what had happened to Yorik and the Followers. 'I, I, I,' she stuttered before terror gripped her again. 'I... wasn't. I... was going to find w-w-wood.'

'For who?'

'Jaeger,' Meena said. 'He, his, he was cold. I... his servant... I offered to help her. She is old.'

Draguta peered at Meena, expecting her lies to reveal themselves, but they didn't, and, in the end, she decided that either she was feeling too weak, or the girl might actually be telling the truth. 'Well, lucky for me,' she smiled, 'for I also require some things. Come inside, I shall write you a list. But you must get them promptly. Leave your wood for another time.'

Meena nodded, her eyes still on her boots as she followed Draguta inside her chamber, waiting while she wrote the list.

Trying not to imagine what gruesome items it would contain.

Finally, Draguta stood, handing the folded piece of vellum to Meena. 'You will bring these herbs to me quickly. I must make a tonic to regain my strength.' She eyed Meena as she twitched before her. 'Find my servants. Morana and Evaine too. Bring them all back with you. We have work to do!' And turning away from Meena, she yawned, heading for the balcony, eager to warm herself in the last rays of the sun.

Meena swallowed, the list rustling in her trembling hand as she hurried to the door before Draguta could make any more requests.

***

Fyn sat on the stool beside Bram's bed.

He didn't know how to feel, and though Bram was unconscious, Fyn was almost too shy to look at him, worried that he would open his eyes and catch him staring. He sighed, overwhelmed by the news that Morac wasn't his father, certain that he should feel relieved. But then there was the real possibility that his actual father might never open his eyes again and discover that he had a son.

Maybe it would be too late for both of them?

'She told you, then?' Thorgils grinned wearily as he pulled over another stool and sat down.

'You knew?' Fyn was surprised.

'I guessed. Only a few days ago, mind. There's a family look, you might say. Still, you're a little weedy to be a true Svanter. So far, anyways.'

Fyn didn't know what to say. He stared at Thorgils as though he was seeing him for the first time.

'Ha!' Thorgils laughed, patting him on the back. 'Wait till Jael hears. You and me, cousins!' He looked at Bram, and his laugh faded away, his uncle's raspy breathing sounding familiar enough to worry him.

'If you want me to take a look at him, you'd better move yourselves!' Derwa grumbled, elbowing her way towards the bed. 'Why don't you take young Fyn back to his room,' she said, pointing a finger at Thorgils. 'Then you can get back to work, doing something useful, instead of sitting here like a lump of cheese!' And she rapped Thorgils on the arm, edging past him.

Thorgils lifted his arm and frowned, standing to help Fyn to his feet. He softened his face as he took one last look at Bram. 'He's a strong man, but he lost his wife and children recently. I think his heart might be broken.'

Derwa looked up at Thorgils more sympathetically now, nodding as she turned to Bram's big chest, holding out her hands and closing her eyes.

***

'There must be something we can do to help?' Edela wondered from her chair by the fire. Ayla perched on Jael's stool, and Eydis was on the floor by Ayla's feet. 'We dreamers are more powerful together than I think any of us realises. And together, we should be able to cause Draguta some problems.'

Ayla nodded, enjoying the silence of Edela's cottage, and the opportunity to sit down. She had been caring for the injured all through the night and for most of the day, and she felt exhausted, but just as eager to see if there was anything she could do to keep them safe tonight. 'Do you have any ideas, Edela?'

'Well, the wall is broken, and the symbol is useless now, so I say we throw away our symbol stones and invite some help. What do you think? Can we reach out to someone? Eydis, your grandmother came to Ayla while she was trying to find her way to you. She came because you dreamed of her. And she was a keeper of the Book of Aurea, wasn't she, so she may be able to help us? Or Ayla, you could try to reach your mother?' Edela's eyes twinkled. She was tired, and her feet still ached, but she felt energised by the idea that they could take action.

It was better to feel as though something was possible than simply fearing that defeat was inevitable. It wasn't. It couldn't be. Not while Jael was still out there with her sword, trying to find that book.

Not while Eadmund was still here in Andala, with them.

Ayla smiled, feeling a renewed sense of hope. 'You're right. We can certainly try. I'll go before it gets dark and gather whatever herbs I can find. I'll bring anything I can think of to help us. Perhaps Biddy can show me where everything is?'

Edela nodded. 'Good! And see if you can find those pesky puppies too. Biddy and I have been trying to catch them all day, but they've been having far too much fun in the snow. I don't want to leave them out there all night, though. Jael would never forgive me!'

Ayla smiled. 'I will. Perhaps you should rest now, Edela? And you too, Eydis. We may have a long night ahead of us. I'll be back as soon as I can.'

'Yes, perhaps you should let your husband know that you'll be staying here tonight? See if Biddy can organise some extra bedding. Though, hopefully, we won't be sleeping much at all!'

***

The wine had helped Draguta feel more alert, so she continued to drink from her goblet, eager to regain her strength. Even though she couldn't taste the velvety liquid, she could feel it warming her insides.

The fire helped too.

Her servants had arrived, and after they'd endured her screeching reprimands, they'd rushed about industriously, brightening the chamber. Now it was warm and glowing with light, and Draguta felt ready to try. She was weak, but she needed to know if it would work.

If what she had seen when she was the dragon was true.

If what she had dreamed was real...

She sat at her table, shivering in anticipation.

Too impatient to gather what she needed, Draguta simply drew her knife across her palm, squeezing her hand together before digging into her wound with a finger, drawing the seeing circle. She closed her eyes and began to chant, feeling her body sway to the slow rhythm of her voice. It reminded her of Thrula, and she felt a burst of anger, extinguishing it quickly lest it dilute her focus.

And then, opening her eyes, she peered into the circle and smiled.

'Hello, Sister.'

***

Meena walked quickly, imagining that Draguta was behind her, barking at her to go faster; picturing what her face would look like if she returned to her chamber late and empty-handed.

Squinting at the list, Meena tried to decipher the odd scrawls, written so hastily that they barely looked like words at all. Finally realising that Draguta was after some bay leaves, she trotted up the path looking for a bay laurel bush. Varna had cared so much about her various herb gardens, but she had made Meena do the work to maintain them, so she knew very well where most things were planted.

The bush she was looking for was hidden away, far off the main path that ran through the winding gardens. Varna had not wanted the kitchen staff to help themselves to her most prized herbs, and the shady spot she had chosen was the perfect place to conceal them. Meena smiled, thinking about how long it had taken her to dig up the secret garden. It had been her favourite. She liked to disappear into the trees and lose herself in the silence, free from the noise of the castle and the square and her grandmother's rasping insults most of all.

Heading into the trees, Meena came to an abrupt halt, surprised to see Evaine Gallas. She was bent over, fiddling with her dress, and when Evaine lifted her head, Meena gasped in horror.

Evaine glared at her. 'What?'

She hadn't cried.

She was too angry to cry. And she didn't appreciate the look on Meena's ugly face. A look so filled with sympathy and pity that Evaine wanted to push her over. She would have if she wasn't worried about falling over herself, and breaking down into a pathetic, sobbing heap.

Meena swallowed and dropped her eyes, not knowing what to say, but knowing exactly what had happened.

'Did *he* send you?' Evaine snapped, finding it hard to talk. Her lips were already swelling, her nose too. She couldn't breathe properly. 'To make sure he hadn't killed me?'

Meena shook her head. 'Draguta did. She wants herbs.'

Evaine frowned, not caring.

'And you,' Meena suddenly remembered. 'She wants you and Morana.'

Evaine tried to smooth down her hair, opening her eyes wide as the pain in her head intensified. 'Good. Maybe she's finally going to bring Eadmund here. And when he comes...' She gritted her teeth. 'When he comes, he will kill that bastard.' And she strode past Meena, desperate to wash the stench of Jaeger Dragos away from every ruined part of her. 'And I will watch!'

***

Thorgils bent over, numb hands on his knees, trying to suck in some air. 'That's a heavy beast!' he panted. 'Even for a man like me. Made by the gods, these arms were!' He straightened up, curling an enormous bicep at his best friend.

'Which puny god made you, then?' Eadmund wondered snarkily. 'The God of Worms? *Is* there a God of Worms?' he asked, winking at Torstan, who laughed, enjoying the indignant look on Thorgils' red face.

It felt nice to have something to smile about.

Thorgils was doing his best not to smile, but he'd enjoyed the insult. Turning around, he readied an insult of his own, but he came face to face with Ivaar, and his good mood vanished.

'Runa said you're to come to the hall.'

Thorgils frowned, trying to see any clue in Ivaar's conniving eyes, but as usual, they revealed little, so he nodded to Eadmund and Torstan, and headed for the hall.

'Are we going to try again before the sun sets?' Ivaar asked coldly, turning towards the now headless dragon.

Eadmund wanted to ignore him and simply walk away, but he reminded himself that it was better to act like the king he was trying to be than a sulking child. 'We go again!' he called to his men who were flopped on the snowy ground, cold and hot at the same time. 'Let's get this dragon out of here!' He looked away from Ivaar, patting Torstan on the shoulder, following him back to the ropes.

Ivaar clenched his jaw, wanting to do anything but bow down to his brother.

Always so smug.

He shook his head, realising that he had to stop caring so much. Time had passed, things had changed, and now he had to find a new future for himself. As Jael had suggested, and Ayla had predicted, if he evened up his ledger, there was a chance his life could be his own again.

So, walking around to the rear of the dragon, away from his brother, Ivaar picked up a rope, waiting for the call.

***

'It's encouraging,' Morac insisted as he cut the almond cake in half, pushing one piece towards his scowling sister, who had just finished telling him about her dream of Draguta and Taegus. 'A start, at least. You know more about her than you did. About how she got the book in the first place.'

'Perhaps,' Morana grumbled, nibbling distractedly on the cake. 'But it does not get us closer to the ritual spell. I must find a way to see that page. I need to read the ritual, or we will never bring Raemus back.'

Morac frowned, reaching for his cup of milk. 'But how will you? If you see it in a dream, how will you be able to remember it when you wake?'

It was a fair point, but Morana dismissed it anyway. 'I'll be able to remember it. You needn't worry, Brother. If I can see it once, I can bring it to my mind as needed, I'm sure. If I can see it just once.' Her dark eyes shone with desperation.

There had to be a way to find that ritual.

Raemus' own son had betrayed him by giving Draguta the book and then abandoning him in the Dolma, refusing to bring him back. And now, the Followers were gone, so she was Raemus' only hope.

And she would not let him down.

There was a knock on the door.

Morac almost dropped his cup as he scrambled nervously to his feet, wondering who it could be. Worrying that Draguta had been outside, listening.

But it was only Meena.

'Draguta wants Morana,' she mumbled, her eyes on the basket of herbs she'd collected. 'She said she has work to do.'

Morana's eyes lit up as she creaked to her feet, leaving the rest of her cake behind. She picked up her own basket, grabbed her long wooden staff, and headed for the door.

***

Draguta was growing impatient, waiting in her chamber on her own, but finally, the door opened, and she smiled in anticipation, ready to begin. But when her servant ushered a battered-looking Evaine inside, all thoughts of what she'd been planning suddenly vanished.

Rising from her chair, Draguta glared at her servant. 'You

will help her, Brill. Tidy her up. Take her down to the baths. Throw away that dress, and find something new, then return her to me.' And without even looking at Evaine, she stalked towards the open door, disappearing without a word.

***

'There!' Aleksander was the first to spot the tiny cottage, hiding far in the distance beneath a smudge of mist in the rapidly darkening wood.

Jael blinked, relieved to see it herself. 'You're sure that's it?'

Aleksander nodded, then sniffed.

It wasn't mist.

'It's on fire!' he cried, digging his heels into Sky, urging her forward.

Jael was right behind him, leaning low over Tig, tucking her elbows in to avoid the spreading branches as they tore down the narrow path towards the burning cottage; the smoke billowing towards them now, quickly clogging their throats.

They pulled the horses to a stop some way before the cottage, looping their reins over a sturdy branch, wanting to keep them well away from the danger.

'Hello?' Aleksander called as he ran towards the cottage, watching the flames engulfing the walls, swallowing the roof. He didn't know her real name. 'Hello? Widow?'

Jael ran to the left, leaving Aleksander to head around to the right. 'Hello?'

They couldn't hear anything but the crackling of the fire as it chewed through the wooden cottage. The flames were so thirsty, and the smoke was so thick that they couldn't get close at all. They met around the back, both of them coughing, shielding their eyes from the stinging smoke.

'We have to get in there!' Aleksander screamed. 'She might

be trapped! She's got the book!'

Jael shook her head, pointing at the cottage as the roof collapsed, sparks flying into the trees. 'It's too late! Move!' And she dragged Aleksander away as the flames exploded in orange and red clusters, rising above them. She could hear the horses whinnying, reminded of how fond Tig was of running away whenever he got spooked. 'We can't do anything!' she coughed. 'Come on!'

Aleksander was reluctant to leave, but they had nothing to put the fire out with, and it was too far gone even if they had. He turned away, following Jael back to the horses as the rain came pouring down.

Jael grabbed Tig's reins, dragging him further into the trees, sheltering them both from the worst of it. Aleksander was soon beside her, holding onto Sky.

They stood there, shivering, dripping, coughing, trying not to let the disappointment crush them.

***

Jaeger lay on his bed, thinking of Evaine, wondering where Meena was. She needed to focus on learning how to become a real dreamer. He was tired of hearing her mundane mumblings about which member of his family had died. He wanted her to find ways to stop Draguta and claim the book for themselves.

The door flew open, banging against the stone wall, and Draguta stepped into the chamber, pale-faced and furious.

'What sort of a king lies abed all day when his kingdom is broken and in need of such urgent repair? When his harbour is not full of the ships needed to conquer his enemies and rule this land? What sort of a *pathetic* king decides to focus his attention on whichever woman he can force into his bed? Taking that which is not *his*!' She was almost spitting with rage. 'Are you even a Dragos, I wonder?' Draguta stopped, inhaling, cocking her head to one side. 'I'm finding it hard to remember why I need you. Why I shouldn't just kill you and find someone else to rule Hest!' She glared at him. 'You will not be required at the Crown of Stones again. You will rule this kingdom as a true king until *I* decide otherwise! And you will stay away from Evaine Gallas!'

Spinning around, Draguta's dress flapped after her as she headed for the door, leaving Jaeger on the bed, his jaw clenched, his hands curled into fists, his temper rising to a boil.

***

Bram had taken a turn for the worse, and Thorgils was holding his breath as he listened to the old healer try to explain how things stood.

'Your uncle,' Derwa muttered, sitting down on the stool. 'He's decided he's done.'

Thorgils tried to protest, shaking his head as he looked from her to Runa, glad that Fyn had been taken back to his bed. 'Bram wouldn't give up in the middle of a fight. This... what we're doing here... he wouldn't give up. He'd want to stay. He'd want to help. You don't know him. He wouldn't just leave.'

'That's what *you* think,' Derwa sighed. 'But he's been strong for everyone, and now he is tired. His body feels weak, so deeply weary. He is ready to go and be with his wife now. His children. He wants peace.'

Thorgils swallowed, scratching his head. 'But if he knew...' He looked at Runa.

'I should have told him,' Runa sniffed, ready to cry. 'I'm so sorry I didn't.'

'No, that's not what I'm saying.' Thorgils struggled to make sense of his thoughts. 'If he knew now. If he knew about Fyn *now*.

Would it make him want to stay? Could we tell him somehow?' He was desperate, grasping for any possibility. 'With serpents and dragons and dreamers and magic books, isn't there some way we could get to Bram?'

Derwa frowned, stroking her white braid. 'Well, yes, I think it's worth a try. Best you find that Ayla. She might be able to help you.'

Thorgils turned to Runa. 'Have you seen her?'

Runa shook her head. 'But Bruno is over there. Perhaps he knows?'

She hadn't even finished speaking before Thorgils was pushing his way through the busy hall in search of Bruno Adea.

***

The rain was so heavy that all they could do was shelter under the trees, getting drowned by it anyway. It was cold too. And when Jael reached up a hand to comfort Tig, she was certain that he was shivering as much as she was.

Her cloak was clinging to her too-small mail shirt, and they were both wet and clinging to her too-small tunic. She closed her eyes, trying to think about something else, though it was impossible to see anything that would help them now.

No Widow. No Book of Aurea.

And if her vision of Andala was real, there was no protection for anyone now.

Eventually, when it was fully dark, the rain eased, and they would have been able to hear one another if they'd had anything to say. The rain had doused the flames, though they doubted there was anything left of the cottage but soggy ash.

'I don't think we can m-m-make a fire,' Aleksander spluttered, shaking his head. Even his eyelashes were dripping. 'Everything's too w-w-wet. Everywhere.'

Jael nodded, too cold to move or talk. She shivered uncontrollably. 'Let's just stay h-h-here then. Wait for the sun.'

It was a miserable suggestion, but Aleksander nodded, still shaking all over after he'd finished. So they tied the horses back around the sturdy branch, took off their wet saddles and sat down, leaning their backs against the generous trunk of an ash tree with its mossy padding for a pillow.

Hoping the sun would hurry.

CHAPTER THIRTY NINE

Ayla bent over, foraging in Edela's herb garden. It was almost too dark to see, but Biddy held a flaming torch near her while she dug in the snow.

Nothing about it was ideal.

Ayla sighed as she revealed another dead plant. 'I'm not sure what more there is to find here. If anything. No one was expecting the snow. There was no time to protect the plants.'

'No, and in all honesty, Edela hadn't been tending to the garden in some time. It was quite neglected before the snow came down,' Biddy admitted. 'But there's another little herb garden I know of, by the kitchen. It's quite sheltered there. Edela helped the cook plant it years ago. Gave her all sorts of advice, I remember. Perhaps we try there? We might find something in the kitchen too.'

Ayla was already up on her feet, nodding eagerly as she brushed the snow from her dress. It was still cold. The sea-fire was all out now. Surely, it was time for the gods to bring back summer?

'Ayla!' Thorgils could see her in the glow of Biddy's torch. 'Ayla!'

Ayla froze, hearing the panic in Thorgils' voice. 'What's happened? Is it Bram?'

Thorgils nodded as he reached her, grabbing her wet hands. 'Please, you need to come and help him. He needs you!'

***

Axl looked from Eadmund to Gant.

They were sitting at a table near the hall steps, beside a flaming brazier, finishing a late supper, though they had talked more than they'd eaten, and their plates were still half full.

Their ale cups had been emptied more than once, though.

'The sickness is a problem,' Gant warned, rubbing his eyes. 'I've seen how it spread in Saala. Rexon couldn't contain it.'

'If it *is* the same sickness,' Eadmund murmured, leaning forward so as not to carry his voice too far. It wasn't the sort of conversation everyone needed to hear. 'Entorp said the Dragos' haven't shown any signs of it yet.'

'No, but three of Ulf's crew are in with the girl now.'

Axl looked troubled. It was bad timing. 'We can't have anyone near them, except Entorp. I think he should stay there, in the sheds, caring for them. What do you think?' He turned to Gant, who nodded. 'With only four needing his attention, he shouldn't be too busy for a while.'

Eadmund was less hopeful. 'There was a bad sickness in Alekka, Bram said. Last year. It destroyed his village. Most of his crew lost their families. Bram lost all of his. I hope this isn't the same.'

Gant frowned, leaning his elbows on the table, resting his chin on his hands. It had been a long day, and they had another long night ahead. 'So do I, but we can't give it much attention yet, not with what might be coming tonight.'

Axl caught Amma's eye as she walked down the hall steps, but he looked away, not wanting to invite her into the conversation; not wanting to worry her further. 'There were a few nights between the serpent and the dragon attack. Maybe the same thing will happen now? It might give Jael and Aleksander time to get back with that book?'

'That would be helpful,' Eadmund said, trying to ignore his

irritation at the mention of Jael's name. 'But now that the fort is broken, they don't need to worry about sending dragons to kill us, do they? Anything will get in through that hole.'

Axl thought of the ravens and the wolves, and he dropped his head, wondering what his father would do; still convinced that Ranuf hadn't really wanted him to be king in the first place.

Gant sensed Axl's discomfort. It had always been so hard for him to live in his sister's shadow. It might not have been obvious to Jael how much Ranuf favoured her, but every one of Ranuf's men knew what he thought of his daughter.

Axl was more like his father than either of them realised, though. And he would make a good King of Brekka; Gant was sure of it now. Choosing to support Lothar had been the biggest mistake of his life, and Gant was determined to make up for it by doing everything he could to help Axl.

Knowing that this was going to be his toughest test yet.

***

Hanna wasn't making any sense, but Marcus kept smiling at her as he held her hand. It felt cold, and he could see his breath puffing out before him in frosty clouds.

She didn't appear to notice as she babbled, her eyes glazed. He could see her brow glistening in the glow of the lamp beside her bed. Marcus tried to focus on her face, ignoring the smell of the shed his daughter was now sharing with three men, who appeared just as ill as her.

Entorp stopped by Hanna's bed, which was really just an old sheepskin and a pile of blankets on the floor. He held out a cup of water. 'She needs to keep drinking. Her lips are starting to bleed.'

Marcus took the cup with a sigh. 'I don't think she can keep it down.'

Entorp nodded. 'I know. It will be hard for her. Why don't we try to sit her up a little? It might make it easier. Just a sip will help.' And kneeling by Hanna, he placed an arm around her back, gently easing her up.

Hanna's eyes popped open, and she recoiled from him in horror. 'What are you doing to me?' she screamed, though she was so dehydrated that her voice was only a broken whisper. 'Get away from me! Where's Aleksander? Where is he? He will save me! Aleksander! Help! Help me!' And she fell limply against her father's chest.

Marcus swallowed, not wanting to look at Entorp; not wanting to see his worst fears revealed to him. He held Hanna firmly, whispering to her. 'Aleksander is coming back. He's coming back to you. You have to hold on for him, though, don't you?' Tears stung his eyes, and he felt his body shake. 'You have to be strong now and wait for him. Be here when he returns.'

Hanna didn't say anything.

Marcus moved her away from his chest, looking down at her face. Her eyes were closed, and he panicked. 'Hanna?'

***

They lay together, wet, tired, and cold.

Aleksander didn't want to move. Jael's head was on his shoulder; she'd stayed that way for some time. Her chest rose and fell steadily against him, and he didn't want to wake her. His entire left side had gone numb, but he didn't move, for if there was a chance that she was dreaming of something to help them, it was worth all the discomfort in the world.

***

Ayla stood by Bram's bed, nodding in agreement as she listened to Derwa. She had always sensed the pain and sadness that Bram had worked so hard to mask with a grin and a twinkle in his eyes.

Derwa peered up at her. 'Jael Furyck did it,' she said. 'Jael went and convinced Edela to come back. Seems like if she could, you can, you being a proper dreamer.'

Ayla nodded, though she didn't feel confident. 'I'll try.' She turned to Thorgils, who appeared to be holding his breath as he stood behind her with Isaura. 'If you can slip off one of his arm-rings. Or, if he has his wedding band? Something to connect me to him.'

Thorgils pulled back Bram's fur and wriggled off his uncle's plain silver wedding band, handing it to the dreamer.

Ayla took the ring, glancing at Isaura. 'If you'd like to, you can drum for me. I'll go back to Edela's cottage and do the dream walk there. It's nice and quiet.'

Isaura was eager to help. She nodded, squeezing Thorgils' hand, trying to get his attention. 'Do you want to come or stay here?'

'I'll stay,' Thorgils muttered, looking at Runa, whose eyes remained on Bram. 'I'll stay.'

Ayla turned to Biddy. 'Can you show me where this kitchen garden is? Maybe we can find some mugwort and dandelion there? Anything to help get me into a trance would be good.'

Biddy nodded, turning away as Isaura left to find her cloak.

'Try not to worry,' Ayla said, smiling at Thorgils. 'I'll do what I can.'

***

They couldn't wake Hanna, and eventually, Entorp had to go and help one of Ulf's men, who had started bellowing in distress. He appeared to be hallucinating too.

Marcus stayed, kneeling by Hanna's side, holding her hand, and when the pain became too much, he grabbed what blankets weren't being used, made himself a little bed, and lay down beside his daughter.

When Hanna had arrived in Tuura looking to meet her father, Marcus had not wanted to acknowledge her. Not at first. As the elderman, it had been his job to keep secrets, and Hanna quickly became his biggest secret of all. Now he was surprised to realise how little it truly mattered. The Following had destroyed the temple and the life he had spent so long making for himself.

And he didn't care in the slightest.

He would sacrifice it and anything else, just to have her well again, to have a chance to be a proper father. She deserved that after growing up without one, and especially after losing her mother.

Marcus closed his eyes and placed a hand on Hanna's arm, feeling the intense waves of heat rising from her, trying to imagine Daala, Mother of the Gods, coming to save his daughter.

***

Eadmund was growing increasingly disturbed by the panicked voice in his head. He had worked hard to focus on the dragon, on the people who needed his help, on thinking about ways to protect them. But his attention inevitably wandered back to Evaine, and he felt himself enter a near-constant state of anxiety. He was on edge, ready to scream, not wanting to talk to anyone in case they interrupted his thoughts.

He wondered if he had the sickness. His brow felt sweaty. His arms were weak, though he had spent much of the day pulling on the dragon. Sighing, he admitted defeat at last. 'I'm going to try and get some sleep,' he yawned. 'I've got second watch tonight.'

Thorgils nodded distractedly, slumped over on the stool by his uncle's bed.

'Runa's giving me her bed in Fyn's room. I think she wants to stay in the hall near Bram, so I'll be in there if anything happens. Just come and get me.'

Thorgils didn't even look around.

Eadmund patted his friend on the shoulder.

'I remember when my father died,' Thorgils said slowly. 'Sitting by his bed. Waiting. Bram nearly died too. You remember?'

Eadmund nodded. They had been ten-years-old. He remembered that summer well. A lot of Osslanders had died.

'When Bram recovered, he tried to cheer me up, tried to make me laugh, saying he'd won the bet with my father over who was the tougher bastard. They'd fought every which way they could to prove once and for all who was the toughest Svanter. And when they were both faced with that sickness, Bram had come out the victor.' Thorgils tried to raise a smile. 'You know what else I heard? Not from Bram, but others said that Bram survived because my father was so unhappy. That even death was better than having to stay married to Odda. They said Bram survived because he was the only one who wanted to live.' Thorgils dropped his head to his hands. 'And now...' he mumbled. 'Now, he doesn't want to live at all.'

***

Morana was surprised by Draguta's lack of interest in her arrival. She expected to be issued orders or handed some long list of ingredients, but Draguta ignored her, leaving her to sit at the round table, awaiting her instructions.

Which never came.

Eventually, Meena arrived, shaking nervously, worried that she had taken too long to gather everything on the list. She looked from Morana to Draguta, sensing the tension in the silent chamber.

'Did you have to go to Saala for my herbs?' Draguta grumbled as she walked in from the balcony.

Meena shook her head, staring at the holes in her boots. 'I couldn't catch a bat.'

Snatching the basket out of Meena's arms, Draguta peered inside. The chamber was bright, and she quickly saw that everything she needed had been found. 'Well, at least you did, in the end.' She looked up as the door opened, and Evaine walked in, looking much fresher in a pale-blue dress, with her hair washed and brushed till it shone. But there was no hiding her bruises. Her face was swollen, and her nose had almost doubled in size. One of her eyes had closed, and her lips were cut. There was a redness to her entire face. Like a rash.

She didn't look like herself at all.

Morana felt a spark of anger shoot through her body, but she didn't move as Evaine trudged towards the table.

'Well, it is not quite how we planned for you to look when Eadmund arrived, is it?' Draguta noted drily.

Evaine's angry resolve suddenly crumbled. 'What will he do?' she panicked. 'When he sees me? What will he do?'

'Who? Eadmund?' Draguta wondered, motioning for Evaine to join them at the table. 'I should imagine he'll do whatever we tell him to. But what he will *not* do is kill Jaeger. He is welcome to try, of course, and no one would blame him. But, for all his very obvious flaws, Jaeger is still my choice to be king. His heirs will rule Osterland one day, so Jaeger is not going anywhere, and nor are you,' Draguta murmured, reaching for Evaine's hand, demanding her attention. 'Not until Eadmund is here to keep you safe. You will remain in my chamber until he arrives.' She held up her other hand to quell Evaine's panic. 'Don't worry, nothing will happen to you while you're in here.'

Evaine's face was aching, and her lips were so swollen that it hurt to speak. She tried anyway. 'But how *can* Eadmund come? You tried before. How can he come now?'

'Ahhh, well, Thrula was not sacrificed in vain. She destroyed the Furycks' fort. And more importantly, she brought my sister out of hiding. She had to reveal herself to help them, and in doing so, she showed me everything I needed to see. No symbol can stop me now,' Draguta smiled, turning to Meena, who stood frozen to the spot. 'Come to the table, girl. It is time for us to see if we can find Eadmund Skalleson!'

***

'How's Bram?' Fyn asked as Eadmund removed his swordbelt, sitting down on the opposite bed with a long sigh.

'The same,' Eadmund said quietly, 'and you should be sleeping.' He wasn't looking for conversation. He needed to be up soon. Bending over, he untied his wet boots, scuffing them off, trying to wriggle some life into his frozen toes. 'You can't help anyone but yourself tonight, so get some sleep, Fyn.' And pulling back the fur, Eadmund fell into bed, his mind instantly filled with pictures of Evaine as he drifted off to sleep.

***

Evaine looked on anxiously, her lips slightly parted, barely breathing as Morana started to chant, hoping that this time it would work.

Draguta smiled calmly, watching Morana, knowing that this time it would most certainly work.

***

'This is a bad idea, Eadmund!' Thorgils warned from the railings. 'A bad idea!' He frowned at Eirik, who was too busy smiling at his son to notice.

'Don't listen to him, Eadmund!' Torstan called. 'You can beat her! Just watch that leg!'

Jael rolled her eyes, tightening her grip on the wooden sword. 'Have they always talked this much? Your big-mouthed friends?'

Eadmund nodded as he paced around in front of his wife, his eyes focused, watching for any hint of movement. 'Always. Not me, though. I prefer to say everything I need to with my sword.'

Jael burst out laughing, jerking quickly to the side as he charged her, stumbling into the space she'd just left. Righting himself, Eadmund spun around as Jael lunged at her husband, cracking her sword against his.

Eadmund stepped back, trying to catch his breath. 'You're quite sneaky.'

'Sneaky?' Jael smiled, moving her eyes to his lips. 'You mean *skilled*? I am, in many ways. Wouldn't you agree?'

Eadmund wasn't about to be distracted. 'Do you try that on everyone you fight?' he wondered, thrusting forward with a low strike which Jael easily parried, spinning away, enjoying herself.

'Only the ones I like.' Dropping to the ground, she swept her leg around, tripping him over before he could jump backwards.

Eadmund fell, rolled, and scrambled to his feet, not letting her trap him.

Eirik cheered, remembering that it hadn't been long since Eadmund had taken half a day to simply roll out of bed.

Jael growled impatiently, walking over to Thorgils, who was leaning on the railings, leaving Eadmund to dust himself off. 'Should I kick him in the head, do you think?' she mused loudly. 'Or in the back?' She kept her eyes on Thorgils' face. It was a dull afternoon, and neither of them needed to squint to see, so when Thorgils' eyes deviated ever so slightly to the right, Jael spun around in a flash, snapping her leg up into the side of Eadmund's head, hoping to find the right speed to knock him over without knocking him out.

She didn't find it.

Eadmund flew sideways, landing in the dirt with a hefty thump.

The Osslanders watching around the Pit roared with laughter.

Eadmund didn't move.

Jael stared at him, wondering if it was just a ploy, but then she saw the blood dribbling from his ear. 'Eadmund?' Rushing forward, she crouched over his still body, before turning back to the railings. 'Thorgils!' she cried. 'Thorgils! Eadmund needs your help! Now! Go and find him! Wake up, Thorgils! He's in danger! Hurry!'

Then Jael was gone, and the Pit was gone. Eirik and Torstan were gone too.

And Thorgils was standing before Eadmund, who lay on the ground with his ear bleeding, Jael's urgent cries echoing in his head.

CHAPTER FORTY

Ayla felt oddly nervous. She had always been able to slip into a trance with relative ease, and she'd done so without the aid of herbs many times. She knew that it was just tiredness tricking her into a lack of confidence.

Adjusting herself on the floor, she exhaled loudly, trying to shut out the voices in her head.

'When Jael came to me,' Edela said, sensing Ayla's panic, 'I heard her. I'm not sure what I thought before, but after she was there, in that cave with me, she was all I could think about. Her voice made me feel less alone. It reminded me of all that I didn't want to let go of. I fought hard to come back because she came to me.'

'Well, I hope I can give Bram as much reason to stay as Jael did for you.'

'You will,' Edela assured her as she retreated into the shadows, sitting back in her comfortable chair, enjoying the warmth of its fur padding against her back.

Glad that she wasn't the one kneeling on the floor.

Isaura started drumming, noticing that Ayla had closed her eyes. Eydis was sitting on the bed, holding onto the puppies. It was quiet now, apart from the crackle and pop of the fire and the sound of her own heartbeat, loud in her ears.

Ayla could feel the paltry bundle of half-dead herbs she had gathered, limp and cold in her hands, but, she thought, taking a slow breath, trying to relax her tension... they would help her.

They would help her get lost and then, hopefully, find her way to Bram.

She smiled sadly, thinking of Bram out on his ship, doing everything he could to save Isaura and the children in that terrible storm. Bram, who didn't know that his second chance was waiting right here for him.

Throwing the herbs onto the flames, Ayla started chanting.

***

Thorgils struggled off the floor with a creaky groan. Pulling on that dragon all day had made him feel like an old man. Quickly checking on Bram, he made his way through the tangle of sleeping bodies and tables, trying to adjust his eyes to the dull light from the low fires. He had no idea how long he'd slept for, but too long was likely the answer.

It had always been the answer, according to his mother.

Frowning, Thorgils wrapped his cloak around his shoulders and reached for his swordbelt. His dream was still with him, but it wasn't how he remembered that day. Jael had kicked Eadmund in the head, but Eadmund had sat up in a grump, annoyed with himself, ready for another go at her. They'd all had to listen to his complaints about ringing ears for weeks afterwards, but there had never been any blood.

Thorgils ducked behind the curtain, shivering. It was cold in the corridor without the warmth of bodies and fires. He quickly found Fyn's chamber and eased the door open, not wanting to wake him up.

Fyn was wide awake, though. He recognised Thorgils' enormous silhouette as it filled the door frame. 'Is it Bram?' he asked anxiously, trying to sit up.

'No, Bram seems the same. I came to check on Eadmund.'

He couldn't see Eadmund.

'He left a while ago,' Fyn yawned, though he wasn't sleepy. He was uptight with worry at the thought that his real father was going to die without ever knowing about him. 'I guess his watch was starting.'

Thorgils nodded. 'I must have slept for longer than I thought. You go back to sleep. And try not to worry. Everyone is hard at work on Bram. He's not getting away from us that easily.'

Fyn smiled, comforted by Thorgils' words.

Thorgils closed the door and turned down the corridor, still half asleep, ready to be all the way asleep, wondering if he could find somewhere more comfortable than the floor. Pushing his way through the curtain, back into the hall, he froze, all the way awake now as Jael's face came rushing back to him.

She had screamed at him, urging him to find Eadmund.

He was in danger, she warned.

He needed help.

And cursing himself for being so slow-witted, Thorgils ran for the doors.

***

'We shall leave her now,' Draguta decided, glancing at Morana, who sat at the table, lost in her trance. 'Your mother will bring Eadmund to us. She controls him now. She always has, I suppose, but now she *is* Eadmund. He will do anything she commands.'

Evaine might have smiled at the thought of seeing Eadmund soon if it wasn't for her aching face and the pain in her heart, not to mention the intense discomfort between her legs. She couldn't decide if she wanted to scream or cry. Reaching up, she felt around her nose, and then the tears came like a torrent, dripping onto the table as she bent her head forward, hiding her face.

'Here,' Draguta said softly. 'Come away and sit by the fire. It's best that you don't ruin my seeing circle. I don't want to have to re-cast it.'

Evaine allowed herself to be led away to a chair in front of the fireplace, where she sat mutely, staring at the flames. It was far too hot to truly enjoy a fire, but something about those mesmeric flames calmed her down.

The thought that Eadmund was finally coming was oddly unsettling.

And as much as she didn't want to relive what Jaeger had done to her, Evaine was desperate to know if she was somehow to blame.

Had she encouraged him? Led him on?

In the end, Evaine sighed, realising that Jaeger would have taken what he wanted even if she'd tried to fight him off with a sword. Nothing was going to stop him, not once he had her alone.

'You!' Draguta barked at Meena, trying to shut out Evaine's droning thoughts. 'You will go back to Jaeger and keep him amused. Entertained. Far away from Evaine!'

Meena gulped, terrified by the thought, but she nodded mutely and headed for the door.

***

'Where's Eadmund?' Thorgils called up to the ramparts by the harbour gates.

He got a few shadowy shrugs back. They were Brekkans, he could tell, but everyone knew who Eadmund was. He had taken on a more prominent role in the fort since Jael had left.

Thorgils quickened his pace, blowing on his hands as he

hurried around the wall, looking up, not seeing any sign of his friend. 'Have you got Eadmund up there?' he yelled to a bunch of Osslanders.

'No!'

Thorgils frowned, sensing movement, and as he turned, his heart pounded at the sight of a familiar shape running towards him.

'What did you *do*?' Thorgils grumbled as Torstan came to a panting stop before him.

They stood in the bright glow of the moon, and Thorgils was quickly aware that Torstan had made an effort to stop Eadmund from leaving.

His nose and mouth were both bloody.

'He punched me, took a horse. He's gone! I couldn't stop him. I tried!'

'Tell Isaura where I've gone!' Thorgils cried, running around the dragon. 'I'll be back as soon as I can!'

Torstan ran alongside him. 'I'm not letting you go after him by yourself! He's not right. Something's wrong!'

'We know that!'

'No, something's *really* wrong this time!' Torstan insisted as they came across Ivaar, who was the last person that either of them wanted to come across at that moment.

Thorgils grimaced, but there was no time to worry about Ivaar. He turned to Torstan, grabbing his shoulders. 'Just tell Isaura. I have to go!'

Ivaar frowned. 'What's happened?'

They ignored him.

'And tell Runa too! Make sure someone's with Bram!' And running again, deciding that Torstan was the worst person to trust to do anything, Thorgils disappeared around the dragon, heading for one of the stable blocks that was still standing, hoping to find a big, fast horse.

***

Bram was on his ship.

Red Ned.

He'd named it for his older brother, who he'd idolised, whose death had shaken him, and who he still missed, even now.

He loved his ship, but not as much as he'd loved his family, so he was sailing to find them. There was no life without them in it, only days that turned into nights and mornings without hope of anything ever feeling right again.

His smile was a trick to fool everyone into thinking that they didn't need to ask him if he was alright. A way to keep them at bay, worrying about other people with bigger problems.

Now he didn't need to pretend. Pretending was so tiring.

Now he could just sail to find his family again. He could be with them forever.

'But what if I said that someone needed you here? Would you abandon them? Run away? Someone like you, Bram? Someone with a heart as big and gentle as yours? I don't think you would. Not you.'

He didn't turn around; she wasn't going to stop him.

'Fyn needs you to come back,' Ayla said softly, walking up beside him, following his gaze towards the horizon as the sun rose, turning the sky a soft, golden pink. 'He's always needed you, Bram. And now you're here, together. You can't leave him. Not when he finally knows the truth. Not when you do.'

Bram frowned.

'Runa never told you about Fyn because she felt as though she'd done something wrong, being with you as she had. But she knew he was yours the moment he stirred inside her belly with his big feet. Morac could never father a child, you see. Fyn was always yours, Bram, but she didn't know how to tell either of you until it was almost too late.'

Bram could feel tears sliding down his hairy cheeks, but he didn't turn around.

'Morac mistreated Fyn because he knew the truth, so your son grew up thinking he was worthless. Wishing he had a different father. One who loved him. Trying so hard to please the one who didn't. Morac punished Fyn, and Runa too. They both suffered at his hands.'

The sea was so calm, yet the ship kept moving forward, edging towards the horizon, but Bram could feel some discomfort now, watching as the sky darkened before them.

'Come back, Bram,' Ayla whispered. 'Come back for your son.'

***

Eadmund had ordered the main gates opened, and Thorgils spent the first part of his journey growling to himself, wondering which fool had followed that order. Eventually, he conceded that it was hard to say no to a king, even if that king was an idiot.

Not an idiot, he reminded himself, shaking his head.

Eadmund was in trouble. Though Thorgils didn't imagine that he would welcome being saved.

Not by him.

***

Eadmund rode without stopping, though he knew that the horse he had taken wouldn't last long at such a punishing pace. As desperate as he was to get to Hest, he wouldn't make it there if he thrashed his horse to death.

Whoever's horse it was.

It certainly wasn't Leada. She was in no condition to ride anywhere. But the horse he had chosen was fast. And Eadmund was determined to ride him until he could be confident that no one was following him, then rest the horse and ride all day. He had no idea how long it would take to get to Hest, but he didn't let that thought take hold. He focused on Evaine, listening to the voice in his head, urging him on. He would be with her soon, it promised.

Soon.

***

Meena had no idea what time it was when she crept into the chamber, but it was dark, and she could hear Jaeger snuffling lightly as he slept. Else had still not moved in, and Meena felt worried about what Jaeger would do to her, reminded of Evaine's bruised face. Her shoulders curled forward, anticipating what might happen if he woke up.

She edged towards the bed, swallowing, saliva flooding her mouth. Then she stopped and took a deep breath, trying to calm her panic. She hadn't remained in Hest to be who she'd always been. She had stayed to help, to get the book away from Morana, and now, Draguta. She was strong enough to survive whatever Jaeger did to her.

She had so far.

And even though her heart raced and her legs shook, Meena started walking towards that familiar bed again, trying to convince herself that all the answers she needed were waiting in her dreams.

***

Aleksander cried out in pain, and Jael jerked awake. 'What? What's happened?' she croaked, reaching for her sword. Confused. Not knowing where they were.

Sitting up. Against a tree. Wet through.

Cold.

Aleksander pulled away from her. The left side of his body had fallen asleep, and moving was excruciating. 'Nothing, nothing. Need to move,' he grunted, deciding that even the sodden ground would be better than leaning back against that tree. He was wet anyway. 'Going to lie over there.'

Jael mumbled and followed him, overcome by the need to stretch out. She glanced around through barely open eyes as they shuffled through the soaking carpet of leaves, certain she'd heard something. But then she remembered the cottage and decided that it was probably just the walls slowly crumbling. The rain had doused the flames, but the building itself wasn't at rest.

Nor were they, Jael thought as she lay down in the leaves and rested her head on her hands, imagining Vella tucked into her chest, keeping her warm.

***

Ayla lay on the floor next to Eydis, trying not to cough. She didn't want to wake anyone. Biddy had aired out the house after the dream walk, shooing the smoke on its way, but Ayla knew from experience that the smoke wouldn't leave her alone for days. It would just sit there, tickling the back of her throat until she was croaking, in constant need of water.

She yawned instead, wondering if she had helped Bram.

She didn't know where those words had sprung from. Runa had certainly never revealed anything to her. Not like that.

Ayla wondered if it was all true.

If it was enough to convince him to come back.

'Ayla,' Eydis whispered, reaching out for her in the darkness.

Ayla pushed away the furry dog who had curled into her chest and grabbed Eydis' hand. 'I'm here.'

'It's Eadmund,' Eydis sobbed. 'He's gone!'

***

Aleksander slept so soundly in the wet leaves that he barely heard the voice in his head. It was familiar, almost comforting now, but he was so tired. Nothing was going to wake him from his sleep.

Not even her.

'The symbol tree. You must find the symbol tree, Aleksander,' she whispered desperately, her voice slowly disappearing into the darkness.

***

Isaura found her way to Edela's door, and when Ayla ushered her inside, she was relieved to see that everyone was up. A fire was blazing, and Biddy was handing around cups of lemon balm tea.

'You again,' Edela smiled, though she looked tired and worried as she sat in her chair, watching the flames dance before her. 'I didn't think we'd be seeing each other so soon.'

'You know about Eadmund, then?' Isaura wondered as she

hurried to the fire and held out her shaking hands. She hadn't stopped shaking since Torstan had banged on her cottage door.

Ayla nodded. 'Eydis had a dream. She saw Morana calling him to Evaine's side.'

Isaura swallowed. 'Thorgils has gone after him.'

'Has he now?' Edela's eyes were wide. 'Well, I do hope Thorgils realises it's not Eadmund he's chasing. Not anymore. He won't hesitate to hurt anyone who gets in his way.' She closed her mouth, realising that tiredness had loosened her tongue. 'But, of course, Thorgils can look after himself, can't he?'

Isaura nodded, not knowing what she thought anymore. She didn't want to believe that Eadmund was lost to Evaine and Morana, but if Thorgils got in his way...

***

Thorgils' horse was thundering across a flat expanse of open land, his path lit by a bright moon and a sea of stars above him. He almost yelled out, certain he could see a shape moving in the distance for the first time. It was very small, but not many things could be moving that fast at night, heading in that direction, he was sure.

Unless, perhaps, it was a wolf?

Thorgils shrugged that thought away, wide awake now in the cool night air, wondering just what he was prepared to do when he caught up with Eadmund.

***

'Why is she bringing Eadmund to Evaine now?' Edela mused,

sipping her tea. None of them were going back to sleep. There was too much to talk about. They had no swords or spears to defend the fort, but they were trying to think of anything they could do to stop Draguta. 'Why now?'

'Because of the symbol. It's not working anymore. None of them are,' Ayla said from the floor.

'Which means that Jael and Aleksander are not safe either. If Draguta could find Eadmund, she will find them too,' Edela murmured.

'And the Widow,' Eydis said thoughtfully. 'The Widow is Draguta's enemy. Draguta wants to kill her too.'

Biddy swallowed nervously. 'But Jael and Aleksander might be with the Widow. Perhaps right now? If she can find one of them, she'll find all of them!'

'Can we do another dream walk?' Isaura wondered. 'Warn Jael?'

Edela shook her head. 'I cannot, and Ayla is too weak. Besides, there is little Jael could do if we warned her now. There is no easy way out of that wood. But don't worry,' she began, trying to comfort herself just as much as everyone else. 'Jael has opened herself up to her dreams now. If anyone is going to sense that something is wrong, it's her.'

***

Meena was standing by Draguta's bed, watching her sleep.

Why?

Panicking, she tried to move, wanting to hurry to the door.

Afraid of waking her.

But her boots wouldn't move.

She held her breath, watching as a hooded figure eased into the chamber, silently closing the door, quickly scanning the room.

Draguta stirred, grumbling in her sleep, rolling over.

The figure froze, glancing around, but, apart from Meena, Draguta was alone.

Her chamber was dark. There was no fire. No candles were burning. But even in the near-total darkness, Meena could see the silvery glimmer as the figure tiptoed towards Draguta's enormous bed, clasping a knife.

Shaking more urgently now, Meena kept trying to move her feet, wondering if she should say something. Not knowing why she was there at all.

She blinked, finally realising that she was having a dream.

Was she?

Creeping to the edge of the bed, the figure jammed the knife into Draguta's neck, drawing it out as she yelped, before plunging it deep into her back. Draguta tried to turn over, to scream for help, but her cries were quickly stifled as the figure left the knife sticking out of her back and grabbed a pillow, covering Draguta's last breaths.

Meena gasped, desperate to tap her head.

She heard a commotion outside the door.

'My lady?'

Meena didn't recognise the voice, but the hooded figure threw away the pillow and quickly felt around for the knife. Drawing the blade out of Draguta's back, it hurried towards the balcony as the chamber door edged open.

'My lady?'

In the darkness, the figure didn't see a low stool placed beside a chair, and it tripped, tumbling to the floor, the knife flying out of its hand, clattering across the flagstones, towards the wall.

Sliding out of sight.

Meena watched as the figure hurried to its feet and slipped through the open balcony doors.

'Are you alright, my lady?'

A man's voice. Meena didn't recognise it.

'One of your servants reported seeing someone enter your chamber. I came to see if you had been disturbed. If anything was wrong.'

There was no answer.

'My lady?'

CHAPTER FORTY ONE

Morning dawned, and it was almost warm.

Aleksander stood, yawning in the dappled early light that was struggling in through the trees. He was wet through, but it almost felt like summer again, and he felt cheered by that. Then he turned towards the cottage in the distance and didn't feel cheered at all.

'So that part wasn't a dream,' Jael sighed as she stood up next to him, her shoulders sinking in disappointment. 'Do you think she was in there?'

'The Widow? I hope not. She would've had a warning, wouldn't she? She seems to see everything bad that's coming for us, so she must have seen what was coming for her.'

Jael wasn't sure, though she was too hungry to think clearly yet. 'We need some food,' she decided, glancing at the pile of ash and charred wood - all that was left of the Widow's cottage now. 'And I think I know where we can find what we need for a fire!' And leaving the horses to eat a big breakfast of soggy grass, she walked down the tunnel of trees towards the cottage.

Aleksander's feet were wet and cold, desperate for a fire, though he felt hesitant about following her. Someone had burned down that cottage. Someone knew where it was. Probably knew who was in it too.

And if that someone could find their way through the Widow's symbols, there was nothing protecting them anymore.

***

'What a delightful morning!' Draguta exclaimed as she walked out onto the balcony, enjoying the bright glow of sunshine spreading across the sparkling harbour. Sighing happily, she squinted, pleased to see that the piers were growing in length. There were no ships yet, but it lifted her spirits to see some progress.

Turning around, she caught sight of Evaine, who had slept on a mound of pillows and furs by the fire, groaning and sniffing all night. She was a hideous mess, though there was little Draguta could do about it now, except try to keep her as quiet as possible.

And far away from Jaeger.

'My dear girl, but aren't you excited? To think that Eadmund is hurrying to your side?' Draguta clasped her hands together as she glided back into the chamber, looking for something to drink. 'Hurrying to you and running far away from his pathetic wife. Isn't that what you've always wanted?'

Evaine was desperate to see Eadmund, but she was suddenly fearful of what he would think of her. What if Jaeger had broken her nose? She was still struggling to breathe and had barely slept because of it. She couldn't see out of one eye and could only imagine how horrific she actually looked.

Eadmund would be revolted by her, surely?

Draguta smiled. 'Eadmund is bound to you. He truly believes that he loves you, so no matter how disgusting you look, he will still want you, I promise.'

Evaine frowned, not comforted by that. She lifted a hand to her face, feeling around her puffy cheeks.

'I shall have my servant go to your chamber. She will bring your things to you, won't you, Brill?' Draguta said, staring at the dour-looking, long-faced creature who was busy making her bed. 'Good! Then you shall organise our breakfast. We will eat in here. And go and find Morana and that useless girl too. We must plan our day!' Her eyes wandered to the book, and she inhaled, feeling it calling to her.

Eager to begin.

***

Meena's dream had woken her well before there was any sign of the sun. It wasn't the only dream she'd had about Draguta during the night, but it had been the most disturbing.

She had lain awake for hours, desperate not to fall back to sleep, which was easy as her mind was jumping with questions.

Who had done it?

Who had killed Draguta?

And what had happened to that knife?

At last, when the sun was up and its bright rays were streaming in through the window, Meena turned to Jaeger and exhaled, relieved to be out of the darkness.

Jaeger opened his eyes, staring at her. 'Did you have any dreams?' he croaked with a sleepy frown. Meena squirmed, but Jaeger grabbed her face. 'Meena?' he growled.

And then, a knock at the door.

***

Eadmund knew he was being followed, so he'd only let his horse rest for the shortest of breaks, leading him to a stream, encouraging him to drink. He hoped that the brief respite would be enough for them both to carry on through the day. He needed to put some distance between himself and Thorgils.

It was definitely Thorgils following him.

That bush of red hair didn't belong to anyone else.

But Thorgils wouldn't stop him.

Nothing was going to stop him from getting to Evaine now. She needed him, and he wouldn't let her down. Eadmund thought of Sigmund briefly, confident that between Tanja and Runa, his son would be well cared for.

Sigmund didn't need him now, but Evaine did. He could feel her panic. It was as though she was in pain, crying out to him.

He had to hurry.

***

Breakfast had been a perfectly charred salmon that Aleksander had caught in the stream running around the back of the Widow's cottage.

They both felt better after eating something hot, though when they returned to the simmering remains of the cottage, any good cheer was quickly extinguished. Sifting through the ashes with long sticks, they couldn't see anything that resembled a person or a book. Everything they touched crumbled. The heat of the fire had been intense, like a well-stacked pyre.

Thanks to the rain, though, it was all wet and soggy now.

'We're not going to find anything,' Jael said, at last, shaking her ashy hands. 'We should leave. Perhaps it was all a trap? Leading us away from the fort so Draguta could attack it? We should get back as quickly as we can.' She turned around, frowning. It made no sense. Why hadn't the Widow seen this coming?

And if she had?

'She didn't come to you, did she?' Jael wondered, throwing away her stick. 'While you were sleeping?'

Aleksander shook his head. 'No.' He threw away his

own stick and followed Jael as she looked around the cottage grounds. The surrounding area was an ashy bog. The sun was trapped above the thick tree canopy, and it felt dark, almost airless.

Jael lifted up her boots which had quickly sunk into the swampy ground. 'I say we go. I can't see anything. Can't feel anything either.'

Aleksander nodded and turned to leave, disappointed.

He spun back suddenly, staring at Jael.

Not at Jael, but at the tree behind her. Squinting, he hurried towards it, placing his hand on the roughened bark, pushing a finger into the indentation.

Following the contours of the shape.

Of the symbol.

And then he remembered.

***

Morana had crept out of the castle while it was still dark, eager to get to Morac's cottage before Draguta found her. She would be required to watch Eadmund until he arrived in Hest, she knew, but she was desperate to dig into Yorik's books before anyone was up. She felt exposed and vulnerable, and Varna's books had revealed little that could help her protect herself.

Not from someone like Draguta.

Whatever she was.

Yorik had liked to talk – far too much – but he'd also liked to read, and Morana knew that amongst his own journals was a vast collection of books that had been passed down through The Following over the centuries. Morac had taken a look for clues about the ritual, but Morana was hoping to find something to keep Draguta out of her head long enough for her to find that missing page in her dreams.

'What happened to you yesterday?' Morac wondered from his stool by the fire. He was still half asleep, having been roused from his bed by his impatient sister while it was still dark.

Morana barely heard him. She was running her finger under a tricky phrase in a book that had captured her attention. Old Tuuran. Not easy for most to understand. Frowning, she turned the page. Draguta was more than just a dreamer, she was sure. But what? 'Happened?' she mumbled, suddenly remembering the mess Jaeger had made of Evaine's face. That wasn't something she could keep from Morac. Evaine was going to look like that for weeks to come. 'Evaine...' she began.

'What?' Morac was instantly on edge, leaning forward.

'Jaeger raped her.'

Morac opened his mouth in horror. He closed it, blinking rapidly, watching as the water bubbled in the cauldron - tiny, hot bubbles bursting towards the surface - and he saw his favourite image of Evaine as a little girl, playing on the floor by his feet.

And he looked up at his sister, ready to kill Jaeger Dragos.

***

Thorgils was hungry, cold, and tired.

And not going to stop.

He'd come too far for that now. Eadmund's horse was faster than his, or perhaps it was that he was heavier than Eadmund? Whatever the reason, he never seemed to gain any ground. Eadmund and his horse were a bobbing speck in the distance sometimes, and often, he lost sight of them entirely.

He'd had to stop and rest, stretch his legs and drink from a stream with his very agreeable horse, but there was little time for anything else. He had no idea how to get to Hest, except to try and follow Eadmund.

***

'How could you forget *that*?' Jael wondered with a grin as they dug into the sinking, wet earth around the tree's roots.

'I don't know. I don't remember dreaming anything. But I do remember those words. Symbol tree. Hopefully, I didn't just imagine it!'

Jael was eager to feel hopeful about something, and she dug around the roots with speed, dirt and wet leaf litter up to her elbows. They had taken one side of the tree each, digging holes until they met in the middle.

But there was nothing there.

'Maybe there's more than one tree with a symbol on it?' Aleksander wondered, already back on his feet, going from one tree to the next, running his eyes up and down the ancient trunks.

Jael stood, flicking the muck from her hands, and frowning, she walked around the broad trunk of the symbol tree. Stopping around the other side, she looked up, noticing an owl stuffed into a little hole. It was speckled, mostly soft brown, blending effortlessly into the tree as if it wasn't there at all.

It blinked at Jael, wide awake, its big golden eyes watching her. She reached up a hand, hoping to nudge it out of the hole, but it didn't move.

Aleksander came to join her. 'No other symbols,' he said, following her gaze, blinking in surprise. 'You don't think?'

'Well, we won't know until he gets out of that hole,' Jael decided, trying to be a little more aggressive with her encouragement. She moved her hand around the side of the owl, pushing him forward.

The owl quickly turned to peck her.

'Ssshhh,' Aleksander soothed. 'Come, come, ssshhh.' And drawing the owl's attention towards his deep, calm voice, he held out his hand, and the owl flew out of the hole, landing on it.

Jael's eyes were as wide as Aleksander's now, but she focused quickly, feeling inside the hole for the book. Gritting her teeth, she pushed herself higher onto her tiptoes, trying not to sink further into the boggy earth, searching every part of the hole.

But there was no book.

There was, however, a scroll, and Jael pulled it out with a triumphant smile.

***

Jaeger grabbed Meena's wrist, yanking her back towards him. 'Wait.'

She didn't like the look in his amber eyes, narrowed as they were.

He flapped his hand at Draguta's servant. 'She'll be there when I'm finished with her,' he muttered, eyeing Brill until she bobbed her head and shut the chamber door. 'You're not Draguta's dreamer,' Jaeger reminded Meena, dragging her towards the bed.

Meena gulped, tripping over her feet as she followed him.

He sat down, patting the fur. 'Tell me about your dreams before you go.'

Meena clamped her mouth shut as she sat down, but Jaeger was staring at her so intensely that she felt her knees bang together in fear of what would come if she didn't tell him something. 'I saw a cave.'

Jaeger leaned towards her. 'What cave?'

'I don't know.'

'And who was in the cave?'

'No one.'

Jaeger grew frustrated. 'Do you want to get rid of Draguta or not? Do you want to get the book away from her or not?' he growled. 'If you don't help me, Meena, if you don't give me more than a useless word or two, how can we do anything?' He put his head in his hands, scratching violently above his ears. 'I have to *do* something!' He couldn't get Draguta's screeching accusations out of his mind. She had been so condescending, so presumptive. Assuming that he was hers to do with as she liked. Like a servant. Not a king.

Assuming that the book was hers. Meant to be with her.

But Draguta was wrong, and Jaeger was determined to prove it. 'Why are you dreaming about a cave with no one in it?'

Meena feared how powerful Draguta was. Would she know that she'd been digging into her thoughts? Would she hear them talking now? But Jaeger had grabbed her wrist, and his fingers were pinching her skin. 'It used to be Draguta's cave,' she whispered so quietly that Jaeger had to bend his head to hear her. 'She lived in it for hundreds of years. It was her prison in the Dolma.' Meena swallowed, her voice almost disappearing. 'It's why she is afraid of the dark.'

'Is that so?' Jaeger released Meena's wrist and smiled. 'She's afraid of the dark, is she? Well, that's somewhere to begin.'

***

The owl flew straight back into its hole as Jael unfurled the scroll, frowning up at the trees, needing more light.

'Over there!' Aleksander urged, pointing towards a ray of sunlight that had forced its way in through the leaves.

Jael hurried towards it, holding up the piece of vellum, reading aloud, though it was a little hard to make out the message. 'I have... hidden the book to keep it... safe. Here is not safe. Follow the map. Get the book, then... hurry back to... Andala. They need you.' Jael turned over the scroll to see that a map had been drawn for them to follow. 'Well, that seems simple enough, I suppose.' She grinned eagerly at Aleksander. 'Let's go!'

***

Jaeger finally released Meena from his chamber, and, after grabbing something to eat from the kitchen, he headed to the ship sheds to check on progress. He was pleased that Meena was finally dreaming about Draguta. It was a start, and hopefully, she would see more soon; hopefully, something to help them take back the book. And then there would be no need for Draguta.

But in the meantime, he was eager to prepare his army, to ensure that his merchants were happy and his fleet was growing.

He was finally ready to be the King of Hest.

***

'Gone?' Axl ran his hands over the well-worn armrests of his throne, looking up at Gant, both of them thinking about Jael. And then the fort. Eadmund had worked tirelessly to organise his men, helping Gant when Axl couldn't. They would miss him.

Though not as much as Jael.

'It's not good for any of us,' Edela muttered. 'We need Eadmund, which, of course, Draguta knows.' She looked around, but there was no sign of Marcus. No one knew more about the prophecy than him, but he obviously had far more important things on his mind with Hanna.

'Do you think they'll hurt him?' Amma wondered from Axl's right. 'Kill him?'

Edela frowned, not sure if she should reveal her fears.

'Grandmother?' Axl leaned forward, placing his cup on the table. 'Now is not the time to keep secrets. We all need to know where we stand. We have to help each other.'

Edela squirmed, realising that he was right, but still not certain that she was. She sighed. 'I have a strong feeling that there would be no fun in merely killing Eadmund. No pleasure to take in such a simple act. Draguta doesn't just want to destroy us. I feel as though she wants to twist the knife. To put on a performance, as she's done with the serpent and the dragon. There are other ways to kill, aren't there? But she wants to make grand statements. Jael is her enemy. I think she plans on torturing her somehow. Using Eadmund to hurt her. Perhaps, kill her.'

Biddy, who had just walked into the hall with Eydis, gasped in horror. 'Eadmund wouldn't hurt Jael. Never!'

Kormac and Branwyn were sitting at the high table, eating their breakfast with Gisila.

'You remember how it was in Tuura, Biddy,' Kormac said solemnly, his face permanently scarred with the reminder of that bloody night. 'Those temple guards would've let us all burn if Eydis hadn't broken the spell. They were bound. Under the control of the dreamers.'

Eydis squeezed Biddy's hand. 'Eadmund is powerless now,' she whispered sadly. 'And Jael is the only one who can help him.'

***

The map was confusing.

Missing a lot of helpful information.

Aleksander and Jael nudged the horses together and took turns spinning it around, trying to see if they were still on the right path.

It was hard to tell.

'I think through there,' Aleksander suggested, pointing to where two trees linked branches, creating a leafy archway.

Jael nodded, tucking the scroll back into her pouch. 'Let's go.' She froze, turning around, shivering. It felt as though someone was standing there, watching them.

'What is it?'

Jael glanced over her shoulder again, watching a breeze lift the leaves on the trees. She shook her head, turning back to Aleksander. 'Nothing. The wood's playing tricks on me, making me hear things.' She smiled, trying to reassure them both, then frowned, noticing that Tig's ears were swivelling back and forth.

'Come on,' Aleksander urged, nudging Sky forward. 'Hopefully, we'll find the stream through there, then we can follow it round to where's she's hidden the book.'

Jael nodded and eased Tig to the right, pointing him after Sky, looking around one more time as the leaves hurried across the path behind her.

***

Morana perched on Morac's bed, near a small table with a bright lamp, reading.

It was an interesting book.

Unexpectedly so.

Morac had left for a walk. He had been too angry to sit still, irritated by his sister's lack of urgency about Evaine. He wanted Jaeger to pay. For him to be held to account for what he had done.

Morana was more circumspect. Jaeger was the king. Unless someone planned on killing him, there was little anyone could do to stop him. Not yet. Not while Draguta was in Hest, and all the plans were hers. In time, things would change, she was sure, but for now, they had no choice but to sit on their hands and wait.

The knock on the door surprised her, but she wasn't inclined to answer it, having just reached a particularly curious passage in the book. 'Who is it?' she grumbled loudly.

There was no reply.

Or was there?

Morana listened, certain she could hear mumbling. 'Little mouse!' she called, rolling her eyes. 'Stop dithering and come in!'

Meena pushed open the door and stepped inside, glancing around, surprised to see only Morana in the room.

'You've been sent to collect me, then?' Morana wondered, not wanting to be collected at all. 'Well, find yourself somewhere to sit because I'm not going anywhere yet.'

Meena didn't imagine that Draguta was going to be pleased about that.

But Morana had her head in the book, following her train of thought, not caring one jot for anything that Draguta may have wanted just then. She ran a finger under the words, almost mouthing them as she read:

After the sisters were beheaded, the Elderman of Tuura took their blood and hair to the gods, who made a magical paste. This paste was given to the Master Blacksmith, Wulfsig, who used it to forge the Sword of Light, the weapon the gods believed would one day be powerful enough to kill the creature Draguta Teros would become.

It was rumoured that Wulfsig kept some of the paste to make himself a knife. He was killed soon after, but nobody ever found the sword or the knife.

Morana looked up at her twitching niece and smiled.

CHAPTER FORTY TWO

'I can't stand it any longer!' Bayla Dragos shrieked, stalking across the hard mud floor of the bare ship shed they had been quarantined in since the night of the dragon attack. 'We are not livestock! How much longer must we be imprisoned in here?'

Her voice was loud and harsh, and it woke Kai up.

Nicolene glared at her mother-in-law. Her son had cried for much of the night, and she'd only just settled him down for a nap.

Karsten frowned at his mother, though he felt the same way. 'Entorp will be back to check on us all soon,' he grumbled. 'Perhaps he'll let us go? None of us has the sickness.'

Berard nodded, eager to find out how Hanna was.

'Of course none of us has the sickness!' Bayla barked, ignoring Nicolene's angry eyebrows and Karsten's rolling eye. 'They just want to shut us away because we're Hestians! Their enemy! You'll see, they'll probably sell us all as slaves if we live through this nightmare!'

'Mother!' Berard had had enough. Bayla had been riled up since breakfast. None of them had slept much, haunted by the memories of the past few days; grief-stricken and scared; displaced and worried about what was coming next.

The shed wasn't comfortable or warm, but with all that was going on in the fort, the Furycks hardly had time to furnish their accommodation in such a way that would please a former

Queen of Hest.

'You need to calm down,' Karsten sighed, holding up a hand as he approached Bayla, who had finally stopped pacing, flopping down onto a stool in defeat. 'There's a dragon out there. They have to move it, repair the wall. There are injured people, homeless people, dead people too. There's the sickness. The serpent broke the harbour, and who knows what's coming next? We haven't come for a fucking visit, Mother!' Karsten bellowed in exasperation, his temper boiling over. '*None* of us want to be in here! *All* of us wish we were back in Hest before any of this happened!' In an attempt to control his tongue, Karsten turned away, coming face to face with Entorp.

Who didn't know where to look.

'How is Hanna?' Berard asked quickly, hurrying forward.

'The same, I'm afraid.'

Berard glanced at Karsten, who looked as troubled as he felt. 'Can we see her?'

Entorp shook his head. 'No, it's best if you stay away. And besides, she doesn't know anyone is there now. She's hallucinating. Not seeing clearly at all.'

'And what about us?' Bayla wondered, striding towards the strange-looking man with the orange hair. 'When will *we* be allowed to leave? I certainly don't want to be locked in here when the next creature comes!'

'Mother!' Berard grumbled, motioning to his nephews and nieces, whose eyes bulged with terror as they huddled together by Nicolene. 'Will you be quiet!'

Bayla followed his gaze to the children, finally clamping her lips together.

'You should be able to leave soon,' Entorp said awkwardly. 'We still only have the three crew members in with Hanna. Hopefully, there'll be no more, though I want to wait one more day just to be sure.'

Bayla frowned, but she didn't speak, and they were all grateful for that.

***

Draguta sat at her table by the fire, smiling as she opened her eyes. 'Does she think that I can't see them? *Me*? Has it been so long that she has forgotten what I can do?'

Morana didn't answer. She had quickly grown sick of the sound of Draguta's voice. Eadmund was being pulled to Evaine's side, and all they could do now was wait for him to arrive, but in the meantime, she saw no need to be stuck in Draguta's chamber, imprisoned with her moaning daughter.

'But where would you go, Morana?' Draguta mused, narrowing her eyes on the black-and-white-haired dreamer. 'If you weren't here with us?'

Morana's face froze, and she cursed her weak mind. 'I was thinking of a walk. Some air.'

'I have a balcony. You are welcome to take all the air you require, whenever you want. You are not a prisoner, Morana, but I do need you close by. A man is following Eadmund. You can feel that. And you must do everything possible to ensure Eadmund's safe arrival. You may be called upon at any time. I need you where I can see you.' Draguta stood, glancing at Evaine, who sat on the bed, staring at the wall, as miserable and hideous as her wild-haired mother. 'Apple?' she asked sweetly, searching through the bowl of polished green apples, looking for the most perfect one.

Evaine shook her head, not turning around.

Draguta smiled, biting loudly into her chosen apple. 'When Eadmund is here, you will thank me for keeping you away from Jaeger. I imagine that once could be considered bad luck, but if it were to happen a second time, one might think you were encouraging him. And how would that make poor Eadmund feel?'

Evaine looked mortified.

Draguta trailed a finger over the symbols she had drawn

around the edge of the table. 'I am grateful that she is leading them to the book, though. It will make things so much easier,' she murmured, biting into her apple again.

***

They followed a meandering stream through the wood. After the downpour of rain, it was mostly flooded. The horses' hooves sucked into the boggy earth, and both Jael and Aleksander kept trying to find higher ground without losing sight of the stream.

It was the most obvious marking on the map they were following.

Jael couldn't shake the sensation that someone was behind them, and as the clouds gathered above the tree canopy, everything suddenly became darker. Quieter too. There was no birdsong. No breeze. Just the constant sucking of hooves in mud, and the blowing of frustrated horses.

Aleksander had the map, and he dismounted, flapping it at Jael. 'We need to walk from here!' he called, trying to lift a leg out of the muck.

'That will be fun!' Jael called back, dropping down to join him in the sinking bog. 'Don't move,' she smiled at Tig, who snorted irritably at her, just as stuck as they were. She lifted a leg and started the slow trek after Aleksander, who had already disappeared around a tree.

Thankfully, the path rose, and they left the mud behind as they forced their way through a tangle of bushes, finally emerging at a little clearing surrounded by an almost-perfect circle of tall pine trees. It was lighter here, and they could see that it was late in the afternoon. The sunlight filtering through the trees was golden, bathing the clearing in a pleasant warmth.

'There!' Aleksander pointed to an old ash tree in the middle of the clearing. Its branches reached out so far on either side of its gnarled trunk that he wondered why they hadn't just snapped off.

It was another symbol tree, oddly covered in owl-filled holes.

A lot of them.

'She likes owls,' Jael noted. 'Any clue as to which one the book is in?'

Aleksander shook his head. 'But this must be it.' He handed the map to Jael, and she could see the circle, surrounding a single tree.

'Well, let's go and wake up some owls!'

***

Draguta sat at her table with her eyes closed.

She was following Jael Furyck.

Watching her.

She could slip into a trance so easily now, Morana noticed. There was no need for herbs or the book or a chant or even a drum. The symbols Draguta had painted around the edge of the table acted like a door for her; a gate that she could open and step through at will.

Leaving Draguta in the trance, Morana walked out onto the balcony, sucking in a welcome breath of fresh air. She was exhausted and had to work hard to keep her thoughts clear of anything that might be pounced upon. It was a constant effort, and she was eager to relax for a moment, taking the risk that Draguta could not remain in a trance and read her mind at the same time.

Evaine leaned over the balcony, staring into the distance, not noticing the giant orange sun sinking slowly into the glittering water. She was downcast, worried about Eadmund, sick with the memories of what Jaeger had done to her.

Morana laughed. 'If I had told you Eadmund was coming two days ago, you wouldn't have stopped smiling. But now?' She scratched her head. 'You must not dwell on what the Bear did to you. Think instead of what Eadmund will do to the Bear when he finds out!'

'Who?' Evaine snapped moodily.

'Jaeger. My mother called him the Bear. She thought he was dangerous, a threat to her beloved Haaron Dragos. And she was right about that,' Morana smiled. 'Right about so much more.'

'But if Eadmund tries to kill Jaeger, what will happen?'

Morana lifted an eyebrow. 'Depends on who's better with their sword.'

'I'm not sure it will be Eadmund.'

Morana cackled, thinking how right she was.

'But what if Eadmund blames me? I shouldn't have gone for that walk with Jaeger. I saw the way he was looking at me. I shouldn't have been alone with him,' she sobbed.

'He's a man,' Morana said bluntly. 'There was little you could do about him taking what he wanted. You're as light as a feather. You're not Jael Furyck! What were *you* going to do to stop him?'

'Well, he is not *just* a man,' Draguta mused as she joined them on the balcony, smiling contentedly. Everything was falling into place, and she felt a welcome peace softening her body. A serenity. A certainty that she was close to achieving her most pressing desire. 'Perhaps Jaeger did indeed bewitch Evaine? He has the power of a god inside him, after all.'

Evaine spun around with speed. 'A god?'

'Oh yes, Valder Dragos, my son... he was half god,' Draguta sighed, her eyes softening in the glow of the late afternoon sun. 'His father was Taegus, the second God of Magic. Raemus was his father.'

Morana tried to feign surprise.

Draguta was too busy reminiscing to notice as she stared at the harbour, remembering the dreams she had shared with her son about what they would build here on this mountainous slab of rock.

Of how they would rule.

Of how she would find a way to bring Taegus back.

***

Bram's breathing was steady.

It hadn't worsened that Fyn could tell, and he was grateful for that.

Eydis sat next to him, wanting to keep him company, but she felt upset herself, terrified about what would happen to Eadmund if he made it to Hest.

'Thorgils will catch him. He'll bring him back,' Fyn tried. 'Don't worry.'

'But how? How will Thorgils catch him? If Eadmund is being controlled by Morana or Evaine, Thorgils will have to hurt him, won't he? How else will he make Eadmund come back?'

Fyn frowned. 'Thorgils wouldn't hurt Eadmund. They're as close as brothers.'

'I know,' Eydis whispered. 'But he can't let Eadmund go to Hest. He won't.'

'Ahhh, my favourite little dreamer,' Derwa smiled as she shuffled over to the bed, stooping low to listen to Bram's chest. 'Hmmm, still here. That's good.'

'Is it?' Fyn wondered eagerly. 'He's not getting worse, then?'

'No, he's not getting worse,' Derwa said. 'He's making up his mind, deciding how it will be, as we all have to, eventually. Sometimes, it feels harder to fight than to just let go, though when you find something to fight for...' She smiled. 'He looks like a fighter to me.'

Fyn looked down at Bram, still in shock.

He wasn't sure that he was reason enough for Bram to want

to stay. Morac had thought that there was nothing worthy about him, and though Jael had given Fyn some confidence, there was still a little boy inside him who felt deserving of Morac's scorn and disgust. It was a deep scar that wouldn't heal, no matter how hard he tried to pretend that he was a different person now.

Eydis reached out, feeling for his hand, and, finding it, she squeezed tightly.

***

The third owl Jael tried was sitting on the cloth-wrapped book, and she pulled it out of the hole with a smile, her body slumping in relief. 'We have it!' she exclaimed wearily. 'We have it!'

Aleksander's face reflected the exhausted happiness on hers. 'You're sure that's it?'

Jael unwrapped the soiled cloth, pulling out a dark leather-bound book. Dropping the cloth to the ground, she flicked through the first few pages. 'Yes, I think so. I hope so,' she sighed. 'Now we can go home!'

***

Thorgils wondered what he was going to do when he caught up with Eadmund.

He *was* going to catch up with Eadmund. Nothing was going to stop him.

They weren't taking his friend away. He wouldn't let them.

But how was he going to convince Eadmund to come with him?

The afternoon was getting old, and Thorgils was starving, but he wouldn't stop until Eadmund did. He couldn't afford to lose the ground he'd gained over the course of the day. He had chosen his horse in haste, but he'd had the good fortune of choosing well. His white stallion had strength, stamina, and a pleasing disposition, and, luckily, he was one of the biggest horses he'd ever ridden.

Thorgils only hoped that Eadmund hadn't been blessed with so much luck. A tired horse would give him reason to stop soon, he knew. And regularly. Glancing up, he could see that the sky was turning deeper shades of blue.

Thorgils spurred his horse on. Thunder, he'd decided, having spent hours amusing himself by trying to think of a name that suited his big-hearted beast. 'Come on, Thunder!' he roared, his red beard flapping as he rode.

***

After two days, they had given up trying to pull the dragon out of the broken wall, and it was now being removed in pieces, which wasn't the most pleasant task. The whole fort was awash with foul odours. The sea-fire smoke was still lingering, and now there was the even worse stink of dead dragon wafting in the air.

Everyone was walking around holding their noses, showing off their blisters, shaking hands slathered in Entorp's salves that Biddy and Amma were busy dispensing from one of the tables in front of the hall steps.

Axl frowned at Gant, turning away from the dragon to pour himself another cup of ale. Summer had returned, and it was pleasant to sit outside again. If it wasn't for the dragon and the threat of Draguta and the Book of Darkness, he would've almost felt happy. 'Any word on the sickness?'

Gant threw back the last drops of his own ale, banging his cup on the table. Sweat was trickling down his brow, soaking his iron-grey hair. He looked at Axl, then Gisila, who sat next to him. 'It's contained for now. No one's died yet.'

'That's good,' Gisila said. 'If only it could stay like that.'

'Unlikely,' Gant warned, thinking of Saala. 'But for now, it's a relief. We have enough to think about without that getting out of control.'

Branwyn trotted down the hall steps with a tray in her hands. 'I have sweet buns,' she smiled, looking around for her sons. 'Still warm, if anyone wants one?'

Gisila shook her head, but Gant grabbed a little bun, popping it into his mouth. 'Right, I'd better get back to it,' he mumbled, trying to swallow. He glanced down at his hands, covered in dried blood, not looking forward to getting up close with the dragon again. It wasn't a task that could be avoided, though. The sooner the giant beast was out of the fort, the sooner they could start making themselves safe again.

'If you see Kormac, tell him to come for something to eat!' Branwyn called as he wandered off. 'Aedan and Aron too!' She offered the tray to Axl, who took a sweet bun, then headed for the other tables full of red-cheeked men and women. Once the ropes had been abandoned, everyone had gotten involved in chopping up the dragon, carrying pieces out to the harbour – even the children.

Axl turned to his mother. 'What would Ranuf do?' he asked quietly. 'What would he be doing now?' He didn't want anyone to hear him, lest they find out that he was no king at all. Barely a man. He didn't want anyone to know what little confidence he had in his ability to lead them.

Gisila could hear the panic in his voice. 'I think Gant would be better placed to answer that. Or Jael or Aleksander, if they were here.' She smiled sympathetically, wanting to say something to ease the sharp lines between his eyebrows. 'He would be bellowing, that I do know. Your father had the biggest voice in Andala. He liked to growl, even when he was happy.'

Axl smiled, remembering. It was mostly for show, he knew.

But you never had to wonder if Ranuf Furyck was displeased with you. 'My leg...' he tried.

'Your leg won't stop you shouting orders,' Gisila said. 'Your father was injured many times. He would still roar from his sickbed. They could hear him out in the square with that voice of his!' She smiled, missing him for the first time in a while. 'I think what Ranuf did best was to make us feel safe. I'm sure there were many times when we weren't, but he made us feel as though he was in control, so we didn't need to worry. I think that's the power of a good king. To command his people in a way that they feel taken care of, and protected.'

Axl took a drink, missing that feeling himself. When Ranuf Furyck had commanded the Brekkan throne, they'd felt invincible.

'Lothar didn't have that,' Gisila added, shuddering. 'He kept us all on edge with his reckless behaviour. He was only ever interested in himself. Every decision he made was motivated by greed. No one felt safe with him as king. No one knew what he would do next. And you could see very well that no one mourned him when he was gone. Not even his own daughter.' Gisila sighed, relieved to be free of her headless husband and his worm of a son.

'Well, maybe Amma didn't,' Axl suggested. 'I doubt Getta would say the same, despite her husband's offer of help.'

'True, and from what I hear, Raymon Vandaal isn't a strong king. His father was a limp fool, much like Lothar, which, I suppose, explains why he got along so well with him!' She patted Axl's arm. 'Don't be afraid, my son. You're the king now. They all know it. They all welcome it. So don't be afraid to pick up your crutch and go and bark at them, if that's the sort of king you want to be.'

Axl looked up as his mother stood.

'I'm going to go and see how Edela is. I can't get her to sit down and rest today, stubborn woman that she is.'

Axl nodded, reaching for his crutch, wondering just what

sort of king he wanted to be.

***

Draguta had returned to her table, transfixed by the seeing circle.

Closing her eyes, lost in the trance.

Watching.

'I can't stay in this chamber until Eadmund returns,' Evaine insisted from out on the balcony. 'It will take days for him to ride here! I need to walk somewhere. I'm not a prisoner, am I?'

Morana wasn't listening. She hadn't been listening for hours.

Evaine had become a droning buzz in the background. And when Draguta slipped into her trances, Morana allowed her mind to wander freely, ignoring Meena and Evaine, trying to remember what she'd read in Yorik's book.

Wondering about the knife.

Had it truly existed? And if so, what had happened to it?

And what had happened to Morac?

Coughing suddenly, she cleared her mind as Draguta walked out onto the balcony to join them again.

'Night will fall,' Draguta shivered. 'Soon. And we must prepare ourselves. We will all be very busy tonight.' She handed one piece of vellum to Meena, who sat on a chair in the opposite corner of the balcony, trying to avoid Evaine, and another to Morana. 'Find these things. We will go to the stones at midnight.'

Meena and Morana looked relieved, happy to leave.

Evaine turned around. 'And me?'

'*You*?' Draguta grimaced. Evaine's face was only getting uglier as the swelling intensified and the bruises deepened, turning all shades of purple and yellow now. 'You will stay here. Brill will watch you.'

Evaine turned back around, clenching her jaw in fury.

Draguta paid her no mind. 'Now hurry along, my little assistants! There is not much to find. Not much that I require, but one item on that list may give you some trouble, Morana. Perhaps your brother will be able to help with that? If, of course, he survives his talk with Jaeger. Silly man.'

Evaine glanced at Morana, her one open eye blinking in panic.

***

Morac had tried to calm down.

The part of him that could still see sense was well aware of the mistake he was making in confronting a king. And not just any king, but a young, strong, giant-sized king with a violent temper.

It would not go well for him, he was certain. And if Morac Gallas possessed one thing, it was an overwhelming instinct for survival. But he couldn't get the picture of Evaine out of his head. The one where she was his little girl, and he was her protector.

Though Eadmund would come soon, Morana had said.

And if he left Jaeger to Eadmund, then perhaps justice would be served?

Perhaps Eadmund was more capable of punishing Jaeger?

But Evaine was *his* daughter. Yorik had never cared about Evaine. Nor had Morana, or even Runa. And Eadmund only thought he loved her because of a spell.

Evaine was *his* daughter, and he wasn't going to let what Jaeger did to her stand. Not without saying something.

So, taking a deep breath, Morac turned towards the piers.

***

Jael and Aleksander had ridden through the wood as quickly as the sodden terrain would allow. At times it felt firm underfoot, and the horses could stretch out on clear paths that had obviously been ridden before. At other times, those paths dried up, and the ancient trees tangled into a blockade, their thick roots spreading and twisting to stop them, forcing them to search for a new route. But they didn't want to stop. Night was approaching, and they were eager to get as far out of the wood as possible before making camp.

As relieved as Jael felt to have the Book of Aurea safely tucked into her saddlebag, she still felt uneasy, wondering what had happened to the Widow. Wondering why her cottage had burned down?

Had someone destroyed it? Tried to kill her? Perhaps succeeded?

Or had she done it herself?

Either way, it appeared that someone knew where to find the Widow, so perhaps Jael wasn't imagining things? Maybe they were being followed?

'Jael! Are you listening?' Aleksander called.

She didn't turn around. 'No, I'm thinking.'

He smiled, riding up beside her. 'We have to stop. Better to find something to eat before night comes.'

Jael nodded reluctantly. 'Maybe we should just find some berries and nuts, though? Not light a fire.'

Aleksander frowned. 'Why?'

'Whoever burned that cottage might have followed us to the book. We don't want to lead them straight to us.'

Aleksander shrugged. 'If someone knew how to find the Widow's cottage, seems to me that they won't need a fire to know where we are.'

'Well, looks like we won't be getting much sleep tonight,

then,' Jael grinned. 'So we may as well have a fire!'

PART FIVE

The Wild Hunt

CHAPTER FORTY THREE

Meena hadn't been able to stop thinking about her dream.

The one where the hooded figure had killed Draguta.

Had that really happened?

She crept along the corridor, knowing that she was supposed to be in the winding gardens foraging for herbs.

But she couldn't stop thinking about her dream.

What had happened after the figure escaped onto the balcony? What had happened to the knife?

Stopping before Evaine's chamber door, Meena swallowed and turned around, glancing up and down the torchlit corridor. Evaine wasn't allowed out of Draguta's chamber, she knew, so no one would be inside, but still, she had the terrifying feeling that Draguta was watching her.

She gripped the door handle, feeling her sweaty palm slip.

Swallowing, Meena turned it and pushed gently, part of her hoping that it would be locked, but the door started to slowly creak open.

'What are you doing?'

Meena bit her tongue, and froze, shaking all over.

***

The sun was sinking into the sea like a fiery orb.

It reminded Morac of sea-fire exploding across the sky. He took a deep breath, ignoring thoughts of sea-fire and battles as he strode towards Jaeger, trying to keep only Evaine in his mind.

Jaeger turned away from the harbour, pleased with the progress he'd seen. Four piers extended from the docks now, and he felt a lift, imagining how quickly his new ships would be moored alongside them. Things were slowly coming together, and it wouldn't be long before he was in charge of a proper kingdom again. Soon he would be a king ready to both defend and attack.

Jaeger frowned, surprised to see Morana's brother walking across the square towards him. His mind quickly turned to food, assuming that Morac had been sent to announce that supper was ready.

He had not.

Morac was vibrating with fury as he stopped just before Jaeger, and despite the king's hulking size and his sharp eyes, he didn't back away. 'I am here about Evaine,' he said, straightening his shoulders and jutting out his chin.

Jaeger looked confused. 'Evaine?' Then realisation dawned. 'And you plan to do *what* exactly?'

'You attacked my daughter!' Morac seethed, wishing he possessed the courage to draw his sword and stab it through Jaeger's evil heart. 'You raped her!'

'Raped?' Jaeger shook his head. 'What do you mean, Morac? Evaine and I, we...' He sounded almost bemused. 'Perhaps she feels guilty for what we did? She's supposed to love Eadmund Skalleson, isn't she?' He started walking back to the castle, irritated that Morac was following him. 'I'm disappointed that she'd accuse me of such a thing, but there was no attack. Evaine was a very willing participant.'

Morac's mouth gaped open. That wasn't what he'd been expecting at all. He swallowed, determined not to be distracted by whatever game Jaeger was playing. 'Evaine said that you raped her!'

Jaeger tried to look concerned. 'You need to speak with her again, Morac. Ask her what truly happened. It's no small thing to accuse a king of rape. It is... shocking to me. Quite upsetting.'

Morac shrank back, confused. He didn't know what to do. 'She is my daughter,' he tried. 'Promised to Eadmund.'

'Is she?' Jaeger mused. 'That's not what I heard. She's not your real daughter, is she? And as for Eadmund Skalleson... he has a wife. She is not meant for him. It was something Morana did. Something decided by people other than Evaine. You might be surprised to learn her real feelings about the matter.'

Morac's frown deepened, and he stepped away.

'But look, here is Morana. Perhaps she can help you get the truth out of Evaine?' And Jaeger strode confidently towards the stooping dreamer, eager to head into the castle for supper. He was starving.

Morana shuffled towards the two men whose shadows lengthened across the cobblestones, impatient to get her brother away from the Bear.

What had he been thinking?

She shook her wild hair, realising that he obviously hadn't been thinking at all.

'Morana,' Jaeger smiled, his eyes as cold and demanding as Draguta's. 'I was just explaining to Morac that Evaine seems to have misled everyone about what happened between us.'

Morana's expression didn't waver, though she could feel an angry heat rising up her body. 'The girl does like to make up stories, so I wouldn't be surprised to hear it.' She eyed Morac moodily. 'We need to go. Draguta has plans for this evening, and I require your help.'

Morac looked at his sister in confusion, and seeing the slightest of twitches in Morana's dark eyes, he clenched his jaw. 'Of course.'

'I assume no one will be coming to the hall for supper,

then?' Jaeger wondered.

'No.'

'Well, all the more for me,' he decided, walking off ahead of them, irritated beyond words. Then he smiled, reminded of how delightful it had felt to claim Evaine.

Perfectly lovely, helpless Evaine.

***

Meena couldn't speak.

Her bottom lip wobbled, and she felt ready to cry as she let go of the door handle and turned around.

'I hear Evaine Gallas is locked in Draguta's chamber. If you're looking for her, that is,' Else whispered, noticing how terrified Meena was.

Meena lifted her shoulders, not knowing what to say.

Else glanced up and down the corridor, lowering her voice. 'Or are you looking for something that has nothing to do with Evaine?'

Meena's eyes widened, and she nodded.

'Would you like some help?'

Meena nodded eagerly, turning back to Evaine's door.

***

Evaine glanced at Draguta as she sat at her round table. She hadn't touched the plate of food Brill had brought her. She couldn't think of food. It hurt to move her face, and her lips were still throbbing. Everything was still throbbing, and she felt so unhappy. Her thoughts jumped all over the place, contradicting each other. She couldn't decide if she was to blame or if Jaeger was. If she wanted to kill him, or if she wanted Eadmund to. If she wanted to leave Hest or stay and claim the throne with Eadmund.

The only thing Evaine knew for sure was that she had been attacked, and she wanted Jaeger to pay for it. But how?

Draguta stared at her, awake from her trance now. 'It makes no sense to starve yourself, Evaine. Eadmund is coming for you. You need to be strong and ready for him. You want to give him some hope that you will recover and return to your lovely self again, don't you? You will only look uglier if you turn to bone.'

Evaine slumped in a miserable heap before the plate of food. It looked appetising, though cold now, and she wanted to cry more than she wanted to eat, but she reached out a hand and grabbed a soggy-looking bean, lifting it to her swollen lips.

'Good girl,' Draguta purred. 'You are stronger than you realise, Evaine. You have come this far, so you can't give up on what you want now! Eadmund will be here soon. Do not despair.'

Evaine nodded mutely. It *was* all that she wanted, and she sat up straighter, determined not to let Jaeger Dragos destroy her dream.

She had waited too long for Eadmund to be hers.

No one was going to stand in her way now.

***

'What were you going to do?' Morana hissed as she walked her brother away from Jaeger, who had headed back to the castle. 'Fight him? Kill him?' She was shuddering with rage. Though Morac was little actual use to her, he was her only ally now, and Morana felt her need for him growing.

'I...' Morac shook his head, wondering what he would have done if Jaeger had turned on him. 'She's my daughter.'

'She's *my* daughter!' Morana reminded him. 'And I shall take care of Jaeger when the time is right. And the time is not right!'

Morac nodded, sighing heavily as he walked along, feeling his heart race, relieved that his sister had come along when she had. 'What's happening tonight?' he wondered.

'Well, I'm glad you asked. We're going to the stones again. You will be coming to drum for Draguta, and there is something she needs you to bring along.'

Morac caught a glimpse of his sister's dark eyes in the last rays of sunlight and shivered.

***

'You're sure it happened in this chamber?' Else whispered, peering under Evaine's bed.

Meena nodded. 'I recognised the arches over the doors when the murderer slipped away. Those monsters' heads. I've seen them in my dreams before.' She frowned, realising that for the first time. 'And this balcony joins onto the next chamber. They must have escaped through there.'

Else struggled back to her feet, adjusting her headscarf, which had dropped over her eyes. 'Well, I suppose Draguta wouldn't have wanted to go back to her old chamber after what happened. No wonder she took Bayla Dragos' instead!'

Meena was crawling around on the cold, rough flagstones, trying to remember exactly where she had seen the knife fall.

Else walked over to her. 'After all these years, though, I imagine someone would have found the knife if it was here. Perhaps even the person you heard knocking on the door?'

Meena sat back on her heels and sighed, red-faced and anxious, realising that she had wasted the time she should have spent looking for Draguta's herbs.

'It was hundreds of years ago, too. I suspect that nothing is as it was back then. Everything in here would have been changed, many times over.' Else held out a hand, helping Meena back to her feet.

Meena scratched her head, peering around one more time. She knew that Else was probably right, and it didn't make sense to keep looking when she needed to hurry to the winding gardens. 'We should go.' And turning to leave, Meena dropped her eyes to her boots, surprised that they weren't moving.

They weren't moving at all.

And lifting her head, she stared straight ahead at an old stone chest.

***

It was growing dark, and Thorgils couldn't see anything but stars and silhouettes now. He didn't know if Eadmund had stopped for the night, but he must have. Even spellbound, he was surely smart enough to care for his horse.

He only hoped that he'd light himself a nice warm fire when he did.

Walking now, and leading a clearly exhausted Thunder, Thorgils took a deep breath, trying to stop worrying about Bram.

Hoping to inhale some campfire smoke.

***

Ayla stopped by Bram's bed to try and tempt Runa into joining her for supper. Axl had ordered the cooks outside, and more people besides, and they had erected large spits which were now turning four of their fattest pigs. He was determined to throw a feast to cheer those who had slaved over the dragon all day, and to say thank you to those who had been tirelessly caring for the injured.

Not to mention the Andalans who had lost their homes and loved ones.

But Runa wasn't hungry. 'I'll just sit here awhile. Perhaps you could see if Fyn would like to go outside? There might be someone who could help him?'

Ayla patted Runa's shoulder. 'I'll find someone. I think he needs some company.' She froze, feeling the tension in Runa's body as she turned around. 'Bram?'

One of Bram's eyelids was moving - just an eyelid - but then a hairy lip too, and soon they could both hear a deep groan.

Runa hurried to her feet, leaning over the bed. 'Bram?' She clasped his warm hand between both of hers.

Bram's eyelids fluttered open ever so slightly before closing.

Ayla smiled, glancing at Runa, who was staring at Bram's face, hoping he would open his eyes again.

'Smells good,' he croaked with a lopsided grin.

***

Jael sighed, sitting back, happy to have eaten something, though the squirrel hadn't had much meat on its little bones, and they'd not wanted to waste time hunting for anything else. She realised now, listening to her still gurgling belly, that that had been a mistake.

'I keep thinking about Biddy's chicken and ale stew,' Aleksander smiled, resting his head against the tree. 'She'd have that cauldron going all day long.'

'Mmmm,' Jael said, salivating. 'She used to make dumplings and cook them on top sometimes.'

'I remember that! They were good.'

'So good.'

They sat in silence for a while, remembering how Biddy had looked after them. Always shooing them out of her kitchen as they tried to steal a taste of whatever bubbled over her fire.

'Should we look at the book?' Aleksander wondered, trying to take his mind off food. 'See if we can find anything useful?'

'You can see like an owl now, can you?'

'There's enough light from the fire and the moon,' Aleksander insisted. 'We can see.'

'When I looked at the other book in Tuura, I couldn't read it,' Jael frowned. 'Still, it's something to do.' And she reached for her saddlebag, pulling out the book. 'It looks like the one Marcus gave me,' she noted, handing it to Aleksander. 'Smells old.'

'It does,' he agreed, moving closer to the flames.

'Don't you dare drop it in the fire! After all we've gone through to get it!'

Aleksander laughed. 'Why would I drop it in the fire?' And he leaned over, trying to shine more light on the pages, but as he did so, something slid out, falling onto the flames. He snatched at it quickly as Jael charged towards him, both of them blowing on the piece of vellum, quickly putting out the corner that had caught fire. 'What is it?' Aleksander asked, handing it to Jael, keeping a firm hand on the book.

Jael bent towards the flames. 'It's a note,' she breathed. 'A note to me.'

***

'What is it?' Else wondered as Meena stepped slowly towards the long stone chest almost completely hidden beneath an ornate tapestry.

It was dark in the chamber now. Neither of them had wanted to attract any attention, so Else had only lit the one lamp, but even that barely gave off any light in such a large room.

But it was enough for Meena.

'I saw that in my dream,' she breathed. 'I'm sure I did.'

Else hurried to the table and picked up the lamp, bringing it over to the chest. Meena turned around, looking back to where the bed was, trying to remember where the hooded figure had tripped over. Turning back to the chest, she dropped down to the flagstones, pushing her arm underneath the narrow gap between the bottom of the chest and the floor. She felt the fluff and dust that had accumulated over the years. How many years, Meena didn't know, but she didn't care as she reached back as far as she could, moving her hand all around, desperately searching for...

The knife.

And gripping her fingers around its cool, smooth hilt, her entire body shivered with excitement.

***

Thorgils was struggling to keep his eyes open now. The darkness was tricking his mind into unwinding, and he stumbled often, not careful enough with his tired feet.

It was mostly hunger, he decided. A man as big as him needed more than a few berries to keep going. If he wasn't so determined to sneak up on Eadmund, he would've tried to kill something for his supper, though he doubted that he'd have much luck being half asleep and thundering about like a drunken beast. Every creature would have scattered long before he approached.

He tried to focus on Isaura.

She would be worried about him, he knew, and he wished

that he was in Andala, keeping her and the children safe. But he was convinced that if he didn't stop Eadmund from getting to Hest, none of them would ever be safe again.

***

Eadmund hadn't wanted to stop at all, but his horse was blowing so hard that he knew it was time to give him a proper break. Hest was a mountainous kingdom, which would be challenging for even the freshest horse, and the terrain would only get tougher the further south he rode. He hoped to come across a village soon; somewhere he could find another horse.

Something to eat too.

Eadmund didn't want to light a fire, drawing Thorgils to him, so he foraged for berries and nuts around the outskirts of Hallow Wood. Though, knowing Thorgils, he'd be far too busy cooking himself a big supper to think about anything else.

Still, it wasn't a risk he wanted to take.

Having finished his very brief meal, Eadmund closed his eyes, leaning his head against a tree trunk, though he had no intention of sleeping. He just wanted to see Evaine.

His breathing slowed as he listened to her voice, urging him to hurry.

But he wouldn't sleep.

***

'Are you alright?' Biddy wondered, furrowing her brow. Edela looked exhausted. 'You're doing too much. It's not long since you were bed-bound, yet here you are, rushing around like you're twenty years younger.'

Edela turned to her, readying a smart retort, but she felt her whole body slump. 'I think I need to go home,' she admitted weakly. 'I need my bed, or, at least, my chair.'

Biddy was surprised. She'd been expecting a fight, but Edela almost leaned against her, and she smiled. 'Well, come on. I'll take Alaric with us. He's been yawning away over there since supper finished. Eydis too. It's been a long few days for everyone.'

Edela nodded, almost too tired to speak. She'd tried to be useful all day: helping the injured, hoping for some visions, trying to think of any way to shine a light on what was coming next.

Worrying about Jael and Aleksander.

Of all the people Edela didn't need to worry about, Jael and Aleksander were at the top of the list, she knew, but they were so dear to her. And so important for helping them all stay safe.

But could they protect themselves?

There were only two of them, all alone in that wood, and thinking about Hallow Wood never gave Edela a good feeling. 'Why don't you grab a little of that cake to take with us,' she murmured, trying to take her mind off her rising panic. 'Eydis and Alaric would probably enjoy a piece or two.'

Biddy nodded as Ido and Vella rushed up to see her, tired themselves. 'Well, it looks like it's time for us to go then,' she smiled. 'If the puppies are here, it's definitely time for bed!'

Edela yawned, looking forward to her own bed, hoping she could slip inside a useful dream. If only she could just reach through the clouds. Straight through. She was certain that answers were waiting for her on the other side.

Edela peered down at Ido and Vella, who stared up at her expectantly. 'You can sleep with me tonight,' she decided. 'If anyone is going to help me find my way to Jael, it's going to be you two.'

***

'Can you read it?' Aleksander asked eagerly.

Jael nodded, holding the vellum as close to the flames as she dared, trying to make out the words. 'My name is Dara... Teros. When I was nine-years-old, my parents died. I was sent away to live with my aunt. My sisters were older. They remained in Tuura. I did not know it at the time, but I was a dreamer. I started having terrible dreams. My sister...' Jael stopped, squinting.

'What?'

'I'm just trying to make out a word... Draguta. My sister, Draguta.'

Aleksander looked at Jael in horror.

Jael swallowed, returning to the note. 'Draguta had been given the Book of Darkness by the God of Magic... Taegus. He loved her and wanted to... make her happy. But the book took her soul and made her evil instead. And I saw what she would become. What she would do. So, I wrote the...' Jael frowned, then looked up in surprise. 'Prophecy. The Widow wrote the prophecy!'

'Go on,' Aleksander urged breathlessly.

Jael tried to find her place. 'I saw you, Jael. You and Eadmund. How you would come together to defeat Draguta. My sister, she tried to destroy the prophecy, and then me. And now she will try... everything to destroy you and Eadmund. She put a curse on me. Made me... immortal like her. Alone. Hiding from the things she had done in my name. You see, Draguta was the real Widow, the one... responsible for all those evil acts.' Jael turned the vellum over. 'Only your sword will kill her now. And only Eadmund's shield will keep you safe while you try. And only this book will protect you both. She will come for me now. I... revealed myself to her when I tried to help Eydis save... Andala from the dragon. But I welcome death. My children and grandchildren are long gone. My... descendants... have cared for me and kept the Books of Aurea safe for centuries. I wrote them with all the... knowledge I have gathered. Every way I know how to fight Draguta is in there. Now it is up to you, Jael. Whatever happens, you cannot give up. It will get harder, but you must not give up while she lives. She can see you now. She is watching. You must hurry back to Andala.'

There was nothing else, though Jael wanted to hear more.

She had so many questions.

Aleksander quickly flicked through the book, wondering if there was another piece of vellum, but there wasn't.

And feeling disappointed, they sat there, staring at each other in stunned silence.

CHAPTER FORTY FOUR

Every now and then, Bram opened his eyes, and when he did, either Runa or Fyn were there, sitting by his bed. He didn't know what to say to them, so he closed his eyes, pretending to be asleep.

They didn't know what to say to him either. He was weak, and it didn't feel right to exhaust him with talking, so they left him to sleep. And eventually, when Bram opened his eyes again, they had gone, and Ayla was there.

Bram felt relieved. She was the one person he wanted to talk to. 'Was it a dream?' he wheezed. 'I had a dream.'

Ayla smiled. 'You did. And hopefully, I was in it.'

Bram closed his eyes, feeling tears coming. 'I wanted to go,' he admitted quietly. 'I thought no one would miss me. Or blame me.'

Ayla squeezed his hand. 'No one would have blamed you, Bram. But you needed to know the truth, just in case you wanted to change your mind.'

Bram didn't say anything; he felt oddly shy. 'So I'll live, then? You're sure? I can't breathe properly,' he croaked. 'Can't feel my leg. Maybe there's no point to me now?'

Ayla burst out laughing, quickly covering her mouth. It was very late, and most in the hall were asleep. 'Do you think we should put you down like a lame horse?' She shook her head. 'Your leg is broken, but it will heal. So will your chest.

Rest some more, and when morning comes, you can see how you feel. But just know that two people have been very worried about you. *They* think there's a point to you.'

Bram felt too strange to talk about that. He changed the subject. 'And Thorgils? Has something happened to him? I haven't seen him.'

'Thorgils is...' Ayla began. 'He has gone after Eadmund. It's a long story.'

Bram frowned, closing his eyes again. 'Well, sounds like just the sort of story I need to put me back to sleep. Start at the beginning, now. I want to hear everything I've missed.'

***

Jael lay on her side, staring at Aleksander. 'So you're one of her descendants, then? The Widow's?'

'Maybe. That could be why my grandmother went to see her. Why my mother told those stories about her.'

'They must have known the truth,' Jael murmured sleepily. 'Who she really was. That she wrote the prophecy.'

'Or maybe they just knew about the books and how important it was to protect them,' Aleksander yawned, shivering. They had kicked dirt over the fire, and now it was smouldering near them. The Widow's note had made them nervous, and they didn't want to lead Draguta to them. 'Maybe she never told anyone the truth?'

'But her sister knows, doesn't she? Which is why she wants to kill her.' Jael caught Aleksander's yawn and closed her eyes, though she didn't imagine that sleep would come.

They were on relatively dry ground, sheltering behind a wall of trees, just off the main path, but a cool breeze hurried the leaves towards them. It was an unsettling sound, adding to the feeling that they were being watched.

'Go to sleep,' Aleksander sighed, trying to ignore his growing sense of unease. 'Let's leave at first light. Or before. I don't want to be in this wood a moment longer than we have to.'

Jael pulled her cloak up to her ear. She had a sudden thought and sat up. 'Give me your symbol stones,' she said, digging hers out of her pouch.

Aleksander handed his over, and Jael threw them into the darkness. He stared at her in surprise, but she was already lying back down, curling into a ball.

'Draguta can find us anyway. And now, so can anyone who might feel inclined to help us.'

Aleksander frowned, thinking of Edela, remembering that he needed to look at her herb garden when he returned to Andala. He yawned. 'Goodnight, Jael.'

'Goodnight, Aleksander.'

***

Morac felt a sense of dread as he walked towards the giant circle of ancient stones. The man he dragged behind him was about his age, but much smaller, and more feeble looking. After his confrontation with Jaeger, he felt shaken, and he hadn't wanted to pick someone who could overwhelm him.

Morac kept the hilt of his sword exposed, watching it gleam in the moonlight, though he wondered what he would do if confronted.

He felt so old and rusty.

'Ahhh, and here is Morac,' Draguta smiled, stepping away from the fire. Everything was finally coming together. She could see clearly now, and what she saw was a path to victory. 'And you have brought me a gift. How very thoughtful!' Draguta strode towards the nervous slave and roughly lifted his chin, looking him over. 'You're no great specimen, are you?' she muttered. 'Yet, that will not matter for my needs.' She turned away, walking past the fire to the sacrifice stone where she had left the Book of Darkness. Picking it up, she motioned for Morac to come. 'Bring him here,' she said casually.

The slave's eyes popped open in terror, and he dug his boots into the wet earth, fighting against Morac, who tightened his grip on the man's arm, dragging him forward. The slave stumbled, falling to the ground, and Morac had to bend down to snatch him before he could crawl away.

'Morac dear, do hurry!' Draguta called over the slave's terrified cries. 'I would like to make a start.' She glanced up at the clear moonlit sky, pleased to see that the gods were behaving themselves. But even if they decided to cause trouble, there was nothing they could do to stop what she had planned.

This spell, she was certain, was weather-proof.

Morac dragged the shaking, pleading man to the sacrifice stone, pushing him down, onto his back. Morana was there, grabbing his other arm. Meena had retreated far into the shadows, covering her ears as the man sobbed, begging for his life.

'You must think of the bliss that awaits you,' Draguta soothed, staring into the panicking eyes of the old slave. 'The true bliss of being sacrificed for a greater cause. I am giving you the paradise of death!' She smiled, thinking how wrong she was. There was nothing good about death.

But life?

Draguta lifted her knife to the pulsing, sagging throat of the slave as he fought against his restraints, slowly touching its tip to the top of his collarbones. She trailed the blade up his neck, moving her head from side to side, inhaling the ripe stench of his fear. And when she found the right spot, she pushed the knife deep into his throat, listening as his screams turned to wet gurgles. 'Turn him over,' Draguta ordered coldly, walking back to the book. 'I need to fill the bowl.'

***

'How's you're head?' Jael murmured as they lay in bed, facing one another. 'Still ringing?'

'*Ringing*?' Eadmund snorted. 'It was never ringing. I barely felt it. You have a small foot. Delicate. Like a little girl.'

'Oh, that's odd. Thorgils said you were complaining about not being able to hear anything over the ringing in your ears from the strength of my powerful foot.'

'Thorgils is obviously the one with hearing problems. Never said that.'

Jael smiled. 'He was right, though, we shouldn't have fought. It's not a good idea to try and kill your husband, especially when you're as deadly as me.'

Eadmund burst out laughing, edging closer, his thighs touching Jael's, expecting her to wriggle away at any moment. 'It's a wonder you can fit your helmet over that big head,' he smiled, bringing his face towards hers.

Jael backed away. 'Big head?'

'Mmmm, but it won't be that big after our rematch,' Eadmund insisted, trying to kiss her again.

'I don't think that will ever happen,' Jael frowned, avoiding his persistent lips. 'You're too fragile. It would be like fighting Edela.'

Eadmund rose up on an elbow, running his finger over the scar beneath her eye. 'Oh no, it will happen. Draguta has promised me, Jael. She said that we will fight again, and next time, I *will* kill you.' He smiled at her with unblinking eyes, staring into hers with a coldness she didn't recognise.

Jael jerked awake, sitting forward, shaking all over.

'What? What is it?' Aleksander mumbled, his tongue stuck to the roof of his mouth. He coughed. 'Are you alright?'

Jael shook her head, her body numb with shock. 'Eadmund has gone. Eadmund has gone to Hest.'

***

Evaine was locked in Draguta's chamber with only Brill for company. It was very late, and there was nothing to do but sleep.

But she couldn't sleep.

Her mind wandered to her son, and for the first time in days, Evaine wondered how he was. Her thoughts about Sigmund were quickly replaced by images of Eadmund, though, and what would happen next. The certainty that he was coming almost made her smile. She felt the pull of him deep within her body, but then a stab of guilt too.

Of shame.

Swallowing, she tried to get comfortable on the floor, imagining what Eadmund would do when he arrived. Wondering whether he would turn and run back to his wife at the sight of her hideous face, or try to kill Jaeger and get himself killed in the process.

Evaine sighed, reassuring herself that Eadmund had no choice but to love her now, no matter what he thought of what had happened.

He was controlled by Morana.

No matter what he wanted now, Eadmund had no choice.

***

Eadmund had the sense that he wasn't alone.

He'd made his camp in a small huddle of trees, his tired horse pulling on some wet grass nearby. He could hear the tiny feet of animals scurrying through the leaves, scratching up tree trunks, calling to each other in the darkness. The breeze was picking up, and he watched as the tree canopy rippled in the darkness, letting through shards of blue-tinged moonlight.

Yawning, Eadmund thought of Evaine, imagining that he was beside her, keeping her warm, protecting her. Closing his eyes, he shut out the noises of the wood. He was too tired to move, finally realising that he needed to fall asleep.

Just for a moment or two.

He planned to leave well before dawn, though, determined to increase his lead over Thorgils, who would surely give up and return to Andala when he couldn't see him anymore.

***

Morana flicked the dead man's blood over Draguta with a hazel switch.

Draguta's eyes were wide with ecstasy as she stood by the fire, under the generous glow of the moon. She held out her arms, her white dress turning red as Morana circled her, chanting, splattering her with the warm blood.

Meena had been forced out of the shadows, and she waited by Morana, holding the bowl for her. She tried not to inhale. The smell of death made her want to run. She didn't know what Draguta was planning, but it didn't matter. She had little choice but to do what was required of her.

Morana finished, handing Meena the bloody switch.

Draguta smiled her approval and stepped towards the circle, indicating for Morana and Meena to join her. 'Take your places, for it is time to begin. Morac, you will drum now.'

***

Eydis was disturbed.

Edela could hear her turning over in her little bed on the floor. She kept whimpering, and Edela wasn't sure if it was time to wake her or whether she was having a useful dream.

Biddy was snoring loudly on the other side of the cottage, and Edela wondered if that was what was disturbing Eydis. It had certainly woken her, and she hadn't been able to get back to sleep.

Sitting up, Edela swung her legs over the side of the bed and pushed her cold feet onto the floorboards, listening to the familiar howl of the wind circling her cottage. Shivering, she reached for a fur, wrapping it around her shoulders. She felt unsettled, and not just because of Eydis or Biddy. Eadmund and Jael were the ones meant to protect them from Draguta, and they were both gone.

And Edela had the sudden fear that neither of them were coming back.

***

Morana felt Draguta leave them.

It was as though she had disappeared into the darkness, leaving only her body behind.

She had no idea where Draguta was going, but she could feel the throbbing of the drum, the murmuring chant rolling over her body. Her lips felt numb. Bright sparks of colour flashed before her eyes.

A howl. A roar.

The beating of a heart.

Morana felt the shock of surprise as her own heart quickened.

***

Tig's ears pricked up as the wind rushed around his legs.

It wasn't the wind that was upsetting him, though, nor the constant rustle of leaves and woodland creatures. It was the noises that weren't familiar at all.

He skittered about, whinnying.

Next to him, Sky joined in.

***

Ayla eased herself out of bed, trying not to wake Bruno.

'Where are you going?' he mumbled.

'Stay there,' Ayla soothed. 'Go back to sleep. I'm just going to check on Eydis.'

Bruno frowned, wondering why she needed to do that, but he was still mostly asleep and didn't speak again as Ayla reached for her cloak and boots, slipping out of their chamber.

***

Jael was sure that she recognised the grove.

The path she followed was overgrown, littered with twigs and leaves and tree roots bursting out of the earth, but Jael could see where it had been walked before, and those well-worn patches led to the expansive trunk of an ancient oak tree. She walked towards it without hesitation, an urgency throbbing in her limbs, propelling her forward.

A deep-blue glow washed over the ground, and Jael could clearly see the woman who emerged from behind the tree. She was tall, with broad shoulders, dressed in leather armour and tight-fitting trousers, tucked into tall boots. Her dark hair flowed loosely past the gleaming silver torc circling her neck.

Jael's frown cleared. 'Furia?'

Furia, Goddess of War, stepped forward and waited, allowing Jael to come to her. 'We cannot help you now, Jael,' she said solemnly. 'We cannot stop Draguta. Her magic is old. Powerful. It is Raemus' magic, and no god can undo it.'

Jael spun around, worried that she could hear something stirring behind her.

'We tried to kill her centuries ago, but the Book of Darkness protected her,' Furia went on, glancing back to the tree whose branches stretched out behind her like long wooden arms. 'She *was* killed, in the end, imprisoned in the Dolma. We didn't know that there was any way out. But she will do anything not to go back there. Draguta is no longer a dreamer. The book changed who she was. And now that she is reunited with it, she is growing more powerful. It is already turning her into that which she wishes to become.'

'And what is that?'

'A god,' Furia breathed. 'Soon, Draguta will become a god, and she will try to kill us all. But she does not have your sword. We had that sword made for you. Your sword is a god killer, Jael, so wake up! Wake up now and fight!'

***

Eydis cried out, rolling onto the floorboards.

Biddy stumbled out of bed, forcing her eyes open, her hands in front of her face, trying to find her way across the dark cottage. 'What? Eydis? What happened?' she croaked, tripping over a whimpering puppy as she made her way towards Eydis.

Edela was already there. 'Tell me, Eydis, what do you see?'

'I don't know,' Eydis breathed, her hands over her face.

'I don't know, but they are coming for Jael and Aleksander. I see them! Now!' She panicked, her throat tight with fear. 'They have to wake up! I couldn't wake them up!'

There was a knock on the door, and they all jumped.

***

Jael rolled onto her back, sucking in a cold breath of night air. Her dream drifted back to her, and her hand snapped to *Toothpick*. The horses whinnied, and she was quickly on her feet, shrugging off her cloak, grateful that she'd slept in her armour.

Aleksander hurried to her, trying to adjust his eyes, wanting to see what was happening.

Unsheathing *Toothpick*, Jael stepped out from behind the trees, cocking her head to one side, certain she could hear a noise. 'What... is... that?' she asked slowly, turning back to Aleksander, shivers racing up and down her spine.

Aleksander followed her through the colonnade of trees towards the path they had ridden down. Shafts of moonlight filtered through the leafy canopy, revealing nothing.

Nothing.

They stood there, sensing the panic of the horses, but not seeing anything.

Then they heard it again.

A strangulated howling. High pitched. Almost wailing. Like wolves.

And then they saw them, rushing through the trees towards them.

***

Biddy opened the door, and Ayla rushed inside to where Eydis sat on the floor, wrapping her arms around the little dreamer, trying to calm her down.

'We have to do something!' Eydis sobbed.

Neither Ayla nor Edela could see what Eydis could, but they both had an overwhelming sense of danger.

'They're in the wood,' Eydis murmured. 'Men. I think they're men. They're running.'

Ayla frowned. '*Men*? An army?'

Biddy wrapped a fur around Eydis' shoulders, kneeling in front of her. 'What army, Eydis?'

'They're not an army,' Eydis said, shaking her head. 'No. They're...'

***

'Dragur!' Jael shouted, running back to their campsite. 'I have to get the book!'

Aleksander planted his feet, firming up the grip on his sword. 'Grab the shields!' he yelled after her.

Jael rushed to grab her saddlebag and froze, not knowing what to do with it. She saw the horses pulling against their ropes in panic, and she ran, untying their reins, slapping their rumps. 'Go! Get out of here! Go!'

'*Jael!*'

Jael could hear the urgency in Aleksander's voice. 'Coming!' she called, and glancing up at the nearest tree, she saw an owl staring down at her. Pushing the owl to one side, she folded up the saddlebag, shoving it into the hole. 'Get back in there!' she told the owl, disappearing to find their shields.

'Jael! Now!' Aleksander screamed.

She heard the clashing of blades, and the high-pitched

screeching of dead men charging. 'Eydis!' Jael cried, shoving on her helmet, grabbing their two shields and running back through the trees. 'Eydis, help us!'

CHAPTER FORTY FIVE

'Dragur?' Biddy blinked, feeling her heart skip. 'You mean *dead* men?'

'More than dead men,' Edela breathed. 'They're warriors. Dead warriors with more strength than any living man.'

'But where did they come from?' Biddy wondered.

'Some believe that Hallow Wood is a tomb to the Tuuran warriors who fought to keep their homes when the invaders arrived from Osterhaaven,' Ayla said. 'Over the centuries, many men were lost fighting for Tuura. And, unlike the Brekkans, the Tuurans have always buried their dead.'

Biddy swallowed, reaching for Eydis' hand. 'Can you see the book, Eydis? Can you help them?'

Eydis shook her head. 'No, the Widow has gone. She can't help us now.'

Edela felt herself panicking, which was unhelpful, she knew. Her body was shaking, and her mind felt fuzzy, but Jael and Aleksander needed help to get out of that wood. 'Ayla, grab the herbs and the drum. Biddy, get the fire going. Eydis, you come with me,' she said, gripping Eydis' hand. 'We need blood. We must draw a circle, and quickly.' And turning around, she started looking for something of Jael's and Aleksander's. 'Hurry now!'

***

Jael spun, throwing one shield at Aleksander, unsheathing *Toothpick* with her free hand. She lashed out with her own shield, slamming the iron rim into the decaying forehead of the dead man who charged her.

He didn't sway.

'Shit!'

'Aarrghh!' Aleksander screamed as he was picked up and thrown against a tree.

'Aleksander!' Jael couldn't help him. There were at least twenty dragur surrounding her. Dead, blue-faced, decomposing creatures with scooped out holes where their eyes should have been. Their jaws gaped open, revealing few teeth, and their limbs swung powerfully, unnaturally, as though they were not attached to their bodies at all. Some had swords: giant, rusted, hammering blades. Some just reached out with their disjointed arms, trying to grab her.

Jael spun around with *Toothpick*, slicing off two forearms, jumping back, out of reach of those searching hands, her eyes everywhere, watching for the next attack.

Aleksander struggled back to his feet, scrambling for his shield, slamming it into the chest of a screeching dragur. The dead man didn't move. Leaning back, he swung the rim into his blue face.

The creature stumbled backwards but kept to his feet and charged.

'Get them down!' Jael yelled. 'Take off their heads!'

She ducked the blows of two dragur, dropping to the ground, slicing *Toothpick* across their ankles as she slid over the wet leaves. They staggered, their bodies jerking, unbalanced, knocking into one another, finally tumbling over.

Jael could smell more dragur behind her. The foul stench of them was overpowering. She rolled away, jumping up, swinging her shield into the neck of one, turning back to hack at the throats of the dragur struggling to get off the ground. More of them were rushing out of the trees towards her, but Aleksander ran forward, sliding on the leaves, dragging his blade across their legs. Jumping up, he kicked out at them, trying to knock them over. The dragur twisted their bodies, righting themselves quickly, lunging for him. Aleksander turned and ran, trying to draw them away. 'Can the book help?' he cried.

'I can't read it! Aarrghh!' Jael screamed as a dragur grabbed her from behind. She dropped her head, curling forward, throwing him over her body. He was heavy, but he fell, and she jabbed *Toothpick* into his filthy throat, pinning him to the ground. He snatched at her ankles, but Jael didn't plan on being trapped on the ground again. She drew *Toothpick* out of his throat, quickly chopping off his head.

Aleksander hid behind a tree, waiting for the dead men to follow him. More were surging through the trees, into their path now. He tried to catch his breath as he waited, then, as they appeared, he swung his sword, cleaving its newly sharpened blade into the first dragur's neck, taking off his head. Throwing his shield into the face of another, Aleksander knocked him off balance, sending the column of dead men tumbling behind him.

'Aarrghh!'

Aleksander left the scramble of bodies, running back through the trees towards Jael, who was surrounded by so many dragur now that he couldn't see her; they were piling on top of her. He looked around, surprised by the bolts of lightning shooting down through the trees. 'Jael!' He rushed in, stabbing the dragur, trying to find his way to her.

Jael burst out of the pile, roaring, slashing *Toothpick* from side to side, her shield lost, blood pouring from a cut in her cheek. The dragur were screeching like birds, their voices piercing her ears, lunging for her, arms outstretched, heads swinging loosely from side to side.

Searching for something.

***

Draguta was growing frustrated. No matter how many of her creatures raced into the fray, Jael and Aleksander managed to fight them off.

They would not stay down.

'The book!' Draguta urged, her voice like a demanding rumble of thunder. 'It's in the symbol tree! Under the owl! Get the book!'

***

Edela had slipped into a trance quickly, holding Vella in her arms with Aleksander's boot and Jael's arm-ring resting on her knees.

She could see them.

It was no dream. She looked around, wondering how to help.

Lightning shot through the trees, setting the abandoned campfire alight. Setting the treetops alight too. 'Jael!' she cried, her voice echoing through the trees like a raven's warning. 'Dragur hate fire!'

***

Aleksander fell to the ground, a stinking, hollow-eyed dead man in his face, and then another, squeezing his throat. He tried to bring up his sword, but they were on his arm.

He couldn't move. He couldn't breathe.

It was like being choked by hands of stone.

He banged his legs on the ground, trying to force himself free, but they were crushing his lungs.

Then he saw a flash of fire.

'Roll!' Jael yelled, swinging the burning log at the dragur. 'Now!'

***

'Who is here?' Draguta roared, spinning around. 'Who is here?' She couldn't see anyone, but she felt as though someone was in the wood, watching. 'Edela? Is that you? You will not stop me!' she snarled, and then her voice changed. It was hissing, slippery, even more insistent now. 'Get that *book*!'

***

Aleksander backed into Jael, who was holding the dragur off with the burning log. The screeching mass of rotting creatures had quickly surrounded them. More and more were surging forward to join the desperate crush of bodies.

'Jael! Get the book! Hurry! Run! You can outrun them!'

Jael could hear her grandmother's voice, but she didn't see how she could go anywhere. She kept swivelling, jerking the flames towards the dragur as they crept closer, then stumbled backwards, shying away from the burning log.

Screeching louder.

'Where are the horses?' Aleksander panted, trying to see over the press of bodies. He lashed out with his sword, hacking into a trio of necks. The injured dragur stumbled away, knocking into one another, but their heads remained attached, and they shook themselves upright, quickly jerking forward again.

'I sent them away!' Jael cried, regretting that decision now. Her eyes flicked to the right, watching a handful of dragur disappear behind the trees, towards their campsite. 'They're going for the book! Take this!'

Aleksander threw away his shield and grabbed the flaming log as Jael slashed her way through the throng of dead men. He swept the log around, taunting the dragur with the hot flames, keeping them away. But they were creeping in from the edges now.

Creeping closer.

***

'Horses,' Ayla murmured. 'We need to find their horses.' She could feel Edela squeezing her hand in agreement.

'Tig,' Edela breathed, remembering the day Ranuf had surprised Jael with her horse. 'Tig.'

He loved Jael more than anything.

'Tig...'

***

Jael's left hand was in the tree, shoving away the owl. Spinning around, she hacked off a dragur's hand as it clamped around her wrist. And then another reached out, and they were scrambling over her, pulling her backwards, and just as Jael got her fingertips to the saddlebag, she slipped, knocked to the ground, dropping it amongst the leaves.

'Aarrghh! Jael!' Aleksander cried from the path.

More lightning lit up the wood, and Jael could see a burst of fire in the distance, but her attention was quickly focused on the dead men clambering over her towards the saddlebag. 'No!' she screamed, wriggling away from them, kicking out, knocking one back into the hot flames of the campfire. She stabbed another through the face, one eye on the creature whose rotting blue hand was just about to snatch her saddlebag. 'You are *not* taking that fucking book!' She spun, chopping down with *Toothpick*, severing his fingers.

The dragur didn't stop, though. He lashed out quickly with his other hand. Jael ducked, leaning back, kicking him in the head. He didn't move, but Jael wondered if she'd just broken her foot.

'Jael!' Aleksander yelled again, his voice muffled now. 'Help!'

***

Meena, Morana, and Draguta sat in the tiny circle amongst the Crown of Stones, holding hands in the darkness. A sudden wind gusted around them, wafting the smell of the dead slave over them, but not even Morac noticed as he drummed rhythmically behind them, lost in the heady fug of the fragrant smoke.

'Up! Up! Up!' Draguta demanded, rising to her feet. 'It is time! Time for you all to rise!'

***

The wood was bright, spears of golden lightning darting through the tree canopy, stabbing into the throng of screeching dragur.

They had knocked Aleksander to the ground, catching fire as they crawled over the flaming log towards him. Aleksander rolled, clambering quickly away from them, feeling their hands on his legs, pulling him back, ripping his trousers, yanking off a boot.

Then Jael was there, her saddlebag over her shoulder, another flaming log in her hand. She threw it on top of the scrambling creatures and ran to find Aleksander, who stuck out a hand. Gripping it, she yanked him out of the pile of burning bodies.

'Run!' Jael screamed, turning down the path.

Aleksander gripped his sword tightly, charging after her. More dragur were coming out of the trees, running after them. 'Why can't they stop them?' he cried, wondering why Eydis and Edela hadn't been able to break the spell yet.

Jael kept running, fearing the answer.

***

Biddy watched as Eydis, Edela, and Ayla sat in the circle before the fire, their eyes closed. She couldn't even hear them breathing. It was as though they weren't there at all. The only sounds in the room were the gentle crackle of the fire and the wind whistling under the door.

Her heart beat in time to the drum she tapped on.

She didn't know what was happening.

***

Jael and Aleksander ran straight down the path. It was as wide as a road, bordered on each side by tall birch trees that had grown into a long wall of silvery trunks over the centuries. Behind them, more dragur were wrenching themselves out of their graves, staggering to their feet, banging into each other in a mad desperation to join the hunt; driven by the one who was commanding them to take the book.

Commanding them to kill those who were trying to escape with it.

But Jael and Aleksander ran fast, their throats burning, their chests heaving.

And then they heard a rumbling sound. Getting closer.

Thunder?

Jael blinked, squinting, trying to see. 'Run!' she bellowed, more urgently now, quickly sheathing *Toothpick*.

And then Aleksander could see them too.

Tig and Sky were galloping towards them.

***

Thorgils swallowed nervously, looping his horse's reins around the thick branch of the nearest tree. He had skirted the edge of the wood, knowing that he had to find somewhere to sleep, but not keen to go too far inside. He didn't envy Jael and Aleksander, who were no doubt stuck in the thick of it still.

Yawning, Thorgils decided that he would just close his eyes for a moment. Hopefully, when he woke, he would be able to find something to eat. Anything to help him on his journey. Maybe a stream too.

He was so thirsty.

But when he turned back to the tree he'd planned to rest his head against, he heard the snorting of a horse. Holding his breath, Thorgils tiptoed quietly back to Thunder, not wanting him to get excited and snort in response. He quickly untied him, moving him away, nearer the entrance of the wood, looping his reins over the branch of another tree.

The carpet of leaves was thick underfoot, and Thorgils hoped it would muffle the sound of his enormous boots. He thought back wistfully to the friend he'd known who would've slept through an army invading the wood.

That Eadmund was no more.

So, taking a deep breath, Thorgils drew his sword, creeping back into the trees.

***

'No!' Aleksander screamed as more dragur lurched out from the trees, rushing for the horses.

Tig was snorting, his nostrils flaring as he ran for Jael, not liking the lightning, nor the strange, shrieking creatures. They stunk of death. He reared up, knocking one dragur in the face. The dead man tumbled out of the way, and Jael hurried to grab Tig's bridle, realising that, though he had reins, he had no saddle. She quickly readjusted her saddlebag over her shoulder, dragging herself up onto his back. Gripping Tig with her thighs, she gathered the reins into her left hand, kicking him sharply. 'Go! Go!'

Tig roared angrily as a dragur grabbed his tail, trying to stop him.

Unsheathing *Toothpick*, Jael turned, leaning across Tig's back, stabbing the dragur through his empty eye socket. He screeched, jerking away. Tig kicked him, and he went down, quickly scrambling back to his feet, joined by five more dead men, but Tig wasn't waiting for anyone else to grab him. He took off, knocking down every creature standing in his way.

Jael glanced over her shoulder, relieved to see Aleksander and Sky charging after them. She could hear Edela's faint voice in her head. 'Ride, Jael! Ride! Ride for home!' Turning back around, her eyes bulged. The dragur had pushed over a tree, blocking their path. But she didn't want to detour, for they needed to get away quickly. Sheathing *Toothpick*, Jael gripped the reins tightly in both hands now, gathering them close to Tig's black mane. 'Go, Tig!' she cried, squeezing with her knees, urging him on towards the fallen tree.

She had ridden her horse into many battles, and for all his stubbornness and skittishness, he was brave in the face of danger.

And so was she.

Jael kicked Tig, sensing that he needed more speed. 'Go!' And Tig rushed for the tree, sailing over it, feeling the branches scrape his belly, scratching his flanks. But he was quickly free of the tree and the dragur, and they were riding now.

Jael listened, wanting to hear Sky behind her. She didn't dare look around, though, not wanting to lose her balance. And then she heard it - a thump of hooves as Sky cleared the tree and thundered after them - and, sighing in relief, Jael dropped her head, driving Tig on.

***

Eadmund walked out from behind the tree into a pool of moonlight.

His sword was drawn.

'Not tired, I see,' he growled at the enormous shadow who stood waiting for him.

'Not tired at all,' Thorgils said calmly, feeling his shoulders tighten at the coldness in Eadmund's voice. He didn't sound like anyone he remembered.

'You should go back to Andala, Thorgils. I don't want to hurt you, but I won't be stopped.'

'You should come back to Andala with me, Eadmund. I don't want to hurt you, but I *will* stop you. You're not going to Hest.'

Eadmund rolled his shoulders and lunged, aiming for Thorgils' arm.

Thorgils blocked his blow. 'Eadmund, stop this!'

'Walk away and I will!' Eadmund roared, slashing his sword towards Thorgils' stomach.

Thorgils jerked away, trying to think of what Jael would do. Feinting to the right, he left Eadmund chasing his sword, shifting his weight quickly, and turning, he slammed his boot into Eadmund's balls.

Eadmund groaned, coughing, trying to keep to his feet, but his body wanted to collapse forward. Gritting his teeth, he straightened up quickly, striking out with his sword, carving it towards Thorgils' face.

Angry now.

***

'Follow them!' Draguta seethed. 'Follow them! And do not stop until you have that book! Until you have killed them all!' She shook herself out of the trance, swaying slightly, opening her eyes. Spinning around, she tried to find what she couldn't see.

Searching.

Listening.

And then she found it.

'You have problems, Morana,' she muttered. 'You will remain here and solve them. Eadmund must come to Hest. Let nothing and no one stand in his way.' And turning from them all, she reached for one of the torches stuck into the ground between the stones, already planning what she would do when she returned to the castle.

CHAPTER FORTY SIX

Morana sat on the ground, alone in the little circle Draguta had cast. Morac and Meena had left, following Draguta back to the castle. The fire burned behind her, still belching out the head-spinning smoke, and Morana quickly slipped back into her trance.

She shut her mind off to Jael Furyck, focusing solely on finding Eadmund now.

She needed to grab that thread and pull it again.

And more.

Morana needed to wind it and move it and control his every thought.

She needed to remove any obstacle that stood in the way of Eadmund getting to Hest.

***

Eadmund's ankle gave way as he stumbled into a shallow hole, but he kept to his feet, clenching his jaw as he swung his sword up to block Thorgils' powerful strike. He roared, ignoring the pain in his twisted ankle, charging forward, crashing straight into Thorgils, knocking him into a tree.

Thorgils barely blinked as his head snapped back, breaking off a piece of bark. 'You're coming with me!' he yelled defiantly, lurching forward, sucking in some air. 'I'm not giving you to them!' Moonlight burst through the tree canopy, and Thorgils could see Eadmund's eyes more clearly than ever before.

He gulped.

Eadmund wasn't there anymore.

Thorgils tried to hold him off with one hand, pushing back against Eadmund's chest, lashing out with his sword in the other. He heard the grunt as he sliced through his friend's tunic. Eadmund stepped back, dipping to the side, aiming his sword at Thorgils' waist. Thorgils pulled away just in time, leaving Eadmund's blade hanging in the air. Growling in frustration, Eadmund jerked upright, elbowing Thorgils in the jaw.

Thorgils stumbled, ducking Eadmund's next blow. Coming back at him, he ignored the pain in his jaw, headbutting his friend with all the force he had. 'Grrrrr!' he bellowed, sending Eadmund flying backwards. Thorgils' ears rang, and for a moment, he could only see out of one eye, but he focused quickly, hurrying to trap Eadmund on the ground.

Eadmund's eyes were closed, and Thorgils worried that he'd killed him, but as he got closer, he saw that his friend's chest was moving. Quickly glancing around, Thorgils tried to think of what he could use to restrain him. He turned back, reaching down to take Eadmund's sword, but Eadmund's eyes burst open, and he rammed his blade into Thorgils' thigh.

Thorgils cried out as Eadmund pulled out his sword, driving it through his shoulder. 'Aarrghh!' he screamed, toppling to the ground as Eadmund hurried to his feet, slipping quickly through the trees.

Running to find his horse.

***

Edela's head dropped forward, and she opened her eyes, trying to catch her breath. The room was bright. Biddy had lit every lamp and built the fire up to a dazzling glow. It was warm, too, though Edela couldn't stop shaking.

'Edela?' Biddy asked, dropping the drum and hurrying to her. 'Are you alright?'

Ayla lifted her head as she emerged from her own trance, checking on Eydis, who was blinking rapidly, not sure what had happened. She felt as though she was asleep, still dreaming.

Ayla turned to Edela. 'We have to get the dragon out of the wall now.'

Edela felt disoriented. 'Biddy, we must go to the hall. Can you find Eydis' cloak and boots?'

Biddy nodded, hurrying to the fire where she'd left them drying.

'But what about Jael and Aleksander?' Eydis panicked. 'How are they going to get out of the wood? Away from those creatures?'

Ayla wrapped an arm around her shoulder. 'They will get out, Eydis, don't worry. The wood is a maze, controlled by the gods. The gods will help Jael and Aleksander. Now, stay still while I put on your boots. We must hurry.'

Biddy held out a hand to help Edela off the floor. Edela smiled gratefully, then frowned, feeling the sudden sense that she'd missed something. It was subtle, though, too faint, and she shook her head, deciding that she was just tired.

***

Morana laughed as she creaked to her feet. 'I never liked you, Thorgils Svanter. You and your bitch mother. Now you will die there. Alone. Knowing that your best friend killed you. Knowing that he is ours now. *Ours*! And soon, he will help us destroy all of Osterland. After he kills Jael Furyck!'

***

It didn't make sense to Axl, but he'd been in such a deep sleep that it had taken a while for Amma to wake him.

'Dragur?' He eased himself down onto his throne, gratefully taking the cup of water his mother handed him. He drank quickly, clearing both his throat and his mind. 'You're sure?'

Everyone in the hall was awake, waiting to find out what was happening.

'The dragur in Hallow Wood have been raised by Draguta. There must be thousands of them,' Edela murmured wearily. She was sitting on a bench, though she felt ready for her bed.

'Draguta has sent them after the Book of Aurea,' Ayla said, trying to catch her breath. 'Jael and Aleksander have it.'

'You think they're coming here? The dragur? And if they do? How can we kill them?' Gant wondered, fearing the answer as he tightened his swordbelt, blinking himself awake.

'I don't know,' Ayla admitted. 'The book would likely have an answer, but we can't find a way to see it. The Widow has disappeared.'

Axl frowned. 'Are Jael and Aleksander coming back?'

'Yes,' Ayla nodded, smiling at Bruno as he pulled back the grey curtain and headed towards her.

'But it will take them days,' Edela added. 'And those things are right behind them. They do not need to rest, but Jael and Aleksander and their horses must. Hallow Wood is not the only place where those dead warriors were buried either. They are everywhere. Perhaps they will all rise now?'

Gant frowned. 'We need to send a message to Raymon Vandaal. He offered his help, and we need it. Now.'

'An army of men will not defeat them,' Ayla warned.

'No, it won't,' Edela agreed. 'But it may hold them at bay while we find a way to protect ourselves again.'

'Find me some vellum!' Axl ordered. 'And someone to take

my note!'

Oleg disappeared behind the curtain, hurrying to Axl's private chamber.

'And we need to get everyone up. Everyone!' Axl shouted, carrying his voice to every corner of the hall. 'We have to get that dragon out of the fort. Now!'

Edela froze, suddenly cold all over. Turning around, she looked towards the hall doors, seeing an unexpected vision of Thorgils standing there.

And he was covered in blood.

***

Jael felt sick.

Her stomach was aching. One of the dragur had struck it with his stone-like fist, and she was worried about what that meant. Gritting her teeth, she bent over, leaning her head against Tig's neck, wanting to shield her face from the wind, wanting to help Tig go faster. They were riding down a welcomingly clear path, with a lighter covering of leaves above them, and the moonlight was brighter than anything they'd experienced so far.

Aleksander, who had been tucked in behind Jael, pulled out and rode up beside her, ducking too late, getting a spindly branch in the face. 'Do you know where you're going?' he shouted over the sound of thundering hooves and snorting horses, and the bone-chilling screeches of the running dragur still following them.

'No!' Jael shouted back, her eyes fixed ahead, ducking and weaving branches and tree roots, balancing safety with urgency. Neither of them could afford an injured horse now. 'We just have to follow the path while it's clear! Wait for the sun to rise. See where we are!'

Aleksander nodded, letting her slip ahead again, turning around as more dragur wrenched themselves out of their leafy graves, trailing after them.

***

'What is it?' Ayla grabbed Edela's arm. 'Are you alright?'

Edela watched as Isaura walked into the hall, Mads on her hip, his face streaming with tears. She swallowed, trying to think, remembering the sensation of being lifted off the ground in that alley; of being carried in Thorgils' giant arms, rocking against his solid chest.

Part of her retained a memory of what had happened.

Of how Thorgils had saved her life.

'Edela?' Isaura froze, worried by the way the old dreamer was staring at her. Ignoring Mads, she placed him gently down on the ground, not taking her eyes off Edela. 'It's Thorgils.' She felt herself starting to shake, tears blurring her eyes.

'Mother, what is it?' Gisila was worried too.

'Thorgils. I... I must help him,' Edela muttered, turning back to Ayla. 'Help me. Back to my cottage.'

'Edela, no, you can't, you're too weak,' Ayla said, feeling Edela shuddering against her, almost ready to collapse. She felt much the same. The trance had worn her out, and the smoke had left her with a strange sense of displacement.

'You can help. We can do it together,' Edela insisted.

'Is he dead?' Isaura panicked, hands over her face. 'Is he dead?'

'Come with us,' Edela said softly, reaching for her. 'Eydis too. We will see what we can do, but we must hurry!'

***

Thorgils couldn't move. He wondered for the hundredth time how he'd ended up with such a troublesome friend.

He had tried limping, dragging himself out of the wood towards his horse.

He was sure that he could still hear Thunder blowing in the distance.

Or maybe it was just the wind?

Thorgils sighed. He felt exhausted and weak, frustrated that he hadn't gotten very far. He'd stopped to rest by a tree, leaning his back against it, tearing his tunic into strips with the one arm that still worked, trying to stem the flow of blood oozing from his thigh. He fumbled, struggling to tie a tight knot with shaking fingers.

It was so cold, he thought fleetingly, wondering if the gods were sending snow again, before realising that it was likely just him.

He started shivering.

***

Arriving back at Edela's cottage, Biddy hurried to build up the fire, which was still billowing pungent smoke, while Edela and Ayla prepared a new circle. Isaura looked on as they made themselves comfortable on the floor and closed their eyes, trying to draw upon their flagging reserves.

Eydis held on to Ayla's and Edela's hands, feeling so sleepy and strange; not sure what she was supposed to do.

Ayla quickly slipped into a trance, looking for Thorgils. She was clasping his lock of hair from Isaura. She could feel Isaura in the room. Her fear was loud, and it helped focus Ayla's mind, and she felt herself drifting into Hallow Wood again. Listening. Trying to see.

She heard a pounding.

Turning, Ayla followed the sound.

It was the steady rhythm of horses galloping down a path.

Not Thorgils.

Shifting her focus, Ayla tried to find Thorgils. She imagined bringing him to her, but she couldn't sense him anywhere. The wood was dark, and the screeching sounds of the dragur were loud, but there was no sign of Thorgils.

'He has his symbol stone,' murmured a voice from somewhere nearby.

Edela, Ayla thought to herself. And she was right. She wouldn't find Thorgils if he had his stone, but she could try to find Jael and Aleksander. She had Aleksander's boot and Jael's arm-ring resting on her knees, just in case.

Feeling as though she was losing the trance, Ayla panicked, spinning around, trying to find those horses' hooves again.

***

Aleksander was riding behind Jael, a large group of dragur trailing behind them. More were squeezing between the trees, jumping out in front of them, throwing themselves at the horses, trying to slow them down. Aleksander wondered why Jael had picked this path as he kicked a screeching dragur in the throat, knocking him off balance, back into the trees. The path seemed to be leading them towards the threat rather than away from it.

Jael spun around as a dragur threw himself at Tig's hind legs. The creature wrapped its filthy hands around one, oblivious to the danger as he was dragged along, banging against the ground. Tig staggered, struggling with the extra weight, and Jael had to adjust her balance so as not to slide off him. She dug in with her knees, sitting back as Tig kicked out at the dead man.

He wouldn't let go.

'Stay straight!' Aleksander yelled, kicking Sky up alongside Tig. Gathering the reins into his right hand, he hung out to the left with his sword, digging his right knee into Sky's belly, jabbing the tip of his blade through the dragur's neck.

The blue-faced creature screeched, dropping to the ground with a thump, rolling away into the distance. Aleksander tugged himself upright, sheathing his sword, falling in behind Tig again.

'Thorgils...'

That wasn't Edela.

Jael swallowed. What did that mean?

Who was that?

The voice faded into nothing, and she didn't hear it again.

But she couldn't stop thinking about it.

***

'No!' Isaura sobbed, rushing to Ayla. 'You have to try again! *Please*!'

Ayla was on her hands and knees, struggling to breathe. The remnants of the smoke and Biddy's revival of the fire had not been enough to keep her in the trance, and she'd slipped out of it just as she spied Jael and Aleksander.

She felt sick.

'I'm sorry, Isaura. I don't think I can.' She glanced at Edela and Eydis. Neither of them could do it. Neither had the strength, and the way she suddenly felt, nor did she.

Tears streamed down Isaura's desperate face. 'But where is he? Please! Ayla, please!'

Isaura was beside herself, and Biddy hurried to her,

wrapping an arm around her shoulder. 'Ssshhh,' she soothed, trying to bring Isaura towards the bed to sit down, but Isaura pushed her away.

'No! No! Ayla!' she begged, rushing back to her. 'Try again. *Please*!'

Ayla couldn't say no, as much as she was convinced that there was no point.

She nodded, swallowing, taking a deep breath. 'Alright.'

***

Jael squinted into the distance, spotting another path.

Two paths.

Which way?

She heard Aleksander bellowing behind her, but she couldn't look around. She could only keep her ears open, comforted by the rhythmic beat of Sky's hooves following Tig's.

They were still there.

'Thorgils. Help Thorgils...'

It was so faint, but now she knew who it was: Ayla.

Jael wanted to pull up on Tig's reins, but she couldn't stop as she approached the second path. Which way?

Which way!

Thorgils...

Eadmund had gone.

But where was Thorgils?

If Eadmund had gone, Thorgils had gone after him.

Jael pulled on the reins, jerking Tig to the right, driving him down a tight, messy, almost-not-quite-a-path path. She spurred him on anyway.

Aleksander blinked in surprise, turning Sky after them.

***

Ayla leaned against Isaura. 'Jael heard me. She'll try and find him.'

No one spoke.

Ayla struggled to her feet, stumbling towards the door, yanking it open and rushing around the side of the cottage. She fell to her knees, retching, bursting into tears.

***

The path widened, and Aleksander rode up next to Jael.

He was starting to panic, convinced that they were digging themselves deeper into the wood. And if they did, soon the dragur would surround them.

Jael wasn't slowing down, though. If anything, she'd increased her speed.

'What's wrong?' he yelled.

She didn't look around. 'Thorgils!' she yelled back, not wanting to think what Eadmund might have done to him. Not wanting to believe that Eadmund was so far gone that he'd hurt his best friend.

Or worse.

Aleksander frowned, not understanding what that meant, but Jael obviously did. He let Sky slip back, kicking out with his right leg, straight through the torn mess that was a lunging dragur's face as they charged on through the wood.

***

Ayla hadn't come back.

Edela was slumped in her chair, eyes closed, entirely spent, but still hoping to see something.

To be of some use.

Biddy dropped a spoonful of honey into a cup of hot milk, hoping it would calm Isaura, who hadn't stopped sobbing. She was so lost in her thoughts that she didn't notice Eydis standing beside her until she started tugging on her sleeve. Turning around, Biddy looked down, but Eydis didn't speak as she pulled her away, towards the door.

'It's Ayla,' Eydis whispered, not wanting to worry anyone. 'Something is wrong with her.'

Biddy glanced around. The cottage was still bright, and she could see very clearly that Ayla wasn't there. She squeezed Eydis' hand. 'Alright, well, you go and sit on the bed by Isaura. Can you do that? Stay away from the fire, mind. And don't trip over Ido. He's right by Edela's chair.' She let Eydis go, hurrying to the door, feeling fear stir in the pit of her stomach.

Opening the door, Biddy peered down the path, but there was no sign of anyone. She frowned, wondering if Ayla had said that she was leaving. But then she remembered how worried Eydis had been, so hurrying down the path towards the wobbly gate, Biddy glanced up and down the moonlit road.

But there was no one there.

Walking back up the path, Biddy decided to get her cloak and go and find some help, but then she caught sight of someone lying in the garden to the right of the cottage.

'Ayla!'

CHAPTER FORTY SEVEN

Jael had no sense of where Thorgils might be, but she was starting to realise that she'd chosen the wrong path. It appeared to be coming to a hasty, dark end. Turning around to Aleksander, she could see that he agreed. They didn't want to slow down, but they didn't appear to have any choice now. She pulled Tig to a stop, searching desperately for any sign of a new path, but the trees were so densely packed around them that barely any moonlight was getting through now.

They could hear the screeching dragur coming closer, scraping their feet across the ground, hurrying like dogs after a fox.

The dragur could smell them. They wanted to kill them.

They wanted the book.

Tig and Sky skittered anxiously, snorting in warning, ears swivelling, not wanting to stay still. Jael and Aleksander struggled to keep them calm as they searched for an opening.

'What happened to Thorgils?' Aleksander called.

'He needs help!'

'*Here*?' Aleksander shook his head; nothing made sense anymore.

'I heard Ayla. I think Eadmund's hurt him!'

'We're stuck!' Aleksander cried, deciding that there was no way out. 'We have to go back through them!' He glanced at Jael, who nodded and switched the reins to her left hand, unsheathing *Toothpick*.

And then Jael saw movement out of the corner of her eye, and she snapped her head to the right. A woman slipped out of view, and suddenly, where she'd been standing, was a clear path. 'There!' But just as she jammed *Toothpick* back into his scabbard, a dragur leaped out of the trees, grabbing her leg, tugging off her boot. Jael pulled Tig around, kicking the dragur in the face, and freeing her bootless foot, she kicked Tig as well. 'Let's go!' Ducking beneath a branch, she urged Tig on, Aleksander pointing Sky after them.

***

Biddy hoped to find Bruno in the hall, but she couldn't see him anywhere, so she grabbed the nearest able man.

Ivaar.

'Help me!' she almost sobbed, breathless after running all the way from Edela's cottage.

Ivaar looked surprised to be called upon. 'What is it?'

'It's Ayla.'

Frowning, Ivaar gripped Biddy's elbow as she stumbled against him. 'Show me.'

***

Thorgils kept trying to force himself awake.

He'd tried to move again, dragging himself across the sodden leaves, desperate to get back to his horse. But all he could see were patches of darkness, and eventually, he'd had to stop, resting against a tree, trying to find enough strength to carry on.

If he could get to Thunder, pull himself up into the saddle

somehow...

But he was shivering and shaking, and now his legs refused to move at all. He felt strange. Dizzy. Panicking, he reached down, pushing a hand inside his leather pouch, searching for the lock of Isaura's hair, wanting to feel it.

Desperate not to be alone.

Finding it, at last, Thorgils wrapped his shaking hand around it, closing his eyes. He saw Isaura, and she had her hand out, calling to him, wanting him to come home to her. He tried to peel open his eyes, but they were so heavy, and when he drifted away, it wasn't Isaura he could see now, but Odda.

Tipping sideways, Thorgils fell to the ground with a thud, the contents of his pouch spilling out onto the wet leaves.

***

Ivaar carried Ayla in his arms, towards the harbour gates.

Biddy hurried just ahead of them, guiding him through the square. Braziers had been lit, but it was still dark and difficult to navigate a path through the maze of tables and people who had been roused from their beds and put back to work getting the dragon out of the fort.

'What's going on?'

Bruno recognised Ivaar and Biddy, and then, Ayla.

'Ayla! What have you done?' he roared, turning to Ivaar.

Biddy grabbed Bruno's arm, trying to get his attention. 'She fell ill. I asked Ivaar to take her to the sheds. I think she has the sickness!'

'What?' Bruno shook his head, trying to see his wife's face in the moonlight. 'Ayla?' But she didn't open her eyes. 'Give her to me!' he demanded.

'You can't carry her, Bruno,' Biddy insisted. 'And this is no time for arguing! Not now. Let Ivaar take her to Entorp. Come with us!'

Bruno shivered, gripping Ayla's hand. It felt like ice. He barely nodded, but he stood out of the way as Ivaar hurried past, following Biddy towards the harbour sheds.

***

Jael and Aleksander weren't being followed now. They hadn't seen any dragur for some time. The wood felt as though it was closing in behind them as they rode, but the path ahead remained clear, and Jael had the growing sense that they were being helped.

She hoped so.

She hoped that whoever was helping them would lead them to Thorgils. She had no idea where they were, let alone where he might be. And then there was the intermittent screeching in the distance, coming from all directions. Those dragur were still out there, somewhere.

Aleksander could feel the sky lightening above them.

Had they been riding that long?

Sky was definitely tiring beneath him. They would have to stop eventually.

Rest the horses. Find water.

They had to get the book back to Andala as quickly as possible, but it was going to be a long journey.

Jael turned around, comfortable enough now to check on Aleksander. He looked as anxious as she felt. Her stomach had not stopped aching, and that made her even more unsettled.

And then she saw the clearest picture.

A white horse was licking Thorgils' face as he lay amongst the leaves beneath the trunk of a majestic moss-covered tree.

'Come on!' she yelled, turning around again. 'I know where to go!'

***

Draguta had not slept since her return from the stones. She felt energised. Instead of depleting her, the spell had invigorated her, and she was eager for more.

She had spent the remainder of the night disappearing into her seeing circle, watching as the dragur hunted the book, chasing Jael Furyck through the wood. The gods might think that they could stop her dead friends, but they couldn't.

She smiled. They couldn't.

Draguta felt calm, confident, ready for what would come next.

'Get dressed. You will join me for breakfast in the hall,' she said to Evaine, who lay on the floor, barely asleep but barely awake either. Draguta's chamber was never dark. It was always hot and filled with light, and it was impossible to sleep for long, especially when her mind kept jumping from Jaeger to Eadmund.

But she opened one eye wide, cringing at the pain in the other.

Desperate to leave her prison.

***

Morning was coming, and the horses were panting, and Jael and Aleksander were tired and struggling to keep their focus.

But morning was coming, and they could see it clearly because they were nearly out of the wood. It made little sense, but Hallow Wood had been a maddening labyrinth and the idea that it was loosening its hold on them, at last, was a relief.

Aleksander was desperate to stop and take a break. He could tell that Sky felt the same, but Jael kept urging Tig on, and he had no choice but to follow her. He wasn't in her head. He didn't know what she was seeing or thinking.

Nor did Jael.

Nothing had come to her since that image of Thorgils being licked by the horse. He was lying in front of a big tree. She kept bringing the picture to her mind as she rode, trying to imagine where he might be. She had seen a lot of light, so he was somewhere near the entrance of the wood, she was sure.

And they were nearing the entrance now.

But where was Thorgils?

***

Isaura left Edela's cottage, wanting to check on the children, trying to take her mind off worrying about Thorgils and Ayla. She'd left Mads with Runa, and she hurried to the hall to find him, remembering how desperately Thorgils had tried to get her son to smile at him.

It hadn't happened yet.

The sky was flushed with pink, red, and purple hues. It was breathtaking, but Isaura didn't notice. She kept her head down, hearing the industrious hum in the distance as everyone worked on removing the dragon. She was so distracted and lost in her jumbled thoughts that she walked straight into Ivaar as he hurried down the hall steps.

He grabbed her arms as she stumbled backwards, peering at her swollen eyes. 'What is it?'

'I came for Mads.'

'Where have you been?'

Isaura burst into tears, rushing past him, trying to stop herself crying, not wanting anyone to see. Not wanting any of it to be real.

Ivaar stared after her before turning into the morning with

a frown, ready to get back to dismantling the dragon.

Trying to stop thinking about Ayla.

***

It was a shadow at first, a blur in the distance, but a moving one, and they both paid attention to it, worried that the dragur had finally found them again.

But as they got closer, they saw that it was, in fact, a horse.

Jael held her breath, sliding off Tig, checking for dragur. She couldn't see any. There were no screeching sounds either.

Running to the horse, Jael grabbed his reins. 'Hello, Gus,' she smiled at the surprisingly familiar face. 'Now, where did you leave Thorgils?'

Aleksander joined her on the ground, stretching out his stiff body as he stared at the horse in confusion. '*Gus*?'

'Thorgils has to be around here somewhere. I saw him lying in front of a tree, in the leaves, but there was a lot of moonlight. He was near the entrance. We need to find him quickly. Look!'

Aleksander's eyes widened as Jael showed him the horse's face. Gus was a white horse with a bloody mouth and cheek. A horse who had been nudging and licking a bleeding man. 'I'll take this side!' Aleksander called, disappearing into the trees to the right.

Jael wished that Gus could just tell them where Thorgils was, and as she thought it, the horse turned around and started walking back to where he'd come from, straight down the middle of the path.

He didn't stop.

Jael cocked her head to one side, watching him go. 'Aleksander! This way!'

***

'Well, isn't this pleasant?' Draguta cooed as Jaeger took his seat beside Meena, who perched awkwardly next to Evaine. 'Our little group. Together again!'

Jaeger had been surprised by the invitation to join Draguta for breakfast, and even more surprised to see Evaine sitting there, beside her. He hadn't expected the sight of Evaine to cause him any distress, but the mess of her face gave him pause.

He was almost disgusted.

With her.

She looked no better than a popular whore after a busy night.

He quickly turned his attention to his plate, happy to see smoked sausages. His favourite. Ignoring Draguta, he grabbed his knife and skewered one, sticking it into his mouth. Ravenous.

Morac had no appetite for breakfast. He had no appetite to sit at the table with any of them. He wanted to take his daughter back to Oss. Back to the moment when he'd agreed to kill Eirik. He wanted to undo it all; to be back with Runa, in their house.

Morana, sitting between her brother and Draguta, felt weary, working hard to keep her mind clear. It wasn't easy; distractions were everywhere. She could feel her brother's tension, her daughter's discomfort, and her own thoughts bursting against their constraints, eager to be considered too. She wanted to think about the book in Yorik's cottage. She wanted to read more about –

'Morana,' Draguta smiled. 'Is Eadmund still on his way?'

Morana nodded.

'How wonderful for you, Evaine dear,' Draguta mused. 'Perhaps we should try and find some sort of balm for your face? Or a scarf? Covering you up a bit might help.'

Evaine felt embarrassed, dropping her eyes to her plate, staring at the sausages and bread, wondering if she might vomit.

Jaeger was two seats away from her, and she wanted to scream and cry and stick her knife through his throat. She wriggled on her seat, feeling the burning pain between her legs, the ache of her face, the humiliation of it all.

She felt dirty. And angry.

Ashamed.

Draguta lifted her goblet, filled to its silver brim with wine, and smiled. 'We have much to look forward to. Much to celebrate!' Lifting the goblet, she drank slowly. 'Much to prepare too. We have an army to build, and an invasion to plan. Tuura is no more, and the end of the Brekkans and the Furycks is coming. Soon all of Osterland will be mine.' She leaned out, looking down the table at Jaeger. 'All mine.'

He scowled at her, wondering what that meant.

'But first,' Draguta sighed, 'we must discuss the small matter of... loyalty.'

The hall was silent. Not even the slaves who lined the walls dared to move.

Everyone was frozen, holding their breaths.

'Meena,' Draguta said, turning to her left. 'You know how important it is to be loyal, don't you?'

Meena bit her tongue in surprise, tasting blood. Her hands shook, and she had to force herself to keep them on her knees.

She started tapping her foot.

'And you, Morana, and of course, Jaeger. Oh, the pain it gives me to have to confront disloyalty. But how can we all stay together when we appear to want such *different* things?'

Draguta's voice was like a cup of poisoned wine: so sweet in appearance, yet so much threat lurked just beneath the surface.

Morana swallowed, as tense as her brother now.

***

Jael followed Gus, Aleksander walking behind her with Tig and Sky.

Gus didn't appear to be in a hurry, but they were as they urged him on, glancing over their shoulders every few steps, searching between the trees, jumping at every sound.

Certain they hadn't seen the last of the dragur.

And then Jael saw the way out of the wood; a clear, open path to freedom. She hurried, urging the white horse on. 'Come on, Gus!' she cried. 'Where is he?'

And then...

'Thorgils!'

Jael ran to the large figure lying slumped just off the path.

He wasn't moving.

Dropping to the ground, she felt Thorgils' neck for a pulse, looking for signs that he was still breathing. Leaning over his chest, she could see the wound in his shoulder, the bloody rag tied around his thigh. His leg was soaked in blood, as was his tunic. He wasn't wearing mail. 'Thorgils?' Tears stung her eyes as she rolled him onto his back, bending over him. 'Thorgils?'

And then she felt his warm breath on her cold face.

***

'Disloyalty is something I abhor!' Draguta spat, her voice hard now. 'To put your trust in someone, only to have them betray you... like Dara. A disloyal bitch if ever there was one.' Sitting back, she felt her jaw clench, her hands tightening around the cool stem of her silver goblet. 'My little sister. I raised her, you know, taught her everything. And look at what she did to me.' Draguta turned her head from side to side, glaring at them all. 'Can you not *see*?' she demanded with frenzied eyes. 'She was jealous of the book! Of how it belonged to me. But it was always mine, always meant for me. You know how that feels, don't you, Jaeger?'

Jaeger didn't look up.

'Dara couldn't accept it, so she wrote her own book, made up a story. Tried to turn everyone against me. She tried to take the Book of Darkness from me! *Me*? As if she ever could,' Draguta snarled. 'All that she knows comes from me! From *my* book! *I* made her immortal! She was my most valuable assistant, and she betrayed me!' She was almost shrieking now, her voice echoing high up to the rafters, crackling with anger. 'She *killed* me!'

Meena blinked in surprise.

'Killed me! Killed her own sister!' She shook her head. 'But you brought me back, didn't you, Morana. You and Jaeger. Your blood, Jaeger. Your skill, Morana. You both worked so hard to raise me. But for what?' She put her hands together, resting her lips on the tips of her fingers. 'Loyalty. If I had tested my sister's loyalty, I wouldn't have been trapped in that fucking cave for three hundred years! If I had tested my sister's loyalty, I wouldn't be sitting here drinking wine that I cannot taste and eating food that may as well be made of cloth! If I had tested my sister's loyalty, I would not be sitting here, needing any of *you*!' And standing, Draguta motioned for Brill to come forward.

Her servant walked towards the table, carrying a tray with a tall pewter jug and five tiny cups. Her hands were shaking.

'So now, before we go any further, it is time to test *your* loyalty,' Draguta smiled, indicating for Brill to serve the table.

The terrified-looking girl placed one small pewter cup in front of each person, and lifting the jug, she filled the cups with a thick, pungent liquid.

'I was far too awake to sleep when I returned from the stones, so I made something for you all to drink. I am most interested in what you think of it. Or, should I say, in what it thinks of you. You see those of you who are working against me, who are planning to betray me... well, this is not the drink for you.' And smiling, Draguta glided across the front of the high table, eagerly anticipating what would come next. 'Drink up, now! If your loyalty to me is as true as you proclaim, you have nothing to worry about at all!'

***

Thorgils was breathing, but he wasn't waking up, and somehow, they had to get him out of the wood and all the way back to Andala.

'You'll have to ride with him. I won't be able to see over his shoulder, but at least you'll stand a chance,' Jael said to Aleksander. 'If we can lift him onto Gus, we can head for Harstad. They have a healer there. We can get a cart to take him the rest of the way home.'

Aleksander frowned. At walking pace, Harstad was days away, and with his extra weight on Gus' back, it would be slow going. Aleksander spun around, hearing the sudden return of the screeching.

And the smell.

The dragur were coming.

'Hurry!' Jael cried. 'We have to get him onto Gus! Now!'

CHAPTER FORTY EIGHT

No one reached for their cups.

Draguta's gaze drifted across the five faces, pausing to enjoy the fear on each one. 'Well, this is disappointing. Will no one prove their loyalty to me?'

Evaine leaned forward, peering at Morana and Morac, neither of whom looked her way. She reached for her cup. Evaine hadn't seen Draguta destroy The Following. She didn't comprehend how easy it was for her to kill.

How much pleasure Draguta took in it.

Morac tensed, watching as Evaine gripped the cup, lifting it to her lips.

Meena shook beside her, certain that she couldn't take her own cup.

She wouldn't.

Evaine glared at Draguta, tipping the unctuous liquid into her mouth. Gagging and spitting, she slammed the cup down onto the table, retching, trying not to vomit.

'Ahhh, the bravest one of all. Not who I expected. Well done, Evaine!'

Those sitting at the table waited to see if something would happen.

So did Draguta.

But nothing did.

Evaine didn't want to drink anymore. She screwed up her

face in disgust, grabbing a sausage from her plate, desperate to remove the foul taste of the potion.

'Now, come, come, if Evaine can be brave, the rest of you can surely join her in proving your loyalty to me. Meena, Jaeger, drink up! Morana, you and Morac too. Pick up your cups and drink. Now!' And her soft voice turned to stone. '*Now*!'

Jaeger clenched his fists.

He was the king here. Of this table. Of this hall. Yet, he was being spoken to as if he were a child. A slave. Draguta's underling.

But *he* was the King of Hest, and he didn't have to drink anything he didn't want to. And he certainly didn't want to drink her stinking potion.

So, shoving away his cup, Jaeger stood, glaring at Draguta.

***

'Hurry!' Jael cried, holding Thorgils in a sitting position while Aleksander organised Gus. Gus was Gant's horse, and Gant took great pride in having a well-trained, impeccably behaved horse.

Gus wasn't like Tig.

He did what he was trained to do.

Aleksander stood to the left of the horse, stroking his face, rubbing his head, whispering in his ear, trying not to panic. He bunched the reins in his left hand and picked up Gus' hoof with his right, still bent over, pulling, easing him gently backwards until Gus started stepping back on his own, getting his feet organised before flopping slowly onto the ground.

Aleksander sighed in relief, patting Gus on the head. 'Good boy.'

And then the first group of ragged, blue-faced dragur appeared, running down the path towards them.

'Quick! Swap places with me! I'll take Thorgils' legs!' Jael yelled as Aleksander hurried around the big horse, trying not to unsettle him. They needed Gus to stay on the ground while they hoisted Thorgils onto the saddle.

'There, there, Gus,' Aleksander soothed as he slipped his hands under Thorgils' armpits, waiting while Jael got a firm grip on his legs.

'On me,' Aleksander said, already feeling Thorgils' dead weight leaning heavily against him.

'Come on!' Jael urged impatiently, watching the dragur running at them.

Hearing Tig whinny nearby.

Aleksander gritted his teeth, taking Thorgils' weight. 'Up!' He thought his back would break. 'Stay there, Gus!' he groaned, watching Gus' white ears spinning around urgently. 'Up!'

Jael only had Thorgils' legs, but it felt like lifting a serpent as she tried to heave them up, over Gus' head. 'Stay there now. Stay there, Gus!' Jael grunted, her attention snapping to Tig, who was whinnying loudly now, panicking as the dragur closed in on them. 'Tig!' she growled sharply. 'You stay there!'

'Higher!' Aleksander screamed, feeling his arms shake as he lifted Thorgils up, watching Jael's eyes pop open with the strain. And then Thorgils was down on the saddle, and Aleksander was quickly sitting behind him, his arms around Thorgils' waist.

Jael grabbed the reins, shoving them into Aleksander's right hand. 'Can you hold them?' she wondered.

Aleksander nodded. He couldn't see over Thorgils' shoulder, but he could hear the dragur getting closer. 'I've got them! Help me get Gus up, then go!' He could hear Sky whinnying, joining Tig, and he hoped that they wouldn't run off and leave Jael without a horse.

'Come on, Gus!' Jael cried, tugging on his bridle, urging him to stand. 'Up! Up!' And she watched as he wiggled, eager to obey, but unused to the enormous weight on his back. 'Hold onto Thorgils!' she called to Aleksander, watching Gus struggle to his feet, wobbling sideways. 'Come on!' she implored, pulling him forward, one eye on the dragur who were almost on them.

***

Draguta's dark eyebrows rose, her red lips clamping together in displeasure. 'You don't think that you should prove your loyalty to me, Jaeger? Why? What makes *you* so special?'

'I am the King of Hest! I will not be bullied by you!' Jaeger roared, striding towards her. 'In my hall? At my table? Ordered about like a nothing? So you can enjoy yourself? Have fun teasing and torturing us as though we're your toys?' He shook his head, his hand hovering near the hilt of his sword. 'Why?' His anger had overridden any caution he should have had. 'What makes you think I need *you*?'

Morana would have enjoyed the spectacle if she wasn't so terrified of what was about to happen. She tried to think of what she could do.

Run out of the hall?

Stick her knife through Draguta's throat?

She quickly swept that thought out of her head. Draguta was too powerful for any of them.

As Jaeger was about to discover.

***

Gus was on his feet, moving slowly towards the gap in the trees that promised an escape from the wood. Aleksander, struggling to keep Thorgils upright, kicked his heels into his flanks, urging him to hurry.

Jael turned back to grab the other horses. 'No! Tig!' she shouted as he charged after Gus; Sky racing after them both. She spun back around, unsheathing *Toothpick*, realising that she had to do something to give Aleksander more time to get out of the wood.

'Furia!' Jael yelled, glancing at the trees, now shaking and creaking in a rapidly strengthening breeze. 'I wouldn't mind some help!'

The first group of running dragur were on her, and Jael skidded along the leaf floor, running her blade across their filthy blue ankles. They stumbled, knocking into each other, struggling to keep their balance.

Jael was quickly back on her feet, checking the gap in the trees where Aleksander had aimed Gus; where Tig and Sky had disappeared after them. 'Tig, you annoying bastard!' Jael screamed. 'Tig! Aarrghh!' And she swung herself around in circles, *Toothpick's* blade high, aiming for the dragurs' throats.

And then she heard it.

That annoying bastard's hooves.

She would know them anywhere.

Ducking the punch of a stone-fisted dead man, Jael stabbed him in the chest, desperate to free herself from the tightening knot of stinking creatures. 'Tig! Come on!'

And then lightning.

Jael froze, gritting her teeth, her eyes on her skittish horse who reared up, slamming his hooves down onto the group of dragur, roaring in anger.

But not leaving.

'Good boy!' Jael exclaimed in surprise as he did it again; as the lightning shot down into the dragur, who peeled away, shrieking in pain, catching on fire; as the trees creaked and cracked and started closing in all around them.

Running for Tig's reins, Jael felt an ice-cold hand gripping her bootless foot, yanking her to the ground, pulling her backwards. 'Tig!' Jael cried, tightening her hold on *Toothpick*, rolling over as she was dragged along the ground. Sitting up, Jael jammed the tip of her blade into the dragur's forehead. He screeched, releasing her foot, and Jael scrambled up, clawing her way through the melee of bodies towards Tig, who was still there, rearing up on his hind legs, ignoring the bolts of lightning and the ear-piercing shrieks of the dragur.

Wrapping Tig's reins around her hand, Jael pulled herself up onto his back, clinging on with her knees as she righted herself and tugged to the left, turning him around. 'Go! Go! Go!' she cried as the dragur charged.

And the trees kept closing in behind them.

***

Draguta stepped back as Jaeger approached, resting her hands by her sides, feeling the slippery coolness of the white silk against her palms. 'It is a mistake to assume that I care what you think,' she hissed, her voice as frozen as her eyes. She smiled. 'It is also a mistake to assume that I need the Book of Darkness or a symbol to hurt you. They are just for show!' And then Draguta wasn't smiling. She flicked her hands, murmuring, her eyes narrowing into deadly slits as she twisted her palms outward, shunting them towards Jaeger.

Meena froze. Even her legs stopped shaking, watching as Jaeger flew backwards, landing on the flagstones with a sickening crack. He rolled away and was on his feet, shaking his head, blinking, dragging his sword from its scabbard. It quickly clattered to the flagstones as his arms were lifted up, then slammed against his sides.

He couldn't move.

Evaine smiled, watching the fear in Jaeger's eyes as Draguta swept her hands around again, sending him flying against the map table at the opposite end of the hall.

Morana glanced at Meena, frowning. 'What do you have?' she whispered hoarsely. 'Give it to me! Now!'

Meena shook her head.

'She will *kill* him,' Morana hissed impatiently, though neither of them cared about that, she knew. 'And then, she will kill us. Do you want to drink that potion?'

Meena blinked rapidly.

'Give it to me. We can stop her together.'

Meena listened to Jaeger's screams as Draguta lifted her hands, watching as he rose, his feet off the ground now, his eyes bursting open as he struggled to breathe.

Digging into her pouch, her hands shaking, Meena pulled out the knife, handing it to Morana.

Morana sat back, taking a deep breath.

Draguta's attention was on Jaeger, watching as he started choking, trying to shake his head, desperate to lift his arms. But he couldn't. Everything was turning dark, as though storm clouds were closing in on either side of him.

'Morana?' Draguta snapped her head around suddenly, inhaling sharply. 'What do you have there?'

Morana stood, hiding the knife in the folds of her black robe, assessing her next move. She couldn't afford a mistake. She stepped away from the table, walking around to face Draguta.

Draguta let Jaeger fall to the ground, turning quickly to Morana, flinging her hand towards her. The knife flew from Morana's hand, spinning across the flagstones, under the high table.

Draguta's blue eyes burst open. 'You too? *You* would try to kill me too?' She burst out laughing. 'Well, I didn't need a potion to show me who I could trust!' And spinning around, she flicked a hand towards Jaeger, who was struggling to his feet, sending him backwards again, before turning to Morana, who stood before her, empty-handed now, stinking of fear. 'But you could have achieved so much if you had given up Raemus,' Draguta cooed. 'For me.'

'You think *you* are worthy of my loyalty?' Morana spat, trying to stave off her terror; trying to keep Draguta's attention focused on her. 'Raemus was everything you are not. He was a god! He didn't seek riches and power. He sought pure darkness, not this vanity!' Morana sneered, pointing at Draguta's dress.

Draguta's anger burned brightly, and she readied her hands to snap Morana's neck, catching a sudden movement out of the corner of her eye.

Meena had run to Jaeger's side. She was bent over him, trying to help him to sit up, crying, sobbing, shaking.

Draguta laughed. 'After all that he has done to you? You *care* about him?' Dismissing the pathetic creature, she turned back to Morana. 'I should have killed you when I destroyed The Following. Now you can join them and Raemus in the Dolma!' she roared venomously, lifting her arms out in front of her, twisting her hands around as though she was holding a rock between them.

And Morana was off the ground, gurgling, her eyes rolling back in her head as all the air was sucked from her lungs.

She couldn't see.

And then Draguta screamed, her eyes bulging in shock.

Spinning around, she glared at Meena and Jaeger, baring her teeth, trying to raise her hands, but she couldn't. She couldn't feel her hands.

She couldn't feel her legs.

Meena could see the knife sticking out of the back of Draguta's head, and she ran for it, ripping it out and plunging it through her neck and then her back. Leaving it there, she pushed Draguta to the ground, panting, retching as Morac hurried to Meena's side, standing over Draguta, his sword drawn.

Jaeger struggled to his feet, stumbling towards them.

But Draguta didn't move.

Her teeth remained bared, her eyes wide open. Her body, sheathed in her white silk dress, lay perfectly still as dark-red blood started to pool around her.

***

They rode all morning across wide-open meadows, veering east, heading for Harstad, eventually coming to a river. And this time, Jael helped Gus to lie down, and once they'd pulled Thorgils off the saddle, lying him on the ground, Gus shook himself up, enjoying the relief of shedding his weighty load. He scampered to the river bank, joining Tig and Sky, who had their heads down, drinking the cool water.

Aleksander rolled onto his back, grimacing, unable to feel his arms, just as grateful for the break as Gant's horse. 'Not sure we're going to be able to convince Gus to lie down again,' he groaned. 'Can't imagine he wants to do that again.'

'Not sure we're going to convince him to come back over here,' Jael smiled, checking on Thorgils, whose wounds were still leaking, not helped by the bumpy ride. 'It's going to be a long journey home.'

'I'm sure we can find a cart in Harstad,' Aleksander said, listening to the imploring gurgles from his empty belly. 'More horses. Saddles. Boots,' he grinned, wondering how they had each managed to lose a boot. They needed rest and food too. Neither of them had slept properly in days, and the exhaustion was starting to bite.

Jael watched Thorgils' face, checking his breathing. She rested her hand on his forehead. He felt cool, which, she decided, was a good thing. Sitting up, she pulled her knees to her chest and rested her head on them, needing to think, but wanting to fall asleep.

'Leave me,' Thorgils croaked.

Jael turned back to him in shock. 'What?'

Thorgils' eyes weren't open, but his mouth was. 'Go. Leave me.' His throat was so dry, he could barely form the words.

Aleksander scrambled to his feet, looking for something he could use to get Thorgils some water.

'I don't think it works like that,' Jael smiled, squeezing her friend's hand. 'You're my loyal oathman, remember? You've sworn an oath to me, so I can hardly leave you behind. Besides, I think Gus has developed quite a soft spot for you.'

'Gus?' Thorgils asked, opening his eyes, grimacing as he tried to move, feeling a stabbing pain in his shoulder.

He stopped moving.

'Gant's horse.'

Thorgils didn't understand. 'Eadmund,' he breathed, almost crying in despair. 'I let him go. I should've... '

'Ssshhh,' Jael said, watching him panic. 'Stay still. Don't worry about Eadmund. We'll get you back to Isaura, and then I'll go find Eadmund.' Jael could feel the dull ache in her belly again; it was getting worse. 'He's not running away from us that easily!' She tried to keep her voice light, not wanting to distress Thorgils further, although she felt an overwhelming exhaustion that made her want to sob.

But there was nothing Jael could do about Eadmund now.

She just had to hope that whatever plans Draguta had for her husband involved keeping him alive.

At least until she could get to Hest and rescue him.

Thorgils felt around for Jael's hand. She gave it to him, and he smiled. 'Thank you... ' he whispered, closing his eyes. 'Thank you, my queen.'

THE END

EPILOGUE

Morac opened the door.

Jaeger stood there with Meena. 'How is she?'

Morac looked worried as he stepped aside, ushering them into the dark chamber. 'The healer has been coming regularly. She is trying to help her.'

Jaeger swallowed as he approached the bed, trying not to inhale. Morana's chamber stunk of piss. He took a stool and sat down, leaving Meena to hover by the fire, not knowing what to do with herself.

There was a lamp by the bed, but its oil was almost gone, and there was barely any light coming from it, but Jaeger didn't need much to see how ill Morana was. He looked up at Morac. 'Has she spoken at all?'

Morac shook his head.

Jaeger turned back to Morana and leaned over, digging under the mound of tangled hair, trying to find her ear. 'Morana,' he whispered, 'you need to open your eyes. We must talk, you and I. About Draguta.'

Meena looked on, wringing her hands, jumping as the fire popped.

Morana's head remained still, but her brow furrowed.

Jaeger was encouraged by that. 'You need to come back, Morana. Now. We're not safe here. None of us are.' He dropped his head and sighed. 'I had a pyre built. I wanted to burn the bitch so there would be no way to raise her again. But when I sent the slaves to get her body, she was gone. There's no sign of her. I've had them searching the city, the catacombs, but there's no sign of Draguta anywhere. I need you to come back, Morana. I have the book. I need you to use it.'

Morana didn't open her eyes, but Jaeger was certain that he'd seen the hint of a smile.

READ NEXT

THE LORDS OF ALEKKA

Books 1-3
(eBook only)

THE FURYCK SAGA

ABOUT A.E. RAYNE

Some things about me, the author:

I live in Auckland, New Zealand, with my husband, three kids and three dogs. When I'm not writing, you can find me editing, designing my book covers, and trying to fit in some sleep (though mostly I'm dreaming of what's coming next!).

I have a deep love of history and all things Viking. Growing up with a Swedish grandmother, her heritage had a great influence on me, so my fantasy tales lean heavily on Viking lore and culture. And also winter. I love the cold!

I like to immerse myself in my stories, experiencing everything through my characters. I don't write with a plan; I take cues from my characters, and follow where they naturally decide to go. I like different points of view because I see the story visually, with many dimensions, like a tv show or a movie. My job is to stand at the loom and weave the many coloured threads together into an exciting story.

I promise you characters that will quickly feel like friends, and villains that will make you wild, with plots that twist and turn to leave you wondering what's coming around the corner. And, like me, hopefully, you'll always end up a little surprised by how I weave everything together in the end!

To find out more about A.E. Rayne and her writing visit her website: www.aerayne.com

Made in the USA
Columbia, SC
15 March 2022